OLIVER PÖTZSCH

The Werewolf of Bamberg

A Hangman's Daughter Tale

Translated by
LEE CHADEAYNE

MARINER BOOKS
HOUGHTON MIFFLIN HARCOURT
BOSTON   NEW YORK

First Mariner Books edition 2015

Text copyright © 2014 by Oliver Pötzsch
English translation copyright © 2015 by Lee Chadeayne

www.hmhco.com

The Werewolf of Bamberg: A Hangman's Daughter Tale was first published in 2014
by Ullstein Buchverlag GmbH as *Die Henkerstochter und der Teufel von Bamberg*.
Translated from German by Lee Chadeayne. First published in English by
AmazonCrossing and Mariner Books in 2015.

Library of Congress Cataloging-in-Publication Data is available.
ISBN 978-0-544-61094-1

Printed in the United States of America
DOC 10 9 8 7 6 5 4 3 2 1

For Olivia, a new member of the large Kuisl family.

Stay cheerful and bright, and give the gray world your laughter.

And, as one says among executioners' descendants: break a leg!

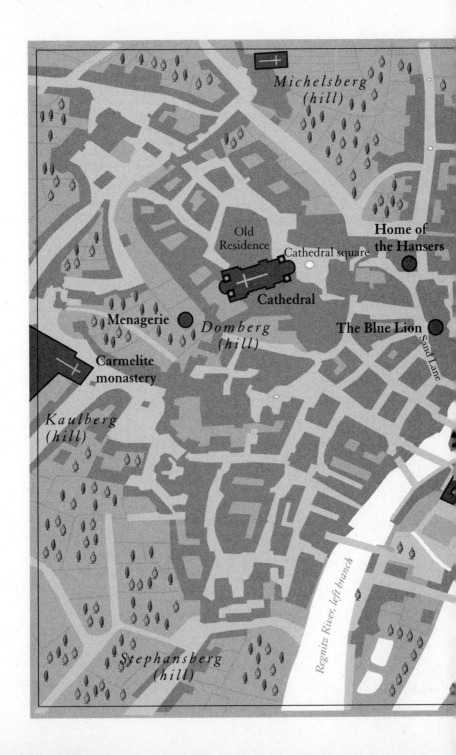

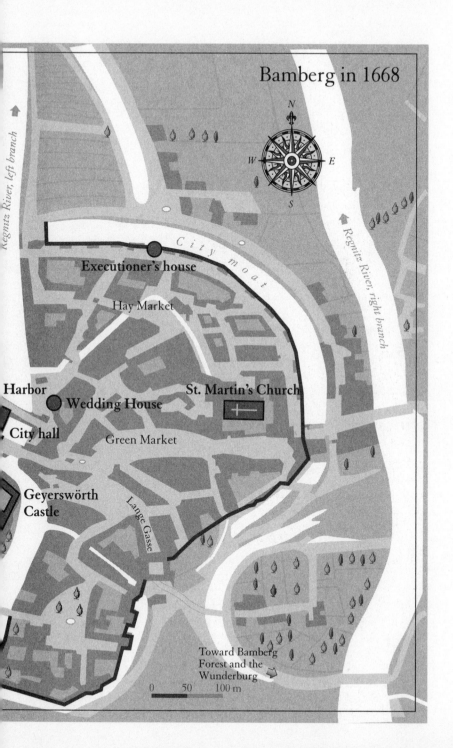

Bamberg in 1668

Regnitz River, left branch

Regnitz River, right branch

City moat

Executioner's house

Hay Market

Harbor

Wedding House

City hall

St. Martin's Church

Green Market

Geyerswörth Castle

Lange Gasse

Toward Bamberg Forest and the Wunderburg

0   50   100 m

Why do we search so diligently for sorcerers? Hear me, you judges, and I will show you where they are. Rise, attack the Capuchins, Jesuits, and all the members of holy orders. Attack them, they will confess. If any deny, torture them three times, four times, and they'll confess. [. . .] If you want more, attack the prelates, canons, theologians and they, too, will confess. How can these delicate, gentle men endure something like that?

—Friedrich Spee von Langenfeld,
Cautio Criminalis, AD 1631

DRAMATIS PERSONAE

THE KUISL FAMILY

JAKOB KUISL, Schongau hangman
BARTHOLOMÄUS KUISL, Jakob's brother, Bamberg hangman
MAGDALENA FRONWIESER (NÉE KUISL), daughter of the
  Schongau hangman
SIMON FRONWIESER, Schongau bathhouse owner and medicus
GEORG AND BARBARA KUISL, twins
PETER AND PAUL, children of Magdalena and Simon
  Fronwieser

CITY OF BAMBERG

MASTER SAMUEL, Bamberg city physician and personal physi-
  cian of the prince bishop
KATHARINA HAUSER, Bartholomäus Kuisl's fiancée
HIERONYMUS HAUSER, Katharina's father, city clerk
MARTIN LEBRECHT, captain of the city guard
ADELHEID RINSWIESER, wife of the apothecary
BERTHOLD LAMPRECHT, tavern keeper of the Wild Man
JEREMIAS, Lamprecht's custodian
ALOYSIUS, executioner's helper and knacker
ANSWIN, collector of rags and corpses
MATTHIAS, night watchman and drunkard

THE ACTORS

SIR MALCOLM, manager and director of a traveling group of
  actors

GUISCARD BROLET, manager of another group of actors and Sir
   Malcolm's major competitor
MARKUS SALTER, playwright and actor
MATHEO, young actor and lady's man

SOME OF THE BAMBERG COUNCILORS

KLAUS SCHWARZKONTZ, cloth merchant
THADÄUS VASOLD, senior council member
KORBINIAN STEINKÜBLER, prince bishop's chancellor
MAGNUS RINSWIESER, apothecary
JAKOB STEINHOFER, wool weaver

CHURCH DIGNITARIES

PHILIPP VALENTIN VOIT VON RIENECK, prince bishop of
   Bamberg
SEBASTIAN HARSEE, suffragan bishop of Bamberg
JOHANN PHILIPP VON SCHÖNBORN, elector and bishop of
   Würzburg, bishop of Worms, and archbishop of Mainz

PROLOGUE

On the day his father died in great agony, Jakob Kuisl resolved to turn his back forever on his hometown.

It was the coldest February anyone could remember. Yard-long icicles hung from the rooftops, the old beams in the half-timbered houses creaked and groaned from the frost as if they were alive, but nonetheless hundreds of people had gathered along the Marktgasse in Schongau, which led from the city hall down to the town gates. Everyone was heavily wrapped in scarves and furs, the richer wearing warm caps of bear or squirrel skin, while many of the poorer had frostbite on their faces or feet that were wrapped in rags, offering only scanty protection from the cold. Silently, but with beady, eager eyes, the residents of Schongau stared as the small group made its way past from the northern town gate on the wide, slush-covered road toward the execution site. Like hunting dogs that had picked up a scent of blood, the crowd followed the condemned man, the four bored-looking bailiffs with the halberds, and the hangman with his two helpers.

At the head of the procession were Jakob and his father, who kept stumbling and had to catch himself on his tall, almost four-

teen-year-old son. As happened so often, the Schongau executioner had been drinking far into the morning hours of the
execution date. Several times in recent years his hand had quivered while carrying out a beheading, but it had never been as bad
as it was today. Johannes Kuisl's face was ashen, he stank of
brandy, and he had trouble putting one foot ahead of the other.
Jakob was happy his father had to perform only a relatively simple strangulation that day. He and his brother, Bartholomäus,
two years younger than himself, could, if necessary, light the fire
around the stake.

Jakob cast a furtive glance at the convicted man, who with
his torn clothing and battered face looked more like a creature
from a dark cave than a human being. In recent years, Hans
Leinsamer had lived like an animal, and today he would die like
one. Most of the Schongauers had seen the old shepherd one time
or another while gathering wood or looking for herbs in the forest. Hans was as dumb as his sheep, bordering on feeble-minded,
but until recently was considered harmless. Only the children
had been afraid of him when he approached with his toothless
grin, muttering as he passed his hand through their hair or handing them a sticky piece of candy. Jakob, too, had met Hans a few
times in a clearing while walking through the woods around
Schongau with his two younger siblings, Bartholomäus and Elisabeth. Lisl, who had just turned three, always held her brother's
hand tightly then, while Bartholomäus threw pinecones at Hans
until he ran away, whining. Their mother had often warned the
three of the homeless tramp, but Jakob always felt pity when he
saw him, while the twelve-year-old Bartholomäus wanted nothing more than to string him up from the next tree as a feast for
the ravens. Ever since Jakob could remember, animals had been
more important to Bartholomäus than people. He would lovingly care for a sick hedgehog, while at the same time Jakob was
helping his father break the bones of a man suspected of stealing
from the offertory box.

Jakob cast a sad glance at the simple-minded shepherd limping along beside them toward the execution site, tied up like a beast. Hans gaped like a cow at the Schongauers, some of whom jeered and pelted him with snowballs and clumps of dirt. He babbled on, whining and sobbing. Jakob suspected Hans was not even aware of why he had to die that day. It was shortly after Epiphany when eight-year-old Martha, the youngest daughter of the Schongau burgomaster, had come upon the old man while she was sledding in the forest. He had pounced upon her like a wolf, without anyone ever being able to say why. Did he want to play with her? Did the speeding sled frighten him? Martha had screamed like a stuck pig. When the other children came running, he had already taken off her clothes. Finally woodcutters in the forest heard the cries, seized Hans, and hauled him off to the Schongau dungeon, where, after torture on the rack, he confessed to the most heinous crimes. For many years he'd lived like an animal, copulating with his sheep, and he reportedly confessed he meant to drag Martha into his wagon, rape her, and kill her.

Jakob looked at the mumbling old man and couldn't imagine how he could have come up with a story like that. And, even less, that there was any truth to it.

In the meantime, they had prepared the execution site outside of town in a large clearing, where, the day before, Jakob and Bartholomäus had gathered a large pile of wood and placed it under the scaffold. A ladder led up to a post in the middle of the scaffold to which the convict was now chained. Out of the corner of his eye, Jakob watched how Bartholomäus admired the execution site, and a feeling of disgust came over him. For the first time, Bartl had been allowed to help his older brother prepare for an execution, and for him it was a great day when Hans was sentenced and the punishment was prescribed. Finally his dream of following in the footsteps of his father and his brother would be realized. Actually, Jakob couldn't understand why Bartholomäus admired him so much. Sometimes he teased his slow-witted younger brother, and in secret he even despised him, but that didn't change the fact that Bartl followed him around like a puppy. Bartholomäus watched Jakob when he cleaned up the torture chamber, knotted the ropes used in hangings, or sharpened the hangman's sword, because once again their father was too drunk to do it. And Jakob knew deep down that some day Bartholomäus would be a better hangman than himself.

Jakob himself had decided years ago not to practice this profession when he grew up, but did he have any choice? Executioners' sons became executioners if they didn't want to hire themselves out as knackers working in a slaughterhouse and buying worn-out, old livestock to slaughter in order to sell the meat or hides. By law, the dishonorable vocations were clearly separated from the others. Their only way out was the Great War, which had been raging in the Reich for years and was desperate for soldiers, honorable or not.

"What's wrong with Father, anyway?" whispered Bartholomäus, who was standing alongside Jakob. The question interrupted Jakob's thoughts. They were standing close to the wood piled around the stake, and the crowd stared at them in anticipation. With a worried look, Bartholomäus pointed to his father, who, despite the cold, was wiping the sweat from his brow as he struggled to keep his balance. "Our dear father can barely stand on his two feet. Is he perhaps sick?"

Meanwhile, the four burgomasters and other high dignitaries had arrived at the execution site. Along with the court clerk and a few hundred spectators, they formed a circle around the three Kuisls and the condemned man. Not for the first time, Jakob had the uncomfortable feeling that his own execution was close at hand.

"There's nothing wrong with Father," Jakob replied in a loud whisper, trying to remain calm as a soft murmur went through the crowd. "He's drunk again. We can only pray he won't set himself on fire by accident."

Bartholomäus shrugged skeptically. "Maybe he has the Plague," he mumbled. "That's going around now. Just look at Mother back home. She's caught it, too."

Jakob rolled his eyes. He hated it when his brother, as he so often did, wrote off all his father's faults. But perhaps, too, it was because father had turned away from Jakob long ago after realizing that his eldest son didn't care to follow in his footsteps. Jakob wished fervently that he could love his father—but he couldn't. Johannes was a drunk and a failure. Long ago, he'd been a great executioner, feared almost as much as his father-in-law, Jörg Abriel, who more than sixty years ago had tortured, beheaded, and burned women in the famous Schongau witch trials. Both Kuisl brothers had inherited from their grandfather those strange, evil books that Bartholomäus loved almost more than his sick animals. Almost every week he would go to his father's room, and the two would take them out of the chest to read. They reminded the family of the great, bloody times when their name was known and feared. But those days were long gone, and in the meantime Johannes Kuisl had become a wreck. People made fun of him behind his back. They were no longer afraid of him, and that was the worst thing that could happen to an executioner.

Unless he was feared, he was nothing.

Now, Jakob saw contempt flaring up in the eyes of many spectators as they looked disapprovingly at the trembling, sweating drinker. Fear gripped Jakob. Twice already his father had almost botched an execution, and the people would not tolerate that again. A bungling executioner quickly landed on the gallows himself.

And with him, sometimes, the entire family.

"Hurry up and be done with it, Kuisl," cried the fat baker,

Korbinian Berchtholdt, whose son Michael had sometimes brawled with Jakob and Bartholomäus. Berchtholdt pointed at the trembling shepherd, who was still standing there muttering to himself, and then at the stake. "Hey, do you want us to do that ourselves, or have your young brats gathered so much wet wood we'll still be standing around here tomorrow?"

Johannes Kuisl reeled slightly, like a willow branch broken in a storm, but then he pulled himself together, grabbed Hans by the collar, and pulled him over to the ladder. Jakob knew now what would follow. Last year he had been present at the burning of a witch. Often the punishment was mitigated by placing a bag of gunpowder around the condemned person's neck or strangling the person first. Dumb Hans also had a few supporters in the town council, and it was agreed the executioner would strangle him with a thin piece of rope before burning—a fast, almost painless way to die if it was done right.

As Jakob watched his father stagger toward the ladder, however, he doubted the strangulation this time would be as fast and painless as they'd hoped. Bartholomäus, too, was noticeably uncertain. With a frozen gaze he watched his father climb the ladder to the scaffold, pushing the blubbering man in front of him.

When they'd almost reached the top, it happened.

Johannes Kuisl lost his grip, waved his arms around helplessly, then fell backward into the slushy snow like a sack of flour and didn't move.

"My God, the executioner is drunk as a fish," someone in the crowd shouted.

Some of them laughed, but from all sides there was an angry murmur that made Jakob's hair stand on end. It sounded like a swarm of angry bees, coming closer and closer.

"Burn him, too, along with the dirty bugger, then we'll finally have some peace in town," someone else called. Jakob looked out over the crowd. It was the master baker, Korbinian Berchtholdt. He turned around to the spectators, looking for support from his audience. "This hangman's performance is a disgrace. It's been like this for years. Even in Augsburg and beyond people make fun of us. We should have gotten rid of him long ago and taken the Steingaden executioner in his place."

"To hell with him! To hell with him!" others were shouting now. First snowballs, then clumps of frozen sod pummeled the hangman. Long pent-up anger suddenly seemed to give way to a single explosion of rage. The court clerk, his face flushed beneath his official headdress, waved his arms ostentatiously, demanding order, but no one seemed to be listening. The four bailiffs who had accompanied the procession stood uncertainly alongside the pile of wood.

Up on the scaffold stood Hans, staring down open-mouthed at the spectacle below. Now the first of the fine citizens of Schongau attacked the executioner with rocks and knives in their hands, and the crowd closed in around Johannes Kuisl like a huge, dark wave. Someone let out a scream, and for a moment Jakob thought he saw, amid all the arms and legs, a dismembered ear lying on the ground. Red blood flowed like sealing wax across the dirty white snow. Then Jakob caught sight of his father's crushed face, one dying eye peering toward him, as more rocks rained down on him.

With a pounding heart, Jakob turned to his younger brother, who was staring disbelievingly at the swirling mob. "We've got to get out of here!" he shouted over the noise. "Quick, quick, or we'll be next!"

"But . . . but . . . Father . . ." Bartholomäus stammered. "We . . . we've got to help him . . ."

"Jesus Christ, Bartl, wake up! Father is dead, do you understand? We have to save ourselves. Come!"

Jakob pulled his horrified brother away from the execution pile, when suddenly they heard a shrill voice behind them.

"There are his brats, running away! Stop them! Stop them!"

Jakob cast a quick glance behind him and saw the crowd of

young hooligans storming toward them down the icy street. In the front of the pack was the baker's son, Michael Berchtholdt, whom Jakob had given a good thrashing just a few weeks ago. Now the skinny weakling finally saw a chance to get his revenge.

"Stop them! Stop them!" he screamed as he picked up a piece of wood from underneath the scaffold and sent it sailing through the air. There was no doubt in Jakob's mind that Michael would beat his head in with it if he were able. This was his chance, and after such an incident no one would ask any inconvenient questions. In any case, the life of a hangman's son wasn't worth very much.

As Bartholomäus just stood there gaping, Jakob gave him a shove that caused him to yelp and stumble forward. Now, finally his younger brother seemed also to comprehend the seriousness of the situation. They ran toward the open city gate, pursued by the howling mob.

Jakob turned off into the narrow lane by the city wall and moments later realized he'd made a big mistake. Their pursuers had split, and some of them had already arrived at the gate up ahead, blocking it. Grinning and swinging sticks in the air, they approached their victims.

"We already got your father," Michael Berchtholdt shouted at his archenemy, "and now it's your turn, Jakob. You and your brother."

"First you've got to catch us," Jakob answered, panting for air.

Out of the corner of his eye he noticed a wagon loaded with barrels standing in front of one of the houses. On a sudden impulse, he grabbed his brother by the hand, climbed on top of the barrels, and pulled himself up onto the low roof. Bartholomäus followed, gasping, and soon they both were standing atop the snow-covered ridge of the roof with a view over the entire town all the way to the execution site. Jakob realized they weren't safe yet. Howls, catcalls, and the sound of running feet let them know the others were hot on their trail. At that moment, Michael Berchtholdt's grinning face appeared above the gutter of the roof.

"And now, you Kuisls?" he snarled. "Where do you think you're going? Maybe fly away like the birds? Or will Bartl, this idiot, send for an eagle to carry you off?"

Jakob looked around desperately. Of all things, they'd picked the house farther from the other buildings than any other on the block. Jakob guessed it was at least three paces, or nine feet, to the next house. He himself had a big, athletic build, and he could make it. But how about his younger brother? Bartholomäus was heavier than he was, and besides, he looked worn out. Just the same, they had to at least try.

Without warning Bartholomäus, Jakob prepared to jump. Vaguely he caught a glimpse of the small lane beneath him, covered with snow and garbage, then he felt solid ground again. He'd made it to the next roof.

Relieved, he looked around at his brother, still standing hesitantly on the ridge of the roof. Just as Bartholomäus was about to leap, Michael Berchtholdt appeared alongside him like a ghost and dragged him back down the icy roof. Other boys followed and started beating Bartholomäus, who screamed desperately for his older brother.

"Jakob, Jakob! Help me! They're killing me!"

Jakob saw the wide eyes of his brother staring back at him. He heard the blows raining down on Bartholomäus — six or maybe seven boys had jumped him. That would be too many, even for Jakob, who with his strength could perhaps have taken on three of them. But even if he jumped into the fray, there had to be someone to warn Mother and little Lisl before even worse things happened. Suppose the unruly mob attacked their house down in the Tanners' Quarter while he was fighting with the street urchins here? Perhaps they'd already set their house on fire. He couldn't waste any time.

But there was something else Jakob was very reluctant to admit, even to himself, something that spun a fine, sticky web around him.

The zeal Bartholomäus had shown the day before while piling the wood around the stake, his constant praise for their choleric father, his cool, dispassionate curiosity concerning the torture of the old shepherd—all of that had increased the contempt Jakob felt for his brother. It was an almost palpable disgust that sometimes caused him to gag, and now, too, it left a bad taste in his mouth.

At this moment it became painfully clear to Jakob that Bartholomäus was just like his father and the whole god-damned family of executioners. Jakob himself had never been one of them, and he wouldn't be in the future, either, no matter how much he'd always longed for his father's acceptance.

Without being aware of it, Jakob had made up his mind.

"Jakob, help me!" Bartholomäus wailed, as the blows continued raining down on him. "Please don't let me die."

For one last time, Jakob stared into his brother's wide, terrified eyes. Then he turned away without saying a word and ran across the roofs of Schongau toward the eastern city wall, where the Tanners' Quarter was located.

Behind him he heard one last high-pitched scream, like that of a dying animal.

He ran faster, until he could no longer hear his brother's cries.

I

Damn! if those people up front don't start moving their asses, I'll grab them by the scruff of the neck and whip them all the way to Bamberg myself."

With a strong curse on his lips, Jakob Kuisl rose from his seat in the oxcart and stared ahead angrily. An entire caravan of all kinds of carts and wagons blocked the narrow pass through the hills and, after a number of sharp turns, ended in a riverbed. The rain was pouring down, and the trees in the dark forest of firs all around were just barely visible. Water dripped from the low-lying branches, and the constant drumbeat of the rain mixed with the many other sounds down at the ford in the river. Pigs squealed, men shouted and cursed, and somewhere a horse whinnied. The muffled roar of the river and the rain drove out most other sounds.

Magdalena frowned as she looked at her father, who was spewing his anger like a volcano. More than six feet tall, he stood out above the carts like a church steeple above a nave.

"Damn it all to hell. I —"

"Can't you see there's something wrong up in front at the ford in the river?" interrupted Magdalena, who was sitting between sacks of grain. She yawned and stretched her back, which ached after having to sit so long. The cold rain had drenched her woolen shawl and she felt a chill. "Do you think we're sitting here in this mess just for fun?"

The Schongau executioner cleared his throat and spat with disgust into the swampy ground on either side of the wagon. "These damn Franks are capable of anything," he growled, now somewhat more calmly. "I keep wondering what hole in the ground all these people came from. There's more turmoil in this god-damned forest than at a proper execution. Where are we, anyway? Didn't they say we'd get to Bamberg before sundown?"

"Well, this ford is the only place you can get across the river in such weather. And, as you see, we're certainly not the only ones," said Magdalena.

Peeved, she turned around. The traffic both in front of and behind them was the worst she'd ever seen in their region, the quiet "Pope's Corner" in the Alps. It had been three weeks since she and her family left Schongau to pay a visit to her uncle Bartholomäus in Bamberg. Since their stop the day before in Forchheim in Franconia, the muddy road had been getting busier and busier. Wandering journeymen traveled from town to town; stooped peddlers struggled under the weight of backpacks full of rudely carved wooden spoons, grinding stones, and cheap knickknacks; while other riders on horseback dressed in fancy clothing hurried by silently in the rain. Most of the vehicles making their way through the forest along the crowded road were simple, canvas-covered two-wheeled carts without springs.

"Hey, what's wrong there up front?" the Schongau executioner called out again, cupping his huge hands to form a mouthpiece. "Are you idiots sleeping up there?"

Now the wagon drivers in front and behind them began to grumble, too, and here and there someone cursed loudly. Magdalena noticed the worried, even anxious glances on the faces of some of the men looking into the forest, which despite the early afternoon hour was beginning to look threatening—as if behind the first few rows of trees night was already falling. Instinctively, a shiver passed up Magdalena's spine.

Probably a wagon got stuck in the mud in the river, that's all. Or a few calves were spooked and didn't want to go on, she thought, trying to comfort herself as she tugged on her father's dirty linen shirt. *So I'd better sit down before I start an argument with someone.*

"It can't be that hard to cross such a narrow part of the river," Jakob said, shaking his head. "These Franks are simply too stupid, that's all there is to it. These stupid drunks would probably get stuck even in a dry riverbed."

The hangman grumbled a little while longer, then finally sat down again and started puffing morosely on the long, cold stem of his pipe. Jakob had used up all his tobacco just as they were leaving Nuremberg, which didn't do anything to improve his mood. The other members of the Kuisl clan were huddled together between the sacks of grain. Magdalena's younger sister, fifteen-year-old Barbara, stared blankly into the steady downpour. Magdalena's boys, Peter and Paul, were scuffling farther back in the wagon, in danger of falling backward into the swamp at any moment. As so often, the younger boy, Paul, had the upper hand and was holding his five-year-old brother in a headlock, and Peter was gasping for air.

"Damn, can't you just once stop fighting?" scolded Simon, who was sitting up front on the coachbox alongside the wagon's owner, a humpbacked old farmer. The long wait had clearly gotten on the nerves of Magdalena's husband as well. Until then, the Schongau medicus had been trying to read a book on medicine for midwives. Though the volume was bound in leather and wrapped in an oilcloth, rain kept dripping onto the pages. Now he put aside the tattered, drenched book and cast a severe glance at his two sons.

"You've been fooling around like that for hours. If you don't stop right away, I'll tell your grandfather and he'll stretch your ears out on the rack. You know he can do that."

"I could also put you both in a shrew's fiddle," Jakob chimed in, ominously. "Then you'll probably scratch each other's eyes out, and we'll finally have some peace and quiet."

"Just stop this nonsense, you hooligans." Magdalena snapped at her husband and father. She pointed at the two boys, who now actually stopped fighting. "Just see the look in their eyes. I think you really scared them."

The children stared at their grandfather for a moment, baffled, then just shouted at one another and went right on brawling. A moment later, Paul, the smaller one, triumphantly held up a handful of his brother's hair. His older, far gentler brother, Peter, almost a head taller than his younger brother, started crying and sought protection behind his father.

"Maybe we should try the shrew's fiddle, after all?" Simon asked hopefully.

Magdalena glared at her husband. "Perhaps for a change you should stop reading so much and pay more attention to your sons. It's no wonder they are always fighting. They're boys, have you forgotten? They're not made for sitting calmly on a wagon."

"Let's just be happy we found someone to take us part of the way," Simon replied. "I myself don't especially want to go to Bamberg on foot. We surely have more than five miles to go, and we don't have enough money to pay for a trip on the Regnitz River."

He stretched and sighed, then grabbed the two boys by the scruff of their necks and climbed down from the wagon with them.

"But, as almost always, you are right," Simon mumbled. "This long wait can drive you crazy." He nodded toward the dark forest on the other side of the narrow pass, where the branches and boughs of the pine trees formed a dense barrier. "I'll take these two little devils for a walk over to the edge of the forest, where they can climb and run around a little. It looks like you'll have to wait here a bit longer."

He gave the two boys a friendly slap, and they started whooping and running up the steep side of the pass. In no time the three had disappeared in the forest, while Magdalena remained behind with her father and bored-looking younger sister.

"Simon is much too easy with the boys," Jakob grumbled. "The little brats deserve a good spanking now and then. When I was a kid, children weren't allowed to misbehave like that."

"How can you say that when you're always giving them candy and putting them up to all kinds of mischief?" Magdalena laughed and shook her head. "You're the biggest kid of all three of you. I'm really anxious to hear what your brother is going to tell us about you and what a rascal you were as a child."

"Ha! What is there to tell? The blood, filth, and death, and all those beatings from my father, the old drunk. That's about all I remember. One minute you're pooping in your pants and sucking your thumb, and the next minute you get chewed up by the war."

The Schongau hangman stared into space, and Magdalena's smile froze. As so often happened when she asked her father about his past, he became even more silent than usual. He hardly ever spoke about his brother, Bartholomäus, who was two years younger than him, and it was only a few years ago that Magdalena had even learned she had an uncle who made his living as the executioner of Bamberg. The letter the Kuisl family had received more than two months ago consisted of just a few prosaic words and had come as a surprise to all of them. Bartholomäus's wife had died some time ago, and now he was thinking about marrying again, and to celebrate this upcoming event he had invited all his relatives in Schongau.

The only reason the Kuisls considered taking such a journey of almost two hundred miles was that Magdalena's younger brother, Georg, had been apprenticed to his uncle in Bamberg over two years ago, and since then, neither Magdalena nor the rest of the family had seen him. This was particularly troubling to Jakob, even though he never came out and said so, and it was the main reason he decided to go.

Out of the corner of her eye, Magdalena looked at her father, who was now in the autumn of his life, as he sat there drawing on his cold pipe. With his wet, gray hair, bloodshot eyes, hooked nose, and scraggly beard, he exuded an aloofness that had grown even stronger in recent years. This did nothing to harm his reputation as the executioner of Schongau. On the contrary, now more than ever Jakob Kuisl was regarded as a perfect hangman: strong, quick, experienced, and blessed with an understanding that was as sharp as the blade of his executioner's sword.

And yet, he's gotten old, Magdalena thought to herself, *old and careworn, especially since the death of his wife. And he misses Georg as well, as I do. They're alike in so many ways.*

"Damn, if those people up there in front don't get their carts moving soon, there will be another accident," said Jakob.

The wagon began to rock again when the hangman jumped down from the sacks of grain. The rat-faced old farmer who had been sitting patiently on the coachbox until then cast an anxious, side-long glance at the huge, angry giant. He mouthed a silent Ave Maria, then turned to Magdalena.

"Good God, tell your father please to sit down," he whispered. "If he keeps raving like that, he'll scare the oxen," he said with a disparaging wave of his hand. "Maybe it would be better for you to continue to Bamberg on foot, as it's not very far now."

"Don't worry, he'll calm down. I know him. Basically, he's a kindly, peaceful man." Magdalena lowered her voice and continued in a conspiratorial manner. "In any case, until he runs out of tobacco. Is it possible you have a few leaves of it?"

The farmer frowned. "Do I look like someone who'd inhale that devilish smoke? The church has condemned it, and for good reason. The stuff comes straight from hell, at least it stinks like it does." He crossed himself and scrutinized the Schongau executioner suspiciously.

With a sigh, Magdalena leaned back and bit her lip. In Forchheim, where she'd given the old man a few kreuzers to take them along, she'd wisely mentioned nothing of her father's trade and had remained silent in other respects, as well. As the daughter of a hangman, she knew that if the pious old man had ever learned he was carrying a real, living executioner and his family, he'd probably run for the nearest church and say a thousand rosaries.

The trip had taken the Kuisls on a large river ferry first down the Lech to Augsburg and then on a smaller river to Nuremberg. Because they ran out of money there, they continued the journey on foot. By now they were only a few miles from Bamberg, and for this reason the delay was even more annoying.

"Shouldn't we first check to see why the wagon train has stopped?" said Barbara from atop one of the sacks of grain farther back. With a bored expression, the fifteen-year-old girl dangled her legs over the side of the wagon. "That would be better than sitting around here listening to Father cursing." She made a face as she played with her hair, which was just as black as Magdalena's. In general, she bore a striking resemblance to her older sister. Barbara had the same bushy eyebrows and dark eyes, which seemed to gaze out sardonically at the world around her. She had inherited both from her mother, Anna-Maria, who had died two years ago of the Plague.

Magdalena nodded. "You're right. Why don't we walk on ahead and see what's happening down at the ford? Let the grumpy old guy sit here and grumble to himself," she replied, winking at her father. "Perhaps we can even find a little tobacco for you."

But Jakob had closed his eyes and seemed to be listening to another, inner melody. His lips formed sounds that Magdalena couldn't understand.

But she suspected that it was, as so often in the past, some long-forgotten war song.

Soon after Simon and his two sons had disappeared into the dense pine forest on the other side of the pass, the shouts of the wagon drivers had become faint and muffled. The ground was strewn with damp, musty needles that swallowed up even the slightest noise. Somewhere nearby, a jay called out, but otherwise a silence prevailed that seemed almost surreal after the noisy wagon train. Even the sound of the rain in the dense forest of firs seemed strangely distant. The boys, too, seemed to notice the almost solemn atmosphere. They had stopped quarreling and held their father's hand tightly.

Simon smiled. As so often, there were times when he wanted to beat the daylights out of the two little pests, but now his heart was overwhelmed by an ocean of love.

"Tonight you'll finally see your Uncle Georg again," he said cheerfully. "The one who always whittled swords for you from oak wood. Do you remember? Perhaps he'll whittle some for you this time, as well."

"Yes! Yes! An executioner's sword," little Paul cried. "I want an executioner's sword so I can cut the chickens' heads off, just like I did in the Stechlin garden. May I, Father, please?"

"Don't you dare!" Simon looked crossly at Paul. He couldn't help thinking of the horrible bloodbath that Paul had inflicted a few months ago on the chickens belonging to Martha Stechlin, the Schongau midwife. What disturbed him more than anything else was the grin on the face of the child who had obviously had a grand time slaughtering the animals, celebrating his first execution like a church mass.

"Is Uncle Georg now a hangman, too?" asked Peter, who was calmer and more thoughtful than his younger brother. Sometimes he seemed far older than his five years. Simon assumed that was due mainly to his tousled black hair and the serious, always attentive gaze whenever he spoke.

Simon nodded, happy for the diversion. "You're right, Peter. Georg is apprenticed to your great-uncle in Bamberg, and when Grandfather gets too old, he will no doubt become the new Schongau executioner."

"And then I'm next, am I?" Paul asked excitedly. "I'll be an executioner someday, too."

"Uh . . . perhaps," Simon replied hesitantly.

Suddenly Peter clutched his father's hand tightly and stopped. "I don't want to be a hangman. Everybody's afraid of Grandfather, and I don't want that. They say he's in league with the devil and brings misfortune." Stubbornly, he stamped the ground with his foot. "I want to run a bathhouse, like you, Father, and be someone who helps people."

He squeezed his father's hand, and without realizing it, Simon returned the gesture. In fact, Peter was already observing his grandfather in executions and could recite the first words in Latin. Unlike his brother Paul, he was fond of poring through the colorful engravings in the Kuisl's family library. He could sit there for hours, passing his little fingers back and forth over the drawings.

He's like me, Simon thought. *But they'll never allow him to become a doctor, not as the son of a hangman's daughter, not in times like these.*

"I smell death, Father. Up there is death."

Paul's thin, bright voice interrupted his daydreams. As usual, when Paul said something horrible, it sounded strangely detached.

"Do you smell death, too?"

"What do you mean by . . . ." Simon started to say, but Paul had already let go of his hand and raced off deeper into the forest.

"Hey, damn it, stop!" Simon called after him. But Paul had disappeared among the trees and paid no attention to him. The medicus cursed, put his older son on his shoulder, and ran with him through the damp undergrowth, stumbling and almost falling several times. Branches struck him in the face, tearing at his leggings.

After a while, Simon heard the gurgling sound of flowing water. The pine trees thinned, and he found himself in a low marshland with occasional birch trees and a dark channel of water running through it, Paul stood alongside the channel pointing proudly at a huge, swollen carcass partially submerged in the water.

"Here, here!" he shouted excitedly. "I found it!"

When Simon got closer, he saw it was the cadaver of a large stag. Its throat had been cut so deeply that the head, with its huge, sixteen-point antlers, hung down into the water and was oscillating back and forth in the current. It's belly had been slit open, as well, and deep, bloody gashes could be seen beneath the wet fur, such as those that might be inflicted by a sickle or a rake.

"What in God's name . . . ?"

Simon set Peter down carefully and walked slowly toward the cadaver. The sweet odor of decay lay in the air. Simon assumed the stag had been dead just a few days, but the worms, beetles, and insects had already begun their work. Paul pulled so hard on the antlers that it appeared the head might separate entirely from the body.

"Just stop that," Simon snapped at him. "We don't know if the animal was sick. Maybe he's giving off poisonous fumes and you could be infected." But even as he said that, he felt foolish. Certainly the stag hadn't died of an illness; it had been ripped apart. The only question was what animal would be able to inflict such a deadly wound on him?

A pack of wolves? A bear?

Simon looked around, trying to think. The silence that just a few moments earlier had seemed so pleasant, now suddenly took on an ominous tone. Even if it had been a huge predator, it was strange that it hadn't devoured its prey at once, or at least dragged it off to hide it somewhere nearby.

Perhaps because it's still around here somewhere?

There was a sound of a snapping branch, as if something large had stepped on it, and suddenly the trees around the clearing seemed to have moved a bit closer. Simon had an uneasy feeling that he couldn't explain: it was as if the forest around them had stopped to hold its breath.

"Peter, Paul," he said, "we've got to go back now. Mama is no doubt worried about us. Come."

"But the antlers," Paul whimpered, tugging again at the decaying carcass. "I want to take the antlers back with us."

"Forget that." The father seized the two boys by the hand and pulled them away from the brook. A trail of blood, slender as a thread, curled through the water. Suddenly the father was overcome by a wave of fear, like a raging storm bearing down on them with thunder and lightning.

Up there is death . . . It smells sweet, like a decaying plum.

"I said we're leaving." Simon forced a smile. "If you behave, I'll tell you what kind of sweets you'll find at the markets in Bamberg. And who knows, maybe Uncle Georg will buy you a few candied apples tomorrow. So let's go."

Grumbling, Paul backed off and followed his father, leaving the rotted cadaver behind. The three of them stomped through the wet marshland, and soon the gurgling of the brook was barely audible from a distance.

A couple of times Simon thought he heard steps behind him like those of a large animal, but every time he turned around, there was nothing there but the dense wall of pines and the rain dripping from their branches. When they finally got back to the pass among the wagons and noisy peasants, his fear was nothing but a slightly queasy memory.

And the stench of putrefaction that clung to his clothing.

Full of curiosity, Magdalena and Barbara walked along the pass down to the ford in the river, with the wagons forming a long line on either side. Mud and feces spattered their clothing, and several times they had to dodge grunting pigs or anxiously bellowing cattle. There seemed to be no end to the long line of wagons.

"I wonder how all of this will manage to squeeze inside the walls of Bamberg," Barbara sighed.

"Don't forget that this is not Schongau," Magdalena reminded her sister. "You should have been with me and Simon in Regensburg, where even the little streets are as wide as the market square at home." She frowned. "But you're right. If things don't get moving soon, we'll never reach Bamberg before dark and the farmers will have to spend the night outside the walls. Tomorrow is butchering and market day, and everyone wants to get there first. It's no wonder people are angry and impatient."

The two sisters hurried past grumbling old women with huge piles of cabbages, apples, and pears, as well as young men staring straight ahead waiting to drive horses forward, and noisy farm owners hauling cartloads of grain to the town market. More than once a little lost goat or calf scurried by.

Finally they reached the ford, where the water, riled up by the rain and the many people passing through, was brown and muddy. A large group of wagon drivers and farmers had gathered there, standing in a half-circle and staring down at something lying on the ground in front of them. Curious, Magdalena and Barbara pushed their way forward until they reached the shore.

Magdalena held her breath in astonishment.

"For heaven's sake," she finally gasped. "What in the world happened here?"

Lying in the water in front of them in the mud was a severed human arm with shreds of what must have once been a white shirt. A few of the fingertips showed little bite marks, presumably from fish, and some strands of torn muscles hung from the forearm. Magdalena assumed that it had been lying in the water for a few days, but certainly no longer than two weeks.

"And I'm telling you again, it was this beast," one of the wagon drivers in the group was heard to say. "This arm is a warning. It eats anyone trying to cross the river."

"A-a beast?" Barbara asked, wide-eyed. "What kind of beast?" She clearly had difficulty diverting her eyes from the grisly discovery.

"You haven't heard of it?" Another wagon driver, with a slouch hat and torn jacket, spat in the muddy water alongside the two young women. "They say a monster is loose here in the Bamberg Forest and has already killed a large number of people. We can count ourselves lucky if we manage to get to town unscathed."

The first wagon driver, a tall, broad-built man of about fifty, resignedly shook his head. "In the city you're not safe, either," he growled. "My brother-in-law lives in Bamberg. He saw with his own eyes how the bailiffs fished an arm and a foot from the Regnitz, next to the Great Bridge. And now this. By all the saints, God protect us and our children!" He crossed himself, and an old woman next to him hastily began to pray her rosary.

"Ah, that is surely very bad," Magdalena began cautiously, "but all the more reason we should move on before it gets dark." She looked over at the treetops, which were already in the shadows. Her thoughts turned to Simon and their two sons, who were undoubtedly still back in the forest. "So what are we waiting for?"

The tall wagon driver looked at her and explained slowly, as if speaking to a small child. "Don't you understand? We cannot cross the ford." He trembled as he pointed at the severed arm. "Can't you see the hand is pointing in our direction, as if trying to warn us? Anyone crossing the river here is marked for death."

"Near Munich there was once a hand alongside the bridge," he said, pointing with his slouched hat and rubbing his unshaved chin pensively. "It was attached with a lead coffin nail to the railing, and a few men made fun of it. They tore the hand off, threw it in the river, then started across the bridge. The bridge collapsed, the river carried the men away, and they were never seen again."

"But . . . but we can't all stand here just because of an arm," Magdalena said, shaking her head. "The wagons are backed up behind us." Nevertheless, she, too, began to tremble when she looked down again at the severed arm that had already begun to decay lying in the mud. What in God's name had happened to the man?

"We are all lost," murmured the old woman standing alongside Magdalena and Barbara. "This is the only place for miles around where you can cross the river. If we have to spend the night here, then God help us. The beast will come to fetch us all." She crossed herself again and looked across to the forest, which meanwhile had grown somewhat darker. The pouring rain showed no sign of stopping.

"Maybe you should go and look for Simon and the children," Barbara whispered to her older sister. "If there really is something on the prowl around here, it's certainly better to stay near the wagon."

Magdalena nodded. "You're right. In just a minute, I'm going to—"

Just then they heard familiar voices behind them, and when Magdalena turned around, she saw to her great relief Simon and the two boys making their way through the crowd. The short medicus looked pale, and there was a slight quiver on his lips.

"Your father said you were down below at the river crossing," he said, pointing behind him as the huge figure of Jakob Kuisl approached. "He's cursing like the driver of a beer wagon because nothing is moving."

"Well, at least we now know the cause for the delay," Magdalena replied. She pointed at the arm on the ground. "People take it for a sign they are not supposed to cross the river, and . . ." She was going to tell Simon the rest, but at that moment her father arrived. Jakob Kuisl paid no heed to those standing around but glanced down and frowned at the severed arm. Then he bent over to have a better look.

"Don't touch it," snarled the wagon driver with the slouch hat. "It will bring misfortune to us all."

"Just because I touch a moldy arm?" Kuisl still had his cold pipe in his mouth, so his words were hard to understand. "If that's the case, then bad luck would follow me like it did Job." Carefully, he picked up the arm and examined it.

"My God, what's he doing?" gasped the second, heavily built wagon driver. "It looks like he is going to smell it."

"Ah, not exactly," Magdalena replied. "It's just that—"

Kuisl interrupted, finally taking the pipe out of his mouth. "This arm belonged to a man who was old and feeble, around sixty, I would say, or perhaps seventy. He was an aristocratic gentleman, or in any case he signed and sealed a large number of documents. Hmm . . ." He held the arm right up to his face, as if about to take a bite out of it. "Yes, no doubt a nobleman whose wife died some time ago and was looking around for a younger partner. He was probably on a trip in search of a woman. But why? He didn't have long to live in any case. He'd been suffering badly from gout, and he had at most one or two years to live." Kuisl nodded, trying to think what it all meant. "By God, this arm can serve as a warning to us not to eat too much fatty meat. Nothing more and nothing less. So now, it has served its purpose."

The hangman threw the arm in a wide arc into the swirling, foaming river, where it quickly sank. The crowd let out a collective shout, as if Kuisl had murdered one of them.

"What . . . what did you do?" sputtered the man with the slouch hat. "The sign . . ."

"What sign? It was just an arm, nothing more. Now let's move before I get really nasty in this awful weather."

As the men along the river stared at him dumbfounded, Kuisl, without saying another word, started back to his place in line again behind the wagons.

"For God's sake, who was that?" one of the wagon drivers finally asked. "A magician? A demon? How can he know exactly who the arm belonged to?"

"Let's just say he's seen a number of severed body parts," Magdalena replied as she turned around. "In this respect, he has . . . uh . . . some experience. So you can believe him." Then she hurried back with Barbara and the other Kuisls to join her father.

They quickly caught up with him as he walked back along the muddy path through the pass, grimly and in haste. Simon now turned to his father-in-law with an inquisitive expression.

"My compliments; that was very impressive," he said, as both he and Magdalena struggled to keep up with Jakob. "How did you know so much about this arm?"

"Good God, because the Lord gave me eyes to see," Kuisl grumbled. "That's all there is to it. You don't need any witchcraft for that, so you can spare yourself all that hooey."

"Come on, just tell us," Magdalena begged him. She knew how much her father loved stringing people along, and she, too, was curious. "Just tell us before Simon starts brooding over it so much he can't sleep."

Kuisl grinned. "I guess I owe him that." As the others walked ahead, he explained.

"The skin was wrinkled like that of an old man, but there

were no calluses on his hands — on the contrary, they were soft as a baby's bottom. In addition, there were spots of ink on the remaining fingertips that had eaten their way deep into the body. Ah, yes, and on one of the very well manicured fingernails there was still a tiny speck of sealing wax. As I said, I have eyes. That's all you need."

"But all that stuff you said about looking for a bride and about gout," Simon persisted, " — what's that all about?"

"Oh, for God's sake, what are you? A bathhouse owner or a quack doctor? Didn't you notice the gnarled joints and the white spots? If you can read books, why can't you read people?" Jakob Kuisl spat on the ground, disgusted. "The joints were so enlarged that I almost didn't see the pale, whitish circle on the ring finger. The man had worn his wedding ring a long time, probably several decades, but had taken it off recently. That's something a man does only when he's out looking for someone else. He was traveling, and probably looking for another woman. But . . ."

Kuisl stopped to think as the wagons in front of them slowly started moving again. Their own wagon, steered by the old peasant, also approached, rattling and squeaking.

"What did you learn?" Magdalena asked. "Is there perhaps something you've kept from us and the others up to now?"

Jakob Kuisl shrugged. "Well, actually there is something that puzzles me. You could assume the man had been murdered, that his murderers left him in the forest, where wild animals finally found him and ripped him apart; and that he came to rest with his arm in the water and was washed ashore today by the rain."

"But that's not what happened," Simon said softly. "Right?"

"No, that isn't what happened. I took a close look at the joint, and there are no bite marks. The arm was severed cleanly. It was no animal; only a person makes a clean cut like that. This poor devil was slaughtered like a piece of meat, but why and by whom? I have no explanation for that."

The hangman shook the rain out of his hair and pulled himself back up onto the coachbox, where the farmer, who had heard the last part of what he said, stared at him and trembled like he was looking at a nightmare incarnate.

They arrived in Bamberg shortly before dusk, approaching the Langgasser Gate. In the last few hours they'd heard wolves howling several times, though very far away in the forests. Nevertheless, the sounds had been enough to make Barbara, in particular, turn white, after the events at the river. Was that perhaps the beast the people were talking about?

At least the rain had finally stopped, though the road was still as muddy and full of puddles as before, so the progress of the wagons had been very slow. The whole area surrounding the city was swampy and full of small rivers, brooks, and canals, especially in the southern part, which was an almost impenetrable wilderness. In the east there were fields and farmland, although now, at the end of October, they were barren and fallow.

Magdalena turned up her nose in disgust, as the odor with which the city received them was so pungent it made them gag. Along the right-hand side of the street was a wide ditch that had dried up just before reaching the gate, forming a thick, foul-smelling morass. Rotten fruit and the cadavers of small animals floated in the puddles. A wide, rotted walkway led across the swamp toward the city wall, where now, shortly before it was time to close the gates, the wagons were backing up. Surely a good number of people in the wagons would have to spend the night in the fallow fields outside of town, a prospect that caused Magdalena to shudder after hearing the gloomy accounts of the wagon drivers concerning their strange finding down at the river. What in God's name was lurking in the forests around Bamberg?

Hastily the Kuisls bade farewell to the old farmer, who was visibly relieved to finally be rid of them, then made their way toward the narrow pedestrian gate next to the vehicle entrance, arriving none too soon. Some time had passed since the bells in the clock towers had signaled the end of the day for the Bambergers, many of whom had been working their little vegetable patches outside of town. The night watchman with his key to the city was standing alongside the gate, beckoning to the last of them to hurry. He looked concerned, almost anxious. He asked the Kuisls briefly why they were there, then quickly closed the door behind them.

"Get moving," he shouted at Barbara, who was at the end of the procession of wagons, giving her a shove. At the same time he pointed at the sun, which had just set behind the western part of the city wall. "Soon it will be as dark here as in hell." He shivered and rubbed his hands together. "Damn autumn nights—the daylight fades faster than you can say 'amen.'"

"If it makes you shiver so much you have to shit in your pants, perhaps you should have become a baker and not a watchman," Kuisl replied with a grin as he passed under the archway that was much too low for him. "Then you'd already be in bed with your wife kneading her fat behind."

"If I were you, I wouldn't shoot off my mouth like that, big fellow. What do you know about this damned city?" The watchman seemed to want to say something else, but then just shrugged and shuffled up the steep stairway to his room in the guardhouse to begin his regular nightly duties.

Magdalena peered ahead at the dark forms where the first houses began. The last time she'd been in a large city was some years ago in Regensburg. At that time, the sun had been shining, it was midsummer, and the size and splendor of the buildings had nearly taken her breath away. On the other hand, there was something depressing about their arrival in Bamberg. That might have been because of the time of year, as now that it was autumn the nights had suddenly turned cool and mist was rising from the moors and settling like a heavy blanket over the roofs of the town, first in little wisps, then in larger and larger clouds. The wide road leading up to the gate quickly branched into a labyrinth of unpaved, winding alleys once they entered the town.

With dark fingers, dusk reached out toward the crooked half-timbered houses, so that Magdalena could only imagine the size of the city. It was said that Bamberg, like Rome, was built on seven hills, and in fact Magdalena could see three dark hills in the west of the city, with the cathedral, the landmark of the city, standing majestically on the one in the middle. Atop the hill on the left the outlines of a large monastery was visible in the fading light of day, and, engulfed in mist, the ruins of a castle. In front of her, Magdalena could hear the rushing of water in a canal or river. At least the stench here was not as overwhelming as by the city gate.

The many carts and wagons that had just a short while ago been backed up behind the city gate were now clattering toward their destinations and finally disappeared in the growing darkness. While Magdalena wandered through the filthy, stinking alleys with her family, she heard occasional laughter, hasty footsteps, or squeaky wagon wheels down some of the alleys, but otherwise everything was quiet. The hangman's daughter was familiar with such quiet nights in Schongau, but for some reason she had imagined Bamberg to be somewhat livelier and happier. The loneliness in the dark lanes had something oppressive about them, something sinister.

Like in a cemetery, she thought, tying her scarf more tightly. *I wonder if the others feel the same way?*

She looked around at Simon and the other members of her family, who were following her sullenly. Peter and Paul in particular were dead tired and whined softly as they gripped their father's hands. Jakob Kuisl stomped ahead of them silently.

"Do we still have far to go?" Magdalena asked after a while in a tired voice. "The children are hungry, and my feet hurt. In any case, I don't like walking for hours through a strange city after nightfall. All sorts of riffraff are wandering about."

The hangman just shrugged. "Executioners don't live in the central market square, and since my last visit a lot has changed." He looked around. "Damned fog. Actually we should just head north here, and follow the city wall."

"The wall is behind us," Simon interrupted, pointing back over his shoulder into the darkness. "I just saw it a moment ago by the little square with the fountain . . ."

"Aha, Herr Son-in-Law will now tell me perhaps where I can find my own brother?"

"Herr Son-in-Law is just trying to help you, that's all," Magdalena interrupted. "But now, as so often, you know better." She sighed. "Why do you men have to be so stubborn when you've made a mistake?"

"I didn't make a mistake—it's just dark and foggy," Kuisl grumbled as he hurried along. "You could have stayed at home. I'm just doing this so I can see Georg again, and certainly not because of my brother, the old stinker. I wondered why he's inviting us to his wedding." He spat in the dirt. "When I think about how the Steingaden executioner is taking over my work in Schongau in the meantime, it makes me sick. It will be a real mess."

As Magdalena walked along behind her father, her vague feeling of anxiety grew. In the narrow, unlit lanes it was already so dark and foggy she could hardly see to the next intersection. Occasionally she heard a whooshing, scraping sound as if someone or something was following her through the little alleys. She turned around to look at the others and could see that Simon and Barbara were also looking around anxiously. She couldn't help but think of the ashen-faced watchman at the tower and his final words.

What do you know about this damned city?

Did the watchman have something to hide? Something that had to do with this beast that the wagon drivers had told them about? The severed arm had belonged to a wealthy citizen. Perhaps a nobleman from Bamberg?

When Magdalena looked once more into the darkness, she suddenly understood where her strange feeling was coming from. It was so obvious, yet she'd not really noticed it until now.

The houses, she suddenly realized. *Many of them are empty.*

And, in fact, the windows on many of the buildings they passed were boarded up. Others were missing a door, or there were black holes where there were once bull's-eye windowpanes. Frowning, Magdalena examined the buildings more closely. The abandoned houses were clearly not the shabby houses of the poor, but of those who'd once been patricians and wealthy citizens. Some of the houses were now nothing but ruins, though some had been rebuilt or renovated. Magdalena remembered all the cranes, pulleys, and sacks of mortar they had passed on their way through the little streets. Simon, too, now seemed to take note of the empty buildings.

"What's going on with all these houses here?" he asked, addressing his father-in-law. "Why are so many of them unoccupied?"

"Well, the Great War was fought here in Bamberg, as well," Jakob replied, stopping at the next fork, trying to get his bearings. "And it was pretty bad. The city was attacked by soldiers more than a dozen times. That may have been twenty years ago, but many Bambergers fled then and didn't return. Some years ago when I was here, things looked even worse. It takes a while for a city to recover from something like that. Some never do, and all that remains of them are a few abandoned ruins with the wind whistling through them."

"But Schongau quickly got over it," Magdalena replied. "Besides, it's mostly the homes of the patricians that are empty."

"I don't care what happened here long ago," wailed Barbara, who was shuffling along slowly at the end of the line. "I'm just tired. Hopefully, Uncle Bartholomäus's house is not a ruin, too. I should have stayed home, where the town fair is going on now, with dancing and—"

"I fear the houses were abandoned for another reason," interrupted her father, who was paying no attention to the younger daughter's whining. "A reason even more dreadful than the war, if such a thing is even possible. I even heard about it far away in Schongau. A grim story."

Magdalena looked at him, puzzled. "And what was that?"

"I think Bartholomäus should tell you about it. I suspect he knows more about it than he wants to." The hangman started walking faster. "Now hurry up and come along before your sister's whining gets the guard's attention."

Silently, he plodded on through the fog, while somewhere beyond the city walls the wolves continued their howling.

Adelheid Rinswieser paused for a moment and listened. The howling of the wolves got louder, like cries of children, long and shrill. The silver disk of an almost full moon was just rising over the pine trees.

The howls of the animals were still far off, deep in the forest. Nevertheless, Adelheid's heart beat faster as she crept through the dense forest of pines and birches outside the walls of Bamberg. It was not at all unusual for wolves to be found in this area. Even twenty years after the Great War, many parts of the country were still devastated and villages abandoned by their residents, and only wild animals remained among the ruins. But no wolves had been seen in the Bamberg Forest. Their fear of people with clubs, swords, and muskets was just too great, and they preferred to relieve their hunger with a sheep or two grazing in the meadows south of the old castle.

Unless their hunger was greater than their fear.

Trembling, Adelheid pulled her coat tightly around her and walked farther into the forest. Now, at the end of October, it was already miserably cold at night. If her husband knew of this nighttime adventure, he surely would have forbidden it. It was also hard for her to convince the watchman at the Langgasser Gate to open the door for her at this time of night. But what the apothecary's wife was searching for could also help the watchman's wife, and thus, grumbling, he finally allowed Adelheid to pass.

Branches snapped beneath her feet as she passed gnarled pines reaching out for her like fingers. In the distance, she could see the watch fires at the city wall, but otherwise it was pitchdark among the trees. Only the moon showed her the way. Once again she heard the howling of the wolves, and instinctively she hastened her pace.

She was searching for the fraxinella plant—*Dictamnus albus,* a rare lily-like flower considered a sure method for aborting unwanted pregnancies. Often young women came in secret to see her or her husband at the court apothecary near the great cathedral on the hill and pleaded with them for a medicine to save them from shame and public humiliation in the stocks at the Green Market. Her husband usually turned away the poor things or sent them to a midwife outside the city gates, as abortion or even assistance with an abortion in the Bamberg bishopric, as in others, was punishable by death. But Adelheid always felt pity for the poor women. Before her marriage with the honorable apothecary Magnus Rinswieser, she, too, had had a few affairs and had gotten into trouble. The old midwife, Frau Traudel over in Theuerstadt, had helped her then with fraxinella, and she felt an obligation now to help others.

The old woman had also then revealed to her that fraxinella should be picked only when the moon was full. The flower was also called witch's flower or devil's plant, and was very rare in this area. But Adelheid knew a secret clearing where she'd picked some of the flowers the year before. Now she hoped to find a few despite the late autumn.

Again she heard the howling of the wolves and realized with a trembling heart that it was closer this time. Did wolves really venture so close to town? Adelheid couldn't help but think of the people reported as missing in Bamberg over the last few weeks. Two women had disappeared without a trace, and old Schwarz-kontz had not returned from a trip to Nuremberg. All that had been found so far was a severed arm and a leg gnawed on by rats, which had showed up in the Regnitz River. Rumors were already going around that the devil was at work in Bamberg, especially since someone recently had seen a hairy creature in the alleyways at night. Until now, Adelheid had always dismissed these reports as exaggerated horror stories, but out here in the dark forest she began to think there might be some truth to them.

Firmly grasping the straps of her wicker backpack, in which she'd already collected some other herbs, she started to run. She didn't have much farther to go. On her left she could already see the moss-covered fallen oak that served to mark her way, and a few hawthorn bushes glimmered reassuringly in the moonlight. Brushing the thorny branches to one side, Adelheid caught sight of the clearing. She took a deep sigh of relief.

Finally. Thank God.

In the silvery moonlight she soon discovered the plants she was looking for on the opposite side of the clearing. The fruit capsules had already burst open, but they still exuded a faint odor, like exotic spices with a hint of lemon. As Adelheid approached the medicinal plants, she quickly put on thin linen gloves that she'd kept in her backpack until then, along with a leather pouch. The seeds of the fraxinella are so poisonous that one has to put on gloves to pick them. The oil that drips from them in midsummer can easily catch fire, which is why fraxinella is also called burning bush. In late autumn only bits of the fruit capsule remained on the withered stalks, but Adelheid didn't want to take any chance. Carefully she picked the few remaining seeds and put them in the little pouch, whispering a few Ave Marias, as old Frau Traudel had instructed her.

"... and blessed is the fruit of your body, Jesus, who was crucified for us ..."

The apothecary's wife made one last quick sign of the cross and stood up. She was about to close the pouch when she heard the howling again.

This time it was very close.

Shocked, Adelheid looked around. Something dark was lurking right behind the hawthorn bushes, which were trembling in the autumn wind. It was a indistinct form, close to the ground, pulsating slightly, with a pair of red eyes shining in the darkness.

What in the world ... ?

The woman wiped the sweat from her brow, and suddenly the red eyes disappeared. Was her imagination playing tricks on her?

"Is someone there?" she asked hesitantly, peering into the darkness. When there was no answer, Adelheid mumbled another prayer, then holding tightly onto the purse, ran across the clearing, making a wide detour around the hawthorn bush. The Langgasser Gate in the east wall was more than a mile away, but long before that the trees thinned out and there were little villages. If Adelheid hurried she could quickly reach the partial safety of the road, where perhaps there might be some travelers even at this late hour. Everything would be fine.

For a moment she thought she heard panting and growling, but when she reached the deer path leading toward the road, all she could hear were the sounds of her own hurried footsteps. In the distance an owl was screeching, sounding almost as if it were laughing at her. Angrily, Adelheid shook her head.

Silly, superstitious woman! If your husband saw you like this ...

As she ran along, she felt angry at herself for being so foolish.

How could she have been scared so easily? No doubt it was only a deer hiding behind the bushes, a wild pig, or a single wolf, certainly nothing to frighten a grown person. Wolves were dangerous only in packs; when they were alone they didn't dare—

Adelheid stopped short. Suddenly her own steps sounded strangely loud to her. The sound was delayed, almost like an echo. She stopped again and noticed that the sound stopped as well.

Tap . . . tap . . . tap . . .

Terrified, Adelheid put her hand to her mouth, realizing what that meant.

Tap . . . tap . . . tap . . . Someone was running alongside her.

Suddenly the sounds stopped, and right after that she heard branches snapping nearby.

"Whoever you are out there . . . come forward!" Adelheid demanded in a choked voice. "If this is supposed to be a joke, it's not funny. This—"

At that moment something came crashing through the undergrowth.

The apothecary's wife was frozen with fear as the creature knocked her down and cast himself on top of her. She smelled animal sweat and the stench of wet fur and began to scream. Her shouts died on her lips, however, as something large and heavy panted and rolled over her.

Oh, God! Help me! This cannot be . . . This is impossible . . . This . . .

A merciful loss of consciousness came over her. A few moments later the howling of the wolves resumed as a dark shadow pulled its lifeless prey into the forest.

Tap . . . Tap . . . Tap . . .

A gasping sound, a last death rattle in her throat . . . then all that remained of the apothecary's wife was a gentle fragrance of fraxinella.

2

JUST AS MAGDALENA WAS BEGINNING TO THINK they'd never find her uncle's house, Jakob suddenly stopped and pointed triumphantly at a two-storied house standing right at the northern city moat.

"Ha! Now look here," he boasted. "My brother's house. A little run-down compared to the last time, but still an impressive place. Bartl must have kissed a lot of asses on the city council to get permission to live in town."

Magdalena frowned as she looked at the lopsided half-timbered house whose paint had been peeling for a long time. A small shed and a stable were attached. The building, shrouded in the fog, was built so close to the moat it was in danger of slipping into the foul-smelling morass at any moment. Nevertheless, it was a stately home. The hangman's daughter couldn't help but think of her father's house in Schongau in the stinking Tanners' Quarter out of town and not nearly as large as this one. She had a vague feeling that her father's barely concealed dislike for his brother had something to do with jealousy.

A thin ray of flickering light came through the closed shutters on the first floor. Kuisl pounded on the massive wooden door, and shortly afterward there was a muffled but still familiar voice that made Magdalena's heart pound.

"Uncle Bartholomäus, is it you?" the voice inquired cautiously. "I didn't expect you back so soon from the torture chamber. Why . . ."

"For God's sake, Georg, it's your own father. So open up, or do you want to keep us all standing out here in the cold?"

The hangman rattled the doorknob, and a muted voice came from inside. Then the bolt was pushed aside and the door opened.

"Georg! Thank God!"

Magdalena shouted for joy when she caught sight of her younger brother, whom she hadn't seen for almost two years. Georg had grown, and the pimples had given way to a dark fuzz on his face. Though only fifteen years old, he seemed much stronger and heavier, almost a smaller version of his father, with his hooked nose, broad chest, and tousled black hair. A smile came over his face, then he shook his head and laughed.

"It looks like my prayers have been answered after all. Uncle Bartholomäus said just this morning that perhaps you wouldn't come to his wedding. But I was sure you wouldn't let us down. My God, how happy I am to see you!" He embraced his father, his twin sister, Barbara, and finally Magdalena. Then he picked up the two shrieking boys and tossed each of them into the air.

"Uncle Georg, Uncle Georg!" Paul shouted excitedly. "Will you whittle another executioner's sword for me?"

"An executioner's sword?" Georg asked, perplexed.

"I told him how you always used to whittle swords," interrupted Simon. "Well, you know how kids are. I'm afraid they won't stop pestering you until they both have swords."

Georg grinned, set the boys down, and shook Simon's hand. "They'll get some, on my honor as a dishonorable hangman," he said, with a conspiratorial glance at Paul. "And if you behave yourself, you can also touch your great-uncle's sword. It's even bigger than the one your grandfather had."

"As if that's all that mattered," Jakob growled. "I can slit open a throat with a kitchen knife."

"Can't you men talk about anything else?" Magdalena said, shaking her head. "Swords, nothing but swords! At least Peter inherited his father's peaceful temperament. Just one like you is all I can take." She sighed and pointed at little Paul, who had just stabbed his brother with an imaginary sword in the stomach.

Simon smiled and put his arms around Peter, who had started to cry.

"Peter is only five, but he can read," he said in a proud tone of voice. "Latin and German, and even a few Greek letters. I taught him myself and with the medicines—"

Jakob finally spoke up. "Can't you even invite your old father to come in, Georg? It's a chilly autumn night, and I think we've stood outside here in the fog long enough. But if you prefer, I can also sleep at an inn."

"Of course not, Father." Georg stepped aside and ushered the family into the living room.

The warmth from the green tiled stove in the corner made Magdalena quickly forget the damp cold and fog outside. The room was homey and neat. Fresh, fragrant reeds were strewn on the floor, and a wide, recently built table provided room for an entire large family. Behind it was the family shrine, with a crucifix, dried roses, and the Bamberg hangman's execution sword. It was, in fact, a little larger than Jakob's sword. Paul at once started to run over to touch it, but Georg laughed and grabbed the tails of the boy's shirt to pull him back.

"You'll be holding it in your hands soon enough," he said, trying to console him. "Why don't you let Barbara take you up to your room instead? It's time for you to go to bed now."

Barbara rolled her eyes and took the two boys, yawning and

only slightly protesting, up the steep stairs to their room. Soon, they heard the soothing sounds of a lullaby.

For a while none of those in the room said a thing, but then Georg reached for the mighty executioner's sword and held it out to his father. "The handle is sharkskin," he said proudly. "When the hangman's hands are sweaty, the leather becomes as raw as a thousand little teeth. As far as I know, only Bamberg executioners have such swords. It would slip out of your hands. Try it."

Jakob shrugged and turned away. "When your hands are wet, it can mean only one thing. The hangman is shitting in his pants, and an anxious hangman is worth about as much as an old toothless whore." He turned around and inspected the room. "But I must say, there have been some changes since my last visit. Bartholomäus really has done well. Who would have thought that the pale, anxious little kid would have turned out this way?"

"Just wait until he marries Katharina," Georg replied. "His last wife came from a family of knackers. Dear Johanna, God rest her soul, died of consumption. She didn't bring much money to the marriage, and there were no children." He sighed softly, then straightened up. "But this time he has a good catch. His new wife is the daughter of a Bamberg court clerk, the dowry is pretty impressive, and Katharina really doesn't look like she's going to waste away anytime soon," he added with a slight smirk. "Well, you'll get to see her soon. She wants a really big celebration, and she's the one who urged Uncle Bartholomäus to invite our whole family."

Kuisl frowned. "Did Bartl get permission from the city council for this? As an executioner, he's not allowed to marry into a higher class."

"He already has the permission, signed and sealed. His future father-in-law is a court clerk and somehow managed to do it." Georg smiled and turned to Magdalena: "A hangman in

Bamberg," he explained, "is something quite different from one in Schongau. We are perhaps not esteemed citizens, but at least no one shies away from us in the street. We are respected. You'd like it here, sister."

"It's no surprise, then, that Bartholomäus lives here like a maggot in the shit heap," Jakob interrupted. "With everything going on in this city, executioners make out as well here as the clergy elsewhere."

Magdalena looked at her father, somewhat confused. "What do you mean by that?"

But Kuisl waved her off. "What's that to me? Where is he, anyway, my esteemed Herr Brother, hmm?"

Georg placed the sword back in the devotional corner, where it seemed like a heathen symbol alongside the roses and the crucifix. "He's still over in the torture chamber. We had a difficult interrogation just yesterday, and he's putting the instruments back in their places. A stubborn thief who is said to have emptied the offertory box over at Saint Martin's . . ." The young apprentice sighed. "All the evidence is against him, but you know how it is. You can't convict anyone without a confession. He didn't confess on the rack, so today we had to let him go."

"I see, a difficult case. Did you have any part in it?"

"My uncle lets me help out with the torture and hangings." He crossed his arms in front of his broad chest. "Different from when I worked with you, where all I could do was scrub the cart used to carry prisoners to their execution."

"Then it's fine by you that they threw you out of town, hmm?" Kuisl bellowed, slamming his hand down on the table so that the dishes rattled. "Don't worry, as the elector's representative, Lechner will see to it that you'll not be coming back anytime soon."

There was an awkward pause, and Magdalena sighed softly. Two years ago, her brother had gotten into a fight with the infamous Berchtholdt brothers and had beaten the youngest of the three half to death. Ever since, the baker's son had a limp, and the court clerk, Johann Lechner, had banished Georg from the city for five years. That had been a hard blow for his father. Since that time, the Schongau hangman went about his duties as best he could, with the drunken knacker at his side, and the hangman's son from neighboring Steingaden had an eye on his job.

"Just outside of town on the other side of the ford, we saw something really strange," Magdalena finally said to change the topic. She told Georg about the severed arm and how terrified the travelers were. "The general mood here is very strange. On Landgasse people are talking about some kind of bloodthirsty beast. Do you know anything about it?"

Her brother hesitated, then shook his head slowly from side to side. "But you should by all means tell the city guard about the arm they found. The way Father described it, it could have been that of Schwarzkontz."

"And who is this Schwarzkontz?" Simon asked.

Georg sighed. "An elderly member of the Bamberg City Council and a clothing merchant who took a trip to Nuremberg more than a month ago and never came back. They say he never got there. And he's not the only one. Two citizens from the town — two women — have disappeared since that time. To top it all, some children playing not far from here found a human arm, and later a leg was found floating in the Regnitz." He shrugged. "Since then, people say there's a man-eating beast prowling around and up to no good. Some people even claim to have actually seen it."

Georg reached for a piece of bread, took a good bite, and continued with a full mouth. "As I said, nothing but rumors. One of the women had an argument with her new fiancé, and Councilor Schwarzkontz ... Well, the road through the Bamberg Forest is dangerous enough even without monsters. Ever since the Great War, any number of marauders and highwaymen hang out there. Just half a year ago, we wiped out a gang there, drew and quartered their leader, and as a warning put their limbs out on display at the road crossings."

"Out in the Bamberg Forest?" Simon interrupted. His face turned a bit paler. "Isn't that the large forest southeast of the city that we passed through this afternoon?"

Magdalena nodded. "Yes, the old farmer who gave us a ride called it that. Why do you ask?"

"Oh, it's nothing ..." Simon hesitated, then sighed and started over. "I went into the forest with the children today and discovered the cadaver of a stag. It was badly mangled. God knows who or what did it."

"Bah! It must have been a few wolves. What else could it have been?" Kuisl reached for the jug of cider and poured himself a cup. "In packs, these animals quickly turn into real beasts. They don't have to be creatures from hell. You're just as superstitious as a bunch of blathering old Schongau washerwomen."

"As reluctant as I am to agree with my stubborn brother, in this case he's damned right."

The voice had come from the doorway, which creaked as it swung open, and in stepped a dour-faced man of around fifty. He was sturdily built and had an almost bald head as large and brawny as the rest of him. He had a bushy beard from which protruded, like two crooked teeth, a hooked nose, typical of the Kuisls, and a prominent chin jutting out like that of a nutcracker. As the man came closer, Magdalena noticed that he limped slightly. His right shoe had a raised wooden sole that thumped with each step he took across the clay floor. Suddenly a wide grin appeared on his face and he spread out his stout arms in greeting as he walked toward Jakob Kuisl. Only now did Magdalena notice the soft and friendly look in his eyes that contrasted so much with his gruff appearance.

"Come give me a big hug, big brother! How long has it been since we last saw each other? Twenty years? Thirty?"

"In any case, damn near an eternity."

"You've gotten fatter, Jakob," Bartholomäus scolded, shaking his finger good-naturedly. "Fatter and puffier."

Jakob grinned. "But you have less hair."

The Schongau hangman rose from his seat and the two brothers embraced. It seemed to Magdalena that this gesture caused them both physical pain. She couldn't help remembering how cross her father became whenever she spoke to him about Bartholomäus. It had to be hard for him to apprentice his own son to his brother, with whom he clearly didn't get along.

"Didn't Georg give you anything to drink but hard cider?" Bartholomäus grumbled in a voice almost as deep as that of Jakob, who was his elder by two years.

"We haven't been here very long," Magdalena replied with a smile. "Anyway, if you haven't seen your beloved brother for such a long time, water from the well is enough." She meant her brother Georg, but evidently her uncle felt she was referring to him.

"*Beloved* brother, yes," he said slowly, in a strange tone of voice, looking at Jakob. "It's been a long time since I called you that." His gaze wandered over to Magdalena.

"She doesn't look much like you, Jakob," he finally continued, "in contrast to her brother, Georg. He's really a spitting image of you. Is she really yours? Well, on the other hand, you can say you're lucky she didn't inherit our nose." He burst out laughing and finally turned to Simon. "And this fine gentleman is your son-in-law you wrote to me about? Not a knacker but in any case a worthwhile person, a medicus and bathhouse owner, so I hear."

"Simon studied medicine," Magdalena interjected. "To marry me he even gave up his title. But his knowledge goes far beyond that of a bathhouse operator."

Bartholomäus grunted disparagingly and kicked the clay floor with his wooden shoe. "And where does it get him? Anyone who shacks up with a hangman's daughter has thrown his lot in with the dishonorable class, and becomes one of them himself. That's the way the law looks at it."

Magdalena was about to respond angrily when Simon took her by the hand and answered with a forced smile: "Well, obviously in your house, too, love won out over class snobbery. It's not every day that the daughter of a court clerk marries a hangman. In any case, I congratulate you on your upcoming marriage. A good catch, it seems to me."

"You're damned right." Bartholomäus grinned broadly, showing his still largely intact set of teeth. "Katharina comes from a good family. Her grandfather was the assistant clerk in the old city administration, and her father, too, became an administrative official. She can even read, and if God grants me children, they will be better off than their father, the hangman. You have my word on that as the sword-swinging, blood-sucking Bamberg executioner." He burst out laughing and pounded the table so hard the pitcher of hard cider almost tipped over.

"You didn't need to make the long trip for my sake," he grumbled after a while, "but Katharina insisted. And once a woman sets her mind on something, she gets it, right? The wedding will be in a week, and, by God, it will be a sinfully expensive party. Katharina is making all the arrangements. Tomorrow she'll be coming at the crack of dawn to check everything out and buy some things. The woman is a whirlwind."

"Apropos of buying things," Jakob interrupted. "Do you by any chance have any tobacco in the house? I ran out of mine while I was still back in Nuremberg."

Bartholomäus snorted. "Still the same vice, eh, Jakob?" He shook his head. "No, I don't have anything like that. But . . ." Suddenly he winked mischievously at Jakob, and for a moment Magdalena thought she could briefly see two twelve-year-old kids planning a prank. "You know what? I have a suggestion for you. Down at the south moat there's a dead horse that no doubt one of the wagon drivers just left there to die. The city council won't allow a dead animal to just lie there longer than a few hours. The damn fools are afraid of poison vapors." He looked at his brother, trying to persuade him. "So what do you think? We can drag the thing into the stable next door in the knacker's cart, and with the money my Katharina will buy you a pouch of the best Augsburg tobacco when she comes tomorrow. I'll give you my word on it."

"*Now?*" Simon replied, horrified. "The two of you want to go out again in the night and the fog?"

Jakob shrugged and walked slowly to the door. "Why not? Is there any better way to celebrate the reunion of two hangman brothers than with a stinking cadaver? If it gets me my tobacco, I'll string up someone for you."

Bartholomäus laughed lustily, but it didn't sound sincere. Magdalena even thought she could detect a bit of sadness in it. Magdalena was in a reflective mood as she watched the brothers leave the room. Even though Bartholomäus was just a bit shorter than Jakob, he seemed to pale in insignificance alongside him.

It took a long time before the thudding of his wooden shoe finally faded away into the darkness.

A half-hour later Magdalena was with Simon up in their room, listening silently to the calm, even breath of Peter, Paul, and Barbara.

Georg had offered to spend nights in the horse stable for the length of their stay. After all the nights they'd spent since leaving Schongau in sleazy flophouses, barns, or in the forest on a bed of brushwood, the accommodations here felt like they were in a royal abode. Their mattress was filled with soft horsehair, a warm, brick-lined stove stood in the middle of the room, and the number of fleas and bugs was tolerable. Nevertheless, Magdalena was having trouble falling asleep. There were too many things going through her mind, and she was anxious to meet her uncle's fiancée.

"What do you think this Katharina is like?" she whispered to Simon. She could tell from the way he was breathing and occasionally shifting around in the bed that he wasn't sleeping either.

He grunted disparagingly. "If she's even a bit like Bartholomäus, she'll be a real shrew. In which case she'll fit right in with this family."

Magdalena gave him a gentle poke. "Are you trying to say that all the Kuisls are ill-tempered ruffians?"

"Well, when I look at your father, his brother, then Georg, I could almost reach this conclusion. In the last two years, your little brother has become a real clod, in any case. I can only hope, that you, too—"

"Don't you dare!" Magdalena tried to sound severe, but she couldn't resist a giggle. "I'll do everything I can, in any case, to make sure our kids don't turn into brutish hangmen's journeymen."

"You'll have a hard time with Paul. He can't wait to chop off someone's head. Peter is quite different, softer, almost like a . . ." Simon paused, but Magdalena completed his sentence.

". . . 'Like a girl,' is what you meant to say. Like the girl that God gave us, then took away again." She turned over and fell silent. Simon ran his hand lovingly over her shoulder.

"She was too weak, Magdalena," he said, trying to console her. "It . . . it was better that it happened so soon. Just imagine if she'd lived even longer—how painful that would have been then. Surely God will give us another chance . . ."

"Just stop!" Magdalena's voice rose, and a soft mumbling came from the boys' beds. It took a while before the room became quiet again. She could feel how Simon, lying alongside her, was searching for the right thing to say. Suddenly her eyes welled with tears and a quiet sob shook her body. Anna-Maria had been her third child. She had come into the world two years ago, just a few months after the death of Magdalena's mother, and had been named after her. Even though Magdalena loved her two boys, it had been wonderful to hold a little girl in her arms wrapped in white linens, with eyes as blue as gentian flowers. Jakob Kuisl had built a crib for his granddaughter, and the old grouch had turned into a loving father in Maria's presence. Simon, too, spent more time with the children then. He'd become a more devoted husband, less concerned with his books and his patients than with his wife, who was weakened by the difficult birth. Maria had been the focus of his life.

And then God had taken her away from them.

It had been one of those fevers that plagued Schongau at regular intervals, first the elderly and the children. Desperately, Simon had tried to fight the fever with leg compresses, mugwort, and chamomile, but the child slipped through their fingers like snow in the sun. They had carried little Maria to her last resting place just a few days after her first birthday. The hurt in Magdalena's soul was still fresh, and occasionally it would break out again.

Just as it had now.

Simon clearly felt it was better to say nothing, and he gently caressed his wife, waiting for the sobbing to pass. Finally she nuzzled up to him again and tried to forget.

"I don't think my uncle is such a coarse fellow as he pretends to be," she said after a while. "He may be just as surly as Father, but there is something soft and very sad in his eyes. Something must have come between the two of them long ago. Maybe it has something to do with his lame leg. Perhaps back then Jakob teased his little brother. A cripple is always an easy target."

"Didn't your father ever tell you anything about Bartholomäus?" Simon asked curiously, glad to have changed the topic.

Magdalena shook her head. "Never. It was like his brother didn't exist. Bartholomäus must have left Schongau soon after Father went off to war as a young man. During the war, Father probably visited him here in Bamberg. Only after Georg had to leave Schongau to find an apprenticeship did the two start corresponding regularly."

"Why does he always talk so much about how well-off the executioners are here in Bamberg?" Simon wondered. "And then this reference to all the abandoned houses in the city, and how he knew why that was so. Why must you Kuisls always make a big secret out of everything?"

"Whatever it is, this city has certainly seen better days. And then these stories about the bloodthirsty monster. You don't believe in that, do you?"

"Of course not," Simon snorted. "Remember all the stories about alleged witches in Schongau, and they were nothing but dumb superstition. But just the same . . ." He paused and looked out the window, worried. The shutters were open a crack, and the pale moon shone into the room through the heavy fog. "Just the same, I feel uneasy knowing that your father is out there prowling around."

Magdalena laughed softly. "You forget he is not alone. Two fierce Kuisls — please! If I were the monster, I'd run away as fast as possible."

She snuggled up to Simon again, and in a few minutes she'd finally fallen asleep.

Soon after the two brothers had left the hangman's house, Jakob became confused and disoriented again in the narrow lanes. In a sullen mood, he stomped along behind his brother, who was pulling a two-wheeled cart smeared with blood and dirt. Bartholomäus kept turning one way or the other in apparently random fashion at crossings, preferring the narrow lanes between houses, where the cart was just able to squeeze through. Out here in the darkness, his limp was barely noticeable.

He's learned to deal with it, Jakob Kuisl thought. *How much effort had that required? How much malice had he been forced to en-*

dure? But, by God, he's really become a tough bastard. I wouldn't have thought he could do it . . .

"Didn't you say the cadaver was over there in the south moat?" Jakob asked finally. It was the first time since they'd left that he addressed his brother. "Why didn't we just take the road along the moat from your house? Wouldn't that be shorter?"

"So the guards patrolling there can ask stupid questions?" Bartholomäus snorted contemptuously. "The cadaver has been there since this morning. I should have picked it up during the day, but I had other things to do, so I'm going to get it now."

"Aha, before the guards discover the thing early next morning and you have to pay a stiff fine." Kuisl grinned. "Now I understand. Well, the main thing is that the tobacco is good."

In addition to his work as a hangman, Bartholomäus had the job of disposing of garbage and dead animals, just like Jakob Kuisl did in Schongau. The authorities attached great importance to disposing of cadavers as fast as possible, because of their fear of plagues. The dead animals were often butchered by knackers who lived outside of town, but sometimes the hangman was responsible for this work, as well.

"You're not going to flay the animal at home, are you?" Jakob asked as they continued their march through the foggy back streets. "I didn't see any scraping knife or other tools in your house, and, moreover, it would stink like hell."

"The city council wouldn't allow it, so I have to take the cadaver out to my knacker's cottage in the Bamberg Forest. There used to be a splendid hunting lodge with a large number of servants nearby, who also were responsible for disposing of cadavers, but since the war that's all gone and I have to do this filthy work all alone. Miserable work and shitty pay," Bartholomäus groaned as he pulled his cart through an especially narrow passage between a pile of horse excrement and other garbage. "We'll take the horse to my stable first, then see what we can do tomorrow."

For a while both brothers were silent, then Jakob carefully broke the ice.

"Listen, I've wanted to thank you for a long time," he began softly, "for taking Georg as a journeyman who—"

"Forget it," Bartholomäus interrupted gruffly. "I don't need your thanks. Georg is a big help to me. He does the work of three or four men and will be a good hangman himself someday." He turned to Jakob and sneered. "Perhaps even here in Bamberg."

"Here in . . ." Jakob looked at his brother, astonished. "You're going to retire and give him your job? That wasn't our arrangement. I need Georg in Schongau. When his apprenticeship is over and he can finally return home, then—"

"Ask him yourself what he wants to do," Bartholomäus interrupted. "Maybe he's had enough of his lying father."

"What did you tell him about me? God, did you—"

A scream from a nearby house interrupted their conversation. Jakob stopped and looked at his brother, listening.

"Who could that be?" he asked. "It's hardly your dead horse."

After some hesitation, Bartholomäus dropped the shaft of his cart and ran toward the place the shouting was coming from, but he turned around once to Jakob as he ran. "Before I fight with my brother, I'm going to beat up a few gallows birds. Come on!"

Kuisl hastened after him. After a few hurried steps, the brothers arrived in a little square surrounded by small cottages with a weathered fountain in the middle. A guard was slouched down at the base of the fountain with a halberd alongside him on the ground, while a lantern at the fountain's edge cast a dim light. He was holding his hand to his mouth and looking around in all directions, horrified. Finally he pulled a clay jug out from under his ragged overcoat and took a long slug.

"Ah, it's just Matthias, the drunken old night watchman." He panted with disappointment and stopped running. "We could have spared ourselves the trip. He probably has had one too many and is about to throw up into the fountain. He used to be a common foot soldier, but now he drinks so much he can hardly stand up anymore." Bartholomäus shook his head. "It's really a shame, the people they have to hire as city watchmen. But the job of a night watchman now is dishonorable, like that of an executioner, and there aren't many people willing to do it."

When Matthias discovered the two men entering the square, he sighed with relief. His face was flushed, full of thick veins, and Jakob thought he could smell brandy on his breath.

He staggered to his feet and stood beside the fountain. "I never thought I'd be so happy to see the Bamberg hangman."

"You scared the hell out of us, Matthias," Bartholomäus replied. "We could hear you shouting clear down at the hangman's house. My brother and I took off right away to see what was going on. And now it's just you and your damned cheap booze. So get moving before I've got to put you in the stocks tomorrow morning at the Green Market."

It didn't seemed to bother Matthias that the hangman's house was much too far away and what Bartholomäus's was telling him had to be wrong, for that reason alone. He tried to keep his composure, something that was clearly difficult for him to do in his condition.

"By all the saints, I swear . . . I'm not drunk," he said, holding up his hand. "At least not so drunk that I don't know what I saw. And I swear I-I saw the monster."

"What monster?" Bartholomäus asked.

"Well . . . the man-eating monster. It was standing here, right before my eyes!"

The Bamberg hangman rolled his eyes. "Now you're starting in with that, too. Isn't it enough that the superstitious women are spreading such foolish gossip?"

"But the monster was here, I swear! I was just about to take a little nap here at the well when I saw the thing come running out of the alleyway. It stopped and stared at me, as if trying to figure out if I'd be a good meal. And then, after what seemed like an eternity, it kept on running, that way, down the other alley." Matthias gestured wildly as he spoke and walked back and forth, wavering slightly. Now he stopped and looked at the two hangmen, wondering.

"You don't believe me, do you?" he asked in a soft voice. "You just think I'm drunk."

"This . . . this monster—what did it look like?" Bartl knew from experience that drunks often had wild visions, especially when tormented by their fears.

"It was hairy, with gray—no, silver—fur," Matthias declared, while casting a quick glance at Kuisl for not understanding what he'd been trying to say. "It had a terrifying set of teeth, long and sharp. At first it ran along on all fours, but suddenly it stood up on its hind legs." The watchman put his hands to his face. "It ran like a human, I swear, like a furry human. Like a werewolf."

"Be careful of what you say," Bartholomäus snapped at him. "Don't be too quick to use words like that. Or do you want to—"

He stopped short when he heard the scream again. At first Kuisl thought it was Matthias, but the scream this time was sharper and at a higher pitch. It came from an alleyway leading to the square and was clearly the voice of a young woman.

The Schongau hangman didn't hesitate for a moment. He ran past the astonished Matthias, and without even turning to look at either of them, disappeared into the dark alleyway. Without the lantern he couldn't see his hand in front of his face, but somewhere he heard a window slam shut and someone shouting in an upper story as the contents of a chamber pot poured down onto the street. Kuisl groped his way along the row of houses, stumbling on a rotten beer barrel that fell over and went clattering down a cellar stairway. As the hangman cursed and tried to run ahead, he slipped on the top step and fell down into a slimy puddle of water. As he scrambled to his feet, he could feel a sticky liquid on his hands whose odor was all too familiar to him.

It was blood.

Somewhere he could hear footsteps running away into the darkness. He looked around, squinting, and could just make out the vague outline of something lying at the bottom of the stairs.

"Whatever you are," he gasped, "man or monster—come out!"

When nothing stirred, he carefully descended a few steps, where he found a body.

It was a young woman lying in her own blood.

"Jakob? Is it you?" a voice called. It was his brother, who had followed him and was now standing at the top of the stairs holding the lantern in his hand, swinging it back and forth. "What did you find down there?"

Jakob held the girl's hand, trying in vain to feel a pulse.

"A corpse," he whispered. "Still fresh. It looks like the poor woman's throat has been slashed. There's blood all over."

"Damn. That's all I need." Slowly, climbing over the staves of the smashed beer barrel, Bartholomäus came down the steps. "Matthias, the old drunk, just took off. Now the two of us will have to report the matter in order not to look guilty ourselves, and I'll have to explain to the city guards what I was doing out here in the middle of the night. Good God!" He stamped his foot angrily. "There are enough people already in the city council who are opposed to my engagement to Katharina and just waiting for a chance to get me. Why didn't this drunken lecher find somewhere else to knock off his woman?"

"A drunken lecher? What makes you think he's one of those?"

"Just come and have a look." Bartholomäus was now standing alongside him on the small, slimy, moss-covered stairway. The entrance to the cellar was blocked by some rough-hewn boards nailed together. Like many other buildings in the lane, the house seemed no longer occupied. Its windows were nothing but dark, gaping holes. The dead girl didn't look like more than sixteen or seventeen and had long red hair that encircled her head like a flame. She was wearing nothing but a simple, close-fitting linen dress, now torn and soaked with blood. Her throat was slit wide open and her eyes stared blankly into the night sky.

"Do you see the yellow scarf?" Bartholomäus pointed to a piece of cloth crumpled up in a corner. "The sign of the Bamberg prostitutes. The Green Market is nearby in the Rosengasse, and that's where the prostitutes usually ply their trade. Evidently the girl and her client weren't able to agree on the price."

"And for that he slits her throat?"

Bartholomäus shrugged. "These things happen. In former days the executioner here in Bamberg was concerned about the prostitutes and protected them, but in recent years the women do that themselves. I keep telling them they ought to at least work under the protection of the whore house on Frauengasse, but some just want to work for themselves," he said as he examined the corpse. "I'm sure I've seen this one here before. Had her nose up in the air and took only rich clients." He looked down at her with contempt. "Well, she certainly was pretty, and it's too bad what happened to her."

Jakob Kuisl bent down and examined the cut on her throat. It wasn't smooth, but ragged, as if the wound had been inflicted by a heavy tool or a claw, and blood was still seeping out. The hangman noticed a strange, barely perceptible odor that reminded him of the urine of predatory animals and wet dogs.

"That's strange," he mumbled. "The wound is actually too large to have been made by a knife. It's almost as if an animal—"

"Now you're starting in with that again," Bartholomäus groaned.

Without answering him, Kuisl took the lantern from his

hand, went up the steps again, and examined the ground. He bent down and held up a piece of her ripped clothing.

"She was probably attacked here," he said to his brother, who had come along behind him. Jakob pointed to some prints in the muddy ground. "There was a struggle, the girl ran . . ." He hesitated. "No, that's not right. Look at the marks on the ground here. Evidently the murderer struck her down, grabbed her by the arms . . ." He returned to the steps. "Then he carried her down the steps and calmly slit her throat. But this odor . . ." Kuisl shook his head, trying to figure out what it was. But he couldn't think what these smells signified.

Except what was the most obvious, and at the same time the most improbable . . .

"What odor? I can't smell anything, but you always had a better nose for these things." He shook his head. "In any case, she's dead. We'll have to alert the guards." He stumbled over one of the splintered staves. "Damn it, they'll probably make us take the girl over to the potter's field outside the city in my cart. We'll have to forget about the horse cadaver," he added, hobbling away. "So let's get over to the guardhouse near city hall as soon as we can and let them know. The sooner we can get this behind us, the better."

Kuisl took a close look at his brother. He was puzzled about the rush. It seemed to him that for some reason Bartholomäus wanted to put this matter to rest as soon as possible. Was it because he feared the criticism of the guards? Once again, Jakob looked down the staircase, where the poor woman was lying in her own blood. Then, with a grim expression, he followed the light of his brother's lantern.

It looked like they'd be transporting not a horse cadaver but the corpse of a young girl through the city. It couldn't be said that the auspices for his brother's wedding were favorable.

3

WHEN MAGDALENA AWOKE THE NEXT MORNING, the sun was already shining brightly, warming her room on the second floor. Someone had opened the shutters wide, emptied the chamber pots, and strewn fresh herbs and reeds on the floor.

How long did I sleep? she wondered, as she yawned and opened her eyes.

She turned to Simon, whose snoring almost drowned out the sparrows chirping outside the window. Barbara was sleeping as well. The bed the two boys were sleeping in, however, was empty. Magdalena began to worry, but at that moment she heard happy laughing coming from downstairs. She also heard a soft, warm woman's voice among them, plus the sound of clattering pots and an oven door squeaking as it was opened and closed. She rose to her feet carefully in order not to awaken her husband and her sister, washed her face quickly in the washbowl in the corner, straightened her tousled black hair, then went downstairs into the living room.

"Mama, Mama!" Peter shouted, running toward her with outstretched arms. "Aunt Katharina is making us some porridge with lots and lots of honey, just as Grandma used to do."

"Aunt Katharina?" Magdalena asked, puzzled. "Where . . ."

Not until then did she see a woman standing out in the hallway by the stove stirring a pot. She was sturdily built, heavy, and seemed a bit larger than life. She appeared to be wearing some woolen petticoats beneath her skirt and jacket so that sweat ran down her slightly pasty red face in streams.

The heavyset woman handed the stirring spoon to Paul, standing alongside her in anticipation, and shook her finger at him in playfully.

"Keep stirring," she cautioned him, "or the porridge will stick to the bottom and the pigs will enjoy a second breakfast."

Her hands had become sticky from the constant stirring, so she wiped them off on her apron and turned to Magdalena with a smile. She beamed with a warmth that made Magdalena like her immediately.

"You must be Jakob's eldest daughter, Magdalena," she began cheerily. "What a great pleasure that you have made the long trip to our wedding. I especially wanted you to come so we could all get acquainted. I must admit that Bartl scolded and grumbled at first," she added with a smile. "He wanted to celebrate just with me and save all the money, but finally the stubborn old guy gave in. I told him I wouldn't tolerate any discord within my future family, and a wedding celebration like this was a good chance to bury any disagreements, even though I still don't know exactly what happened between the two old grumps."

She tipped her head to one side and looked closely at Magdalena. "Well, I must say that you don't take after the Kuisls. I had not expected such a beautiful woman."

Magdalena laughed. "Then just wait until you meet my younger sister, Barbara. When the young fellows here in Bamberg see her, their eyes will pop out. Fortunately she inherited neither the nose nor the build of our father," she grinned. "Only his feisty temper."

"Oh, if she's anything like your uncle, this will be an exciting week." The chubby woman gave Magdalena a hearty kiss on both cheeks. "I'm Katharina, as you no doubt already know. Make yourself at home here. I hope I didn't wake you up, since I've already aired out and cleaned up the rooms a bit. It's already after eight." She flashed a big smile. "This house has been in need of a woman's touch for some time and urgently needs someone to get things in order."

Magdalena sighed and rolled her eyes. "You're telling me? Ever since my mother died, Dad's place is like a pigsty. Men should really not be alone for too long." She looked around. "Where is Dad, anyway?"

"He and Bartholomäus had to pay a visit early this morning to the town manager in city hall. It seems some poor woman was killed last night in a dark alleyway, and Bartholomäus and your father were witnesses. Georg is here, too," she said, gesturing toward the living room. "But let's not begin the day with such dark news. Drink this—it will get you moving again. It's an old recipe of my grandmother's, with crushed clove and a little pepper." Katharina gave her a cup of steaming hot mulled wine diluted with water. With an approving look, she pointed at little Peter sitting at the other end of the table, leafing through a book on anatomy. "Smart lad you've got there. Went straight to Bartl's study, took out a big book, and has already told me some things about bloodletting and checking the urine." She laughed. "Just like a little medicus. He must get that from his father."

Magdalena nodded and took a gulp of the hot mulled wine. It tasted wonderful, both sharp and sweet and not too strong. But she couldn't help thinking of her father, evidently in trouble again.

Trying to change the topic, she asked, "When will the wedding take place?"

"This Sunday, in just five days. Just imagine, even though your uncle is the executioner here in Bamberg, the city gave him permission to celebrate it in the Wedding House—that's the addition to the large tavern over in the harbor. They'll give us a room there. Nearly a hundred guests are invited." Katharina smiled. "I assume my father has made use of some of his influence with the city councilors. As you know, perhaps, he's one of the city clerks."

Magdalena nodded her agreement. It was unusual that a hangman was allowed to celebrated his wedding just like any other shoemaker or tailor. In many parts of Germany, executioners were shunned and in the streets people went out of their way to avoid them, as they believed a hangman could bring misfortune just by looking at him. Magdalena couldn't help remembering what her brother, Georg, had said to her the previous evening.

You'd like it here, sister.

Secretly she watched Katharina, who was now humming as she dashed through the room, sweeping cobwebs from the windows. Bartholomäus's fiancée was in her midthirties, and it was a wonder she was still unmarried. Though she wasn't especially beautiful, and clearly was too fat, Magdalena could appreciate what her uncle saw in his fiancée. She was a good catch, strong and healthy, and her friendliness was genuine and contagious. Magdalena was surprised that such a nice person could tolerate a grouch like Bartholomäus.

But that's just the way it was with Mother and Father, it occurred to her, and she smiled mischievously.

"What are you thinking about?" Katharina asked, but at that moment the steps began to creak and Simon and a very sleepy-looking Barbara entered the room. Katharina greeted the new arrivals just as warmly has she had Magdalena but then stopped when she smelled something burning.

"Oh, God, the porridge," she cried out, running out into the hallway. "I shouldn't have left the boy alone at the stove."

Simon sat down at the table alongside Magdalena, took a piece of bread, and dunked it in the wine.

"It seems she's not an old battle-axe, as you suspected," he said with a smile between bites, and gestured with his head toward Katharina.

Magdalena shook her head. "No, certainly not. Clearly, Peter and Paul like their new aunt, too. At least up to now they haven't played any tricks on her, and it's already eight in the morning. That's pretty unusual." She grinned, but then her look suddenly became very serious. "On the other hand, Father seems to have a problem."

She quickly told Simon and Barbara what had happened to Jakob and Bartholomäus the night before.

Simon groaned and passed his hand through his hair. "It's enough to drive you crazy. No sooner has your father come to town than the first cadaver shows up."

"Oh, come now, there was one even before we set foot in town. They're attracted to him like bees to honey, but perhaps that's the way it is for hangmen."

Simon took another piece of fresh, delicious-smelling bread that Katharina had no doubt baked earlier that morning. "Well, this time at least it appears he's not suspected of being the perpetrator, like back in Regensburg," he said with a full mouth. "That alone is progress."

Magdalena remembered with horror her time in Regensburg six years ago, when her father had been suspected of murder, tortured, and could only be saved at the last moment. Shortly after that, she and Simon had married.

"I at least don't want to sit around here all day waiting for Father and Uncle Bartholomäus," said Barbara, who up to this point had been sitting around listlessly playing with her hair. "I want to see something of the city." She turned with a pleading voice to Magdalena. "How about our going down to the marketplace together?" Her eyes sparkled expectantly. "Please? I've never been in such a large city, and now in the light of day it doesn't look as scary as it did last night."

Magdalena gave her a conspiratorial wink. "I don't know

any reason not to. Unless . . ." With a questioning look she turned around to Katharina, who was just entering the room hand in hand with Paul, who had porridge smeared all over him. "Unless my future aunt needs me today to help with preparations for the wedding."

Katharina waved her off with a laugh. "If you can do a little shopping for me, feel free to leave the boys here and go exploring in the city. I hear that my future brother-in-law needs some tobacco. It stinks at least as bad as burned porridge." She opened a window to let the smell out. "Well, it looks like we'll have to make a second breakfast."

Simon quickly stood up and carefully looked through some books lying on the table next to Peter.

"Many thanks for the bread and wine, Katharina. If you don't mind, I'll take this chance to visit my old friend Samuel." Magdalena frowned, but he looked to her with pleading eyes. "You know that I also came to Bamberg because of him. He is now a respected physician and apparently even treats the bishop himself. I hope I may be allowed to have a look at some books that have just appeared. There are a few interesting new theories about the circulation of blood . . ."

"Just stop." Magdalena rolled her eyes with annoyance. "It would be nice if your interest in books brought in some money from time to time. Other bathhouse owners do bloodlettings without giving much thought to circulation."

"Other bathhouse owners are quacks," Simon replied bitterly.

"Now just stop fighting," Katharina interrupted. "Enjoy the day, each one in your own way. I don't want to see any sad faces around me so soon before my wedding." She led the two boys over into the pantry. "And you two can help me now to stir a new pot of porridge. Let's see if we can find some more honey."

Magdalena smiled at her younger sister. "It looks like this could really be a nice day." She stood up and buttoned her bodice.

"Well, then, come along before there's nothing left to buy but mushy cabbage leaves."

Jakob Kuisl's stomach growled so loudly he thought for a moment some monster had crept up behind him. It was late in the afternoon and several hours since he'd had his last skimpy meal. He stopped for a moment, wiped the sweat from his brow, and now, cursing under his breath, went back to helping his brother pull the filthy, foul-smelling cart through one more narrow lane alongside the city moat.

He wanted more than anything else just to sit back and smoke his pipe, but they'd been working since early morning and hadn't returned to the hangman's house, where his future sister-in-law would, he hoped, be awaiting him with the promised tobacco.

It had been a long night. They'd followed their orders and taken the corpse of the young prostitute to the office of the city guards, but the captain on duty, by the name of Martin Lebrecht, was not available so they just left it with the regular guards. They'd also tried to see him earlier that morning to inform him of what had happened that night, but he was suddenly busy with other things. Kuisl had the vague feeling that the guards and especially their captain had something to hide. Finally he'd picked up Georg, then left with him and Bartholomäus to take the dead horse out of town. Georg had stayed in the Bamberg Forest helping the knacker flay and butcher the cadaver, while Jakob and Bartholomäus headed to city hall with the empty cart, where the two executioners were finally going to be cross-examined as witnesses.

After a few more bends and dead ends, Bartholomäus reached a shed near the river and pushed the cart in between two rotted boats stacked inside. He wiped his hands on his apron and headed for the stone bridge nearby that led straight to the city hall.

"The shed belongs to Answin, the rag collector, who delivers his goods to the paper mill farther down the river," Bartholomäus explained. "We're good friends. The cart can stay there for a while," he said with a grin. "The noble gentlemen aren't so happy to see us and our filthy work and only wish we could make ourselves invisible." He cast a critical eye at Jakob. "You should wash off a bit in the river before we go over to the city hall. It's quite possible my future father-in-law will be there. As one of the clerks he sometimes helps out in the guardhouse. It won't put our family in a very good light if he sees you like this."

"That's all I need — my little brother telling me when to take a bath," Kuisl growled, and he kept stomping forward. "Nobody asked me to give them a report, and if the gentlemen want to question me, then they'll just have to smell me as well."

Some worn steps led up to the bridge, which was crowded with people at this hour. Patricians with bulging purses rushed by on their way to the financial sector by the cathedral; two Benedictine monks walked slowly by in silent prayer on their way to their monastery on the Michelsberg; while some children climbed around on the stone parapet. When the boys and girls saw the Bamberg executioner, they began whispering to one another anxiously.

Without paying attention to those around him, Jakob suddenly stopped and stared up at the huge structure before them. He couldn't help but wonder what builder would ever have had the crazy idea to build something in the middle of the river. The Bamberg city hall stood on a tiny island and hung out over the river on all sides like an overgrown mushroom. The wide stone bridge connected it both to the north and south shores, and upstream there was an additional bridge. The Regnitz rushed past the point of the island, where a small building huddled up again the main structure. It almost looked as if the little building could break off at any moment and plunge into the river.

Bartholomäus did not seem to notice his brother's amazement as he stood alongside him, pointing to the building.

"It stands right between the two parts of town," he explained. "As Bamberg continued to grow, the citizens on this side of the river built the new city over there, and ever since then, they've been quarreling with the bishop." He spat into the foul-smelling water below. "With the city hall, they're telling the bishop he can kiss their ass. And they get bolder every year."

He continued toward the building, and Jakob followed over a narrow path along the shore to the defiant little building clinging to the south side of the city hall that was evidently the office of the city guards.

Bartholomäus turned to speak to his brother. "Captain Martin Lebrecht is not a bad fellow," he said. "He often asks for my advice when his men have to extricate the corpse of a starved beggar or some other poor creature from the mud and garbage of the city moat." He frowned. "But I can't figure out why he wants to see us both at the same time. We told the guard everything last night."

Two sleepy guards were leaning on their halberds in front of the guardhouse. When they saw Bartholomäus, their faces darkened.

"Isn't it enough that they brought a bloody corpse to the guardhouse and sent us off on a wild chase looking for the devil? Now the hangman is coming to pay us a visit," said the older one, making the sign of the cross. "So much disaster has rained down on us since yesterday that I can't even pray anymore." Dark rings had formed under the watchman's eyes, and it looked as if he'd spent a long, sleepless night.

"What devil?" Bartholomäus asked. "And who are you looking for?"

The guard just waved him off. "None of your business, hangman. Get out of here."

"It certainly is our business," Bartholomäus replied curtly.

"The captain sent for me and my brother. So just let us through before he gets impatient."

"Your brother?" The second guard, a short, mousy, nervous-looking fellow, regarded Jakob wide-eyed. "Do you mean we now have *two* hangmen in the city?"

"It looks like you need them," Jakob jested, "with all the filth and vermin here."

Without another word, the two brothers pushed their way past the guards and entered the chief's office. An older, powerfully built officer was having a conversation with a gray-haired, potbellied man. They were standing next to a table looking at a bundle of personal things wrapped in a sheet. Alongside this was a smaller bundle, also wrapped in a cloth. Jakob knew at once what was underneath the sheets, as there was an odor he was all too familiar with in the air.

The stench of decay.

When the chief noticed the new arrivals, he raised his head, and a thin smile spread over his lips. Just like the guards outside, he looked pale and weary, and black stubble covered his angular face. Jakob assumed the man in front of him was Martin Lebrecht, the captain of the Bamberg city guards.

"Ah, Master Bartholomäus," he exclaimed with relief. "Please excuse me for not having any time for you earlier, but there were . . . well . . . some things that had to be taken care of." He hesitated briefly, then pointed with a sigh to the portly gentleman on his right who was wearing the simple garb of a clerk and nervously rubbing a roll of paper in front of him with callused fingers. "I'm sure I don't need to introduce you to Master Hieronymus Hauser."

Bartholomäus nodded. "I'm glad to see you, esteemed father-in-law. Katharina, by the way, is well and rearranges the furniture in my house every day. Soon I won't even be able to find my way around my own room."

The fat man smiled. "You can forget about calling me 'father-in-law' until the week after the wedding," he replied, shaking his finger at him playfully. "And don't tell me I never warned you about Katharina's compulsion for cleaning."

Jakob was amazed to see the degree of collegiality and respect the men showed each other. Here, the hangman appeared to be one of the local authorities, unlike in Schongau, where he had to live outside the city walls and was avoided by everyone. But then he suddenly thought about the whispering children over on the bridge.

It will always be so; some things never change.

"And I assume this is your brother?" asked Hieronymus Hauser, turning around to Jakob with a smile and extending his ink-stained fingers. Kuisl shook hands with some embarrassment. Now he regretted not having washed off in the river earlier. "Welcome to the family," said the clerk. "We were surprised you came. It was just last week that I learned Bartholomäus even had a brother."

"We Kuisls don't talk very much," Jakob explained hesitantly.

Hieronymus laughed. "Indeed! But my daughter compensates for that three times over. It was one of her fondest wishes to have all the members of the Kuisl clan sit down sometime at a table. Even if it means, so I've heard, bringing together two obstinate executioners who are always quarreling with one another," he added with a smile.

Martin Lebrecht, who had been standing next to them feeling somewhat embarrassed, interrupted: "May I ask you to put off the family matters until later? We're here today to discuss a very important matter." He looked intently at the two hangmen. "First, you must assure me that everything we discuss here today is confidential. We will keep minutes and then bury them in a mountain of documentation. Have I made myself clear?"

Bartholomäus and Jakob nodded, and the captain took a deep breath.

"Then take another look at the corpse you found and tell me exactly what happened yesterday."

He pulled away the sheet lying on the table. Hieronymus gasped softly, while the two hangmen looked down with interest at the naked corpse. They had seen too many corpses and too much sorrow in their lives, but just the same, anger started welling up in Jakob.

She's just a little older than my Barbara . . .

The red-haired girl in front of them was as pale as parchment. Something had ripped open her throat so that her neck was just one gaping wound. Even more gruesome to look at, however, was the thin cut Jakob had not noticed the night before beneath her bloody dress, a cut that extended down her breastbone. It looked just like the incisions the Schongau hangman sometimes made himself on hanged criminals in order to study the body's internal organs. Clotted blood had formed along the incision, where a fat blowfly buzzing loudly alighted and starting crawling down toward her navel. The girl looked like a doll that had been torn to pieces and clumsily stitched back together.

"Who would do anything like that?" asked a horrified Hieronymus Hauser after a while. His pasty face had suddenly turned gray and he took a deep gulp.

"Well, that's the reason I wanted to hear more about what happened last night," Martin Lebrecht replied. "The girl was evidently a whore. An unhappy client probably slit her throat, but what about this here?" He shook his head in disgust and turned to Bartholomäus. "When you brought me the corpse last night, I discovered the incision at once and decided not to have the girl taken to potter's field, as I usually would. That would only have started rumors, and we have enough of those in the city already." He stopped to think. "In addition, look what the rag collector, Answin, brought to me early this morning. He fished it out of the Regnitz just a few hours ago." Lebrecht pulled aside the second, smaller sheet, revealing the pale leg of a woman. It seemed to have been in the water for some time, as rats and fish had already been nibbling on it.

"This is the third body part we've found this month," the captain continued.

"The fourth," Jakob interrupted.

Martin Lebrecht looked at him, obviously confused. "What are you saying?"

"I said, 'the fourth.' Yesterday evening, just before we arrived in Bamberg, we came upon a right arm that had been washed ashore from the river." In a few words, Jakob Kuisl told him about their discovery in the Bamberg Forest. "Evidently it belonged to a man about sixty years old who did a lot of writing . . . and had gout," he said finally. "The fingers were all gnarled."

"Hmm, that could indeed be from Councilor Schwarzkontz, who has been missing for four weeks," Lebrecht mumbled. "Did he have a ring on his finger?"

"It looked like he used to wear one. I found a pale circle on his finger, but the ring was gone."

The captain thought for a moment and nodded. "That must have been the ring with the city seal. Schwarzkontz was known to have worn it wherever he went."

For a moment, Kuisl closed his eyes and cursed himself for being such a fool. He was so certain the man had worn a wedding ring that he'd ignored any other possibilities. Now he realized how rash his judgment had been.

You never stop learning. Not even in your old age. Well, at least Magdalena won't hear anything about it . . .

"The arm you found brings the total to four body parts," Lebrecht continued, "some male, some female. I assume that at least both arms belonged to Klaus Schwarzkontz. His son Walther was able to recognize a scar on one of them, and he is sure it was his father's arm."

"Just a moment." Bartholomäus stared in confusion at the captain. "The left arm belonged to Councilor Schwarzkontz? But—"

"I know, what you're going to say," Lebrecht interrupted. "If Klaus Schwarzkontz was slain by highwaymen somewhere in the forest, what in the world is his left arm doing here in Bamberg?"

"The entire area around the city is full of small rivers and streams," Hieronymus interrupted. "It's quite possible that one of the body parts was carried here by the water. Wild animals ripped up the corpse and—"

"This wasn't any wild animal," Kuisl retorted crossly. "I saw the arm, and someone had been working on it with a knife or an axe."

"Well, isn't that just fine. One more riddle." Lebrecht groaned, then began counting off on his fingers. "Including Klaus Schwarzkontz I have three missing people and a bunch of body parts, and now the apothecary Magnus Rinswieser comes to me early this morning whining and complaining that his young wife has vanished into thin air. Guards saw her entering the forest near the city late at night." He took a deep breath. "But as if that's not enough, now the old drunk Matthias is running through town telling everyone he saw a hairy monster that walks on its two hind legs last night. This . . . this idiot!" Lebrecht rubbed his bloodshot eyes, and again Jakob Kuisl had the feeling that the captain was withholding something from them.

"I immediately put Matthias in the city jail to sober him up," Lebrecht continued, "but by then the whole city had heard about it. Until now, isolated reports could be discounted—a tragic accident, wild animals, marital discord, what have you—but when this gets out . . ." He paused for a moment, pointing at the girl's mutilated body. "When this gets out I'll have to report the matter to the prince bishop whether I like it or not. And we all know what that means . . ." His final words hovered in the air, fraught with meaning. Finally Lebrecht continued. "So, for God's sake, tell me exactly what happened yesterday. I pray to God we can find a natural explanation for all this."

Bartholomäus cleared his throat, then started talking. Occasionally he brought Jakob into the picture, and the latter responded in a few words.

"So there was a struggle," the captain summarized. "The girl tried to defend herself, but the murderer struck her down, stabbed her, and, for whatever reason, slit her throat. It's clear up to this point, but what caused the incision in her chest?"

"May I have another look at the corpse and the leg?" asked Kuisl.

Martin Lebrecht looked at him suspiciously. "Why?"

"My brother is skilled in medicine," Bartholomäus tried to explain. "It was always the case. It runs in the family. I'm the only black sheep in this respect."

Jakob nodded almost imperceptibly. Like many other executioners, he knew how to torture and kill but also how to cure. The medical knowledge of the Kuisls was known far and wide, but his brother Bartholomäus was never interested. Bartl was good at doctoring animals and knew a lot about horses and dogs, but people, Jakob assumed, only appealed to him when they were already dead.

The captain stepped aside and motioned for Kuisl to step up and take a closer look at the cadaver. "Go right ahead. You certainly are welcome to try, though I don't think you're going to find out anything I haven't seen already."

First, Jakob turned to the severed leg, which had been lying in the water for several days and was already in such bad shape that it was impossible to say anything more about it, except that it probably belonged to an elderly woman. It was also not possible to tell if the leg was severed with a knife or had simply been ripped off. Before turning away, Kuisl took one last look at the toes. He stopped suddenly, then stood up again and looked all around him.

"Two of this woman's toenails have been ripped off," he said.

"What?" Martin Lebrecht frowned. "Are you trying to say she has been tortured?"

"I can't be sure of that, but what point would there be otherwise in pulling someone's toenails out? So she wouldn't have to cut them again?"

"And perhaps because the rats have had a feast on the corpse?" Hieronymus Hauser suggested, without any reaction to Kuisl's sarcastic remark.

Jakob Kuisl shook his head. "Believe me, my brother and I know what it looks like when someone's nails have been pulled out. We've done it ourselves often enough, haven't we, Bartholomäus?"

Bartholomäus nodded silently, and Jakob had the feeling that the two others were distancing themselves a bit from him and his brother.

After a while, he bent down over the girl's corpse and began sniffing noisily, his huge nostrils flaring out like sails. Again he noticed the strange musty odor that he had wondered about the previous night. Now it was far fainter, barely perceptible.

"What in the world is your brother doing?" the horrified captain whispered.

"He . . . well, he has a good nose, a sensitive one," Bartholomäus tried to explain. "Sometimes he smells things that no on else can. Almost like a bloodhound."

The others remained silent as Kuisl examined the wound in the neck more closely. The edges were frayed, as if the murderer hadn't used a sharpened knife, but a saw or a jagged sword.

Or claws?

Kuisl put the thought aside and concentrated on the cut to the chest. Pulling the edges of the wound apart, he noticed that the breastbone had almost been cut in two in one place. Evidently the murderer had stopped what he'd been doing because he'd been disturbed. The wound was in the upper third of the breast-bone, directly above the heart.

He paused.

Was that possible?

"Why are you stopping?" asked the clerk, who had been watching him with great curiosity up to that point. "Did you find anything?"

Jakob hesitated and shook his head. "Just a hunch. But too vague to say . . ."

"Now come out with it," his brother interrupted. "Always this mystery! That's what I couldn't stand about you back then, even if you were usually right," he added, grumbling.

"Speak up," Martin Lebrecht insisted.

"The perpetrator had cut through the skin and evidently wanted to open the chest with a saw, or something like it," Kuisl said finally, as he turned to the circle of onlookers. He pointed at the clean incision. "This, unmistakably, is the work of a skilled workman. My brother and I probably disturbed him, and the question is why he was doing that."

"And what do you suspect?" Hieronymus asked.

"The deep incision is right at the level of the heart," Kuisl replied. "I, myself, have made incisions like this in order to ex-amine the inner organs of a body. I think . . ." He hesitated. "Well, I think the murderer wanted to cut out the girl's heart."

For a while no one said a word, and the only sound was the constant rushing water of the Regnitz. Finally Martin Lebrecht cleared his throat.

"It doesn't matter whether or not this is sheer nonsense," he finally said. "One thing must be clear: this assumption is never — I repeat never — to be mentioned outside the walls of this guard-house. If the bishop gets wind of this, great misfortune will come to this city — a misfortune like the one known all too well by the older men among us." He cast a gloomy look at Bartholomäus.

"If that should happen, Master Bartholomäus, I promise you there will be much for you to do here in Bamberg." His voice failed him. Finally he continued in almost a whisper. "God in Heaven, will this horror never end?"

"If I'd known that our new aunt was sending us out after so many things, I would have thought twice before coming along on this shopping trip." Groaning, Barbara pushed past the many displays in the Fischgasse, where brook trout and slimy perch were thrashing about. A huge catfish glared scornfully at the two women, while mussels and river snails soaked in wooden tubs next to the displays. It was already past noon, but the hustle and bustle of the marketplace showed no sign of ending.

"We promised Katharina," Magdalena said in a stern voice, "so stop complaining. Besides, the only thing we still need now is the crabs for this evening, and then we'll be done."

"Yes, after we've bought thyme, carrots, cabbage, onions, eggs, stockfish, a jug of muscatel, half a pig of bacon fat, Father's tobacco . . ." With a sigh, Barbara sat down at the edge of a well and splashed some water on her face to cool off. "How many markets have we been to today? I stopped counting hours ago."

"You insisted on seeing the marketplace." Magdalena grinned. "Aunt Katharina likes to cook, and surely we can get a few recipes from her."

"I didn't come to Bamberg just to sit by the stove and exchange recipes. Besides, I don't want to get as fat as Aunt Katharina, and—hey, wait for me."

Magdalena had turned away with a shrug and continued down past the many stalls on Fischgasse toward the harbor. Their shopping trip had indeed taken the two hangman's daughters through half the city. They'd gone from the Green Market in front of St. Martin's Church to the fruit market, the milk market, and finally down Butcher's Lane. The city seemed much friendlier to Magdalena now than it had on their arrival the night before. The streets were wider and also cleaner than in Schongau, and some of them were even paved. Gaily colored, half-timbered houses, breweries redolent of malt, and a huge number of small churches and chapels bore witness to the rich heritage of this seat of the archdiocese of Bamberg, formerly one of the mightiest cities in the Reich. It was clear, however, that Bamberg's best years lay behind it. The two women again and again came across abandoned houses and ruins that looked like festering wounds between the other buildings. Not for the first time, Magdalena asked herself why people had simply abandoned their magnificent homes.

Up to that point, they had been strolling only through the new part of the city, a large area standing like an island surrounded by two branches of the Regnitz. The old part of the city, where the canons and the bishop resided, lay on the other side of the canal, where a cathedral was built atop a hill, the highest point in the city. The two sections of town met in the harbor, not far from city hall. Huge river rafts, flat-bottomed boats, and small barks traveled serenely past the houses there. More ships lay at anchor at the piers to pay their tolls before proceeding to Schweinfurt or Forchheim. A wooden crane was unloading crates from one of the rafts, and the air smelled of algae, fish, and stagnant river water. Men shouted, laughed, and cursed, as fishwives offered their slippery catch to passersby.

Magdalena went to a booth off to one side and bought the river crabs that Katharina had asked for. Her basket was now filled to the top, and Barbara also had a heavy bundle to carry, with carrots and bunches of leeks sticking out of their wrappings.

"So that's it," Magdalena said with relief. "Let's take the things as quickly as we can to the hangman's house before Aunt Katharina gets impatient, and then—"

She was interrupted by a drumroll and a squawking fanfare of rusty trumpets, and when she turned around, she saw a group of men down at the harbor with drums and wind instruments. They wore colorful, threadbare costumes and powdered wigs on their heads like those now in fashion at German and French courts. In the middle was a beanpole of a man, who with great ceremony unrolled a parchment.

"Are these actors?" asked Barbara with surprise. "I've never—"

"Sh!" Magdalena whispered, while the gaunt man began a speech in which he enunciated each word like a traveling priest with a strange accent Magdalena had never heard before.

"Citizens of Bamberg, hear and be amazed," he proclaimed. "The venerable troupe of Sir Malcolm, which has traveled widely and to great acclaim in performances in London, Paris, and Constantinople, has the honor of performing in this city tragedies and comedies unlike anything the world has ever seen before. Beginning tomorrow, come to experience love and murder, nobility and villainy, and the glory and fall of royal dynasties. We offer for your enjoyment music, dance, burlesque—in short a true feast for the eye and ear in the large ballroom of the Wedding House . . ." The man pointed dramatically to a multistoried building beyond the harbor square. "Our first play will be given there tomorrow afternoon, at a cost of just three kreuzers per visitor. Anyone missing it will regret it for a long time."

"The Wedding House," Barbara whispered. "Isn't that where the celebration for Uncle Bartholomäus and Katharina will be? Can we go there right now, Magdalena? Let's see what's going on there."

Magdalena chuckled as she watched her younger sister stare longingly at the actors. A large crowd of people had gathered around the group and began to cheer. It grew louder when men began doing cartwheels and juggling balls. One of them, a handsome young fellow, glanced at the two young women and smiled. He had matted, jet-black hair and was tanned, almost dark-skinned, with sinewy muscles standing out from beneath his tight-fitting linen shirt. Magdalena grinned as she saw her little sister running her fingers through her curls in embarrassment as they watched the antics of the two actors.

Once again, Magdalena realized how little she herself had seen of the world, despite her thirty years. Occasionally, troupes of jugglers also came to the provincial town of Schongau and performed their little tricks and dances and made crude jokes. Many of them came from lands beyond the Alps, and they played short comical scenes wearing masks on their faces. But a troupe that presented obviously longer stories on stage was new to Magdalena.

There was a long roll of drums, then the trumpets sounded again, off tune, and the troupe moved slowly back toward the Wedding House.

"Come, let us see where they've set up their theater," Barbara pleaded again. "Just for a few minutes."

"But what about all these things we've bought?" Magdalene asked.

"We'll take them along." Barbara was already making her way through the crowd toward the entrance to the Wedding House. "Half an hour one way or the other doesn't matter."

With a sigh, Magdalena followed. She was going to object, but she couldn't deny that the theater had an almost magical attraction for her, as well.

As soon as the two young women entered the wide door of the Wedding House they could feel the coolness of the huge walls. It was almost as if winter had already arrived here. Shivering, Magdalena looked around the spacious area, where kegs of wine, bales of cloth, and crates were standing around. Some servants were unloading a cart that had made its way from the harbor to the building entrance. Farther back, the room opened into a interior courtyard that evidently belonged to a large tavern. The two girls could hear the shouting and quarrelling of some revelers, and somewhere a fiddle was being played very badly. In a domed area, a wide, winding stairway led to the upper floors, from which people could be heard hammering and sawing busily, and a roll of drums could be heard now and then.

"I think the actors are somewhere up there," Barbara said, and started running up the stairs so fast that Magdalena had a hard time catching up with her. The basket in her hand was full to the bursting point and getting heavier with every step.

On the second floor they indeed found the troupe. Almost the entire area was a huge dance floor surrounded on three sides by a gallery with a walkway. At the opposite end, several actors were standing on a stage normally used by musicians. They were setting up a structure whose purpose Magdalena didn't understand. After a few moments she spotted the tanned youth again, now sweaty and wearing an open shirt, doing gymnastic tricks and putting together a two-part pole at eye level, dividing the stage in half. Magdalena was amused to see that Barbara had spotted him, as well, and was once again playing with the locks of her hair.

"Ah, I see the ladies are admiring our equipment," a voice behind them said suddenly. "Good gracious! You two would truly make charming queens."

Magdalena turned around and saw the haggard man who had given the dramatic speech earlier. His body was wrapped in a long, black coat that fluttered like a scarecrow's. He was pale, poorly shaven, and had dark eyes that appeared to bore into everyone he spoke with. Strands of a cheap wig curled like dead snakes down to his shoulders. When the man noticed the women's hesitation, he bowed slightly.

"My dears, I completely forgot to introduce myself," he continued in that strange, soft accent that Magdalena had noticed before. "My name is Malcolm. *Sir* Malcolm, to be exact. I am the director of this outstanding theater group." He pointed to the men on the circus wagon and bowed. "We strive to entertain you.

Or, as Shakespeare once said, 'All the world's a stage, and all the men and women merely players.'"

"Shakespeare? Entertain?" Barbara's mouth opened wide in amazement. "I'm afraid I don't understand . . ."

The gaunt man's laugh sounded like the bleating of a billy goat. "Tell me, you beautiful ladies have never heard of William Shakespeare or Christopher Marlowe? Well, then you can count yourself lucky, because Sir Malcolm's group of itinerant actors is the best, the most sensational, and"—he gave a conspiratorial wink and lowered his voice—"and surely the most risqué in the whole of Germany." His smile was so broad that Magdalena was able to see and admire a row of astonishingly sharp, white teeth behind it. "I would in any case be delighted to welcome you to one of our next performances, perhaps tomorrow afternoon, when we shall present Christopher Marlowe's *Doctor Faustus*. You surely have already heard of our legendary production?"

"Well, I'm not sure . . ." Magdalena started to say, struggling for words. "What kind of play is it?"

"*Doctor Faustus*? Oh, it's an ancient tale of a learned man who made a pact with the devil. Lots of hocus-pocus, smoke, and goose flesh. Sometimes the people run out of the theater screaming because they're so terrified." He bared his teeth, like a wolf. "In other words, they love it."

"And the devil also appears in it?" Barbara asked, curious.

Malcolm nodded. "I play that part myself, and in all modesty I must say there's no more diabolical devil in the entire empire. Markus plays the part of the old man, Faust, and Matheo plays the beautiful Helen of Troy. "Markus, Matheo! Come here! I've found two admirers of our art."

Two of the men working on the stage looked over at them. Barbara's eyes sparkled on seeing that one of them was the suntanned youth. The other was a pale man of around forty with a strangely magnetic, melancholy look. Magdalena thought she could sense in his gaze a glimmer of infinite sadness. Both men jumped down from the stage and approached them.

"Matheo comes from an old Sicilian family of jugglers," Malcolm explained, as Barbara tugged excitedly at her linen dress. "He can juggle balls like no one else and plays with us the part of either the handsome hero or the beautiful girl." He lowered his voice and whispered, "It's true that you see nowadays more women taking women's roles, but here under the auspices of the bishop we thought it better to stay with things the way they are. We don't want to do anything to spoil our relation with His Excellency, of course."

"Certainly Matheo is quite qualified to play either role — the handsome hero or the beautiful maiden," Magdalena said with a grin, and looked at her sister. "What do you think, Barbara? Don't you think he'd make a beautiful girl?"

Barbara rolled her eyes as if Magdalena had just said something terribly embarrassing, but Matheo just laughed and curtsied.

Magdalena now turned to the pale man that Sir Malcolm had referred to as Markus. "For the role of an old scholar you are astonishingly young," she said, curious.

The man smiled, but the sadness in his eyes remained. "You have no idea what a little makeup can do, and sometimes I really do feel very old." He nodded toward the haggard director. "Sir Malcolm is a miserable slave driver."

Malcolm let out a bleating laugh. "I pay my slaves damn well. And besides, soon everyone will be talking about you, not just in Bamberg," he said, turning serious again. "Markus Salter is not only an actor, he is also our playwright," he continued. "We take the original plays of William Shakespeare and Christopher Marlowe, and Markus gives them . . . well, the necessary polish."

"Aren't the plays good enough by themselves?" Barbara asked.

"Well, for the general public they're sometimes just too difficult and dry, so we cut out the long monologues and concentrate on the funny parts and, above all, the bloody passages. Many of the pieces have not yet been translated into German, and Markus worries about that, as well."

"I butcher Shakespeare's plays by turning them into bloody spectacles for the masses," Markus sighed in despair. "Carefully constructed pentameter, beautiful images—for that the world itself clearly has no taste nowadays. The more blood, the better. But I, myself, have written my own pieces that—"

"Yes, yes," Malcolm interrupted, "that would be enough to make Shakespeare cry, I know, or simply put him to sleep. I'm afraid you're boring the ladies, Markus. Just like your plays. We can't afford experiments. After all, I have a whole troupe to feed," he said, clapping his hands. "But now it's time to get back to building the stage. Will you excuse us?" He bowed to Magdalena and Barbara and stomped off toward the stage, not without first casting a final, reproachful look at his two actors.

"Old slave driver," Markus mumbled, and followed him, while Matheo paused a moment and winked at Barbara.

"Then can we look forward to seeing you again at tomorrow's performance? We'll put aside a few seats for you up in the gallery. *Ciao, signorine.*"

"*Ciao,*" Barbara said, flickering her eyelashes as Matheo, in one single, flowing movement, climbed back onto the stage. Magdalena grinned at her sister.

"*Ciao?*" she asked with a frown. "Is that the way a Schongau hangman's daughter says good-bye, or are you an Italian contessa addressing her prince just before their wedding?"

"You . . . you are a rude, stupid old biddy, do you know that?" Barbara snarled, now once again in her familiar tone of voice, as she ran for the exit. Magdalena followed her, laughing, but her sister was so fast that she lost sight of her going down the stairway in the central dome.

• • •

Barbara was positively foaming at the mouth. As she ran out into the square by the harbor, she thought of a dozen choice curses for her big sister. How Magdalena had humiliated her! She still treated Barbara like the little girl she used to read bedtime stories to and took with her to pick blueberries, though she was now fifteen. Fifteen! An age at which other young women married.

For example, to good-looking, sun-tanned lads like Matheo.

But in the next moment she saw what a fool she was. She couldn't really understand what was going on inside her. In her conversation with the attractive young man she suddenly felt so incredibly foolish, simply ridiculous. She felt as if he could look right through her. Didn't he flash her this strange smile, as if he could read her thoughts?

She slowed her pace as she gradually calmed down. Her frantic flight was actually pretty stupid. What had really happened? Actually, Magdalena had just teased her a little. Probably this harmless teasing was just the drop that caused the barrel to overflow. The long trip, the bizarre severed arm on the riverbank, then her happy reunion with Georg . . . The stress and excitement was probably just too much for her. She hadn't seen her twin brother for two years, but his greeting the night before had seemed cool to her. Yes, Georg had been glad to see her, but she thought he would be spending at least the next day with her. Instead, he went out to flay an old horse, and she went shopping for her future aunt.

The things they'd bought . . .

All of a sudden, she stopped. She had left her packages up in the Wedding House! Should she turn around? Surely then she would meet her big sister, and she had no desire to talk with Magdalena. She was still too ashamed because of her bad behavior. In any case, Magdalena had probably picked up the packages of onions, tobacco, and herbs and was on her way back to the hangman's house. She could put it out of her mind and keep going.

She looked around to see where she was. She had left the noisy harbor behind and was walking down a wide street toward the city moat. On an impulse, she turned into a narrow lane lined by houses crowded closely together. The roofs almost touched, so that only a few rays of sunlight reached the ground. There was no more crying of fishwives to be heard, and the only sound was that of a faraway church bell.

Barbara soon realized she had gotten into a real labyrinth. In all directions there were intersections and forks in the road leading to shadowy squares and niches. Here and there were stinking, gurgling ditches that, after a few feet, disappeared under a small bridge or house. Only once in a while did she see any pedestrians, but she was too afraid to ask for directions. Strangers weren't welcomed anywhere, she knew from her experiences in Schongau.

She was about to take a turn into another side street when she felt a burning sensation between her shoulder blades, a gnawing and itching, as if someone was watching her. She turned around and just caught a glimpse of a gray, indistinct figure scampering over one of the low-hanging roofs. She heard a scratching sound, and a roof shingle fell directly at her feet.

"For heaven's sake . . ." she said, but then fell silent on hearing a thumping sound coming from the house in front of her.

Somewhere inside, a door squeaked.

As she examined the house more closely, it occurred to her how deserted it seemed. The shutters were askew, the paint had flaked off, and the roof had partly caved in so that the exposed rafters looked like gnawed-off ribs. This had to be one of the abandoned houses they had all noticed the night before.

Now sounds could be heard inside. Someone was running down the stairs.

Or perhaps some thing, Barbara suddenly thought.

She thought of the horror stories about the beast, and all the severed body parts that had been found both in and outside of the city.

At that moment she felt very alone and forsaken.

"Is-is someone there?" she asked in a hoarse voice.

Even though everything inside her was screaming for her to run as fast as she could, she moved forward as if on an invisible string in the direction of the cellar window. As the hangman's daughter, Barbara had inherited from her father not just his obstinacy and love of books but also his notorious curiosity.

I don't actually have to go inside, she thought, *just have a quick look.*

With a pounding heart, she stepped to the window, whose rotted shutters were hanging open. It was so high she had to pull herself up onto the windowsill. In front of her she saw an empty room with parquet flooring made of oak, which had been partially torn up, presumably for use as firewood. The ruins of a tile stove were scattered about, moldy rags were lying in a corner, a rusty candelabrum was—

"Hey, what the hell are you doing here? Snooping around?"

A guard's face had appeared so suddenly in the window that Barbara screamed, let go of the windowsill, and fell back into the dirt. She stared open-mouthed at the guard, who was wearing a metal helmet and a rusty chain-mail shirt, and for a moment took him to be a furry beast.

"Don't you know these abandoned houses are off-limits, you filthy brat?" he added. Now a second, older guard appeared alongside him and placed his hand on his colleague's shoulder.

"Take it easy," he said, trying to calm him down. "Back when we were kids, we were also curious and wanted to know what was going on in the abandoned houses. The girl certainly wasn't up to any mischief."

"You know exactly what the captain said," the first man whispered in a hoarse voice. "No witnesses. Suppose—"

"Sh!" The older man pulled him away from the window. "You already said too much."

He smiled and turned to Barbara. "And you, scram. There are no treasures or ghosts here, only garbage and rats." Suddenly he frowned. "Who are you, anyway? I've never seen you before in Bamberg."

"I . . . I'm just visiting my uncle," Barbara replied, scrambling to get up on her feet. "Sorry to disturb you. I'm leaving."

She ran down the narrow, shaded lane as the guard ran after her, shouting.

"Hey, little girl! Which uncle do you mean? Stop!"

But she didn't stop; she kept on running until she finally saw sunlight in front of her again. As she stepped out of the labyrinth of gloomy lanes, she was relieved to see she had reached the city moat. It stank of decay and feces, but at least she had the sun in her face again.

She arrived at the hangman's house shortly thereafter, and by then the incident with the guards was nothing but a distant memory.

Just as Magdalena was running out of the Wedding House on her way to the harbor, she remembered the package that Barbara had put down earlier beside the stage. That little brat was so angry at her older sister that she'd forgotten it.

"Damn, is it really my job to look after everything?"

She cursed as she ran back through the portal and up the stairs. If she showed up at the hangman's house without the things she'd bought, Katharina would be very disappointed — to say nothing of her father, who was impatient for his tobacco. She walked out onto the dance floor, grabbed the bundle, and hurried back out, intending to give her saucy little sister a good tongue-lashing. The actors were too busy to notice her.

Just the same, Magdalena had to smile. It looked like Barbara in fact had fallen for the sun-tanned youth.

She's growing up. It won't be long before she'll start driving Father crazy with stories about her boyfriends. And why won't the old man just treat her the same as he did me?

On the stair landing, she suddenly heard a mumbling voice coming from a room off to one side. Curious as to what it might be, she turned and saw a room full of old chests and theater props. Markus Salter, the playwright, was standing with his back toward her, leaning over a small trunk, whispering in a trusting tone, almost as if speaking with a child. When he noticed Magdalena standing behind him, he closed the trunk quickly and turned to her. He looked as if he'd been caught doing something not permitted.

Magdalena raised the basket and package apologetically. "I didn't mean to disturb you; I just forgot something, and then I saw . . ."

There was a scratching and scraping in the box, and something was squealing softly. Markus appeared to be thinking for a moment, but finally he uttered a sigh of resignation and stepped aside.

"May I introduce you to Juliet? But promise not to tell Sir Malcolm about this."

Magdalena looked puzzled. "Juliet? I'm afraid I don't understand . . ."

Without answering, Markus lifted the lid and pulled out a small, wriggling bundle of fur. It took a while for Magdalena to realize it was a ferret. She laughed with relief.

"This is Juliet?"

Markus nodded and lovingly petted the squirming little animal. "I found her last spring in the forest, along with her brother, Romeo. The two were the only ones in their litter to survive. The others were probably eaten by wild boars. That old philanderer Romeo unfortunately ran away some time ago, but Juliet stayed with me. She's rather friendly, just see."

Markus opened his hand carefully, and the ferret climbed up

his right arm to his shoulder, where it sat down and scrutinized Magdalena with beady red eyes. There was an animal intelligence in its gaze that reminded Magdalena of a rat. On the lookout, and in a strange way . . .

Evil?

Magdalena shook her head and Markus looked at her, wondering.

"What's the matter? Don't you like ferrets? They're pretty smart. You can easily train them to chase rats." He shrugged with the other shoulder. "Unfortunately, Sir Malcolm can't stand animals — ferrets, martens, weasels, all the little creatures that live in the forest . . . He says they transmit diseases. What nonsense. I think he's just afraid of them."

"Well, they are in need of a place to live," Magdalena replied hesitantly. "Ah . . . especially when they've been domesticated."

"If Sir Malcolm finds Juliet, he'll put her in a sack and throw her into the river. Please don't tell him anything." Markus petted the ferret still sitting on his shoulder like a kitten. "I'm hiding her here among the stage props until I can find a better place for her. I've really become very fond of Juliet."

Magdalena smiled. "I'll be as silent as the grave, I promise." After a few moments she asked, "How long do you intend to stay here in Bamberg?"

"Probably all winter." Markus put the squirming ferret back in her trunk and closed it carefully. "That's what all itinerant actors do. In the winter it's too cold to get around. Just last May we were here in Bamberg, and evidently the bishop liked our performances, as he has given permission for the troupe to spend the winter here this year. The innkeeper here in the Wedding House is very cordial. He's reserved the dance floor for our practices and performances and provided a few rooms where we can spend the night." He grinned. "Of course, it brings him business, too. During the performances people drink as if there was no tomorrow."

Magdalena suddenly had an idea. "You say you were in Bamberg once before?" she asked. "Do you happen to know anything about all these abandoned houses in the city? We noticed them as soon as we arrived yesterday evening. It seems rather . . . weird."

"The abandoned houses?" He appeared to hesitate. When he continued, his eyes looked a bit sadder. "Indeed, they do seem strange — silent witnesses to an enormous crime, perhaps the most violent this part of the country has ever seen."

"What sort of crime?" Magdalena asked.

Markus looked at her, perplexed. "You really must be from someplace far away if you never heard of the Bamberg witch trials. That was more than forty years ago. I myself was just a kid at the time and lived with my parents and siblings in Nuremberg, forty miles away. But even there everyone was talking about the horror that took place here." He leaned forward and lowered his voice, as if he didn't want anyone to hear. "Hundreds of innocent people in Bamberg and the neighboring towns were accused of witchcraft and put to the stake — men, women, and children. Some were just simple people, but some were noblemen, a few were burgomasters, and there was even a chancellor. The prince bishop and his henchmen were beside themselves with rage, and nobody could stop them. Not even the pope and the kaiser . . ." He paused and looked into the distance. "What a tragedy. The events at that time would really have been good material for a play, an especially bloody one."

"And the homes of the people condemned at that time are still empty?" Magdalena asked in disbelief.

Markus shrugged. "For a long time people thought the houses were haunted. It was said that the innocent people who were tortured and burned would wander as ghosts through their former homes. Then the homes fell into disrepair, and now it's probably just too expensive to restore them." He sighed. "Bamberg really has its best years behind it, and I'll be happy when we can leave the city again in the spring."

Magdalena looked out the window down at the marketplace, where the fishwives were still loudly extolling their wares. The late afternoon sun shone down mildly on the Regnitz, where a small boat was sailing calmly toward the city hall, while in the background the mighty spire of the cathedral rose up into the mist and low-lying clouds. Everything appeared so peaceful, but it seemed to Magdalena that since her visit to the market, a gray shroud had descended over the city. Even from up here she could see some of the burned ruins, the gangrenous wounds of a dying city. War, plagues, witch trials—would Bamberg ever recover from the many horrors of past years?

Suddenly Magdalena felt a chill in the cold building, and goose flesh appeared on her bare arms. She picked up her basket and package and bowed slightly.

"I enjoyed meeting you, Master Markus," she said, "even if your story was a rather sad one. Until tomorrow, then, at the performance." Suddenly her face broke out in a smile. "Oh, and say good-bye to Juliet. Perhaps I'll bring her some treats on my next visit."

Magdalena turned and hurried down the stairs toward the wide portal. Not until she reached the bustling harbor did warmth gradually return to her arms and legs.

4

FOR THE FIRST TIME IN WEEKS, SIMON FELT TRULY liberated.

The medicus and bathhouse owner wandered aimlessly through the narrow lanes, breathing in the smells of the city that were perhaps not pleasant but in any case very interesting. The prevailing stench of garbage and feces did not completely mask the smell of the river water, the sour wine, and the ever-present beer in the taverns, and as he passed through one of the many market squares, he even thought he could smell a faint scent of clove and nutmeg in the air.

In recent years, Simon had felt more and more confined in Schongau, and it was primarily for that reason he had decided to close his prosperous bathhouse for a while and accompany the Kuisls on the long trip to Bamberg. He understood the risk of doing this, as a second bathhouse had opened in town and in the last year even a new doctor had set up business. Simon considered the man a complete charlatan, but that didn't keep people from buying highly overpriced and worthless tinctures and medications from him — all because he had studied in the exotic city of Bologna on the other side of the Alps.

As Simon strolled through the little back streets, dodging

carts and passersby and struggling in vain to avoid stepping into the deep piles of garbage in his new, freshly polished leather boots, his thoughts wandered back to Ingolstadt, where he had studied long ago. That's where he had met Samuel, who came from a Jewish family that had converted to Christianity years ago. Samuel was smart and well-read, but just like Simon had a fondness for a good jug of wine, expensive clothing, and, above all, gambling — a passion that had led the two young students to many a disreputable tavern and had finally cost Simon his expensive place at the university. After just three semesters he had spent all his money on drink and gambling and had to return home to Schongau — a failure for which his father, the Schongau medicus Bonifaz Fronwieser, had never forgiven him.

Nor had he forgiven himself.

Samuel, on the other hand, had enjoyed great success. Since that time, he'd become the official doctor of Bamberg and on occasion had even attended the prince bishop in letting his blood. The two former students had corresponded occasionally, and Samuel, who was still single, always inquired about Simon's family. For this reason, Simon was immediately excited when they received the invitation to visit Bamberg. He wanted to finally see his old friend Samuel again and hoped to hear about the latest advances in medicine that might be useful to him in Schongau.

Furthermore, Simon enjoyed — more than he wanted to admit to himself — wandering by himself through the little alleyways of Schongau. He loved his two boys, but they could be incredibly tiring, especially Paul, a little hellion who tended to break out in temper tantrums. Simon hadn't told his wife when he would be back, so he was free to enjoy these precious moments visiting the many churches and chapels, buying a package of his beloved coffee beans in the spice market — despite the outrageous cost — and shopping for clothing material.

As Simon strolled past the church of St. Martin, he saw a young girl whose hair had been shorn, standing by the church portal. She was wearing braids of straw and holding in her hand a wooden tablet informing passersby that she'd had a casual affair with a young man prior to her marriage. Some of those passing by spat on the ground in front of the girl, while others regarded her with pity. Simon's face darkened, and he couldn't help thinking how he, too, and Magdalena had been exposed to mockery and hatred in Schongau before they were finally permitted to marry.

It's always the same. Bathhouse owners, amateur doctors, and hangman's children . . . we'll always be shunned as dishonorable, all our lives. Probably even in the sophisticated city of Paris they'd be singing lewd songs making fun of us.

After stopping several times to get directions, Simon finally stood in front of the so-called Burgher's Enclave adjacent to the distinguished Jesuit college near the Hay Market. Several buildings surrounded an elegant interior courtyard full of flowers and fruit trees. Simon had learned that the head city clerk as well as the city physician were housed there. As he pondered the freshly roofed buildings, carefully pruned apple trees, and meticulously clean yard, he couldn't help but think of his own wretched bathhouse back home.

Perhaps Father was right, after all. I'm just a miserable failure.

Then he thought of Magdalena, the boys, and all the exciting things that had happened since then, and his gloomy feelings evaporated.

Excitedly Simon knocked on the door that he had been directed to, and waited. After a while he heard footsteps, and an elderly woman, presumably Samuel's housekeeper, opened the door. The woman was haggard, severe looking, unusually tall for a woman, and had her hair tied in a tightly wound bun. She cast a disapproving glance down at the short bathhouse owner in his rumpled clothing.

"The doctor is not in," the haggard old woman snarled. "If you have an ailment that needs tending, come back tomorrow."

She scowled. "Wednesday mornings Master Samuel also treats common people."

Simon choked back the nasty reply on the tip of his tongue. "I'm an old friend of his," he replied with a smile. "Where could I see him now?"

The housekeeper pursed her lips. "People like you wouldn't be admitted there. Herr Doktor is over at Geyerswörth Castle with His Holiness, the bishop. One of his . . ." she hesitated, "uh, chambermaids, has a woman's ailment that only Master Samuel is able to cure. But that's no business of yours."

"Aha, a chambermaid. I'll wager she's a bit younger, prettier, and no doubt more affectionate than the chambermaids of an ordinary city physician. Well, in any case, good day to you."

While the housekeeper was still frowning and trying to figure out the meaning of what he'd just said, Simon had already turned away and left the Burgher's Enclave. As so often when people alluded to his low social standing, a rage rose up in him that was hard for him to control. Once again he swore to himself that his children and grandchildren would someday be better off than their father, who despite all his talent had made it no further in life than that of a dishonorable bathhouse owner in a backwater town. Would things have turned out differently if he'd completed his studies in Ingolstadt? Would he, too, have become the personal physician of a duke or bishop?

Simon was still seething as he turned into a small lane leading to the hangman's house on the city moat. Then, on the spur of the moment, he decided to give it a try after all and go to Geyerswörth Castle to look for Samuel. There was no reason for the old woman to have turned him away so rudely, as his clothing, though a bit rumpled, was still quite appropriate. His petticoat breeches and smart feathered hat had cost him a fortune. Simon attached great importance to his appearance, trying to make up for his small stature.

At the next corner he inquired about the way to the castle

and was directed toward the left branch of the Regnitz. Soon he could make out, a bit upstream and not far from the city hall, a long island on whose northern half stood a magnificent building decorated with oriels and little towers. Stained-glass and lead-lined crown-glass windows reflected the light of the afternoon sun. It looked like a slightly smaller version of a royal hunting lodge. Suddenly Simon was no longer so sure he should ask to see his friend Samuel in this splendid building.

Summoning up his courage, however, he strode across the bridge to a large portal with two oaken wings where the bishop's guards stood on duty. Meanwhile, he'd straightened up his clothing a bit, and the soldiers who looked him up and down were not hostile toward him.

"Is the city physician available?" Simon asked, endeavoring to sound both blasé and accustomed to giving orders.

One of the guards frowned. "He's inside with one of the girls. Why do you ask?"

"Well, uh . . . he forgot his package of Bengali fire beans." On an impulse, Simon held up the small purse of coffee beans he'd just bought. "Without these, the patient's treatment will probably be ineffective. I need to take them to the doctor as soon as possible."

"Bengali fire . . . what?" The folds in the guard's forehead deepened. "Do you think that will help cure the accursed French disease the girl has?"

Simon smiled inwardly. Now he at least knew what the bishop's so-called maid was suffering from. The French disease, also known as syphilis, was a contagious and extremely dangerous sexual infection often leading to madness and eventually death. It was especially feared in the royal courts, as there was practically no cure. The bathhouse owner shook the bag so that the beans rattled inside.

"A cure is possible only with the use of Bengali fire beans," he announced solemnly. "They come directly from the East Indian islands, and the prince bishop paid a fortune for them. They're effective only for one hour, and after that they start going bad."

"For heaven's sake!" It was clear from the look on the guard's face that he was thinking what was in store for him if the bishop had any reason to complain. "Then get yourself in right away. The Jew must have forgotten to bring his medicine," he grumbled softly, but Simon had already slipped by him and entered the shaded inner court of the palace. He could feel the suspicious gazes of the other guards like arrows in his back, so he decided to hurry along with his head held high, toward a stone archway that appeared to lead to the back of the castle.

As soon as he'd passed through the arch, he stopped, overwhelmed by the sight in front of him. Before him lay a large park with lines of green hedges bounded by two branches of a river. Some bushes were shaped in the form of animals, others stood in waving rows, and some had leafy tops. Between the rows there were beds of all kinds of roses, many of which had faded. In the middle of the park stood a fountain with graceful statues and a bronze stag with holy water spraying from its antlers. Colorful, exotic birds chirped in a nearby aviary, and next to it was a gleaming hothouse containing dark-green lemon trees. After all the filth and stench outside in the alleyways, this scenery seemed so bizarre that Simon almost thought he was dreaming. A loud voice calling his name finally brought him back to the present.

"My God, Simon! Tell me it's really you."

From a balcony with steps leading into the castle, a tall man came running toward him. He was wearing a broad black cloak and a pointed hat, making him look like a magician, and his arms were spread out in greeting. Not until the man had drawn closer did Simon recognize the friendly face, slightly hooked nose, and bushy eyebrows. His hair had thinned and he had a few more wrinkles around his eyes, but otherwise he looked just like he used to.

"Samuel!" Simon replied with a laugh.

They embraced warmly, and for a moment, the park with the fountain, the hedges, the exotic birds, indeed all of Geyersworth Castle was forgotten.

"You should have sent me a messenger to tell me you were coming," Samuel chided him, raising his finger playfully. "I was worried something might have happened to you on your long trip."

Simon sighed. "I'm afraid you overestimate my financial means, Samuel. I'm just a simple bathhouse owner who can't afford a messenger on horseback." His gaze wandered, half in wonder and half with envy to the castle towers. "You, on the other hand, evidently are a regular guest of the Bamberg prince bishop."

"And shoot enemas up his fat ass," Samuel laughed, waving him off. "The life of an esteemed city physician is not always as pleasant as people think. You know, of course, that the richer the patient, the more difficult he is to deal with. At present I'm treating not so much His Excellency as I am one of his playmates . . ."

"The one suffering from the French disease, I know," Simon interrupted.

Samuel grinned. "I see you haven't changed. Curious and sly as an old Jew. I don't even want to know how you got wind of this highly secret information, nor how you slipped by the guards of the bishop's summer residence," he added with a playful threat.

"Well, let's just say both in the same way," Simon responded with a smile. But then his face darkened. "The French disease is a horrible scourge. I remember that years ago my father had some cases to treat, and all the patients died. Is just the girl infected, or the prince bishop, as well?" He lowered his voice and looked around to see if anyone might be listening.

Samuel shook his head. "Probably not, even if naturally that is Philipp Rieneck's greatest worry at present. I spread quicksil-

ver all over the girl's body to stop the disease, and the young thing
screamed like a stuck pig. If the syphilis doesn't drive her mad,
then possibly the treatment will, but what can I do? I don't know
any other treatment." He sighed sadly. "That's the reason why
we've quarantined the patient here in Geyerswörth and not in
his palace up in Mengersdorf where the prince bishop resides in
the cooler months." Samuel smiled with tightly pursed lips. "The
screams remind His Excellency too much of his own mortality,
though today, at least, he condescended to come and visit her. After all, she'd been until very recently his favorite concubine."

"Did you ever try using the potion made from the guaiac
tree?" Simon inquired. "I read about it just a few months ago.
The great humanist Ulrich von Hutten, in an experiment on
himself—"

Samuel laughed. "I see in this regard as well you haven't
changed—always in search of the newest treatment methods,
and perhaps you are right. I'll . . ."

He fell silent as two elegantly dressed men accompanied by
several guards appeared beneath the archway and starting walking toward them. With a sigh, Samuel removed his hat and motioned to Simon to do the same.

"What a schlimazel," Samuel muttered, falling back into the
Yiddish jargon of his childhood. "The prince bishop and the suffragan bishop both at the same time. I am spared nothing. Let's
just hope these two high-placed gentlemen don't both want to be
bled at the same time, so I can return home before the morning."

He bowed deeply, and Simon, hesitantly, did the same.

A deep, booming voice greeted the city physician: "Ah, my
dear Samuel." The cleric was large, had long, elegantly waved
gray hair, and a goatee, likewise gray. His garb was that of a nobleman, with only the cap on his head revealing to Simon that
the man standing before him was none other than the prince
bishop in person. He appeared to be about fifty years old.

"So how is treatment going for my beloved Francesca?"

Philipp Rieneck asked with concern. "When I visited her this morning, the poor creature was beside herself. She didn't even recognize me, her father confessor." Only now did he notice Simon, and his eyes turned to tiny slits. "Have you perhaps shared our little secret with one of your servants?"

Samuel shook his head vigorously. "Of course not. This gentleman is the renowned physician Simon Fronwieser, a professional friend and esteemed doctor from the Munich area. We're just discussing other treatment possibilities that won't be as painful as quicksilver."

The bishop seemed to be thinking it over for a moment but finally nodded his head. "Very well, good, anything is better than this screaming. Sometimes it's so loud it goes right through you. But one thing has to be clear." He looked Simon up and down sharply. "It concerns medical confidentiality — or I will soon be pleased to hear *your own* screams, Mister . . . Tell me your name again."

"Fronwieser," Simon quickly told him in a rasping voice. "Simon Fronwieser." He still couldn't come out with the words of the bold lie Samuel had just told, elevating him to the status of a certified physician. "You . . . you can depend on me."

"Very well. I see we understand each other." The prince bishop flashed a friendly smile. Then he pointed to the elderly gentleman at his side, who, like himself, was wearing ecclesiastical garb and was no doubt the suffragan bishop. While Philipp Valentin Voit von Rieneck was in charge of both the worldly and spiritual administration in Bamberg, the suffragan bishop concerned himself only with affairs of the church. He had the tonsure of a monk and a piercing gaze that Simon could feel going straight through him.

"Well, my dear Master Samuel," Philipp Rieneck continued, turning to the doctor as his face darkened. "There's bad news. Suffragan Bishop Sebastian Harsee has just informed me of another gruesome find reported to His Excellency by well-informed friends in the city guard. Evidently an arm belonging to the missing city councilman Schwarzkontz has been found out in the Bamberg Forest. Dreadful, isn't it?" Rieneck shivered. "The old city councilman was always such a strong pillar in the house of God."

"This same Lord God will watch over him," Samuel replied. "Probably the poor man was torn to bits by wild animals in the forest."

"Or something else," the suffragan bishop interjected. His creaking voice reminded Simon of the crunching sound of rotted wood.

Samuel looked at Harsee in bewilderment. "Something else? What do you mean by that, Your Excellency?"

"As His Eminence has just indicated, this is not the first finding of a severed body part," Harsee replied sharply. "And missing-persons cases are mounting. Apparently, the wife of the apothecary has disappeared, as well. But that's not all." He continued in a whisper, "I have just learned that last night a large, furry creature was sighted in the city walking on its hind legs. It is said to be as large as a man, with long, pointed teeth."

"A furry creature with long, pointed teeth?" Samuel stared at him open-mouthed. "But . . ."

"One of the night watchmen saw it, and the brave man reported it to me just this morning," Harsee interrupted. "There is no doubt."

Prince Bishop Philipp Rieneck, who was standing beside him, cleared his throat nervously. "I told the suffragan bishop immediately that I think the entire matter is . . . well, pure fantasy. Evidently the witness is an old drunkard. Unfortunately, the man told other people about it, and the rumor is now coursing through the taverns. The church fears unrest."

"Rightly so," Sebastian Harsee noted. He straightened up as if about to deliver a long sermon. "Together with the earlier reports of men and women who have vanished and these gruesome findings of severed body parts, I come to a serious, though logical conclusion."

"And what would that be?" Samuel asked hesitantly.

"Well . . ." The suffragan bishop paused briefly for dramatic effect before continuing in a whisper: "It's not out of the question that a werewolf is afoot in Bamberg."

For a moment, the men remained silent, and all that could be heard was the splashing of water in the fountain.

"A werewolf?" Simon finally ventured. "But . . . that's such nonsense."

Then he bit his tongue. He actually had meant to keep his silence, but the suspicions of the suffragan bishop had completely flustered him.

Sebastian Harsee gave him an indignant look, as if he'd been disturbed by some hideous sound, then turned back to the Bamberg city medicus.

"The existence of werewolves has been proven. The *Malleus Maleficarum,* or *Hammer of Witches,* that treatise used by the Inquisition, which cannot be praised highly enough, and other books written by eminent scholars, provide ample proof of that. There were many trials against magical creatures, especially in France, but also here in the German countries. The last of them took place in Landshut and Straubing just a few years ago." Harsee's voice began to rise and assumed a priestly tone. "Just like the witches, werewolves are evil men who have entered into a pact with the devil, who gives them a mantle of wolf's hide, transforming them into horrible, hairy beasts with a ravenous appetite for all living things. I have studied the scholarly treatises about them and am certain that a werewolf is prowling the streets of our city."

The prince bishop had until then remained silent and seemed to be struggling with his emotions. Finally he cleared his throat.

"I must admit that I've had my doubts, but now, as rumors are spreading and more and more people claim to have seen this beast—"

"Something like that is not uncommon," Samuel interjected. "A person thinks they've seen something, and at once ten others are there to boast they've seen it as well. If we investigated every rumor, we'd probably not be able to save ourselves from all the witches, werewolves, and other magical creatures."

"But what do you say about the many missing persons and the horribly dismembered bodies?" Philipp Rieneck shook his head. "I'm afraid I can no longer close my eyes to all of this, even if I wanted to. People are becoming restless, and if this continues, I won't be able to find beaters for my hunting trips, because no one will dare to go into the forest anymore." He sighed. "Moreover, in just a few days His Excellency the elector's representative and bishop of Würzburg, Johann Philipp von Schönborn, will be paying us a courtesy visit. He is one of the most powerful men in the Reich and a friend of the kaiser, and we cannot allow any unresolved, horrible acts to mar this occasion. I have therefore decided, with great regret, to call together a commission to investigate these matters more closely." Rieneck pointed to Harsee, who was standing alongside him, his arms folded and with a grim look on his face. "Suffragan Bishop Harsee will head the commission, and I would also like to have you join the group, Master Samuel. After all, everything needs to be scientifically verified. Bamberg cannot afford to be placed once again in a bad light."

Simon had no idea what the prince bishop meant in his last sentence. He cast a questioning look at Samuel, but Rieneck had already turned back to address the city physician. "I'd like to discuss a few details with you. Alone." He glanced briefly at Simon. "Your friend will certainly be able to find his way out by himself."

"Of course." Simon bowed deeply and was about to hurry off when Samuel held him back.

"When this nonsense has passed, I'd be glad to have a glass of wine with you," he whispered in Simon's ear so that those around them couldn't hear. "Let's say tomorrow afternoon at my house?"

Simon nodded imperceptibly, then headed toward the exit. When he turned around again, he saw Bishop Philipp Rieneck walking along the row of hedges with Samuel, in animated conversation.

Only the suffragan bishop was still standing in the same place, watching Simon suspiciously, as if wondering if a short, brash doctor might be in truth a dastardly werewolf.

A few hours later, in a far less hospitable place, Adelheid Rinswieser, the wife of the apothecary, stared at the flickering wick of a small candle, which was about to go out. Her voice was hoarse from screaming, and her bones and muscles ached from the leather straps tying her to the bench. She could only move her right arm and used it to reach for an earthenware cup of water standing on the ground alongside her, which she used to wet her fingers and moisten her lips.

Where am I? How did I get here?

The cell she was in was square, stuffy, and smelled of sour wine and the feces of rats, which scampered now and then across the dirt floor, squeaking. Most of the time there was a leaden silence, as if she'd been buried somewhere in the bowels of the earth. Now and then Adelheid heard the screams of the other woman, and then she knew it was starting again.

When is it my turn? Oh, God, when?

Adelheid had long ago given up calling for help, and the only sound coming from her mouth was an occasional whimper. She had no idea how long she'd been lying down here. The last thing she could remember was that crackling sound when the creature threw itself upon her in the forest—that and the odor of the wet fur. After that she had awakened in this cell with a headache like that from drinking a bottle of brandy. On one side of her head, above the temple, a large bump was throbbing.

Since then, the dreary hours dragged on. There was no window, not even a crack where light might penetrate into the damp chamber, and the only light came from a tallow candle that cast dancing shadows on the walls. The only sounds she could hear were the occasional shrill screams of the other woman. Adelheid had never seen the poor woman but assumed she was in a room at the other end of the hall. Adelheid feared this room more than anything else.

The torture chamber.

Shortly after she had regained consciousness, a man wearing a hangman's hood led her there in chains. Even now, she shuddered when she thought of all the strange instruments she'd seen there. Though Adelheid didn't know what most of them were, she suspected they all served the same purpose, to inflict as much pain as possible on a human being. Her suspicions were confirmed by a hastily sketched drawing on the walls of the chamber. They were drawn on strips of cloth that hung down from the ceiling, like the flags of an evil kingdom, and they showed images so horrible that even hours later she was still gagging with fear.

Adelheid remembered the image of a man riding astride a sharp wooden cone, his mouth opened wide in agony, and the face of a woman whose jaw was propped open by an iron clamp while her tongue was cut out with a knife. A third image showed a naked, red-haired girl lying on the rack while a masked hangman poured water into her mouth through a funnel. Other torture victims wore bronze boots full of pitch, were hung from the ceiling like slaughtered animals, or driven with pitchforks into the rushing, dark waters of a river. The images in the chamber showed a more horrible vision of hell than anything she'd seen in the Bamberg Cathedral, and Adelheid still had no idea what her offense had been.

What agony is in store for me? Oh, God, let me lose my mind first, so I no longer can feel the pain. Or am I perhaps already mad? Is this hell?

The man had not removed his hangman's cap and at first spoke not a word, not breaking his silence until they were in the torture chamber. His voice had been firm and matter-of-fact, and he'd kept asking the same questions:

Confess, witch! Who taught you your magic?

Who are your brothers and sisters?

Where do you meet? In the forest? In the cemetery? Up in the old castle?

Where do you meet on Witch's Sabbath?

How do you brew the drink that makes you fly?

Confess, witch, confess, confess, confess . . .

There was nothing Adelheid could tell him — she'd just shaken her head and pleaded for her life. But he had continued asking the same questions, his voice an unending torrent of words.

Confess, witch, confess, confess, confess . . .

Then he'd taken her back to her cell and whispered in her ear one final, strange sentence:

This is the first degree . . .

Adelheid knew from stories she'd heard that suspects were always first shown the instruments of torture. Often that by itself was enough, and they confessed out of sheer terror. But the apothecary's wife had no idea what to confess to, and the man had brought her back without saying a word, tied her to the bench again, and left her alone.

What the second, third, or fourth degree might be, she could now hear in the next room.

From deep within the walls she heard a high-pitched scream, and groaned softly. There was no doubt that the torture was continuing in the chamber. The screams of the other prisoner faded in and out, but for some reason Adelheid knew the man would not inflict pain on her until the other woman was dead.

Hang on, whoever you are. Hang on as long as possible.

A while ago Adelheid had made out some bits of words amid all the screams — shrill calls for help, pleading, praying, but since then the words had begun to sound like the whimpers of a mad person.

And they became weaker and weaker.

Hang on.

Adelheid closed her eyes and mumbled a quiet prayer as the screams seemed to pierce her like needles.

Hang on!

"Damn, this is tobacco the way I love it. Black as the devil's hair and sweet as the ass of a young whore."

His eyes closed, Jakob Kuisl sat in the Bamberg hangman's dining room puffing on his pipe as dark clouds of smoke rose to the ceiling. The foul-smelling tobacco seemed to transform the hangman into a more peaceful, sociable creature. The others present rubbed their stinging eyes and occasionally coughed but accepted that as the price they had to pay.

The fading light of autumn had turned to night several hours earlier, and the Kuisls were sitting together around the huge oaken table while Katharina cleared away the bowls, plates, and tableware. From the ingredients Magdalena and Barbara had brought back to her from the Bamberg markets, Bartholomäus's fiancée had conjured up the most delicious meal Magdalena had eaten in months. Now she was sitting across the table from her father, feeling full, relaxed, and tired, watching as he blew smoke rings of various sizes across the room. The boys, Peter and Paul, were already asleep after Barbara had told them a long bedtime story.

Outside, the autumn rain beat against the shutters and the

wind howled like a wild beast. With dread, Magdalena thought about the previous night and the terrible events her father and Uncle Bartholomäus had just related to them.

"And someone really slit open this poor girl's chest in order to take out her heart?" she asked in the ensuing silence. "For heaven's sake, who would do such a thing?"

"What rubbish," growled Bartholomäus, who was sitting at the table off to one side, whittling a piece of pinewood. "Your father just made it up. The perpetrator probably just took a swing at the poor child to shut her up."

"But what about the toenails that were ripped out on the foot the captain showed us?" Kuisl interrupted. "Did the perpetrator just take a wild swing there, too? This is one too many coincidences for me."

"Well, even if that's the case," Bartholomäus said, casting a dark glance at Jakob, "I really can't understand why you have to tell us all about it here, Jakob. The head of the city guards expressly—"

"What I tell my family is none of your damn business," Kuisl interrupted, nodding toward Georg and Simon. "Georg already knows about it; I told him. He'll take it to his grave with him, and my son-in-law may be just a bathhouse owner, but he knows a thing or two about medicine. So why shouldn't I ask them for their advice?"

Magdalena couldn't help laughing. "Good God, wonders never cease. This would be the first time you asked my husband for advice," she said, turning to Simon. "Right?"

Simon just shrugged. He was warming his hands on a cup of hot coffee, the brew that did the most to stimulate his thinking, as Magdalena knew. "In any case, I don't believe this crime can be kept secret very long," he finally said. "By now, half the city already knows about the hairy monster."

"You're right," said Georg, stretching. The long, strenuous day clearly had tired him out, as well. "I was in the Bamberg

Forest today, and later went over to Saint Gangolf to pick up a few dead sheep. Even there, people are talking about this beast, and they think it can only be a werewolf." He shook his head. "If the prince bishop learns about this . . ."

"Unfortunately, he already has," Simon interrupted with a sigh, "from his own suffragan bishop, Sebastian Harsee. Do you know him? He's really a disagreeable fellow."

He briefly told about his meeting with Master Samuel and the dark suspicions expressed by the suffragan bishop.

"They want to put together a council to consider if it's really a werewolf," Simon concluded, "even though this Harsee bastard has already made up his mind. Thank God that Samuel will also be a member of the commission—at least one enlightened voice in this crowd of superstitious and bigoted agitators."

"But suppose it really is a werewolf?" Barbara asked anxiously. After helping Katharina clear the table, she sat down alongside her brother, Georg, and looked around at everyone. "In any case, people have disappeared, severed body parts have been found, and then this furry creature . . ."

"And don't forget the horribly mangled cadaver of the stag that Simon told us about yesterday, and the talk by people who have traveled through the forest," Magdalena interrupted, turning to her father. "There may be nothing to it, but isn't it possible some beast is really lurking around Bamberg and causing this trouble? It doesn't have to be a werewolf. Maybe it's just a large wolf, or—"

"Good God, just stop this!" Bartholomäus shouted, pounding his knife into the table. "I don't want to hear anything more about this in my house. Werewolf? Bah! These are horror stories that only sow hatred and discord, as if we didn't already have enough of them in Bamberg." He stood up, and stomped off to the downstairs bedroom, slamming the door behind him.

"What's the matter with him?" Simon asked. "You might almost think tobacco doesn't agree with him."

"You'll have to excuse him." With a sigh, Katharina took off her apron and sat down in her fiancé's empty chair. With a silent but disapproving look, she stared at the knife in front of her jammed into the top of the table, still quivering. "You're not Bambergers," she said softly, "and don't know what this city went through back then, when they burned hundreds of accused wizards and witches here. Bartholomäus just doesn't want to go through all that again."

"Even though as the Bamberg hangman it would bring him a lot of business," Jakob replied sullenly. Then he started counting on his fingers. "Let's see: if Bartholomäus receives two guilders each time he tortures a person and ten more for every witch put to the stake and burned, that would amount to—"

"You! You just can't bear the fact that your brother is more successful than you are," Georg burst out angrily. "Admit it, Father. Our uncle has really made something out of himself here in Bamberg, and now he's marrying the daughter of a city clerk while you in Schongau are still cleaning garbage from the street. And that gets under your skin."

Kuisl looked down at the reeds on the floor and spat. "Better to have your feet in the shit than to crawl up the perfumed asses of the noble gentlemen. By the way, that's no way to talk to your father. What has your uncle taught you in the last two years?"

"More than you in ten."

"Enough of this, now." Katharina had jumped up and was glaring angrily at the father and son. "Perhaps some of you have forgotten, but we'll be celebrating a wedding soon, and I want you all to get along. The reason I invited you to Bamberg was so Bartholomäus could finally become reconciled with his relatives. After all, we're one family." She pointed at Georg. "And you will excuse yourself, at once. That's no way to speak to your father."

For a while no one said a thing. Finally Georg nodded. "Very well. I'm . . . I'm sorry, Father."

Jakob Kuisl remained silent, but Magdalena could see how

he was struggling with himself. He crushed his pipe stem between his teeth while exhaling little clouds of smoke like a smokestack. Finally he nodded as well, but still not a word escaped his lips. Magdalena decided to change the topic and turned to Katharina.

"Was Bartholomäus the Bamberg executioner back then, during the terrible Bamberg witch trials?" she asked.

Katharina stared at her, at a loss. "I'm not sure. At the time I was just a baby. If he was here then, he must have been just a young assistant, so it was no fault of his."

"We hangmen are never at fault," Jakob Kuisl said, between two puffs on his pipe. "Even if the noble gentlemen wished we were. We are just the sword in their hands."

"So Bartholomäus's worries are really justified." Simon was thinking it all over as he slurped his strong-tasting brew. He, too, seemed glad that the quarrel between the father and the son had been put aside, at least temporarily. "If they really set up a commission because of this werewolf, it won't be long before the first burnings at the stake take place," he continued. He turned to Kuisl. "Think of Schongau. Wasn't it your grandfather back then who beheaded and burned more than sixty women in this ill-fated witch trial? The whole town went crazy."

"That was a long time ago," Kuisl growled. "The times were different."

"Really?" Magdalena looked at her father, mulling it all over. "For my part, I pray that men have changed since that time. But I'm very skeptical. Even if—"

A knock at the door interrupted her words, and a shiver ran up her spine, as if something evil was lurking out there, demanding to be let in. The other members of the family looked questioningly at one another.

"Don't worry," Katharina said, trying to calm them down. "That's just my father. He insisted on picking me up personally today. After everything that has happened in the last few weeks, he doesn't want me to walk alone through the dark back streets." She opened the door, and in stepped a portly gentleman wrapped in a heavy woolen cape with a hood, from which the rain dripped in little rivulets to the ground. A lantern dangling from his hand cast a dim, flickering light around him. Magdalena couldn't suppress a smile. Katharina's father looked as if someone had dumped a barrel of water over him, shrinking his clothing so it sat tightly on him all over his body.

"Horrid weather outside," he remarked, shivering. "Wouldn't even allow a dog outside in this weather."

"Let's hope it's too wet and cold for the evildoers as well," Katharina responded with a smile. "You don't look like you could scare him off very easily."

She pointed at the others at the table. "But even in such terrible weather, we mustn't forget our manners and greet our guests. This is my father, Hieronymus Hauser. You already met Jakob earlier; behind him is Magdalena and her husband, Simon, and between them, that pretty young lady is Georg's twin sister, Barbara."

Hauser bowed politely, then he winked at Barbara. "I can't say you look very much like your brother, but that isn't necessarily a disadvantage."

Jakob Kuisl laughed grimly. "You're right, Master Hauser. Barbara is more like her mother."

"Well, with regard to corpulence, I'm more like my father," Katharina lamented, rolling her eyes playfully. "I can count myself lucky that Bartl prefers bigger women." She stretched, and rubbed her tired eyes. "Excuse me, but the day has been long and at the first light of dawn tomorrow we need to go back to preparing for the wedding. I'm afraid we must leave."

Hauser nodded. "Yes, I think we must. The night watchman is just going by outside along the moat, and I'd like to join him.

These autumn nights feel a bit eerie to me . . ." He shook himself and turned to Simon. "I'd like to continue our talk sometime in the light of day. They say you know something about books, and I have some at home that might interest you."

Simon looked up at him, delighted. "Oh, of course. What are they, what . . ."

Magdalena yawned loudly. When Simon started talking about books, there was usually no end to it. "Katharina's right, it's already late," she said as she stood up. "Besides, I promised to help Katharina tomorrow."

"I'm so glad for the help," her aunt smiled. "We must pick out the material for my dress and cut it to size, and given my figure, it will take a couple of rolls. Thank you very much, Magdalena." She clapped her hands as if trying to scare off an evil spirit. "A little sleep should do everyone some good and drive away the gloomy thoughts, so let's hurry and get to bed." She shook her finger in mock admonishment. "And remember, no more quarreling in the family. After the wedding you can rip each other to shreds, for all I care."

Hauser frowned. "I hope there will be no occasion to do that. Or is there?" He looked all around. "Where is Bartholomäus, anyway?"

Katharina brushed off the remark lightly. "Oh, he's just gone off to sulk a bit. It's nothing serious, Father, believe me. I'll tell you all about it on the way home."

She put on her coat and hugged Magdalena once more. "Take care that Bartl and your father don't squabble too much, will you?" she whispered. "It would be the best wedding present you could give me."

Magdalena nodded silently, and with one last nod, Katharina and Hieronymus Hauser stepped out into the rain.

Everyone at the table rose, each heading for their own bedroom, except for Jakob Kuisl, who remained, puffing rings of smoke and watching them rise slowly toward the ceiling. When Magdalena turned around one last time to look at her father, she felt as if she were being pursued by hordes of strange, hairy, creatures with long fangs.

Then the beasts slipped out through cracks in the windows and disappeared into the night.

5

THE YELPING OF THE HOUNDS ECHOED THROUGH the forest—a hoarse, endless, nerve-racking howl that got on Jakob's nerves. It grew louder, then suddenly died away, then morphed into a growling and whimpering as the knacker Aloysius finally tossed the bloody pieces of meat they'd been begging for into their kennel.

The Schongau hangman watched with interest as the hounds, almost twenty in number, fought over the food. Most were agile hunting dogs with black, shiny coats, and a few were brawny mastiffs kept in their own kennel next to the others. All the animals were muscular and well-fed, baring their fangs as they growled and tore at the large pieces of meat until all that was left of the horse carcass was a few hairy scraps.

"Good dog, good dog," said Aloysius cheerfully, as if talking to a few little lap dogs. "Here's a little more for you. Enjoy it!"

He wiped his bloody hands off on his leather apron, reached for a bucket of steaming innards, and tossed the contents into the enclosure. The dogs pounced on it, barking loudly. Kuisl had met the dour hangman's journeyman the day before, when he and Bartholomäus and Georg delivered the horse cadaver. Since then, two dead goats and a pig had died of some mysterious disease. To avoid a possible epidemic, the law required all cadavers to be brought to the knacker in the Bamberg Forest as soon as possible for processing and disposal.

As so often, Jakob Kuisl was fascinated to see all the ways a dead body could be put to use. The horsehair was used to fill mattresses or to make sieves and cheap wigs; the hooves and horns were ground into a powder and spread over the fields as fertilizer; and the boiled, foul-smelling fat was used in making expensive, sweet-smelling soap.

We turn garbage into gold, he thought, *and they pay us with rusty pennies.*

There was actually no reason for Kuisl to return to the Bamberg Forest that day, though he was curious to find out about this so-called beast. Even more, though, he had been driven by his longing for his son, whom he hoped to find here. He and Georg had never talked much with one other, yet there was an affinity between them that had not faded away in all those years. Despite the great distance between them, Jakob had always felt close to his son, and that's why the quarrel the other day had disturbed him more than he even admitted to himself. What was it, again, that Georg said?

You just can't bear the fact that your brother is more successful than you are . . .

Is that what it was? Was he really jealous of his younger brother, the one he'd despised so much back then — little Bartl, who'd been a bit more slow-witted than he himself, who'd looked at every torture as an interesting experiment and had been able to get along better with animals than with people.

Or does meeting him remind me of the guilt I can never wash away?

A foul smell stung his nose. When he turned around, he saw his son, Georg, along with Bartholomäus, stirring a large steaming kettle of lye that hung over a fireplace in front of the knacker's house. The one-story blockhouse was solidly built and as

large as a small but formidable castle. In addition, there were a
few sheds, a dog kennel, and a smoking coal pile. Taken together,
the buildings formed a defensive area surrounded by fences and
thorny hedges standing in a large clearing in the middle of the
forest.

"Well, what do you think of my dogs?" With a slight limp in
his gait, Bartholomäus walked over to his elder brother and
pointed proudly at the hunting dogs yelping and panting as they
fought among themselves for the last scraps of food. "It took forever to train them, but they're fast, untiring, and do everything I
tell them. They're the best hunting dogs anywhere."

Jakob frowned. "And *you,* a hangman, go hunting?"

Bartholomäus laughed and waved dismissively. "Of course
not. I only train them for the Bamberg prince bishop. He's crazy
about dogs and other animals. His Excellency is very happy with
me, above all because I tend to his beloved menagerie. I feed the
bears there and clean out the cages." He grinned and rubbed his
thumb and forefinger together. "His Excellency pays me quite
well for my work. In a few more years, perhaps I'll buy a larger
house somewhere near the Green Market."

"Just be careful then that the people don't set your expensive
house on fire," Jakob warned him. "People don't like it when dishonorable folks like us come into money and become their
equals."

"Maybe in Schongau, but things are different in Bamberg."
Bartholomäus pointed at Georg, who was still standing alongside the boiling kettle and stirring it with a long stick. "Ask your
son. He likes the way he's treated here." A faint smile passed over
his lips. "And your daughter Barbara would no doubt like it
here, too."

"What do you mean by that?"

"Well . . ." Bartholomäus paused for a moment, then nodded
in the direction of Aloysius, who was standing in the kennel surrounded by the dogs. The knacker was wearing a long leather

jacket smeared with blood and dirt, and a glove on one hand that one of the dogs had just sunk its teeth into. "Aloysius has been looking for a wife for a long time," Bartholomäus continued in a soft voice. "He isn't the handsomest fellow in the world, but as the Bamberg knacker and hangman's journeyman, he makes a good living. In addition, he's loyal and reliable. When I'm not here, he does all the work of the knacker by himself here in the forest—flaying, grinding bones, caring for the dogs . . . A little feminine companionship would be good for him."

Jakob laughed loudly. "You don't know my daughter, Bartl. She's got a mind of her own. Years ago I tried to marry off Magdalena to my cousin in Steingaden, but she couldn't be talked out of marrying her Simon."

Bartholomäus shrugged. "Just think it over. Other hangmen's daughters would love to have an offer like this."

"It's enough for you to try to change Georg," Kuisl grumbled. "For heaven's sake stay away from Barbara. We're here to celebrate a wedding, and then everyone will go their own ways. That's what we agreed to." Jakob turned around, but his brother's sharp voice held him back.

"That's what you do best, isn't it, Jakob? Go your own way, and not concern yourself with others."

"How dare you . . ." Kuisl flared up, but at that moment Aloysius approached with another bucket of fresh guts. The knacker, whose face was scarred by pockmarks, greeted them with a brief nod.

"I'm going out back, master," he mumbled into his stubby beard. It was clear he was missing some teeth.

"Do that," Bartholomäus replied, "and remember the bishop needs the mastiffs tomorrow for his bear hunt, so wash and comb their fur so they don't embarrass us."

Aloysius grinned. "Very well, master. They'll shine like bridled white horses." Humming a tune, he disappeared behind the shed.

"Do you have more dogs?" Jakob asked.

Bartholomäus looked at him, puzzled. "What makes you think that?"

"Well, Aloysius won't be eating the entrails in the pail himself, will he?"

His brother laughed loudly, and Kuisl thought he briefly detected a nervous twitch around his mouth.

"Ha! My apprentice will eat any damn thing and is a bit strange, but he doesn't go that far," Bartholomäus said in a raspy voice. "No, those are the stinking remains of the cadaver. We've dug a hole behind the house six feet deep where we bury the garbage, on orders from the bishop. We can't leave anything lying around here. The noble gentlemen have a fear of poison vapors."

He pointed at the large blockhouse and the buildings standing around it, all apparently new. "The animals in the forest, especially his hunting dogs, are extremely important to the bishop, and that's why he had this large house built here. Before the war the house of the bishop's master of the hunt stood nearby, but now it's just a ruin with the wind whistling through it. People say it's haunted. Well, stories like that at least scare poachers away," Bartholomäus grinned. "The bishop's new master of the hunt prefers to live in the luxurious canon's quarters, and I can do whatever I please here."

"Whatever you please . . ." Jakob nodded. "I understand." He looked over at his son, who at that moment was scooping fat from the kettle. "How much longer do you need Georg today?" he asked, trying to sound as casual as possible. "The womenfolk in my family are going to the theater to watch those silly people prancing, dancing, and singing. That's not for me. I thought that Georg and I might perhaps go for a stroll in the forest . . ."

"He'll surely be busy for a while with the boiling, and the leather needs to be sent to the tanner today. I'm afraid there's no time for that." Bartholomäus forced a thin smile. "But feel free to ask him if he wants to talk with his father later on about old times."

Kuisl was about to give him a blunt response, but then he waved his hand wearily.

"Maybe it's just better to go our own separate ways for a while. Georg and myself, I mean, but also the two of us. See you this evening, dear brother."

"Hey, where are you going?" Bartholomäus shouted gruffly, as Jakob was leaving.

Kuisl turned around. "I need some peace and quiet and some fresh air. The foul odor here is too much for me."

"Then you're heading in the wrong direction. There's nothing to see there, just the place where we bury the garbage."

As if to confirm Bartholomäus's response, the servant Aloysius at that very moment came around the corner of the building with empty buckets in his hands. He looked at Jakob distrustfully and, spreading his legs apart, blocked Jakob's way.

"One could almost think I'm not welcome here." Kuisl growled. "Some family this is."

He hesitated briefly, then headed for a small gate he'd noticed at the far end of the clearing and leading from the yard out into the forest. Without turning around again, he started walking toward it. He entered the forest, where the sudden silence at once calmed him down a bit. Just the same, inwardly his spirit was in turmoil. He kept thinking of Bartholomäus's words.

Ask your son. He likes the way he's treated here. And your daughter Barbara would no doubt like it here, too.

Kuisl knew his brother was right. His children would probably have a better life here than at home in Schongau. Perhaps Georg would someday even marry a woman from a higher social class, just like Bartholomäus. But Jakob also knew the real purpose of these offers from Bartholomäus.

He wants to destroy me. After all these years, he still cannot forget . . .

A narrow, almost overgrown deer path ran along the fence behind the buildings and then deeper into the pine forest. The musty odor of wet needles mingled with the burning smell from the knacker's fire behind him, while overhead the clouds hung so low they grazed the upper branches. Though it was only noontime, dusk seemed to already be settling over the forest.

Jakob Kuisl had gone some distance when he suddenly heard a long, drawn-out growl. At first he thought it came from the dog kennels, but then he realized the knacker's house lay already far behind him. He stopped and listened.

Again, he heard something growling, deep and threatening—but more important, very nearby.

Instinctively, Jakob Kuisl reached for the long hunting knife hanging on his belt, pulled it out, and looked around carefully. Then he took a few steps forward but immediately stopped again, as he heard a crackling sound nearby.

Just a few steps in front of him, a ghostly figure scurried through the bushes. The thicket obscured his view, and all he saw was the vague apparition. But the figure was very large and growled deeply and angrily like a veritable hound of hell.

"What in the world ..." he muttered, holding his hunting knife up and ready to strike.

But as fast as the figure had appeared, it vanished again. There was one last rustling in the bushes, suggestive of some large, furry creature, and then the spirit had vanished. Jakob waited awhile before cautiously moving on.

Who or what was that?

His heart beat faster and his worries about Georg, Barbara, and his younger brother suddenly receded into the background. The hangman thought of the severed arms and legs, the dead whore in the watchman's office, and the strange odor emanating from them.

The odor of a wet beast of prey.

For a moment, Jakob was no longer sure whether or not he

believed in the existence of werewolves. But then his reason won out. Deep in thought, he pulled out his cold pipe, put it between his teeth, and plodded onward. This creature might have been a large wolf, perhaps a wild dog, but certainly it wasn't what his imagination had been leading him to believe.

Or maybe it was?

Kuisl picked up his pace. Perhaps the creature would pay him another visit. But this time, he'd be ready.

Wide-eyed, Magdalena sat in the sold-out ballroom of the Wedding House, staring at the stage, where Doctor Faustus screamed as he was taken off to hell.

The figure of the scholar was shrouded in clouds of smoke, and thunder rumbled through the room as the man condemned by God slowly sank into the earth while the devil danced around him, laughing. An older woman seated next to Magdalena groaned and fainted while the man seated on the other side of her, presumably her husband, did nothing to help her, spellbound by the events on the stage. Cries of horror could be heard in the hall, and many people in the audience clenched their fists or gripped their beer mugs in fear. The same people who had been carousing gaily just a few hours ago now seemed to have turned to stone. When Magdalena turned around briefly, she saw her younger sister standing behind her, pale and wiping the tears from her eyes.

"Oh, God," Barbara gasped, chewing on her fingernails, "it's . . . it's so horrible!"

While the men in the Kuisl family went about their usual business and the two boys spent the day with Katharina and her goodies in the kitchen, Magdalena and her younger sister had attended the matinee theater performance in the Wedding House. Ever since yesterday, when the theater director, Sir Malcolm, had invited them, Barbara had been beside herself with excitement, and Magdalena, too, had been eagerly looking forward to the performance. For almost three hours they'd been immersed in a world the two young women had never thought was possible.

Along with Doctor Faustus and the devil, they had traveled to Rome, where the devil played tricks on the pope, and they had witnessed the notorious sorcery at the court of the Habsburg emperor — how people were suddenly made to grow antlers on their heads and angels from heaven actually came swooping down to earth. When finally the beautiful Helen of Troy from Greek mythology appeared in person and Doctor Faustus promptly fell in love with her, Magdalena and Barbara were overwhelmed. The two of them watched helplessly as the scholar, who had wandered off the straight-and-narrow path, could not be saved even by the love of the beautiful Helen and was dragged mercilessly down to hell, condemned to eternal damnation.

Magdalena knew of course that Doctor Faustus was in fact the playwright Markus Salter, and that the devil with the horns on his head and the black and golden robe was none other than Sir Malcolm. Still, she broke out in goose flesh and her heart beat faster as demons dressed in scarlet robes and wooden masks tugged at the doctor's clothes until all they held in their hands were bloody shreds.

It's magic, Magdalena thought, *and yet it isn't. Is it a miracle . . . ?*

Finally Faustus had disappeared completely into the ground, and while the devil laughed and danced through the mist, the curtain squeaked as it was pulled closed.

For a moment the crowd just stood quietly in the great hall, then scattered cheers went up that soon turned into thunderous applause. Beer mugs and hats flew into the air, while toward the back of the room windows had been opened and women leaned out, fanning themselves. The curtain rose again and the performers came forward to take a bow. Some drinking cups flew in the direction of Sir Malcolm, whom many in the audience evidently still regarded as the devil, while the director dodged the mugs with a smile, apparently proud of the confusion between himself and the character he had played.

Not until the curtain had fallen for the third time did the people slowly make their way down the steps and out of the building, where it was already late afternoon. Magdalena realized she had completely lost track of time. She looked up at the stage, which now, without the costumed actors, music, and the loudly declaimed verses, looked cold and lifeless. The magic had vanished. In one corner of the room an old man was sweeping up broken beer mugs while a dog licked up the sweet-smelling puddles.

"Let's go backstage to visit the actors, shall we?" Magdalena suggested.

By now, Barbara had recovered, but her nose was still a bit pale, and she couldn't quite control her voice. "That . . . that's a wonderful idea."

Magdalena smiled. "You just said before you thought it was terrible, so which is it, terrible or wonderful?"

"Both at the same time."

The two sisters had long forgotten their little quarrel of the day before. With a nod, Barbara headed for the front of the room, where a wooden staircase on the left led up to the stage and behind a curtain. Magdalena followed and was startled when Sir Malcolm suddenly appeared between the folds of the curtain. Sweat had rolled down over his white makeup, smearing it and giving him an almost diabolical appearance with his black and gold costume and the plaster horns on his forehead.

"I hope you enjoyed the performance," he said with a slight bow.

"You were splendid." Barbara replied. "The people were practically bewitched."

"Oh, just don't let your bishop hear that." It was the voice of Markus Salter, who had changed his clothes and was approaching the two young women. "If the rumors going around are right, quite a few people believe a werewolf is afoot in the city. It would be a shame if His Excellency thought it was connected with our group of actors."

"Oh, they'll figure that all out, just wait and see." Sir Malcolm smiled and waved his hand dismissively. "We can easily explain our little tricks." He pointed at a hole in the stage floor with white dust around the edges. "Doctor Faustus disappears in this heap of flour, our angels fly on ordinary ropes, and our thunder, too, is homemade." He laughed as he pounded on a thin metal plate leaning against a wardrobe closet. Barbara was startled and put her hands to her ears.

"In any case, it isn't the worst thing in the world for us if people come here to be entertained because of all the dreadful things going on out there," Sir Malcolm continued, as the thunder gradually died away. "Tomorrow we're performing a comedy called *Vincentius Ladislaus,* and then people will have something to laugh about. I will be playing the part of the brave Vincentius, Markus will be the duke, and Matheo the beautiful Rosina. Believe me, Matheo is the most beautiful girl from here to the Far East. Isn't that so, lad?"

As if on cue, the sun-tanned Matheo jumped out from behind the curtains. He had taken off the dress of the beautiful Helen but still had some makeup on his face, making him even more attractive, Magdalena thought.

At least for a fifteen-year-old girl, for whom men were still nothing more than crude, beer-guzzling ogres, she thought, as she glanced secretively at her younger sister. Barbara let out a soft sigh and gripped the curtain tightly.

"I stepped on the hem of the dress a few times," Matheo said with a laugh. "One more step and the beautiful Helen suddenly would have been standing there naked."

"Oh, I know a few people who wouldn't have minded seeing that," Magdalena replied with a slight smirk. She suppressed a cry of pain as Barbara stepped on her foot. Matheo grinned and returned the compliment with an affected courtesy, then turned to Barbara.

"Are you coming tomorrow, as well?" he inquired with genuine interest. "At the next performance I will need someone to throw balls to me to juggle. Would you perhaps like to do that?"

"You mean . . . me?" Barbara squeaked. "Oh, certainly, if—"

"If time permits," Magdalena interrupted. "We have to help get ready for a wedding this week."

Matheo put on a disappointed face and turned back to Barbara. "Oh, your own, perhaps? Best wishes."

"Oh, no!" Magdalena replied with a laugh for Barbara, who was at a loss for words. "Our uncle is getting married. Incidentally, right here in the Wedding House . . . but oh, God," she continued, slapping her forehead, "with everything going on here, I almost forgot. My aunt had some things she wanted me to ask the innkeeper. I suppose he's over in the tavern."

"You can spare yourself the trip." Sir Malcolm pointed at a huge man who had just entered and was walking toward them. "He's right here."

The man approaching them with wide-opened arms was extremely fat. It looked almost as if a mountain of flesh were making its way through the room. He had a huge mane of red hair and snorted and wiped the sweat from his brow with a large cloth.

"Damn, Malcolm," the fat man panted. "These steps will be the death of me yet. I should have set you up over in the tavern. Don't forget, I'm no longer as slim and trim as I used to be."

"Well, you couldn't have accommodated anywhere near as many people over there," the director replied with a smile, "nor sold as much beer, either."

The fat man roared with laughter. "Right you are. After a few more performances like this, my cellars will be empty. But I must congratulate you, Malcolm. People say the devil was really here in person at the Wedding House."

"With regard to the wedding . . ." Malcolm pointed at Magdalena and Barbara, who were standing off to one side. "These two young ladies want to talk to you about their uncle's wedding. He's, uh . . ."

"Bartholomäus Kuisl," Magdalena interrupted, trying to sound casual. "The Bamberg executioner."

Markus Salter gasped, and for a moment both Sir Malcolm and Matheo were speechless. Until then, Magdalena had avoided mentioning her father's vocation, but now she saw no reason not to. They could just go ahead and gossip; she was accustomed to it.

The innkeeper's resounding laugh finally broke the awkward silence.

"Ha, ha! You see, young lady," he said, extending his huge hand and vigorously shaking hands with Magdalena, "some people are more afraid of an executioner than the devil. My name is Berthold Lamprecht. I'm the innkeeper of the Wild Man, right next door to the Wedding House. I've known your uncle for a long time. It's an honor for me to host his wedding to the beautiful Katharina."

"An honor?" Magdalena looked at him, puzzled. "Excuse me, but this word sounds unusual to someone in a hangman's family."

"I don't care what other people say," replied Lamprecht, waving his hand dismissively. "Your uncle has a hard job, and it's said he does it very well. Why, then, shouldn't he marry just like other people?"

"That's very kind of you." Magdalena smiled. Perhaps her brother was right after all, and this city was the promised land for families of executioners.

"I'm here to make some requests for my aunt," she said finally. "She'd like wine, beer, sausages, sauerkraut, and bread, and some pastries, as well.

Lamprecht nodded. "Of course. But first I have a message for the actors . . . an unsettling bit of news." His face darkened.

"I've been told that another group of actors arrived in town this morning and have taken lodging in the Grapevine Inn."

"A *second* group of actors?" Sir Malcolm's jaw dropped. "But the bishop assured me . . ."

Lamprecht shrugged. "The bishop changes his mind as often as he uses the chamber pot. It seems to be a French troupe directed by a certain Guiscard Brolet. Do you know him by chance?"

"Guiscard!" Malcolm's face suddenly turned as white as chalk. "The old snake in the grass. He steals and copies materials whenever he can get his hands on them. A charlatan! He probably thinks he can settle down here for the winter and spy on us. But he's mistaken."

"I can't imagine that the bishop in this city wants to put up two troupes of actors," Markus Salter thought aloud. "He has enough trouble already with his suffragan bishop, who considers our work blasphemous," he said, turning to Sir Malcolm. "Remember our performance for His Excellency a few months ago, when he suggested a possible permission for us to spend the winter here. The suffragan bishop's stared at us with a look that could kill."

"Naturally there will be only *one* actor's troupe in Bamberg, and we are the ones." Malcolm stiffened, like a soldier at attention. "I will ask today for another audience, and then the prince bishop will have this swindler whipped and chased out of town." He turned to Magdalena and declared with a theatrical voice, "Tell your uncle, the executioner, that he'll soon have some work to do."

"I'd be happy if we were just allowed to stay in the city," Matheo murmured. "Just imagine what it would be like to have to wander through the countryside in the winter . . ." He shuddered. "It's all the more important, then, that the audience tomorrow goes well and that the people like us."

The innkeeper, Berthold Lamprecht, nodded. "I agree."

With a smile he turned to Magdalena and Barbara. "But now let's turn our attention instead to the beautiful ladies. After all, a wedding ceremony is something very special, isn't it? Especially when it's the hangman who is getting married." He turned around, looking for someone.

"Jeremias!" he bellowed. "There's work for you here. Come here, you lazy fellow. Did you fall asleep while you were scrubbing the floor?"

A stooped figure came shuffling out of a corner of the room, with a little dog jumping around at his feet. It was the old man Magdalena had observed cleaning up earlier. As he approached, Magdalena shuddered instinctively. The man was completely bald, and his head and face were heavily scarred. All that was left of his two ears were tiny stumps, giving the poor fellow the appearance of a smooth egg, but in the midst of all these horrible wounds were two sparkling, friendly eyes.

"Don't be afraid," Berthold Lamprecht said. "Jeremias comes from a family of charcoal burners. When he was a child he fell into a pit of burning lime, which is responsible for his appearance. Many people are superstitious and don't want anything to do with him; they think he's a monster, but with me he has a job."

"You can go ahead and call me a monster, if you like," Jeremias told Magdalena and Barbara with a smile. His voice sounded soft and pleasant. "I'm used to it. Just please don't call me mincemeat, even if sometimes Biff here thinks I am." The little dog jumped up and licked his hands. Not until then did Magdalena notice that the little dog had a misshapen paw. He was a cripple, just like his master.

"Jeremias is something like the good soul of this house," Lamprecht continued. "Cleans, picks up after us, but above all takes care of our books." The innkeeper grinned. "For that alone, he's earned his pay. You can go over to the tavern with him, and he'll carefully note down what you need."

Jeremias nodded enthusiastically, and Magdalena and Barbara followed him hesitantly down the stairs into the tavern the Wild Man. The dog limped along, barking happily. A small but solid door next to the main entrance led into a large room, where several notebooks lay on a table. A large birdcage hung from the ceiling, and inside it a few sparrows were chirping merrily, while on a narrow bed an old cat dozed, apparently not disturbed by either the birds or the barking dog.

"My kingdom," Jeremias said proudly, spreading his arms. "It's small, but at least no one disturbs me here." He shrugged. "The children in the streets outside can sometimes be very annoying with their mean words. I'm happy to have found peace and quiet here." The old man groaned as he bent down over a notebook and dipped his quill pen into an inkwell. "So, what exactly do you wish to order?"

Magdalena gave him the individual items just as Katharina had asked, while Barbara bent over to pet the little dog, which whined and panted happily. When she looked up again, she noticed a few books in a rickety bookcase alongside some bottles and jars.

"William Shakes . . . Shakespeare," she said, looking puzzled as she deciphered the writing. Then her face brightened. "Ah, Shakespeare! Is that the fellow that Malcolm's playwright Markus thought so highly of? Do you read theater pieces?"

The old man smiled. "I actually bought a few of them just last year from a traveling book salesman. They are especially popular translations into German, published here for the first time under the name William Shakespeare. This Shakespeare is a celebrity in England, though all that anyone knows about him here are his plays. But I'm afraid they don't appeal to me: there's too much blood and heartache, and no numbers or balance sheets at all. You're welcome to visit me and have a look . . ." He hesitated and looked at Barbara, puzzled. "But can you read — I mean more than just a few letters?"

"As you probably heard earlier, we come from a hangman's family," Magdalena explained. "We have to read. After all, we deal with medicines, and our knowledge of that often is found only in books."

Jeremias nodded, and for a moment he seemed to be a bit surprised. "I understand. Well, if you come from a hangman's family, you no doubt know how it feels when people go out of the way to avoid you." He pointed at the books. "I taught myself how to read. It's consolation during all those lonely hours. Very well . . ." He clapped his hands, and Magdalena saw they were also scarred. "I'm afraid I have to take care of some wine that's being delivered. The wagon no doubt is standing outside the door." He smiled as he turned to Barbara. "And, young lady, my offer stands. If you want to read theater pieces, you are always welcome here. Biff likes you, and I always rely on his judgment."

The little dog ran to its master, jumped up, and barked as Jeremias petted him. Barbara curtsied, then turned to run after Magdalena, who had already stepped out into the yard.

"What a poor fellow," said Barbara after they were back at the harbor. "He really does look like a monster."

Magdalena shrugged. "You see, the nicest people can look like beasts, and the evilest of people sometimes have the faces of angels. Never rely on outward appearances." She picked up her pace. "And now let's quickly get home before the rascally boys drive good Aunt Katharina completely out of her mind."

When Simon knocked on the door of the Bamberg city physician the next day, it took only a few moments for the door to open. Once again, it was the haggard old housekeeper, but in contrast to their meeting the first time, she was noticeably friendlier.

"Ah, the old friend from the university," she said in a saccharin voice. "Excuse me . . . but if I had known . . ."

"Of course." Simon pushed past her into the house. "Where can I find the doctor?"

"He . . . he's over in his study. Follow me."

They walked down a freshly plastered hallway. On his right, Simon got a brief glimpse into a room furnished with exquisite chests of drawers and stools. The walls were decorated with splendid tapestries, and though it was just after noon a cheerful fire was already burning on the hearth. Simon sighed softly to himself. He wondered again if he might have enjoyed such comforts if he hadn't broken off his studies in Ingolstadt.

But then I probably would never have met Magdalena and would be married now to the daughter of some boring Munich burgher who would spend the whole day nagging me and trying to stop me from reading . . .

All morning he'd been looking through Bartholomäus's little home library, which, except for a few writings on veterinary medicine, contained nothing of interest. Simon's greatest joy had been teaching his son Peter to read, and the five-year-old had made astonishing progress. Little Paul, meanwhile, had gutted fish with Katharina for supper, and working with a knife seemed to be in his blood. Magdalena and Barbara were now probably at the theater performance they'd looked forward to so much; the children were playing with Katharina in the hangman's room; and Simon could finally pay the visit to Samuel that he'd promised the day before.

The housekeeper knocked quietly on a door at the end of the hallway, and Samuel answered, smiling broadly.

"Ah, Simon, I've been waiting for you," he said, greeting him with a firm handshake. "Do come in." He turned to the elderly housekeeper. "And Magda, please no more patients today."

The housekeeper nodded silently, then walked away with a majestic bearing, leaving the two men alone.

Simon looked all around the room, impressed. The walls were lined with bookshelves on three sides filled with books right up to the ceiling. Heavy books, notebooks, and roles of parchment were piled on the floor and on a side table, as well.

Simon could sense jealousy welling up inside him. The Schongau bathhouse owner loved books above everything else. What he wouldn't have given to someday have a library like this.

"I'm sorry things are such a mess here," Samuel said, "but I've spent half the morning trying to learn more about this accursed werewolf. We need to be well prepared, after all, when we attend the bishop's council," he said with a smirk.

"We?" Simon looked at him, puzzled. "What do you mean, *we?*"

"Well, perhaps you remember. You are no less than Doctor Simon Fronwieser, the learned physician from Munich, an experienced and well-traveled gentleman, as I described you again yesterday to the prince bishop." Samuel grinned from ear to ear. "I've urged His Excellency to invite you to the meeting of the council."

Simon shook his head. Suddenly it felt terribly hot in the overheated room. "I don't know if that's such a good idea. If they find out that—"

"Oh, how would they learn about that?" Samuel interrupted. "Munich is very far away. Besides, I really value your curiosity and insights, Simon. Come on." Samuel looked at his friend, pleading. "You can't leave me alone with this gang of superstitious priests. Anyway, I have a little surprise for you." Bowing like a magician at a carnival, he reached behind the books on the table and pulled out a little silver pot. When he removed the cover, a tantalizing odor spread through the room.

"I hope you still like coffee the way you used to during our time at the university," Samuel said, pouring them both a cup. "This is a very special, aromatic blend from Turkey. I order it at sinfully expensive prices directly from Genoa. It will help us to separate pure superstition from crystal-clear logic." He grinned. "Maybe I should bring a little packet of it to the pious suffragan bishop."

Hesitantly Simon raised the cup to his nose and sniffed. The fragrance was divine. He sighed and shrugged his shoulders.

"This is pure and simple bribery. You really know how to talk me into this, Samuel."

Simon made a dour face, but inwardly he was thrilled by the chance to take part in the meetings of the council and eager to see what proof the members of this commission would offer for the existence of a werewolf.

But I'll be sure to keep my damned mouth closed, he resolved, *so no one gets it into their head to learn more about the world traveler and scholar Doctor Fronwieser. If I don't watch out, I'll be hanged by the brother of my father-in-law for fraud.*

Simon tasted the bitter brew, and almost at once felt the stimulating effect. This coffee was incomparably better than the dried beans he'd bought in the market the day before.

"Really excellent," he acknowledged. "Bitter, as it should be, though I sometimes wonder if something creamy or sweet might be used to balance the bitterness — warm milk, for example, or that expensive sugar from the West Indies, the way the Arabs are said to do . . ."

Samuel laughed. "You haven't changed. Never content, always looking. That's exactly what these crusty old councilors need."

The steam from the coffee pot spread through the room, and soon the two friends were talking about old times. Simon told about his life as a medicus and bathhouse owner in Schongau and his marriage to Magdalena, which had cost him his standing in society.

"Believe me, Simon, a high social standing can also be a prison." With a sigh, Samuel took another sip of coffee. "Count yourself lucky that you were able to start a family and have a wife at your side who loves you. Look at me." He pointed at all the costly books on the shelves and the expensive furniture around them. "What good is all the money if the only woman in this house is a withered old housekeeper who jealously watches the few rendezvous I have? I'm almost afraid I'll never find the right woman in my life." He waved his hand. "But enough of this complaining. I'm afraid it's time to talk about a much more serious topic." He set down his cup and reached for one of the books on the side table. It was bound in leather and not printed but handwritten in a flowing script with colorful pictures and drawings. The city doctor opened to a page in the back, where a number of headless men were drawn with faces in the middle of their abdomens. Other figures had duck beaks instead of mouths, or colorful, shimmering fish tails instead of feet.

"Megenberg's *Book of Nature*," he explained. "For hundreds of years the standard work about all living things. You are no doubt familiar with it. Konrad von Megenberg devotes one chapter completely to animal men, or human animals, and also describes the werewolf, though his description is very vague." He turned to another page showing a wolf standing erect while it was eating a child. Only the poor child's feet protruded from the wolf's mouth. Simon couldn't suppress a shudder.

"There have no doubt been stories about werewolves for as long as there have been people to tell them," Samuel continued. "I've read about them in German legends, where the word *wer* stands for 'man.' The Roman historian Pliny the Elder also mentions such wolf-men. They are always hybrid creatures imbued with enormous strength because of a pact they have made with the devil, and kill sheep and cattle, just as wolves do. In their wolf-like form they cannot control themselves: they keep killing and devouring their prey and are practically invincible."

"Practically?" Simon asked, curious. "That means there are ways to defeat them?"

Samuel shrugged. "Well, it is said that a potion made from the highly poisonous flower, the wolfsbane, commonly called monk's hood, can kill them. Others swear by silver bullets. It is safest to completely burn their bodies." He snorted disapprovingly. "I suspect this is the method Suffragan Bishop Harsee would prefer. He can cite as his authority *The Hammer of Witches* and a few more recent writings. Scholars, however, are not in complete agreement whether the werewolf is really transformed or if the change is just a perfidious illusion. On the other hand, no one denies their existence. To dismiss it as nonsense would be tantamount to blasphemy."

Simon looked again at the drawing of the wolf-man devouring the child and shook his head.

"Do you think there really are such creatures?" he asked. "To tell you the truth, I've never seen a werewolf, a real witch, or a sorcerer, even though most scholars are convinced they exist."

Samuel grinned. "Interestingly enough, a few hundred years ago, people were put to the stake for saying witches and sorcerers *did* exist. Times have changed. But have they really, as far as the werewolf is concerned?" He walked to the bookshelf and took out a little book containing a number of old, crudely drawn engravings, among them a wolf on its hind legs attacking a child. Other illustrations showed a chase with hunting dogs, a trial, and finally an execution in which the head of a wild-looking old man was chopped off while he was tied to a wheel. Simon put the book down with disgust.

"The execution of Peter Stump," Samuel explained, sipping contentedly on his cup of coffee. "Years ago you could buy this print at any fair for a few kreuzers. Almost a hundred years ago in the vicinity of Cologne, they say Stump killed two pregnant women and thirteen small children. He ate the brain of his own son before he was finally caught and executed. The case was a sensation all over the Reich, but there were many more like it. Just a few decades ago in France, hundreds of so-called werewolves were tried and burned, and in Franconia there were werewolf trials, as well. The last case I heard of was just a few years ago." The physician set his cup down carefully on a pile of books. "Everyone talks about witches and charlatans, but most people are much more afraid of werewolves."

"You didn't really answer my question," Simon quickly replied. "Are there werewolves—or not?"

Samuel remained silent for a long time, then began to speak hesitantly. "For some years I've been a member of the Academia Naturae Curiosorum, a circle of honorable men who are dedicated to scientific research into the natural world, and believe me, Simon, this world contains more wonders than you can even imagine. I've seen the tusk of a real unicorn . . . there are camel leopards in Africa with necks as long as trees . . . and washed up on the shores of our oceans, eyeballs have been found as large as pig heads. So I can't rule out the existence of what the common folk call werewolves. Perhaps they are just especially large, aggressive dogs; perhaps they are men who have been turned into monsters by a cruel fate—who knows? But I'm afraid that the pursuit of such a monster here in Bamberg will hurt many innocent people. That's just what we saw during the last witch trials. In any case, we'll have to proceed very carefully in the council."

"Which you have invited me to join as a famous scholar without asking me," Simon replied with a smile. "I hope no one expects me to cite references from the standard works in this field." His face turned serious again. "And it would no doubt be a good idea for you to tell me once again what's been going on in Bamberg the last few weeks, so I don't make a complete ass of myself before the council."

"Very well, then." Samuel took a deep breath. "It all began about four weeks ago, when the venerable councilman Klaus Schwarzkontz set out on a trip to Nuremberg—a trip from which he never returned. Most people thought he had been attacked somewhere in the forest. These things happen. As luck would have it, some children found his left arm in a pile of garbage down by the Regnitz but still within the city walls."

"His right arm was found in the forest along the shore of a swampy branch of the river," Simon interjected. "My father-in-law thought it had been severed cleanly with something like an ax." Simon had told his friend earlier about the strange finding in the Bamberg Forest.

"Whatever." Samuel shrugged. "In any case, two weeks later Barbara Leupnitz, the beloved wife of the miller, disappeared after she'd left on a visit to relatives in neighboring Wunderburg. And, as you told me, two severed legs belonging to a woman have been found in the city since then. Whether they belonged to the miller's wife or someone else, we can't say."

"The toes of one of the legs appeared to show she was tortured. And then there is the corpse of the young prostitute whose torso had been ripped open," Simon mused, sipping on his coffee. "This werewolf's behavior is becoming stranger and stranger."

"Indeed," Samuel replied. "Very strange. The people started to take notice, in any case, when only a few days after the disappearance of the miller's wife, another prominent citizen, Johanna Steinhofer, also vanished. Johanna is the granddaughter of the late Julius Herrenberger, an esteemed city councilor. Just prior to her disappearance she had a quarrel with her husband, who was younger than she." Samuel rubbed his temples. "And now the highly regarded wife of the apothecary Rinswieser has also vanished."

"Is it possible these cases have nothing at all to do with each other?" Simon interrupted. "A robbery, wild animals in the forest, a young woman who runs away after a quarrel with her husband . . ."

"And the severed limbs that have shown up in the city? The signs of torture? The furry beast inside the city walls that the night watchman told us about?" Samuel shook his head. "Something strange is going on here, Simon, and if it's not a werewolf, then it's something else. A werewolf would of course be the simplest solution for many Bambergers. A monster like that would be capable of anything." He stared at Simon. "Dear friend, it's not just as a joke that I want to bring you along with me to the council meeting. You have a sharp mind and were always skeptical of supernatural things. Please help me solve this riddle. Otherwise, I fear the worst for our city."

Simon set his cup down. Suddenly, not even the coffee he loved so much appealed to him, and he had a queasy feeling in his stomach. "I'm afraid you're overestimating my intelligence, Samuel. I don't know how I can—"

Suddenly, he was interrupted by angry shouts coming from the street.

Silently, Jakob Kuisl slipped through the streets of Bamberg with Georg and Bartholomäus at his side. He'd spent half the day in the forest alone, but the odd, shadowy figure that he had come upon did not appear again. He'd returned to the office of the city guards, where Bartholomäus as well as his own son Georg had given him a cool reception. Now he was walking along the stinking city moat with the others back to the hangman's house, where hopefully a good meal would be awaiting them. Kuisl had told no one of his strange encounter.

He was trying to sort out the events of the last two days— the dead prostitute with the slashed-open chest, the strange odor emanating from her, Captain Lebrecht's report about the missing persons, the various body parts, the growing rumors of a murderous werewolf . . . But as hard as he tried, he wasn't able to make sense of it all. In addition, his thoughts kept turning to his son, Georg. As he watched him walking like an old friend alongside his brother, Bartholomäus, he felt deeply hurt.

Just what did Bartl tell him about me? Does he know everything?

"Katharina promised to make some fish chowder," Bartholomäus said, breaking the silence as they moved on past the dilapidated houses along the moat. "I love fish chowder. Let's just hope she's gotten around to it, with all the things she has to do to prepare for the wedding." He grinned. "In any case, I'm eager to see her wedding dress. The material cost a pile of money."

"No wonder, given how big she is," Kuisl grumbled.

Bartholomäus broke out in a loud laugh. "It's true; if you marry Katharina, you don't need any more soft comforters in bed during the night. But she's a good soul, and I love her, believe it or not."

"Her? Or her money?" Jakob asked.

"You may have a point, but it's still no business of yours." Bartholomäus shot back. "This marriage may make it possible someday for me to buy my citizenship. Other hangmen before me have been able to do that."

"And where does it get you?" Kuisl retorted gruffly. "People will still shy away when they see you coming."

"Just ask Magdalena or Barbara how they feel being cursed all the time as hangman's brats." Georg, who was alongside them, spoke up. "Believe me, Father, if they could, they wouldn't waste any time —"

He stopped suddenly on hearing angry shouts coming from a narrow lane that led down to the marketplace. A moment later, an elderly man in tattered clothing and an unkempt beard came running out of the lane. He looked around anxiously but at first didn't notice the three men in front of him. He bumped against Kuisl's broad chest and fell over.

"Hey, what's the rush?" the Schongau hangman asked. "You haven't been up to some mischief, have you?"

Gasping for breath, the man struggled to his feet and grabbed Kuisl's shirt. "Oh, God, no, help me!" he panted. "They're . . . they're going to kill me. They . . ."

Only now did he notice Bartholomäus and Georg, and he winced. "Oh, no, the Bamberg executioner and his journeyman. Did they call for you? Now I'm as good as dead."

"Take it easy, now ..." Bartholomäus started to say, but at that very moment an angry mob burst out of the lane. There were almost two dozen of them, some armed with pitchforks and scythes and others just with clubs. When they saw him standing alongside the three hangmen, they stopped with a triumphant look on their faces.

"Aha! The hangman has already caught the beast," shouted an old farmer at the front of the group. "Let's go; let's take him away right now to be burned. There are plenty of bales of straw over at the Hay Market."

"What's going on here, folks?" Bartholomäus asked in a threatening tone. "Speak up, and be quick about it. Exactly what did this fellow do?"

"This is the werewolf!" cried a skinny man standing farther back in the crowd, in a shrill voice. "We'll make short work of him before he attacks any more of us."

"What makes you think he's a werewolf?" the Bamberg executioner asked.

"Can't you see?" A third man spoke up, a young wagon driver with broad shoulders and a broken nose. "This is Josef Hartl, the shepherd in the Bamberg Forest. Day after day he's out there with his animals. Karoline Furtwängler swears to God that he makes an ointment that he can rub onto himself to turn into a werewolf."

"But that's just a salve I rub onto the sheep's inflamed udders," Hartl retorted, wringing his hands. "Haven't I told you that a thousand times?"

"Ha! And how about the strange herbs you used to sell at the Green Market?" the older farmer hissed. "Admit it, we've seen you slinking into the city to peddle your magic tinctures and turn everyone into werewolves."

"That was arnica and ground oak bark for the sick horse belonging to the tavern keeper at the Grapevine. The horse has scabies, that's all." Josef turned to the Bamberg executioner. "Master Bartholomäus," he pleaded. "You know me. You yourself have bought ointments and herbs from me for your dogs."

Bartholomäus nodded. "Indeed I have, and I don't think —"

"Just look at his eyebrows," the skinny man shouted again, pointing at the trembling shepherd. "They have grown together in the middle — a sure sign that he's a werewolf."

"If that's the case, then all three of us are werewolves," Jakob Kuisl growled. "We have bushy eyebrows, we sell ointments and herbs, and, by God, when I see dumb-ass farmers like you, I can howl like a wolf and devour you, too." He took a threatening step forward. "Now get out of here, every last one of you, before things really do get violent."

"Who are you to boss us around, stranger?" the husky-looking wagon driver asked.

"He's my brother," Bartholomäus replied, and stepped between the two men. "And just incidentally a lot tougher than any of you. If you want to have Josef Hartl, you'll first have to deal with us Kuisls. All right, now, who's first?" He cracked the knuckles of his right fist and the people stepped back.

Finally the powerfully built wagon driver stepped forward, swinging a club as he ran toward Jakob. "You son of a —" he started to say, but at that moment the Schongau hangman hit the large man in the stomach, sending him sprawling onto the ground, gasping for air. As he tried to get up again, Georg kicked him for good measure.

"Just stay right there on the ground, big fellow," Georg said, shaking a finger at him. "That's the safest place for you right now."

In the meantime, a few other men had drawn closer with their pitchforks, flails, and scythes and started threatening the three Kuisls with clubs and swords, but at a safe distance. Josef

Hartl had taken refuge behind his protectors, where he cowered against the wall of a house, crying.

"Oh, God, they'll kill me, they'll kill me . . ." he kept repeating.

Jakob, Bartholomäus, and Georg stood shoulder-to-shoulder warding off the attacks as best they could. Shouts, gasps, and heavy breathing combined to make a sound reminding Kuisl of the war. He had not yet reached for his large hunting knife, knowing that once blood was shed, he might wind up on the gallows himself.

And who is going to hang me? he thought. *My own brother?*

In a rage, another large man came running toward him, whom Jakob tripped, then he punched another attacker in the nose so hard the man sank to the ground, moaning. Nevertheless, one blow hit Kuisl in the face, and warm blood ran down his cheeks. The fight was dirty and mean, and Jakob knew that in the end they would lose. There were simply too many attackers, and they had heavier weapons. What should they do? Flee and abandon the old shepherd to his fate?

Just as Kuisl dodged another blow from a scythe, a commanding voice nearby rang out.

"You will stop at once, or I'll have you all thrown into the city dungeon on orders of the prince bishop."

Jakob looked up in astonishment and saw some figures emerging from another small side road. There were a half dozen city guards armed with pikes and halberds. The man who had just spoken stood directly alongside them wearing the official robe and hat of a doctor. Behind him, Kuisl spotted a smaller, somewhat foppishly clothed young man who appeared to be trying to hide behind the guards.

The hangman, relieved, raised his hands in a gesture of surrender.

"Damn, I would never have thought I'd be so happy to see my son-in-law!" he called out. Then he turned to his astonished attackers. "Didn't you hear? Drop your weapons before these two learned gentlemen stab you to death with their letter openers."

Simon stepped out from behind the guards and gave a smirk. "In return for our having saved your lives, dear father-in-law, you will keep your mouth shut."

"Saved my life? Since when have I had to ask you for help in a fight . . . ?"

"Perhaps you can put aside your family squabbles until later," said the man standing alongside Simon. "We really have more important matters to attend to now." Then he turned again and in a firm voice addressed the milling crowd.

"Haven't I made myself clear? Hurry up and leave. You know me. I am the prince bishop's personal physician. Shall I report you are being insubordinate? You know very well that rioting in the city is forbidden." He pointed at the shepherd still standing alongside the wall of the house, frozen in fear. "Whether this man has broken some law is up to the court to decide, not you. So move on, and let the law take care of this."

Grumbling, the crowd dispersed, one person after another. They picked up the injured and carried them off, not without turning around a few times with threatening glances. When the last steps had died away, the physician took a deep breath.

"That was close," he said softly, and turned to Jakob. "You really should thank your son-in-law for this. He's the one who called the guards. Otherwise, we would probably have no executioner here in Bamberg anymore, but only a murderous, pillaging mob. Take the poor fellow down to the Langgasser Gate. It would be best for him to stay away from Bamberg for the next few weeks."

"But if he in fact is a werewolf . . ." one of the soldiers demurred.

"For God's sake. How stupid are you, anyway?" the doctor interrupted. "It takes more than grease and herbs to be a werewolf. I give you my word as the personal physician of the bishop, that this man is no monster. And now, off with you."

The guards left with the shepherd, who was still trembling all over, and Jakob Kuisl wiped the blood out of his eyes. "You have a pretty influential friend on your side," he said appreciatively to Simon. "I'm guessing this Doctor Samuel is your old school friend." He grinned at the two former classmates. "And your years at the university were not a total waste."

"Well, I hope I haven't exceeded my authority," Samuel murmured. "Though I do have some influence here in the city, when His Excellency the bishop learns I ordered the release of a man suspected of a crime, I can expect a reprimand—if the suffragan bishop in person does not skin me alive first."

"But you saved a person's life," said Georg, who, except for a bloodied lip, appeared uninjured. "I think it was worth it," he continued, casting an admiring look at his father. "You beat the crap out of them. It's hard to believe you're already over fifty."

"It was nothing to beat up a couple of wiseass farmers," Kuisl growled. "And my rude son, too, if he doesn't keep his mouth shut." But even as he complained, a warm feeling of affection pulsed through him. The ice between him and his son seemed finally to have thawed.

"Do you know what, Jakob?" Bartholomäus chortled. "This fight reminds me of when we were kids and how the sons of old Berchtholdt would sometimes beat us up down by the Lech River. That was always a real blast. I think we should do this more often. It's what bonds us together."

Simon shook his head in disbelief. "I always knew I'd married into a strange family," he mumbled, beating the dust from his badly rumpled petticoat breeches. "But in any case . . . it's time for us Kuisls to go back home. My youngster, I believe, has caught us some fish for supper, and if we wait any longer, he'll be angry. That's worse, by God, than any fight in the streets."

• • •

A few hours later, after night had fallen like a black shroud over Bamberg, two stooped figures snuck over the Rathaus Bridge toward the new section of town.

One of them was as tall and broad as a bear and wore swords, hunting knives, and a loaded wheel-lock pistol on his belt. Cautiously, the huge man stopped at every crossing and looked around before waving to the other man to follow. The hesitant man bringing up the rear was short and crippled, stooped with age, and visibly in pain as he moved forward, clutching his cane. Nevertheless, the old city councilman Thadäus Vasold insisted on paying a visit to his old friend at this unaccustomed hour.

The old man trembled all over, but that had little to do with the cool autumn night. Shivering, he closed the top button of his expensive woolen coat and followed his husky guide warily through the labyrinth of alleys that spread out below the cathedral. The friendly giant was Hans, Vasold's most loyal servant, who had also served as a coachman to his father, scion of an old patrician family. After the realization at an early stage that Hans, though blessed with enormous size and strength, had the intelligence of a doorstop, Vasold had often taken him along on his trips as a bodyguard. The giant might not have been the brightest, but he was discreet, and robbers, thieves, and highwaymen always ran off when they saw him coming.

Vasold hoped this would also be the case with werewolves.

Naturally, the patrician could have paid this visit officially during the day, but Thadäus Vasold wanted to prevent others from hearing about their conversation. Even after so many years, some people might have drawn the right conclusion, and Vasold wanted to attract as little attention as possible. Thus he had decided to make a far more dangerous trip in the dead of night.

In his callused hands, big Hans carried a tiny lantern to help them find their way through the night. The lantern was just bright enough to form a flickering circle of light for the two men, beyond which lay nothing but the fog and darkness.

Vasold cursed softly to himself. How often had he urged the council to put up lanterns in at least the larger squares in town, as various large German cities had already done. But the council had repeatedly put him off because of the cost, and possibly for fear of starting a fire, and thus he, Thadäus Vasold, one of the most esteemed and oldest patricians in Bamberg, had to find his way like a thief in the night, stumbling over garbage, rotten barrels, and pieces of wood lying around, and nearly shitting in his pants with fear.

When his old friend and colleague on the city council, Klaus Schwarzkontz, had not returned from a trip to Nuremberg a few weeks ago, Vasold had at first not been at all worried. On the contrary, Schwarzkontz had been one of his major competitors in the wool business, and now that just meant more business for him. But since then, more and more people had disappeared, and gradually Thadäus Vasold was beginning to suspect something horrible. Perhaps he was mistaken, but if the various pieces of the puzzle fell together, there was something there — something reaching far back into the past and touching upon an especially dark part of his life.

Was that possible? After all these years?

After the apothecary's wife, Adelheid Rinswieser, had disappeared without a trace, Vasold had struggled with himself for a long time before deciding to pay this nocturnal visit. Secretly, the patrician hoped his friend would try to calm him down, laugh at his fears, and together they would raise a toast to old times. Vasold feared nothing more than the idea that his friend might have come to the same conclusion.

And he suspected he had.

And what will we do then? Lock the doors and hope that the shadow passes? Pray? Go on a pilgrimage? Plead with God for forgiveness?

"What's the matter, Hans?"

Vasold's loyal servant had suddenly stopped in his tracks, so that the patrician, lost in his thoughts, almost bumped into him. The huge man was standing there like a monument of stone, his hand on the loaded pistol still hanging from his belt.

"I don't know, master. I thought I heard something," he murmured.

"And what did you hear?"

"A . . . well, a growling and scraping sound. It came from the entrance to the house here."

Trembling, Hans pointed to a shadowy niche on their left, and Vasold felt as if a fist were slowly squeezing his heart.

The house was one of the many dilapidated buildings that had been standing vacant for decades. Ivy had wound its way up the unplastered walls, the windows were boarded up, and rotten beams of wood and clumps of rock lay in front of the wide door. Only now did the old patrician notice that the once splendid portal with its inlaid wood and carvings was open a crack. Inside, a form, even darker than the darkness, was undulating back and forth. Somewhere a stone fell off, crashing to the ground, and now Vasold heard it, too—a long, sustained growl, deep and evil.

"There it is again, master," Hans whispered.

Thadäus Vasold had never before seen the big man scared, not even when he confronted two marauding mercenaries in the Bamberg Forest, but now he was shaking all over.

"These werewolves . . ." he groaned. "People say they love fresh blood, they slowly tear their victims apart, first the arms, then the legs, then—"

"Damn it, Hans, I didn't bring you along to tell me all these foolish horror stories," Vasold replied hesitantly. "Go take a look and see who or what it is."

"As you say, master." The large man pulled himself together, drew the loaded wheel-lock pistol, and carefully approached the doorway. He spoke a silent prayer.

At that moment, the door opened with a loud grating sound

and a figure appeared, so horrible that Hans uttered a cry, dropped his weapon, and fell to his knees.

The creature looked like a wolf as it slunk toward them on its hind legs. In the darkness of night, it looked taller than a man, and it had black fur and long fangs that flashed in the light of the lantern that Hans had dropped on the ground.

"God in heaven, help us!"

The voice of the huge man was suddenly high-pitched and whining, like that of a girl. With a final horrified scream, he scrambled to his feet and raced away down the street, disappearing into the darkness.

Thadäus Vasold wanted to call after his servant, but his voice failed him. Terrified, he stared at the creature that was approaching him with its long claws. The lantern on the ground flickered slightly, casting dancing shadows on the wall, making the creature look larger and larger the closer it came.

"Please . . ." Vasold croaked, paralyzed with fear, clutching his walking stick, and watching wide-eyed as death incarnate approached. "Please, spare me. By God, I'll give you anything you want. I'll . . ."

Only at the last minute did the old patrician realize what he'd completely overlooked in his anxiety.

He knew this house, and he knew also who had once lived here.

I was right. But why . . .

Vasold's thoughts scattered like snowflakes in a storm as the creature pounced on him with a contented snarl.

In the distance, the servant's shrill cries for help rang out, but the councilor couldn't hear them anymore.

6

"Gentlemen! Silence, please! Silence!"

Simon sat on a hard wooden chair at one corner of the huge council table, listening and watching attentively as some of the most venerable citizens of the city fought with one another like street urchins. The meeting had started just a little over half an hour ago, but tempers were already at the boiling point. Men in lavish patrician garb shouted at one another, some were about to come to blows, and yet others were just sitting quietly at the table shaking their heads, as if they couldn't understand the atrocious spectacle. Even Suffragan Bishop Sebastian Harsee, the chairman of the hastily convoked council, could think of nothing better to do but pound his little gavel on the table again and again while casting furious glances around the table.

"Quiet!" he kept shouting, "Quiet! Is this the way distinguished citizens of our city behave? One more time, quiet, or I'll have the room cleared!"

Simon and Samuel glanced at one another peevishly. At an ungodly hour of the morning a messenger with a look of annoyance on his face had pounded on the door of the Bamberg hangman's house to take Simon first to the castle complex and then, with Samuel, to the city councilor's offices. They walked past the church and then toward the municipal offices and into the council room, where the suffragan bishop had unexpectedly scheduled the first meeting of the so-called Werewolf Commission immediately after the morning mass. In addition to Simon and Samuel, a half dozen city councilmen were present, as well as a scholar from the Jesuit seminary in the nearby St. Martin's Church, two doctors of law, the bishop's chancellor, and even the dean of the church, who was attracting attention with his loud prayers and laments.

The occasion was indeed serious. The night before, the Bamberg werewolf had apparently struck again, and his victim was no less than the venerable patrician Thadäus Vasold, at the age of nearly eighty the oldest member of the council. Vasold's servant had seen the monster with his own eyes, though there was not a trace left of the councilman himself. The growing fear of the citizenry as well as that of the scholars in the council chamber had soon led to a great commotion in the room.

"And I'm telling you," insisted one of the councilmen, a gaunt, elderly man wearing an old-fashioned ruff collar, "it's time for us to shut the town gates. This werewolf is prowling around just outside the walls. Two charcoal burners saw him in the forest just yesterday. And he can come and go in our city as he pleases."

"And what good is that going to do?" snarled another patrician with fat, drooping cheeks. "Do you know what that will do to our businesses if we don't allow anyone into town? Anyway, the gates were closed last night, and the beast still managed to get old Thadäus."

"Let's not forget the monster has magical powers," replied one of the jurists in a solemn voice. He cleared his throat and started reading from a large book lying in front of him. "According to *Formicarius,* considered the authoritative work in the field by the Dominican scholar Johannes Nider, werewolves can assume any shape, animal or human. Who knows . . ."—he paused theatrically and looked around the table—". . . perhaps the werewolf is sitting right here at the table with us."

Loud shouting broke out again, and two patricians were about to pounce on the scholar.

"One last time, silence! For God's sake, silence!"

The suffragan bishop pounded the table with his gavel again, to no effect. Harsee looked pale and unkempt, and Simon thought he could detect a nervous twitch around his mouth. Nevertheless, his eyes still glared out from beneath his monk's tonsure with the same evil intensity as when Simon met him the first time in the palace garden.

It was Master Samuel who finally managed to bring an end to the uproar—with a simple trick.

"Let us all pray for our friend Thadäus Vasold," he intoned loudly, while making the sign of the cross. "I believe he deserves our thoughts and prayers. Or does someone think differently?"

The members of the council paused in their squabbling and finally started praying quietly while still casting suspicious glances at one another.

"Amen," the suffragan bishop finally said, relieved, and licked his dry lips before continuing in a piercing voice. "Dear members of our committee, we may hold different opinions as to the exact nature of this werewolf, but at least there is no doubt this beast actually exists, given what happened last night. Vasold's servant saw this monster and unequivocally recognized it as a werewolf."

"Just like the drunken watchman two nights before," Samuel murmured so softly that no one except Simon heard him. "And Vasold's servant is just as dumb, as everyone in the city knows. He'll think a calf is a werewolf, if you just keep asking about it long enough. But no one here is thinking about that."

"Is there something you wanted to tell us, Master Samuel?"

asked the suffragan bishop sharply. "Or are you just talking to your learned friend?"

The physician shook his head. "I was just saying that the people we've heard from so far are not the most reliable eyewitnesses, but I must confess that the honorable councilor Vasold is already the fifth resident to have vanished. In any case, we must find out why these people have disappeared."

"Listen, he must *confess*." With a sarcastic smile, the suffragan bishop looked around at the attendees. Once again, Simon noticed the dark circles around his eyes.

"In this regard, it might be interesting for members of the commission to know," Harsee continued smugly, "that Herr Doktor released a suspect yesterday on his own authority, a shepherd from the Bamberg Forest who has been peddling magic potions here in the city. A few concerned citizens reported that to me shortly before our meeting."

The crowd began to murmur and hiss, and many of those present glared at Samuel.

"The magic positions were arnica and crushed bark from oak trees," the physician replied. "Harmless ingredients. Both are used in the medical treatment of animals, as the learned Doctor Fronwieser seated alongside me can confirm."

Simon was stunned when Samuel turned toward him to confirm that statement, but finally the little medicus and bathhouse owner nodded, trying to sound as wise and professional as possible.

"Ah, indeed. I have written a paper about that myself," he said: "'On the Nature and Growth of Medicinal Plants, with Special Emphasis on Coltsfoot, and its Effects, as Well as on Arnica, and . . .'"

"Very well, very well," Harsee waved him off peevishly. "We don't need a complicated monologue, but just a brief opinion of its effects. It's quite possible they were just harmless herbs, but a thorough questioning of the suspect would have been appropriate."

"Your Excellency, what do you know about this troupe of actors that has been visiting here for the last few days?" asked the provost of the church, a gaunt, anxious-looking man with a pinched face. "The people who come to me for confession have told me some dreadful stories. They tell me of satanic incantations on the stage, and even today, on our sacred day of rest, they portrayed a devil dancing. Could it be possible that the werewolf has been attracted here by this witchcraft?"

Sebastian Harsee nodded. "That's an important consideration, Your Excellency. These magical doings performed under the pretense of edification are a thorn in my side, as well," he said with a sigh. "But unfortunately the prince bishop doesn't look at it that way. Along with his many beloved animals, his great passion is the theater, and I've even heard that a second troupe of actors recently arrived in Bamberg. His Excellency is considering offering them the permission to spend the winter in Bamberg, as well. In any case, we'll have to keep a close eye on these immoral persons."

"Keep an eye on them? Is that all we're going to do?" Trembling with anger, a middle-aged councilor rose to his feet. He was wearing a gray coat on which a mortar and pestle were depicted — the emblem of the apothecary's guild. "This is the monster that presumably ripped my Adelheid apart like a deer, and you are going to do nothing more than *keep an eye* on things?"

"Why was the woman roaming about in the forest at night?" a younger councilor hissed under his breath. "She was probably gathering magic herbs there, and I wouldn't be surprised to learn she was somehow working with the werewolf and up to no good."

The apothecary wheeled around. "What did you just say?"

"What did I just say, Master Rinswieser?" the other man replied, looking around for support from the others. He was wearing the fancy clothing of a nouveau riche dandy and seemed quite sure of himself. "Well, your Adelheid watered down those tinctures. Word gets around."

"How dare you, Master Steinhofer?" He stormed across the room to the younger man. "If only Adelheid's father could hear that. He and your own father were once members of the council, they were friends, and now you denounce his daughter as a witch, you . . . you . . ."

"Don't forget that my beloved Johanna has also disappeared," his opponent interrupted, playing with his goatee. "And that was just after she'd bought some strange tincture from your wife."

"And I heard she ran pell-mell away from you after an argument in which chairs went flying through the air," the apothecary shot back. "No doubt she couldn't stand being around you anymore. By the way, you don't seem too concerned that your young wife has simply vanished into thin air. Did you marry her only for the dowry?"

"That's slander!"

The two men were about to come to blows when the bishop's chancellor suddenly stood up and spread his arms, trying to calm them down. With his enormous rolls of fat, he looked more like a tavern keeper than one of the highest dignitaries in Bamberg.

"My dear colleagues," he began jovially, "we must not quarrel. I think I have a solution. Even if His Excellency, the venerable Prince Bishop Philipp Rieneck is not among us, I believe we can speak on his behalf. We, uh . . . should think about setting up an inquisition."

"An inquisition?" Master Samuel frowned. "Why do we need that? Don't we already have this Werewolf Commission?"

"I believe the honorable chancellor is completely right." Sebastian Harsee smiled, and it seemed to Simon that the suffragan bishop was quite happy with the direction the meeting had taken.

A quick glance at the chancellor even made him think that this move had been prearranged.

"Forty years ago, at the time of the Bamberg witch trials," Harsee continued, "quick action was called for in order to get control of the many suspects, so an inquisition composed of only a few members was set up, with the task of deciding who had to be tortured. Their conclusions were presented to the prince bishop, who signed their death sentences."

"Only a handful of people are to make the life-or-death decisions?" Master Samuel shook his head in dismay. "But what, then, is the purpose of this commission . . ."

"I suggest a vote," the suffragan bishop interrupted. He looked around the table, his gaze resting for some time on one attendee after another. "All those present are naturally above all suspicion. None of the accusations made here will be considered; we are concerned only with the strangers in the city. The actors, for example, but also gypsies and other itinerant people. I will personally appoint the members of this commission if necessary—naturally only with the blessing of His Excellency, the prince bishop. Are all in agreement?"

For a while, silence prevailed. The bishop's chancellor was the first to raise his hand, followed by the young dandy with the goatee, and finally all the others. Only Samuel and Simon sat there motionless.

"I see there are only two objections," the suffragan bishop finally concluded, taking out a silk handkerchief to wipe the sweat from his bald head. "Well, that's more than enough, especially since one of the two objectors is not even from this town," he added smugly. He turned to the chancellor. "I ask you to please inform His Excellency the prince bishop of our decision. I'm certain he will approve."

The chancellor nodded. "I believe you are right, Your Excellency." He reached for his glass of wine and offered a toast to the others. "Here's to our city!"

"To our city!" the others replied, raising their glasses as well.

While the councilors and scholars drank deeply from their wineglasses, Simon felt as if a rope were slowly tightening around his neck.

Though she was walking ankle-deep through the garbage in the streets, Barbara felt like she were walking on a cloud. Together with Matheo she strolled through a narrow, muddy lane that ran from the Green Market to the Lange Gasse. There was an odor of hops and smoked meat in the air, freshly washed clothing hung from the windows, and in a doorway children were playing with a top.

Sir Malcolm had given his actors time off after the performance, and for an hour the two young people had been walking through Bamberg like a husband and wife on a Sunday afternoon stroll. Matheo had stopped now and then at one of the many market stalls, bought a few little things, and, like a gallant gentleman from a good family, had given the delighted Barbara some tasty tidbits to eat.

As casually as possible, Barbara reached out for Matheo's hand and let him help her jump over a large puddle in the street. The day was certainly the finest she'd ever had. Alongside her walked the first boy she really loved — not one of those uncouth Schongau farm boys who thought it was a sign of affection to run after her reciting one of their obscene poems, nor the feeble-minded knacker's son from the neighboring town of Peiting who had only three teeth left in his mouth, stank like a barrel of tannic acid, and actually hoped to marry soon. No, this boy was like something out of one of those wonderful storybooks that Magdalena had always read to her at bedtime. Matheo was muscular, tanned like a Turkish prince, with mysterious, sparkling eyes and a healthy set of white teeth that gleamed when he laughed. And he was smart and funny. At that moment he took another playful bow, mimicking a dandy at the royal court.

"My dear lady, allow me to guide you safely through this dubious part of town," he said in an artificially pompous tone, pointing to the left, where the lane opened into a broader avenue.

"Dear lady?" Barbara grinned. "No doubt you have forgotten the family I come from. Or are we still play-acting?"

"Isn't all of life a stage?" he replied with a wink.

Their act that morning in the Wedding House had been a great success. It was actually Matheo's act, and Barbara had only tossed some balls and hoops to him from time to time. But the act was well received, the audience laughed, and at least for a short while they'd forgotten their fears. In her excitement, Barbara had hardly given any thought to the werewolf that was once again wandering the streets of Bamberg during the night. While the audience was applauding at the end of the piece, Matheo had called her up onto the stage, and she'd bowed to the audience, whose applause washed over her like a pleasant summer rain.

Now Barbara started dreaming of becoming an artist someday, too. Even as a very small girl she'd enjoyed clowning around and getting dressed up. Was this perhaps the chance she'd yearned for to escape the dreary, predestined life of a hangman's daughter? She would rumble through the country in a wagon and make people laugh or cry. Weren't actors just as dishonorable as knackers and hangmen? So, in fact, she'd remain true to her class. But what she didn't know was how to break this news to her family. She suspected that her father would definitely not be excited about these plans.

"Another prune?"

Matheo handed her the small, shriveled fruit, interrupting her thoughts. They were just passing the barred windows of the city prison on the Hellergasse, and Barbara couldn't help thinking that her uncle occasionally whipped convicts here before dragging them off to the gallows or the place where they were to be beheaded. Matheo seemed to have noticed her worried look.

"Has your father ever had nightmares because of all the executions?" he asked, lifting his crumpled hat back over his neck. He had a southern accent but spoke German extremely well. "I can imagine he also has to torture or hang people sometimes and feels sorry for them, doesn't he?"

Barbara shrugged as she put the prune in her mouth and slowly chewed on it. For a while they were both silent.

Finally she swallowed the fruit and said, "He doesn't talk to us about his work, ever. Actually, none of us knows how he really feels. Maybe Mother did, but unfortunately she's dead." Her face turned grim. "My brother, Georg, will probably become the Schongau executioner after my father is gone, and he, too, is stubborn and doesn't talk much. It's in our blood, no doubt, at least for the men. Uncle Bartl is the same way." She sighed and wiped her mouth. "But let's talk about nicer things. For example, how you became an actor." She cast him a sideways glance as they turned onto a wide, paved street.

Matheo grinned. "There's not much to tell. I was an urchin on the streets of Sicily, without a father, and with a mother who was a drunk and happy when I ran away. I joined a group of jugglers, and it seems I had talent. In any case, Sir Malcolm discovered me at a fair in Siena, and since then I travel the country with him." He laughed. "Until now I've usually been the beautiful girl in his troupe, but recently my voice has become too deep, and I'm starting to grow fuzz on my face. Here, feel it."

He took Barbara's hand and ran it across his scratchy chin. She got goose flesh on her arm.

"Yes . . . yes you are," she said haltingly. "Then another fellow will soon have to play the girl."

Matheo waved her off. "Not until recently have women been allowed to play the female parts, though the church doesn't actually condone it. But what does it matter? I prefer playing the role of the lovesick young man, anyway."

"That's something I can well imagine."

The last few minutes Barbara had been walking along as if

in a trance, and when she looked up, she saw they were close to the Lange Gasse, alongside a wild garden in the middle of the city. Beyond the garden was a larger building whose walls were in ruins and overgrown with blackberry vines. Between the piles of stone Barbara saw some wild apple trees with a few shrunken apples still on its branches.

"Let's go and get ourselves a few apples." Matheo winked at her. "Perhaps we can rest a bit in the shade of the trees. The guards aren't especially happy if people wander around back there, but don't worry, they won't catch us."

Barbara couldn't help thinking of her last encounter with the guards when she'd been looking into the abandoned house, but the look in Matheo's big, brown eyes convinced her.

"Rest a bit?" she laughed. "Why not? I do feel a bit hot." In the next instant it occurred to her that it was the end of October and because of the cold she was wearing a thin woolen coat over her blouse. "Ah, I mean I'm a bit tired after the performance. Perhaps we should really sit down for a minute."

Matheo had already pulled himself up on some protruding stones and offered his arm to help her. She climbed over the wall, and after just a few steps it seemed they were far from the street. A few sparrows chirped in the branches, a light wind was blowing, but otherwise all was quiet. Matheo was still holding her by the hand.

"A beautiful spot," she said hesitantly, looking over at the larger building, the back of which was only a stone's throw away. A second wall separated the wild area from a well-tended garden that evidently belonged to the stately property. "So peaceful, yet in the middle of the city."

"It was probably not always this beautiful here," Matheo answered softly. "Our playwright, Markus Salter, told me about it during our last visit to Bamberg. The people who live here call this place the 'Druid's Garden.' Even just forty years go there was a building right where we are now standing in which alleged witches were examined and tortured. The so-called House of the Inquisition. Did you ever hear about it?"

Barbara shook her head silently, and Matheo continued.

"It all started when the son of the burgomaster was found with a book about Doctor Faustus. The book was confiscated."

"The same Doctor Faustus that Markus Salter played on the stage?" Barbara asked.

"Yes," Matheo nodded. "The fourteen-year-old boy thought it was a genuine book of magic and started randomly accusing people of witchcraft. Soon a wave of arrests began, to which the boy himself fell victim. Evidently there were so many suspicious people then that the dungeons in Bamberg couldn't house them all, so they had to build this accursed house here." He pointed at the overgrown garden. "There were cells, torture chambers, stalls, even a chapel to hear confessions, and a courtroom. But everything was hidden from view, so that people didn't learn about it. The Bambergers didn't know exactly what was going on here. Shortly before the Swedish invasion, they released the last prisoner and very quickly tore down the building, probably because it reminded them of their own guilt."

Matheo sat down on an old tree stump. "By then hundreds had already died. In the neighboring town of Zeil they had even built a huge oven in order to burn all the alleged witches. Isn't that dreadful?"

Barbara looked around anxiously. A cloud had passed over the sun, casting a dark shadow on the garden. Between the violet heather and the apple trees, she could make out the remains of the building's foundation, individual, rectangular rooms, and here and there rusty nails and rotten beams eaten away by the ravages of time. Suddenly, the garden no longer seemed so beautiful.

"It's good that those days are gone forever," she finally said.

Matheo nodded grimly. "Let's hope they don't return, but if this hysteria about the werewolf continues, then perhaps you'll soon need such an inquisition . . ." He shuddered as if trying to drive away the evil thought. Then he beckoned for Barbara to come over and take a seat alongside him.

"I think we're a good couple," Matheo began hesitantly, after she'd taken a seat on the tree stump. He laughed with embarrassment. "I . . . I mean in the theater, naturally. I think you really have talent. The people look wide-eyed when they see you, and you have a natural charisma."

"A natural charisma?" Barbara moved a bit closer to Matheo. "What does that mean?"

"Well, that means—"

At that very moment the angry voices of two or three men could be heard coming from the well-kept garden behind them. Matheo stopped and frowned.

"I'll eat my hat if that isn't the voice of Sir Malcolm," he mumbled. "What's he doing here?" Quickly he stood up and ran back to the rear wall.

Barbara sighed and followed him. She didn't know what would have happened if she'd sat with him a bit longer under the apple tree, but she really wanted to find out.

Meanwhile, Matheo had discovered a chink in the wall where he could look through and observe what was happening on the other side without being discovered. Excitedly he waved to Barbara.

"It really is Malcolm," he whispered, "along with a few other men. I'm afraid that one of them is this Guiscard that our innkeeper was telling us about, and this garden belongs to an inn— probably the one the accursed Frenchman is staying in."

Barbara had also found a crack in the wall to look through. She saw a pretty little orchard with tables and chairs scattered around, though in late October none of them were occupied. Underneath the trees stood the English producer surrounded by three men Barbara didn't know. Two of them were wearing rather shabby-looking clothes and were pointing their swords threateningly at Sir Malcolm. The third man was wearing a wig, like Sir Malcolm, and a bright red jacket covered with gleaming copper buttons. Judging from his stiff lace collar and a hat jauntily pulled low on his face he was no doubt a nobleman. When she looked again, Barbara noticed the many wine stains on his clothing and poorly mended rips in his shirt and stockings.

"*Tout de suite!* Take back those words at once," he shouted at Sir Malcolm. He spoke with an artificial-sounding French accent that made him seem affected and feminine. Barbara could now see, too, that he was lightly made up.

"*Il y va de mon honneur,*" the Frenchman continued loudly, pounding his chest dramatically. "Have you not understood me? If you lie like that again, I'll order my men to punch you full of holes like an old wine pouch."

"Ha! I'd like to see you try," Sir Malcolm snarled back. "You are a bad man and a thief, Guiscard. Unfortunately the theft of theater pieces is not punishable by law, or you'd have long ago been sent to the gallows." The English producer puffed himself up. "*The Doge of Venice* belongs to *my* troupe. It was written personally for us by the great playwright Markus Salter, and now you are on the road, peddling it like a common merchant. You haven't even done much to change the title: *The Dome of Venice.*" He laughed maliciously. "What nonsense. As if the dome in this piece played any major role."

Guiscard waved him off. "It sounds good — that's the main thing. Besides, you know yourself that with a few chases, sword fights, and broken hearts, the story could take place anywhere."

"Then you admit you stole the piece from us?"

The Frenchman smiled. "Didn't you just say there's no law against taking theater pieces? As soon as they're written down, anyone can use them. And now, *excusez-moi.*" He tried to push his way past Malcolm. "We will be having one more rehearsal, and I'm certain that *The Dome of Venice . . .*" he said, emphasizing every word, followed by a smug pause, "well, this performance in the Grapevine Tavern will be a great success, followed by many others. The bishop has invited us to spend the entire winter in Bamberg."

"He signed a document giving us the exclusive right . . . you frog eaters." The gaunt Sir Malcolm stood more than a head taller than Guiscard. Like a scarecrow that had just sprung to life, he pushed his arch-enemy to the ground.

"Murder! Murder!" Guiscard cried out theatrically, clutching his chest as if in the throes of great pain. "Men, save me from this cowardly assassin."

Now the two huge men took up their swords and attacked the English producer, who fought back, darting from one table to the next.

"We must help Sir Malcolm," Matheo whispered, "or they'll skewer him alive."

"But how . . ." Barbara started to say. But Matheo had already climbed over the wall, and his hat went flying off. On the other side he picked up a heavy branch and attacked the men. He struck one of the huge men from behind, who screamed and fell to the ground. The other turned away from Sir Malcolm and looked at Matheo in astonishment.

"What in the world are you doing here, you wimp?" he growled. "You've gotten yourself into a lot of trouble, little fellow."

"I know him," cried Guiscard, who meanwhile had struggled to his feet and was leaning on one of the tables with an anguished expression. Breathing heavily, he dabbed his forehead with a silk handkerchief. "That's the pretty boy in Malcolm's troupe. Beat him black and blue. And let's see then if he can still play the part of the young hero." He smirked. "Without the handsome hero there's no play, and thus no permission from the bishop. *Compris?*"

Guiscard's helper had meanwhile struggled to his feet. Along with the other guard he rushed at Matheo, who looked in vain for a way to escape. He was still holding his weapon in his hand, but it was trembling noticeably.

"One more step, Guiscard, and I'll send my whole troupe after you," Sir Malcolm said in a threatening voice as he sought protection behind a tree. "Then you'll be lucky if you can leave this town on all fours."

Guiscard Brolet let out a shrill laugh, like that of a little girl. "And just where is your oh-so-brave troupe? I see here only a weakling, a mere youth with a big mouth."

"We're here," a high voice replied. "And now get out before we have to spill any blood."

Astonished, Guiscard looked toward the wall, where Barbara was still hiding, and his helpers stopped fighting, as well.

Barbara had spoken up almost instinctively, and now she was thinking feverishly about how she could help her friend. She couldn't fight herself, and it would no doubt take too much time if she called the guards—if they would even be interested in a fight between two actors. Finally, she did something she'd always had fun doing even as a child.

She disguised her voice.

"You heard the lady, get out, you dirty frogs," she growled, trying to sound as rough and deep as a barroom brawler.

"Before we break your legs, you filthy Frenchmen," she grumbled in an even lower pitch with a Swabian accent.

"Come on, let's get them!" Barbara shouted then in a brighter, breaking tone, sounding like a real Bavarian. "There are only three of them. This will be a bloodbath."

She threw a few stones over the wall, then quickly grabbed Matheo's hat, still lying in the flowers, pulled it far down over her face, clambered to the top of a rock pile near the wall, and started bombarding Guiscard and his men with stones. One of them shrieked loudly when one hit him right in the temple.

"Damn, there are a number of them over there," he whimpered, ducking down like a whipped dog as he ran over to the back door of the inn. The second thug was also hit in the shoulder by a rock and looked around anxiously. He, too, ran off when he noticed the hat of his supposed attacker on the other side of the wall.

"Monsieur Brolet, come quickly!" he called to the theater director. "We must get some reinforcements. There are too many for us."

"*Sacrement*! You cowards." With another French curse on his lips, Guiscard struggled to his feet and ran after his two bodyguards, who had already disappeared inside the building.

"You'll come to regret this, Malcolm! You'll regret it," he shouted again in the direction of the English theater producer, who was still hiding behind the tree. "We'll see you again, and then the bishop will allow only one troupe of actors here in Bamberg. And that's us!"

He slammed the door to the tavern with a loud thud.

For a while there was not a sound in the garden, then Sir Malcolm stepped out from behind the tree and turned to his comrade-in-arms, who was gasping for air.

"Well, Matheo, how many warriors did you really bring along with you? And why don't they come out from behind the wall?"

Matheo was still standing there, his mouth open in amazement. Suddenly he broke out in a loud laugh, shook his head in disbelief, and began clapping his hands.

"*Mamma Mia,* that was the best performance I've seen in a long time," he exulted, as tears of laughter ran down his cheeks. "This girl is a natural."

Sir Malcolm looked at him in astonishment. "Girl? Which girl? I don't understand a word you're saying."

Matheo clapped a few more times, then called out, "Barbara, you can come out now. The play is over."

Hesitantly, Barbara peered over the wall, still wearing Matheo's hat, but her pale face showed how terrified she really was.

"Have they . . . have they left?" she stammered.

Sir Malcolm seemed puzzled at first, but then his face broke out in a wide smile.

"*She* is our men?" he asked. "A whole troupe of actors played by one girl behind the wall?" He bowed deeply. "On my honor, young lady, if that was meant to be an audition to convince me of your abilities, you have come across better than any actor before you."

Barbara had to catch her breath. "Audition?" she asked softly. "I'm afraid I don't understand."

Sir Malcolm grinned. "I can see in your eyes that you have the talent befitting an actor. Have you ever thought of appearing on the stage? Well? Now that Matheo is too old, we need some-one new for the leading female role." He sighed with satisfac-tion. "Matheo and you would be perfect for the roles of Romeo and Juliet. There's never been a more perfect couple."

Barbara suddenly became weak in the knees. She wanted to reply, but in contrast to before, she was now speechless.

"I . . ." was all she could say. "Matheo . . ."

With his arms wide open and his body quivering with emo-tion, Sir Malcolm approached her. "Milady, welcome to my troupe. So much talent positively cries out to be an actor on the stage. I can't pay much, but I promise you, you'll have the whole world at your feet."

The apothecary's wife, Adelheid Rinswieser, listened to the screams echoing down the corridor from the room at the other end. They sounded like the howling of a beast, but she could tell they were made by a man. They were occasionally interrupted by a soft murmur when the stranger asked his questions. And even though Adelheid couldn't quite hear the voice, she knew what it was saying.

Who taught you the art of magic?

Who are your brothers and sisters?

Where do you meet? In the forest? In the cemetery? Up in the ruins of the old castle?

Where do you go on the Witch's Sabbath?

How do you make the drink that lets you fly?

Confess, witch, confess, confess . . .

Confess . . . Confess . . . Confess . . . Confess . . . Confess!

"Oh, God, I don't know anything," the victim shrieked. "Who are you? What do you want from me, you devil?"

Adelheid wished she could hear the answer to that, as she still had no idea why the stranger had locked her up here. Why her? And why this constant questioning and torture in the horrible chamber? The man had to be crazy, a deranged murderer, and they had all become his victims by sheer coincidence. There couldn't be any other reason.

Or could there?

The screaming of the young woman had stopped the day before. Was she already dead? Wounded? Unconscious? Adelheid didn't know, but evidently the stranger had found another victim, and the chalice had not yet been passed on to her.

Again there was a loud scream, and Adelheid froze with fear. She couldn't help thinking of the beast that had attacked her — the tapping in the bushes, the odor of wet fur. Was this perhaps nothing but a ghost, a figment of her imagination? Were the stranger and the beast one and the same? Or was there not just a madman prowling around out there, but a beast obeying his commands?

"On my honor, yes. I'm a witch. Yes, I have kissed the devil's anus. Yes! . . . Yes! . . . Yes! . . . Anything you want, just please stop. Stop. Stop. Stop!"

The victim's voice sounded a bit higher now, and Adelheid felt she was about to vomit. Her fear felt like a little rodent gnawing its way through her bowels.

When is it my turn?

Curiously, the stranger had spared her until now. He'd come back into her cell twice again, but he hadn't taken her back to the horrible torture chamber, just brought her a new candle and stared at her silently through his hangman's mask. Adelheid thought she could see his body trembling softly. Then he'd dashed out again, almost like a man possessed, and had bolted the door behind him.

A few hours ago, the stranger had turned his attention to the male prisoner, and Adelheid was shocked to realize it had brought her relief. Relief and at the same time guilt.

I'm happy that it's someone else. Oh, God, forgive my sin!

She tugged at the chain that for some time had shackled her to the wall of the cell. Recently, the stranger hadn't bothered to attach the leather straps, so that now she could at least sit up and even walk around a bit. The pain in her arms and legs had eased off a bit, so she could shake her arms and legs and massage them to get the blood flowing again. How long had she been in this cell? Day and night merged into one viscous clump, but despite everything, she'd not given up. In the endless hours between the stranger's visits, she constantly thought of how she might escape. She'd turned over all the possibilities in her mind and finally come to a conclusion.

Perhaps there was a way, but to do that, she'd have to wait until the man came back again and took off the chains to lead her to the torture chamber.

It would, no doubt, be her last chance.

Adelheid Rinswieser took a deep breath, closed her eyes, and tried to retreat into herself, to a place where she could escape the screams and the fear.

• • •

"The tanners are invited to the wedding, and so are a few of the Bamberg fishermen, and a whole family of weavers distantly related to Katharina, and — you'll hardly believe this — even Aloysius, that stubborn hangman's servant in the Bamberg Forest. Ha! Something like that would never happen in Schongau. But the tavern keeper at the Wild Man, a fellow by the name of Berthold Lamprecht, doesn't give a damn about what people say and is going to let Uncle Bartholomäus have the party, though not in the main hall but in the little room off to one side. The city councilors have more to worry about this year than making a fuss about *that*."

Jakob Kuisl was silent while his daughter Magdalena babbled on. Late in the day, the hangman, his daughter, and grandchildren took an afternoon stroll. They were walking behind a wagon slowly making its way toward the city across the wide, wooden Sees Bridge, whirling up clouds of dust as it went. They'd spent the last few hours in Theuerstadt, a part of town northeast of the city, where many farmers grew onions and licorice. Both products were well known not just in Bamberg but in the area all around the city, often earning the locals the sobriquet of "onion heads." But out there in the country around the monastery of St. Gangolf, where the streets became wider, the houses smaller, but the people friendlier and above all, cleaner, there were farms where vegetables were grown as well as many fruit trees and different kinds of flowers, most of which, however, had already withered at the end of autumn.

Katharina had asked Magdalena to find flowers to decorate the tables at the wedding, but it seemed to Jakob that the conversation with the old toothless flower woman would go on forever. After that, the hangman had let Magdalena wheedle him into looking around in Theuerstadt for asters, stonecrop, and autumn crocuses and ordering the flowers from the gardener for the coming Sunday — a decision Kuisl had by now regretted. He took consolation in the fact that here in Bamberg no one knew him. In Schongau, an executioner who was more interested in the fragrance of violets and pansies than in the security of the noose on the gallows would surely have been laughed out of town.

But it wasn't just his visit to Theuerstadt that was a total disaster; it was the entire trip. He'd come here for only one reason — to finally see his son Georg again after two years, only to see that his uncle had completely spoiled him. Georg had become rebellious and impudent, but even worse, he stood up to his own father and defended his uncle. The fight in the street the day before had brought them somewhat closer together, but Georg's attitude revealed to Jakob that Bartholomäus had told him more than he'd wished.

"I don't know what all this fuss is about the wedding," Jakob grumbled, struggling to make his way across the wooden bridge behind the agonizingly slow carts, holding both boys by the hand. Below them, the right branch of the Regnitz flowed along lazily. "Your mother and I didn't need to have any big party back then; there wasn't any money for it anyway. We invited the midwife, Stechlin, the knacker and his servant, and the night watchman — that was all, and we all had a good time just the same, without all these so-called friends, cousins, aunts, and uncles, who just want to hang around all day eating the free food."

Magdalena looked at her father and scowled. "Didn't you want to have your sister and brother there for the celebration?"

"Ha! Ask Bartl. He never would have come to my wedding."

"But why?" Magdalena took her father by the arm and stopped for a moment. "Something happened between you two. Don't you want to tell me?"

"Maybe some other time. I'm tired now, and if I'm not mistaken, we still have one more thing to get for my future sister-in-law. So come along."

Jakob pulled himself away and stomped ahead, through the

Bamberg Gate and down the little lane leading to the Fisherman's Quarter north of the city hall on the left branch of the Regnitz. Magdalena and the children followed at a distance.

In fact, they had promised Katharina to ask the furrier about finding them a piece of fox fur for the hem of her wedding dress. Jakob's sister-in-law had given them precise directions, but it was difficult to find the right house in the labyrinth of tiny, winding streets, many of which ended at the water's edge. Water rushed past the dilapidated piers, where the boats bobbed up and down in the current. Many of the half-timbered buildings had boat sheds opening onto the river, and the air was heavy with the smell of rotting fish and moldy nets spread out to dry between wooden poles on the docks and balconies.

Several of the fishermen eyed Jakob Kuisl cautiously as he stepped out of an alley leading straight to the piers. In front of a small half-timbered house on the left, a number of leather hides fluttered in the wind, slapping noisily against the wall of the house, where a bloody deer hide had been hung on a wooden frame to dry. Jakob turned around to Magdalena.

"This is probably the house," he said. "It would be best for you to stay outside on the pier with the children, so they don't fall in and drown. I'll be right back."

He knocked, and a small old man immediately opened the door. He had a wrinkled, unshaven face that was barely visible under his bearskin cap, and he gave off a moldy smell more familiar to Jakob than that of violets and pansies.

"What do you want?" growled the old man. "Did Johannes the leatherworker send you? Tell that greedy bastard I'm not finished with the tanning, but just the same, I'm not going down one kreuzer on the price."

"Katharina, the fiancée of the Bamberg executioner has sent me," Kuisl responded. "She needs a nice fox fur for her wedding."

"Ah, the wedding of the executioner." The man grinned, revealing his three remaining teeth. "A lot of tongues are wagging because the innkeeper of the Wild Man is letting the hangman celebrate in his place. But we all stink the same when the devil takes us away to the dance." He giggled. "I'd have to know. I'm the furrier here in town, after all. Come in, big fellow."

He motioned for Jakob to enter the cottage. The hangman had to duck to get through the low doorway. A magnificent bearskin hung over a chest, empty eye sockets staring at the hangman, and below them a huge mouthful of sharp teeth, while furs of martens, weasels, and polecats lay on a table in the middle of the room, next to some scraping knives, and a string of rabbits hung by their ears from a stick over the oven. There was a smell in the room of the wild, the hunt, and death.

"And are you sure Katharina doesn't want badger fur?" the old furrier asked, rummaging about in some furs on the table. Finally he pulled out a beautiful black piece and waved it in front of Kuisl's face. "That's much more impressive and still is one of the furs that people in her social caste are allowed to wear." He stopped and looked suspiciously at the Schongau hangman. "Who are you, anyway? I've never seen you here before."

"Just a member of the family," Kuisl replied curtly. Then he shrugged. "Katharina wants a fox fur, so that's what I'll bring her. What does it cost?"

The little old man waved him off. Putting the badger fur aside, he reached into a trunk containing some musty-smelling, rather shabby-looking remnants. "Keep your money, big fellow. It's never a bad idea to stay on good terms with the future wife of the executioner, is it? Anyway, fox is not an expensive fur like ermine." He handed Kuisl a reddish fur full of holes. "Here, take it. The creature got caught last week in one of my rabbit traps. It was foaming at the mouth and snapping in all directions before I killed it. If you ask me, the thing had rabies, a terrible sickness going around in the forests now. My brother-in-law's nephew was bitten a few years ago by an infected fox, and now . . ."

He paused when he saw Kuisl leaning over the trunk and pulling out another fur. The hangman held it in his hand, thinking. It was dark gray, had a long tail, and sharp claws on its paws.

"Why are you interested in the wolfskin?" the old man grumbled. "I can't imagine Katharina wants to have the big bad wolf decorating the hem of her wedding dress." He waved him off, giggling. "That's just something for poor people. I'm happy I was able to sell five of them all at once just a few days ago. Who knows how long they would have otherwise just been rotting away here?"

"*What* did you do?" Kuisl stared at the furrier as if he'd just seen a ghost.

The little old man shrugged, not knowing quite how to answer.

"Well, uh, I also found that a bit strange because no one actually wants to have wolfskins. They say it brings misfortune. Especially now, when this werewolf is supposed to be prowling around the city. But if someone offers you a good price for these old, battered things, you don't ask. I still have two of them, and if you want—"

"What did the man look like?" Jakob interrupted.

The old man pushed his fur cap back on his head and started thinking. "I can't remember very much, which is funny, actually, because I usually have such a good memory for these things. Hmm, wait . . ." His face brightened. "Now I remember. He had a beard, a kind of floppy hat, and was wearing a broad cape. Exactly!"

Kuisl spat on the floor. "That describes about every other person you bump into on the street. Can't you remember anything else?"

"Unfortunately not." The only man frowned "Why is it so important for you to know that?"

"Thanks for the fox," said the hangman, without answering the question. Then he put down the wolf's hide and headed toward the door with the mangy fox fur. Suddenly he turned around. "Oh, and if this man drops by again, get in touch with me over at the executioner's house. As you said, it's never a bad idea to stay on good terms with the hangman."

"You still haven't told me who you are," the furrier replied, and his little eyes flashed suspiciously. "How do I know you're not just random punk that the executioner is about to string up on the nearest tree?"

"I'm the hangman's brother, and I string up people myself— punks and sometimes guys who are too curious."

Then Jakob Kuisl turned away, stooping down to get through the doorway, like a giant leaving a dollhouse.

Outside, Magdalena had to watch the boys closely to make sure they didn't push each other off the dock. For a while they'd been playing hide-and-seek among the skins and furs fluttering in the wind, but now they'd started tussling with one another alongside the rushing water. Though Paul was the younger of the boys, the two were about the same size, and as usual, Peter was losing. Soon his brother had dragged him toward the water and out onto the pier.

"Mama, Mama! Paul's going to drown me like a witch," Peter cried.

"For heaven's sake, can't the two of you ever play like . . . like . . ."

Magdalena was about to say "girls," but caught herself just in time. Sometimes in her dreams or in moments of reflection she could see herself telling stories to a little daughter sitting on her lap, as she once had with Barbara. Then the pain and sorrow at the loss of her child came back again, and even now she could feel a burning in her throat. She loved her boys with all her heart but still felt there was something in them she couldn't know. Peter took after his father, and Paul . . . Well, there were days when she almost feared his temper tantrums.

She ran after the boys and pulled them apart. Luckily, she still had some licorice left from the gardens around St. Gangolf's, and she gave a stick to each of them. Soon they were busily sucking on them and the fight was forgotten.

Impatiently Magdalena looked back at the furrier's house. Why was her father staying so long? For a moment she regretted not going with Barbara to the theater performance that day, but Katharina had asked for her help. And she had a bad conscience for leaving the children with their aunt every day, even though Katharina clearly enjoyed having them. Surely, she wished for some of her own. Why had it taken her so long to find a husband? She came from a good family, and though she was a bit overweight, she was always smiling and was an excellent cook. Magdalena knew that executioners had a hard time finding suitable wives. Bartholomäus could count himself lucky that . . .

A creaking sound tore her from her reveries. Carefully she turned around and noticed a figure just two piers away, behind one of the fisherman's nets that was hung out to dry.

It was no doubt a man, as he was wearing a floppy hat and a wide cloak, and she also thought she could make out a beard. At first she thought he was just one of the many fishermen living in that part of town, but then she noticed he wasn't working on the nets but just standing there, clearly observing her and the boys. Was he perhaps a robber waiting for dusk to fall so he could attack her in a dark alley? The man seemed strangely familiar to her. She looked up anxiously at the sky. The sun, a glowing ball of fire, was setting behind the Michelsberg to the west, and shadows were already falling over the city. She wondered where her father was.

She was about to walk over to the furrier's house when the door swung open and out came Jakob Kuisl holding a fox fur looking like a dirty rag in his hand; he had a thoughtful look on his face.

Magdalena took a deep breath of relief and slowly started walking over to him, trying to look as inconspicuous as possible.

"Do you see the man with the floppy hat over there behind the nets?" she said in a soft voice. "I think he's watching us."

Jakob Kuisl squinted and finally nodded.

"Yes, I see him, and I'd like to have a little talk with him, man-to-man, if you know what I'm saying," he added with a growl. He turned to leave, but Magdalena held him back

"Father, whatever you have in mind, just remember you're not as young as you used to be, and I'm worried that you—"

"Damn it," he interrupted angrily. "The day my daughter starts worrying about my age is the day I'll willingly go to my grave. But first I have a few questions I want to ask that fellow over there. You wait here."

Silently he disappeared behind a frame holding a large beaver pelt. For a brief moment she could hear the sounds of his receding steps, but then all fell silent. Magdalena sighed and shook her head.

"Your grandfather is as stubborn as a mule, and an idiot, do you know that?" she said to the children, who were still peacefully sucking on their licorice sticks, their legs dangling from the pier.

"You say the same thing about Georg," Peter replied, "and about Dad, as well . . . and about the wagon drivers in Schongau who are always playing cards and getting drunk down at Semer's Tavern. Are all men stubborn mules and idiots, Mama?"

Despite her annoyance, she couldn't keep from smiling. "Well, most of them, but your grandfather much more than the rest. I hope he doesn't hurt himself."

Hiding behind the drying racks, Jakob Kuisl disappeared behind the furrier's house, then slunk down a cluttered alleyway parallel to the river, and from there back to the other piers. Some children playing in the street looked up anxiously as the grim giant hurried past them in his flowing cloak.

Kuisl's thoughts were racing. Ever since he'd seen the wolf pelt in the furrier's trunk, he had a strange suspicion, so strange it might even be correct. Especially after learning that a stranger, just a short time ago, had bought a whole bunch of wolf pelts from the furrier.

Could it be possible?

He wanted to get to the bottom of this as fast as possible. If the man hiding behind the nets really turned out to be the stranger the furrier had talked about, that would explain a lot of things.

But if it's really him, why did he come back?

A muddy path led from the lane down to the pier where the man had just been standing. Kuisl stayed close to the wall of the house. From the corner of his eye he could see a few fishermen watching him suspiciously from their boats out on the river, but he couldn't let them distract him now, and taking a deep breath he stepped out into the open.

The stranger was still standing behind the frame holding the fishnets, but in the gathering darkness it was hard for Kuisl to see more than the vague outline of a man wearing a floppy hat and an overcoat. Slowly, the hangman walked along the path, the only access to the pier, so the man wouldn't be able to escape. Unless he decided to fight. But Jakob had been in many fights, more than most people.

"Hey, you," the hangman said, addressing the stranger. "Stop. I need to have a word with you."

When the man saw he'd been discovered, he froze like a cornered animal. And then he did something Kuisl never would have expected.

He jumped.

It was a full three yards to the next pier, almost ten feet, but the man landed safely on the creaking planks. For a moment it

seemed like he might fall backward, but then he got his balance
again and ran down the pier toward the shore. Kuisl was startled
to see that the stranger had a slight limp. He knew only one person in Bamberg who limped—and that was his own brother.

That's impossible, he thought. *Or maybe it isn't . . .*

Cursing, he turned back and ran through the little alleys full
of rotted rowboats put up on jacks, handcarts, and barrels of fish.
The man with the floppy hat had a lead of at least twenty paces,
and Kuisl had to remember what his daughter Magdalena had
said earlier—he wasn't so young anymore. In a fight he could
count on his experience, but in running, the younger folk were
better. Nevertheless, he'd already gained a few yards on the
stranger, when suddenly the man turned sharp right and ran
back down to one of the four piers.

"Now I've got you," Kuisl panted.

He ran toward the pier as fast as he could and only at the last
moment saw what the other was planning to do. A small rowboat was tied to one of the posts, with the oars tossed carelessly
into the stern. In one fluid move, the man jumped in, pulled out
a knife, and quickly cut the rope. Just as Kuisl reached the end of
the pier, the boat cast off and started floating down the river with
the current. The distance between them grew from one second to
the next.

There was no time for Jakob to reflect. He just kept running,
and with a final sprint, jumped into the water toward the boat,
and . . .

. . . missed.

He hit the cold water with a loud splash, the waves closed
over him, and in the next moment his clothes filled with water
and threatened to pull him under. As he thrashed about wildly,
Kuisl pulled off his heavy coat, and only then with powerful
strokes could he make his way back to the surface. Breathing
hard and paddling to keep afloat, he looked around in all directions.

The boat was drifting slowly down the river and was already some distance away. Jakob watched as the stranger put the oars in the oarlocks and pulled vigorously.

Then the boat disappeared around the next bend in the river.

The man with the floppy hat was breathing heavily as the small, half-timbered houses in the Fisherman's Quarter, with their balconies and piers, slowly receded. Night was falling over Bamberg, but the shadows did not fill him with happy expectations, as usual, but something approaching fear. His foot hurt, and his whole body shivered. Evidently, to add to his misery, he'd sprained his ankle jumping off the pier. That was nothing critical, but it showed him he was not invulnerable.

For the first time he'd been not the hunter, but the hunted.

He cursed himself under his breath for returning to see the furrier, but on his last visit he'd taken a liking to the beautiful furs, and for that reason planned to buy the two last pieces in order to continue his search for prey. For now, he enjoyed the musk-like odor and softness of the furs. When he wrapped them around him, he felt like someone else. The apothecary's wife had given him them to try on for the first time. They were like a second skin wrapped around him and protecting him and turning him into some sort of monster.

Something that inspired fear in people, as much fear as he had known back then.

But then he'd made an unforgivable mistake. It had given him a feeling of power to observe unnoticed, practically invisible, a potential victim, and this thrill had almost caused his ruin. He bit his lip nervously. His coat, floppy hat, and fake beard might conceal his true features — but he'd have to be very careful.

The buildings along the river were thinning out, just a few more sheds, an old mill, then the forest began, the wilderness, the realm of the beasts — a realm where more and more he was beginning to feel at home.

Old Schwarzkontz had broken down faster than any of them, and he was the first to die. The first woman also confessed quickly—her heart stopped beating from the fright—and he disposed of the corpse in the usual way. But he learned quickly. The young woman who was his next victim had survived four questionings before she, too, finally died.

For the first time, he felt pity, a feeling that he immediately suppressed. Pity was weak, and he could never show weakness. Just the same, he kept putting off the torture of his next victim, the apothecary's wife. Each time he looked into the woman's eyes, a shudder came over him, and he felt disgusted with himself.

Fortunately, though, he had come across Thadäus Vasold the night before.

The old fool had fallen into his trap in just the right place. It warmed his heart to see his wrinkled face frozen in horror. The feeling of revenge had been so sweet, like thick, golden honey. Now the old man was all tied up in the house, awaiting his next interrogation.

Confess, witch, confess . . .

The old man had been the fifth.

But his greatest satisfaction was yet to come. For a long time he'd been waiting to carry out his boldest plan. It couldn't be much longer.

Just three . . .

The man listened intently and could hear a long howling coming from the forest across the river. It was like a greeting of closeness, of intimacy—of home. Something he'd not experienced before.

The wolves were accepting the man as one of their own.

7

THE NEXT MORNING, THE KUISLS SAT AROUND
the table in the hangman's house, spooning the warm barley porridge Magdalena had made for them earlier that morning from
a large communal bowl. The wedding was only two days off,
and until then everyone had their own daily chores to do or
helped in the preparations.

Bartholomäus had already been down to the city moat with
Georg, where the Bamberg City Council had given him the
thankless task of shoveling out garbage that had been clogging
the moat—one of the responsibilities of the city executioner that
Bartholomäus hated even more than the occasional torturing of
criminals. Jakob had promised to help him that day, but first
there were a few loose shingles in the adjoining shed that had to
be replaced. Magdalena planned to bake bread for the week with
Barbara, while Katharina had to help her father with his paperwork at city hall.

The two boys were, for a change, playing tag peacefully with
a few of the neighboring children outside in the alley, so that the
Kuisls could enjoy being by themselves again for the first time in

a long while, even though Georg was missing, and there seemed to be trouble brewing.

Magdalena blew on the porridge in her wooden spoon to cool it off a bit, though her mind was occupied with thoughts of the strange man her father had tried to catch the night before. Finally, Kuisl had turned up, soaking wet and without his coat, by the furrier's house, and Magdalena could tell from the way he looked that even the slightest query would cause him to explode like gunpowder—so she'd held her tongue.

"You still haven't told us why you ran after that stranger," she finally asked. "You were frozen when you got back here yesterday, and you're lucky you didn't come down with a cold." She shook her head. "Falling into the river, at your age. Besides, your overcoat cost a lot of money. Do you know—"

"When I need a nurse, I'll tell you." Kuisl snorted angrily. "You're worse than my beloved Anna used to be, God rest her soul." For a moment he stared into space, then continued, speaking quickly. "But in any case, I'll tell you what happened yesterday. The furrier described a man to me who'd bought five wolfskins from him last week, and this description seemed to match very closely the man who was watching you."

Magdalena frowned. "Wolfskins? But why . . . ?"

"There are too many werewolf stories going around town now to suit my taste," Kuisl interrupted. "When someone goes out and buys five wolf pelts, I get suspicious, especially when he tries to run away from me. I'd like to know what he's doing with them. Perhaps he's making himself a big coat out of them, a coat he can hide under . . ."

"Just a minute. Do you think this fellow bought the fur so he could dress up as a werewolf?" asked Simon, putting down his spoon. "But why would he do that?"

"To spread fear in the city? So no one recognizes him when he goes out to murder people? I don't know." Kuisl shrugged, then started rummaging in the pocket of his trousers, looking for his tobacco pouch. "Perhaps there really is a werewolf causing trouble around here. I've heard that some of them clothe themselves in pelts in order to look like animals."

"So you believe in werewolves?" Simon asked skeptically.

"I've seen so many evil and crazy things in my life—so why shouldn't there be werewolves, as well? Or at least men who seriously believe they're werewolves." Kuisl opened his tobacco pouch and began filling his pipe with the dry leaves.

"Lots of poor creatures live in the forests," he continued. "Crazy people rejected by society who are more animal than human. Long ago, I myself had to break a man on the wheel who'd lived in the forest since childhood. During the great famine of 'forty-nine, he began hunting people to kill and eat them, especially children who'd run away from home. Their flesh was the most tender, he confessed later on the rack. Was he a werewolf?" Kuisl picked up a burning piece of kindling to light his pipe and began puffing with enjoyment. "I don't know. But in any case he was a danger to people and, for this reason, had to be put down."

"Here in Bamberg, the case is not as clear," he continued. "I'm afraid this Werewolf Commission under our unholy prince bishop will simply pick up some random person and have him tortured, just to find someone to blame." Simon had already told them about the first meeting of the commission the night before, and their intention of finding a supposed perpetrator and dispatching him without any further ado.

Kuisl grinned. "Good for Bartholomäus. Maybe he'll have his new hangman's house earlier that he'd even dreamed of."

"You are disgusting, Father. How can you even say anything like that about your own brother?"

Astonished, Magdalena looked over at the bench in the corner where Barbara was sitting. Until then, she'd been sitting silently in the corner, as if daydreaming and paying no attention to the conversation. Since two nights before, Magdalena thought she'd detected a faint smile now and then on the lips of her little sister. Barbara hadn't told her much about the performance with Matheo and the other actors, but that wasn't necessary. Afterward, she was gone for a long time, and Magdalena thought she knew with whom. Until then, she'd only told Simon about her suspicions, and he'd cast a knowing look in her direction.

Now, the smile was gone from Barbara's face. "Georg is right," she continued angrily, glaring at her father. "Ever since we've been here in Bamberg, you've been saying mean things about your brother. What did he do to you? You . . . you're just jealous because he's more successful. And because, unlike you, he found another wife."

Jakob slapped her hard on the cheek, and though she didn't cry, Magdalena could tell she was having trouble holding back her tears.

"You don't talk to your father like that, understand?" he growled. "Not you, and not your impudent brother, either. What do you know about Bartholomäus and me?"

"Yes, what do we know?" Magdalena said in a soft voice. "Actually, nothing, because you don't tell us anything."

"And that's the way it's going to be. Don't poke your nose into things that are none of your business. And now, I'm going over to the moat to help your accursed uncle shovel shit. That's better than sitting here and listening to you going on and on."

Jakob was just about to get up from the table when the door flew open with a loud crash. Georg was standing in the doorway, completely out of breath.

"They . . . got him," he panted.

"Who did they get?" Magdalena asked, puzzled.

"Well, who else? The werewolf," Georg replied, his eyes flashing. "I saw with my own eyes how the guards led him away. They found his wolf pelt, and a few citizens recognized him, too. But they say he won't confess. Uncle Bartholomäus and I are going to put the screws to him as soon as possible."

Barbara put her hand to her mouth. "Oh, my God! Who is it?" she asked anxiously.

Georg grinned. "One of those group of actors by the name of Matheo, a little Italian-looking guy. If you ask me, I knew right away that something was fishy about these actors."

For a long time, no one said a thing, and Georg looked from one to the other, puzzled.

"What's the matter?" he asked. "Did I say something wrong?"

Magdalena looked at her sister, who was so shocked she couldn't say a word, while Simon, standing alongside her, just stared at the floor. Jakob, the only one who didn't know about their special friendship, just shrugged.

"Well, now the hunt is on, no doubt," he grumbled. "But there's nothing you can do about it. It's always the same: they need someone to blame, the faster the better, and as I said, it pays off for Bartholomäus, too, you'll see . . ."

"Matheo is innocent!" Barbara suddenly shouted, in despair. "There's no way he's a werewolf. And anyone who says that is . . . is . . ." She broke down sobbing, and collapsed on the bench.

Magdalena took her gently in her arms and started talking to her softly, as if to a child.

Georg just stood there in the doorway, his mouth wide open in astonishment.

"You know this little punk?" he finally asked. "But why . . . ?"

"Well, Georg, I'm beginning to feel like the two of us are the village idiots," Jakob said, folding his arms in front of his broad chest. "Perhaps someone in this esteemed family can explain this to me, hmm?"

Simon cleared his throat. "Well . . . I don't know the details, but it appears that Barbara and this Matheo . . . well, they have some sort of close relationship . . ."

"She's in love with the guy. Is that so hard to understand, you dopes?" Magdalena looked up briefly as she continued to hug her crying sister. "We were at the theater performance two days ago," she continued, a bit more calmly, "then yesterday she was at the Wedding House again and no doubt was helping Matheo a bit during the performance. She told me they were standing together on the stage . . . and since then the two have no doubt become closer . . ."

"My daughter stood on a *stage?*" Jakob shook his head in disbelief. "With these wandering rogues and pickpockets?" He clenched his fists angrily. "Good God, can't we leave you women alone for a minute without you going out and doing something to embarrass us?"

"These actors are almost as dishonorable as hangman's families," Magdalena answered dryly. "In that sense, Barbara is staying true to her social standing."

"And to make matters worse, you're sticking up for her?" Kuisl laughed grimly. "Do you think she should marry the boy?"

"Well, at the moment this Matheo won't marry anyone, because he's sitting in the dungeon and suspected of being a werewolf," Simon interjected hesitantly. "And unless there's a miracle, your brother and Georg will no doubt be interrogating him."

"Monster! You monster!" Barbara jumped up suddenly and charged at her twin brother, hammering his chest with her little fists. "If you harm even a hair on his head, I'm no longer your sister. I'll . . . I'll scratch your eyes out, I'll . . ."

"Barbara, Barbara! Just stop, please." Georg tried to grab her arm, but each time she wriggled away. "What do you want me to do?" he wailed. "Even if you think this man is innocent, the new Inquisition Commission ordered me to question him and torture him. There's nothing more I can do for him."

"You . . . you beast! You ogre! To hell with all executioners." Beside herself with anger, Barbara kept beating her brother's chest. Finally, Jakob Kuisl stepped in between them. With one hand he seized Barbara's wrist and held it in a vise-like grip, and with the other hand he gave her a resounding smack in the face.

Barbara fell silent at once and glared at her father while trembling all over. The blow seemed at least to have quieted her down a bit.

"Now you listen to me, Barbara," Jakob began in a slow, firm voice. "You're striking the wrong person. Georg has nothing to do with the fact that your Matheo has been put in the dungeon. And there's nothing he or Bartholomäus can do but torture the fellow. After all, he's the executioner in this city, and you know what that means."

He let go of her and walked over to the executioner's sword hanging in the devotional corner of the room. Barbara stood in the middle of the room, as if turned to stone, her lips pressed together in two thin lines. "It's our living; it's what we do," Jakob continued, pointing to the sword. "We didn't go looking for it. God put us here in this place." He tried to sound comforting. "But I can talk with Bartholomäus. If Matheo is submissive, there are means of expediting him as painlessly as possible into the hereafter."

"Is that what you're suggesting?" Barbara asked in a toneless voice. "That you kill Matheo like . . . like a sick mongrel, even if you yourself don't believe he is this werewolf?"

"You heard your father," Georg replied. "We're just the tools, and —"

"Then let me tell you this, you . . . you *tool*," Barbara interrupted, slowly backing toward the door. Her voice was now sharp and cold, not at all like that of a fifteen-year-old. "I'm going now, and I won't come back until you get Matheo out of prison." She looked at her father. "I know you can do that. You've helped other people before. If he doesn't get out, Sir Malcolm's troupe will soon need someone new who can play the role of the girl, and that will be me, for God knows I have talent."

The door slammed shut, and the rest of the family just sat there, motionless.

"It looks like we have serious problems now," said Simon, breaking the silence. He sighed. "There's one thing I know for certain: Barbara is serious. After all, she's just like the rest of you, an accursed, stubborn Kuisl."

Down in the crypt of the Bamberg Cathedral, Suffragan Bishop Harsee knelt before a simple stone altar and struggled to commune with God. That was not so easy, as the large, whitewashed church was crowded with worshipers even on weekdays. Smaller masses were being held in the side aisles and individual chapels, pious sinners waited to speak with their confessor, and some beggars used the church pews for a short nap before the sexton came and roughly poked them to wake them up.

Sebastian Harsee closed his eyes, trying to ignore the loud sounds around him as best he could. In the last few days, his headaches had been getting worse from all the noise. How he hated this constant racket. Hadn't the Savior himself ejected the merchants and loud salesmen from the temple? If it was up to Harsee, this cathedral would be a place of silent reflection. Anyone wanting to hear God had to be silent and obey.

But silence and obedience had always been hard for the people of Bamberg.

The suffragan bishop crossed himself, then lay down on his belly on the cold stone floor and spread his arms out—a gesture of obedience he had loved even as a young man. Most people were lacking in humility, especially these ambitious patricians who increasingly took a stand against God and were followers of the vile god Mammon. Simple folk were for the most part devout, but even some of them rebelled from time to time against the holy Catholic Church and the divine order. Recently, Harsee had heard that the Bamberg executioner would be celebrating his marriage in the Wedding House, just like an honorable man.

The council had approved, apparently because his father-in-law was employed there as a lowly clerk. These were exactly the subtle, insidious changes that Harsee detested so much. After all, God had assigned a place to everyone in life — kaiser, bishop, tradesman, farmer . . . and hangman. To call that into question was heresy. Well, if things were headed in this direction, Harsee would know how to prevent this wedding celebration.

And, indeed, things were heading in this direction.

Harsee couldn't help thinking of events forty years before, when there had been a short period of sincere faith in Bamberg and the church had regained its former strength in the struggle against witchcraft. Hundreds of people had been put to the stake in Bamberg, and though even Harsee hadn't believed they were all witches and magicians, the strict regiment had led the citizens back into the flock of the prince bishop, and for that, no sacrifice was too great. Harsee smiled and pressed his cheek against the cool stone floor.

The Lord will know his own . . .

Back then, at the time of the trials, he himself had still been a young theology student, but with the help of his father, the venerable councilor and zealous Catholic Johann Georg Harsee, and a few loyal supporters, it had been possible to liquidate the enemies and turn Bamberg into a New Jerusalem. The power of the ambitious patricians had seemed broken, and the prince bishop had regained the upper hand. With the House of the Inquisition and the special Witches Commission they had created a perfect *purgatorium,* a court that was able to separate the true from the false, purify souls, and condemn useless bodies to the flames.

But then came the war, and with it the heretical Swedes, who put an end to the promising experiment. The prince bishop fled into exile in Austria, and gradually the patricians regained the upper hand in Bamberg. The present bishop, Prince Philipp von Rieneck, was weak and interested more in palaces, formal gardens, and his exotic animals than in preserving the faith.

But now God had presented him, Suffragan Bishop Sebastian Harsee, one of his most loyal servants, a new instrument that would drive his wayward flock back onto the true path.

A werewolf.

Briefly, Harsee shifted around again to scratch a sore on the right side of his neck. Something had bitten him there a few days ago, probably while he was sleeping. The wound was small, but it was weeping, and the itching was damned unpleasant. For some time, he'd been thinking of consulting Master Samuel, but after the bishop's personal physician had attacked him in the council meeting, he didn't think that was appropriate anymore. Well, no doubt the itching would just go away eventually. The suffragan bishop closed his eyes and concentrated again on what was important.

When the first reports came in of missing people, Sebastian Harsee hadn't thought much of it—a case for the civil authorities, nothing more. But suddenly there was talk of a hairy beast; new rumors surfaced, and that set the ball rolling. Harsee didn't have to do anything but steer it in the right direction.

The disappearance of Thadäus Vasold, a good friend of his family, had disturbed him, however, because back in the old days, Vasold and his own father had joined in fighting the enemies of the church. The council member had been one of their own, much more than fat old Klaus Schwarzkontz, who had also been a former colleague of his father. In recent years, Schwarzkontz had indulged much more in worldly matters, and his death seemed to Harsee like a just punishment. Vasold's cruel abduction and probable death, on the other hand, frightened Harsee. Evil was close at hand, and he thought he could even smell the werewolf's foul breath.

Harsee pressed himself even harder against the stone floor, as if trying to be joined together as one with the cathedral, subsumed into the body of the church. He began to feel dizzy, as so often in recent days, as if a slight fever was spreading over his body. He couldn't get sick now, not when he was so close to his goal.

He remembered with relief how quickly he'd been able to track down the beast that morning. The first troupe of actors had attracted attention through their demonic presentations in the Wedding House, and he'd personally given the order to raid their quarters and search for evidence the first thing the next morning. And, indeed, stored in a trunk they'd found a few wolf pelts sewn together, which the impersonator could slip into at night to look like a beast. What else was necessary? Even the leader of this troupe of charlatans and vagabonds had been horrified. But Harsee was sure that would not be the last case, and he would see to that. Forty years ago, it had also started with one witch, and by the time it was over, there were hundreds.

The Bamberg suffragan bishop kissed the dusty stone floor, then he stood up, thanked the Lord God, and climbed the stairs up from the crypt to the cathedral, each step an agony for him. Cold sweat ran down his back, and the accursed little wound on his neck began to itch again.

No doubt he had really caught some kind of fever, and he sent a brief prayer to heaven asking God to protect him from sickness in the coming weeks.

It was high time for him to find the next werewolf.

Brooding darkly, Jakob Kuisl sat in the devotional corner of the hangman's house, cracking his knuckles. He had the strength of a bear and a sharp mind, but seldom had he felt as helpless as when his youngest daughter ran away.

First Georg, and now Barbara, as well. What would my beloved Anna have said to all of that? Oh, Anna, how I miss you.

Furious, he pounded the table with his hand, and the other members of the family, who had been sitting quietly alongside him, cringed.

"What in hell is wrong with that girl?" Kuisl ranted, to let off steam. "Gets involved with a traveling actor and threatens me as well. I'll drag her back to Schongau by the hair."

"Oh, and then? Are you going to tie her down there by her hair?" Magdalena asked. "You know Barbara. I'll bet my life she'll run away on you again if you don't help her now. She's crazy about the fellow, and neither words nor force will do any good."

"She'll come to her senses, don't you think?" Georg asked hesitantly.

Magdalena shook her head. "You menfolk don't understand anything about that. If you let Barbara down now, we'll lose her forever, and I'm as sure of that as the fact I'm sitting here now."

Kuisl laughed dryly. "So what do you think I should do? Go to the dungeon, tell the guards that Matheo is innocent, and simply bring him back with me? Or just knock them around a few times?"

"You can at least have a talk with your brother," Simon interjected. "There are ways of delaying the torture, drawing it out, and you know that better than I do. Think of Stechlin back then."

The hangman was silent and just sat there grinding his teeth. In fact, almost ten years ago he had saved the Schongau midwife Martha Stechlin from the worst torture by using ruses and subterfuge to put off the torture again and again. But that had been in his hometown, where he knew the councilors and was better able to weigh the possibilities. Here, though, his brother was the hangman. What would Bartholomäus say if Jakob proposed he do the same?

He certainly would hold it against me.

"I know that Uncle Bartholomäus doesn't like to torture," Georg finally said, after thinking it over, as if reading his father's mind. "He finds torturing horrible, just like the long executions. I'm sure if he could, he'd just stay in the Bamberg Forest caring for his dogs and for the bishop's menagerie. If we can convince him that this Matheo is really innocent . . ."

"He's innocent," Kuisl interrupted. "and there's no question about it. These actors have not been in town more than a few days, but the first of the missing persons was discovered more than a month ago. And there's a connection between all these cases, even if I don't know yet what it is. In any case, it can't be the actors, it must be someone who's been in or around the city for some time."

Simon frowned. "You're right, but no matter how logical that is . . ."

"I know," Kuisl snorted. "That doesn't mean the councilors sitting around on their fat butts are going to care a whit. If you want to, you can explain anything by calling it witchcraft, and this damned commission wants to please the Bambergers by finding a culprit. They won't point to anyone living here, if they can get their hands on such a fine scapegoat as Matheo. Even if we drew out the interrogation, sooner or later they'd put Matheo to the stake, as sure as the 'Amen' in church."

"Unless we can find the true perpetrator." Magdalena sat at the table, her arms crossed, looking expectantly at the others. "Come now," she continued, "it wouldn't be the first time that we've hunted down a criminal."

"Except that this time the evildoer is a werewolf." Simon weighed his head in his hands. "Or at least someone dressing up as one, if you are to accept your father's assumptions." Suddenly his face brightened. "This wolf pelt that they found in Matheo's possession. Isn't it possible that the real perpetrator planted it on him to deflect suspicion from himself?"

Magdalena nodded. "It's possible. In any case, someone needs to talk to Matheo. Perhaps he himself knows who might be behind this."

"That's something Uncle Bartholomäus and I can do," Georg

replied hesitantly. "Provided my uncle agrees." He sighed. "In any case, I'll do anything to try to bring my sister back, even though I still think this actor is a dubious character."

"Someone also has to go and look for Barbara," said Jakob as he struggled to his feet, snorting. "Not that she's going to do anything to harm herself. Perhaps I, myself . . ."

"Certainly not! You'll do nothing of the sort," Magdalena replied, patting her father on the arm. "You've caused enough trouble here with your boorish behavior. This is a woman's job." She smiled grimly. "And as chance would have it, I think I know where Barbara is hiding."

8

𝕸AGDALENA HURRIED THROUGH THE NARROW streets of Bamberg, pondering the dreadful news she'd just heard. Young Matheo was suspected of being the werewolf everyone was looking for. At the breakfast table, she'd looked into her sister's eyes and saw how her world was collapsing. She could understand Barbara's anger and grief all too well, and she knew how mercilessly the wheels of justice would start turning now. For Matheo to have even the slightest chance, they'd have to quickly find the real beast and inform the council. Was that even possible?

With a billowing skirt, she ran along the foul-smelling city moat and from there southward, where at this hour crowds of merchants and farmers were coming from the Green Market. She made her way past market women hawking their wares, and coachmen loudly cursing their horses, until she'd finally reached the harbor and the Wedding House. She suspected Barbara would seek shelter with the actors. There was no one else in the town that she knew, and ever since Barbara had helped Sir Malcolm and his colleagues in the performance the day before, they were on friendly terms.

Magdalena ran up the stairway to the Wedding House, taking two steps at a time. When she arrived breathless at the top, she found the actors gloomily sitting around on the floor among the ransacked piles of boxes and crates. The floor was covered with costumes, some of them ripped apart; one of the backdrops had been slit lengthwise, and everywhere there were the muddy shoeprints of the guards who had wreaked havoc like marauding bandits.

When Sir Malcolm raised his head and saw Magdalena, he smiled sadly.

"Ah, see who's here—the beautiful hangman's daughter," he said in a melancholy singsong. "Well, I fear we shall not be able to perform for you today, my dear," he lamented, pointing again to the chaos all around them. "First, we shall have to clean up here, and then we'll see if we can play again here in Bamberg."

"What happened, anyway?" Magdalena asked, still out of breath from running.

"The guards came this morning and turned everything upside down," Markus Salter explained in a tired voice as he crouched down on a trunk alongside the director. He was even paler than usual, and there were dark rings under his eyes. "Each of us has his own trunk in which we can store our costumes and belongings," he continued. "They ransacked everything, and in Matheo's trunk they found the wolf pelts. I have no idea what the lad was planning to do with them."

"Did he admit they are his?" Magdalena asked.

Markus shook his head. "No, he denied everything, and to tell you the truth, I can't make any sense of it, either. But the guards didn't care; they just took him along, and now I hear there are a number of witnesses who claim to have seen him in town dressed as a werewolf."

Sir Malcolm sighed. "Yes, it looks like the boy has a dark secret, a dark soul that he concealed from all of us."

"Are you saying you really *believe* that Matheo has something to do with this beast?" Magdalena looked at Malcolm wide-eyed, but he just shrugged.

"Who can look into another man's soul? I only know I have to protect my troupe. If we'd defended Matheo, they would have taken us all along. We still have the blessing of the prince bishop, but that can quickly change—particularly now that this cursed Guiscard has arrived in Bamberg with his own troupe." Sir Malcolm rolled his eyes, then he intoned in a dramatic voice: "Sometimes a person must be sacrificed for the good of the rest, do you understand? I think we should soon dedicate a play to Matheo, some heroic epic, perhaps *Henry the Fifth*."

"But . . . but . . . that's disgusting. Is that what you all think?" Magdalena looked around, horrified, but saw only indifferent expressions. Some of the actors turned away and stared at the floor, as if there might be something interesting to discover there. Only Markus Salter returned her gaze.

"I'm afraid Sir Malcolm is right," he finally said in a soft voice. "There's nothing we can do to help Matheo, and remember, those wolf pelts were in his trunk. None of us can figure out how they got there."

"Haven't you wondered if someone might have planted them there?" Magdalena replied sharply. "Possibly the guards themselves because they had to find someone to blame. And who would be a more obvious choice than a dishonorable foreigner whom nobody will miss?"

Icy silence followed. Magdalena waited awhile before continuing. "Anyway, I'm not here for Matheo, but for my sister. I already know that my father is not at all happy about how close Barbara and Matheo are. Now tell me the truth: did she come here to hide out?"

Sir Malcolm shook his head. "Unfortunately no, though she would be welcome here anytime. I must tell you honestly that we even offered her a job yesterday. The girl has real talent. And

now, since Matheo . . . uh . . . is no longer with us, we need someone for the women's roles, in any case."

"She was serious?" Magdalena caught her breath, realizing
what Barbara had meant with her strange, veiled hints. "Do you
idiots have any idea what my father will do to you if he hears
about that, you . . . you . . ." She shook her head, unable to say another word. Then she stormed out of the hall.

When she was already on the stairway, she heard a voice behind her.

"Magdalena, wait!"

Markus Salter came running after her. "I saw your sister," he
called. "She was down in front of the Wedding House, and it appeared she was coming up to see us, but then she suddenly turned
around and went over to the Wild Man. Maybe you'll find her
there."

"The Wild Man?" She frowned. "What in the world does
she . . ." But then she put her hands to her head. "Naturally. Why
didn't I think of that before?"

She was about to hurry on, when Markus put his hand on
her shoulder again.

"Magdalena, believe me," he pleaded, "I am very sorry about
what happened to Matheo, and your assumption is correct. The
trunks were in the room next door, and the guards could easily
have put the pelts into Matheo's chest."

"If they were in the next room, anyone could have done it,"
Magdalena mused. Then she stopped short. "Just a minute. Sir
Malcolm spoke about this other troupe of actors. I wonder if one
of them could have planted the pelts in Matheo's chest in order to
do away with a troublesome competitor?"

Markus Salter nodded hesitantly. "You're right, I didn't even
think of that. Sir Malcolm and Guiscard Brolet had a nasty fight
yesterday, and Matheo was also involved in it. This French tramp
and plagiarist certainly wouldn't stop at doing that in order to
get us out of the way." His face darkened. "I'll go and talk with

Sir Malcolm about that right away, but I doubt he'll go to the prince bishop to plead Matheo's case. What proof does he have that Guiscard is the culprit?"

Magdalena sighed. "You're right; that will be difficult." Suddenly an idea came to her. "Oh, and by the way, did they find your dear little pet, the ferret, in their search?"

"Juliet?" Markus smiled. "Fortunately not. The guards were so happy to find the wolf's pelt that they got a bit careless after that." He looked darkly at Magdalena. "But you won't go to Sir Malcolm or the city guards . . ."

"Believe me, Master Salter, at the moment I have much more important things to do than to worry about a pet ferret," Magdalena interrupted. "And now, please excuse me; I'm looking for my sister."

She found Barbara sitting on a bed in the little room occupied by the director right next to the tavern, leafing through a dog-eared copy of Shakespeare's works translated into German. It seemed almost as if Barbara expected her sister. She closed the book and looked at her with sad, red eyes, swollen from crying.

"This Shakespeare really knows how to make someone cry," Barbara said softly. "The play is about Romeo and Juliet, who come from two quarreling families, the Capulets and the Montagues. The lovers die at the end because they can't marry. Perhaps that's the way it has to be with a great love."

Magdalena sat down alongside her and hugged her. She could imagine how Barbara felt. No doubt this Matheo was her first real love, and now he was locked in a dungeon and could expect a slow, painful death. Magdalena doubted this was a good time for her to become involved in a book of tragic love stories.

"I spoke with Father," she said. "He said he'd do everything he could to gain Matheo's freedom." That wasn't quite the truth, but she was certain God would excuse this little white lie.

Barbara shrugged defiantly. "Ha! What can he do? He's not

even from around here. The only ones who can torture people here are my uncle and Georg."

"You know what Father can do. It wouldn't be the first time he helped an innocent person obtain justice. And Georg, too, is going to talk to Uncle Bartholomäus."

Barbara looked at her hopefully. "Then . . . then you also think Matheo is innocent?"

"Of course. We all think so. The family will not abandon you."

She embraced her sister again, when suddenly the door opened and in the doorway the scarred face of Jeremias appeared. Magdalena flinched at the sight of the terrible scars. At the old man's feet, his crippled dog danced around and then hobbled toward Barbara to lick her hand.

"Ah, I see the two ladies have already found each other," Jeremias said with a smile, as his mouth twisted into a horrific grimace. Then he turned to Magdalena. "I found your sister in the yard crying and offered her my room as a temporary shelter. I hope that's all right." He pointed to some vials standing on a shelf in his tiny, cramped room. "I gave her a little St. John's wort and valerian—that calms the nerves."

"You know about medicine?" Magdalena inquired curiously.

Jeremias rocked his head from side to side. "Well . . . a little. One learns all sorts of things in a long life." He made a gloomy face. "In any case, that's a sad story your sister told me. The poor lad."

Barbara started to cry again, and Jeremias stroked her hair sympathetically. "Well, it's not the end of the world; there's still time to do something. There's a regular, proscribed procedure in a trial. First, there's the accusation. Then, the hangman shows the accused the instruments of torture, probably even several times. That's the first stage, and then . . . ."

"Thank you," Magdalena interrupted, fearing that Jeremias

was about to explain all the details to her sister. "We ourselves know all about the different stages of torture—after all, we come from a hangman's family."

"Oh, excuse me, I forgot." For a moment it appeared Jeremias was about to say something else, but then he just gave a kindly smile. "Well, then there's nothing I have to tell you. I just wanted to say there are still some things that can be done. You mustn't give up hope—ever." He sighed. "Even though this accusation is especially serious. The whole city is already swept up in this madness. A werewolf?" He shook his head. "As if Bamberg hasn't already had enough bloody trials."

"You're probably referring to the witch trials held here forty years ago," Magdalena replied. "Were you in Bamberg at the time?"

Jeremias nodded grimly. "I was a young man then, and saw things . . ." He paused, as if trying to shake off some terribly memory, and only then continued. "It always begins with just one incident, but then it's like an avalanche, more and more cases, and finally half the city is condemned. That's the reason they had the accursed Inquisition House built, with its dungeons, torture chambers, courtrooms, and a chapel for the last confession. Above the entryway was the statue of Justitia, as if there was ever any justice in that dreadful place. It was always a question of power." He shrugged. "A wave of prosecutions is just what the powers wanted in order to dispose of their enemies."

"What do you mean by that?" Magdalena asked, frowning.

"Well, back then it didn't just affect the poor and the dregs of society; there were many decent patricians among them, even a chancellor and some mayors with their wives and children. Entire families of city councilmen were wiped out. Looking back on it, it becomes evident it was mostly a redistribution of power." Jeremias walked over to the birdcage in the middle of the room and tossed a few crumbs to the sparrows. "When positions became free, others could move up, do you see? The dead person can no longer be a troublesome competitor." He brushed the remaining crumbs from his scarred hands.

"Do you think something like that could happen again?" Barbara gasped. "Then Matheo would be just the first pawn in the game, with many other higher-placed people to follow."

Jeremias shook his smooth, oval head. "I didn't say that. But in any case, two venerable councilmen—Herr Schwarzkontz and Vasold—have already disappeared. Who knows, perhaps soon a patrician will be suspected of being a wolfish magician and tearing his own colleague to bits. Some people would be very happy if that happened."

"You forget that this time a lot of very strange things have happened," Magdalena replied. "Corpses with severed body parts have been found, and many people have also seen this beast. It's no doubt different this time. There is something or someone prowling around out there, so there's every reason for people to start looking for a perpetrator."

"You're right; I'm just talking nonsense." Jeremias bent over to pet Biff. "Anyway, we ought to be thinking about your sister instead of these dark, forgotten times."

"I'm not going back, if that's what you mean," Barbara said, crossing her arms defiantly in front of her chest. "Not until Father really tries to get Matheo released." She glared at Magdalena. "And if you squeal on me and tell Father where I am, then . . . then I'm leaving with Sir Malcolm and the other actors, going far, far away and never coming back. Because I've got—"

". . . talent, I know," Magdalena sighed, finishing the sentence, "for something or other." She stood up and stroked her little sister's hair again.

"Don't worry, I'll just tell Father you are well, and if I know him, he already has a plan to help you." She looked sternly at Barbara. "But do me a favor, will you? Don't read so much of this sentimental nonsense. It's not good for you. You are Barbara Kuisl and not a princess or noble lady. Do you hear me?"

As the morning fog began to rise over the Bamberg Forest, a solitary person could be seen trudging determinedly down the muddy road. The few people coming toward him looked down and passed without greeting. The man didn't look like anyone who would return a greeting, in any case, and his whole being exuded something threatening and unapproachable.

Jakob Kuisl was angrier than he'd been in a long time. To make matter worse, he'd forgotten his tobacco in the Bamberg hangman's house. He was actually supposed to be helping his brother clean the city moats, and that would have been his chance to tell Bartholomäus about the lad that he and Georg would soon be torturing. But the fast-moving events required intensive thought, and that was something he could best do in the forest, if necessary even without tobacco.

The Schongau hangman was torn in two directions. Actually he no longer had much interest in hunting down scoundrels and solving crimes, especially in a city that was no concern of his. In addition, he'd become too old for such adventures. In his recent fight with the Bamberg street mob he could hear his bones creaking. He wished he could just leave town that day along with his whole family and return to Schongau. But now his beloved Barbara, his youngest child, had run away, and Kuisl knew that the little one was just as stubborn as the rest of the family and she'd carry through on her threat. Barbara wouldn't return to him until he'd helped this rascal Matheo. But how, for God's sake, could he do that? Who or what was this monster lurking around Bamberg?

Kuisl was certain that something was out there. There were missing people, severed body parts, people had seen a furry monster in the streets, and he himself had come upon the horribly disfigured corpse of the young prostitute whose attacker had evidently tried to rip out her heart. The strange musky odor emanating from the corpse allowed only one conclusion: the girl had in fact been attacked by a wild animal.

Was that possible?

And then there was that man he'd seen the day before in front of the furrier's house who had presumably bought five wolf pelts there. Was it conceivable that the stranger had dressed up in these wolfskins to spread panic in the city? Or was the secret hidden somewhere here in the Bamberg Forest, where Kuisl in fact had seen a strange, large beast two days ago? But above all— could the limping stranger have been his brother? Magdalena had also told him later that she thought she'd seen the man somewhere before.

To find an answer to this last question, the hangman had set out into the forest after breakfast to pay another visit to the knacker's house.

A thin column of smoke rising above the trees showed him the way, and after a good hour he'd finally reached the fenced clearing. A cool breeze was blowing, and Kuisl was glad Katharina had given him one of Bartl's old coats the night before after he'd lost his own in the waters of the Regnitz.

Just as before, a fire was burning in front of the huge log house and Aloysius was apparently boiling the bones of some cadaver. The wind turned suddenly, and Kuisl held his nose in disgust. To the right of the log house was the dog compound. The dogs had scented the new arrival much earlier and now broke out into loud barking and jumped up against the fence.

"Good day, Aloysius," Kuisl called out amid the racket. "What you're stirring there stinks all the way to Bamberg."

The hangman's journeyman looked at him suspiciously, then set down the stirring pole and wiped his hands off on his apron.

"The master's not here," he grumbled, without responding to Kuisl's remark. "He's over in the city cleaning out the moats."

The hangman saw the innumerable pockmarks on his face, only partly concealed under his stubbly beard, and couldn't help remembering how just two days ago Bartholomäus had suggested his servant as a possible husband for Barbara.

Well, perhaps a better choice than some vagrant actor.

"I know Bartl isn't here," Kuisl retorted. "I'm just looking for some sweet cicely that Katharina needs to make cakes for the wedding. Do you have any idea where I can find it?"

"Recently, it's been dangerous to go out there alone to search for herbs," Aloysius replied. "Lots of wolves out there." He turned his head to one side and pointed to a few stiff cadavers lying nearby on some pine branches. "I caught these right around here with a few wolf traps. You've got to be really careful . . ." His words hung in the air like a vague threat.

He's not as dumb as he looks, thought Kuisl.

With a shrug, the hangman walked over to the dog compound, where the bloodhounds and mastiffs had calmed down a bit. They ran nervously back and forth behind the fence, and some whined while others growled at the visitor.

"Nice dogs you have," Kuisl said with admiration. "Well-fed and cared for — and smart. I bet they can be easily trained. They belong to the bishop, I've heard. Does he ever take them out hunting?"

Aloysius nodded silently.

"It's really a shame. They ought to be taken out more often," the hangman continued after a while, then he cast a conspiratorial glance at Aloysius. "It's a big forest here. One could easily take them out hunting without the sovereign getting wind of it. Bears . . . wolves . . . deer . . . Come now, tell me — don't you and Bartholomäus itch to take them out sometimes?" He paused for a moment. "Or perhaps . . . someone else?"

"Only the lords are permitted to go hunting," Aloysius answered stiffly, as if reciting the words from memory. "Poachers are hanged. As an executioner you really should know that."

Kuisl nodded. "Of course, of course."

He walked along the fence examining the mastiffs that, with their black, shining pelts and red chops, looked like the hounds of hell.

"Besides, all the dogs are branded with the bishop's seal," the servant continued, his voice now sounding a bit nervous. He walked over to Kuisl and pointed to one of the young hounds lying near the gate, panting. When it saw Aloysius, it came over to him, whimpering happily, and licked his hand. The seal of the Bamberg prince bishop was in fact branded on its right side near the foreleg — a lion and a diagonal line.

"Each of the dogs is branded like that soon after birth," Aloysius explained. "The bishop's master of the hunt carefully records all the new births. They're an expensive breed, and he can't miss a single one."

"Are you trying to say it's impossible to steal these dogs?" Kuisl inquired.

The servant grinned. "Precisely. It can't be done. When a nobleman loses one of his charges in the hunt to a bear or a boar, we hear about it and take charge of replacing it. There are strict procedures for all that."

"Well, too bad," Kuisl said, shrugging. "I thought I might be allowed to take out a few dogs . . ."

"Out of the question," Aloysius interrupted. "And now, excuse me, I have to go back to my bones." Suddenly he stopped and a grimace spread across his face. It took a moment before Kuisl realized it was a smile.

"They say your younger daughter is a real beauty," Aloysius said, now in a much milder tone of voice, "and the master tells me she still doesn't have a husband. I'd like to meet her sometime. Perhaps we can talk about that during one of our hunts." He broke out in a loud, nervous laugh, and Kuisl felt the hair rising on his neck.

Maybe the actor isn't such a bad choice, after all, he thought.

"I'll see what I can do," he replied.

Aloysius nodded, then returned to his simmering kettle and left the hangman by himself. Kuisl examined the bloodhounds and mastiffs a bit longer, then finally strolled toward the log house and the buildings behind it. Immediately Aloysius stopped stirring the kettle.

"What are you doing there?" he asked suspiciously.

"Well, I thought you might have some more dogs in back to admire," Kuisl replied, with feigned innocence.

"These up here are all we have. The only thing in back is the place we bury the waste. It's not a good place—it stinks to high heaven."

"Well, if that's the case, I won't bother you any longer."

The hangman raised his hand in farewell, then headed through the front gate and back onto the path heading toward the city. Singing an old army song from his mercenary days, he trudged on.

His visit had gone differently than he'd expected, but he'd learned a few things. He hadn't asked about the branding marks, but Aloysius was eager to tell him all about them, as if quickly trying to dispel all suspicions. And why had he flared up when Kuisl wanted to see the building in back? Was something hidden there?

Something smells bad here, and it's not just the garbage.

He had gone about half a mile when he met a group of men coming toward him from the city. They were carrying scythes, pitchforks, and clubs and were marching in step like a group of soldiers. As they drew closer, Kuisl could see they were simple Bamberg workers, but their stride had something pompous about it, something artificial, as they looked all around from side to side where the dense stands of firs formed a kind of wall.

Kuisl stepped to the side of the path to let the group pass, but the first man suddenly stopped and looked at him suspiciously. Only now did the hangman see they were the same men who had chased the unfortunate shepherd through the city two days before. The man in front was the wagon driver whom Kuisl had beaten over the head with a club right at the beginning of the fight.

"Who are you and what do you want?" one man asked in a loud, brash voice.

Kuisl sighed under his breath.

Well, isn't this just great? This is the last thing I need.

"You know who I am," he answered. "I had the pleasure of meeting you a few days ago, so stop this nonsense and let me by, or we'll both do something we regret."

The tall, broad-shouldered wagon driver acted as if he hadn't recognized Jakob until then.

"Ah, of course," he exclaimed. "The brother of the Bamberg hangman. How delighted I am to see you again," he said, turning around to his friends. "Standing here all by himself, he doesn't look so big, does he? Almost as if he'd shrunk."

The men laughed, but their leader stood up straight and threw out his chest.

"We're the Bamberg citizens' militia," he declared. "If the city council and the bishop can't do anything to protect us from this werewolf, we have no choice but to do it ourselves."

"And that's the reason you're running around like rabbits in the forest?"

"You'll soon regret your fresh remarks," the man hissed. "We're looking for suspicious characters—charcoal burners, shepherds, people who steal wood . . . The forest is full of such riffraff, and it's quite possible a werewolf is hiding among them. They can change their appearance, but with holy water we will be able to view their true form." He shook a little bottle hanging on his belt as if it were a deadly weapon. Then he jutted out his chin in a defiant gesture and demanded, "So tell me again. What are you doing here?"

"I went to visit the knacker. Is that forbidden?"

The man grinned. "No, it's not forbidden, but it makes you look . . . suspicious." He stepped closer to Kuisl and began sniffing.

"Do you smell this, too, men?" he asked with a sneer. "It has the smell of a wild beast, of dirt and feces, and hmm . . . yes, a bit like sulfur. Phew!" He held his nose tightly. "So either this is a werewolf or a hangman who's never taken a bath."

The men grumbled, while Kuisl closed his eyes and tried to keep a cool demeanor. He couldn't let them get under his skin, even though he suspected the wagon driver wouldn't stop needling him. The last time Kuisl had sent the powerful man sprawling to the ground with a single blow and made him look foolish in front of his friends. The wagon driver wouldn't pass up this chance to pay the hangman back in kind.

So let's get it over with . . .

Jakob reached for the cudgel hanging on his belt. There were six of them, but if he was fast enough, he could get the best of the leader and perhaps one or two others. Then he could seize the moment of surprise to flee into the forest. But he wasn't as fast as he used to be, and once again he could feel the ripping of his tendons as if on a rack. Probably they'd catch him, and then . . .

"What a lovely autumn day," a loud voice behind him suddenly proclaimed. "Much too lovely for a quarrel. Don't you think so, men?"

He turned around and saw his brother coming down the path from the knacker's house.

But how . . .

By now, Bartholomäus had already reached the group of men and placed his arm around Jakob in a friendly gesture.

"My brother came to visit me in the forest," Bartholomäus said. "Is there a problem?"

The wagon driver and the other men were clearly disappointed. They could have easily done away with Jakob; he was from out of town and no one would miss him. Bartholomäus, on the other hand, was known in town. If he disappeared or was beaten and made a cripple, there would be unpleasant questions.

"We have the right to question any suspect," the leader snapped. "Your brother is a dubious character; we don't want him in our city. We want him out of here."

"If anyone should get out, it would be you," Bartholomäus shot back.

The wagon driver picked up his cudgel and seemed about to throw caution to the wind. "You damn bastard," he shouted. "I'm not going to let some dishonorable person—"

"Just stop, Johann," one of the men interrupted. He was an older farmer with small, rat-like eyes that darted around nervously. "I wouldn't take on two hangmen. That can only bring bad luck. It's bad enough that we had to come across the men here in the forest."

He turned away and murmured a quiet prayer. Now the other men hesitated as well, and some in the rear made a sign to ward off curses and bad magic.

Kuisl grinned. Even back home in the "Pope's Corner" there were many superstitions concerning the executioner. Now, for once, it seemed to be an advantage to be a social outcast who was allegedly in league with the devil.

"Your friend is right," he growled. "If anyone touches me, they will have seven years of bad luck for everything they set their hands on. Their children will become sick and their wives will be dry and infertile, I swear to you as surely as I am an accursed hangman." He stepped forward with a threatening look in his eye, and the men murmured to each other anxiously. Their leader, the powerfully built wagon driver, also seemed uncertain.

"Very well," he said. "Today I'll just give you a warning, but if we meet alone in the forest the next time . . ."

"That's enough, you windbag, now step aside." Kuisl squeezed past him and left with his brother. Soon they were alone on the path through the forest.

Bartholomäus shook his head. "'Your children will become sick and your wives dry and infertile'? How did you think up that nonsense?"

Jakob grinned. "Should I have painted my face black and shouted 'boo' to scare them? Sometimes it's an advantage when the people are afraid of you. You probably know that just as well as I do, brother."

Bartholomäus chuckled, then he looked suspiciously at his brother. "Aloysius says you're asking dumb questions," he said. "Why?"

"Why don't you tell me what you're doing in the forest when you should be in town cleaning out the moats."

"That doesn't concern you." Bartholomäus suddenly turned and hobbled along ahead, as if trying to avoid bothersome questions. "Georg has already started shoveling, and there's enough time for me to take a break."

"Forget about the shoveling. There are much more important things to do."

Something in Jakob's voice caused Bartholomäus to stop in his tracks. He turned around to Jakob, who told him briefly about the alleged werewolf Matheo and his relation to Barbara. Bartholomäus frowned, and Jakob thought he detected a nervous twitch in his eyes.

"And the girl just ran away on you, and you don't know where?" Bartholomäus finally asked with a sneer.

Jakob nodded. "She won't come back unless I help her Matheo. I know myself that's impossible, but I have to at least show her I've tried a bit." He sighed. "You and Georg are going to start torturing the boy soon, and you know there are ways to postpone the torture or at least make it bearable. Potions, certain methods . . ." He paused, waiting to hear what his brother had to say.

Bartholomäus sneered. "You really expect me to help you, with everything there is between us?"

"You won't be helping me, you'll be helping Barbara. She's your niece, after all." Kuisl stopped to think for a moment, then continued. "Besides, I can hardly believe that Katharina would want to see a member of the family refuse to come to your grandly announced wedding out of defiance or grief. What do you think?" He looked at his brother innocently. "Shall I tell your fiancée you refuse to help Barbara?"

"You bastard," Bartholomäus hissed. Then he took a deep breath and answered: "Very well, then, I'll see what I can do. For the sake of Katharina and her family."

He turned away and hobbled down the muddy path, dragging one foot behind the other like a reluctant animal. But then he turned around again to his brother with an angry look.

"And you will stop meddling in other people's business. What I'm doing here in the forest is my business. Understand? Otherwise, I'm going to hurt this Matheo so that he whimpers and howls like a real werewolf."

"I hope your relationship with the prince bishop is as good as you told me," Simon said as he strolled along the east side of the Bamberg Cathedral with Samuel. On their right was a large market square surrounded by a number of half-finished buildings that would eventually be part of the prince bishop's palace. Workers hauled sacks of mortar or lifted large blocks of stone with pulleys onto the shaky scaffolding. Sweating profusely, horses pulled a cart of plaster up the steep hill leading to the cathedral for the ornamental plasterwork.

It had been Simon's idea to pay a visit with Samuel to the prince bishop. Perhaps the only way to postpone the trial would be for the prince to intervene. Simon didn't believe there was much hope, but they had to seize every possible opportunity to save Matheo—and Barbara. Samuel was skeptical at first, as well, but finally his friend persuaded him. It was already late afternoon, a milky autumn sun hung low over the city walls, and the forests and swamps in the distance were shrouded in fog.

"Well, ever since I started caring for the bishop's concubine, and above all for his persistent digestive problems, I've actually become something like a friend to him," Samuel replied, after they'd gotten past the noisy building site. He sighed deeply. "Alas, the word *friend* doesn't mean very much to Prince Bishop Rieneck. His best friends are still the animals in his menagerie. To be honest, he's not much of a ruler, and the suffragan bishop long ago seized control over spiritual matters."

Simon looked downcast. "Then I see a gloomy future in store for Bamberg. This Sebastian Harsee seems to me to be a real fanatic."

His friend nodded, "Harsee's father was one of the driving forces in the witch trials, and even back then, he himself was heavily involved, as well. In Harsee's eyes, Bamberg is a den of iniquity that needs to be cleaned up. He'd like to make it into a sort of City of God, full of well-behaved, timid believers who go to church and praise the Lord all day long. But don't underestimate him. He's very intelligent and above all very hungry for power."

Now they had gone around to the back of the cathedral. Behind it was a park in a little hollow surrounded by a high wall. Just as at Geyerswörth Castle there were neatly trimmed bushes and hedges and an artificial waterfall pouring into a basin, and from that into little brooks and canals. Here and there were individual cages and aviaries of different sizes, from which chirping, warbling, screeching, snarling, and an occasional growling could be heard.

"The prince bishop's menagerie," Samuel said to his astonished friend as he pointed to the cages. "Here's where the bishop spends most of his time. If you have a request, this is a good place to ask. He's usually in a good mood here."

As they walked along a small, gravel path winding its way

down to the little valley, Simon was amazed to see the many creatures in the cages and aviaries. There were gaily colored birds of paradise with long, bushy tail feathers, a brown bear running around in circles, strutting peacocks, tame dwarf deer, and strange wrinkled turtles with round shells that trundled away. An enclosure with a dead tree in the middle seemed to be empty, but in the next cage, fuzzy little animals were screeching, shaking the bars of their cage, and glaring at the curious-looking two-legged creatures. They looked like little people, and their faces reminded Simon of skulls painted with chalk.

"For heaven's sake, what are those?" he asked with a mixture of astonishment and horror. "I've never seen creatures like that."

"Oh, those are called squirrel monkeys," Samuel explained, as they continued down the path. "They come from the New World and are presents from the Bavarian elector Ferdinand Maria. The bishop also has a few capuchin monkeys and some great apes that sometimes are brought to state functions to entertain the nobility with their climbing and dancing. At present Rieneck is trying to acquire something called a rhinoceros—a monstrous animal. The king of Portugal once had one, but it unfortunately drowned in a storm at sea. And there's also here a—" Samuel stopped short, as another cage, full of pheasants, appeared behind a bush trimmed into the shape of a sphere. In front of the cage, wearing a purple cape, stood a powerful-looking figure throwing feed to the birds.

"Ah, that's His Excellency," the doctor continued, turning to Simon with a determined look. "It's now or never. Let's hope the bishop has had a good day."

Two armed guards suddenly appeared from behind the bushes, and when they caught sight of the strangers, they reached suspiciously for their halberds. But now the bishop had also seen Samuel and Simon. He gave them a friendly smile and waved for the guards to leave.

"You fools! Can't you see this is my very honorable personal physician? Leave us alone." He put down the silken feedbag he'd been holding and reached out his hand with the bishop's ring. "Master Samuel, what a pleasure. I hear that the mercury treatments you prescribed are working wonders for my beloved Francesca. I'm very grateful."

"But I am indebted to you for permitting me to act as the personal physician of such a magnanimous ruler." He bent down to kiss the bishop's ring, then glanced at his friend as a silent admonition for him to also show his reverence.

"Well, I see you have brought your esteemed colleague," Rieneck said, and continue to smile as Simon put his lips to the gold signet ring. "I hope he is enjoying his stay with us in Bamberg."

"Ex-extremely," Simon croaked, struggling to his feet. "A beautiful city, and the new bishop's palace up on the cathedral square will soon be the jewel in your crown."

God, what drivel is coming from my mouth, he thought. *Must one be such a bootlicker to serve the mighty?*

The bishop nodded. "Indeed it is, even though some unfortunate incidents have marred the overall picture recently." He turned to Samuel. "I have heard a suspect has already been found in this werewolf matter—a fellow from one of these groups of itinerant actors." He shook his head. "What do think of it, Doctor? Did your commission come to the conclusion that he is really a werewolf?"

Suddenly, the squirrel monkeys behind them let out such a loud scream that Simon winced.

"That's exactly the reason we wanted to speak with you, Your Excellency," Samuel began in a somber tone. "In our opinion, it is very doubtful that the suspect is guilty. This troupe of actors had not even arrived in the city at the time of the first missing-persons cases. The only evidence is a few wolf pelts they found in the young man's room. That's all."

"Hmm, I think Harsee views it differently. He thinks that questioning the lad would lead us to other werewolves."

"I, on the other hand," said Samuel, "fear a mass panic like what we saw at the time of the ill-fated witch trials. The boy will name everyone he can think of, and the citizens are already troubled enough. We shouldn't be too hasty."

Philipp Rieneck seemed lost in thought for a while, then reached for his silk bag of feed and went back to caring for his pheasants, uttering comforting cooing sounds from time to time.

"I'm extremely saddened that the guards seized this actor," he said after a while. "I had been looking forward so much to a performance by the troupe in Geyersworth Castle, especially since the bishop of Würzburg announced he would be stopping by for a visit the day after tomorrow, but if even more actors—"

"The boy is innocent, without question," Simon replied, then was shocked to realize he'd just interrupted a real live prince bishop. Rieneck looked at him indignantly.

"I'm certain that the Inquisition Commission just founded by Suffragan Bishop Harsee will come to a different conclusion," His Excellency replied coolly. "And if my information is correct, the good bishop did not request your participation nor that of City Physician Samuel in this narrower circle that will decide who is to be tortured."

"But *you* will make the final decision," Samuel answered gently. "All we ask you is to postpone the torture a bit. We are in the process of collecting evidence that can lead us to the real culprit."

Simon swallowed hard. Up to now, all he had told his friend was that they were hoping to save an innocent person from the claws of justice. Samuel had really stuck his head out in making his last assertion, and it was clear to Simon that his friend was risking the loss of his good reputation and perhaps even his position as the bishop's personal physician.

"The real culprit?" Rieneck frowned. Suddenly he seemed

unsure of himself. "Do . . . do you have any suspicions as far as the beast is concerned? Do any of the witnesses claim to have seen anything else?"

"You know that I don't have a very high regard for these so-called witnesses," Samuel replied. "The night watchman was drunk as a skunk, and the rest is probably just idle talk. In my view they're just figments of the imagination on the part of a few pompous idiots. We have some missing people here, and someone is responsible for their abduction. It isn't necessarily a werewolf."

"Not a werewolf? Well, if you think . . ." The bishop continued feeding the pheasants, but evidently he was mulling it over. Finally he turned back to his guests with a broad smile.

"Perhaps you are right, Doctor. If this young fellow is questioned, he'll probably accuse his colleagues of being werewolves just to save his miserable life, and I can forget about my visit to the theater. Since my good friend Johann Philipp von Schönborn, bishop of Würzburg, is unfortunately no friend of the inquisition, we shall have to postpone the torture until after the performance." Then he threw the bag away and rubbed his chubby hands together. "In addition . . ." He hesitated briefly, then continued, animatedly: "In honor of the bishop's visit, there won't be just one performance, but two. After all, he's a real imperial elector."

"Two performances?" Samuel asked, confused. "I'm afraid I don't understand."

Rieneck gave a sly grin, like a small child. "Well . . . I was so stupid as to give permission to another theater troupe to take winter quarters in our city. The manager comes from the beautiful country of France and somehow was able to wrap me around his finger with his sweet, honeyed words. Supporting two troupes of actors in a modest bishopric like Bamberg is clearly beyond our means. Our suffragan bishop, Harsee, is at times a bit zealous and keeps pestering me about the first group." He rolled his eyes, but then nodded cheerfully. "All right, then, we'll have a contest. Two performances, one by each troupe, performed for His Excellency the Würzburg bishop and all the citizens of Bamberg. The one putting on the better performance will be permitted to remain in the city. Well, what do you think? Isn't that a splendid idea? It kills three birds with one stone: I politely dismiss one of the two groups, impress the elector, and gain the good favor of the Bambergers. For years they'll remember this friendly gesture by their monarch."

He scrutinized his guests' faces like a cook who had just suggested an especially strange menu.

"Ah, a splendid suggestion, Your Excellency," replied Simon. "So there's some hope for Matheo?"

The bishop frowned. "Who is Matheo?"

"The young lad sitting in the dungeon accused of being a werewolf," Samuel explained.

"Ah, I see. Well, yes, then, he will be spared until after the performance, as I said—an acceptable solution for all concerned." The bishop seemed extremely pleased with himself and turned to Samuel with a smile. "I owe it to you for having suggested this marvelous idea, Doctor. It will be a great pleasure for me to greet you and your friend at the performance."

He reached for his sack again and dismissed his guests with a wave of the hand without even looking at them again. "And now, farewell. I must go to feed my dear monkeys. This menagerie takes a great deal of my time."

"Damn it! You know where Barbara is. Now tell me right away, or—"

"Or what?" Magdalena gazed at her father serenely. "Are you going to torture me on the rack if I don't tell you? Pull out my fingernails or put on the thumbscrews? Hmm?"

"I'd be happy just to give you a good spanking, and it's too bad you're too old for that now."

Grumbling, Jakob waved her off and fell into a gloomy silence. He leaned back on the wooden bench in the Bamberg hangman's house, lit his pipe, and disappeared in a cloud of smoke. A steady rain pounded against the closed shutters. Simon, sitting next to Jakob, tried again to calm them down. He had returned from his audience with the bishop several hours ago, and now night had fallen.

"Magdalena promised Barbara not to tell you where she was hiding out," Simon said in a pleading voice. "If she breaks this promise and you bring Barbara back here by force, she'll run away again the first chance she gets. That's pointless."

Jakob remained silent, clouds of tobacco rose like bad spirits toward the ceiling, and a tense atmosphere reigned all around the table. Magdalena could scarcely bear it.

Why must Father always be so stubborn? she thought.

The aroma of ham, beans, and millet still hung in the air, and the large pan from which the whole family had scraped the last bits of supper stood empty in the middle of the table. The children, Peter and Paul, the only ones in the group not depressed, were playing with the cat on the living room floor, which was strewn with rushes, and from time to time Simon had to step in when they pulled the cat's tail or held a burning stick of kindling against its fur.

During the meal, Kuisl had kept quizzing Magdalena, hoping to find out where her younger sister might be hiding out, but she had remained stubbornly silent. Meanwhile, Bartholomäus, chewing loudly and smacking his lips, had polished off the rest of the stew without saying a word. Magdalena was certain that Katharina would cure him of these bad manners after the wedding, but for now his fiancée demurely spent the night near the harbor gate with her father.

After a while Georg cleared his throat. "My uncle and I were in the dungeon of Saint Thomas's Chapel in the Old Residence next to the cathedral late this afternoon," he began in a confident voice, no doubt trying to cheer everyone up. "That's where they put the prisoners especially important to the bishop. We took a quick look into Matheo's cell, and he's doing well, considering the circumstances. If what Simon said before is correct, then nothing will happen for the next few days. But of course the boy is terribly frightened."

Simon had already told the rest of the family about the prince bishop's plan to schedule a competition between the two groups of actors, and also that Matheo's torture would not begin until after the decision. In that respect, Simon's visit with the bishop hadn't been entirely in vain, even if Magdalena knew they had won just a short reprieve.

"Were you allowed to speak with Matheo?" she finally asked her younger brother.

Georg shrugged. "Only very briefly. He swears he's innocent, but he suspects someone—"

"Guiscard and his troupe, I'll assume," Magdalena interrupted. "That's not so implausible. After all, Matheo had a fight with his men the day before, and the room with the actors' chests was accessible to anyone. Guiscard no doubt hopes that others in Sir Malcolm's group will be suspected of being werewolves—especially since Matheo will soon be tortured." She turned to her uncle. "Will you help us delay the torture until we've found the true culprit?"

Bartholomäus wiped the remains of the stew out of his beard and grinned scornfully. "Ha! Do you really think you can run around through the streets of town and catch this werewolf—or whatever it is out there—and you will get your Matheo back?" He shook his head. "You can forget about that. Even if you found out who or what was behind all these missing-persons cases, the hunt will go on. That's what happened during the witch trials. Now the big cleanup is at hand."

"And you'll make good money because of it, won't you, Bartl?" said Jakob from behind a dense cloud of tobacco. "Every burning at the stake will bring you at least ten guilders. Tell me, was this fine house bought with the death of all those witches back then? Was it one of the many buildings standing empty because their owners are no longer alive? A good deal for a hangman — isn't that so?"

"How dare you!" Bartholomäus pounded the table so hard that the two boys were frightened and ran over to their mother. His voice trembled slightly, and once again Magdalena noticed that her uncle wasn't really the tough fellow he sometimes pretended to be. "Who the hell are you to pass judgment on me, Jakob?" he raged. "You've killed at least as many people as I have."

"Not one of them was a witch, Bartholomäus. Everyone I executed died for a good reason — or if not, at least I didn't extend their suffering unnecessarily. Can you say that of yourself?"

Bartholomäus clenched his teeth. "Damn it, I had nothing to do with those damned witch trials. I came to Bamberg just after that. The job was free, because . . . because the old hangman simply ran away, disappeared without a trace, after he'd tortured and executed hundreds of people."

"And still, his work clings to you like a curse," replied Jakob.

Suddenly, Bartholomäus leapt up and seemed about to grab his brother by the throat.

"That's him! The big, smart-ass brother who could do everything better," he shouted. "If you're so damn smart, Jakob, so self-satisfied, tell your loving children the story of how you ran away then. Do you know how old I was then, Jakob? Or have you forgotten? Twelve! Our sister, little Elisabeth, was just three. And you just ran away, abandoned us."

"I had my reasons."

Magdalena looked at her father and frowned. Jakob suddenly looked unsure of himself, nervously sucking on his pipe.

"Abandoned?" she repeated. "You never told us what happened back then when you left Schongau, Father. Why did you—"

At that moment there was a loud pounding on the door.

Everyone held their breath for a moment, then Bartholomäus shouted, "Who's out there?"

"It's me, Katharina. Please open the door!"

Her voice failed and turned into a long lament. Bartholomäus jumped up at once and rushed to the door. He opened it and she rushed into his arms, sobbing. She was soaked with rain and completely out of breath, as if she'd run all the way.

"What happened?" Bartholomäus asked in a hoarse voice. For the first time, Magdalena saw something resembling fear in his eyes. When she didn't answer but just continued sobbing, he began to shake her. Now the two boys started to whimper and whine.

"Katharina, won't you just tell us?" the Bamberg hangman shouted over the general commotion. "What in hell's name happened?"

"They . . . they've forbidden it," she finally gasped. "Simply forbidden!"

Bartholomäus looked at her, perplexed. "Who has forbidden what?"

"Oh, God, I think I know," Magdalena whispered to Simon, who like all the others in the room was staring in bewilderment at the large woman.

"What do you think? The wedding feast," Katharina replied in a choked voice. She pulled out a large handkerchief and blew her nose loudly. "Those fine people in the city council have turned down our celebration in the Wedding House. My . . . my father just returned from the city hall, where they gave him the news. A dishonorable executioner may not celebrate a wedding in a public building, on orders from the suffragan bishop."

"This damned Harsee," Simon mumbled. "I should have guessed. This bigot thinks the world will come to an end if someone has a party."

For a moment there was silence in the room except for Katharina's muted sobs and the whining of the two boys. Bartholomäus shook his head with obvious relief.

"My God, and I thought . . ." he groaned. Then he looked sternly at his fiancée. "Why didn't you wait until tomorrow to give us this news? Do you have any idea how dangerous it is to run through the streets after nightfall? God knows what might have happened."

"But don't you understand what that means, Bartholomäus?" Katharina lamented. "We have to call it all off. The musicians, the food, the wine, the table decorations . . ."

"Then just celebrate here in the hangman's house," suggested Jakob, still sitting on the bench, smoking. "Just like me and my Anna. Anyway, it's a lot nicer and cozier. Who needs all that pomp and ceremony?" He shook his head. "They didn't forbid the marriage, just the celebration in the Wedding House, didn't they?"

"I'm reluctant to agree with my brother, but in this case he's right," Bartholomäus grumbled. "All this celebrating is so hideous, anyway. We'll just uninvite most of the guests, and you can cook a tasty stew for us; there will be one or two mugs of beer, and then—"

Whatever else he had to say was drowned out by Katharina's renewed sobs. The two Kuisl brothers looked at each other, at a loss, and Georg frowned, as well.

"I'm afraid you men don't understand," Magdalena said. She rose to her feet and embraced her future aunt, who again broke out sobbing. "Katharina has already put a lot of time and effort into preparations for the wedding feast. This rejection is a slap in the face to her. Just having to uninvite all the guests offends her sense of pride . . ."

"She'll have to get used to that if she marries into the family of a hangman," Jakob growled.

"Is there no chance we can persuade the council to change their mind?" Simon asked, but Bartholomäus waved him off.

"You can forget about that. The council will never get involved in a controversy with the suffragan bishop on such a trivial matter."

"Trivial?" Katharina glared at him. "This is no trivial matter. My God, it's our wedding," she shouted, her face darkening. Magdalena had never before seen her so angry and determined. "In any case, I'm not going to celebrate my wedding in this stinking room — at least not until everything else has been tried," she said, ready for a fight. "I'll ask my father to bring up the matter again. Maybe . . . maybe we'll have to take the small room in the Wild Man. That would be a compromise, but we'll just have to put off the wedding until that's all straightened out. Perhaps the suffragan bishop is just upset now about this werewolf, and soon—"

"Postpone?" Jakob took the pipe out of his mouth. He looked a little pale around the nose. "You mean to postpone the wedding? We can't just stay in Bamberg forever."

"If what I'm hearing is correct, you'll have to stay around here longer anyway on account of your stubborn daughter," she replied stiffly. She had apparently regained her former self-confidence. "It's no longer a question of a few days more or less."

She turned to her future husband. "I'm going to spend the night here in your room, without you, as is proper, and you'll move upstairs to the attic. Tomorrow we'll figure out what to do next. And, Bartholomäus . . ." Katharina said, taking the hem of her skirt and wiping the remains of the potluck stew from the beard of the astonished hangman, "you need to take a bath more often, or even after our wedding you'll often be going to bed alone. Good night to you all."

She sniffed once again, wiped the last of the tears from the corners of her eyes, then holding her head high, walked over to the bedroom and slammed the door behind her.

Jakob grinned and winked at his brother. "Do you know what, Bartholomäus?" he said as he lit his pipe again. "I like your fiancée. She's just like my Anna, God bless her soul. Why should you be any better off than I was?"

About an hour later, Simon and Magdalena lay upstairs in the attic listening to the snoring of Jakob and Bartholomäus coming from the next room. Peter and Paul were sleeping next to them on a straw mattress and pillows filled with horsehair. In the darkness, Simon could just see their outlines. The older boy clung to the younger one, as if trying to shield him from all the dangers of the world.

It was in such moments that Simon thought of little Marie, who had been taken from them so soon, and he suspected that Magdalena did, as well.

She had propped herself up on the bed and was watching the children, lost in thought. They were quiet for a long time, and now she whispered, "I hope that Katharina can still have children despite her age. She'd really be a good mother."

"Sure . . . sure . . ." Simon nodded, half dreaming. There was something he absolutely had to discuss with Magdalena. He didn't know if this was the right time, but perhaps there really was no suitable time for it.

"This wedding . . ." he began hesitantly. "The fact that Katharina is now putting it off is . . . ah, so unfortunate . . ."

"But completely understandable," Magdalena interrupted. "If it were me, I'd try everything before I'd celebrate here in this stinking hole. Remember our own wedding, after Secretary Lechner had given his permission as representative of the elector."

Simon couldn't suppress a smile. The wedding then was only possible because he'd given up his status as a doctor in training. Only as a simple bathhouse owner would he be allowed to take the hangman's daughter as his wife. They'd had to celebrate in one of the simpler taverns in Schongau, not in the refined Star Tavern, but nevertheless in good style with a lot of wine, a roast suckling pig, and a half dozen musicians. The party had cost a fortune, and because of it Simon had had to sell a few of his beloved books.

"I can really understand Katharina," Magdalena continued, "and Bartholomäus is just as uncouth as our father. No doubt both of them would rather have just two guests—a big keg of beer and a pot of onion stew. With those two, they at least wouldn't have to strike up a conversation."

Simon sighed. "But your father is right. We can't stay here forever. We've already been away for nearly a month. My patients will start going to the new doctor in town, and if I don't go home soon, they'll never come back and I will have to close my bathhouse."

Magdalena looked at him darkly. "What are you trying to say? That we shouldn't stay for the wedding?"

"Ah, well . . ." Simon waffled. "If it's going to go on much longer, then I think, in fact, that—"

"That's out of the question." Magdalena lay back down on the bed. "Until Barbara is back, we can't leave, and Barbara will hide out until Father can think of something to do for Matheo."

"Do you realize what that means?" Simon could feel the anger welling up inside him. Didn't anyone ever think of him? "Both your father and I have work to do in Schongau," he grumbled. "Do you want us to lose our jobs? Have you even thought about what Secretary Lechner will say if his hangman and the local bathhouse owner stay a few more weeks here in Bamberg?"

Magdalena tried to calm him down. "It doesn't have to be weeks more. Katharina didn't ask for more than a few days postponement, and Father will never go without Barbara, that's for sure."

"Well, great." He groaned as he sank back into the pillows. "Every day here costs me a fortune. Why do we always get mixed up in these crazy adventures? All I want is to be an ordinary, respectable bathhouse owner."

"Evidently God has other plans for you." Magdalena grinned and kissed his forehead, but then she turned serious. "I want to know what it was that came between Father and his brother back then. Whatever it was, it really hurt Bartholomäus." She sighed. "Sometimes I think I really don't know my father."

"You're not the only one. Nobody knows him." Simon took a deep breath and closed his eyes. "He probably doesn't even know himself."

The old patrician's house at the foot of the cathedral mount groaned and moaned like a huge animal. In the last few hours, the rain had increased, and the wind had gotten stronger, from time to time rattling the shutters with gusts of wind, as if loudly demanding entry.

The house's owner, Agnes Gotzendörfer, sat alone in the living room, wrapped in heavy woolen blankets. It was a cold night at the end of October, and the wet logs burning on the hearth gave off only a small, bluish flame. Agnes's legs were suffering from gout, and the constant clattering of the shutters got on her nerves.

The old patrician's widow had never liked this house—it was too large, too drafty, and the stone flooring in the entryway and the kitchen were cold as ice even in midsummer. In addition, it was hard to find servants, as the simple folk were still firmly convinced the old house was haunted. It used to be that Agnes just shook her head on hearing that, but on nights such as these, she herself believed in evil spirits.

Especially since these nightmares had come to torment her.

Her late husband, the once so influential city councilman Egidius Gotzendörfer had acquired the property at a bargain price more than thirty years ago. It was one of the houses standing empty after the great wave of persecution and the subsequent witch trials. Once it had belonged to the Haans, a venerable patrician family in the city. Dr. George Haan had advanced to the position of chancellor, and the family owned several properties in the city, but suddenly the Haans had been suspected of witchcraft, and one by one the hangman had tortured, beheaded, and burned the family at the stake.

Quite a few people claimed to know for certain that their souls still wandered restlessly through the house. And in fact, for several weeks Agnes had felt pursued by these souls. She saw them in her dreams and was chased and tortured by them. As a child, Agnes had always feared ghouls and ghosts, the horrible bands of murdered people who, especially on raw winter nights, swooshed through the air with their dogs, horses, and other beasts.

In her nightmares, these creatures reached out for Agnes and dragged her down through a whirling vortex into the deep.

Another strong gust of wind shook the shutters, frightening the old patrician woman. Agnes Gotzendörfer lived alone in this huge house; her children and family had died or moved to other cities. Lisbeth, the only maid, had long ago gone to bed. She was a lazy, garrulous old maid but the only person who agreed to work in the haunted house. Agnes couldn't stand her, but at the moment she wished she were here to keep her company. The nearly eighty-year-old woman felt more or less secure here in her own four walls, but now a cold fear was creeping up her spine, a fear that even all her blankets couldn't keep out.

Just an hour ago, long after the night watchman had announced the curfew, Agnes had heard quick footsteps in front of the house, and through a slit in the shutters she recognized Katharina, the daughter of the city clerk Hieronymus Hauser. Agnes's husband Egidius had often called upon the young Hieronymus to take minutes of the meeting, and because of this, Agnes also knew his chubby daughter. What was the woman doing in the street at this hour? Agnes had heard she would soon be marrying the Bamberg executioner, a gloomy fellow who, it was said, drank the blood of his victims and sold magical amulets.

Perhaps even some that could turn their owner into a were-wolf?

Agnes felt a chill and huddled down even deeper into the woolen blankets on her armchair. Her maid had told her that in the marketplaces the only thing people talked about was this horrible werewolf. It was said to have killed a countless number of people, and evidently a militia had already assembled, since no one trusted the city council or even the bishop anymore. Agnes knew that Lisbeth liked to exaggerate, but she herself had heard of the missing people from other patrician widows she had spoken with. Among the missing were Klaus Schwarzkontz and Thadäus Vasold—two old city councilors her husband had known before his death ten years ago. They had sat together on various commissions and had both gotten rich, powerful, and fat. It seemed that the werewolf would stop at no one and stole and ate everything it could catch—rich and poor, young and old, men and women . . . It was quite possible fat Katharina would be next. Why did this stupid woman have to run through the streets at this hour? It would be her own fault if—

A soft rapping interrupted Agnes Gotzendörfer's thoughts. At first she couldn't say where it was coming from—her hearing wasn't what it used to be—but when she finally figured it out, the hair on the back of her neck stood up.

The knocking came from one of the shutters.

It was one of the shutters facing the street and had become louder, so that Agnes could no long brush it off as a figment of her overworked state of mind.

Knock . . . knock . . . knock . . .

"Is someone there?" she called out in a hoarse voice that broke apart and crumbled like an old, moldy rag. But even as she spoke those few words, she had a suspicion that no one would answer. Instead, the knocking began again.

Knock . . . knock . . . knock . . .

She closed her eyes, struggling to think, as her heart pounded wildly. She'd better call Lisbeth, but Agnes knew the maid was a deep sleeper and her bedroom was on the top floor, just underneath the roof. No doubt Agnes would have to go up and get her, but she was eighty, and going up stairs was getting harder for her by the week. The stairway was steep, the steps smooth, and just last month she had slipped and just managed to grab the banister in time.

In her nightmares, Agnes saw the shadows of restless spirits trying to push her down the stairway, again and again.

Knock . . . knock . . . knock . . .

When the knocking began again, Agnes made a decision. She would look through a slit in the shutters and see who or what was outside, then she could still decide whether to call for help. She really had nothing to fear, as there were thick bull's-eye windowpanes between her and the street, and beyond them solid iron bars to protect the property from burglars. Only then came the shutters. No one, nothing, could break in here.

Agnes pushed her blankets aside, rose from her armchair, and hobbled carefully on her swollen legs toward the window. Her heart was pounding so hard that her chest ached. As she approached the window, she thought she heard a faint sound, like long nails scratching against the shutter.

Or claws?

Trembling, she summoned up all her courage and opened the window just a crack, carefully reaching through the iron bars until she felt the bolt for the shutters. Pushing it aside, she looked out into the night through a narrow slit. In the pouring rain and darkness, it wasn't possible to see anything clearly. She squinted. And only then did she see it, standing a few steps in front of the bars, as if behind a clouded lens. The thick window glass distorted it somewhat, so it looked grotesquely large, much larger than a man. Otherwise, there didn't seem to be much that was human about it.

What in the world . . . ?

The next moment the window with the bull's-eye window-pane exploded into a thousand pieces. Rain poured into the room, the curtains fluttered like flags in the wind, and behind the bars and the wide-open shutters a monstrous creature, like something from a nightmare, rose up.

Agnes's nightmare.

The creature was a man and yet not a man: it seemed to walk on two legs, but hair covered its entire body and it had a monstrous head atop a neck that was far too small. She peered into the dead eyes of a bear, or was it a wolf? Atop its skull was a set of horns dripping dark water or blood, and below the head it had the black, soaked pelt of a horse or dog.

The creature looked as if the devil had cobbled together all the animals of the forest into one evil creature, in defiance of God.

And it let out a howl, high-pitched and loud.

Finally it raised its huge paws and reached through the bars toward Agnes Gotzendörfer. In its right paw it held a mangled human hand that had been chewed off.

The thought flashed through the widow's mind: *The creature from my nightmare. The ghosts of those who have been murdered. They are back. The beast has come to take me away.*

That was too much for the old patrician woman. Her heart, which had been beating so strongly, suddenly stopped, and blood rushed through her skull like a raging, black torrent. She felt one, last, stinging pain, then collapsed on the floor lifeless, like a puppet.

The beast growled and rattled the bars for a while, as if trying to break them in two, but finally it gave up and slunk away through the alleyways, where it soon disappeared in the raging storm.

As the storm subsided, a few drops of rain, blown into the ancient house by a final gust of wind, fell onto Agnes's face, twisted into a frozen grimace of terror.

Then, once again, silence fell over the house.

9

Barbara sat on a bed in Jeremias's little room, leafing dreamily through the works of this so highly acclaimed William Shakespeare. She had found a slender volume on the bookshelf about an old king who decided to distribute his realm among his three daughters but ended up giving it all to the two unworthy sisters. In his stubbornness, this King Lear reminded Barbara of her own father. She didn't understand everything in the play and often skipped pages, but nevertheless the play led her into another world, far from her current problems.

God knew she truly had enough of them.

When Magdalena visited her the day before, Barbara had briefly pulled herself together and appeared strong, but after her sister left, she broke down sobbing again. Matheo, the first boy she really thought she loved, faced gruesome torture and execution—and if a miracle didn't occur, it would be her own brother and uncle who killed him. By running away from her family, Barbara had tried to put pressure on her father. But was there anything at all he could do?

In her anger, she had first decided to seek shelter with the actors, but then it occurred to her that was the first place Magdalena would come to look. After she'd wandered aimlessly for a while in the courtyard of the Wedding House, the crippled Jeremias had offered to take her in, but she knew it was only a matter of time before someone would find her here. She was almost relieved that it was Magdalena who found her. She needed someone to whom she could pour out her heart. Old Jeremias was certainly a nice man, but he was no substitute for a real friend.

Barbara had already considered returning to the Bamberg executioner's house, but there she would have felt even smaller and weaker than she did now. For a fifteen-year-old this was all simply too much. But then she remembered this Juliet from the other play by Shakespeare. The girl from the Capulet house had been only thirteen and, God knows, had gone through a lot more than herself. So Barbara clenched her teeth and wiped away her tears.

Jeremias had been very kind to her. He'd let her sleep in his bed while he slept in the tavern's pantry. From time to time he'd come over to her to try to cheer her up or bring her a soothing drink of lime-blossom tea, but she realized she couldn't stay here forever.

Sooner or later she'd have to make a decision.

She knew she'd either have to return to her family or join the group of actors. Ever since Sir Malcolm had declared she had "talent" she felt a constant restlessness inside her. Finally, she saw a real possibility of escaping the preordained life of a hangman's daughter. She wouldn't have to marry any filthy, stinking knacker or hangman's apprentice while suffering in silence and bearing him a half dozen children. No. She'd see the world! This longing in her had grown stronger ever since she began leafing through the dog-eared book of plays. At times, Barbara whispered some of the passages to herself, at first haltingly, then more and more fluently, until the florid language positively rolled off her tongue. Now, once again, she was reading some lines from King Lear that especially appealed to her.

> *Good my lord,*
> *You have begot me, bred me, lov'd me; I*
> *Return those duties back as are right fit,*
> *Obey you, love you, and most honour you.*

"Ah, wonderful! That is music to my ears."

When Barbara heard the voice, she looked up in embarrassment expecting to see old Jeremias, but it was Sir Malcolm standing in the doorway with a wry look on his face. The haggard old director was so tall his head almost touched the ceiling. He bowed deeply.

"Didn't I say you have talent? When I hear you read these lines, I think how right I was." He opened his arms wide and looked up, as if the heavens had opened. "A star is born."

Barbara frowned. She was embarrassed that Sir Malcolm had surprised her, and furthermore, it troubled her that the director had found her in Jeremias's room. Who else knew about this place except for Jeremias and Magdalena? Perhaps her hiding place could not be kept secret much longer.

All the more important that I make up my mind soon . . .

"A star?" she asked finally. "I'm afraid I don't understand."

Sir Malcolm sat down alongside her on the bed and patted her on the knee. "Excuse me for just bursting in here. To tell you the truth, it was Markus who told me about your hiding place. He no doubt saw your sister coming in here yesterday. Be assured, I'll be as quiet as the grave. But now to something else . . ." He paused briefly and smiled at her expectantly. "I have good news for you, Barbara."

Barbara's heart started to pound. "Matheo!" she burst out excitedly, jumping up from the bed. "Did they let him go?"

"Matheo? Ah, unfortunately not." Malcolm at first seemed puzzled. "But you can be sure we all are praying very hard for the young man. No, no, the news actually concerns you."

Barbara slumped over again. "What do you mean?" she asked in a soft voice.

Malcolm nodded excitedly. "I have the great pleasure of informing you that you will soon be given a very important role to play in Sir Malcolm's theatrical group. You will be playing no less than the beautiful Violandra in the extremely popular comedy *Peter Squenz*. So what do you say about that?"

It took Barbara a moment to catch her breath. "I'll be playing in one of your pieces here in Bamberg?" she finally managed to say. "But . . . but I've never done anything like that."

Sir Malcolm demurred. "Everyone begins sometime. Besides, you have talent, as you've just proved again." He hesitated. "Ah, in addition, women's roles are difficult to fill. Most men are too large or too fat. And after the regrettable loss of Matheo . . ."

"Stop right there," Barbara interrupted angrily. "You want me to take Matheo's role? Never! Who do you think I am? That would almost make it seem I'm happy he's wasting away in a dungeon."

"Believe me, Barbara, this is what poor Matheo would want you to do. I'm absolutely sure of that." Sir Malcolm nodded with a sad, earnest look. "Unfortunately, the bishop did not accept my suggestion to simply banish Guiscard's miserable group of jugglers from the city. Instead, His Excellency decided to hold a contest between our two groups." Malcolm briefly described the bishop's plan, as Barbara turned paler and paler.

"If we lose, we'll have to spend the winter somewhere outside the city," the director concluded, nervously patting Barbara's thigh with his long, sinewy fingers. "A lot depends on you now, as I have no one else in the group to assume the female part."

"Do you mean . . . I'm to play personally in front of two bishops in this palace down by the river?" Barbara asked in a toneless voice. "On a real stage before all these noble ladies and gentlemen?"

"Well, at least it's not a public performance, so you won't have to be afraid someone from your family will recognize you and drag you off the stage."

Barbara took a deep breath. "And when will this contest take place?"

Sir Malcolm cleared his throat, embarrassed. "Uh . . . tomorrow night."

"*Tomorrow?* But I don't even know the play yet, much less my part. How can I do that?"

"Oh, there's no magic to it. Just keep thinking of Cordelia's noble words in *King Lear* . . ." Sir Malcolm rose to his feet and pressed his hand dramatically to his chest as he declaimed in a loud, majestic voice.

> *"We are not the first*
> *Who with best meaning have incurr'd the worst."*

Then he hobbled hastily over to the door. "If you would be so kind, follow me into the hall, and we'll begin the rehearsal at once."

"Gentlemen, the meeting has come to order."

Suffragan Bishop Harsee tapped his gavel on the polished oak table and looked around as the last of the murmured conversations died away.

Simon sat with Master Samuel at the far end of the large oval table in the council room of the Old Residence. One after the other, the Schongau medicus and bathhouse owner scrutinized the faces of the honorable council members, who appeared gray and anxious. In contrast with the last meeting, the mood now was not aggressive, but gloomy. No one shouted, and all of them—the Jesuits, the scholars, the chancellor, and the dean of the cathedral—stared at the Bamberg suffragan bishop as if he alone could bring them salvation.

But Sebastian Harsee himself did not seem in the best of moods. He was pale and kept wiping beads of sweat from his brow with a silk handkerchief. He also kept nervously scratching an itch on his neck.

Just like the meeting two days ago, this one had also been convened on very short notice. The reason was that the old patrician widow Agnes Gotzendörfer had been found dead early that morning in her house. This by itself was no reason for the emergency meeting—the dearly beloved Agnes was almost eighty years old—but the gruesome circumstances of her death had further stirred anxiety among the citizenry. Evidently, a window in her house had been smashed in, tracks had been found in the road right in front of the house, and the face of the deceased was frozen in horror. In addition, a severed human hand presumably belonging to Thadäus Vasold had been found on the front steps. In any case, his signet ring was found on one of the fingers. Since then, all of Bamberg was in an uproar.

"Dear fellow citizens," the suffragan bishop began in a measured tone, "it appears now that we are no longer safe from the powers of Satan even inside our four walls. The case of poor Agnes Gotzendörfer makes that clear. Now's the time to act quickly, to find the hideout of these terrible beasts, and to mercilessly eradicate them."

"B-beasts?" replied the dean of the cathedral, quaking. "So far, all we've talked about is a single werewolf."

"But we caught him and locked him up yesterday," said one of the council members, the apothecary Magnus Rinswieser. "Don't tell me this fellow has escaped."

Harsee shook his head. "No, no, he's safely locked away in the dungeon of Saint Thomas's Chapel. We'll begin with the torture soon in order to learn more, but as I said, it is . . ."—he sighed——"... this fellow is no doubt just the start, and there are presumably a number of others who have sold themselves to the devil. The death of Agnes Gotzendörfer proves there are other monsters lurking around."

"What do you mean when you say you'll *begin with the torture soon?*" a council member with a goatee sneered. It was the wealthy young wool weaver Jakob Steinhofer, whose young wife had also disappeared. "Why haven't you started already?"

"Well, the venerable prince bishop wanted to hear the judgment of the doctors of law before he makes his decision," replied Sebastian Harsee, raising his eyebrows scornfully. He pointed at the two earnest-looking scholars sitting across from him. "But that will be in the next few days, won't it?" Harsee cleared his throat. "I'd like to stress here my difference of opinion with the prince bishop in this regard. The Inquisition Commission, consisting of the legal scholars, the dean of the cathedral, and yours truly have clearly expressed our recommendation regarding the torturing of this subject. The prince bishop, however, has the last word, and he has said he doesn't want to have anyone tortured without proof. Besides, at the moment, His Excellency is much more interested in the theater and his menagerie. In summary, he asks for a delay because of the scheduled visit of none other than His Excellency, the bishop of Würzburg tomorrow evening. He surely wishes to avoid any religious dispute and is yielding to the wishes of his great colleague and neighbor. Well, then ..." Harsee waited for his words to die away in the hall while regarding the angry faces with amusement.

Simon smiled grimly. *You know how to bring people over to your side,* he thought.

"'Tortured without proof'?" Jakob Steinhofer spoke up, angrily. "How many reasons does one need to have to make this fellow talk? My dear Johanna was mauled to death by this beast. Two city councilmen are among the victims, and now the respected widow of the patrician Gotzendörfer, who for so many years guided the destiny of this council—"

"To say nothing about my dear Adelheid," the apothecary chimed in with a quavering voice. His face was ashen and his eyes full of tears.

"One could almost say this werewolf has very good taste," Master Samuel suddenly interrupted from the far end of the table. All eyes turned to him and Simon. It was the first thing the doctor had said.

"What do you mean by that?" asked the pale, bloated chancellor Korbinian Steinkübler, staring at Samuel distrustfully with his tiny, porcine eyes. Simon had learned from his friend that Steinkübler came from one of the richest families in the city. He had obtained his position after a long struggle and was known for his absolute loyalty toward the prince bishop.

"Well, please excuse my rude way of putting it . . ." Samuel raised his hands in apology. "What I meant to say was, it's striking how many of the victims come from the patrician class." He started counting them off on his fingers. "Two aging former councilmen, a patrician widow, the wife of a council member, and a young married woman . . ."

"You forget the nameless prostitute and the miller's wife," the chancellor interrupted harshly. He leafed through the papers in front of him. "A certain . . . Barbara Leupnitz. You can hardly classify her or the whore as patricians." He smiled peevishly.

Samuel nodded. "You are right . . . but nevertheless . . ."

"What's the point of splitting hairs like this?" the suffragan bishop inquired impatiently. He rose to his feet and angrily looked at the city physician while beads of sweat dripped from his forehead. "Yes, there are patricians among the victims, but these werewolves stop at nothing and spare no one. It's quite possible that the faithful come together in the Bamberg Forest, and if we don't strike soon, their numbers will continue to grow.

Therefore . . ." Harsee paused, gripping the table tightly, as if he was about to collapse. But then he got control of himself again, and continued. "Therefore, starting today, guards—along with a courageous group of citizens—will patrol the forests in order to locate suspicious subjects. A so-called civilian militia has already come together, because they evidently no longer trust the prince bishop . . ." He paused for a moment for his words to sink in, then continued. "In addition, I'm considering announcing a reward for any information leading to the apprehension of a werewolf. We will destroy this brood of vipers!"

Pale and bathed in sweat, he took a seat again. By now, Simon was certain that Harsee was coming down with a bad fever, but his sympathy had its limits.

"If you offer a reward, you'll surely get a lot of tips," the Schongau bathhouse owner mused, "but you have to wonder if these tips won't just be made up. For money, people can see a lot, even werewolves."

"Are you saying the Bambergers would lie?" the young councilor Steinhofer flared up.

"Well, a lie can take many forms," Simon replied. "Sometimes there is nothing more to it than an assumption."

"Just stop this nonsense," the suffragan bishop growled, visibly exhausted. "The reward will be offered, and that's the end of the discussion. His Excellency, the prince bishop, already agreed, and the civilian militia will also officially begin its duties today. As soon as we find the suspects, the inquisition subcommittee will convene to recommend torture and execution." He sneered slightly as he once again mopped the sweat from his forehead. "I'm sure that this time His Excellency, the prince bishop, will agree. He cannot afford opposing his flock in the long run. And now excuse me." Looking even paler, Harsee struggled to stand up. "Recent events have been for us extremely . . . strenuous. The meeting is over."

He stood up, pulled his black robe around him, and struggled toward the exit.

A bit later, Simon and Samuel were strolling across the great square in front of the cathedral, where the construction work on the bishop's palace proceeded unabated.

"What did you mean before when you said that for the most part patricians and their relatives are the victims?" Simon asked his friend.

Samuel shrugged. "It's just one piece of the puzzle, nothing more. Suppose these murders were not committed by a wild monster but by someone trying to target the ruling class? Did you ever think about that?"

Simon stopped to think, puzzled. "But why would anyone do anything like that?"

"I don't know. I only know there is a struggle for supremacy in the city, an attempt to do away with competitors, and, as you know, the end justifies the means." Samuel nodded sadly. "Take for example this chancellor Korbinian Steinkübler. He paid a lot of money to obtain his new position, and I know that some patricians, among them the missing old councilor Thadäus Vasold, were not at all happy about that. Many would have preferred to have Sebastian Harsee in that position. He comes from an esteemed family, and his father before him was the chancellor."

"By the way, Harsee didn't look at all well in the meeting today," Simon said, frowning. "He appears to be seriously ill, probably some kind of fever."

"Which brings me to the dean of the cathedral," Samuel replied. "For a long time he's had his eye on the position of suffragan bishop. Did you see his expression just before that when Harsee nearly broke down? I'm sure he'd like to see him dead." Samuel shook his head. "Believe me, Simon, this council really is one big gang of cutthroats."

"So you think this werewolf is a hired killer sent to dispose of any competitors?" Simon mused, rubbing his chin. "That could be so for the two councilors, but how about the prostitute and the miller's wife, or the apothecary's wife and the Gotzendörfer widow? The latter two come from patrician families, but they're women and not competing with anyone for an appointment."

Samuel sighed. "You're right, of course. As I said, it was just a thought, and even if my suspicion was right, things are moving in a different direction now. See for yourself."

They were just passing the front portal of the cathedral, where a city guard was nailing a piece of paper to the door. A large crowd had already gathered around, while another guard loudly proclaimed the text of the announcement.

"The city council will do everything in its power to stop the activities of the beast in this city," he cried. "All able-bodied citizens are summoned to report to the city hall, where a city militia will soon be established. Information leading to the capture of the werewolf will be rewarded at the rate of five guilders for each suspect." The crowd broke out in cheers, and a number of them headed down to the city hall, shouting and rejoicing.

The two friends walked by, shaking their heads. "I fear we'll soon have many more werewolves here in Bamberg," said Samuel. "When this is all over, the prince bishop will be lucky if there are enough councilmen left to govern the city."

Adelheid Rinswieser huddled down in the corner of her room waiting to hear her captor approaching.

He'll be coming to get me soon. The moment is almost here . . .

Since the day before, she'd been both yearning for and fearing this moment. She knew that only the death of the other prisoner—that poor creature who in the last hours of her life had screamed, cried, and finally just whimpered and moaned—made her own escape possible.

My only chance.

Yesterday, the screams had continued all day, interrupted only by occasional murmuring, then abruptly, around evening, they had stopped. Shortly after that, Adelheid had heard a door slam and something being dragged along the ground, as if a heavy body were being carried away. Then it turned silent again.

And Adelheid waited.

The apothecary's wife was still chained to the wall and couldn't move more than a few steps. There was a rusty lock around her right ankle that until now had resisted all her efforts to open it. She knew that when the stranger came to drag her into the horrible chamber, he had to open this lock. He'd done it once before, shortly after he'd abducted her, when he'd taken her to view the chamber. At that time she'd been too weak to offer any resistance. He'd wound a leather strap around her neck and led her there, her hands in manacles, like a whipped animal. This time, things would be different; she would know how to defend herself.

Adelheid had a weapon.

Just yesterday she'd beaten her earthenware cup against the wall so that, in addition to the many small pieces, there was an especially long, large shard. The man saw the broken pieces and brought her a new cup, but he hadn't noticed the largest piece lying in her bed under the straw. It was pointed and sharp, like a small dagger. Adelheid reached for it and made a fist so the sharp point protruded between her index and middle finger.

She'd use it to slit the man's throat.

She trembled and tried to calm herself by reciting simple Bible verses.

"The Lord is my shepherd, I shall not want . . ."

The verses helped to get her wildly pounding heart under control and fill the long hours of waiting. Adelheid counted the hours using the small, flickering tallow candle that the man came in regularly to replace. Recently, she thought she'd heard birds chirping or dogs barking, and one time even an angry growl. Was that perhaps the beast that had overpowered her? But it could also be her imagination playing tricks on her. Otherwise, an oppressive silence prevailed, like a heavy blanket stifling everything, interrupted only by her own voice.

> *"He makes me lie down in green pastures.*
> *He leads me beside still waters . . ."*

Suddenly she heard a door close. Steps drew nearer, became louder, and stopped outside her room. Then a key was inserted in the lock and the door squeaked as it opened.

Adelheid tried not to scream when she saw the man with the mask in the doorway. In the light of the flickering candle, all she could see of him was a dark silhouette.

"Now it's your turn, witch," he said, his voice sounding astonishingly tender. "We will now begin with the second degree. Are you ready?"

"Please, please . . ." she whimpered, turning toward the wall and secretly placing the shard in her hand. She tried to act as defenseless as possible. "I don't know what you want from me . . ."

"You will soon find out."

She could hear his shuffling feet in the dirty straw as he approached. He touched her gently, then wrapped the leather noose around her neck, pulling it so tightly she could barely breathe.

If I move, he'll tighten it all the way. I must be fast—faster than he is.

She was still turned away from her tormenter, whimpering and moaning to lull him into a false sense of security, while she listened to the rattling of the chains. Now the man reached for the lock, and she could hear the squeaking of the key as the lock opened and the chain fell to the floor . . . *Now!*

Adelheid turned around. For a brief moment she couldn't

see exactly where the man was in the dim light. He was kneeling on her left, where the chain was attached to the wall. Shouting furiously, she attacked, and at the same time could feel the noose tightening around her neck. Before it could completely cut off her airway, however, she was already on top of her torturer.

"You . . . you devil," she gasped.

She raised her fist with the splintered piece of the cup, ready to strike, while the man under her lashed out at her, trying to escape. He was much stronger than she, and she could feel his powerful arms trying to push her away. The whites of his eyes shimmered through the slits in the hood, and Adelheid thought she saw fear welling up in them.

"You devil!" she screamed again.

With a final, furious scream, she swung at him with the shard, but in that moment he released his grip on her, and when the shard was a mere hand's breadth from his throat, he blocked her blow with his arm. With sweat streaming down her face, Adelheid reached under the mask of her opponent to scratch his cheeks or stab him in the eyes with her fingers, but she only managed to hit his hood. She clutched at the mask, pulled it . . .

. . . and tore it from his face.

The shock at the fact that the horror suddenly had a face caused Adelheid to hesitate just an instant.

It was the instant that cost her her freedom.

The man pushed her away like a dirty bundle of rags. Adelheid hit the wall behind her, bloodying her back as she slammed against the large stones, and the shard fell from her hand. Then she felt a strong pull, and the leather noose tightened around her neck.

Squinting, Adelheid saw the man standing over her pulling on the strap. She gasped for air, desperately, in vain. She clawed at the noose around her neck, but the leather had dug itself too deeply into her skin. Colored circles danced before her eyes, faster and faster, and then came the darkness . . .

This is the end . . . This is . . .

After what seemed like an eternity—or was it just seconds?—Adelheid emerged from a sea of darkness. She gasped and gagged, and in fact, wonderful cool air now entered her lungs. She reached for the strap, trembling, but it hung loose around her neck.

But why . . .

Suddenly she heard someone sobbing softly. It seemed to come from far away. Shortly before losing consciousness, Adelheid summoned up her last bit of strength and turned to see the man crouched in a corner.

His hood lay beside him on the floor, and he was crying like a small child.

Then Adelheid finally collapsed.

Simon rushed as fast as possible from the cathedral mount to the new part of town. He absolutely had to speak with Magdalena again about the postponement of the wedding. After the meeting in the council chambers, he'd had a brief conversation with Samuel, who agreed he shouldn't leave his bathhouse in Schongau closed much longer. Samuel himself had patients to see all day, so their discussions about the werewolf had to be put off to the next day.

When Simon finally arrived at the executioner's house, the only one there was Jakob Kuisl, who was sitting at the table smoking and brooding. Before him on the table lay a small tattered book, which he quickly shut when he saw Simon coming.

"Where are the others?" Simon asked in astonishment, as he looked around the empty room.

Jakob Kuisl shrugged. "Bartholomäus and Georg have some stuff to do over at the council chamber. I'm sure you know that last night an old patrician's widow died under mysterious circumstances. Now the noble gentlemen have announced the hunt, a number of arrests are expected, and the city dungeon is being put in readiness for them. I can't tell you where Magdalena and the two children are."

He opened the book again and began to read, as if Simon were not even there. The bathhouse owner was familiar with that sort of behavior from his father-in-law and took no offense. It only meant that Jakob Kuisl was deep in thought, and for that he needed tobacco and complete silence.

Simon sat down silently on the bench next to the hangman. While pouring himself a cup of watered-down wine, he glanced over curiously at the dog-eared book. He recognized it at once— Lonitzer's herb almanac, an illustrated work found in every hangman's personal library. Apparently the little book belonged to Bartholomäus and came from his collection in the adjoining room. On the page to which the book was opened was a high-lighted article with notes in the margin, but Kuisl's hand was on top of the book and Simon couldn't see anything else.

After a while the hangman put the book aside angrily and glared at Simon.

"How in the world am I going to concentrate when someone is staring at me the whole time?" he growled. "So what is it? If you have something to say, then say it, and don't squirm around here as if you'd soiled yourself."

Simon smiled. Sarcastic grumbling from Jakob Kuisl was his way of extending an invitation to talk about something.

"I was only wondering why you were suddenly so interested in plants," he replied. "Does that by chance have anything to do with this mysterious werewolf? Are you perhaps looking for an herb that will protect you from such creatures?"

"Bah, humbug! Wolfsbane or Saint John's wort can give you confidence, perhaps, but can they really protect you? No." Kuisl frowned. "The only thing that can help you is your reason, and that's just what's missing here in Bamberg."

"Then you don't believe in the werewolf? Earlier you weren't so sure."

Jakob Kuisl rolled his eyes impatiently, then turned to look Simon directly in the face. "I believe my own eyes and my common sense," he said in a firm voice. "In this city, someone is abducting and killing people in a very cruel manner. Some people claim to have seen a furry creature, some in the city, others out in the forest, and someone bought a whole bunch of wolfskins from the furrier . . ."

"Wolfskins found among the possessions of the unfortunate Matheo," Simon continued, absorbed in his thoughts. "Magdalena thinks that anyone could have put them there. Perhaps it was someone from that other group of actors."

"Perhaps. And perhaps by someone who was beginning to feel the heat and needed a scapegoat to deflect the suspicions."

Simon frowned. "What do you mean by that?"

Kuisl slowly expelled the smoke from his pipe and held three chubby fingers up to Simon's face. "There are three possibilities. First, there really is a mad beast out there. Second, there's a madman out there, also a sort of beast. Or . . ." He paused and leaned back in his chair. "Or there's somebody smart out there following a plan. I'm sitting here with my pipe, thinking, and asking myself what kind of plan that could be."

Simon nodded. "My friend Samuel has some interesting ideas about that. What do you think of this?" He told Kuisl briefly about the meeting that morning and Samuel's assumptions about the council members. "Perhaps there really is a struggle for power among the patricians," the bathhouse owner concluded. "Someone is trying to do away with his enemies and is ready to accept the deaths of other completely innocent people. Perhaps the suffragan bishop, perhaps the chancellor, or one of the noblemen on the council . . . ?"

"And to do that he kills the wife of an ordinary miller and a prostitute to cover his tracks?" Kuisl spat into the reeds on the floor. "A daring plan. But there's something wrong with that picture. Only two of the six missing or dead people were actually council members; the rest of them don't fit in that category."

Simon sighed. "Samuel said that, too. But do you have a better idea?"

"Perhaps I would have come up with something a lot sooner if you didn't always interrupt me." Growling, Kuisl picked up the little book again. "But, yes, I have an idea. There's something I can't get out of my mind . . ." He squinted. "The dead prostitute had a . . . strange odor, like the smell of a beast of prey . . ."

Simon felt the hair on the back of his neck standing on end. "A beast of prey?" he repeated anxiously. "And you're only mentioning that now?"

"Because I refuse to believe in a werewolf. But yes, it was the stench of wet fur." Kuisl said. "It took a few days to figure out where I've smelled that before."

"But if the prostitute smelled like a beast, that would mean that perhaps, after all, a werewolf—" Simon said. Kuisl cut him off with an angry gesture.

"For God's sake, just forget the werewolf. You're driving me crazy with your superstitious drivel." The hangman pointed at the highlighted section of the book in front of him. "There is only one herb that smells just like a beast of prey. Because of all this nonsense about the werewolf, I've overlooked the most obvious thing. But when you think about it . . ." Kuisl grinned as he always did when he was about to spring a surprise.

Simon drummed his fingers nervously on the table. He hated it when his father-in-law tortured him like this. "Just get to the point," he pleaded. "Why do we always need to beg you to tell us what's on your mind? What kind of herb is it?"

"Well, as a bathhouse owner you really should know that. It's henbane, also known as stinking nightshade or dog's piss root," Kuisl elaborated with obvious satisfaction. "It's found in many witch's brews because it's said to have magical power, but primarily, it's used as a strong anesthetic. Along with opium, mandrake, and hemlock it is often used in sleeping sponges—things you no doubt have heard of."

"Sleeping sponges?" Simon asked, perplexed. In fact, he did use such sponges himself occasionally. Soaked in narcotics, these sponges were placed over a patient's face during operations to calm them down or, if necessary, make them unconscious. It was extremely hard to adjust the dosage—a bit too much of the liquid, and the patient would never wake up.

"Do you think someone drugged the prostitute first and then killed her?" he asked breathlessly.

Kuisl nodded. "Probably not just the prostitute. It had to be someone who knew a lot about medicine. The right quantity to use on a sleeping sponge is actually something known only to members of four guilds, in my opinion." He counted them off on his fingers. "Doctors, bathhouse owners, midwives, and . . ."

"Hangmen," Simon gasped.

"Indeed. I've used sleep sponges a few times myself to relieve a condemned man's pain. It's a drug preferred by hangmen and their journeymen. Anyone who understands suffering and death must also know about healing."

Simon stared at the highlighted paragraph in the book describing the recipe for preparing such a sleep sponge. "I'm assuming *you* aren't the person who highlighted this paragraph and entered the notes in the margin?" he whispered.

Kuisl shook his head. "That was Bartholomäus; I know his handwriting." The hangman knocked the dead ashes out of his pipe, stretched, and slowly rose to his feet like a giant who'd been sleeping for a long time in his cave.

"I'm afraid I'll have to ask my brother and his servant Aloysius a few very unpleasant questions."

"Morning is breaking, the sun will soon . . . uh . . . will soon . . . set."

"*Rise.* The sun will soon *rise!* Damn it, is it so hard to read from a script?"

Sir Malcolm tore at his hair, staring at Barbara, who was standing along with four other actors on a sort of balcony above the stage. Barbara could feel a knot in her stomach, and blood rushed to her head. They'd been rehearsing all morning, and by now she'd begun to doubt she really had that wonderful talent that both she and Malcolm thought she had. Her role was actually not that large. At first, Barbara had even felt disappointed to discover she had so few lines to speak.

By now, even those few lines seemed too much for her.

"Morning is breaking, the sun will soon rise," she declaimed loudly this time, looking up at the ceiling as if morning had indeed arrived.

Sir Malcolm nodded contentedly, then turned to Markus Salter, who was standing in a threadbare red cape alongside Barbara.

"Ah, behold, and be appalled. Speak of the wolf, and he will come. What will . . . what will . . ." Now Salter also stumbled in the text, and Sir Malcolm rolled his eyes as angrily as if he were a wolf himself.

"Good Lord, Markus," he fumed. "How many times have we performed this play? Five? Ten?"

"It seems like a hundred," Salter groaned.

"Then I really don't understand why you're so distracted. As the king, you have fewer lines than any of us. Just what's wrong with you lately? Always tired, apathetic, late for rehearsals . . ."

"I had to rush to get all the costumes and props," Markus replied in a soft voice. "And then at night I have to retranslate Shakespeare's *Titus Andronicus* and this complicated *Love's Labour's Lost.* Do you have any idea how difficult it is to find the right rhymes?"

"No, I don't. But I do know something else. None of you have understood yet that this is the most important damned performance of the entire year." Malcolm glared at each of the actors, one by one. "If we mess up this time we'll be spending the winter in some barn with the oxen and asses. Is that clear to all of you?"

Apologetic murmurs could be heard coming from the actors before they continued, with Sir Malcolm interrupting frequently to correct something or roll his eyes theatrically when someone forgot his or her lines.

Barbara took a deep breath, concentrating fully on her next lines. They were performing *Peter Squenz,* a comedy by a certain Andreas Gryphius. She'd scarcely had time to sit down and read the play through. It was about a group of simple-minded workers who performed the play *Pyramus and Thisbe* for the king and his court—and failed in a comical fashion. Barbara's role was that of Princess Violandra, and she had little more to do than to flutter her eyelashes, look pretty, and occasionally say something funny. Sir Malcolm took the main role, that of the shoemaker Peter Squenz. Barbara observed with amazement how he could turn himself into a simple-minded clown using just a few gestures, all while making it look so natural and easy. It seemed he could assume the part of almost any character at will. Stuttering like a toothless old farmer, he had just bowed submissively to the king in the balcony.

"Herr . . . Herr King! There are lots of f-f-f-fools at your court."

The more Barbara thought about their performance the next morning at Geyerswörth, the queasier her stomach felt. Malcolm had promised her a splendid costume that would be made especially for her that evening. The old one was in the actors' wardrobe wagon, which had been in an accident just outside Bamberg and fallen into the river. For the rehearsal she wore her simple gray dress with a soiled bodice. Her legs were trembling, and she didn't feel at all like a princess but more like a housemaid who didn't know what she was supposed to be doing.

I never should have agreed to do this, she thought.

But then she thought of Matheo, languishing in a dungeon not far away. Sir Malcolm had told her again that Matheo would certainly have wanted her to play the part that night, if only because the actors needed warm, safe quarters for the winter.

"Peace! Peace! *Pax vobis*! Aren't you ashamed of yourself? Back away, back away!" Sir Malcolm cried in his role as Peter Squenz, as an actor dressed in a tattered lion costume crawled across the stage on all fours. Barbara could only hope the bishops had a sense of humor.

"Master Lion, be gone," Sir Malcolm intoned while covering his eyes in a dramatic gesture. "Be gone from—"

At that moment there was a loud clatter outside one of the windows. Barbara turned around just in time to see a falling shadow through the bull's-eye glass.

"Damn! Those are surely Guiscard's spies," Sir Malcolm shouted. "To hell with them!" With amazing agility he jumped down from the stage, ran on his long, gangling legs to the window, and opened it.

"Scoundrels!" he shouted, shaking his fist. "It won't do you any good, Guiscard. We're better than you!"

When Barbara ran to the window, she saw a ladder that had fallen over down below in the courtyard of the Wedding House, and alongside it a man struggling to his feet while rubbing his arms and legs before hobbling away. She could see Guiscard hiding in one corner of the courtyard. The French theater director sneered.

"Aha! *Peter Squenz. Mon dieu,* what a trite, dull piece," he crowed with his feminine-sounding French accent. "For that, the bishop will surely give you quarters—in the pigsty. That's the best place for this farce."

"We'll see about that, Guiscard. Get ready for a very, very cold winter. Then you'll have all the time in the world to make up your *own* pieces, you ignorant, thieving fool."

Malcolm closed the window and took a deep breath, as if trying to pull himself together again.

"Do you think then that he'll also perform *Peter Squenz*?" Markus Salter asked, sounding worried. "If Guiscard puts on his play for the bishops ahead of us, we've got a problem."

Malcolm waved him off and suddenly didn't look angry or excited anymore. "Oh, he's rehearsing *Papinian*. That mush is so boring it wouldn't even lure a sleeping dog out from behind the stove, so don't worry."

"*Papinian?*" Markus Salter asked him in surprise. "How do you know that?"

Malcolm grinned like an old crocodile. "Well, if Guiscard can spy, so can I—the difference being that I haven't been caught." He shrugged innocently. "It was my idea, by the way, for Guiscard to put on *Papinian*."

Now Barbara looked surprised as well. "Your idea? But how . . ."

Malcolm put his finger to his lips and gave a conspiratorial wink. "Sh! We don't know if he's listening in," he whispered. He walked to the window and peered out cautiously, and only then continued, with a smile. "Well, I gave a guilder to a talented young man in the bishop's guard to tell Guiscard confidentially that *Papinian* was the favorite piece of His Excellency."

"And that's not the case?" Barbara asked

"Not exactly. The bishop *hates Papinian,* a deadly boring piece about an intrigue at the Roman emperor's court. Unlike Guiscard's group, we've been in Bamberg before and inquired, of course, about what his Excellency likes." Malcolm's smile broadened. "Prince Bishop Philipp Rieneck likes silly love stories, especially when there are animals in them. I'm sure he'll find our *Peter Squenz* extremely amusing. And now," he said clapping his hands, "let's get back to our rehearsal, my darlings, so that the comedy doesn't turn into a tragedy. We haven't won yet."

. . .

Deep in thought, Simon was sitting in the Bamberg executioner's bedroom studying the drawing in Lonitzer's herb almanac. It showed the dirty yellowish flowers of the henbane plant as well as some of the black seeds that always reminded the bathhouse owner of mouse droppings. A note was scrawled alongside:

Anesthetic sponge? Additional ingredients: poppy, mandrake, hemlock . . .

Goose flesh prickled on Simon's neck. Jakob Kuisl had left a while ago to find his brother and ask him some questions. Was it possible that Bartholomäus or his journeyman Aloysius had anything to do with the terrible murders? Where had they been the last few nights? In the house of a self-made werewolf? Simon didn't know Bartholomäus well enough to judge. The Bamberg executioner was as grim and reserved as his brother, even though he seemed a bit more tactful. Was he hiding something? What made him seem so gloomy? Was it just this strange animosity he felt toward his brother?

Simon frowned as he moved his finger back and forth across the page, lost in thought. Up to now he'd always trusted his father-in-law's judgment, but this time he wasn't really sure that Kuisl was right. Perhaps there were other reasons Jakob had been so distrustful of his brother. The strange odor of the dead prostitute and the scribbled notes in the herb almanac weren't enough to explain it.

Simon poured himself another glass of diluted wine and leafed through the little book, pondering the illustrations of the mandrake, the highly poisonous hemlock, and the poppy seeds. He loved these illustrations; they gave him the feeling that nature, despite all the hardships it put in your way, was understandable and could be explained.

He awoke suddenly a while later. The wine had made him sleepy and he had forgotten the time. It was nearly noon, and Magdalena and the children had still not returned. Where were they, anyway? This city was worse than a busy, humming beehive. But then it occurred to him that Magdalena had probably gone to see Katharina to console her on account of the botched wedding plans. Perhaps there was some news and the council had allowed at least a little party in the small room of the Wild Man.

Hastily, Simon smoothed his jacket and splashed a little water on his face from the washbowl in the corridor before setting out for the cathedral mount, at the foot of which the Hausers had a little house near the river. Simon had accompanied Katharina home once before and exchanged a few polite words with her father about books, so he quickly found the tiny house, which was directly alongside a noisy tavern. Behind it stood the Michelsberg, a hill with small paths leading up from the valley through the vineyards to the monastery. It was clear that houses in this part of town belonged to well-off citizens, and Simon wondered how the Hausers could afford living there.

She's really a good catch for Bartholomäus, he thought, *if the wedding actually takes place.*

He knocked and Hieronymus Hauser opened the door. The fat scribe was pale and unshaven, wearing a long, worn coat with billowing sleeves, and looking haggard and strained. He appeared about to shout angrily at his visitor when he recognized Simon, and a smile spread across his face.

"Ah, the bathhouse owner from Schongau," he said. "This is certainly a surprise. Did you perhaps come to talk with me about books?" He hesitated briefly when he saw Simon's troubled gaze. "I hope you're not going to tell me you'll be heading back home early because of this unfortunate wedding matter."

"Uh, no," Simon replied. "That's not . . ."

Damn, this is probably not the best time to bring that up, it occurred to him at the same moment. *Why is Magdalena never here when I need her?*

"I'm looking for my wife," he said instead. "Is she perhaps here with Katharina?"

Hieronymus shrugged. "No, sorry, she's not here, though my daughter could really use a little consolation." He pointed behind him with his thumb. "She locked herself in her room upstairs and is crying her eyes out, the poor thing. It's really a disgrace. Just recently a half dozen of the most influential councilors told me they approved of the celebration in the Wedding House. Bartholomäus's profession may be offensive to some, but in all these years he has had an excellent reputation."

"Wasn't there anything else you could do to persuade the council?" Simon asked. "Maybe a smaller party?"

Hieronymus waved him off. "Ever since the werewolf started threatening the city, everyone dances to the tune of Suffragan Bishop Harsee. Nobody wants to be on bad terms with him." Lowering his voice, he pointed out into the street, where a merchant was passing by, pushing a cart. "Especially since starting today there's a reward being offered for any clues," he whispered. "Now everyone is afraid his neighbor will turn him in because of some trivial matter." Hieronymus looked gloomy. "God help us. It's just like it was almost forty years ago."

"Were you working as a scribe back then?" Simon asked curiously.

"Indeed, and it was a terrible time." He sighed, a chill went up his spine, and he rubbed his fat belly. "But why are you standing out there in the cold? Come in, and warm yourself with a glass of mulled wine."

Simon smiled. "I already had enough wine today, but I'll accept your invitation anyway. I'll have to wait in any case until my wife shows up."

Hieronymus winked at him. "I think I have some freshly ground coffee. Katharina says you're wild about this new brew."

Simon's heart beat faster with joy, as he hadn't had a sip of it since his visit to Samuel, and he needed it to think, just as Kuisl needed his tobacco. "Well, uh, that would be very kind of you," he replied, "but I don't want to impose." Hieronymus had already taken off down the hallway, and Simon followed him full of expectation.

Hauser's house was small but neat and clean. The oaken floor had just recently been scrubbed and polished, and the walls were freshly whitewashed and decorated with pretty little tiles. Everywhere Katharina's hand was evident. Hieronymus Hauser's wife had passed away some years ago, and since then his daughter saw to it that the house got a good cleaning every day.

"Please excuse my appearance," Hieronymus said as they climbed a narrow staircase up to the second floor. "Nowadays I spend almost all my time in my study in the attic. The council has ordered me to recopy a huge pile of old, barely legible financial records." He sighed. "If there is a hell set aside for scribes, I can imagine what it looks like. Well, at least I can work at home."

They entered a warm room decorated with colorful wall hangings. In a corner a cheerful fire flickered on the hearth. Hieronymus offered Simon a stool upholstered in fur, then disappeared in the next room for a while before returning with a steaming pot and two small, dainty cups. Simon raised his eyebrows, knowing that these new drinking vessels were extremely expensive.

"Here, too, this devilish concoction is becoming more and more popular," Hauser said, as he made himself comfortable on another stool, took a slurp of the black brew, and let out a groan of satisfaction. "The suffragan bishop has banned it because it comes from unbelievers and is said to instill heretical thoughts. Fortunately Sebastian Harsee is not yet able to look through the walls of your house." He grinned. "That bigoted zealot would do that, too, if he could."

"You were talking earlier about your time as a scribe during the witch trials," Simon began cautiously. "So were you able to watch those trials personally?"

Hieronymus nodded gloomily and, as if suddenly seized

with a chill, wrapped his chubby hands around the tiny cup. "You could say that. At that time I was just a very young, simple apprentice, but they needed everyone they could get, as many members of the council had also been accused. A few times I even served as a scribe in that notorious Inquisition Commission that sat in judgment on the accused. I saw how some people were sent to the dungeon, based only on the testimony of a jealous neighbor, where they were tortured and burned."

"And there was nothing you could do about it?" Simon asked.

"What could I have done? Anyone who challenged the Inquisition Commission was found guilty of witchcraft himself. I was ... afraid. Besides, for God's sake, I was only the scribe. I took the minutes, that's all." Hieronymus paused. His fat lips wobbled as he remembered.

"Sometimes it was hard to understand the defendants," he finally said in a soft voice. "They ... they screamed and whimpered, and in the end all they did was moan. No one can describe this moan, much less write it down."

Hieronymus had put down the cup of coffee. The conversation had clearly shaken him. His face was gray, and he seemed to have temporarily forgotten his visitor.

"I'm sorry, I'm not accusing you of anything," Simon said, trying to console him. "It's just sometimes hard to understand how ..." He struggled to find the right words, and an embarrassing silence followed.

Suddenly Simon had a thought. Hieronymus was probably just a lower-level scribe, but certainly he knew all about the influential people in town and their intrigues — then, as well as now. Maybe he had some thoughts about what the dead and missing people of the last few weeks had in common.

He cleared his throat. "My friend, the city physician Master Samuel, has an interesting assumption," he began in a firm tone. "He thinks that perhaps there's no werewolf out there at all, just someone who wants to do away with some of the council members, who are possible competitors. What do you think of that?"

Hieronymus seemed perplexed for a moment, but in any case the unusual question seemed to have brought him back to his senses. Lost in thought, he rocked his massive head from side to side. "Hmm, I admit I don't really believe in a werewolf," he replied finally. "No more than I believed in witches at the time. But are you suggesting that all of this is just a cold-blooded series of murders designed to get rid of some of the patricians? Let me think . . ." He stood up and walked back and forth in the room, holding his fat, unshaven chin in his hand.

"Thadäus Vasold and Klaus Schwarzkontz were powerful figures in the city council no doubt, even if they were long past their prime. Their deaths did in fact make room for newcomers in the city council. Egidius Gotzendörfer has been dead for long time, but his widow certainly still had influence. But as to the others . . ." Suddenly the scribe fell silent, his fat body stiffened, and Simon could see that his right hand was trembling slightly.

"No, no," he finally said, almost a little too fast, as he continued to stare thoughtfully into the fire. "I'm afraid there's nothing I can do to help you, Master Fronwieser, as much as I would like to." He shuddered, as if to cast off a bad dream, then turned to his guest with a nervous smile. "And I also have other things to do than to get involved in such intrigues. That's a risky business nowadays." He stiffened and pointed toward the door. "I'm afraid we'll have to continue our conversation some other time. I have to go to the city hall, where I have a lot of paperwork waiting for me that can't be done at home."

Confused, Simon got to his feet. "Well, that is a shame. If you see Magdalena . . ."

"I'll tell her you were here." Hieronymus held out his hand, which felt soft and flabby. "I'd be very grateful if your wife could try to cheer up my Katharina a bit. And now farewell."

Simon barely had time to finish his coffee, and moments later he was standing outside in front of the clerk's house.

Up on the Michelsberg Magdalena sat on a bench set out for pilgrims and looked down at the bustling life in the city below. Her children were playing hide-and-seek between the bushes above the vineyards. She took a deep breath and only now noticed how refreshing the air was up here. Down in the narrow streets there was a strong stench of smoke, feces, and rotting vegetables even now in the colder month of October, but up here a brisk but icy wind was blowing.

After Simon had left unexpectedly early this morning to attend the council meeting, she decided to take a walk with the children in the countryside. Since Katharina's wedding had been postponed indefinitely, she didn't need to help her aunt with the preparations in the wedding hall. For a while she strolled with the boys along the Regnitz, then on a whim decided to climb to the top of the Michelsberg to visit the grave of Saint Otto and pray for Katharina. Before God all men were equal, and Magdalena was sure the Lord would make no distinctions between honorable and dishonorable people. He certainly would have no objection to a hangman celebrating in a middle-class wedding hall. But here on earth the ruler was not God but the church, which had once again shown her family that a hangman was nothing but dirt in their eyes.

My children must have a better life than us, Magdalena thought as she watched Peter and Paul playing. *No one must be allowed to forbid them from getting married just because they are considered dishonorable.*

She sighed softly. Magdalena completely understood Simon's wanting to get back home to Schongau. On the other hand, she couldn't leave without Barbara, and it didn't appear her little sister was going to let anybody change her mind anytime soon. If there was only some way she could help Matheo. The prince bishop's decision to postpone the torture until after the theatrical competition gave them a little time. She earnestly hoped her father, but especially her uncle, would think of something by then. As the Bamberg executioner, Bartholomäus was probably the only one who, though he couldn't spare Matheo's life, could at least save him from the worst pain.

After a while, she stood up, called for the boys, and together they walked back down the narrow pathway that wound its way through the vineyards. The little pilgrimage path ended at the Sand Gate, near the river. Magdalena considered paying a visit to Katharina and her father, who didn't live far from there, but then decided against it. It was already after noon, and the children at her side were hungry and fussy. Surely Simon would be waiting impatiently for them in the hangman's house, and perhaps he'd have news from the city council meeting about Matheo and his trial.

As Magdalena walked briskly through the Sand Gate and from there across the city hall bridge, she noticed that a huge crowd of people had gathered down by the harbor on the opposite side. She heard shouts and jeers and, at regular intervals, loud cheering. As she approached the crowd, she could see that the people had assembled around the cranes usually used to load the ships. At that very moment a crane was lifting something up into the air.

What in the world . . .

To her horror, she saw it wasn't a barrel or a crate but a bearded man in plain-looking clothes hanging on a rope and dripping with water. The rope was tied around his waist, and he was kicking and thrashing about like a fish on a line. His body was lowered toward the river, and people broke out in cheers as he gurgled and disappeared again beneath the waves.

"Mother, what are the people doing?" Peter asked anxiously, while his younger brother Paul watched the scene, clearly amused.

"I'm not sure, Peter," Magdalena replied. "But whatever it is, it isn't good."

The hangman's daughter was familiar with such scenes in Schongau and other cities. Occasionally, bakers who made bad bread were put in a cage and dunked a number of times in the water until they nearly drowned. They called that "baker's baptism," and it was one of the less harmful punishments an executioner had to carry out. Magdalena also knew, however, that her grandfather would take convicted child killers to a pond outside the Schongau city walls and hold them under water with a long pole until they were dead. The spectacle here at the harbor also seemed something like an execution. She looked around but couldn't find either Bartholomäus or Georg. At the edge of the crowd, two guards were leaning against a barrel of pickled herring, watching the sight before them, not certain what to do. Magdalena ran over to them.

"What's happening here?" she asked.

The soldier just shrugged. "The man is an itinerant peddler," he replied, picking his nose. "He was hawking wolf's claws as a protection again these werewolves, but people say he's one himself."

"'People say . . .'" Magdalena frowned. "And for that they practically drown him?" She poked the guard angrily in the chest. "Where are the officials, anyway? Where is the executioner? The man at least has to be questioned."

The guard just smiled, unsure of himself. "Oh, come on, he's not going to die, and even if he does, so what? He's just a stranger in town. You can understand what the people are doing. They're terrified because of this werewolf." He looked at her suspiciously. "And who are you? I don't think I've seen you here before."

"I am . . ." she started to say, but her answer was swallowed up in a deafening roar from the crowd. They were cheering now, as the peddler was dunked in the water again. Evidently the man couldn't swim, as he just thrashed about with his arms and finally, with a loud cry, slipped beneath the water. After what seemed like an eternity, two strong young men standing by the crane laughed and hoisted him back up again. The man was noticeably weaker and he was having trouble moving.

"Damn it! Do something," Magdalena shouted at the guards. "The poor fellow almost drowned."

When the two just waved her off with a bored gesture, she made up her mind. She'd have to get her uncle. As the executioner, Bartholomäus surely had some standing in town, especially when it came to executions. Perhaps he could put an end to this activity.

Magdalena knew that at this hour Bartholomäus and Georg would likely still be at work in the city dungeon, where they would be cleaning and preparing the cells to receive possible additional suspects. The dungeon was in a small lane not far behind the Wedding House, but with the two small boys it would take her much too long to get there, and by then the peddler would probably be dead. She quickly looked around, and her gaze fell once again on the Wedding House.

Barbara.

Her younger sister could surely keep an eye on the two boys for a short time. Magdalena knew there was a passageway in the Wedding House leading to the Wild Man Tavern and from there to the street behind.

Without paying any further heed to the guards, she made her way, holding both boys by the hand, past the shouting and cheering crowd until she finally entered the open door of the Wedding House. Once she was inside the courtyard, things were noticeably quieter. Breathlessly she knocked on the narrow door next to the entrance to the tavern, and after a while it opened. She was greeted not by her sister, however, but by an astonished Jeremias. It appeared he had been sleeping.

"Magdalena?" he asked, rubbing his eyes. "Why are you so out of breath?"

"I have no time for long explanations," she gasped. "Is my sister here?"

Jeremias shook his head. "Unfortunately not. She's upstairs with the actors, but she'll soon be coming back. It seems that Malcolm is very pleased—"

"Do me a favor," Magdalena interrupted. "Please keep an eye on my two boys for a while. I have to go and see my uncle. It's urgent." She turned to Peter and Paul, who were staring at the crippled old man with a mixture of fascination and horror. "This is Uncle Jeremias," she said. "He may look a bit strange, but he's very nice, and he's got some exciting stories to tell. You stay here with him for a while, and I'll be right back."

"Uncle, why did someone pull off your skin?" Paul asked.

Jeremias sighed and sat down to explain, but Magdalena was already gone and out of earshot.

She ran through the tavern past astonished revelers, knocking a beer stein over, and finally slipped through the back door, finding herself on the street in back. From there, she turned right and soon reached the city dungeon, a gloomy, one-story building with barred windows that she'd seen before on her trips to the market. At the entrance, she almost bumped into Georg, who was just leaving. He looked tired and his shirt was filthy—evidently he had just finished his work inside.

"Georg," Magdalena called out with relief. "How fortunate I am to meet you. I'm looking for Bartholomäus."

Georg frowned. "Why are you all so concerned about Bartholomäus today? Father was out looking for him, and he didn't come back until a quarter hour ago. And now you've come here doing the same."

"Because I need him urgently to save a life." Speaking hurriedly, she explained to her astonished brother what was happening down at the harbor.

"And there are no city authorities there?" he asked in astonishment. "No burgomaster, nobody from the city council?"

Magdalena shook her head. "Only two guards who don't want to get involved. We have to work fast or they'll drown the poor man like a kitten."

Georg paused to think. "Well, Uncle Bartholomäus left a while ago to go to the knacker's house in Bamberg Forest. Damned if I know why he's been going out there so often in recent days. Father followed him, and it looks like they had a fight. Father looked very, very angry." He looked at her with a grim expression. "And in the meantime, Uncle Bartholomäus left all the dirty work for me."

Magdalena kicked the door, furious. "Damn! When you hangmen are needed, you're not there." She hesitated. "Perhaps you can do something yourself to make sure everything is all right down at the harbor."

"Me?" He stared at her wide-eyed. "I think you're vastly overestimating what I can do. I'm just an ordinary hangman's servant."

"But someone has to help this poor man."

Georg sighed. "Very well, I'll tell you what I'll do. I'll go to the guard's office at city hall. The chief, Martin Lebrecht, is a good man, and if anyone can help you, it would be him. As much as I'd like to, there's no more I can do."

He embraced his sister again, then ran down the street toward the city hall and disappeared around the corner.

Magdalena took a deep breath. Georg's idea seemed the right thing to do, she thought, and perhaps help would come in time for the poor fellow down at the river.

She was just about to run back to Jeremias and the children when she remembered what Georg had just said about her father. He'd just been there and evidently had another quarrel with Bartholomäus. Why couldn't the two of them get along? Jakob's taunting words directed at his brother had gotten meaner in recent days . . . and they needed Uncle Bartholomäus urgently in order to help Matheo. If the two brothers had a falling out, Bartholomäus would most likely refuse his help, if only out of defiance. Magdalena knew her father and how quick-tempered he could be. She absolutely had to stop him from doing something in anger that they would all regret later.

She thought it over briefly, then her decision was made. If she hurried, she might still catch up with her father and try to cool him down a bit. She'd leave the children in Jeremias's care for the time being, where they'd be well cared for.

With brisk steps she set out toward the Langgasser Gate, from which a muddy road full of puddles led into the fog-shrouded Bamberg Forest.

She hoped it was not yet too late.

Simon stood in the street in front of the Hauser's house, still perplexed at how quickly he'd been asked to leave. He heard the shouting and jeering coming from down by the river but paid it no heed. He was pondering instead what might have caused Hieronymus to usher him out so suddenly. Evidently, the scribe had remembered something — something to do with the many missing people. Perhaps Hieronymus had suddenly become nervous, or — Simon stopped short.

Perhaps there was something he needed to check out.

Simon decided to hide around the corner and wait awhile. And in fact, it wasn't long before the door to the scribe's house opened and Hieronymus Hauser stepped out into the street. The scribe looked distraught; he hadn't buttoned his overcoat and evidently had forgotten his hat. He panted and puffed as he hurried down the street, then soon turned right, where a steep stairway led up to the cathedral mount. Simon followed at a safe distance, occasionally pausing as the fat old man stopped to catch his breath.

Finally they had reached the cathedral square. Hieronymus

quickly crossed to the other side and hurried on toward the Old Residence, where Simon had been with Samuel early that morning. Now Hieronymus entered the building.

Simon hesitated briefly, then decided to take a chance. If Hieronymus discovered him, he could still say he'd left something behind in the council chamber. As soon as he slipped through the portal he bumped into a burly guardsman.

"What are you doing here?" the man growled, examining the little bathhouse owner up and down. "At present the Inquisition Committee is meeting to make a decision about additional suspects. That's strictly confidential. I didn't know you were invited."

"Ah . . . no," Simon replied. Then he pulled himself together and his voice became firmer. "As a consulting scholar, I sit on the Werewolf Commission, which you no doubt have heard of. That's strictly confidential as well," he added with a conspiratorial whisper.

"That may be so, but the committee in session now is the Inquisition Commission."

Simon cursed under his breath. The guard before him appeared just as stupid as he was obsequious, a dangerous mix. He decided to change his tactics.

"Well, I actually just need to speak with Master Hieronymus, the city scribe," he said with a friendly smile, and winked at him. "You know, the fat fellow. He just entered the room. Was he perhaps appointed to take minutes for this extremely important Inquisition Commission?"

The guard frowned. "No, he just went over to the bishop's archive." He pointed to a stairway behind him leading up to the next floor. "That way."

"Ah, the archives," Simon replied, pleased. "Then surely I may—" He was about to walk past, but the guard blocked his way with his halberd. "Only the scribe and the chancellor are permitted to enter the archive," he growled. "Do you have permission from the bishop?"

"Unfortunately not." Simon smiled innocently and raised his arms. "Well, then I'll just wait outside for Master Hauser. Have a wonderful, watchful day."

He went out into the street, where he finally could let out a loud curse. How he hated this guard who was so obsessed with the bureaucracy. People like him would be the downfall of civilization. Well, at least he'd found out that Hieronymus had some business to attend to in the bishop's archive. Did it have anything to do with their case?

Wrapped up in his thoughts, Simon strolled back across the cathedral square toward the executioner's house. He hoped Magdalena would be waiting there for him.

They had a lot to talk about.

IO

THE FOG THAT ENSHROUDED THE FORESTS AROUND
Bamberg every year at this time was lifting. Clouds drifted like
gigantic, ghostly sheets through the treetops, where the mois-
ture gathered on the red and yellow leaves and came trickling
down. Kuisl's boots splashed through the leaves and made a gurgling sound as they sank ankle-deep into the moss and decaying
foliage.

Unlike the last time, he'd decided to approach the knacker's
house from the rear. He had no idea what his brother might be
doing at this hour in the forest, but he didn't want to give him
any opportunity to avoid a conversation.

And, God knew, there was certainly a lot to talk about.

After Jakob had learned from Georg that Bartholomäus had
left for the knacker's house, he had immediately set out to find
him. In recent days, he'd grown more and more distrustful of his
younger brother. The notes in Lonitzer's herb almanac had been
the last straw. Was it possible Bartholomäus was making sleep
sponges to anesthetize the victims of the supposed werewolf?
The accusation sounded so appalling that at first Jakob thought
it out of the question. But then he remembered all the other

strange things that had occurred in the last week — the stranger he'd seen in the cloak and floppy hat near the furrier's house. He'd limped, and from a distance seemed vaguely familiar to Magdalena. Bartholomäus had always brushed off the werewolf stories, almost as if trying to discourage Jakob from looking into it any further. He was always wandering around the forest without any explanation, and his servant, Aloysius, also seemed to be hiding something. Twice already, Jakob had tried to approach the back of the knacker's house, and each time had been harshly rebuffed. Was something hidden there that he wasn't supposed to see?

Well, this time he wouldn't let himself be put off. He made a wide circle around the clearing and approached the house from the rear. He heard dogs barking happily nearby, as someone evidently had approached the front gate from the other side.

He cursed under his breath as he crept toward the sheds that were now visible between the trees. There was no wall or fence on this side, which was unnecessary in any case, as a dense thicket of prickly hawthorn bushes made passage impossible. When the hangman tried to squirm his way through, thorns reached out and tore at his clothes like long claws. After one or two paces, it was clear he wouldn't make it. He freed himself from the thorny branches and started walking alongside the bushes. Suddenly, he caught sight of a natural, knee-high tunnel in the bush, concealed under a covering of ferns and ivy. It looked like some animal had made its way through it just recently.

He crouched down on all fours and crawled through the bushes, cursing softly to himself as the thorns tore at his clothes. The sleeves of his shirt ripped open, thorny branches scratched him in the face, thistles clung to his beard, but finally he made it through to the other side.

When he stood up, he found himself behind one of the sheds at the rear of the cabin. The happy barking had stopped and he heard a low, angry growling close by.

It didn't come from the dog compound.

He looked around. A sickly sweet odor from a pit several paces away on his left almost made him throw up. He could see scraps of fur and bones lying beneath a cover of white lime, and a black cloud of flies buzzed over it.

The garbage pit. At least in this respect Aloysius had not been lying.

Holding his breath, Jakob turned to the two nearest sheds. One of them was nothing but a hastily nailed together shelter for storing wood. The other building was considerably larger, built of thick pine boards with a solid-looking door on the side and narrow slits at eye level around the exterior.

That was where the growling was coming from.

Kuisl approached the door warily. He could see fresh footprints in the mud leading from the blockhouse to the shed and beyond. It was evident that someone had been here just a few moments ago. The hangman saw a bolt with a rusty padlock, but on closer inspection realized the recent visitor had not closed it carefully and the bolt had not been slid over all the way.

Perhaps he intends to come right back.

The angry growling became louder, deep and threatening, almost like that of a bear. Kuisl removed the lock from the bolt, placed it carefully on the ground, then began to slowly push the bolt aside.

Something scratched at the door.

He paused, then opened the door a tiny crack. Even if it was dangerous, he simply had to see what was in there. It was quite possible this *something* was the answer to many of his questions.

Suddenly, he heard a sound behind him, and out of the corner of his eye saw a knotty cudgel coming at him. Instinctively he ducked, so that the blow hit him not on the back of the head but only on his shoulder. It came down with full force, however, so that it knocked him to the ground like a fallen tree, as mud and wet leaves splattered his face.

Before the stranger behind him could deliver a second blow, the hangman turned on his back and lifted his feet to kick his attacker. His eyes were covered with mud, but he could feel he'd scored a direct hit. His attacker groaned and fell over backward.

Kuisl wiped the mud from his face, blinked his eyes, and saw Aloysius lying in front of him, whimpering and clutching his groin. Alongside him lay the club he'd use to strike the hangman.

"You rotten bastard," Kuisl panted. "Just who the hell . . . ?"

"Watch out! The door!" shouted a voice.

At the same moment, Kuisl saw his brother Bartholomäus jump out from behind the shed. Though he had a limp, the Bamberg executioner was as fast as the devil. He threw himself against the door while something heavy pushed on it from inside, barking and growling loudly. The door opened a crack, and Kuisl saw a ghostly white body with two red, glowing eyes.

"Quick! Help me," Bartholomäus shouted.

Jakob scrambled to his feet and shook himself, as if trying to forget a bad dream, then pushed with all his weight against the door to close it. With a gasp of relief, his brother bolted and padlocked the door. The angry barking continued for a while, and the door and hinges shook, but they didn't give way. Finally, the only sound was a soft growling and the moaning of Aloysius, who had managed to get back onto his feet.

"What in the world was that?" Kuisl panted when he got his breath back.

"That?" Bartholomäus wiped the sweat from his forehead. "An alaunt, or, actually, two of them. If I hadn't gotten here in time, they would have torn you apart like a baby deer. That would have been a fitting punishment for your curiosity."

"An alaunt?" Kuisl tried to ignore the deep growling behind him. "What in God's name is an alaunt?"

"It's perhaps the most beautiful race of dog that God ever created. Strong, fearless, many with snow-white fur, the perfect hunting dog." Bartholomäus took a deep breath, and his tone of voice softened. "Unfortunately, they almost died out in recent centuries. A few are still said to be living today in the Spanish Pyrenees. The alaunts were once the war dogs of an ancient tribe and are the ancestors of most large hounds today, such as the powerful molossers and the mastiffs that we keep here for the bishop . . ." he said, pointing to the dog compound and beaming with pride. "But the alaunts are the strongest and largest of them, with a body the size of a calf. I've been able to raise a litter of the hounds." He looked lovingly toward the shed, where the growls turned to whimpers and happy barking. Evidently the dogs recognized their master's voice. "Brutus, Damian, and Cerberus. They are my pride and joy."

"You just said there were two dogs in there," Kuisl said in a soft voice. "Tell me . . . where is the third?"

Bartholomäus hesitated for a moment, then threw his hands up with a sigh. "Oh, what does it matter? Sooner or later you would have figured it out anyway. Yes, the third dog ran away — my dear Brutus, the largest of them. Aloysius left the door open briefly while he was feeding them, and the damn thing ran off through the hawthorn bush and was gone."

Jakob remembered the large white form he'd seen in the forest a few days before, and its strange growl — and the hair on the back of his neck stood on end.

"Are you telling me a beast like that is wandering through the forest out there killing animals and people only because my little brother has become a dog breeder?" he asked, trying to sound calm.

Bartholomäus rolled his eyes. "I know what you're going to say — that Brutus is this werewolf. That's what a lot of people would think if they knew about him. That's the reason I haven't told anyone and have been looking for him together with Aloysius. We've already gone as far as the river near where the hunt master lived, sticking our noses in all the caves and root holes.

He's got to be somewhere. Right, Aloysius? We'll find him, if not today, certainly very soon."

He turned to his servant, who meanwhile had drawn closer and was still holding his groin, his face contorted with pain. Aloysius nodded meekly.

"Believe me, Jakob," Bartholomäus pleaded. "Brutus has nothing to do with these horrible events. No doubt he's killed a few animals in the forest, and he might be dangerous to a person walking alone there, but remember—some of the victims were killed in the city, and their severed limbs were found in Bamberg. That can't have been Brutus. How would he have gotten into the city? Furthermore, he escaped only about a week ago, and these murders began much earlier. Believe me, he's somewhere here in the forest."

Jakob nodded hesitantly. It sounded like Bartholomäus was right. That would explain why both his brother and Aloysius had tried to keep him from looking behind the house, and why Aloysius had declared so emphatically that no one could steal the bishop's hunting dogs.

"I assume the bishop knows nothing about the dogs you are breeding?" he asked.

His brother nodded. "If Philipp Rieneck knew, he'd certainly take the three and lock them up in his menagerie along with the apes, peacocks, and parrots. The bishop loves rare animals, but in one of those miserable cages the poor animals would surely die. I know what I'm talking about. It's my job to clean out the cages and feed the animals. The bear is a mere shadow of his former self, and the old gray baboon is getting meaner every year because he has no companion to play with . . ." Bartholomäus pinched his lips, and there was a hint of suspicion in his eyes. "In fact, he seems to take as much interest in the animals in the menagerie as in his own hunting dogs. And certainly more than in the many missing people." Jakob had to wonder if his brother would ever feel as much love for Katharina or his future children as for his dogs.

"Why did you highlight the entry on sleep sponges in Lonitzer's herb almanac?" Jakob suddenly asked.

Bartholomäus looked at him in astonishment. "Why did I . . . ?" he started to say. He paused, then shook his head in disbelief and laughed. "Come now, Jakob. Don't tell me you really thought I drugged the young prostitute and then killed her. How could I have done that? After all, we were together when we found them. Please."

"Perhaps you didn't kill her," Jakob replied hesitantly, "but that doesn't mean you couldn't have prepared the sleep sponge. The prostitute smelled of henbane, and you know as well as I do it's often a hangman's job to prepare and use that poison to calm the condemned prisoner in his final hour. So tell me why you highlighted that entry."

"Good God, how suspicious you are, Jakob. I'm your brother. Have you forgotten?" Bartholomäus was working himself up into a fury. "But you were always like that. You don't trust anything I do, and always think the worst of me. Haven't you ever thought that I might have noticed that strange odor myself? I'm not as stupid as you think. I, too, wondered about that odor, and that's why I highlighted the entry. But no, you think right away I must be a murderer." Bartholomäus glared at him with hate-filled eyes. "You haven't changed at all, Jakob—always so impressed with yourself, always the cleverest guy in town. But it's all just for show, and behind it there's nothing but hollow words."

Jakob fell silent. He was convinced he'd made a mistake. In his distrust of his own brother he'd made up a mental image of Bartholomäus, a caricature that had nothing to do with reality. Jakob remembered how he'd pursued the stranger in front of the furrier's shop. He'd had the impression that the man had a limp, but he'd only noticed that *after* the man had jumped over to the other dock. Probably the stranger had just twisted his ankle then, and the fact that the man looked familiar to Magdalena was probably just a coincidence. Still, Jakob had suspected that the stranger was his brother.

Bartholomäus is right. I'm a fool, a damned fool.

Still, he couldn't bring himself to apologize; he opened his mouth, but not a sound came out. Then he said in a calm voice: "If you don't catch this beast soon, Bartholomäus, it's going to kill someone, if it hasn't done so already. It could be the cause for at least a few of the missing persons, the apothecary's wife, for example, who clearly got lost here in the woods." He looked at his brother calmly. "You should ask the civilian militia for help in the search."

"So they can kill Brutus and take Damian and Cerberus away from me? Never. Aloysius and I will find that naughty runaway, and then . . ."

"Good Lord in heaven, it's not a naughty runaway, it's a dangerous beast," Jakob interrupted angrily. "Can't you see that?"

"You're not going to tell me what to do." Bartholomäus was screaming now, and Aloysius carefully stepped to one side. "Maybe there was a time you could push me around, big brother," Bartholomäus continued in a rage, "but that time is long past. You're a coward. Georg has known that for a long time, and soon Magdalena and Barbara will know it, too."

Jakob swallowed hard and his face turned white. "So . . . so . . . you told him?"

Bartholomäus flashed a sardonic grin. "Of course. You can be sure his image of his father is badly tarnished. I've already told you Georg wants to stay here with me, and once Barbara has gotten over her infatuation with this young rogue, she'll probably consider staying herself. Especially when she hears what a traitor—"

"You . . . you rotten scum."

Without giving it another thought, Jakob charged at his

brother. They grabbed one another, fell to the ground, and wrestled, first one, then the other appearing to get the upper hand.

"I'll shut your filthy mouth," Jakob hissed. "I should have done that a long time ago."

He raised his fist to take a swing, but suddenly Bartholomäus squirmed out from under him like a slippery fish. He reached for the cudgel lying on the ground next to him and, like a madman, hit his brother as he lay on the ground.

"What's done is done!" Bartholomäus shouted. "And you can't undo it. Now the whole family is going to know."

"Like hell they will."

Jakob reached for the cudgel, ripped it out of his brother's hand, and flung it far away, almost hitting Aloysius. For a long time the servant had been anxiously watching the two combatants and hadn't moved. The two Kuisls fought now like two twelve-year-olds, rolling in the mud, spitting out leaves and dirt, and for a moment Jakob remembered how they used to fight then, forty years ago, in almost the same way.

Just before I left, he thought gloomily.

The fight was ending. Even after all those years, Jakob was still stronger, and Bartholomäus lay on the ground, beaten. Jakob clenched his fist, ready to bash him between the eyes, when suddenly a familiar high-pitched voice rang out.

"Stop at once! By God, if Mother knew you were fighting in the dirt with your own brother. Shame on you both, you foolish men."

It was Magdalena. She was standing alongside the dog shed, her arms crossed and her eyes ablaze.

She stared at the two grown men fighting with each other and didn't know whether to laugh or cry. Her father was over fifty, and his brother not much younger. The two were covered with mud and leaves, their clothing ripped, and despite their ages, they looked like two little kids. Alongside them, distraught, stood the pockmarked servant Aloysius. The whole scene was unintentionally comical, though Magdalena could see the blood lust in the eyes of both brothers and knew it was deadly serious and no joke.

Where does this hatred come from? she asked herself. *What happened between the two back then?*

Even though Magdalena had run after her father as fast as she could, she hadn't caught up with him until now. At some point along the way he must have left the road and made his way through the forest. In any case, there were no longer any footprints in the muddy road. And then, even before she'd reached the knacker's house, she'd heard the angry shouts and realized at once that there was a serious fight in progress. She ran across the clearing to find her father and uncle fighting like two mongrel dogs.

"Is this the way you settle an argument in the family?" she chided them angrily. "Just stop it, and start acting like grown-ups."

Her anger helped her drive away her fear. If her father beat up Bartholomäus, then the latter would hardly be willing to help them. Everything was just as she had feared.

"Father, you . . . you stupid ox," she shouted. "Just stop right now. If not for my sake, then at least for Barbara's."

This message got through. Jakob rolled off his brother and stood there groaning and wiping the bloody, dirty hair out of his eyes. His hat lay alongside him on the ground, beaten and ripped.

"This doesn't concern you," he growled. "This matter is between Bartholomäus and me."

"Oh, but it certainly does concern her," Bartholomäus hissed. Now, he, too had gotten up, swaying slightly, dragging his crippled leg behind him. "It's time she learned the truth."

Magdalena frowned. "About what?"

There was an embarrassing silence, and Jakob turned his eyes away from her. Finally he looked at Bartholomäus.

"Tell Aloysius to leave," he said.

Bartholomäus nodded and gestured to his servant. "Go and attend to the dead cow in front of the house," he said. "This is a family matter."

"But the dogs—" Aloysius started to say.

"Get out of here, I said!"

Silently, Aloysius withdrew, not without casting one last, anxious look at his master. Bartholomäus wiped the blood and snot from his beard, then cast a questioning glance at his brother.

"Shall I tell her, or do you want to?"

Jakob shrugged and finally took a seat on a nearby woodpile covered with fungi and took out his pipe. "Just go ahead," he grumbled. "Spit it out so you can have some peace of mind."

Bartholomäus took a deep breath and also sat down on a woodpile. He was visibly exhausted by the fight, and his hands were trembling.

"I'll now tell you the story of our family," he said to Magdalena. "The whole story, from the beginning. What do you know about your great-grandfather?"

Magdalena hesitated. "My great-grandfather? His name was Jörg Abriel. He was an executioner, like everyone in the family."

"He wasn't just any executioner," Bartholomäus corrected her. "He was the best and most famous executioner in the whole country. He would go with his family anywhere he was needed. He had a coach, horses, servants, and his reputation preceded him wherever he went. He was the one who broke the whole, notorious Pappenheimer family on the wheel in Munich, and impaled them, and in Schongau and Werdenfels he beheaded and burned more than a hundred women suspected of witchcraft in 1590. It was rumored that Jörg Abriel could recognize witches from a distance; he could smell them. Well, it's possible that was so . . ." Bartholomäus grinned and paused briefly before continuing. "After all, he was a witch—a warlock—himself."

Magdalena looked at him in disbelief. Many times, her father had told her and also her siblings about the notorious Jörg Abriel. But what Bartholomäus told them now was new to her.

"My great-grandfather was a . . . a warlock?" Magdalena asked. "What do you mean?"

"We don't know exactly, but his wife, that is your great-grandmother Euphrosina, dealt with magical elixirs and amulets. In addition, Jörg Abriel kept some magic books containing, it was said, all the magic sayings he had forced out of the witches when he tortured them. I saw those books myself when I was a child — bound in the finest calfskin and with silver fittings, a true feast for the eyes. They were considered the most valuable and truest books on magic that ever existed."

"Don't these books exist anymore, then?" Magdalena asked.

Bartholomäus shrugged regretfully, and his gaze darkened. "Unfortunately not. Your dear father burned them after he abandoned us, and only told me about it much later."

"Because they were the work of the devil," Kuisl interrupted. Up to that point he had remained silent, but now he could no longer restrain himself. "Written with the blood of a hundred innocent women. They disgusted me."

"They were our family's heritage," Bartholomäus snapped. "Even if you were the firstborn, you had no right to do that." He turned back to Magdalena. "Your father had a great responsibility thrust upon him at that time, but he failed. Our father was a good hangman until he started to drink." He stared blankly into space. "That happens to many hangmen tormented by their dreams. Some even go mad. Father couldn't stand it, either, and finally —"

"He was a failure and a drunk," Jakob interrupted. "And you've never understood that, Bartholomäus. He beat our mother black-and-blue, and us, too. Yes, I loved him and respected him, but then I saw him as he really was. I didn't want to become like him. Ever."

Bartholomäus nodded grimly. "And for that reason you put

your tail between your legs and just took off—not without first destroying the magic books, our family's heritage—and you simply abandoned us, your younger brother and sister. I was only twelve, Jakob, and Lisl just three, and when you left, Mother had a bad fever. Do you remember? She never recovered, but it wasn't her sickness that did her in, it was her grief. What were you thinking?" He lowered his voice and repeated, "What, in God's name, Jakob, were you thinking?"

Magdalena watched her father in silence, but he turned away and just stared at the ground. She knew that as a young man he'd given up his vocation as a hangman and gone off to war, but Jakob had never told them what had happened to his brother and sister. All she knew about Aunt Elisabeth was that she'd gone to live with a midwife after the death of her parents, then grew up with her brother Jakob when he returned from the war, and later went to Regensburg to live with a bathhouse owner. She hadn't heard about Bartholomäus until just a few years ago. Her father had put up a great wall of silence concerning his immediate family.

Now, for the first time, Magdalena understood why.

Suddenly, Bartholomäus got up from the woodpile and raised his right trouser leg. Magdalena could see an old, whitened scar starting at his ankle and running up his leg.

"Take a look at my leg, Jakob," he said. "Take a good look. This here is your doing. When you left me alone on the roof after Father's death, with all those bloodthirsty villagers . . . I jumped. I didn't make it to the other roof; I fell. Like a brick. My leg splintered, and the broken pieces stuck out like fish bones. The old bathhouse surgeon, that wheezing old bungler, sawed on it for a while and just made everything worse. Since then, I've been a cripple, Jakob. Because of you."

"Father," Magdalena asked hesitantly. "Is this true? Please talk to me. What happened then?"

Jakob cleared his throat, then slowly and haltingly began to speak.

"Your grandfather was a drunkard, Magdalena," he began. "Toward the end, it was impossible to put up with him. He beat us, he squandered the little money we had, and he bungled the executions. People in town grumbled and gossiped about the only descendent of the famous Jörg Abriel, who had been such a feared executioner." His grimace turned into a scornful smile. "Everybody hates us hangmen, but at least they respect us. No one had any respect for your grandfather, and when, for the third time, he turned the scaffold into a bloodbath, they stoned him to death, like a beast. Both Bartholomäus and I were there as helpers, and we were barely able to get away . . ."

"Damn it, Jakob!" Bartholomäus interrupted, "you were the older of us two. You knew how an execution was supposed to go. You should have helped Father. But no, you stood there like a pillar of salt. My big, beloved brother, the one I looked up to—you were so afraid you almost shit in your pants. And at the end you just left me behind in the dirt while the Berchtholdt brothers attacked me."

"There was no way out. When will you finally understand?" Kuisl paused, and when he continued, the words came gushing out. "Yes, I left you behind on the roof. I had to warn the others, Mother and Lisl. Old Berchtholdt and his people were already on the way to our house. The two were just able to hide in time. And if the court clerk—"

Bartholomäus interrupted him. "But it was a few weeks later that you abandoned us . . . all of us. You just took off." His voice was bitter.

"Because I was disgusted with you . . . with Father, the whole place. I didn't want to turn out like my father, nor my grandfather. Yes, I took the magic books along and burned them, and then I took off and went to war. Away from you, from the family, from our reputation that stuck to us like blood on our fingers. Damn it! I wasn't even fourteen."

"You abandoned us," Bartholomäus repeated in a trembling voice. "Can you imagine what it was like to live in a place as children of a dishonorable hangman who had been stoned to death? We were helpless and exposed every day to harassment and bullying. When Mother finally died of grief, little Lisl went to live with the midwife in Peiting, and later I traveled around doing odd jobs. They were hard years, Jakob, and not until I arrived here in Bamberg did I finally get a job as an executioner. I'd almost forgotten you." He broke out in a bitter laugh. "And then one day during the war you came by here. You'd done well; you were a sergeant then, a strong, robust fellow, and just as arrogant as before. I can't forget how you turned up your nose when you entered my stinking hangman's room."

"That's not true," Jakob mumbled.

"No doubt you thought we'd just shake hands and all would be forgotten," Bartholomäus continued, as if he hadn't heard his brother. "But it's not as simple as that. The whole time I hoped you had kept the magic books; I thought you'd taken them away and hidden them somewhere, but then you told me you'd burned them like so many dry leaves. I'll never forgive you for that, not for that and not for this, either," he said, pointing to his crippled leg. "Some wounds never heal, Jakob. Never."

"But you took Georg as your journeyman," Kuisl replied in a muted voice. "I thank you for that, Bartl, even if you cannot forget."

"Do you know what I always asked myself?" Bartholomäus said after a while. He pulled his trouser leg down again and sat down alongside his brother. "Why did you go back to being a hangman? Why did you come back to Schongau instead of staying with the troops? From everything I've heard, the Steingaden executioner did a good job standing in for you."

Jakob stared up into the treetops, as if he might find the answer there.

"I found the woman I loved," he said finally, "and war is an unending, bloody business, no place for small, crying children. I needed a place where I could stay and support my family." He looked at his brother sadly. "And the only thing we Kuisls ever learned was killing. We're masters at that. If people have to be killed, it should at least be done by people who can do it in the best and most painless way. That's what the war taught me."

Jakob took a deep breath. Now that it was all in the open, it was as if a great storm had finally passed.

"And Georg knows everything?" he asked.

"Everything." Bartholomäus nodded. "I told him last year. It seemed to shake him up a lot." Then he smiled. "Evidently it's in our blood that in our family we have to disappoint one another again and again."

A great stillness came over the clearing, and only from far off the sound of a cuckoo could be heard. Magdalena was silent, as well. Her father, who had always seemed so big and strong to her, now appeared very old and vulnerable. He sat on the woodpile, a cold pipe in his mouth, gray and stiff as a weathered tombstone. And at this moment she felt a love for him stronger than anything she'd every felt before.

"You . . . you have not disappointed me, Father," she said softly. "On the contrary. But it's good that . . ."

She cringed when she suddenly heard a deep growl from the shed just alongside her.

"For heaven's sake, what was that?" she asked anxiously.

Her father smiled wearily. "That's an alaunt, or rather two of them. Your uncle's pets." He sighed and began filling his pipe. "I'm afraid we'll have to put aside the old family matters at least for the time being. There's a whole lot of catching up to do."

· · ·

A while later, Magdalena was sitting between her father and her uncle on the wet woodpile, going over in her mind everything she had just heard. She kept looking at the shed, where growling and occasional scraping and scratching could be heard against the wooden wall.

"Well, at least we probably know now what the wild animal was that killed the stag Simon and the two boys discovered in the forest the day we arrived," she finally said. "Let's hope this animal wasn't responsible for killing a few people, as well. In any case it probably isn't the werewolf we're looking for."

Bartholomäus sighed. "I don't understand why Brutus didn't come back. He has everything he needs here." Ever since the conversation was no longer about the family, but only about his runaway dog and the werewolf, he had calmed down. It looked like the two Kuisl brothers had declared a truce, at least for the time being.

"I can do without your beloved pet for now," Kuisl responded grimly, puffing on his pipe, from which little clouds of smoke rose heavenward. "At the time I only had a glimpse of him, but that was enough for me. The beast is as big as a calf."

"Bigger," his brother grinned. "The three alaunts eat half a horse between them every day." Suddenly he paused and raised an eyebrow. "Ah, that's something that might interest you. A few wolf pelts were found in Matheo's possessions, weren't they?"

"And what about it?" Magdalena asked.

"Well, yesterday a whole bunch of pelts were stolen from the knacker's house—everything we'd made from a few weeks of slaughtering—hides of horses, cows, but also a stag, a few dog hides, and even an old bearskin full of holes."

"I knew it!" Jakob smacked his forehead. "It was that stranger hanging around the furrier's. That son of a bitch bought the wolf pelts and was using them in town. And when things got too hot for him, he hid the pelts in Matheo's room . . ."

"And he came here to the knacker's house to get new ones,"

Magdalena added. She nodded, thinking it over. "It certainly could have happened like that, but why did he do it, and above all, who was it? We don't have the vaguest idea about that." She sighed. "And as long as we don't have any culprit to present to the bishop, more people will have to die, and not just Matheo."

She briefly told her uncle and her father about the mob down at the river and the poor peddler who had probably already drowned.

"I'm afraid this is just the beginning," Magdalena concluded. "It will be just as it was in these witch trials. Then, too, there were hundreds of victims before things finally settled down. The executioner really had his hands full."

"If you think I'd dirty my hands with this, you're wrong," Bartholomäus chimed in angrily. "I know that the victims in these trials are usually innocent. That's nothing a hangman ever wants to do, even if he makes good money at it." He wiped his mouth nervously. "The previous Bamberg executioner went crazy—from guilt, it was said. He walked off into the forest and no one ever saw him again. I took his place, but only after it was all over." Bartholomäus looked at his brother and Magdalena, in despair. "Believe me, I wouldn't do that. Three times I've hanged convicted thieves, I've tortured a confession out of a man who robbed a church offering box, and broken an arsonist on the wheel—that I can do. But a wild-goose chase like this . . ." His voice failed him. "Well . . . I supposed I'd have to. Jakob, you know yourself what happens to hangmen who can't perform. They wind up swinging from a tree themselves."

Jakob nodded. "True, that's our job. People are always glad to find someone to do the dirty work for them."

"Then help us find the real culprit," Magdalena said to her uncle. "Perhaps we can still stop this madness."

Bartholomäus gave a despairing laugh. "Nobody can stop the madness—not once it has started. They have their first were-wolf—this Matheo—and you can be sure I'll torture a hair-raising confession out of him. The suffragan bishop will badger him and torment him until he turns into a real, howling werewolf."

"A real werewolf . . ." Jakob Kuisl took another deep drag on his pipe and sent a few smoke rings up into the autumn sky. His forehead was deeply furrowed, as always when he was thinking hard. "A real werewolf . . . Of course. We need a real werewolf," he murmured.

Magdalena looked at him, puzzled. "What are you saying?"

A small smoke ring pushed its way up through a larger one as Jakob's face broke out in a broad smile. "Yes, that might work," he finally said, mostly to himself.

"For God's sake, what are you talking about?" his brother scolded. "That's one thing I've always hated about you—this constant, arrogant secretiveness."

Magdalena sighed. Just like her uncle and Simon, too, she hated it when her father tortured her like this. "Now come on, spit it out," she demanded. "What are you going to do?"

"If we want this madness to stop, we've got to present a real werewolf to the people," he replied calmly. "Then they'll be happy, and the pursuit will perhaps come to an end."

"A *real* werewolf?" Magdalena stopped short. She'd hoped her father would find a way out, but now she was more confused than ever. "And who would that werewolf be?" she asked gruffly.

"Matheo."

"Matheo?" Magdalena shook her head in horror. "Have you lost your mind? People already think the poor fellow is the werewolf. Barbara will never come back to us if—"

"For God's sake, let me explain, you cheeky little tart," Kuisl replied angrily. "Yes, we'll rescue Matheo from the dungeon, but we'll make it look like he'd changed himself back into a werewolf, with fire and brimstone and thunder, and all of that. Matheo will disappear, and in the cell all that will remain is the wolf. A dead one, that is. The werewolf everyone was looking for died in the dungeon, killed by the incense and all the prayers.

And the hunt will be over." Grinning, he pointed behind him, where Aloysius was still busy flaying the dead cow. "Your servant trapped a few wolves in the forest just yesterday. One is enough for our little trick. It just has to be big." Kuisl looked around, waiting to hear what everyone thought. "Well, what do you think?"

Magdalena was at first too surprised to say anything. Her father's plan was so bold and absurd that her first thought was just to reject it, but then, slowly, she came around and seemed to like the idea.

Primarily because she couldn't think of anything better.

"It might work," she mumbled. "It's very risky, but it might work."

"Nonsense," Bartholomäus snapped. "People will never fall for anything like that. And even if they do, how do you intend to get the young man out of the dungeon, huh?"

"With your help," his brother replied.

Bartholomäus laughed. "With my help? I'm afraid you don't understand how hard that would be. I can't . . ."

"Do you have the key to the dungeon in Saint Thomas's Chapel — or not?" Jakob interrupted him curtly.

"Well, as the Bamberg executioner, I do have the keys to all the dungeons." Bartholomäus shrugged. "But you forget the guards. The dungeon is in the old courthouse, right next to the city council room, and it's teeming with guards."

"I know what might be a good time," Magdalena interrupted excitedly. "Tomorrow evening is this great competition between the two groups of actors in Geyerswörth Castle. Simon told me that on that day His Excellency the elector and bishop of Würzburg will be arriving with his entourage, and for that occasion, they'll need every available man in the castle. It's possible the dungeon up on the cathedral mount won't be so closely guarded then."

Bartholomäus waved his hand dismissively. "That only requires two or three guards. If you somehow get rid of them, you'll immediately arouse suspicion, and people will figure out that somebody came and freed Matheo. And I'll be the first one everybody suspects."

"Damn!" Magdalena kicked the woodpile. "Bartholomäus is right; that won't work."

"Oh, but it will. We have to just adjust the plan a bit . . ." Jakob knocked the pipe out and stuck it in the pocket of his ripped jacket. He thought for a while longer and finally continued, nodding happily. "The werewolf will at first overwhelm the guards as it flees, before finally dying in a fight with them. They have to believe they're fighting a real monster." He grinned. "Believe me, it's a story the silly guards will be telling their great-grand-children."

"Ah, and if I refuse to help you?" Bartholomäus suggested again. "What then?"

Kuisl shrugged. "Then Damian and Cerberus will no doubt spend the rest of their days in the bishop's menagerie alongside bad-tempered apes and half-starved bears. Yes, I'm afraid someone will tip off the authorities."

"That's . . . extortion," Bartholomäus muttered. "You're extorting your own brother."

"It's not extortion; I'm just making you do something for your own good. After all, I'm your big brother, and I can do that." The hangman stood up and slowly started walking back to the knacker's house. "Now let's go up front and let Aloysius find us a nice big werewolf. And it has to look terrifying. If I have to, I'll file down his teeth to make them even sharper myself."

Tormented by violent chills, the Bamberg suffragan bishop, Sebastian Harsee, lay in his bed and cursed the devil and all the archdemons for sending this fever at such an unfavorable time.

The fever had come on a few days before, and since then Harsee had felt dizzy and exhausted. His headaches were so severe, it felt like his brain was riddled with large needles, and he had completely lost his appetite. Until now, the illness could be relieved with infusions of hot linden blossom tea and iron self-discipline, but that morning something odd had happened. As Harsee was preparing to drink the freshly brewed tea, a horrible aversion had come over him. He forced himself to drink it, immediately threw it up again, and from that moment on his aversion to every liquid just increased. Actually, he should have just stayed in bed. Then he learned of the death of Gotzendörfer's widow and, bathed in sweat, had attended the meeting of the city council and later the inquisition committee. With his last ounce of strength, he'd finally dragged himself back to his room adjacent to St. Martin's Church, and since then had lain in bed shivering and with chattering teeth.

Sebastian Harsee clenched his fist and pounded the bedpost so hard that the pain at least made him forget his headache for a moment. He couldn't get sick now, not when everything was going his way. For half his life, he'd waited for this werewolf. The devil had finally come to Bamberg spreading fear, and fear was the glue that held this city together. Finally, his flock had gathered around their shepherd; finally they turned to the Lord God in their despair. With the help of this werewolf, Harsee would succeed in doing what had been denied to him and his followers almost forty years ago—to turn Bamberg into a City of God. And now, this accursed illness had confined him to his bed.

In addition, the bishop of Würzburg, Johann Philipp von Schönborn, an elector of the realm in person, had announced his arrival the next evening. Together with the Bamberg bishop, Schönborn would be attending this ridiculous competition between the two theater groups that His Stupid Excellency had naively thought up in order to impress his powerful neighbor.

Harsee shook his head angrily as a new wave of pain racked his body. It was finally time for him to take the reins of leadership firmly in hand in this city. His bishop was so enamored of

his menagerie—his monkeys, bears, peacocks—and all his
other useless pastimes, that it was quite possible he would soon
retire to his estate in the country and turn over the rule to the cathedral chapter. And Harsee had already softened up the cathedral chapter, gaining their trust. Finally, he, Sebastian Harsee,
the most devout servant in the vineyard of the Lord, would be
the man of the future—a powerful adversary of the depraved
worldliness spilling over from the neighboring bishopric of
Würzburg.

Harsee and Würzburg's Bishop Schönborn had for a long
time shared a deep aversion for each other. Unlike the Bamberg
suffragan bishop, Johann Philipp von Schönborn had always
been a vocal opponent of witch trials, which he had forbidden for
years in the Würzburg bishopric. Harsee was well aware that
Schönborn would do everything he could to limit Harsee's hard-
won influence, a project that was all the more threatening to
Harsee because Johann Philipp von Schönborn was not only the
Würzburg bishop but at the same time the bishop of Worms,
archbishop of Mainz, and, as elector and friend of the kaiser, one
of the mightiest men in the entire Reich.

Sebastian Harsee groaned and clenched his teeth as another
bout of shivering came over him. He had to be there, at all cost,
to stop this coward Schönborn from talking to Rieneck about the
werewolf trials. In the worst case scenario, Schönborn might
even talk the Bamberg bishop out of holding the trials. His whole
plan was in danger if he didn't recover soon. At least he'd been
able to prevent this miserable executioner's reception in the Wedding House. A hangman dancing with honorable citizens—that
contradicted the divine order and every sense of morality. It was
really high time to lead this city back on the right path.

There was a knock on the door, and an anxious servant entered, bowing and scraping.

"What is it?" Harsee asked crossly, dabbing the cold sweat
on his forehead.

"You . . . you asked for the bishop's physician, Your Excellency," the servant answered, looking down at the floor. "He has just arrived."

"Well, then, send in that Jewish quack doctor, so that he'll at least earn his exorbitant salary."

The servant disappeared, and Harsee licked his dry lips. He'd delayed a long time before calling Master Samuel. As a pious Christian, he couldn't stand the Jews, even though Samuel's family had converted long ago. In addition, Bishop Rieneck put blind trust in the doctor. Ever since the doctor had started treating the bishop's mistress for the French disease, His Excellency had become more and more attached to the quack. Harsee feared that Samuel would secretly give the bishop false advice; after all, the doctor was also an opponent of the werewolf trials. He should never have allowed him to serve on the committee.

And from the very outset he disliked the doctor's friend, this dubious little scholar whom he brought with him to the meetings. Who was he, anyway? Some sort of imposter? Well, as soon as he recovered, he'd make inquiries. Perhaps he could use this acquaintance to make a noose for the Jewish doctor.

There was another knock on the door, and Master Samuel entered with a shamelessly casual bow. He was carrying a large, worn leather bag.

"Your Excellency, you called me?" he asked, looking at Harsee with concern. "You didn't look well today at the council meeting. It appears you have a fever."

Harsee nodded, with visible impatience. "It doesn't take a doctor to see that," he mumbled. "I called for you so you could do something for me, and quickly. Can you?"

"That depends entirely on what's ailing you. Tell me exactly how you feel."

Annoyed, Harsee told the doctor about his stabbing headaches, vomiting, and dizziness. Master Samuel listened silently and finally opened his leather bag, which had dozens of little pockets and compartments. After looking around, he pulled out a long wooden stick.

"For heaven's sake, what is that?" Harsee mumbled. "A cooking spoon?"

"It's a tongue depressor, Your Excellency. I'd like to have a look at your throat, and that's why I need this instrument. Would you please open your mouth?"

With a shrug, the suffragan bishop let himself be examined. Master Samuel pressed his tongue down and seemed to put it all the way into the back of his throat.

"*Harrummff...*" Harsee croaked.

"Say again?" Samuel pulled the stick back out of the bishop's mouth.

"I said spare me this newfangled treatment," Harsee groaned. "If you'll bleed me properly, it'll get better."

Samuel frowned. "In your present condition, I'd strongly advise against that. You're already weak enough. A bleeding could kill you."

"Kill me? Ha!" Harsee shook his head, and again a stabbing pain passed over his forehead. "I just have a fever, that's all. If you can't bleed me, then find something else to do so I can get out of bed by tomorrow night at the latest. You know yourself that the bishop of Würzburg is coming to visit us, and I must be there."

"I'm sorry, Your Excellency, but the bishop will have to do without you," the doctor replied calmly. "Absolute rest is the only thing—"

"Damn it all! I-I order you to..." Sebastian Harsee tried to get out of bed, but his body was again racked by a spasm of pain. He fell back, groaning, and allowed Master Samuel to unbutton his shirt and place an odd-looking wooden horn against his chest. The doctor put his ear up to it and appeared to be concentrating intensely.

"What . . . what are you doing there?" the suffragan bishop gasped. "What sort of devilish instrument is that?"

"It's an instrument I invented to check a patient's heartbeat," the doctor answered as he put it back in his bag. "Yours is much too fast. You shouldn't get so excited."

Samuel was carefully palpating the patient's chest when, suddenly, he stopped.

"What's this?" he asked, pointing to a little scab on his patient's neck.

"Oh, that? Nothing important." Harsee waved him off. At that moment the spot began to itch badly again, and he scratched it hard. "Something probably bit me there. It just won't heal, that's all."

Samuel fetched another strange instrument from his magic bag, a large glass lens with a handle, and looked at the wound more closely.

"Do you know what kind of creature that might have been?" he asked.

"No idea." Suspiciously the suffragan bishop studied the lens. "Something must have bitten me during the night, perhaps a god-damned rat. Who cares?"

The doctor looked at him somberly. "There's a red circle around the wound. I don't like that at all. You should have put a bandage on it right away."

"If I need a bandage, I'll go to a bathhouse," Harsee growled. "I don't call the bishop's personal physician for that. Just tell me what to do about the fever and these damned headaches."

Samuel was still examining the wound and he appeared to be lost in his thoughts. Finally, he straightened up.

"Well, I'll brew a potion for you out of elderberries and thistles. That will lower the fever. In addition, I'll give you some willow bark for the headache." Samuel pulled out a little bottle of a brownish liquid. "I always have a little bark essence with me. I suggest you take a few spoonfuls right away dissolved in wine . . ."

The suffragan bishop demurred. "Put it on the table over there. I don't feel like drinking it right now."

Samuel looked at him with concern. "But you should drink a lot. That's important."

"I said I just don't want to," Harsee snapped. "The very sight of any liquid makes me sick to my stomach. So get that stuff out of my sight."

With a shrug, Samuel put the little bottle down on the table, then turned back to his patient.

"If you really want to get better, I can only advise you to drink a lot. And you absolutely must stay in bed the next few days. You are seriously ill, Your Excellency."

"Just let me worry about that." Harsee forced a grin; he had calmed down somewhat. "I assume the bishop also invited you to the play tomorrow evening, as the two of you understand each other so well . . ." he added smugly.

Samuel nodded. "Indeed he has, as well as my friend Simon Fronwieser. It's a great honor."

"Ah. You see? If something happens to me, there will be two capable doctors available. I'm as safe as in the bosom of Abraham."

Samuel sighed with resignation, then stood up and packed his bag.

"I can't order you to do anything," he said, shrugging. "Do what you think is right, Your Excellency. I just thought you wouldn't be especially interested in worldly theater plays, anyway."

"Believe me, the action that evening won't be just on the stage," the suffragan bishop replied dryly. "Politics is also involved, without any prepared text, and I want to be sure to be there and play my part." He winked, but what he'd said sounded like an order. "And now, farewell. I'll wait for my medicines, and until then I have no need for you here, Jew."

Master Samuel seemed to flinch on hearing the final words but excused himself silently with a stiff bow. Sebastian Harsee waited for the door to close, then let out a long, loud moan. His headache was killing him.

Absent-mindedly he scratched the scab on his neck until he felt the blood on his fingertips.

At least the itching took his mind off the fever.

"A runaway dog?"

Simon looked at Magdalena, astonished. Night was falling, but his wife and the two Kuisl brothers had returned to the executioner's house only a few minutes before. Young Georg had been there for a while already and was chatting with the young medicus. Simon had also learned from him what had happened down by the river. Georg had finally been able to alert the guards in city hall, and the unfortunate peddler was saved at the last moment. He was now sitting in the city dungeon awaiting his fate.

Actually, Simon had intended to tell the others about his strange encounter with Hieronymus Hauser, but what Magdalena told him now sounded so peculiar that he kept his own story to himself for the moment.

"I never believed that Bartholomäus had anything to do with this sleep sponge," he said, casting a sympathetic glance at the Bamberg executioner, who was sitting with folded arms at the far end of the table. "Well, at least we know now what killed the stag we discovered in the Bamberg Forest as we were coming to town, and also why some people say they've seen a monster out there." He shook his head. "It was just a dog."

Magdalena smiled grimly. "Believe me, you can't think of it as just an ordinary dog. It's more like a—" she started to say, when her father interrupted her rudely.

"It's a monster of a beast," he growled, "as large as a calf and with long teeth. Even if it isn't the werewolf we're looking for, it's still some sort of monster."

"You don't know Brutus," Bartholomäus objected. "I raised him since he was a little pup. He wouldn't do anything to hurt you; he's just playing."

"Damn it, that's the last straw." Jakob pounded the table with his fist and glared at his brother. "Your beloved Brutus probably killed two people, Bartl. If we didn't have so many other problems now, I'd report you to the authorities."

"You'd turn in your own brother?" he snarled. "That would be just like you."

"That doesn't have anything to do with snitching, you simpleton. We have to protect people from this beast. Now just shut your mouth before I do it for you."

Simon sighed softly as he looked at the two brothers. Just a while ago it seemed they'd get along with each other. Magdalena had suggested they were on speaking terms again after their discussion of things that had happened a long time ago. But evidently their enmity ran too deep.

"You mentioned before that there was a way we could help Matheo and Barbara," said Simon, turning to his father-in-law to try to put an end to the awkward topic. "What was your plan?"

"Bah! That's no plan; it's a suicide mission," Bartholomäus scoffed. Then he turned silent and leaned back on the bench, sulking.

Jakob cleared his throat, then briefly explained what he wanted to do. Simon and Georg listened silently while cold sweat poured down Simon's back.

"You mean we'll just pretend we've caught a werewolf?" Simon shook his head in disbelief. "Do you really think you can get away with that?"

"No, of course it's not going to work," Kuisl growled, "because every damn one of you is so chicken-hearted. God, if during the war, I had—"

"Let's not get started about the war again, Father," Magdalena interrupted. Then she turned to the family, trying to calm them down. "I know the plan sounds absurd at first, but it might succeed for just that reason. If we all work together."

Simon frowned. "The bishop has invited me to the performance tonight. This Sebastian Harsee is a very distrustful man; he always looks at me with suspicion. If I don't go—"

"Just stop worrying, you sissy. I have another job for you," his father-in-law interrupted, "one where you won't trip over your own feet or get any dirt on your fine clothes. You're a friend of this Jewish quack, aren't you? We need a few ingredients from him that Bartl doesn't have in the house—poppy seed oil, mandrake, henbane, and hemlock."

Simon stopped short. "Henbane and hemlock? But they're all—"

"Ingredients for a sleep sponge, right," Kuisl nodded. "If the werewolf can use them, so can we. That way, we'll get rid of the guards. The stuff isn't very reliable. The men will just be dazed, and not for very long. Everything that happens will seem like a dream to them." The hangman flashed a mischievous smile. "And let's make sure it's a real nightmare." He turned to his son. "Georg, you go over to the furrier's and see if you can get some cheap furs and skins."

"Furs and skins, right." Georg nodded hesitantly. "But why . . . ?"

"Don't you get it?" Magdalena said, looking around impatiently. "Father and Uncle Bartholomäus are going to dress up like monsters so the guards will think a real werewolf is attacking them. Later, when they wake up, a large, dead wolf will be lying next to them. They'll think it's the real werewolf that had attacked them before."

"And where are we going to find this wolf?" Simon wondered.

Magdalena pointed toward the door. "In the shed next door.

A real beast that Aloysius caught in one of his traps. Rigor mortis will have set in already, but in their excitement the guards will never notice." She winked at her uncle. "After all, they'd just been attacked by a ferocious werewolf."

"Hold on just a moment." Bartholomäus bent over the table with a threatening look in his eye. "Maybe I'll give you the key to the dungeon, fine, but there's no way I'm going to wrap myself up in a stinking animal hide."

"Think of your darling little pet," Jakob said in a grim tone. "You want to keep her, don't you? So help us. It's as simple as that."

"Just stop this." Magdalena looked at her father angrily, then turned to Bartholomäus in a conciliatory tone. "You're doing it for Barbara. She is your niece, after all. Besides, you've said yourself you don't want this werewolf trial. If we can present people with a dead werewolf, perhaps we can still stop this madness. Katharina would surely want the same thing."

"Keep Katharina out of this. It's bad enough that you bring me into it." Bartholomäus bit his lip and seemed to be struggling with himself. "Very well," he finally said. "I'll do it. But if anything goes wrong—"

"It's not your fault," his brother interrupted. "Understood." He turned around to Simon. "Do you think you can talk your Jewish friend into giving us a few more ingredients?"

Simon thought for a moment. "It depends. What were you thinking of?"

"Brimstone, charcoal, and saltpeter." Kuisl grinned again. Despite his age he sometimes seemed to Simon like a kid thinking up new tricks.

"All three ingredients are used separately as medications," the hangman explained, with visible satisfaction, "but together they make up the most devilish stuff man has ever thought up: gunpowder. At the end, we want to give our werewolf a send-off that all of Bamberg will be talking about, don't we?" He clapped his hands. "We don't want to cover anything up. Besides, sulfur stinks so much, they'll think the beast came straight from hell. Matheo will get out of the dungeon, and no one will suspect my brother of having opened the door."

Magdalena nodded. "So this is the way we're going to distribute the work: Simon will get the necessary ingredients today from Doctor Samuel; Georg will go to the furrier for the furs and hides; and tomorrow night, Father, Uncle Bartholomäus, and I will sneak down to the dungeon in the old courthouse."

Simon looked at his wife, confused. "Why you? I thought . . ."

"At first I wasn't especially crazy about the idea, myself," Kuisl interrupted, "but Magdalena convinced me that she could perhaps distract some of the guards. We don't know how many there are. If there are only two or three of them, Bartholomäus and I can manage, but if there are more, we'll have a problem."

"Damn! If something goes wrong, you'll all be hanged as heretics and devil worshipers," Simon groaned. "Do you all realize that?"

"I think they'd rather break us on the wheel and cut our guts out," Jakob replied. "That's what they used to do in Schongau. What do you think, Bartholomäus?"

His brother nodded. "They could also boil us in oil, which is what they sometimes do with warlocks and counterfeiters, but to do that they need a competent hangman. It will be hard to find one so quickly. Perhaps the Nuremberg executioner?"

"Just stop that," Simon groaned. "That . . . that's dreadful." He turned to his wife. "Magdalena, I won't allow you to be part of this madness."

But Magdalena just shrugged and turned away. "Oh, come, Simon. We've survived all sorts of adventures together. And besides, you forget that most of the guards will probably be down at Geyerswörth Castle. Nothing will happen."

Simon closed his eyes and rubbed his temples. Why did he have to have married such a stubborn, rebellious woman?

I can only hope that our sons turn out a bit more like me. But at least in Paul's case, I already have my doubts. He shuddered.

In the excitement he'd completely forgotten to inquire about the children. "And where are Peter and Paul?" he asked, frowning. "They're not at Katharina's house. She's there with her father, crying her eyes out."

Magdalena squeezed his hand. "Don't worry, they're being well cared for. The old tavern keeper over at the Wild Man is keeping an eye on them and telling them exciting stories. I looked in on them a while ago, and they're fine. I just thought it would be better for us to have a good talk and not be distracted." She looked over at her younger brother and smiled. "But as soon as Georg gets back from the furrier's, he'll be a good uncle and care for them. Won't you?"

Georg folded his arms in front of his chest and jutted his chin forward. "Hey, that wasn't what we agreed on. Magdalena gets to go along with Father and Uncle Bartholomäus to free Matheo, and I'm supposed to stay home caring for the kids and singing lullabies? That's not fair."

"Damn it, Georg. You're only fifteen," Kuisl growled. "It's bad enough that Magdalena is involved in it. You'll stay here, and that's my last word."

Georg was going to object, but when he saw the severe look on his father's face, he kept quiet. After a moment's silence, Bartholomäus cleared his throat.

"There's something else I've got to tell you," he began cautiously. "Before I started out for the Bamberg Forest this noon, I was down at the river. I spoke with the rag picker, Answin, on account of the filth in the moat. Answin also has the job of making sure the Regnitz stays more or less clean, so I thought he could help me to clean the moat, too."

"And?" Kuisl asked harshly.

"Well, this morning Answin fished another body out of the water. I only got a brief look at it, and it's in bad shape, but I think it's Thadäus Vasold — you know, the missing council-man."

"Damn!" Jakob jumped to his feet. "Why didn't you say that before? We must have a look at the body. Every victim has something to tell us about the murderer. Now Answin has probably taken it to the guard's office in city hall."

Bartholomäus shrugged. "Not necessarily. Sometimes he keeps the body, especially if it is in such bad condition as Vasold is, and the guards come to him and inspect the corpse there before it's buried."

"Then let's pay a visit to Answin as soon as we can, before it gets dark." Kuisl was already halfway out the door. "I don't think we'll be allowed to examine the corpse, as we did the last time, if it's already in the hands of the guards," he said, rubbing his huge nose. "And I'm convinced this dead man has a story or two to tell us."

Without another word, he disappeared into the street.

A short while later, Simon and Magdalena were sitting alone at the table. Bartholomäus had followed Jakob down to the river, and after sulking awhile, Georg had started on his way to the furrier's. On his way back, he'd pick up the two boys in the Wild Man. For the first time in a long while, Simon was sitting together undisturbed with Magdalena: there were no whining children and no grumbling father-in-law to constantly tell him what to do.

The sweet smell of resin came from a few logs crackling on the fireplace, and Simon suddenly noticed how hungry he was. He'd had nothing to eat that day except for a skimpy breakfast before the council meeting. He walked over to the stove, cut off a few slices of smoked sausage hanging from the chimney hood, put them onto two plates along with some bread, then pushed one plate down the table to Magdalena, who immediately started eating.

For a while they ate silently while Simon tried to gather his thoughts. There was so much to discuss that he hardly knew where to begin. Magdalena was still firmly determined to stay for the wedding that had been postponed indefinitely. Perhaps now, however, everything would happen much faster than they'd expected. Once Matheo was free, there would be no reason for Barbara to hide from her father, and perhaps they could soon leave for home.

But it's also possible we'll be branded as witches and conjurers of werewolves, then quartered, and boiled in oil.

Suddenly, he lost his appetite. He poured a cup of diluted wine for his wife and himself, then took Magdalena's hand. "Are you really sure you want to go through with this?" he asked. "If something goes wrong tomorrow night . . ."

"Nothing will go wrong," Magdalena snapped, and pulled her hand away. "Besides, a family always has to stick together, no matter how tough things get. That's something you'll have to learn if you want to become a real Kuisl." She gave him a wan smile. "I'm especially happy that Father and Uncle Bartholomäus will work together to get this poor fellow out of the dungeon. Perhaps that will help, finally, to end their hostility."

"You dropped a few hints before," he said. "Did you finally learn what came between the two of them long ago?"

Magdalena nodded gloomily. "Oh, yes, I know. Perhaps I even know more than I want to."

Hesitantly, she told Simon about the death of her drunken grandfather and her father's sudden flight from Schongau.

"And he simply left Bartholomäus and little Elisabeth behind, all by themselves?" He frowned. "Just what was he thinking?"

"He was still just a boy, Simon. And he didn't want to become an executioner. I can understand what he did," she said with a dark face. "I had the impression that Uncle Bartholomäus was bothered even more by something else . . . something to do with our family, with my great-grandfather's legacy."

"What sort of legacy?" he asked, surprised. "I've never heard anything about that."

But Magdalena just shook her head. "I'll tell you about that some other time. It's . . . a family matter." She hesitated, then nodded with determination. "Most of all, I'm glad we've put all this madness behind us." Then she looked at him with curiosity. "But you haven't told me anything yet about what happened this morning in the council meeting."

Simon sighed and shrugged. "Actually, nothing of importance, except that the suffragan bishop evidently has some sort of fever coming on. Also, they've offered a reward to anyone who can provide a tip about other suspects. You can imagine how many werewolves we'll have in Bamberg before long." He took a sip from his cup, then paused. "But after that, something really strange happened. It has to do with Bartholomäus's future father-in-law. That's why I didn't want to talk about it before, when your uncle was here. Perhaps he would have gotten angry and refused to help us."

In a low voice he told Magdalena about his visit to the Hausers, his conversation with Hieronymus, and the latter's strange behavior.

"He went straight over to the old courthouse, and from there probably right to the bishop's archive," he said finally.

"The bishop's archive?" She stopped to think. "What do you think he was looking for there?"

"Well, it's possible it didn't have anything to do with us. But perhaps it did. Who knows. But it appears he was going to check something in the records."

"Do you think we could find out what that was?" she asked.

Simon laughed, at a loss. "I'm afraid that would be hard to do. If the archive is as large as I think, there are thousands of files there. It would be like finding the proverbial needle in a hay-stack." He shook his head. "Hieronymus would have to tell us himself, and he probably won't do that."

He pushed the cup aside with a sigh and stood up. "It's time for me to pay a visit to Samuel and ask him for the necessary ingredients for your cloak-and-dagger operation." One last time, he gave Magdalena an earnest look. "And then let's all pray this hocus-pocus doesn't send us all to an early grave."

"Damn it all, won't you wait?" Jakob heard the voice of his brother behind him and the typical scraping sound as Bartholomäus dragged his crippled leg through the mud.

Jakob stopped and turned around. "Have you decided to come along after all?" he asked crossly.

"You ... you don't know Answin," Bartholomäus gasped, completely out of breath, as he caught up with his brother. "If I'm not there with you, he won't tell you a damn thing."

"I'd make him talk," Jakob grumbled, as he stomped ahead through the narrow lanes that were already in the shadows on this autumn afternoon. Despite his grumpy reply, Jakob was basically glad that Bartholomäus was coming along, not only because he really did have a better chance of learning something from the rag picker if his brother came with him, but also because he still felt rather moved by his earlier confession in the forest. As young children, he and Bartholomäus had played together a lot; they'd practiced beheadings using carrots hung on strings, they'd run through the forest with wooden swords and had watched when their father took down the huge executioner's sword and polished it on a large grindstone with a leather strap. Jakob had never loved his younger brother — they were too different — but there was still a bond between them, even now, after all the years. Their fight in the forest had shown Jakob once again that one can't run away from his own family.

You take them in, wherever you are . . .

Since those days, he'd visited Bartholomäus only once in Bamberg. That was during the Great War, when Jakob was a sergeant under General Tilly. He'd learned by chance that a certain Bartholomäus Kuisl was the executioner in Bamberg, and since the army was passing by near the city, he wanted to make sure that this Bartholomäus was actually his brother. Their conversation was short and gruff, because Jakob had expected something like an absolution for running away, but there was no forgiveness, and he felt his younger brother had cut the ties with him.

But that wasn't the main reason their parting had been unamicable. It all went back to their grandfather, Jörg Abriel, the most famous and most feared of all the hangmen in the German Reich.

Jakob had told Bartholomäus that he'd burned Abriel's magic books shortly after he left, without knowing how much these books had meant to his brother. Bartholomäus had reacted with horror and revulsion on hearing that Jakob had simply consigned the family's most valuable heritage to the flames.

What Jakob had really done with them, Bartholomäus would never know, as Jakob had sworn to take that secret with him to the grave.

Bartholomäus had never forgiven his older brother for the destruction of their heritage, and ever since then, Jakob had looked down condescendingly on his younger brother, who was earning good money in Bamberg, but cared little for the wisdom and logic of medicine. Instead of that, he had decided to seek salvation in ancient grimoires, or books of black magic.

They parted ways, but then Jakob had become a hangman himself, and out of necessity sent his son Georg to serve Bartholomäus as an apprentice. Suddenly he himself couldn't tell right from wrong.

"When we're with Answin, I'll let you do the talking," Bartholomäus said, putting an end to Jakob's dark musings. "He's a little peculiar. It must have something to do with his job."

"The man is a rag picker," Jakob replied. "What's so peculiar about that?"

"Well, you have to understand that Answin doesn't just collect rags. The Regnitz washes all kinds of filth ashore, which he has to fish out. A lot of things get stuck in the mill wheels and weirs that otherwise would have settled to the bottom of the river and disappeared forever." His face darkened as they walked through the busy alleys. "Every year there are at least a dozen corpses among them — people who've suffered some tragedy and jumped in the river, some suicides, and often people who have been robbed and murdered. The city guards go to visit Answin regularly. He's not just a rag picker, but a corpse fisher, and he makes good money doing it."

Jakob frowned. "How does he do that?"

His brother stopped and pointed down at the river that wound its way between some warehouses and markets like a black stinking ribbon. Behind it was the cathedral mount and the other hills.

"Often, the victim's relatives are looking desperately for the corpse in order to give it a decent burial," he explained. "Answin is their last hope. For each corpse he fishes out he demands three guilders, and rich people pay even more. He's fair, even with his corpses."

By now they'd reached the bend in the river that separated the old and the new parts of the city. The city hall lay nearby on the right, and on the left were the piers and jetties, with boats tied up and bobbing in the current in the last light of day. Jakob remembered leaving the knacker's wagon there almost a week ago when he and Bartholomäus were on their way to city hall. Two rowboats sat on jacks in an open shed near the piers. Alongside one of them, a filthy-looking man with matted, flaming red hair was applying caulk to some holes in the hull with a spatula.

"Good day, Answin," Bartholomäus said.

The rag picker raised his head, and Jakob could see he was blind in one eye, with black scabs covering the encrusted tissue. With his good eye he regarded the two suspiciously.

"Who's the guy with you?" he asked cautiously. "I've never seen him before."

"My brother, who's come all the way from Schongau. He's here for the wedding."

Answin grinned. "For the reception that is probably not going to happen, according to everything I hear. Too bad; I would have fished a few nice clothes out of the river for myself."

"So you can come to my party stinking like an old catfish?" Bartholomäus laughed. "Perhaps it's just as well it will probably be a smaller group." Then he turned serious. "But I'm not here to make small talk with you. I came to ask about the corpse you found in the river. Is it still here?"

"That councilor?" Answin nodded. "Of course. He's not going to run away."

Now that Jakob was standing right next to him, he noticed the rag picker had an old, familiar smell about him — not very strong, but nonetheless overlaying everything.

The smell of rotting corpses.

"I informed the city guards some time ago, but so far no one has taken the trouble to stop by," he said. "Apparently they've got their hands full. Chief Lebrecht has looked pretty damned upset recently. I'd like to know what his problem is. Well, whatever . . ." He snorted. "Just this noon, a few guys tried to drown some poor fellow over in the harbor, and now the guards are checking a few tips they got concerning this damned werewolf." The rag picker lowered his voice and looked around carefully with his one eye. "The whole city is one huge hornet's nest. If this doesn't stop, I'll have a lot more corpses to fish out of the river."

"Can we have a look at him?" Bartholomäus asked.

"Sure, sure." Answin put the bucket of caulk down on the

floor and walked down to the river. "He hasn't gotten any better, though. If the guards don't come soon, he'll start falling apart."

They followed him to the shore, where a dock led out into the water, then walked over moldy, rotten planks to a place where there was a sort of wooden tub alongside the dock, hammered together out of rough boards. Something in it was bobbing up and down, and Jakob at first took it to be a bunch of rags. He had to look twice before realizing it was a corpse floating face-down. The body was clothed in a wet black overcoat that was moving slowly back and forth in the water.

"I use this tub for keeping eels and sometimes a dead body," Answin explained. "Both of them keep better in cold water. Why are you interested in this corpse, anyway?"

"Oh, that's a long story, Answin," said Bartholomäus, winking at him. "I'll tell you some other time, who knows, perhaps over some fine pastry at our wedding reception, if we ever have one."

"Mmm, pastry, delicious. I like it most of all with lingonberries." The rag picker licked his lips. The sight of the corpse and the foul stench rising from the tub despite the cool river water seemed not to trouble him. He looked at Jakob curiously as he climbed down a slippery ladder to the tub and tugged at the corpse's overcoat until it finally turned over on its back. Cold eyes, like those of a dead fish, stared up at the hangman.

Jakob cringed. The dead man was at least seventy years old, his gray hair curled in the water like seaweed, and the skin was white and bloated. His trousers, jacket, and shirt were in shreds, his right hand was missing, and Kuisl could see that the fish and crabs had already started nibbling on the body. But that wasn't what horrified him so much.

It was the signs of torture visible all over the body.

He couldn't help but think of the woman's leg he had examined in the guard station that had also showed evidence of torture. Bartholomäus, standing on the dock alongside him, seemed also to have noticed the wounds. He gasped, sucking the air in through his teeth.

"Good Lord, all kinds of torture were used on this person," he said, nodding partly in disgust and partly in recognition. "His fingernails were pulled out, there are burn marks on his legs, an arm wrenched out. Whoever did this knew how to inflict pain. Do you think they chopped his hand off while he was still alive?"

Answin laughed softly. "I have to admit, at first I thought you were the one who did it," he said, turning to Bartholomäus. "It looks a hell of a lot like the work of an executioner, and the only one I know is you."

"The work of an executioner, indeed . . ." It was the first time Jakob had spoken. Carefully, he unbuttoned the dead man's shirt, trying not to think about the sickly sweet, fishy odor.

"It's hard to say how long he's been in the water," he mumbled, thinking it over. "But judging from the decomposition, it can't have been very long. I can't find any clear cause of death. It's possible he simply died as a result of the torture." Carefully, he began removing the man's overcoat. The shirt underneath was in shreds.

"Look at this," Bartholomäus said suddenly, pointing to the dead man. "The welts on his back. They come from a leather whip, without question. People call that 'the Bamberg torture,' because it's mainly used here." He shrugged. "I myself prefer to hang the bastards up by their wrists, tie stones to their feet, then hoist them up. That's the old way."

"So our werewolf is a real expert," Jakob said softly. "Where do you think he learned that?"

"Well, in any case, he had a lot of practice," Bartholomäus replied. "If this madman is responsible for all the missing and the dead, this here would be his seventh victim. How many are yet to follow?"

Jakob turned away from the horribly mangled corpse and looked at Answin.

"Exactly where did you find the corpse?" he asked.

The rag picker scratched his nose. "This one got tangled in the water wheel of a paper mill." He pointed to the north. "You know, the mill on the right branch of the Regnitz, not far from Saint Gangolf, outside the city walls."

"Aha! I thought it had come ashore here on the left branch of the river," Bartholomäus chimed in.

"No, it didn't, and it surprised me, too, because most of the corpses have been found on the left branch, where there are far more mills for them to get caught in."

"Hmm." Jakob frowned. "That means the perpetrator dumped the body outside the city, somewhere along the right branch of the river. But why did he do that? After all, according to the servant, Thadäus Vasold was attacked by the werewolf in the middle of town. That's what Simon told me. So, this monster took him out of Bamberg. Why?"

Again, Jakob turned to the rag picker. "Didn't you find any other parts of the corpse in the water?"

Answin shook his head. "Only a leg and an arm. The second leg was lying in a huge pile of garbage near the river. Children found it while they were playing."

"If it was so near the river, it's possible it was in the water earlier and some dog picked it up and took it there." Kuisl ground his teeth, thinking. "Where did you find the arm and the leg?"

Answin pointed to the north again, to the right branch of the river. "They were entangled in the pillars of the bridge. There are a few shallow places and islands in the middle of the river, where it's easy for things to get hung up. I told the guards right away." He picked at his teeth, looking bored. "But there wasn't much to see; clearly, animals had been chewing on them, and one arm and a hand had been ripped off, probably by wolves or who knows what."

Jakob poked at the corpse one last time, and it turned around slowly in the water, then he climbed up the ladder again to the pier.

"First, a few body parts, and now a whole corpse," he said when he got back up on the dock, "and all of them found in the right branch of the river. Somebody must have disposed of them there, then the fish and other animals did the rest." He nodded, still lost in his thoughts. "I myself have also fished people out of the Lech who committed suicide. If they get tangled in the weirs or are found by wild animals, it can easily happen that only parts of these poor souls are ever found. There's nothing magical about that."

"You're forgetting the victim's hand." Bartholomäus pointed down at the corpse again. "I've heard that was found in front of widow Gotzendörfer's house, so clearly the hand didn't come from the water. And didn't you find an arm in Bamberg Forest when you were coming to town?"

"That was on the bank of a smaller river. The whole area there is crisscrossed by brooks and rivers, as far as I can see, so it's possible the arm was dumped somewhere else and drifted there."

"And Vasold's hand in front of widow Gotzendörfer's house?"

Jakob spat into the dark water. "If you ask me, somebody intentionally put it there to cause a panic. And they succeeded."

Bartholomäus frowned. "But who would do anything like that? And why?" He kicked a rotted post. "Damn it, this all reminds me of the witch trials back then. I didn't arrive here until just after the old hangman's sudden disappearance, but according to what I heard, everybody was afraid, just like now."

"Just like now . . ." Kuisl stared into the distance with a furrowed brow. "Just like now," he repeated.

He was about to say something else, when the sound of marching feet could be heard coming down one of the side streets, and moments later about a half dozen city guards appeared. At the head of the group was the commander of the guard, Martin Lebrecht, who looked even more bleary-eyed than the last time they'd met in the guard station. When he recognized the two hangmen, he stopped, surprised, and removed his helmet.

"Master Bartholomäus," he said with annoyance. "What are you doing here?"

"Ah, I was just about to ask Answin if he could help me and my brother clean the moat," he replied, a bit awkwardly. "And now he's shown me his latest find." He pointed at the corpse behind him. "You'll be sad to learn that it's the body of city councilor Thadäus Vasold. He's clearly recognizable."

"Damn. As if I didn't already have enough to do." The sergeant closed his eyes briefly, as if struggling to get hold of himself. "Answin already suggested to me that might be the case, and I must admit I suspected we would eventually find Vasold's corpse—especially since his hand was found early this morning."

"I thought you would've come a lot sooner," grumbled Answin, who was leaning against a post on the dock some distance away. "I've been waiting for you all day. Evidently the discovery of a city councilor's corpse doesn't mean much to you."

Martin Lebrecht sighed. "Believe me, Answin, I would have come earlier, but all hell has broken loose out in town. Ever since the suffragan bishop offered a reward for any tips, we're swamped with accusations. I'm just coming back from the home of old Ganswiener up on the Kaulberg who swears that his neighbor turns into a hairy monster every night and barks like a wolf. It just so happens that Ganswiener has had an eye on his neighbor's property for years." The sergeant groaned loudly. "He's a damn liar, but just try to prove it. If I don't take his report, he'll run straight to the suffragan bishop, and in the end they'll say I'm a werewolf, too. And then tomorrow," he continued with a desperate laugh, "His Excellency and the elector the bishop of Würzburg will be arriving, and I've got to reassign the guards, so there will be no mishaps. Aside from all that, I've got to—" He stopped short, then shook his head in frustration. "In a word, I really don't know whether I'm coming or going."

He looked at the two hangmen, trying to think. "But since the two of you are already here, can you at least say what killed old Vasold? His servant swears to God he was attacked by a werewolf, but perhaps the old man just fell in the river and drowned after a night of carousing."

"I hardly think so," replied Jakob with a grim smile. "From the looks of him, he might have been attacked by a half dozen werewolves."

Martin Lebrecht turned as white as a ghost. "Oh, God. Is it that bad?"

Bartholomäus nodded. "Worse. And now, farewell."

Before leaving with Jakob, the Bamberg executioner pointed at Answin again. "Don't forget to give the corpse fisherman his reward. It's said whoever declines to pay him his money will be the next one the river carries away."

He gave the rag picker a secret wink, then continued walking with his brother down the stinking Regnitz, where dead branches and leaves seemed to reach out like long fingers as the river carried them away.

When Simon knocked on the door of the Bamberg city physician's house that evening, it wasn't the arrogant old housekeeper who opened the door, but the master of the house himself. Samuel looked overworked and was pale and unshaven, but when he saw Simon, his face brightened.

"Thank God!" he cried in relief. "I thought at first you were another one of those patients coming to ask me for a magic potion to protect them from werewolf bites."

Simon frowned. "Are there people like that?"

Samuel let out a pained laugh. "There were three of them

here already today, and it's Magda's day off, so she's not here to turn away this superstitious riffraff. One of them even demanded a silver wolf's tooth. I sent them all packing, telling them I was a university-educated doctor and not a magician or charlatan." He groaned. "But since I come from a Jewish family, they probably consider me an especially gifted doctor. Sooner or later one of them will probably turn me in as a werewolf." Samuel gestured for Simon to enter. "Oh, but excuse me. Do come in. I still have a little freshly ground coffee, if you'd like."

Soon the two were sitting in Samuel's little study, slurping the bitter black drink. The doctor gave Simon a worried glance.

"It's really bad, what's going on out there since the suffragan bishop offered this reward," he lamented. "I've heard there were nearly a half dozen arrests already today, and that's surely just the beginning."

Simon nodded. "I'm worried, too. If you ask me, the only real werewolf in this city is the suffragan bishop himself. He's infecting everyone else with his rabid hatred."

Samuel laughed softly. "A good comparison, but at least we won't have to worry about Harsee for a while. He's got a bad fever that will keep him in bed for a few days at least, even if he doesn't want to admit it." The city physician suddenly turned serious. "I visited him just this afternoon. He's really sick, with severe headaches, joint pain, sweating . . . and something else . . ." He hesitated for a moment, then told Simon about the little wound in his neck.

"Actually, that's nothing to worry about, but there's a red ring around the wound that I don't like at all," he concluded.

"Probably it's just become inflamed," Simon speculated. "Do you think it's somehow related to the fever?"

Samuel frowned. "I don't know, but there's something strange about it. In addition, he refuses to drink anything; he says every time he drinks something, he throws it up." Simon shook his head. "I wanted to look it up in my books, but I couldn't find anything." He sighed, took a sip of coffee, and turned to Simon with a smile.

"If I know you, you didn't just come to drink coffee with me," he said with a twinkle in his eye. "So, what's on your mind?"

Simon took a deep breath. He'd been wondering for a long time whether to let his friend in on the plan, but finally decided against it. If something went wrong, it was better for as few people as possible to know about it. He didn't want to burden Samuel unnecessarily.

And there was another matter he'd been troubled about for days, but he kept putting it out of his mind until just now.

"What I'm going to tell you now may sound a bit strange," he began hesitantly, "but believe me, I know what I'm doing." He ran down the list of ingredients his father-in-law has asked him to get from Samuel.

For a moment, Samuel just stood there with his mouth open. "Mandrake, henbane, poppy seed oil, and hemlock . . ." he finally said, shaking his head. "Damn it, Simon, what's that for? Magic incantations? Are you trying to conjure up your own werewolf?"

Simon smiled weakly. "Something like that, but believe me, it's for the good of the city and has nothing to do with magic. On the contrary. Nevertheless, for the time being it's best for you not to know anything more about it."

Samuel leaned back and looked at Simon suspiciously. "You're asking quite a lot of me. You want me to give you all these strange ingredients but won't tell me why?"

"Because I don't want to put you at risk unnecessarily. Understand . . . if it all works out, you'll be the first to know."

After a while, Samuel nodded. "Very well, but only because it's you. I have most of the ingredients over in my office. Poppy seed oil and hemlock I'll get from the court apothecary, but that shouldn't be any problem. I'll just tell them I need the ingredients for a new medical procedure. As the bishop's personal physician, I can do things like that." He leaned forward. "When do you need them?"

Simon swallowed hard. "Ah . . . tomorrow?"

"Tomorrow!" Samuel looked at him in astonishment. "But tomorrow is the bishop's reception. I thought you'd be coming along with me."

"I don't need them for myself, but for a . . . a friend," Simon replied hesitantly.

Samuel rolled his eyes. "Very well, I'll go to the cathedral mount first thing tomorrow." But then he shook his finger threateningly. "But make damn sure I don't know what you're going to do with it."

"Oh, don't worry about that. I'm sure the news will quickly . . . um, get around." Simon set his cup down, squirmed restlessly in his seat, and blushed. "There's one final favor I have to ask of you," he said in a halting voice.

Samuel groaned. "For God's sake, what else do you want?"

"It concerns the reception tomorrow night in Geyerswörth Castle," he began. "Many noble gentlemen will be there, even the bishop of Würzburg, an elector, no less. You have introduced me as a widely traveled scholar, and in fact I'm able to put on a pretty good act. It's just that . . ." He looked down at his sweaty shirt and filthy petticoat breeches. "I'm afraid I've got nothing suitable to wear. Do you have perhaps . . ."

His question was drowned out by Samuel's loud laughter.

"Simon, Simon," the doctor finally replied, wiping the tears from his eyes. "You haven't changed at all — still the same proud dandy as back then when we were in school." He rose from his seat. "Let's go and have a look in the closet. You're not exactly my size, but I'm sure we'll find something that will make you the best-dressed scholar in all of Bamberg."

II

THE BISHOP OF WÜRZBURG ARRIVED THE FOLLOW-
ing afternoon with a large entourage.

Since early morning, people had been standing at the wooden
bridge by the town gate to welcome and show homage to His Excellency the elector. This display was not completely selfless. Johann Philipp von Schönborn was a good-natured but above all
generous leader who liked to throw coins and small gifts to the
crowds who came to meet him on his trips. Accordingly, the
crowd was large at the bridge, and everyone wanted to be standing in the first row.

Magdalena stood somewhat to one side with the children.
The boys had climbed a scraggly willow tree with a good view of
the proceedings. Though they had no idea who or what a bishop
was, they were clearly enjoying the excitement as well as the fragrance of candied apples and chestnuts that street vendors were
roasting over glowing coals and hawking to the crowd. Magdalena, too, couldn't help smiling. The fear of the werewolf, the
paralyzing horror that lay over Bamberg like a dark cloud,
seemed to have lifted, at least for a while.

Actually, Magdalena had wanted to help her father and uncle prepare the tincture for the sleep sponge, but Peter and Paul

kept grabbing the henbane and hemlock from the table and throwing it around, and Jakob was getting angrier and angrier. After little Paul had almost taken a sip of the opium juice, the hangman lost his temper and Magdalena hastily left the house with the children. Now she was standing near the busy bridge, each of the children was holding a slice of apple in his hand, and she could reflect in peace on the plans they'd made.

At first, they sounded so far-fetched that she couldn't decide if the idea was crazy or simply a stroke of genius. Tonight they'd actually create a werewolf, a fiendish monster on which the people of Bamberg could vent their anger.

The tense mood in the city was evident here, as well, among the people in the waiting crowd. Two young journeymen in front of her kept whispering and turning around cautiously to make sure no one was listening.

"... and early this morning they came to arrest Jäckel Riemer, that drunk tower guard in the church," one of them whispered. The speaker was wearing the kind of hat traditionally worn by raftsmen on the river. "They say that the sexton at Saint Martin's Church saw him at night in the cemetery, digging up corpses to eat."

"Bah!" the other journeyman replied with disgust, shaking his head. "You just have to hope this will all be cleared up before the whole city goes mad."

"What are you trying to say?" the raftsman asked suspiciously. "You mean to tell me you don't believe in the werewolf?"

"Oh, I do," his acquaintance assured him. "It's just that . . ."

He was struggling for the right words, when suddenly there was the sound of a trumpet on the bridge. A wave of applause followed, and the journeyman was clearly relieved that instead of replying to his friend, he could acknowledge the bishop's arrival. "Look, the noble visitor has finally arrived. What gorgeous horses. We haven't seen anything like this for a long time."

At that moment they indeed heard the clatter of hooves, and shortly thereafter saw the team of six horses crossing the bridge. The two lead horses were wearing plumes, and their silver harnesses glittered in the noonday autumn sun.

"Mama, Mama!" Peter shouted, "Look, here comes the kaiser."

Magdalena smiled. "Not exactly the kaiser, Peter, but someone who's almost as rich and powerful. He's the bishop of Würzburg, a real, living elector, who takes part in naming the king of the Reich."

"I want to see the elector, too," Paul said, sitting on the branch below so that the crowd blocked his view. He climbed a bit higher as she watched with trepidation, but then she turned back to the sight before them.

They're growing up, she thought. *I'll have to get used to it.*

Royal guards with gleaming breastplates rode before and behind the coach, and one was holding up the flag of the Würzburg bishop. Behind them came a line of smaller coaches, no doubt conveying lesser clerics and courtiers. When the coach, with its team of six horses, passed Magdalena, she briefly caught sight of an older, bearded man inside, with long gray hair, smiling benignly, and waving out the window.

The applause and cheers became louder as the soldiers took out leather pouches containing small coins and threw them into the crowd. The journeymen in front of Magdalena caught a few of them.

"Three cheers for the Würzburg elector!" the raftsman shouted. "Three cheers for the elector!" But after the coach had passed, he turned crossly to his neighbor. "He's getting greedier and greedier. The last time there were a few guilders among the coins, and now look at this. Only a few piddling kreuzers."

"The guilders and ducats are for our Bamberg bishop," his friend responded with a grin, "so he can finally finish building his residence up on the cathedral mount. The word is that Johann Philipp von Schönborn isn't here just for fun. He'll no doubt have to lend his colleague a big sum of money again."

The other raftsman bit his kreuzer to check it. "But they'll also have time for amusement. Have you heard? Two troupes of actors will be performing tonight. It will be a long night."

"If the werewolf doesn't come first and run off with two fat bishops."

The two sauntered off, laughing, and Magdalena felt her good mood dissipating. The conversation had reminded her again of their scheme that night, and she felt a lump in her throat. Would the sleep sponge work? And how far along was her father in preparing the gunpowder? Simon had gone off to visit his friend Samuel that morning to get the rest of the ingredients. No doubt he was still in the executioner's house with the two Kuisls stirring the highly explosive mixture, and the three men would certainly have no need for a couple of rowdy boys.

On the spur of the moment, Magdalena decided to visit Katharina and offer her some consolation. Simon had said she had gone off to her father's house to grieve the cancellation of the wedding reception.

"Shall we go and visit Aunt Katharina?" she suggested to the two boys, winking her eye. "Who knows, maybe she'll make you porridge again with lots of honey."

She didn't have to ask twice. Peter and Paul were wild about the motherly Katharina and especially her cooking. As quick as two little squirrels, they scurried down from the willow and pushed their way with their mother through the crowd that was starting to break up, now that the Würzburg bishop had passed on his way to the cathedral mount, though the cheering could still be heard in the distance.

After a while they crossed the city hall bridge and soon were standing in front of the Hausers' house. It was Katharina herself who answered the door after a few knocks. Her eyes were red from crying, but the sight of the children brought a smile to her face.

"Peter! Paul! How glad I am to see you. Come in, I've just taken some buttered apple fritters out of the oven. I think you'll like them."

In fact, there was a heavenly aroma of warm apples and hot butter throughout the house, and the children stormed into the kitchen hooting and cheering, where Katharina served them a whole tower of the sweet pastries. While the boys sat at the table, eating happily, Magdalena had a chance to have a quiet conversation with Katharina.

"When I'm unhappy, I often stay in the kitchen," Katharina said with a faint smile. "Cooking still is the best way for me to forget my cares. You should feel free to come and visit me more often."

"I can't tell you how sorry I am about the wedding," Magdalena replied, holding Katharina's hand. "In any case, we'll stay awhile longer in Bamberg, and if necessary, we'll just have a smaller party."

Katharina nodded. "I'm so grateful for that. Thank you." She stared off into space, and there was a pause during which the only sound was the children's chewing and smacking their lips.

"Do you know how long I've been waiting for this wedding?" Katharina finally continued in a soft voice. "People in Bamberg thought of me as a dried-up old maid who'd never find a man. Too old, too fat . . ." She sighed. "There were a few men earlier, but when the time came, they always ran off."

"And then?" Magdalena asked.

"Then Bartholomäus came along." She smiled and her eyes began to sparkle. "I met him down at the fish market when he offered to carry my heavy basket. Most people steer clear of him. He's the Bamberg executioner, after all, and people don't want anything to do with him. But I've seen what kind of a person he really is: he can be very warm-hearted, you know."

Magdalena laughed. "Up to now, he's kept that well hidden from me, but of course, you know him better."

"Well, that's the way he is." Katharina rubbed her chubby fingers, which were sticky from baking, and looked down. "At first, everyone opposed this marriage — my father, my friends ... Being married to an executioner — what can be worse than that? It would be better to die an old maid. But I got my way, even with my father." She laughed sadly. "I was even able to talk my father into a big, expensive reception, even though Bartl was so reluctant at first. He said he didn't want anything more to do with his family than absolutely necessary. But do you know what?" She winked at Magdalena. "I think in the end he was proud to show his big brother what he'd made of himself here — the big house, the marriage with a clerk's daughter, a good dowry, a beautiful wedding reception ..." She sighed deeply. "But at least the last of those is not to be."

They both fell silent for a while, then finally Magdalena asked. "Was your father able to make any progress with the city council? He was going to put another word in for the wedding reception."

Katharina shook her head. "He hasn't gotten to it yet. In the last few weeks he's seemed lost in his thoughts, almost constantly up in his study because he has to copy some old lists for the city. I was getting used to it, but since yesterday I've not even been able to talk to him. He keeps leaving the house without telling me where he's going. I really wish I knew what's wrong with him." She shook her head. "Just this morning I was up in his room to clean up, and I'm telling you, it looks like lightning has struck the place. He didn't even look at me, and he just shouted at me to get out."

Magdalena remembered what Simon had told her about Hieronymus Hauser. Was it possible that his preoccupation had something to do with yesterday's conversation?

"Simon was here yesterday to visit your father," she said

carefully, "and he learned that Hieronymus attended the witch trials back then as a young scribe. Do you think all this werewolf business has upset him?"

Katharina seemed to be thinking it over. "Hmm, it's possible. That was before I was born, but I know that upset him very much. He sometimes dreams of the torturing that he had to witness, as the scribe, in order to document the statements. Then he screams in his sleep. But he doesn't want to talk about it." She shrugged. "Just like everyone else in Bamberg, as if they wanted to forget and bury what happened then."

"Simon thinks he saw your father in the bishop's archive after their meeting." Magdalena added. "Is it possible he was looking for something there? Something having to do with events back then?"

Her aunt was silent for a while, then she picked up one of the crispy apple pastries and took a bite. "Unfortunately, I just don't know," she said, as she kept chewing on the fritter. She gestured apologetically. "Excuse me, but I think the constant crying has made me hungry." After she'd finished, she continued. "It would be best for you to ask my father yourself. He probably won't be back from his office until late afternoon, but you can stop by and see us again then."

"This isn't a good day," Magdalena replied hesitantly, "as I have other things to do." She pointed at her two children. "I just wanted to ask you if you could look after the boys for a while. Simon is visiting the bishop today, and Father and I have some things to discuss with Georg. It's been such a long time since we've seen each other . . ."

Magdalena cleared her throat, embarrassed. She'd made Uncle Bartholomäus promise not to tell Katharina about their plans for that night, and she looked desperately for some explanation. The idea of leaving the children in Katharina's care had just occurred to her. Actually, she'd already asked Georg to do that, but he hadn't been especially fond of the idea. And after asking him again several times that morning, his reply was still gruff and noncommittal. Evidently he could not get over the fact that Magdalena was being allowed to take part in freeing Matheo that evening, and he wasn't.

Katharina appeared to accept her vague excuse, but then she gestured apologetically. "You know I love your boys, Magdalena, but on this particular evening I can't do it. Believe it or not, my father is also invited to the bishop's reception, and he even managed to get an invitation for me." She smiled faintly. "He thought that would cheer me up a bit. Such a celebration will just make me think of my own wedding reception, of course, but I can't turn him down. It's a great honor for our family. Only the better classes of citizens are invited." She hesitated. "Many members of the city council will be there, and Father still hopes he can do something about the wedding reception."

"I understand." Magdalena nodded. "Then you've got to go."

She looked over at the two boys, who had by now wolfed down their apple fritters and turned their attention to the pot of butter, which they were taking out and smearing in each other's hair.

"I think it's time to take the kids back to their strict grandfather so he can tweak their ears a bit," she said with a grin, then she stood up and embraced Katharina. "Good luck to you. You'll see — everything will work out."

As she left the house with her two boys, she wasn't sure if her last wish hadn't been directed primarily at herself.

At about the same time, a man was sitting somewhere along the banks of the Regnitz, daydreaming and staring out over the water. Branches and leaves floated past him, and occasionally dirty rags or the cadaver of a small animal. Farther up river there had been an autumn storm, and brown whirlpools formed in the water, making the leaves dance around until they finally sank and popped up again downstream.

Nothing disappeared forever; it all eventually returned to the surface.

He flung a branch out into the river as far as he could and watched it drift along like a ship pitching and rolling in the waves. Briefly, he felt the urge to jump in after it and end his own life. He felt empty, so empty, but he still had to complete his plan — he was almost finished.

Just two more to go . . .

It was only a day ago that the clever woman had ripped his hood from his head. She'd seen his face and thus sealed her fate. Now she was tied up again in the cell, and he wouldn't let that happen to him again. He had briefly lost control of himself, of the entire situation, but now his decision was firm.

He would not waver again.

He had in fact, even before the previous day's event, considered letting the woman live. It had gotten harder and harder for him to torture and kill the women, while with the two old men, he felt nothing but elation with every blow, every squeeze of the tongs, every turn of the wheel.

When old widow Gotzendörfer died of fear, he'd even felt a sense of relief. He'd walked up to the window to terrify the old woman, but also in the hope she'd open the window for him. When he'd seen the solid iron gate in front of the window, he was almost ready to give up, but then the mere sight of him and the woman's own weak heart had been enough to kill her. It had been a clean death, and he hadn't had to hear this screaming again.

The screaming . . .

The man shook, as if trying to cast off the memories. But it was in vain: they'd eaten their way too far inside him. Just the same, since the young woman had seen his face, she would have to die, too. She'd almost gotten away, and what he'd been planning for so long would have been doomed.

Now he'd gotten control again.

Even if things didn't work out just the way he intended. He'd been waiting too long to carry out his clever plan. At first, he thought it was ingenious. He would conquer his foes with their own weapons, he'd create a monster in their midst and at the same time crush his worst enemy. But still the long-awaited change had not occurred. It seemed like God still had the power to control life and death.

The man closed his eyes and murmured an old Bible verse, something that had been with him all his life.

Vengeance is mine, I will repay, says the Lord . . .

He decided to wait a few more days. By then he would have his next to last victim. And besides, he had to think about what to do with the woman. He didn't want her to suffer more than necessary, but nonetheless he'd have to get rid of her somehow.

The man gazed into the river, where the cadaver of a fox was drifting by.

The river consumed everything; it had swallowed the others, and it would also take the woman. A quick blow, the silence after that, the lonely trek through the forest, and everything would be as it was again.

He stood up and walked away.

Soon it would be over.

"No, damn it! The trunk goes on the right; the stairs are on the left. Shall I break a leg when I try to climb the stairs to the stage for my first scene? Is that what you want?"

His face as red as a beet, Sir Malcolm was running back and forth between his actors, unpacking some of the props and costumes. They were in the so-called festival hall of Geyerswörth

Castle, where the two performances were scheduled for that evening. To get there, Barbara and the actors had to first make it past a well-guarded gate and then another door to the interior court, which was just as well guarded. The guards had been watching them with a mixture of disgust and tense anticipation, as if they were exotic animals — a look that the young hangman's daughter from Schongau was all too familiar with. The vocations of executioners as well as actors were regarded as dishonorable, and anyone engaged in that line of work was reviled by the good citizens of the town. Just the same, everyone expected a technically perfect and above all entertaining performance from both troupes.

It was still more than five hours before the performance, but Sir Malcolm already seemed at the end of his rope. Barbara couldn't help wondering how he would be just before the curtain rose.

Will he explode? Go through the roof? Murder us all?

As Malcolm continued his rant, she looked up dreamily at the vaulted ceiling of the festival hall with its paintings of flowers and strange beasts, which, along with the stone columns, gave her the feeling of being in an enchanted forest. The tingling sensation in her stomach became stronger. When she first noticed it the day before, she thought it was the sign of indigestion, but some of the actors assured her it was quite normal. Stage fright, they called it, a sickness that could only be cured by a successful performance.

Looking around at her colleagues, Barbara noticed that some of them were reciting their lines in a low voice as they moved the trunks around without paying any heed to Malcolm's temper tantrums. Evidently they were accustomed to their director's outbursts.

"And go and get Salter," he shouted. "The dress rehearsal will begin in an hour, and we can't wait for everyone to get here."

"Uh, you yourself sent him to the Bamberg tailor this morning to pick up the princess's costume," said fat Matthäus, who would be playing the part of the joiner Klipperling in the play. Barbara had come to know the older actor as a good-natured fellow who had almost as many problems memorizing his lines as she did.

"And then you wanted him to look around for some metal for the king's crown," the fat man reminded his director. "The last crown started to rust long ago."

"Ah, that's right." Sir Malcolm nodded absent-mindedly. "Well, let's hope the lad will get back in time."

"I hope so, too," a snide voice suddenly said from behind one of the columns in the back. It was Guiscard Brolet, who stepped forward and looked into one of the open trunks full of colorful costumes. "You have exactly two hours for your last rehearsal, Malcolm," he continued while fanning himself with a threadbare, dirty lace handkerchief. "Not a minute longer. Then it's our turn. That's what we agreed on."

Sir Malcolm slammed the cover on the trunk and scrutinized his competitor angrily. "Don't worry, Guiscard, we don't need any longer than that. In contrast to your group, we're neither amateurs nor thieves."

Guiscard sighed. "Always the same old story," he sneered in his French accent. "Well, we shall see which piece the prince bishop prefers. I happen to have learned from a reliable source that he's especially fond of Gryphius's *Papinian*." He shrugged. "Your crude farce, on the other hand . . ."

"*Papinian!*" Malcolm replied, putting his hand to his forehead. "Why didn't I think of that myself?" He trembled with anger, and if Barbara hadn't known better, she could have sworn that Sir Malcolm was just hearing for the first time about the piece Guiscard had picked out. In fact, it was a plot of Malcolm's own making.

He's really a pretty good actor, she thought, *on stage as well as in real life.*

Guiscard grinned. "As I said, I have my sources. And you can rest assured His Excellency will be horrified by your *Peter Squenz*. I have that from trusted sources, as well."

Sir Malcolm managed to turn white as a sheet. He ran his hand through his hair in feigned despair, and Barbara had to wonder if he wasn't overdoing it a bit.

"I didn't think about that," he muttered. "You're a slippery character, Guiscard."

"But somehow you managed to be scheduled after us," Guiscard replied darkly. "I have no idea how you managed to arrange that with the bishop's court. But that won't help you, either, Malcolm." He let out a diabolical laugh. "Especially since one of your key actors is missing. Or so I hear."

Sir Malcolm's face became as red as a beet, and Barbara could see at once that he was no longer play-acting.

"I swear, Guiscard," he hissed, moving a few steps closer to his competitor. "If I find out you're behind Matheo's arrest, then God help you."

Guiscard waved him off. "Always this histrionic talk. Save that for the stage." He pointed at the trunks that still hadn't been unpacked. "Until then, it appears you have some things to do, but remember . . . two more hours. After that, I'll personally make sure the guards throw you out."

Waving his lace handkerchief in the air, he left the festival hall, humming a little French tune. Sir Malcolm waited a minute, then clapped his hands triumphantly.

"*Mon dieu,* zees I know frem a reliable soorce," he mimicked, running his hand through his hair in a feminine gesture. "Ha! He'll be looking around for another job, the sucker. Isn't that right, people?"

Some of the actors grinned, but Barbara looked serious. "Did he really arrange Matheo's arrest?" she asked. "Perhaps the wolf hides come from his people, and we'll have another nasty surprise this evening. This Guiscard seems capable of anything."

"Do you think a real werewolf will interrupt our performance?" Malcolm shook his head and grinned. "I don't think the old fellow has that much imagination. Believe me, the bishop will doze off during the first play and wake up the moment our play begins. It will be a great triumph for us."

He was spreading his arms in a dramatic gesture, when suddenly the door to the hall burst open and Markus Salter entered. As usual, the young man looked tired and pale. He was carrying a tightly wrapped bundle.

"I had to run all over town looking for a tinsmith to cobble a crown together for just a few kreuzers," he complained, glowering at Malcolm. "You didn't want me to spend any more than that. We put a little gold-colored paint on it and stuck on a glass stone with wax. We need to make sure it doesn't get too warm or the stone will fall down on your nose, but otherwise everything looks good."

He unwrapped the bundle and picked up a sparkling object that looked like one of those magnificent crowns Barbara had only seen before in stained-glass church windows. The other actors clearly liked it, and even Malcolm, who was usually so critical, nodded his approval.

"So it was worth the wait," he said, patting Markus on the shoulder. Then he pointed at the bundle. "And the dress for our new princess?"

Markus grinned, and suddenly his face brightened. "In this dress," he said, winking at Barbara, "even an empress could attend a reception. Everyone will fall in love with you in this dress."

Carefully he opened the bundle, taking out a red dress embroidered with lace and with glittering metal buttons.

It took Barbara's breath away. "It's beautiful!" she gasped. "May I try it on?"

"Please do," Malcolm replied, motioning toward the dress. "After all, we want to see how our princess Violandra looks in it."

Carefully, Barbara slipped into the dress, and it fit perfectly. She was happy to see how all the other actors looked at her in astonishment.

"Ah, yes, fine feathers make fine birds," Sir Malcolm murmured. "You actually do look like a princess. It's hard to believe you're actually the dishonorable daughter of a hangman." He stopped to think for a while, then clapped his hands. "But even princesses have to learn their lines," he continued in a stern voice. "So please, everyone, take your places. Let's begin the rehearsal, before Guiscard comes snooping around here again."

Georg was bored standing with his two nephews along the left branch of the Regnitz and watching as the children threw one stone after another into the water. Magdalena had handed the children over to him just an hour ago, but it already felt like an eternity. It was late afternoon, but night seemed endlessly far off.

"Look, Uncle Georg, see how far I can throw," Peter called, as he skipped a stone out into the river. Georg nodded approvingly and grumbled something unintelligible as his thoughts drifted away like the water in the river.

Watch the kids while the others are planning a daring escape from the dungeon . . . Damn, this is a woman's job. Barbara should be doing this.

Then he remembered they'd gotten dragged into this only because of his love-stricken twin sister, and his anger rose. Even as a small child, Barbara always had gotten her way with their father, maybe because she was smarter than her twin brother and could read and work with the healing herbs far better than he could—skills that almost always impressed Father more than a flawless execution or a quick confession. And no matter what Georg did, Father always found something to complain about and to criticize. Then when he accidently beat old Berchtholdt's boy so badly that he crippled him and was thrown out of town, he was depressed and angry when he first arrived in Bamberg to live with his uncle. He would lie in bed many a night, sleepless and cursing his fate, but then he realized how free he felt in this city, far away from Father. His uncle respected him as a hangman's apprentice and asked him to do things his father never would have allowed. And so Georg gradually became an adult. Then, a year ago, Uncle Bartholomäus told him how his father had fled Schongau as a young man and abandoned his family. Since then, the great monument had started to crumble.

Bartholomäus had invited him to stay in Bamberg, and Georg felt truly comfortable here. Why should he return to little Schongau and a grumbling father who even after he became an old man would probably still be pushing him around? Why should he put up with that when he could have a far more appealing career here? Bartholomäus had assured him more than once that he could follow in his footsteps as the Bamberg executioner. But he had to put all these considerations aside now, because his sister once more was getting her way. And on top of it all, he had to play the part of a nursemaid. It was enough to drive a person crazy.

"I'm cold," little Peter whined, rubbing his fingers as he stood alongside him. He no longer seemed interested in throwing stones. "Let's go back to our great-uncle, can we?" he begged. "Or to Aunt Katharina. She has such yummy apple fritters. Please!"

"We can't go back to your great-uncle, because you just fool around," Georg grumbled. "And we can't go back to Aunt Katharina, either. Your mother told me to walk around Bamberg with you for a while, so let's do that."

"But I don't want to walk around the town," little Paul wailed. "It's so boring. I'd rather go back to old Jeremias. He has a sword just like Uncle Bartl only smaller. And a slingshot, too. I want to play at old Jeremias's place."

"Oh, yes, let's go to visit Jeremias," Peter pleaded as well. "He'll tell us more stories. And his little dog can even do tricks. Please, please, let's go there."

Georg sighed. He'd picked up the children the night before in the Wild Man and had met the old crippled custodian. This Jeremias looked like a monster but was really a good-natured fellow. He'd told the boys stories and let them play with all sorts of stuff in an old trunk. The children hadn't even wanted to go home.

"Jeremias won't be thrilled if you go and bother him again," Georg said, shaking his head, but suddenly the idea no longer sounded so far-fetched. He himself was cold and bored and had no desire anymore to keep watching the boys throw stones while listening to their complaints.

"Fine, we can ask if he has time," he said begrudgingly.

The children broke out in cheers and tugged at his hand. Georg grumbled a bit, but he'd made up his mind. They walked along the muddy towpath along the river and finally reached the harbor and the Wedding House. The boys laughed as they ran through the door and the inner court until they were finally standing before Jeremias's door. Out of breath, Georg knocked, and a moment later the astonished custodian was standing in the doorway.

"Oh, you again?" Jeremias laughed. "Rascally bunch! Tell me, would you like to hear more stories?"

"Oh, yes, please, Jeremias," Peter said. "Can we come in? Uncle Georg said we could. Please, please?"

Georg shrugged. "Well, I only said we could ask," he said, embarrassed. "Their parents are really busy right now and I thought . . ."

"You thought why should I put up with these rascals when that crippled Jeremias has nothing to do," he interrupted with a grin. "But you're right about that. The sound of children laughing is a medicine for me, something I can never get enough of. So come on in."

With loud shouts, the boys stormed into the room with the birdcage hanging from the ceiling and the shelves full of books. They ran to a trunk in the corner and immediately began pulling things out of it. Georg caught sight of a musty old blanket, a few wooden dolls, a battered helmet, and a sword with a handle that had broken off, which Paul immediately picked up to use as a weapon. They laughed as they tussled with the crippled dog that Georg had seen on his last visit. Meanwhile, old Jeremias sat down on the straw mattress.

"Would you like to have a venison pie?" he asked, handing Georg a steaming plate that had been lying on a shelf. "I just brought them from the kitchen. They taste wonderful."

"Thanks, I've already eaten." He declined with a wave and a slight smile while furtively examining Jeremias's scarred face. The sight made him sick to his stomach. He remembered men from the Schongau leprosarium whose faces had been disfigured in the same way. Unlike the custodian of the Wild Man, those poor devils had to live outside the city because people were afraid of catching the disease. But Jeremias, too, lived a very secluded life.

The old man seemed to sense Georg was looking at him. He winked, and his face contorted into a grimace.

"You'd better watch out if you ever work with unslaked lime," he said. "One careless moment and you'll never find a woman who wants to marry you." He laughed mischievously. "I made advances to your two sisters, but I fear it was in vain."

Georg stopped short. "Do you know Barbara, too?"

Jeremias hesitated, then he nodded. "Oh, yes, she was here once with her big sister. She was very interested in my library." He pointed to a shelf in the back of the room, where Georg could see a row of large books. He struggled to read some of the titles, among them books of medicine he'd seen in his father's collection, but also some he didn't recognize, then he shrugged and turned away.

"Books aren't my thing," he replied. "I prefer to work with my hands."

Jeremias smiled. "I know your family, Georg, and believe me, I respect your profession."

Georg looked at his two nephews, wondering. As usual, it was Paul who had cornered his older brother with the broken sword handle while the dog barked excitedly at both of them.

Someday they'll be executioners, too, he thought. *Soon I'll be taking Peter along to his first execution.*

But then it occurred to him he'd probably be staying in Bamberg.

Or maybe not? What do I want, anyway?

To get his mind off things, he stood up and wandered along the shelves, on which some full vials and crucibles stood alongside the books. Little boxes were labeled in Latin, and Georg read the names *Hyoscyamus niger, Papaver somniferum,* and *Conium maculatum.* His blood ran cold as he remembered how his father tried to drill some Latin into him—without much success. That, too, was better with Uncle Bartholomäus. His uncle was only interested in Latin terms when dealing with herbs for curing diseases in animals.

"This is quite a medical library," Georg finally said, turning to Jeremias. "There's almost as much here as in my father's library in Schongau."

"Well, I know a bit about medicine—the sorts of things you learn in the course of a long life," the old man responded. "Sick people visit me, especially those so poor they can't afford a doctor or a barber surgeon, and I can earn a Heller or two that way, too," he winked conspiratorially. "Just don't tell the city council, or the honorable Magnus Rinswieser and the other members of the Bamberg Apothecary's Guild will see to it that I spend the rest of my days in a dungeon."

Georg laughed. "I think the council has bigger things to worry about right now."

"Indeed." Jeremias nodded sadly. "This matter of the werewolf is serious. People never learn. '*Homo homini lupus,*' as we learned from the playwright Plautus. 'Man is a wolf to man.' In those cruel witch trials back then, they attacked one another like animals. Yes, I remember them as if they were just yesterday." But then he brushed the thought aside. "But why am I telling a young fellow these old stories. I'm sure you want to go off and have a good time. So go ahead, leave."

Georg looked at him, amazed. "What? Go?"

"Isn't that what you wanted to do?" He grinned. "Drop the boys off here so you can knock about town a bit. So, be off with you."

"Well, actually . . ." Georg was about to say something, but then he burst out laughing. "I'll admit, you've seen through me. And it looks like the children would rather stay with you than with me anyway." He pointed at Paul who was happily hacking away at one of the dolls with the broken sword, and Peter, who was looking at illustrations in one of the old books, leafing through it attentively. "I'll be back in two hours," Georg said. "All right?"

Jeremias cut him off. "It doesn't matter if it's three hours. Most of the guards are down at the castle for the bishop's reception, so you can go home after curfew without being thrown into the stocks. And now, off with you, at once."

Georg thanked him with a smile, then bid good-bye to his nephews, who hardly even paid attention to him.

Moments later he was standing out in front of the Wedding House. Night was falling, and for a moment he considered returning to the executioner's house. He suspected, however, that his big sister wouldn't be happy with how he'd shirked his responsibilities, so he started drifting aimlessly through the alleyways.

He crossed the city hall bridge, which was still open at this hour, and turned off into the section of town near the Sand Gate, where he could hear noise and laughter. Here along the river below the cathedral mount there were almost as many taverns as houses. The Bambergers liked to drink and carouse, especially on a holiday like this when an important visitor was in town. Georg had once heard there were more breweries here than in any other city in Franconia. Everywhere he turned, he could hear music and the clinking of beer mugs.

The party was especially raucous in the Blue Lion Tavern, famous for its smoked beer — which took a little getting used to. Georg had often been here to fetch a jug of beer for his uncle. As the Bamberg executioner, Bartholomäus Kuisl was not especially welcome in the taverns, so he preferred to drink alone at home. Georg, on the other hand, had always enjoyed the atmosphere in the Blue Lion, even if he hadn't frequented it much lately. He stopped to think.

Well, why not?

He was just fifteen, but with the dark fuzz on his face and his imposing size, he looked considerably older. In addition, as a hangman's journeyman he was nowhere near as well known as the Bamberg executioner himself. He'd always wanted to stop here and have a beer. He thought some more as he fingered the few coins in his pants pocket, his pay for the week.

I think I've earned it . . .

Pulling himself together, he opened the door latch and entered the noisy tavern. The odor of fermented mash, smoke, and hot sauerkraut drifted toward him; someone was plucking the fiddle, and people were shouting and laughing. The noise enveloped him like a soft cocoon, and in the back he noticed an empty seat. He pushed his way through the crowd with his broad chest, took a seat at the scratched wooden table, and ordered his first beer.

It would not be his last.

In the meantime, the first guests had arrived in Geyerswörth Castle.

Simon stood off to one side with Samuel, watching the activity in the inner courtyard. Yesterday, his friend had lent him a new pair of petticoat breaches, a clean shirt with a lace collar, and a strikingly handsome, dark-green jacket that was actually a bit too large but looked much better on him than the dirty street clothes he'd taken for the trip. He was also wearing a flashy hat with a red feather, an expensive accessory that he'd bought from the Bamberg hat maker with the last of his money. After all, the reception and the theater performance that day were to honor a German elector, and he didn't want to embarrass himself by looking out of place.

Crossing his arms, he leaned against an ivy-covered fountain, where water flowed from the mouths of nymphs, and observed the Bamberg citizens strolling by, nodding to each other with a smile and making pleasant conversation. The constant chatter, laughter, and clinking of glasses made it hard to believe there was a werewolf just outside the city gates striking terror into people's hearts. In spite of the open fires burning in iron pots all around the city, it was uncomfortably cool and damp at the castle. Simon couldn't help but think of Magdalena, who, along with her father and uncle, was making final preparations for freeing Matheo.

And all this while I'm visiting the theater. Well, my father-in-law told me straight out that he didn't need me. Let's see how the cranky old man gets along without me.

Nevertheless, Simon was having a hard time concentrating. What if the guards up on the cathedral square surprised Magdalena and the others in the act? He could only hope the Schongau hangman was still the old swashbuckling brawler he knew from earlier adventures.

"Almost the entire city council is here," Samuel whispered, standing next to him dressed in the black coat of the Doctor's Guild. "Strange, isn't it? All these people who have been struggling to cast off the yoke of the church fall to their knees as soon as the bishop of Würzburg arrives."

"They say that Johann Philipp von Schönborn is very open-minded and tolerant of worldly things," Simon replied, sipping on his glass of cool white Sylvaner. He was happy for this diversion. "I expect a few strong words from him about the werewolf panic here in Bamberg."

"Ha! I'm not even sure Schönborn knows about it. Our own bishop will no doubt do everything he can to cover it up. After all, he wants to stay on good terms with his Würzburg colleague. "He needs him to—" Samuel stopped short on hearing cheers suddenly coming from the entrance to the castle. He turned toward the sound and squinted, trying to see something through the crowd of the many visitors.

"Well, speak of the devil . . ." he mumbled. "The noble gentlemen have arrived. It's about time."

Now Simon could see the bishop's legates, a small group of clerics and some courtiers, who fluttered around the bishop like moths around a candle. When the pompous-looking courtier stepped briefly to one side, Simon caught a glimpse of Bamberg's Prince Bishop Philipp Valentin Voit von Rieneck, and alongside him an elderly gentleman with wavy gray hair and a bushy beard. He smiled good-naturedly while representatives of the Bamberg citizenry stepped up to him and bowed to him and their own sovereign. Behind the two bishops stood an ashen-faced Sebastian Harsee. His skullcap had partially slipped off his bald head, he staggered a bit, and he kept taking out his handkerchief to dab the sweat on his forehead.

"Didn't I tell him he'd have to stay in bed?" Samuel whispered. "Just look, Simon. The man is running a fever. But no, he won't listen."

"There was something else about his illness you wanted to check," Simon replied in an undertone. "Did you find anything else?"

Simon himself had been thinking about the illness of the suffragan bishop, especially the red circle around the wound on his neck. He'd taken some books from Bartholomäus's library, but the Bamberg executioner was not as interested in medicine as his brother. Almost all his books were about curing animals, and they were of no help to Simon.

"Unfortunately, I've been busy caring for the bishop's mistress for the last few days," Samuel answered with a shrug, "and haven't had much time to deal with Harsee's illness, but I think—"

"Master Samuel!" cried Philipp Rieneck, interrupting the conversation. Evidently the Bamberg bishop had just discovered his personal physician in the crowd. "So here you are. I'd like to introduce you to our friend Johann Philipp."

Samuel sighed softly, then took the surprised Simon by the arm and led him to the front row, where they both knelt down before the elector.

"This is a great honor for me, Your Excellency," Samuel said, bowing reverently, "and also for my friend Simon Fronwieser, a widely traveled scholar who even in distant Munich has heard about your wisdom and kindness."

Simon cringed. Once again, Samuel was lying through his teeth, this time to one of the most powerful men in the Reich. Out of the corner of his eye he could see Harsee, trembling and watching it all.

He suspects something, Simon thought. *Perhaps it's just as well he's so sick . . .*

"Philipp Rieneck has told me about your wondrous cures,

Master Samuel," the Würzburg bishop replied in a deep and pleasant voice. "They are said to be a bit unusual but nevertheless effective. It seems you have been very helpful to a young woman Philipp cares greatly about."

"Ah, a loyal servant, nothing more," the Bamberg bishop interjected. "But it is indeed true that Master Samuel is caring for her at the moment with great success. Just this morning I spoke with her and . . . ah . . . took her confession."

"Perhaps you could use your expertise to help our dear brother Sebastian," Schönborn said, turning to the shivering suffragan bishop, who was as white as a corpse. "You don't look well at all, my friend."

"Oh . . . I'm . . . managing," Sebastian struggled to say. "A slight fever, nothing serious. Didn't . . . want . . . to miss the performance. If only I could get rid of these damned headaches. But of course, our Savior also had to suffer."

He struggled in vain to smile. Meanwhile, the Würzburg bishop had turned back to Samuel, who, like Simon, was still kneeling before him.

"But do stand up, dear Doctor," he said warmly, "and your friend, too."

After the two had gotten to their feet, Schönborn continued: "I'd like very much to hear your opinion on one matter, Doctor. I have heard that a werewolf is prowling about here in Bamberg and magically abducting his victims." He frowned. "As you may know, we don't think much of this hocus-pocus in Würzburg, something I've debated often with my friend Philipp. Isn't that right, Philipp?" He glanced at the Bamberg prince bishop, who laughed stiffly. "On the other hand, such creatures appear again and again in stories and reports, and now here in Bamberg," Schönborn continued. "Tell me, dear Doctor, is there an explanation for this, as far as you know?"

The entire courtyard fell strangely silent, as visitors halted their conversations. Simon looked at Philipp Rieneck, who politely nodded as if encouraging him to respond, though his eyes were as cold as ice. Right behind him stood Sebastian Harsee, who despite his fever suddenly looked very threatening.

If Samuel wants to continue practicing in Bamberg, he's got to be very careful about what he says now, Simon thought. *Sometimes it's a real advantage to be just a barber surgeon in Schongau.*

"Well . . ." Samuel said hesitantly, "a thorough answer to this question would probably not be appropriate for this large audience. But let me assure you that I and my learned friend," he said, giving Simon a friendly pat on the shoulder, "have come a long way toward finding an answer. We already have reached some tentative conclusions."

"That would really be of great interest to me," Schönborn replied with a smile. "But you're right. The first of the two theater performances will begin soon. Perhaps we'll have time to debate this topic afterward."

"Ah, indeed. It will be my pleasure."

Samuel bowed one last time, then stepped back into the crowd with Simon, while the suffragan bishop eyed them suspiciously.

"Good God, what are these tentative conclusions?" Simon whispered. "If Schönborn asks you about them later, you must have something to say."

"Hopefully I'll think of something by then," Samuel replied. "What should I have done? If I question the existence of the werewolf, I'll fall out of favor with my prince, and if I support it, I risk my reputation as a doctor and scholar and will lose favor with one of the most powerful men in the Reich."

"A really impossible situation." Simon nodded sympathetically. "Let's hope the two plays are so boring we'll have time to think about a compromise. Shall we enter?"

They entered the great festival hall of the palace with the other guests, passing through a low doorway. In the back third of the room, a stage had been constructed of spruce wood, with stairs leading up to it and a red curtain in front. The room was illuminated by hundreds of candles, giving a lifelike appearance to the paintings of plants and animals on the vaulted ceiling.

In the first row there were fur-upholstered seats for the two bishops, the suffragan bishop, and some of the leading patricians. The rest of the audience, as usual, had to stand. Behind them, stairs led up to a gallery, where Simon and Samuel managed to find room standing along the railing with a good view of the stage.

The excited murmurs in the audience stopped abruptly when the Bamberg prince bishop gave a sign to one of his servants, who blew a fanfare on his trumpet, then took out a long parchment roll and began to read.

"Honored guests, noblemen, and gentlemen of Bamberg. It is with great joy that His Excellency Philipp Valentin Voit von Rieneck welcomes to the hallowed halls of Geyerswörth Castle his beloved friend, the archbishop of Mainz, bishop of Würzburg and Worms, a prince of the Reich, defender of the Faith, and close confidant of the German kaiser — the honorable Johann Philipp von Schönborn . . ."

While the servant reeled off the usual tributes, Simon's eyes wandered over the audience, where he caught sight of Hieronymus Hauser and Katharina, whom he had overlooked earlier in the milling crowd. Magdalena had told him that the Hausers were also invited to the reception. Katharina had put on her best dress, and her father wore a coat and vest like a real councilor, but he too looked almost as pale as the suffragan bishop. He seemed distracted and kept turning around carefully as if looking for someone in the audience. In the next moment, though, he seemed completely lost in his thoughts.

I wonder if it has anything to do with our conversation yesterday? Simon thought.

By now, the herald had greeted all the important guests by name and had started explaining the rules of the theater competition.

"In his infinite kindness, our bishop has decided to offer winter quarters to a group of itinerant actors," he proclaimed. "Since there are two groups in Bamberg this year, a competition will decide which one will be permitted to remain in the city. Each group has selected a short piece to perform for us now, and after that the bishop will choose the winner. The two pieces are entitled . . ." — he looked down at his parchment roll — "*Papinian* and *Peter Squenz,* both from the pen of the esteemed author Andreas Gryphius. Good luck to everyone."

One last time he played the fanfare on his trumpet, then the candles in the audience were extinguished, bathing the stage in a warm light. The curtain rose, and out stepped a pale, made-up, somewhat feminine-looking actor who spread his arms and turned toward the two bishops while declaiming the prologue in a slight French accent.

"Those who climb over everyone else, then loook down prouuudly as reeech people at how pooor people behave," he began in a fervent voice, pronouncing each vowel in a peculiar way . . . "As ooonder heeem a Reich gooz uup in flaames, or theere the miiighty waaves cooover the feeelds . . ."

Simon wasn't familiar with Gryphius's *Papinian,* but it was soon clear it was very melodramatic and yet also very boring. It concerned a courtier in a Roman royal family who stood between two feuding emperors, brothers who eventually killed each other. There was also an almost endless number of characters in the play but only a limited number of actors, so that each actor played multiple parts, and Simon was soon completely confused.

Well, at least we have enough time now to think about what we're going to say to the Würzburg bishop, he thought.

And indeed, in a few minutes his thoughts wandered, while

up in front the actors declaimed, whined, and died. How was Magdalena doing? Was she already up on the cathedral mount with Jakob and Bartholomäus, preparing to free Matheo? If that was the case, the tower guard would surely have already sounded the alarm . . .

Now and then he glanced at the two bishops in the first row. While Johann Philipp von Schönborn listened attentively, observing the action on the stage, Prince Bishop Rieneck appeared extremely bored, shifting back and forth in his chair and even yawning loudly one time. Moments later he demanded a glass of wine, which startled the actor playing Papinian on the stage. Other guests followed the example of their leader and began talking or loudly clinking their glasses, while the actors continued to struggle through their lines.

The person most distracted from the performance on the stage, however, was the suffragan bishop, Sebastian Harsee. He was having difficulty even sitting up in his chair, and he occasionally slumped forward but then caught himself at the last moment. He appeared to be in great pain, kept putting his hands to his head, and Simon wasn't certain he would be able to hold out through the two performances.

After what seemed like an eternity, Papinian finally spoke his final lines.

"Receeve my innocent bloood, and show meercy to thiiis innocent empire."

He bared his naked chest to the executioner, and as he uttered a death rattle, the curtain came down. There was some restrained applause, but also a few boos. The garishly made-up leading man grimaced, stepped forward with the cast, and curtsied effeminately in response to the nonexistent ovations.

He was mercilessly booed off the stage, and from behind the curtain the sound of trunks and heavy props being moved around could be heard. Finally, the curtain opened again and Simon saw the second group of actors in threadbare costumes, among them a skinny beanpole of a fellow with a wig, evidently the director of the troupe. From talking with Magdalena, Simon knew he was an Englishman by the name of Sir Malcolm. There was whispering in the crowd, as naturally most of the guests knew that the werewolf who had been caught came from this group of actors. Simon's heart began to pound.

They must be very good to have avoided any hint of suspicion . . .

But it soon became clear that Malcolm's people had chosen the right piece to perform. Two actors played the parts of stupid workmen rehearsing a play for their king and his entourage and getting involved in all sorts of foolishness. Sir Malcolm proved to be a superb comedian. The mood of the audience also became much more relaxed as people laughed and slapped their thighs. The Bamberg bishop laughed loudest of all, causing the audience to burst out laughing even louder.

After a while the clueless workers exited the stage to loud laughter and applause, and the second act began with the entrance of the king and his retinue. A dainty maiden in a red dress — no doubt the character mentioned previously, the beautiful Princess Violandra — walked alongside the monarch. A murmur went through the crowd, as it was unusual for women to appear on the stage.

The young child is quite beautiful, Simon thought. *She almost reminds me a bit of Magdalena.*

He couldn't help admiring her grace and noble bearing as she stepped to the front of the stage. For the first time her face gleamed in the light of the candles.

"We all enjoy comedies and tragedies," she said in a clear, bright voice, her right hand trembling just a bit. "Which type do you wish to see?"

Simon was stunned, and a muffled cry escaped his lips. He knew the voice.

"What in the world . . . ?" he gasped.

The stunning Princess Violandra was none other than Barbara.

Night had fallen over Bamberg and the gates of Geyerswörth Castle, and the autumn fog rose from the river, embracing the city and soon the hills around it, enveloping everything in a damp, billowing comforter, with only a few church spires rising above it.

Under the protection of darkness and fog, three disguised figures slunk toward the cathedral mount, each holding a large wrapped bundle. They avoided the main streets and took long detours to avoid the local night watchmen. When the bell of the church struck eight, they could hear the watchman's call somewhere nearby, but his steps receded, so they pressed on up the hill until finally they reached the vast, deserted cathedral square.

Magdalena pushed her headscarf down inside her collar and looked around, squinting while her eyes grew accustomed to the dark. On the left, the towers of the cathedral rose up like long black shadows, while on her right was the new building site for the royal residence, with only the two rear wings of the building so far complete. Faint music could be heard coming from the city below, but otherwise it was as silent as a tomb.

"We're too early," Magdalena whispered, out of breath from the steep climb and the bundle she was carrying. "We should have at least waited for the next ringing of the bells. How do we know there aren't a few night owls still roaming around?"

"The sooner this is over, the happier I'll be," Bartholomäus growled. "Besides, this is the best time, believe me. Most of the guards are still down at the reception in the castle, but later they'll return with the two bishops when they come here to sleep. And the good citizens are carousing in the taverns." He gave a dry laugh. "The Bambergers drink and party for any reason at all, even if it's just the visit of some bishop."

"We need a place to change," Jakob Kuisl grumbled, looking

around the cathedral square. "Here we're as easy to see as the devil's naked ass."

"Don't worry, I know where we can go," his brother replied. "Follow me."

With Bartholomäus leading the way, they slipped along the walls of the cathedral, then, just before reaching the Old Residence, they turned left into an alleyway so dark they could barely see anything. After a few paces, Bartholomäus stopped, set down his bundle, and drew back the lantern shade so that for the first time since leaving they had a bit of light.

"We're safe here for the time being," Bartholomäus whispered. "I've checked this out. The only one pulling guard duty tonight is Matthias, the old drunk." He turned with a wide grin and looked at his older brother. "You remember . . . the old booze-hound from our first nighttime expedition. I stopped by earlier and brought him a bottle of brandy. Right now he's no doubt off in dreamland. But of course that doesn't apply to the guards in front of the Old Residence."

"We'll send them off to dreamland, as well," Jakob replied. "And now stop talking so much and give me the pelt."

Bartholomäus unrolled his bundle, which contained a number of animal hides along with some pots sealed with beeswax. Magdalena, though standing a way off, could smell the odor of decomposition. She, too, was carrying a bundle of pots and pelts. Her father had dragged the almost one-hundred-pound wolf, wrapped in nothing but a thin cloth, up to the cathedral mount. Now he threw it down in front of them like a sack of stones.

If we mess this up, they'll break us on the wheel right here in the middle of the cathedral square, Magdalena thought. *But we won't mess up. We mustn't.*

Carefully she opened one of the pots, which gave off a pungent odor, and with trembling fingers immersed two of the larger linen rags into it until they were completely soaked. They hadn't been able to find real sponges at the market, as they were too rare and too expensive, but Magdalena hoped they could get by with what they had. Her father had worked for hours that day to get the proper mix, and finally they tried the potion on a stray dog, which immediately fainted, collapsed, and only regained consciousness more than an hour later. That was no guarantee, however, that it would have the same effect on the guards.

"Well, how do we look?" Jakob asked, interrupting her thoughts. His voice sounded strangely muffled, as if he were underneath a blanket. "Will we pass for werewolves?"

Magdalena looked up, and it hit her like a bolt of lightning.

In front of her stood two horrible creatures that looked like a hellish mixture of man, wolf, bear, and fox. As in an ancient ritual, both brothers wore wolf skulls on their heads, making the huge men appear even taller than they already were, and the hides of stags and bears wrapped around their necks made them look much wider, as well.

In the flickering light of the lantern, Magdalena stared into the empty eye sockets of the wolf skulls. Though she knew they were just her father and her uncle, she had difficulty suppressing a scream.

"That stuff stinks like the Plague," panted the creature on the left. It was Uncle Bartholomäus, and he tugged angrily at the hides. "If I have to run around in this getup much longer, I'll throw up on the guard's shoes."

"Pull yourself together," the werewolf next to him said. "Your servant Aloysius doesn't smell much better."

"I don't know how I ever let myself get roped into such a crazy thing," Bartholomäus complained as he staggered back and forth like a drunk in his hides. "Besides, I can hardly see anything underneath this wolf's head." He tugged at the skull tied in place under his chin by a leather strap. "I'll be lucky if I don't run right into a wall."

Bartholomäus tugged harder on the skull, but Jakob grabbed his arm and pulled it down.

"Just keep thinking of your dogs, my dear brother," he whispered. "You don't want to lose them, do you? So don't back out now."

"For God's sake, you bastard. I'm . . ."

"Stop it right now, you two," Magdalena interjected. Her voice was so loud she was afraid someone might have heard her. But all remained calm.

"We all want to see the end of this werewolf frenzy," she continued in a softer voice, and looked pleadingly at the two men. "We certainly don't want anyone to suspect afterward that Uncle Bartholomäus gave us the key, and we can only do that if we present the Bambergers with a dead werewolf on a silver platter. Here it is," she said, pointing at the cadaver on the ground, "so let's put an end to all of this, and no more threats, Father, do you understand?"

The creature mumbled something unintelligible from under his fur pelt.

"I asked if you understand me," Magdalena persisted.

"Yes, yes, all right. I won't make another sound if that guy keeps his mouth shut, too."

Magdalena took a deep breath, then handed each of the brothers a cloth soaked in sheep's blood and then some sulfur from the little wooden boxes, the tinder, and the gunpowder.

"So let's begin," she said quietly. "From now on, there's no going back."

Down below in the Blue Lion at the foot of the cathedral mount, Georg had learned one of the great maxims of drinking. The more beer you guzzle down, the better it tastes. That was especially true of Bamberg beer brewed with smoked mash, which always gave it a slight taste of cold ashes and ham. By now, Georg was on his fourth mug, and he felt great.

Behind him, a hot fire was roaring in the tile stove, which caused sweat to run down his forehead. In one corner, three men were drinking and singing an old Frankish melody, and Georg noticed himself instinctively humming along. As a child he'd often had a small beer to drink, which was supposed to be healthier than the polluted water, which was used only for washing and cooking. The beer here, however, was dark and strong . . . very strong. Finally Georg understood why men always wanted to patronize the taverns. Something as splendid as this beer couldn't really be appreciated in silence and alone. You needed company. As he tapped the table with one hand to the beat of the melody, he chugged down his mug of beer and beckoned to the hefty woman behind the bar, who smiled and set down another freshly filled mug in front of him.

"You're the executioner's boy, aren't you?" she said with a wink. "Don't worry, I won't tell anyone. I recognized you right away when you came in. You're a splendidly built lad."

Georg grinned sheepishly He wanted to reply but couldn't think of what to say. It was strange: just a while ago the woman at the bar had appeared very old and fat, but since the last beer, she suddenly seemed to have gotten younger and more attractive. She probably wasn't much older than Magdalena.

Magdalena . . . the children . . .

Georg was startled at the thought.

"What . . . what time is it?" he asked, dazed. "How long have I been here?"

The woman shrugged. "No idea. Two hours, maybe." She winked at him. "Don't worry, we don't have any closing time, if that's what you're wondering. All the taverns are open later on account of the reception for the bishops. Why are you asking?"

Georg stared into the foam on his freshly served beer, trying to think. Something came to mind, fleetingly, and then it was gone. It had something to do with Jeremias and the children, but all he could remember was Jeremias saying he could also stay away longer than two hours.

Just one more beer—it's right here in front of me. It would be too bad to let it spoil . . .

Not until then did he notice that the woman was still standing next to him. He pushed a few coins across the table.

"Thanks very much," he mumbled, "but after this beer, I've really got to go home."

"Of course," she replied with a smile. "That's what they all say."

With a laugh, she turned away, and Georg put the mug to his mouth.

As the black brew dripped from his lips, he struggled to remember what had gone through his mind before. Once again, the thought flashed through his mind.

Jeremias . . . the children . . . the sword . . .

But the beer washed the memory away, and soon his head sank down onto the table.

A short time later he was snoring peacefully to the beat of the music.

"That surely is a kindly wall that doesn't hold me back . . ." Barbara was just saying up on the stage of the festival hall, but the rest of her lines were drowned out in a chorus of laughter and applause.

The applause was like a soothing, warm wave washing over her and at the same time filling her inside. Barbara rolled her eyes theatrically and stepped back a pace in order to make room for the other actors in the scene. Her initial trembling and the rumbling in her stomach, which the actors had called stage fright, had disappeared as if by magic, making her feel as if she were in seventh heaven now. She was not just acting the part, she *was* the princess Violandra. It seemed like with this splendid dress she'd been able to leave her old life behind her. The theater gave her the opportunity to be anything she wanted. She was no longer a dishonorable hangman's daughter, but a princess, a queen, or a beautiful young woman waiting for her lover. There were so many roles to play. And it was clear that the people here loved her. They laughed at her few lines, and when she gracefully skipped to the front of the stage, they whistled and cheered. It was just fabulous.

After some hesitation, Sir Malcolm gave her more lines than he had planned at first, no doubt because he'd noticed in the rehearsals the effect she had on the men in the audience. In addition to the part of the princess, Barbara now also played the prince and the queen. The play within the play, the drama *Pyramus and Thisbe* takes place at the king's court, with the simpleminded workers first to appear. One of the actors represented a wall through which Pyramus and his beloved spoke. The woman played one of the male roles with an artificial, high-pitched voice and exaggerated fluttering of her eyelids. The audience applauded wildly.

"You loose, immoral wall!" the mythical Pyramus cried. "You roguish, thieving, frivolous thing!" Then the wall and the hero came to blows, causing a wave of loud laughter in the audience.

"Well, I'd not want to be the wall in this play," Barbara continued in her role, and the people groaned happily.

Since it was dark in the hall, she couldn't see beyond the first few rows where the nobles were sitting. The Bamberg bishop was wiping tears of laughter from the corners of his eyes, and the man alongside him, evidently the bishop of Würzburg, appeared greatly amused as well.

It's a hit, Barbara thought. *Sir Malcolm will surely win the competition, and Matheo . . .*

The thought of Matheo made her stop short, reminding her of how she'd run away from the executioner's house and Magdalena's promise that her father would certainly do something to help them. Did he already have a plan? Or would her family abandon her and Matheo?

"God forbid, what. . . what . . ." she stuttered, forgetting her lines and shifting from one leg to the other. Malcolm cast a disapproving glance at her and suddenly seemed not at all happy.

"What's the meaning of this?" he whispered so softly that no one else could hear.

"What's the meaning of this?" she finally exclaimed. But no one else noticed her momentary lapse, since at that moment another workman appeared on the stage holding a painted shield bearing a carelessly scribbled image of the moon.

"Noble queen, this is the moon," said Sir Malcolm, quickly falling back into his role of Peter Squenz, then turning to the cheering crowd to acknowledge their applause.

The play continued, and after the moon came another workman wearing a threadbare woolen blanket over his head, meowing like a cat and representing a lion. The audience was abuzz now, and the room seemed to seethe and tremble like a pot of boiling water. Barbara looked down and saw an older cleric in the second row wearing a monk's cowl. He appeared ill and was swaying back and forth in his chair with his face buried in his hands and his mouth opened in a scream, though Barbara could hear nothing in the general tumult. Was the man ill, or was the noise and heat just too much for him?

There was no time for her to ponder that question, as the action on the stage required her full concentration. Assuming that his beloved Thisbe had been attacked and eaten by the lion, the foolish Pyramus had taken his own life. Just the same, he continued chatting merrily with the laughing public. Barbara shook her head in feigned annoyance.

"You can't just have the corpses get up like that and give speeches," she scolded.

Sir Malcolm, playing the part of both a worker and a clumsy director, shook his finger. "Pyramus, you're dead, you should be ashamed of yourself," he chided him, with a wink of his eye.

"You can't say anything. You just have to lie there like a dead pig."

At that moment there was a loud crash and banging sound in the audience. Barbara looked down from the stage and saw the sick cleric fall off his chair. Most in the audience hadn't noticed and continued laughing and cheering, but the two bishops turned around to look. With concern, Archbishop Schönborn stood up and beckoned for a servant to come over, while his colleague, Philipp Rieneck, just shook his head in annoyance, evidently angry at the interruption.

Many in the audience were still unaware of the incident, and they stepped aside reluctantly as two men approached from the rear of the room. One wore the typical hat of the Doctor's Guild, the other, who was noticeably shorter, a wide-brimmed hat with a red feather.

"Simon," Barbara whispered. "But why . . ."

"Damn it, what's going on?" whispered Sir Malcolm, standing alongside her. "Come, come. It doesn't matter what's going on down there, the show must go on."

With a loud, somewhat forced laugh, Malcolm turned to the public and regained their attention.

"Before I was a *prologus,* so now I am an *epilogus,*" he declaimed, bowing deeply.

That was as far as he got, for at that moment there was a piercing scream in the hall. It came from one of the servants who had just bent down to the sick man who lay writhing and quivering on the floor. His monk's cowl lay alongside him, and a thin stream of blood trickled across his bald head. Suddenly the sick man jumped up from the floor and began waving his arms and dancing around wildly. The wheezing sounds that came from his mouth sounded brutish and inhuman.

For a moment, he turned toward the stage, and in the flickering light of the candles Barbara could see his face. It was pale like that of a corpse, and his eyes bulged out of his head. The worst thing, however, was his lips. They were so thin as to be almost invisible, and between them was a row of sharp, yellow teeth much larger than those of an ordinary human. Foaming spittle dripped from his teeth onto his cassock, while the creature, clearly possessed by the devil, let out a long, brutish cry and rushed at Simon, who was paralyzed with fear.

"My God, it's the werewolf!" the terrified servant shouted, stepping back a few paces and knocking down some of the others as he fell to the floor. "Our suffragan bishop is a real werewolf! Oh, God be with us, the devil is in our midst!"

Then the entire hall erupted in chaos.

12

Up ON THE CATHEDRAL MOUNT THE FOG HAD BEEN getting thicker and thicker. The damp air made Magdalena's clothes cling to her, as if trying to prevent her from getting any closer to her father and uncle.

Matheo was imprisoned in St. Thomas's in the Old Residence, a huge enclave on the cathedral square surrounded by high walls on all sides. Years ago, kaisers, kings, and bishops had resided there, and meetings of the parliament had been held there as well. Now the Old Residence was not much more than a large horse barn and arsenal, but the meeting room for the city council and the former main room of the castle gave evidence of the great power centered there in the past.

The three of them passed by a chapel recessed into the wall, then sneaked quietly by the council chamber until they reached the so-called Schöne Pforte, or "Beautiful Gate," which served as the entrance to the old enclave. During the day, there was much hustle and bustle as people entered and left — workers, coachmen, and soldiers on patrol on the opposite side, where construction was proceeding on the new bishop's residence. But at night, and in the heavy fog, practically no one was around; just two lonely guards stood watch at the gate, tightly clutching their halberds, as if struggling not to keel over with boredom and exhaustion. The only light was a single lantern hanging on a hook on the wall, swaying back and forth in the wind. The cathedral bells struck the ninth hour.

"We have to get by the two of them; we can't avoid that," whispered Bartholomäus, sweating profusely under his werewolf costume. "And then there are probably some more guards inside—I have no idea how many tonight. I hear that the captain has a unit he can call up for special occasions. If they're busy down in the city now, perhaps we'll have an easier job of it."

"One thing at a time," Jakob grumbled, turning to Magdalena. "It's important to get to them before they can sound the alarm, or our beautiful plan is going fall apart at the very beginning. Is there anything you can do to distract the fellows for a while?"

Magdalena smiled and batted her eyelids. "That shouldn't be too hard for me." She swayed her hips suggestively from side to side. "What do you think?"

"For God's sake, don't overdo it," her father scolded. "What would Simon think? A little flirting should be enough."

"Believe me, a little flirting won't get very far with these men. I'll have to pour on the charm."

Without any explanation, Magdalena pulled a yellow scarf out from under her jacket and tied it around her head. Adeptly, she pulled her bodice down so far that her breasts almost popped out.

"Damn it, girl, you're not going to . . ." he started to say.

But Magdalena had already stepped away from the wall and started swaggering toward the entrance. Soon she stepped into the light of the lantern, and the guards looked at her suspiciously.

"Hey, you," they called to her. "What's the matter with you? Don't you know it's way past curfew?"

"Some people don't even start work until after curfew," she

cooed, smiling and swaying her hips as she drew closer. Only then did they see the yellow scarf over her head, which identified Magdalena as a whore. The fatter of the two guards grinned lewdly.

"Aha, Hans, just look, we have an important visitor," he said, bowing slightly. "It looks as if the beautiful lady has lost her way. The Rosengasse is, as far as I know, down below near Saint Martin's."

"That can happen easily with fog like this," said his colleague, a pimply youth who surely had not yet touched many women in his young life. Lewdly he stared at Magdalena's low neckline. "But since she's already here . . ."

"You know, we could arrest you and throw you in the dungeon," the fat man said to Magdalena, shaking a finger at her in jest. "Fortunately, there's already someone there whom you surely don't want to meet, unless you like to have sex with animals." He let out a dirty laugh.

"I'd much prefer a couple of strapping lads," she replied, fluttering her eyelids. "What would you say if I gave you two handsome boys a special price, hmm?" She stroked her bodice, and the young man gaped sheep-like at her.

"Well, we've got to stand guard here until the shifts change," he said hesitantly. "Maybe later . . ."

"Later, I'll be back to turning tricks on the Rosengasse." Magdalena smiled. "Besides, who's going to notice? As far as I know, the captain and the other guards are down at the castle. They just left you two poor devils up here?"

"You forget our three colleagues in the Old Residence," the fat man chimed in. "But you're right, it's not fair. The people down below are having a party, drinking and watching the play, and we're standing around here in the damp and the fog, tired and ready to drop." He grinned. "Ah, but I know what we can do. One of us will stand here to guard the gate while the other can go over to the little alley next to the cathedral with you and see what you have to offer. We'll switch off."

Magdalena gave him her sweetest smile. "What a wonderful idea. I should have thought of that. So, which of you two handsome lads will go first?"

Even before she had asked, she was sure it would be the fat one. She walked ahead, swinging her hips back and forth while the heavy man followed, groaning and snorting. He left his halberd behind, leaning against the wall.

The guard grinned expectantly. Soon, he was sure, he'd get to use his other lance.

In the meantime, skinny Hans remained standing in front of the gate, imagining vividly what he would soon be doing with the woman.

Hans was seventeen years old and actually he'd never seen a naked woman before, with the exception of his mother, of course, an old, fat linen weaver, but it wasn't a pretty sight. With trembling lips, he imagined the shapely woman with the wild black locks, and how he would soon slip his hand under her skirt. What was there to find down there? Friends had told him the strangest stories about the female sex organs; they spoke of a quick little mouse hiding there, but they probably were just pulling his leg. Well, he'd soon find out. Hans had five kreuzers in his pocket, and that should suffice for a first voyage of discovery.

He listened anxiously, full of expectation for his turn that was about to come. Suddenly he heard a muffled cry that probably came from fat Jonas, his father's friend and colleague. Was that part of this great secret? People shouted when they made love? He'd heard that also from his mother, who in years past had rolled around with his father under a sheepskin blanket in the room. This was the only heated space in the house, so the eight-member family had to use it as a common bedroom. Their parents' bed was separated from the children's beds by nothing more than a thin curtain full of holes, and sometimes Hans had the feeling his mother was crying with pain. Now, as well, what he heard were not shouts of rapture, but rather . . . panic? Yes, they were clearly cries of horror. Was that also part of the game? And what were they doing there all this time?

Shivering, Hans rubbed his cold fingers together. A year ago, when he'd taken this job with the city guards, he thought he'd find real adventure. But for the most part what he did was pick up drunks in the streets and stand guard for hours on end until his feet were killing him. And if the captain was putting together an elite squad for some secret mission, as he did just a few days ago, he naturally couldn't be part of that. It was driving him mad.

Hans was just wondering whether to leave his post for a moment to see if everything was all right, when he heard a scraping sound behind him, as if someone in large boots were shuffling over the pavement. Was it that fat Jonas? That was strange, since he had gone off in the other direction. So who . . . ?

Hans turned around and let out a long squeal. Actually, he tried to scream, but what was standing in front of him was so horrible that his voice failed.

It was a huge hairy creature with a foul odor towering two heads above him. With dead eyes it stared down at him, as a deep growl and finally human sounds escaped from its lips.

"Ach . . . curses . . . I can't see . . . Damn!"

Hans whimpered, his hand went limp, and he dropped his halberd on the ground. He hadn't understood exactly what the monster said, but there was no doubt in his mind this creature in front of him was the slender lad imprisoned in St. Thomas's who'd changed back into the monster who'd killed so many people and now had escaped the dungeon. Surely he'd already killed fat Jonas and the prostitute as well, and now it was his turn.

"Please . . . please spare my life," he whimpered, throwing himself down in front of the werewolf. "In the name of all fourteen holy saints in our hour of need, please . . ."

He got no further, as a shadow swept down on him. Suddenly Hans felt something soft with a strong, bitter taste being placed over his face.

The thought raced through his mind: *The werewolf's jaws. He'll rip my lips off and eat them. Oh, Holy Mother of God . . .*

Then he felt heavy and sank into a dark fog that smelled of old, musty animal hides. The werewolf had swallowed him whole.

"Damn! That could have easily blown up in our faces. Why didn't you get rid of the fellow sooner?"

Jakob stood alongside his brother pointing to the unconscious guard at their feet.

"Because I can't see a damn thing under these hides," Bartholomäus replied. "Just be happy I found his face so I could put the sleeping sponge over it."

"Pull yourselves together, both of you. Do you want to wake up everyone in the Old Residence?"

It was Magdalena, approaching them from the narrow alley and speaking in a hushed voice as she looked around. The two brothers looked quite fearsome, like two demons wrestling for dominion in an endless battle in hell.

Or like two old grouches always criticizing each other, she thought. *When this is all over, I hope I won't have any Kuisls to put up with for a while.*

But then it occurred to her that she was in fact a Kuisl herself.

How did Father put it in the forest yesterday? You can't pick your family . . .

After Magdalena had lured the guard into the lane, her father had come down on him like a ton of bricks. The man could only utter a brief cry before Jakob pressed the sleeping sponge in his face. The guard had twitched and groaned briefly but then fell silent. The potion seemed to have worked. But then they heard the other guard wailing and crying and they ran over to the gate, where Bartholomäus had already gotten things under control.

"Well, so far so good," Jakob said with satisfaction, turning to his brother. "I hope you remembered the keys."

They were standing in front of the Beautiful Gate, made of stone and surrounded by several figures and statues of Mary. On the left, next to the larger gate intended for wagons was a smaller gate. Bartholomäus searched under the furs and finally fished a rusty set of keys out of his pocket.

"These keys are for the gate, Saint Thomas's Chapel, the torture chamber, and the dungeon down in the city," he whispered. "They'll take us anywhere we want to go, but you still have the guards, and I just don't know how many of them there are."

"The fat guy mentioned three guards at the Old Residence," Magdalena whispered.

Kuisl cursed. "That's just one too many, unless . . ." He stopped short, then pointed at the whore's cloth in Magdalena's hair.

"Give it to me; it's a thorn in my side, in any case."

She handed him the kerchief, and he quickly opened the pot of henbane and dunked the cloth in it. Finally, he gave it back to her. "If things really get tough, you'll have to take on one of the guards yourself. With this, you won't need to use your wiggling behind and fluttering eyelashes."

She smiled as he handed her the sharp-smelling cloth. She noticed before that the sight of his daughter as a whore had enraged him. Still, Jakob had to admit to himself that her plan had worked. His grumbling and growling now was just a peculiar, Kuisl-like compliment.

"Once I unlock the door," Bartholomäus warned his two

companions in a low voice, "you'll have to work fast. The guard-house is over on the right, behind the gate, and it's quite possible the guards are still around. The next building on the street is the Chapel of Saint Thomas, and that's where we have to enter. Are you ready?"

Magdalena and her father nodded, and Bartholomäus silently entered through the small gate.

Sebastian Harsee's fingers dug like claws into Simon's arms, and his face was only a hand's breadth away. With madness in his eyes, he glowered at Simon as the spittle dripped in long strings from his teeth. Simon struggled to keep his distance from the crazed bishop. Was he mistaken, or were Harsee's teeth in fact longer than before? Perhaps it was just that the muscles in his face were in spasms and his lips contorted in a horrible grin.

That must be it, Simon thought. *There must be some logical explanation. Or is this perhaps a nightmare? Was Barbara's appearance on the stage just a hallucination?*

Once more the suffragan bishop let out a ghastly howl. He seemed to be trying to seize Simon, who finally managed to pull himself free of the quivering creature, gasping, as what almost looked like a magical circle formed around them. Behind Simon, people were shouting and screaming, frantically trying to escape through the narrow entranceway into the courtyard, and somewhere there was the sound of a window breaking. Simon grabbed hold of one of the chairs, stood up, and tried to catch his breath.

Not until then was Simon able to think through everything that had happened. Until just a short while ago, he'd been standing up in the gallery of the Geyerswörth festival hall with Samuel, staring in disbelief at his fifteen-year-old sister-in-law in her debut performance as an actress. He had to confess that Barbara was excellent in her role, though they never could allow her father to hear about this activity. And right in the middle of the thunderous applause, the suffragan bishop had collapsed. Simon had rushed forward with Samuel to help, and then his worst fears were realized. Sebastian Harsee had turned into a werewolf.

"My God, who would ever have thought this possible?" asked Philipp Rieneck, the Bamberg bishop, pointing with a trembling finger at Harsee, who was still convulsing on the floor. "Dear Brother Sebastian is himself a werewolf. Holy Mary, help! Who else in Bamberg has the devil taken away?"

He looked around in a panic as half-crazed citizens, clerics, and courtiers ran screaming past him.

"Guards, guards, over here!" Rieneck shouted shrilly. "Help your monarch!"

Out of the corner of his eye, Simon could see his friend, Samuel, stuck in the crowd, desperately trying to make his way to him. Farther behind, Martin Lebrecht, captain of the city guards, appeared with drawn sword, accompanied by two anxious-looking guards.

"Here is the werewolf!" Rieneck shouted. "Come here, quickly! Kill him!"

At the same moment, Sebastian Harsee began to howl again and froth at the mouth, which made his lips look more and more like those of a wild beast. He tried to stand up but couldn't. Panting and twitching, the suffragan bishop lay on the floor groaning like a dying animal.

"Doctor, doctor, do something," shouted Johann von Schönborn, standing petrified alongside his colleague. "Whatever is wrong with this man, he urgently needs your help."

"He doesn't need any help—he's a werewolf," Rieneck shrieked. "Quick, Captain, get rid of him before he can destroy any others."

In the meantime, Samuel had succeeded in getting to the howling suffragan bishop, but so had Martin Lebrecht. The captain of the guard raised his sword and was about to strike, but Samuel held him back.

"Stop!" he shouted. "Can't you see he no longer poses any danger?"

In fact, Harsee's convulsions had diminished. He struggled so hard to sit up one more time that Simon feared he might break his back, then he finally fell silent. The wound on his head, evidently caused by his fall, was no longer bleeding so hard.

"Is he dead?" Philipp Rieneck asked anxiously after a few moments.

Carefully, Samuel leaned down to the sick man and listened to his chest. He shook his head.

"It looks like he's lost consciousness, though his eyes are wide open. So it can also be a spasm, and he'll be able to hear everything around him just as if he were fully awake."

"What a dreadful thing," Simon whispered.

In the meantime, the theater had emptied out, broken shards of glass and crockery lay all around, the curtain in front of the stage was torn, and the actors had all vanished. Through the broken windows, excited voices and shouts of the city guards could be heard coming from the courtyard below.

Bishop Johann von Schönborn turned to Martin Lebrecht, who had put his sword back in its sheath.

"It appears you will no longer be needed here," said the Würzburg bishop, who, in contrast to his colleagues, had settled down somewhat. "It would be best for you to go outside and calm people down."

"At your command, Your Excellency."

Lebrecht saluted, then withdrew with the two visibly relieved guards and headed down to the courtyard. Once all the men had left, Philipp Rieneck turned to his colleagues and addressed them in a trembling voice.

"For a long time now," he began hesitantly, "I've had my doubts about these werewolf stories, and I thought it was about time for good brother Sebastian to get hold of himself. I didn't stop him because . . . because . . ." He fell silent.

Because you don't give a damn about this city, Simon thought. *The only thing you care about is your menagerie and your mistresses.*

"But I must confess that Brother Sebastian was right," Rieneck finally continued in a firm voice. "And what's worse, this werewolf seems able to turn even honorable people into werewolves." He shuddered with horror. "If he can take away my God-fearing suffragan bishop, he can even take me . . . and . . . you, too."

He pointed at Johann Schönborn, who frowned and stepped back a pace, as if fearing that the pure terror that had seized his colleague might be contagious.

"I'll admit I don't have any explanation for this, myself," said Schönborn, shaking his head and pointing at the paralyzed body of the suffragan bishop, whose wide-open eyes were still staring blankly into space. "Only the learned doctors can help us here. What do you think, Master Samuel?"

"It's surely too early for a definitive diagnosis," replied Samuel, still kneeling alongside the sick bishop and checking his breathing and heart beat. "But judging from the way the suffragan bishop was twitching and thrashing about, it could be epilepsy, or perhaps these spasms can be attributed to Saint Vitus' dance."

"Do you think Harsee has caught Saint Anthony's Fire?" Simon asked.

The medicus had seen that illness many years ago in Regensburg. A bluish mushroom that sometimes grew on grain could cause hallucinations, spasms, and at times paralysis, which could lead to death. Simon looked down in horror at the contorted face of the suffragan bishop, who seemed to be staring back up at him.

"Saint Vitus' dance can have many causes," Samuel explained, "including angel's trumpet and other magical herbs.

Sometimes people dance around in a religious ecstasy, but some people say the twitching comes from a spider bite, for example, from a tarantula . . ."

"The wound in his neck," Simon interrupted excitedly. "Do you remember? Could that be a spider bite?"

"Perhaps you're right." Samuel pulled down Harsee's robe at the collar and took another look at the wound with the red halo. "No doubt it's a bite," he said with a frown, "but for a spider it's really too big, and besides, there are no tarantulas here. As far as I know, they are found much farther south, in southern Italy."

"Aha, then he was no doubt bitten by a werewolf," Rieneck cried out. "Did you see Brother Sebastian's teeth? They were pointed and long. And foam was dripping from them onto the ground."

"That can be caused by cramps," Samuel assured him, "which distend facial skin, giving the impression that the victim has long teeth." He stood up and wiped his hands on his jacket. "I can't tell you any more now, but we should keep a close eye on him." He shrugged and turned to Simon. "Can you help me take care of him?"

Simon had gone to fetch a jug of wine and a piece of material from the theater curtain to wash Harsee's head wound and apply a temporary dressing. As he approached the sick man with the jug, something strange happened. Suddenly the suffragan bishop once again started quivering, tossing his head back and forth and rearing up as if the very sight of the wine were painful to him.

"See! A sign," Philipp Rieneck said. "He is terrified on seeing the blood of our Savior. Sprinkle him with holy water so he will lose his power. With witches that's supposed to be a sure-fire method."

Now Johann Schönborn also seemed uncertain. "I've never seen anything like this before," he mumbled. "Perhaps we really ought to try using holy water."

"Nonsense." Samuel's voice was so low that the bishops couldn't hear him, but he turned to Simon, frowning.

"I must admit this is strange," he said softly. "As I told you, he refused to drink anything yesterday."

"Indeed," Simon nodded, thinking. "He wouldn't drink a thing, and for that reason I don't believe he went into convulsions on account of the blood of our Savior. See for yourself . . ." He looked around until he found a jug of beer that was still unopened and approached the sick man, who once again started to quiver and writhe around. After a while, Simon put the jug down again and turned to the two astonished bishops.

"Since transubstantiation and Communion have never taken place with beer, I can only assume that he'll react that way toward any kind of liquid." He smiled wryly. "It appears he would react that way even if it were apple juice."

"But why?" asked Johann Schönborn, shaking his head. "This is all very mysterious." He turned to Samuel and looked at him sternly.

"Before the performance you said you had certain suspicions concerning this werewolf. I think it's time for an explanation, my dear Doctor."

Samuel took a deep breath. "Well, it seems that . . ." he began hesitantly, "some of the, uh . . . literature suggests that . . ."

At that moment there was a loud clap of thunder and shouts of terror from the crowd out in the courtyard. Prince Bishop Philipp Voit von Rieneck fell to his knees and folded his hands in prayer.

"Holy Mother of God!" he wailed. "Now we've angered the heavens as well with your heretical scholarly words. Will this madness never cease?"

Up in the Old Residence, three other guards experienced the worst nightmare of their lives that night.

Outside it was cold and damp, and the guards had decided to while away the hours of their shift with a friendly game of dice in the guardhouse. The captain was down below in Geyerswörth Castle, and the second-in-command had the job of guarding the bishop's palace. So who was there to tell them they couldn't enjoy one or two little games and a well-deserved beer?

"Here's to fat Jonas and the kid, freezing their asses off out at the gate," said red-haired Alvin with a grin, lifting his mug. Earlier, he'd been able to get hold of a keg of strong, malt-flavored Märzen beer. "Brrr, on a night like this I'm glad I didn't pull guard duty down in the cathedral square."

"Do you think there's really a werewolf prowling around out there?" asked the second guard, a pale, pasty-faced fellow whose eyes kept flitting anxiously back and forth.

"Ha! I'll bet you're shitting in your pants, Eberhard." With a loud laugh, Alvin wiped the beer foam from his lips. "Haven't you heard? We have the werewolf in custody, and he won't attack anyone now." He lowered his voice. "But just between us, if you ask me, this fellow in Saint Thomas's is no werewolf. Just look at him — such a wimpy guy, crying his eyes out and praying to all the saints. And you think that's a werewolf? I'll eat my dick if . . ."

He stopped short on hearing a sharp knock at the door.

"I hope to hell that isn't the captain checking things out," grumbled Manfred, who, as the eldest, was in charge. A former mercenary in the Great War, Manfred had known some tough taskmasters, and Captain Martin Lebrecht, though considered very cordial, was known to be a snoop. He had this special unit you could be assigned to at any time . . .

"Quick, hide the dice and the keg," he ordered in a whisper. Then he went to the door, slid back the bolt, and carefully pressed the door handle. A cold blast of air ripped the door open, but there was no one there.

"Is someone there?" Manfred called out into the darkness. When there was no answer, he turned back to his buddies with a grin. "It's probably just Jonas trying to play a trick on us. Just wait, I'm going out to whip his fat ass. I'll be right back."

He stomped out and was soon swallowed up in the darkness. For a while, the two others heard his footsteps, then a thud, and something fell clattering to the ground.

"What . . . what was that?" Eberhard asked anxiously.

"Aw, probably just the wind," Alvin replied. "What else could it be?" But his voice sounded far less confident than before. "Manfred?" he called loudly. "Manfred? Hey, damn it, where are you?"

With a groan, he stood up, straightened his armor, and staggered to the door, muttering a stream of dark threats.

"I'm telling you, if you guys down at the gate are messing around with us, you've got something coming to you. I'll stick my halberd into you so deep you'll never find it, and then . . ."

He'd just reached the open door when a huge black shadow swooped down like a bird, pulled him to one side, and disappeared with him into the night. Moments later there was a muffled cry, followed by a gurgling sound, then silence. Everything happened so fast that Eberhard only now comprehended what he'd just seen. He held his hand to his mouth, trembling.

Good Lord in Heaven, the shadow had a fur pelt . . . a wolf pelt.

Now he heard the sounds of steps approaching the door.

"Oh, my God!"

Eberhard dug his fingers into the top of the table as an enormous beast entered the room. It was so large it had to stoop to get through the door. All that stood on the table was a single flickering candle, and Eberhard could only guess the size of the monster, but he saw claws, he saw the fur, and he saw the head of a wolf.

"The werewolf," he moaned. "He . . . he . . . escaped."

"And now he has come to get you, and take you with him to hell," the monster said.

Then it growled and attacked the screaming guard.

Jakob removed the bitter-smelling cloth from the mouth of the unconscious night watchman and stowed it away carefully in the bundle he'd brought along. They mustn't leave anything behind that would give them away.

"What do you think? How much time do we have?" asked Magdalena, entering the guardhouse and looking around carefully.

Jakob shrugged. "No idea. Perhaps until the next hour strikes—or less. It's hard to measure out an exact dose, and the guards at the gate outside will naturally wake up sooner."

"Time is short." Magdalena tugged at her father's pelt and ran out into the courtyard with him. "So let's hurry over to Saint Thomas's."

Outside, the two other guards lay on the ground not far from a fountain. Magdalena was relieved she didn't have to press a cloth over anyone's mouth. The men would probably have put up a fight, and the anesthesia wouldn't have been as effective, but Uncle Bartholomäus and her father had done their work with the same calm, quick, and almost painless perfection they'd employed as executioners beheading criminals.

"You could have left out the last part," Magdalena whispered as they ran along.

Her father looked at her, perplexed. "Which part?"

"Well, that about hell. Who told you werewolves can talk?"

"Who told you they can't, hmm?" he replied with a grin. "You told us yourself to play our roles to the hilt, and I like to play the role of the bad boy."

Meanwhile, they'd reached the old chapel of St. Thomas, a tall five-story tower with a wooden stairway leading to the upper stories. Bartholomäus waited impatiently with his lantern in front of the solid doorway on the first floor.

"Here you are," he snapped. "I was beginning to wonder if you were having a beer with the guards."

"Believe me, when this is all over I'm going to have more than one," Jakob replied. "Now open up."

Bartholomäus pulled a key ring from his pocket and unlocked the iron bars reinforcing the solid oak door. They were confronted with the nauseating stench of feces, mold, and rotten food. Magdalena turned up her nose and followed Bartholomäus, who held up the lantern to show them the way. Behind them, Jakob ducked and entered the room.

"This used to be a chapel," Bartholomäus whispered, "but for many decades it's been used as a dungeon while the bishop likes to come to Saint Catharine's Chapel on the floor above to pray. Sometimes he no doubt hears the cries of the prisoners from up there, but that doesn't seem to upset His Excellency." He looked around the dark vault, then in a slightly louder voice said "Matheo? Can you hear me? Where are you?"

"Here . . . here I am," came a weak voice from a corner in back. Bartholomäus raised the lantern, and now Magdalena got a better look. It was a low, vaulted stone room with soot-smudged walls covered with messages from innumerable prisoners. Rats on the filthy straw-covered floors squeaked and fled into the dark corners. Massive, chest-high wooden stocks with two holes on the top and two on the bottom stood there, and in the last stock, just beyond the light from the lantern, something was moving.

"They locked the fellow in the stock," Jakob growled. "They must be pretty damn afraid of him, though from what I've heard, he's just a little squirt."

As they approached the last stock, Magdalena could finally make out Matheo. He was even thinner than she remembered; his shirt and trousers were ripped, there were bloody welts all over his body, and his right eye was swollen shut. His hands and feet had been placed in the holes in the wooden block and chained together so that the boy could scarcely move, and his back was twisted into an unnatural position. A chill went down Magdalena's spine. How long had Matheo been in the stock? Two days? Three? He had to be suffering great pain.

"Have you come . . . to get me . . . hangman?" he asked in a broken voice. The block was positioned in such a way that he couldn't see who had just entered the dungeon.

"Yes, I'm coming to get you," Bartholomäus replied, "but not for the gallows. This is your lucky day, young fellow. See for yourself."

"What . . . what do you mean?" Matheo gasped.

Bartholomäus stepped forward, and only now could the boy see the Bamberg executioner. The young man uttered a faint cry.

"I'm dreaming . . ." he said in a fading voice, "I must be dreaming. Oh, God, that's not possible."

His head fell to one side, and his eyes stared blankly into space.

"You idiot," Jakob snarled at his brother. "Couldn't you have told him you're only wearing a disguise? Look what you've done. Who's going to explain that to Barbara?" He rushed forward and held a finger to Matheo's jugular. "It's lucky for you," he remarked, "the boy is simply unconscious. With the way you look and smell, he could have just as easily had a stroke."

From under his pelts, Bartholomäus growled disdainfully. "It's probably better this way. If he were awake he'd just make trouble for us. And given how light the prisoner is, I wouldn't mind carrying him all the way to Würzburg."

"It'll be enough if we just get him to your house," Magdalena interjected. "And now, let's get out of here before the guards outside wake up."

"Not so fast. First we have to take care of the necessary hocus-pocus."

Jakob put down his bundle, took out a few little containers, and in a few hasty strokes sketched a black hexagram on the floor with a piece of coal.

"The Seal of Solomon," he whispered in a feigned tone of piety. "A powerful magic symbol, at least if you believe in it. It's said Solomon used it to conjure up angels and demons. So why not a werewolf?"

In the middle of the star-shaped seal, Jakob placed a wooden dish that he filled with yellow kernels, then set fire to it with a burning stick of kindling lit off of a guard's lantern. The contents began to give off clouds of smoke.

"My God, what a smell," Magdalena said, coughing and holding her hand over her mouth and nose. "Is that really necessary?"

"You can't cast the spell without sulfur. An ancient witch's rule." Her father blew a puff of air into the bowl, and another cloud of smoke rose toward the ceiling. "Believe me, in my life I've had to question a lot of witches, and at the end they always mention sulfur—not because it's so, but because that's what the inquisitor wants to hear. Sulfur goes with Satan like holy water goes with the dear Lord." He stood up and wiped his hands off on his stinking fur cloak. "Bartholomäus, you can carry the little shrimp," he said. "Magdalena, take the lantern. I'll wait at the gate outside for our big surprise." He grinned. "We don't want the guards to forget our werewolf."

They exited the dungeon, though the way out was hard to find because of all the smoke. The unconscious guards were still lying outside in the courtyard alongside the wolf's cadaver that Jakob had been wearing earlier. Once again, Magdalena admired the impressive specimen her uncle had been able to trap. Rigor mortis made the cadaver appear even larger than it already was.

"We'll put him right under the gate," Jakob said, "along with a nice little farewell gift."

They ran across the courtyard to the open gate, where Jakob

set the carcass down and unpacked another little container, which, like the previous one, had a wax seal. This time, however, it had a little hole on the side with a fuse sticking out. The hangman looked around, set the container down in the courtyard far enough from the unconscious guards and the wolf cadaver.

"We want to make sure they have a story to tell about their terrifying battle with the beast from hell. Hand me the lantern," he said, turning to Magdalena.

Carefully, Jakob lit a stick of kindling and held it to the fuse, which immediately started hissing, with a spark quickly approaching the container.

"And now, we must all run quickly," he said. "I was almost going to say *like the devil.*"

When they'd gotten halfway across the cathedral square, there was a thunderous explosion behind them, and shortly afterward they heard the cries of the guards.

They ran as fast as they could until they reached the foot of the cathedral mount. Gasping for air, Bartholomäus directed Jakob and Magdalena into a narrow, unlit side street, where he finally placed the still unconscious Matheo on the ground.

"How is he doing?" Magdalena asked softly.

"Better ask how *I* am doing," Bartholomäus groaned. "The kid is heavier than he looks."

Her father bent down to the injured boy and examined him quickly. "The guards gave him a bad beating, and the stocks have crushed his joints," he said finally. "Also, he badly needs a cup of wine to get his strength back, a little black-currant salve, and something to eat. But he'll survive."

And in fact, at that moment Matheo began groaning and moving restlessly back and forth.

"Can you hear me, Matheo?" Magdalena asked. The boy nodded hesitantly, and Magdalena continued. "It's me, Magdalena, Barbara's sister. We rescued you from the dungeon."

"But . . . but the werewolf . . ." Matheo murmured.

"That must have been just a bad dream," Magdalena replied, not wanting to go into any long explanation.

Far above them, on the cathedral mount, excited shouts could still be heard, but they were soon drowned out by Bartholomäus's loud laughter.

"Be quiet," Jakob whispered to his brother. "We're far from being out of the woods yet. If they catch us here wearing these pelts, you might as well start drawing and quartering yourself right now."

"Oh, come now." Bartholomäus waved him off dismissively. "They've got other concerns up there now." He grinned and nudged his older brother. "I've got to admit I had no faith in your plan, but it really worked. With all this hocus-pocus no one will figure out that I opened the dungeon for you. And perhaps the good citizens of Bamberg will be satisfied with their dead werewolf." His eyes sparkled merrily. "That reminds me how when we were kids we stole three skulls from the Schongau City Cemetery and put them in the windows of the pastor's house. Do you remember? You spoke in a deep voice, and I . . ."

"Do you hear that?" Magdalena interrupted.

Bartholomäus listened, then he frowned. "I hear shouting. So what?"

"Yes, but it's not coming from the cathedral mount, but from the city," Magdalena answered. "Something must have happened there."

"Damn, she's right." Jakob quickly took off the stinking pelt. "Quick, get out of these rags before the people discover us. It sounds like perhaps a fire has broken out, and then the whole city will wake up."

After some hesitation, Bartholomäus also removed his wolf's costume. They wrapped everything up in a big bundle that Jakob tucked under his arm.

Magdalena bent down again to Matheo, who seemed to be falling back to sleep again. "Can you walk?" she asked with concern.

When Matheo nodded, she turned to the two Kuisl brothers. "It would be best if you could support him on both sides, like a drunk. That way we won't attract so much attention."

With Matheo in the middle, they slowly walked down to the end of the lane, then turned in the direction of the Michelsberg, where everything was still calm and dark. Shortly thereafter, they arrived at the muddy tow-path along the Regnitz. Jakob took the bundle with the pelts, the old rags, and empty containers, and threw them as far as he could out into the river, where it bobbed along on the surface for a while and finally sank.

"I feel much better now," Jakob groaned, wiping the sweat from his brow. "I sweated like an old pig under that pelt."

"We just need to make sure nobody smells us," his brother replied with a grin, "or they'll put us in a dog kennel."

In the meantime, Magdalena had walked out onto a rickety dock and from there looked over at the eastern part of the city.

"Geyerswörth Castle is brightly lit," she whispered excitedly. "That's where all the noise is coming from. But I can't see a fire anywhere." She sighed. "I hope nothing has happened to Simon at that bishop's reception."

"Well, at least the boys are safe at home with Georg," her father replied in a reassuring voice. "They probably went to bed long ago. Let's hurry home to Bartholomäus's house, and perhaps on our way there we'll learn what happened."

With the groaning Matheo between them, they hurried along the towpath toward the lower city hall bridge, where despite the late hour they could see a number of people running back and forth. The shouts had now become much louder.

"In any case, we won't have to worry that anyone will stop us for being out after curfew," Bartholomäus growled. "It looks like all of Bamberg is out and about."

Up on the bridge, the Bamberg executioner stopped the first passerby he met. It was one of the guards responsible for keeping order in the eastern parts of town. He was running with a lantern in his hand toward the city hall.

"Hey, Paulus!" Bartholomäus called out to him. "What's going on? No decent Bamberger can sleep with all this noise."

The guard stared at him absent-mindedly. He didn't seem surprised that the city executioner was up at this late hour, nor did he wonder about the groaning lad in the dirty clothing who was supported on the other side by another huge man. Evidently he had other things on his mind at the moment than to lecture an apparently drunk fellow who had no doubt just been sick to his stomach.

"Haven't you heard?" the guard snapped. "In Geyerswörth Castle, the suffragan bishop himself turned into a werewolf and is attacking one citizen after the other. The news is spreading like wildfire. I'm going to get reinforcements to try to calm people down. Everybody is going wild."

"The . . . the suffragan bishop is a werewolf?" Magdalena couldn't contain herself. "Who told you that?"

"On my honor, I saw it myself," he affirmed. "I was in the festival hall with our captain, when the beast—" He stopped short. "Excuse me, I meant naturally the suffragan bishop . . . well . . . when he attacked a friend of our city doctor."

"A friend of the city doctor?" Magdalena gasped. "Was it perhaps a little guy with a feather in his hat?"

"Uh, yes." The guard finally seemed to notice her. "Do you know him? He must be a stranger here—in any case I've never seen him before. Well, now that the werewolf has bit him, it's probably curtains for him."

"Bitten by the *werewolf*? My God, we've got to get to the castle right away and . . ." Magdalena was about to run away, but her father held her back.

"You're not going anywhere like that, and certainly not

alone," he whispered to her. "As a dishonorable person you can't enter the castle, anyway. If worst comes to worst they'll suspect you of being in league with the devil. Look around. The whole city is in an uproar. We'd best get Matheo to a safe place and see if the children are all right."

Magdalena stopped to think. She would, in fact, have difficulty getting into the castle, and besides, Simon had told her that Samuel had introduced him as a famous and widely traveled scholar. Even if she succeeded in getting through to Simon, she could hardly say she was his wife. In addition, she was worried about the children. The whole city seemed seized by panic, and she could only hope Georg hadn't let the boys out of his sight.

"Very well," she responded hesitantly. "Let's first go to have a look at the children."

They all ran over the bridge together, leaving the befuddled watchman standing there, wondering what this strange group was up to. From all sides, curious people came toward them heading for the brightly lit castle. Others seemed to have just come from there and were excitedly telling their fellow citizens what they'd seen.

"I swear by Saint Barbara, our dear suffragan bishop turned into a terrifying werewolf," a stout elderly woman cried out, raising her hands imploringly toward the night sky. "I saw it with my own eyes; he has long teeth and even longer claws, and now he's out in the city looking for victims. Jesus, Mary, and Joseph! Get yourself and your children to safety. Pray, or we will all be lost."

Some of the braver young men had armed themselves with cudgels, pitchforks, and burning torches and were heading toward the castle.

"We must help the guards kill the beast," one of them was shouting, evidently one of the journeymen of the dyer who had his workshop down by the river. "Up on the cathedral mount, the guards have already killed another werewolf—a huge beast.

The battle must have been awful." Magdalena saw that the journeyman was one of the men who'd nearly lynched the peddler at the harbor the day before. In a raucous voice he was trying to stir up his friends.

"Surely we'll find even more werewolves in the city," he cried. "Follow me, friends!"

The grim-faced young men marched past the three Kuisls and the semiconscious Matheo, without paying any attention to them.

"Good Lord, has everyone gone mad?" Jakob Kuisl murmured. "If the city guards don't step in, they'll all kill each other."

"Your beautiful plan is all shot to hell in any case," Bartholomäus snapped. "With the suffragan bishop and the dead wolf up in the palace, all hell has broken loose here, no thanks to you. I'll no doubt have more torturing and executions than I can handle. Why did I ever get involved in this?"

"No one could have foreseen that on this very night the suffragan bishop would go mad," Jakob shot back. "But at least in all the turmoil no one will suspect you gave us the key to the dungeon." He glared at his brother. "Besides, now you can't blame yourself for not having done enough. Isn't that what you always wanted — to be a good executioner? Now you can prove it."

"Ha! You've still got the same fresh mouth as always. Just wait, I'll . . ."

Bartholomäus prepared to take a swing at his brother but noticed at the last moment that there was something standing between them. Matheo. With a grunt of disgust, he lowered his arm.

"Once again I have to wonder why I ever invited you to my wedding," Bartholomäus grumbled. "I hoped you would have changed, Jakob, but you're still the same old smart-ass."

Jakob spat on the ground. "Don't forget you're not the one who invited me, but Katharina, because she wanted to have peace in the family."

"Well, she sure made a mess of it."

Magdalena turned her eyes away while the two men bickered back and forth. Finally she'd had enough.

"For God's sake, can't you ever think about anything but yourselves?" she asked. "May I remind you that you're carrying a wounded man who needs your help and probably has a headache listening to all your whining?"

"You don't talk to your father that way," Jakob growled, but now in a calmer voice.

"And you don't talk to your brother that way, either," she replied. Bartholomäus started to snicker, but she glared back at him. "That goes for both of you."

Silently they continued through the dark city, along the foul-smelling city moat, while the shouts behind them gradually faded away. Finally they arrived at the executioner's house, which lay in total darkness. Magdalena looked up suspiciously at the second-floor windows.

"It looks like Georg has already gone to bed," she said with a frown. "There's no light up there."

They opened the door and stepped inside. The house was cold, with only the odor of dead ashes in the air.

"Georg?" Magdalena called out. "Peter? Paul?"

When there was no reply she took the lantern and ran upstairs—but soon returned.

"They're not here," she said. "Where in the world can Georg have gone with the children? I hope nothing has happened to them."

Nor to Simon, she thought suddenly, and a chill suddenly ran down her spine. Not until then did it occur to her how bitter cold it had become in the last few hours.

"Perhaps Georg took the children to the castle to see what's going on there," said her father, trying to console her. But he, too, seemed slightly shaken.

Magdalena nodded hesitantly. "Well . . . maybe you're right. We'll just have to wait and see."

They lit a warm fire in the stove and sat down at the table. Jakob busied himself with the injured Matheo, who seemed to have a high fever and kept waking up screaming from bad dreams. The hangman gave the young man some strong brandy mixed with valerian and St. John's wort, until Matheo finally calmed down.

Bartholomäus huddled down on the long bench, cracked his knuckles, and kept looking at the executioner's sword, hanging as always in the devotional corner of the room alongside the crucifix.

"How many werewolves do you think they'll catch tonight?" he asked in a soft voice. "How many men and women will scream their confessions to me on the rack that they're in league with the devil? How many will I have to put to the stake?"

"Perhaps now you have a better understanding of why I left Schongau back then," Jakob said, as he placed a bandage coated with a yellowish, pleasant-smelling ointment on Matheo's ankle. "I always preferred healing to killing and torturing." He chuckled. "But they give us people to heal only after we've inflicted pain on them."

Bartholomäus shook his head. "It wasn't right, Jakob, and you can't make it better with the same old explanations. You had responsibilities then, as the elder. We were helpless, and you abandoned us—" He stopped short. After a while, he continued in a soft voice, staring blankly into space.

"I always loved animals more than people. Their souls are good—without malice or hatred. My first wife, Johanna, was just like that, like a sweet little fawn, not the brightest, but sweet. When she died on me, of consumption, I thought there was nothing more to come . . . but then came Katharina."

Again there was a long pause.

"You will marry Katharina; it will all work out," said Magdalena, trying to console him as she anxiously awaited the next ringing of the cathedral bells.

Where are the children? she wondered. *Where is Simon?*

Bartholomäus laughed out loud. "Do you think Katharina will still want to marry me if I turn into a killer? Up to now I only had to deal with thieves and robbers. There was also a woman who killed her child. I managed to arrange for her to be beheaded rather than drowned miserably like a cat. But what we're facing now will be bad, very bad. Many innocent people will die, just like back then during the witch trials . . ." Once again his gaze wandered over to the executioner's sword with the strange, sharkskin handle.

"As the story goes, the Bamberg executioner at the time, a certain Michael Binder, went mad after all the torturing and burning," he said in a flat voice. "One day he just left town and vanished, and that's why his position was open for me. Who knows, perhaps after all this I'll turn as mad as Binder and disappear in the forests. Then Georg will be the new executioner." He gave a bitter laugh. "It will start all over again, an eternal cycle. We take the guilt upon ourselves until we can no longer stand it."

"Unless you step out of the circle," Jakob murmured. "I at least tried, back then. But I came back."

In the silence that followed, the only sound was Matheo's occasional restless moaning. Finally, Magdalena stood up and walked aimlessly back and forth in the room. The far-off sound of bells could be heard coming from the cathedral.

"It's midnight, and Georg and the children still aren't here," she said, rubbing her freezing torso. "We don't know how Simon is, either. We should go out and look for them. But where? In the castle? It seems to have calmed down a bit there. Just where could they . . . ?"

She stopped short, and suddenly her eyes lit up. "I have it!" she cried out. "With old Jeremias in the Wild Man, of course. The children enjoyed so much being with him yesterday. Perhaps Georg couldn't figure out what to do with the two rascals, so he went there with them. And then they forgot what time it was."

And then they met Barbara there, she was thinking. *That's got to be it. Georg found his sister again, and they lost track of the time.*

She still hadn't told her father where Barbara was staying. She wanted to keep her promise until Matheo was brought to safety.

"Still in the Wild Man at midnight?" Bartholomäus said and shrugged. "Do you really believe the kids are there?"

"Well, it's at least a possibility." Magdalena hurried to the door. "I'm going to go there right now . . ."

"How often do I have to tell you you're not going anywhere alone tonight," her father interrupted gruffly. "God knows what these self-appointed guards are doing now. If you go at all, I'm going along."

"I thought you were going to the castle to look for Simon there," Magdalena replied.

Bartholomäus stood up. "I can do that." He nodded toward the sleeping Matheo. "I'll just take the lad here up to the bedroom. With his fever and all the brandy Jakob gave him, he's sure to sleep soundly for a few hours, then we'll have to think about what to do with him later."

Magdalena looked at her uncle gratefully.

"Thank you," she said.

Bartholomäus grinned, but his eyes looked sad.

"This is perhaps the last time for a long while that I'll be able to do something good. I hope God will remember me for this later on." He gestured impatiently. "And now let's get moving before I change my mind."

Magdalena nodded to him and then disappeared into the night.

Georg was dreaming of dark malt beer flowing slowly from a giant barrel and spreading across his head. All he had to do was to open his mouth and the delectable fluid would completely fill his body.

But then the color of the beer suddenly changed: instead of brown, it was now red, and Georg could taste blood. He was in danger of choking to death on the huge stream of blood, and through the deluge of red he heard cries now; someone seemed to be calling to him. Then he felt someone shaking him roughly, the blood disappeared, and all he felt now was a pounding in his head. "Hey!" he heard a voice saying. "Wake up, we're closing. Let's go, you drunk."

Georg opened one eye and stared into the pasty face of the tavern keeper, who suddenly looked as old and fat as he remembered her from earlier that night.

"Get out, boy!" she yelled. "Get out of here before people start wondering what happened to you. All hell has broken loose outside."

"Hell . . ." he mumbled, nodding slightly. Like hell — that's how he felt at the moment.

"They caught a couple of werewolves in the city," the woman continued. "One of them, they say, is the suffragan bishop himself. The whole city's gone crazy. So move along." She gave him a shove and he almost fell off the bench. "I want to close before one of these self-appointed guards shows up and starts wrecking my place."

"Werewolves? Suffragan bishop? I don't understand . . ." Georg struggled to get up from the table and staggered toward the door. The tavern was deserted, and only a few puddles of beer were there as a reminder of the earlier crowd of partiers.

Georg almost fell over once, but the tavern keeper caught him and helped him get his balance.

"You'd better stay on the main streets," she told him, "or find a few other late-night revelers to take you home. It's a strange night. God knows who or what is lurking around out there." She crossed herself, closed the door behind him, and Georg found himself alone on the street.

He took a few deep breaths and rubbed his tired eyes. The cool night air helped him sober up a little. There was a small fountain at the next corner, and he staggered toward it. First he just splashed a little cold water on his face, then he stuck his head all the way in, like an ox at a trough.

The stinging cold water brought him more or less back to his senses. He shook the water from his hair, then cautiously looked around the deserted streets. The only light he could see came from the second floor of the tavern. Everything else lay in darkness.

Georg frowned. The bar woman had said something about captured werewolves. One of them was possibly the wolf's cadaver that his father, Uncle Bartholomäus, and Magdalena had left behind for the guards up in the old castle. So it seemed Matheo was able to escape. But what about the other werewolves, and what did that all have to do with the suffragan bishop?

He heard loud voices in the distance, perhaps night watchmen calling to one another. Georg shook his head, still clouded by alcohol. It would be best for him to pick up the children and get home as fast as possible, and . . .

Georg's heart skipped a beat as he remembered how he'd ended up at the Blue Lion. He'd left the boys with Jeremias. That was hours ago. Unless he was really lucky, Magdalena had long ago come back home and would be sick with worry. She'd scratch his eyes out if he told her what happened. There was nothing he could do about that; it was the price he'd have to pay for getting drunk. At least the children were in good hands with Jeremias.

Jeremias . . .

Georg was about to continue on his way toward the city hall bridge, when he stopped again. The name of the old custodian started him thinking. One thought that had been stirring in his alcohol-befuddled brain suddenly popped out. Standing there at that moment, in the cold autumn night, with freezing hands and water streaming from his hair, it all became clear.

He had seen something.

Something very suspicious that, now, after the fact, brought all the pieces of the mosaic together to form a clear picture.

Jeremias . . . the children . . . the sword . . .

Georg began to run.

In her cold, dark prison, Adelheid, the apothecary's wife, made preparations for her imminent death.

She knew her death would come sooner or later in the form of that man whose hood she had ripped off the day before in her escape attempt. She just didn't know the exact hour.

Or how she would die.

Her heart raced as she thought of all the instruments she'd seen in the torture chamber, which had brought death to so many others before her. The rack, the sharp-pointed cone, glowing hot tongs, bronze boots, arm and leg screws . . . Which one would the man use first? Which one last?

The last candle had gone out hours ago, and since then the man hadn't brought a new one. Darkness enveloped her like wet black soil, and she felt as if she'd been buried alive. By now, she was sure her prison had to be somewhere in the forest. From time to time, as if through a heavy woolen blanket, she could hear the muffled chirping of birds, and when the wind was blowing especially hard outside, the cracking of branches. Since her eyes could see virtually nothing, her other senses became all the more intense. She could smell the hard dirt floor, the mold on the walls, the tiny feces that the mice left in their nests and passageways. Sometimes she even thought she could hear the sound of the roots growing all around her—a constant cracking and crunching—but that was probably her imagination.

Then there was the cold. In their house in Bamberg, the Rinswiesers had a cellar where they stored beer and other perishable items. In the winter, Adelheid's husband cut blocks of ice from the frozen Regnitz, which he stored deep under the house to keep things cool. Adelheid called this the "ice hole," and it was as cold there in the middle of summer as in mid-February. She never stayed longer there than absolutely necessary.

And now she'd been lying here for many days in just such an ice hole. And it would probably be her grave.

She was surprised that the man hadn't returned. There was still a tiny spark of hope in her. She couldn't stop thinking how the man had cried the day before—an almost childlike sobbing. Or was that already the day before yesterday? It seemed he intended to take her to the horrible torture chamber, but then he changed his mind. When she recovered consciousness, she found herself shackled to the wall like an animal awaiting slaughter. Her throat was sore from the leather noose he'd used when he almost strangled her, and it was hard for her to swallow. The clay cup next to the bed had fallen to the floor, so she was tormented with a terrible thirst that got worse by the hour. But until now, he had spared her. *Why?*

Suddenly the thought came to her that perhaps the man hadn't spared her at all but had chosen the worst of all tortures for her.

He'd just let her rot away down here, in this icy hole.

In her dark, cold grave.

"Help! Help!" she screamed. "Is anyone there? Anyone at all?"

But her throat was so sore and dry that her cries turned into a muffled rattle. She coughed and vomited sharp, acidic mucus.

I'll slowly freeze here and die of hunger and thirst. How long will it take? Two days? Three? Longer?

She struggled to sit up, but the leather straps were tied so tightly over her chest that they took her breath away every time she moved.

Adelheid closed her eyes and tried to stay calm. She wasn't dead yet, and she would fight to the end. There was still hope. If the man left her down here to die like a wounded animal, it would be the end for her, but if he came back, she would appeal for his sympathy. He had cried. She didn't know why, but he had feelings. Since she'd seen his face, he was no long a monster, but a person. Perhaps at that moment he'd viewed himself again as a person. Did he perhaps regret what he had done?

On the other hand, Adelheid also knew he couldn't really allow her to live now. She had seen his face; she would recognize him.

If only for that reason, she had to die.

"Help!" she cried again, but stopped when the pain in her throat became too severe. She broke out sobbing, though she knew that the tears were draining the last bit of fluid from her body.

How long would it be? How long? ... How—

Suddenly, through her crying and wailing, she heard a soft sound. Adelheid froze, in shock. Yes, something was there. Definitely. A scraping and scratching, and it came from somewhere above her.

"Is someone there?" she asked excitedly.

The scratching continued. Now she realized it came not from the ceiling, but from near the top of the wall. Was someone digging down to her? Had they finally found her?

"Here!" she cried out in a hoarse voice. "Here I am! Here ..."

What happened then made her fall silent for a moment.

Something up there was growling loudly and deeply. There was an ugly rattling and a deep rumble, as if the mythical Cerberus, the Hound of Hell himself, had awakened from a long sleep.

My God, the monster! It's outside. It's digging down to me.

Adelheid held her breath. The scratching and scraping that until just a moment ago had sounded so promising, suddenly had become an evil sound from the bowels of the earth.

Suddenly she noticed a slight brightening in the room. It took some time for her to realize that a tiny ray of moonlight was coming from the same corner as the sounds through a slit in the wall. Evidently there was a window up there that had been covered by soil, and now someone or something was digging its way down to the window.

Again she heard the terrifying growl.

She cringed. If it was an animal, it had to be very, very large, and it was trying to dig its way down to her.

The beast. God in heaven, protect me. Holy Saint Georg, protect me.

13

WITHOUT STOPPING TO CHECK IF ANYONE WAS following him, Georg ran through the dark streets of Bamberg. A horrible thought had seized him with such force that at first he rejected it.

You're just imagining things. Stay calm. Try to think things through, like Barbara or Magdalena would . . .

But the more he thought about it, the more anxious he became. The very possibility that his assumptions might be correct made him run faster and faster. He needed certainty. Perhaps it would have been better to ask his father for advice first, but now there was no time for that. Besides, who was to say he was right? It was quite possible he was just imagining things and would make a fool of himself in front of his father and the others. It was better, then, for him to reach his conclusions by himself. At least his fear had sobered him up somewhat.

Gasping for air, Georg ran through the deserted fish market toward the Wedding House, whose outer gate was still open. Normally, two guards were stationed here, but evidently they had more important things to do tonight. No doubt they were off somewhere hunting werewolves. Georg wished he could learn more about it, but first he had to make sure the children were safe.

He entered the dark interior court and turned right, toward the door to Jeremias's room. He took a deep breath and listened, but couldn't hear a sound—no voices, no cries of children. He knocked timidly.

"Who's there?" came a voice from inside after a while. Georg thought it sounded nervous and tense.

"It's me, Georg," he whispered. "I'm sorry it got so late."

A bolt was pushed aside and Jeremias's scarred face appeared in the opening. He was smiling broadly.

"Ah, it's only you," he said with relief. "I thought something had happened to you. The guards have been reporting the most horrible things about what's going on in the city." He winked. "But looking at you, it seems you've been quenching your thirst a bit too much. The first time you really got drunk, eh? Well, that can be terrifying." He opened the door. "Come on in, I'll help you get yourself together again."

Georg entered the room and looked around. There was only a single candle burning on the table alongside a board with chess pieces on it. The draft coming through the open door made the cage with the sleeping birds swing back and forth gently, and a mangy cat was dozing on the bed. He couldn't find the children anywhere.

"Where are the boys?" Georg asked anxiously.

Jeremias pointed toward a small door on the left next to the bookshelves. "I took them over to the bench alongside the stove in the tavern. It's nice and warm there, and after the guards came and threw everyone out, it was quiet and empty. Biff is watching them, so you don't have to worry." He pointed toward the bed with the straw mattress. "It would be better for you to spend the night here with the children. No doubt you've heard what's going on out there tonight."

Georg nodded absent-mindedly. He sat down on a stool by the table, while Jeremias busied himself at a little tile stove in one corner. Finally, the crippled old custodian turned around and handed Georg a steaming cup.

"Here, drink this," he said. "It's hot small beer mixed with honey and a few strong herbs—the best cure for the aftereffects of the accursed devil's brew."

"Bless you." Georg gratefully took a sip. It tasted sweet and at the same time bitter, and in fact did clear his head a bit.

"Do you play chess?" Georg asked after a while, pointing to the chessboard on the table. "Who with?"

Jeremias laughed. "In any case, not with Peter yet, though the little fellow has a really good head on his shoulders. No, I play against myself." He winked at Georg. "Believe me, I'm a merciless opponent."

Georg gave a wan smile, and his gaze wandered over the medical books on the shelves, then farther to the chest on the floor with whose contents the boys had been playing so excitedly that afternoon.

I was right, he thought, his heart pounding. *At least as far as the medical books are concerned, my memory wasn't deceiving me. And for the rest . . . well, we'll see.*

"This is really an impressive library," Georg began hesitantly. "I just now realize my father has almost the same books."

"Really?" Jeremias raised his eyebrows. "Well, there aren't a lot of really good books about medicine. I'm sure you know that—"

"Lonitzer's herb almanac, for example," Georg interrupted, pointing to a rather thin, dog-eared book whose title, nonetheless, was easy to recognize on the book's spine. "Uncle Bartholomäus has one of these, too. It's a book consulted often by hangmen, because it contains many recipes on how to dispatch the condemned man quickly and above all painlessly into the hereafter. At least that's what my uncle told me." Georg hesitated for a moment. "There are also some instructions on what to do to a condemned man to break his resistance."

Jeremias suddenly pricked up his ears. "Ah, indeed?" he said with surprise. "What, for example?"

"Well, it just happens my father told me of one method just recently," Georg replied, his voice trembling a bit. His head felt dull and heavy, but he kept a careful eye on Jeremias. "There's the so-called sleep sponge. It's often used in surgical operations, as well, to sedate patients. My father thinks the victims of this werewolf were drugged first, to make them easier to take away and kill. Are you familiar with this sleep sponge?"

"The werewolf sedates streetwalkers and then rips open their rib cage? Is that what you're thinking? Very original. Your father must be a very imaginative hangman." Jeremias chortled, and the scars on his face seemed to spring strangely to life. Then he shrugged. "To get back to your question, perhaps I have indeed heard about this sleep sponge. But unfortunately I don't know anything more about it."

"Really? That surprises me. After all, its main ingredients are standing right there on your bookshelf." Georg pointed at the crucibles and vials. "*Hyoscyamus niger, Papaver somniferum,* and *Conium maculatum.* The first time I was here, I couldn't make any sense of the Latin names, but later, in the tavern, they occurred to me—henbane, opium, and hemlock." He smiled between clenched lips. "I may not be as smart as Barbara, but sometimes I remember the seemingly most insignificant things. It must be true that alcohol doesn't always make you dumber. Sometimes it helps you to figure things out."

For a long while the only sound was the soft chirping of the birds in the cage. Some had been awakened by the conversation and were flapping their wings excitedly.

The crippled custodian with the scarred face continued looking at him cordially, but Georg thought he noticed an anxious flicker in the man's eyes.

"I've always recommended alcohol as a means of healing," Jeremias said finally. "It can be amazingly effective, especially if the patient is unaccustomed to it. The same is probably true for the sleep sponge." He folded his arms and leaned back on the bed. "I have a certain feeling that alcohol has provided you with additional insights. Is that the case?"

Georg nodded. "Indeed." He took another sip of the stimulating drink before continuing. His voice sounded more confident now.

"I told you before that my Latin was not so good. I always hated it when Father pestered me about it. But there's no getting around the fact that hangmen have to learn Latin. Most of the books on healing are written in this language, and that's the way we earn most of our money—with healing, much more than killing. So every day I had to translate Latin with my father, and I've actually remembered some of it. Barbara was always better, of course." He looked at Jeremias approvingly. "Your Latin is, by the way, excellent, as far as I can judge. Recently you've spoken Latin with me several times. *'Homo homini lupus*— "man is a wolf to man."' Do you remember? Those were your words."

Jeremias smiled and raised his hands disarmingly. "Very well, I'll admit I speak a respectable Latin, and I have a few herbs that I really shouldn't have, but so far your reflections have led you to no conclusions, and that surprises me. Is there anything more ... any conclusions?" he asked, playfully shaking his scarred head.

Georg sipped his drink and thought some more before continuing slowly, as if he were groping forward, word by word.

"My father always told me when we were learning Latin that when you get lost, sit back and look at the whole sentence, not just the individual parts. They only make sense when you take them all together. With you, too, I've been looking at the whole thing and had a part I just couldn't fit in anywhere—at first."

"And what would that be?"

"A sword."

Jeremias looked at him, astonished. "A sword? I don't understand. For the first time, you're actually making me curious."

Georg pointed at the old battered trunk in the corner. "Well, when I brought the children to you, they went to play back there by the trunk. Paul was crazy about a short sword he found there. It was actually just the handle and the lower part of a blade that had broken off . . . dull and scratched. At first I didn't pay any attention to it, but then I remembered what Paul had said to me when we were out by the river. He was very keen on going to see you. 'He has a sword just like Uncle Bartl, only smaller.' Those were his exact words, and at first I didn't know what he meant by that. But now I do."

Meanwhile, Jeremias had gone over to the old trunk, opened it, had taken out the broken sword, and was holding it reverently in his hand. It was a "great" sword—a two-hander—dull and rusted, and its handle was just as rough and gray as on the day it was forged.

"The handle is of sharkskin," Georg whispered, "Isn't that right? A handle only found in Bamberg executioners' swords. I always admired Uncle Bartholomäus's sword. Even if you are anxious and your hand is sweaty, every drop will run off, and your hand won't slip when you deal the deadly blow. I always wanted to have a sword like that. You have one, at least a broken part of one. Why?"

"Why don't you tell me," Jeremias replied. His eyes had lost their cordiality now. He looked sad and very, very tired, almost as if he'd aged years in the last few minutes.

Georg placed the cup down on the table and stared at the cripple for a long time. "I asked my uncle once how he'd become a hangman in Bamberg. After all, he was a stranger here, and almost always the firstborn son of the previous hangman is given the job. The hangman before him, however, had no children."

"No, he didn't," Jeremias said in a soft voice.

"After the witch trials, the hangman disappeared without a trace," Georg continued. "Nobody ever saw him again, though I think people were also somewhat relieved. His name was Michael Binder. As the Bamberg executioner, he took upon himself the weight of their guilt. He had tortured and executed almost a thousand people on the orders of the bishop and a special inquisition committee, and then he simply disappeared. And with him, the guilt."

"The guilt remains," Jeremias replied. "It can't be washed away, not even with caustic lime. The good citizens cannot, and the hangman certainly cannot, either. He must continue to live with this guilt, especially with the one . . ."

Georg could see tears welling up in the custodian's face, and suddenly, he felt sorry for him.

"What kind of guilt do you mean?" he asked hesitantly.

Jeremias smiled sadly. "You'll be a good hangman someday, Georg. I can see, believe me. Good hangmen are like sharp swords. They relieve suffering, if possible. Just a whoosh of air, and it's done. Be careful not to think too much about it. With the thinking come dreams, bad dreams." Jeremias groaned as he returned and sat down on the bed with the sword handle. "Especially when you are torturing someone, your mind must be as clear and clean as a freshly forged sword. The screams, the pleading, the wailing must all bounce off you, have no effect. But sometimes you can't do it. Perhaps you will know some of the victims, not well, but you've met them and greeted them on the street. They are neighbors, casual acquaintances, the tavern keeper where you've always ordered your beer, the midwife who helped your wife deliver her child. This isn't a large city, and to some degree everyone knows everybody else. And the day may come when you must torture and execute someone you . . ." — he hesitated — ". . ..you really love. This guilt stays with you forever."

"My God." Georg looked at him, horrified. "You . . . you . . ."

"Carlotta was sixteen," the old man continued, staring blankly into space while his fingers clutched and kneaded the sword handle. He seemed lost in his own world. "She was the daughter of a well-to-do linen weaver. Our love was clandestine. No one was to learn of it. But we swore we would get married someday. As a sign of my affection, I gave her a dress of pure fustian, as soft as goose down. Toward the end of the third wave of persecutions at the time of the Great Plague, the tavern keeper of the Bear's Claw claimed he'd seen my Carlotta dancing with the devil in the parish cemetery at the time of the full moon. In those days, lots of people danced with the devil," Jeremias said with a dry laugh. "The trial didn't even last half a day, then they handed Carlotta over to me. I can still remember her wide-open eyes. My hands trembled, but I did my job, as always. They asked her about the people she knew, and every time I applied the tongs to her, I thought she would speak my name. But she didn't. She just looked at me the whole time with her big, brown eyes, like those of a sweet little fawn . . ."

"Did you burn her at the execution site?" Georg finally asked, breaking the silence that followed.

Jeremias shook his head. "She hanged herself in the dungeon with a rope made of the dress I'd once given her. Perhaps she wanted to spare me the sight of the execution . . ." He laughed bitterly again. "The sinner spares the hangman from having to kill her. What irony. The devil really had a time with us."

"What happened then?" Georg asked.

"I couldn't live with this guilt. That very night I smashed my executioner's sword and fled from the town. I found shelter in an old shack built by a worker at a limestone quarry near Roßdorf in Bamberg Forest and cried my eyes out. Then I decided to end my life and wipe all memory of me from the face of the earth. So I poured the unslaked lime in a trough, added water, and jumped in. But the pain was too great. I couldn't bear the same pain I'd inflicted on others. I wandered through the forest, half-blind and screaming in agony, hiding in stables and barns, until finally Berthold Lamprecht found me and took me in."

"The innkeeper of the Wild Man," Georg added with a nod.

"And a good Christian, God knows. He's a distant relative of mine, the only one who knows who I really am. The young people in Bamberg don't know me, of course, and the old ones just regard me as an old, scar-covered cripple. None of them ever recognized me on the street, and if anyone started giving me a closer look, I pulled my hood over my face and moved on. I'm just a monster, and monsters have no past." Jeremias bared his teeth. In fact, with his scarred head and deformed face he looked so horrible that even Georg could not help feeling repelled.

"Back then, Berthold went to the executioner's house and fetched some of my things, among them this god-damned, broken sword . . ." he said, weighing it in his hand like a feather. "Then he gave me work and this room that I've lived in ever since like an ugly beast inside a mountain. I kept the sword, God knows why. Perhaps so I would never forget my evil deeds and always remember my beloved Carlotta . . ."

Tears ran down his scarred face, and he cried silently, as the birds in the cage above his head, now fully awake, began to chirp cheerfully. Georg was sure he'd never met such a lonely man.

And yet, I have to ask him this one last question . . .

"Do you know what I still find strange?" Georg said after a while. "As I told you earlier, sometimes little details stick in my mind. That happens to me often when I'm talking to people, and it did this time as well. When I mentioned the sleep sponge before, and Father's assumption that the werewolf uses it to stun his victims, you laughed. You said my father was an imaginative fellow if he thought a werewolf would sedate a prostitute and then rip open her rib cage. Well . . ." He paused and stared intently at Jeremias.

"What are you trying to say?" the old man asked, as he wiped the tears from his face. "What about it?"

"I never said anything about prostitutes nor a ripped-open rib cage, and I don't think you could have heard about it. My father told me that Captain Martin Lebrecht wanted to keep these matters absolutely confidential. Basically, there's only one other person who would know about it." He paused for a moment, then continued: "the murderer."

Again there was a tense silence. Finally, Jeremias threw the sword into a corner, where it clattered to the floor. There was a glint in his tired eyes, something devious, like a wild animal at bay.

"Enough of this game of hide-and-seek," he hissed. "So you know, very well. You can be proud of yourself, I really underestimated you." He seemed to be thinking it over, then he gave an evil smirk. "But your knowledge will do you no good."

Georg could feel his hair bristling on the back of his neck, and at the same moment he knew he'd made a tactical error. He should have gone to his father with this and at least have kept this last question to himself, but now it was too late.

"What . . . what do you intend to do?" he asked cautiously.

Jeremias pointed to the cup in Georg's hand. "I said before that alcohol can have an astonishing effect, among them that it can easily cover up an odd taste." He pointed to the back of the room. "It was no accident that the little jar of *Conium maculatum,* poison hemlock, was back there on the shelf. I thought I might have a chance to use it again."

Georg's heart suddenly started pounding. "You *poisoned* me?" he gasped.

Jeremias shrugged. "Well, poison is a strong word for it. I'd say I've seen to it that we'll keep this little secret to ourselves." The man who was once the Bamberg executioner, Michael Binder, watched Georg intently. "Can you feel anything yet? The effect usually begins in the feet, and from there the paralysis travels up through the whole body. When it reaches the heart, that's the end."

Georg tried to wiggle his toes, and in fact, he felt a slight tingling creeping up toward his lower legs.

"You are a devil," he groaned. "And I thought . . ."

"That I'm just a kind old man?" Jeremias waved dismissively. "You still have a lot to learn, Georg. I've executed hundreds of men, so do you think one more or less matters? Yes, I killed this young prostitute, Clara. Believe me, I regret this crime every hour of every day, but that doesn't mean I'll let the unruly mob out there tear me to pieces because I'm a werewolf. Because, by God, that's just what they would do. Look at me." He pointed at his disfigured face. "I'm a monster. They won't find anyone else to fill the role better than I do."

"Then you're really not the werewolf at all?" Georg asked, confused. The tingling had already reached his thigh.

"Am I? Or am I not?" Jeremias sighed. "My dear Georg, you thought you were so clever. But some things are simply a bit more complicated. I'm no kindly old fool, but I'm also not the devil. Like most people, I'm probably something in between, and I cling to life, just like you yourself, no doubt."

With a smile, he took a fist-sized brown clump from the bookcase, which Georg didn't recognize at first. It was evidently some sort of dried plant.

"The famous rose of Jericho," Jeremias explained. "The first crusaders brought it to us from the Orient. Though it appears dead, it will turn green and begin to bloom again when you water it. Wise men call it Mary's hand, and its curative powers are legendary." He picked off a bit of the dry material and crumbled it into a cup. Then he walked over to the small stove, where a kettle of hot water was standing, and filled the cup.

"Just a bit of Mary's hand, and a few other ingredients that only I know, will stop the spread of the poison," he continued. "Not for long, only about a day, and then the hemlock's deadly poison will take effect again." He smiled and handed the cup to

Georg. "This is my suggestion. You will hold your tongue, and in return you may visit me and pick up the antidote every day until I reveal the other ingredients to you, and then you will leave Bamberg forever. I'd call that a chivalrous offer, wouldn't you?"

Georg tried to move his toes, which seemed almost paralyzed now. He nodded hesitantly, then reached for the steaming cup. He had made his decision.

You are a Kuisl, and don't forget that . . .

"A chivalrous offer," he repeated. "Especially since it comes from an unscrupulous murderer. But I'm afraid I cannot accept it."

Without saying a word, he threw the steaming hot contents straight into Jeremias's face.

The old man fell to the floor screaming and holding his hands over his scarred skin.

"Are you crazy?" he shrieked. "I have offered you your life, and you—"

Georg jumped at him and started to choke him. "No one extorts a Kuisl," he hissed. "No one. As a former executioner you should know there are ways to make you talk. You will tell me at once the ingredients, then I'll take this shriveled plant and . . ."

At that moment, someone crashed through the door and with brute force tossed Georg to one side.

In the meantime, Barbara was in both heaven and in hell.

She was crouching in a back corner of a hothouse in the castle garden, where she had fled in order to escape the growing chaos in the city. The building was at the far end of the park where the canal and the left branch of the Regnitz came together on each side of the garden. Exotic trees grew there, reaching to the ceiling and bearing fist-sized orange fruit, which gave off an intoxicating fragrance. Brightly colored birds chirped as they fluttered amid the dark green foliage. The fragrance was so intense and enticing that Barbara had already bitten into one of the fruits, which was so terribly bitter, however, that she spat it out again.

She assumed it was one of those so-called Seville oranges. She had learned from her father that the expensive blossoms of these trees were occasionally used in herbal medicines and perfumes. They actually grew only in southern regions, but now, in the autumn, a good fire was rumbling in a stove in the middle of the pavilion and providing the necessary warmth.

Closing her eyes, Barbara tried to rest a bit. It was warm, the air was fragrant, and she was safe, at least for the moment. Still, she felt trapped in a nightmare.

She had been sitting here for over an hour, and she still couldn't comprehend what had happened. After Suffragan Bishop Harsee changed into a werewolf, she fled out of the building in the general chaos. The citizens of Bamberg had already begun hunting down the actors, whom they now regarded, after what they had just seen, as witches and magicians. The good-natured Matthäus had been their first victim. Barbara had turned away as his cries for help turned into an almost inhuman scream. Despite the warmth in the pavilion, Barbara's whole body was trembling. Where was Sir Malcolm? Where were Markus Salter and the other actors? Had the mob of people torn them to pieces, as they probably had Matthäus? Were their corpses already dangling from the trees in front of the castle?

She struggled to get her thoughts together as the birds fluttered around overhead. The aromatic smell of the orange trees helped her at least to calm down a little. Had her father and Uncle Bartholomäus managed to free Matheo, as Magdalena promised they would?

Matheo . . .

As soon as she thought of him, tears welled up in her eyes. Ever since Matheo had been taken prisoner, her feelings had been in turmoil. Yes, she thought she loved him, but how could she know what love really was if she'd never experienced anything like it before? She was only sure of one thing: she had to help him. And there was something else she'd come to realize in the last few hours.

She wanted to go back to her family.

Ever since she'd been separated from Magdalena, her twin brother Georg, her father, and the other Kuisls, she felt like a part of her was missing. Why had she run away? She'd behaved like a fool. In any case, she couldn't go back now to old Jeremias. No doubt the guards were ransacking the Wedding House looking for the actors.

It was high time to go home.

After what seemed like an eternity, the noise outside gradually subsided. She could hear occasional shouts, but they were probably just the night watchmen. She got up, cautiously approached the door, and peeked out through a crack into the darkness. Seeing nothing, she slipped out into the cool night air of the garden.

She crept barefoot across a gravel path that wound its way alongside a labyrinth of hedges. Everywhere on the lawn stood bushes trimmed into the shapes of animals and geometric figures, which in the nearly complete darkness looked like huge monsters. The statues around the fountain in the middle of the park appeared to be following Barbara with their eyes.

After a while she stopped and turned around, squinting. The garden was enclosed on three sides by a high wall that rose up just a few steps in front of her in the darkness. On the fourth side was the castle, through which she had entered and which was also the way out to the city. It seemed too risky to her to go back. No doubt the gate to the courtyard had long ago been closed.

So, over the wall, she thought.

She was fearful about doing that, as she remembered the castle grounds were surrounded on both sides by water. Even if she succeeded in getting over the wall, she'd have to swim. She didn't even want to think about how cold the water would be in late autumn.

Looking for a way out, she continued groping along through the darkness. On the left a huge log house appeared, and inside it there was a pounding and a sound of rushing water. She'd seen a number of small canals filled with water around the pavilion and in the garden, and she assumed the building housed one of these fashionable new water pumps. The building stood right against the wall, and was covered with ivy, so for a halfway experienced climber it would be an easy matter to scramble up.

Barbara didn't hesitate for a moment. She grabbed hold of the thin vines and pulled herself up bit by bit until she was atop the roof with the rumbling machines beneath her. Now the top of the wall came up only to her waist. She pulled herself up and looked down at the narrow, fast-flowing Regnitz on the other side. She was a good swimmer, but she couldn't tell how far the current would carry her. At worst, she could land in one of the many water wheels just a short distance down the river and be ripped to shreds.

Do I have any choice?

Barbara murmured a short prayer, then jumped feetfirst into the rushing water.

It was so cold that it took her breath away, and the current drove her toward one of the mills, whose wheel was squeaking and groaning as it turned in the water.

The river water stank of rot and decay and tugged at her as if with a hundred arms, seemingly reluctant to give up its prey. Nevertheless she fought against the current, getting closer and closer to the opposite shore.

Finally she grabbed hold of a slippery shrub along the shore and pulled herself up on it. Gasping for air, she scrambled up the steep bank and looked for refuge behind a few splintered barrels.

In front of her was a dark street littered with horse droppings. Everything seemed calm, and the only thing she heard were the bells in the distance striking the eleventh hour.

Barbara leaned against one of the barrels and tried to catch her breath. Her whole body shook and her teeth chattered with the cold, but she had made it. Now she just had to get back to the executioner's house. Her father would probably give her a good whipping, but she'd accept that punishment in return for a cup of hot mulled wine and a firm embrace from her big sister.

They'll excuse me. A family always forgives.

Carefully she sat up and got her bearings. The city hall had to be in front of her, somewhere on the right. There was also a bridge there that she could take to get to the newer part of the city. Hastily, she picked up the dripping hem of her skirt and set out on her way.

Just as she reached the next corner, a mob of young men armed with scythes, pitchforks, and torches came running out of a side street. They appeared just as surprised by the sudden meeting as she was, but their hesitancy didn't last long.

"Hey, isn't that the cute princess from the troupe of actors?" one of them shouted, pointing at Barbara's torn dress. Instinctively, she cringed. In the excitement she'd completely forgotten the expensive red dress, and now she felt it was practically glowing in the dark.

"Just have a look at this," another young man said, ogling her breasts beneath the soaking dress. "Looks like the dirty little water rat has been taking a bath in the city moat." He looked down at her condescendingly. "Tell me, did you meet with the other witches? You can't deny it. We've already caught a couple of you, and they all admit they changed the suffragan bishop into a werewolf. So speak up."

Barbara immediately understood that further discussion was pointless, so she did the first thing that came to her mind: she turned and ran down the street as fast as she could. The young men ran after her, shouting.

She zigged and zagged a few times, then darted off into a narrow lane. Not until it was too late did she notice that the way led steeply uphill, probably to the Kaulberg adjacent to the cathedral mount, a labyrinth with many tiny houses, stairways, winding lanes, churches, and chapels. Barbara struggled for breath as the young men behind her bellowed triumphantly and drew closer.

The lane became steeper and narrower, and now Barbara had completely lost her way. Evidently the men had split up, as she could now hear the sounds of running feet on all sides.

They're surrounding me. Like wolves chasing a young deer, they're closing in on me.

Suddenly the lane widened, and before her she saw the dark outlines of a monastery. She hesitated for a moment, looked around, then ran across the market square to the large portal of the monastery church. Building cranes and scaffolding stood all around, just as they did in front of many other church buildings in the city. The entire square was one huge construction site, with piles of stone blocks and sacks of mortar, which served as cover as she stooped down and ran toward the monastery. If she could make it into the church, she had some chance of evading her pursuers. As in all churches and monasteries in the Reich, the right of asylum applied in Bamberg as well. Anyone who entered the protective interior would be safe.

With her last bit of strength, she rushed toward the gate and shook the doorknob frantically.

But the door was locked.

Furiously she pounded the massive wooden door. That simply wasn't possible: a church was supposed to be open at all hours of the day and night. Evidently, the monks in their fear of werewolves and marauding militias had locked the door.

She looked around and could see the light of torches entering the square and drawing closer. In desperation she stormed toward a building crane in the middle of the square where she could see the dark outlines of a large pile of sand. Perhaps she could find someplace to hide there.

She quickly scrambled up the pile, damp from the evening fog, and was almost at the top when the sand beneath her suddenly gave way. She reached out wildly in all directions, but found nothing to hold on to and rolled back down the slope into a pit at the foot of the sand pile. Face-down, she lay there in the mud.

This is the end, she thought.

And indeed, she heard the shouts of the young men, this time very close by. They were somewhere on the construction site.

She crawled away from the pile, from which the sand was still trickling down, and suddenly she caught sight of a tunnel supported by wooden beams. It appeared to have been dug by the workers looking for the necessary sand for their building. She crept toward it, ducked down to get inside, and at once was enveloped in darkness as black as the grave. The tunnel was waist-high but noticeably narrower at the far end. Nevertheless, she kept moving forward until the shouts behind her were muffled and finally faded away.

She lay there panting and listening.

Everything was quiet, and evidently the men had given up the chase.

Barbara decided to wait. It was possible her pursuers were still outside. As the water dripped down onto her hair, she thought she could literally feel the weight of tons of soil and sand above her.

Just as she was about to crawl back out of the tunnel, something attracted her attention — a tiny ray of light coming from the far end. Was there possibly another way out?

Barbara decided to go and see. If it really led to the outside, she would be a good distance from the men who were probably still looking for her at the construction site. She crawled forward on all fours, and the light, which seemed to be coming from one side of the tunnel, actually got brighter,

In about another fifty or sixty feet she reached the end of the tunnel, where on the right several slippery, worn steps led into a larger tunnel. At first the steps were covered by fallen rocks, but after a few yards there was an area of solid, smooth stone. The dim light came from a low doorway apparently leading to a room above.

Holding her breath, Barbara slowly moved toward the light. Upon entering the room, she found a single, smoking torch revealing the outlines of several dust-covered crates and trunks, with a figure in a brown threadbare monk's habit cowering between them. The man's face was scratched and full of bloody welts, and he was so pale he appeared almost transparent. Still, Barbara recognized him at once.

It was the playwright, Markus Salter.

When he caught sight of her, the haggard man winced, then a tired smile spread across his face.

"Greetings, Barbara," Salter said, raising a shaking hand. "I thought they'd finally caught up with me, but evidently Providence has allowed the two of us, at least, to escape this madness." Tears ran down his bloodied face. "I don't know where God is, but tonight he has clearly abandoned Bamberg."

The blow that struck Georg was powerful yet not especially painful. Nevertheless, it was hard enough to hurl him back into the corner of the little room, where he came to rest with his head against the wall. A strange odor, which Georg couldn't place at first, was in the air. Then he recognized the stench of a beast of prey and decay.

A werewolf. Jeremias has conjured up a werewolf.

Trembling, he turned around only to look straight into the angry face of his father.

"What the hell are you doing, beating up a crippled old man, eh?" he shouted. "I don't know what happened here, but my son doesn't beat cripples, do you understand?"

His heart pounding wildly, Georg stood up and wiped his mouth where his father had slapped him. Alongside Jakob stood Magdalena, her arms crossed and staring angrily at Georg.

"Good God, Georg, what are you doing here at Jeremias's house at this hour of the night?" she scolded. "Do you have any idea how worried we've been? And where are the children? They should have been home and in bed hours ago."

"The children are next door in the tavern," he croaked. "They're all right. In contrast to me."

"What is that supposed to mean? Speak up." His father pulled him to his feet. "Say something."

Georg pointed at Jeremias, still lying on the floor, panting for breath. His scarred face was bright red from the hot water Georg had flung in his face.

"He's no defenseless cripple," Georg said angrily. "He's Michael Binder, the man who used to be the Bamberg executioner. He's a murderer and probably the werewolf we've been looking for. He . . . he poisoned me with hemlock."

Sheer terror seized him as he felt the strange tickling that had already traveled up to his thighs.

"He has an antidote." He turned excitedly to Jakob and Magdalena, who stood there gaping at him. "The rose of Jericho. He's the only one who knows the exact formula. We must force him to give it to us, or I'm done for."

Jakob dropped down onto a stool, which creaked perilously with the sudden weight. The hangman shook his head, at a loss.

"Murderer . . . antidote . . . rose of Jericho . . ." he mumbled. "Damn it, Georg, how much have you had to drink? I can smell your breath from here."

"But it's the truth," Georg insisted. "Jeremias is a murderer; he admitted it himself. And he poisoned me. Here." He pointed to the cup of hemlock still standing on the table. "He gave me the hemlock in this cup."

Jakob picked up the cup, and his huge hooked nose disappeared for a moment in the cup as if it were an autonomous creature acting on its own. He sniffed a number of times, then shook his head.

"I'll eat a witch's broom if there's hemlock in this." he said calmly. "Hemlock smells like mouse droppings. This here is actually . . ." He stopped to smell the cup again. "Cinnamon, honey, hmm, probably cardamom, a pinch of pepper . . ."

"And a few cloves from far-off India," Jeremias interrupted. He'd gotten to his feet again and sat down unsteadily on the bed. "And don't forget the sinfully expensive muscat. The brew is a so-called hippocras, brewed according to the original recipe of the Greek physician Hippocrates—a strong and, by the way, very delicious spiced wine that is not at all poisonous."

"But . . . but you told me yourself it contained hemlock. Now I'm completely confused." Georg's gaze wandered back and forth between Jakob and Jeremias. "And I can feel this tingling . . ."

"Do you really, Georg?" Jeremias asked with a mischievous smile. "Or is it possible it's just your imagination?"

Confused, Georg wiggled his toes, and indeed the tingling seemed to have almost completely disappeared. How was that possible?

"The fascinating power of suggestion," Jeremias said. "With a little showmanship you can make people believe anything. Healing powers as well as deadly ones. Your father surely knows as much about this as I do."

"And the rose of Jericho?" Georg asked hesitantly, though he already suspected what the answer would be.

"The rose of Jericho is a pretty, though expensive knick-knack," Magdalena said with a shrug. "When you water it, it turns green, but I've never heard that it was a strong antidote for anything. If you'd paid a little more attention to Father back home, you'd know that."

Georg tore his hair in anger. He'd thought he was so smart, and now it appeared he'd made an ass of himself again in front of his father and big sister. Furious, he turned around to Jeremias. "You . . . you did that only so I wouldn't run out of here, didn't you?"

Jeremias raised his hands apologetically. "And it worked. Believe me, Georg, that one murder was enough for me." His face turned dark. "I'll roast in hell for that alone."

"I think you owe us an explanation," said Magdalena, looking at him suspiciously, "but first I want to see my children. And perhaps someone else," she added ambiguously.

Jeremias pointed toward the little door next to the bookshelves. "Georg was right: the two boys are sleeping peacefully in the next room. But please assure yourself."

Magdalena opened the door and disappeared. When she returned, she was visibly relieved. "The boys are fine," she declared. "To judge from the smears around their mouths, at most they have had too much plum jam to eat. The one I'm really missing, however, is Barbara."

"Barbara?" Jakob looked at her in surprise. "This is getting even more confusing. Are you saying that Barbara was here the whole time? Damn it. Damn it . . ." He was getting ready to explode, but Magdalena cut him off.

"None of that matters anymore," she said. "Now that we've brought Matheo to safety, I would have come tomorrow in any case and brought her home," she said. Turning to Jeremias she asked sternly, "So where is she?"

Jeremias sighed. "Actually, Barbara was with the actors most of the time, and I haven't really seen her. She left to go to the castle this morning with the actors. Perhaps she was helping the other actors with their costumes."

"Just wait till I get my hands on her," Jakob growled. "But we'll take care of that later." He turned back to Georg. "And now it's high time you told me what happened here."

Georg took a deep breath, then lowered his head and told him about getting drunk in the Blue Lion, but also all the things he'd seen and how he'd been able to make sense of it in the end. He told him about the ingredients for the sleep sponge he'd discovered in Jeremias's room, the amazing knowledge Jeremias had of Latin, and the broken executioner's sword, but most important, he told him about Jeremias's confession that he was Michael Binder, the former executioner, and that he had just recently committed a murder.

"He himself confessed to having killed the young prostitute," Georg said finally. "Only the murderer could know about the ripped-open rib cage. Jeremias is the werewolf you've been looking for."

Jakob had listened silently the whole time, and now he turned to Jeremias, still sitting on the bed, rubbing a cool ointment on his red, scarred face.

"Is it true what the boy said?" the hangman asked.

Jeremias sighed. "Only part of it. Yes, I killed Clara, but I'm not the werewolf. You must believe that."

"Then we'll have to hear more," Kuisl replied. He took out his pipe and lit it on a flaming wood chip he fetched from the stove. Soon, fragrant clouds of smoke were ascending toward the ceiling, dispelling the rotten stench of the beast of prey that had been clinging to his clothes.

"So speak up," Jakob demanded. "Or must I first ask my brother to throw you on the rack and torture you with thumbscrews?"

Jeremias winked mischievously. "Believe me, when it comes to the rack and thumbscrews, you youngsters could still learn a lot from me." But then he turned serious.

"It's just as Georg told you. Indeed, I was once the Bamberg executioner, Michael Binder, but Michael Binder is long dead and gone. He died almost forty years ago in a trough full of unslaked lime. Since then, I'm Jeremias. But I was never able to wash away the guilt weighing on me at that time . . . just my old name." The old man sighed deeply, and there was a strange rattle in his throat. "I could never forget the sight of my beloved Carlotta, the woman I loved. . .and drove to suicide. An image of her follows me in all my dreams. And then, about a year ago, this young girl appeared, who was the very image of Carlotta."

"Do you mean the young prostitute?" Magdalena interrupted.

Jeremias nodded. "The first time I saw the girl, she came to me to abort a child. Prostitutes know about my knowledge of healing and visit me in secret. Ever since then, I couldn't forget the girl. Her . . . her name was Clara. I went to her and told her I only wanted to touch her, nothing more. At first, she was disgusted, but I gave her money, lots of money, and she gave herself to me. I often visited her in the brothel in the Rosengasse, and once I persuaded her to sleep here with me." A blissful smile spread across his face. "It was the most wonderful night in almost half a century. We talked a lot, just as I had talked back then with Carlotta—mostly inconsequential things, the way new lovers do. I was a fool. A stupid old fool." He pounded his forehead with his fist before continuing.

"In a moment of weakness, I told Clara my secret. I told her that in my former life I'd been Michael Binder, the hangman of Bamberg." His face darkened. "The next day she demanded money, and later, even more. She threatened to turn me over to the officials."

"Why would that have been so bad?" Georg asked. "After

all, you didn't do anything illegal back then, you were just the hangman."

Jeremias smiled. "That's just it, I was the hangman," he responded. "Remember, at that time, not only ordinary people, but more important, many patricians and councilors were being burned at the stake. Their families swore bloody revenge. I can still see them standing there alongside the flaming stake and pointing at me." He shuddered. "They could never call the ones responsible to account, as they were too powerful. But believe me, they would have taken out their anger on me, and they still would do it today, because I'm just a simple hangman."

Jakob grumbled his agreement and took another drag on his pipe. "You're probably right. It's so easy for them to vent their anger and guilt on us, and that's why they need us — to kill, and to heal sometimes, too, so we can relieve them of their undesired offspring. And afterward, in the street, they look away, and behind our backs they make the sign of the cross."

"What happened with this young Clara?" Magdalena asked.

Jeremias took a deep breath. "Once, when I had no money to pay her, I went to her and asked her to stop it. But she just laughed at me, and said she'd go to Captain Martin Lebrecht the next day to report me. She called me a stupid cripple and told me all the things the patricians would do to make my life hell. At that moment, I knew I had to act." He stopped short. "I thought about all the ways I could hurt her, and got the idea of using the sleep sponge, which I had used on criminals in the past. The very next night, I lay in wait for her and pressed the sleep sponge over her face. She cried once, then fell to the ground. She didn't even feel the blow that smashed her skull."

"But the rib cage," Georg whispered. He was both fascinated and repelled by Jeremias's cold-blooded description of the young girl's murder. "You cut open her rib cage. Why?"

Jeremias shrugged. "There were people who'd seen me with Clara, and I was afraid someone might get the wrong idea. An old man, an unrequited love . . . so I made it look like this were-wolf had sunk its fangs into her." He winked at Jakob. "And all of you were fooled by it."

Georg now looked at the old man in disgust.

Is this what happens when you kill hundreds of people? How sick and unfeeling can you get?

For the first time he felt nothing but revulsion for the voca-tion of the executioner.

But this is probably what I'll have to do someday . . .

The little room was now almost completely filled with smoke from Jakob's pipe, and through the gray clouds, Jeremias's scarred face looked almost like a ghost, a spirit from a long-for-gotten past.

The silence in the room was broken by his question, uttered in a soft voice. "Are you going to hand me over now to the guards?" Jeremias asked.

"I'm not a judge; I'm just a hangman like you used to be," Jakob replied hesitantly. "God knows, there was a lot of pain in your life, but I'm sure that at least the great judge of us all will see to it that you pay for this deed in eternity. And you will pay more than any of the others you have killed, because at least this one time you were able to make your decision freely. And you chose the path of darkness."

"I know that," Jeremias replied gloomily and waited to see what his visitors would do next. "So you'll let me go?"

"I'm not sure yet," Jakob said. He puffed on his pipe and seemed completely lost in his own thoughts. "It depends on what else we learn. Perhaps even with your help." He stared at Jere-mias sharply. "Do you swear you have nothing to do with the other murders?"

The old man held his hand to his skinny chest. "I swear by all the saints and the Holy Mother of Jesus."

Jakob waved dismissively. "You can forget all that rot. I al-ways thought there was something fishy about the murder of the

young prostitute—the odor of henbane, her ripped-open chest
. . . It didn't seem to fit with the others."

"But the other victims were also badly mangled," Magdalena
interrupted. "They'd been tortured, dismembered . . ."

"The werewolf," Georg whispered, making the sign of the
cross.

"Good God, just stop talking about this damn werewolf,"
Kuisl scolded. "Can't you see that someone is playing us for
fools? Jeremias used this horror story, as did someone before
him. But who? And why?" The hangman frowned. "Well, at
least we know this prostitute doesn't belong with the others. She
was the stone in the mosaic that didn't fit. If we put this aside,
who's left? Who . . ."

Jakob reached out for the chess pieces still lying on the table
alongside the chessboard, mulling everything over.

"The first victim was probably this Klaus Schwarzkontz," he
mumbled, without taking the pipe out of his mouth. "An old
Bamberg city councilor." He placed a white castle on the board.
"Thadäus Vasold was also an old councilor, and the old lady Agnes Gotzendörfer was the widow of an influential patrician, as
well . . ." Another castle and a black queen followed. "So here we
have three people connected by the power they had in the past."

"But there were also some rather young women," Magdalena chimed in. "The apothecary's wife, Adelheid Rinswieser, for
example, whose husband is also on the council. And Simon said
that the fiancée of another young councilor also disappeared, a
certain Johanna Steinhofer."

Jakob placed two white knights alongside the black queen
and the two rooks. "Look," he said. "It's just a thought: if you
leave the prostitute out of the picture, it's just a struggle between
patricians and their families. The only conclusion, then . . ."

Georg cleared his throat. "Father?" he asked softly.

Impatiently, Jakob turned to face him. "For God's sake, what
is it?"

"Uh, you forget there was one more woman who has disappeared," Georg replied timidly. "A simple miller's wife by the name of Barbara Leupnitz, who lived in the Bamberg Forest. Her husband is certain one of the dismembered arms belonged to her. After Councilor Schwarzkontz, she was the second victim."

Jakob set down another white pawn alongside the other figures. "So, not one of the patricians. I thought the veil was lifting."

"Well, perhaps it is, after all."

It was Jeremias, lying on the bed and groaning. Evidently, the pain in his face had subsided. Now he stood up, shuffled over to the table, and stood there thinking about the six figures on the chessboard. He reached out with his gout-plagued fingers for the lone white pawn, then turned to Georg with a questioning look.

"Did you say the miller's wife is Barbara Leupnitz?"

When Georg nodded, Jeremias continued, lost deep in thought: "I knew her father well. A certain Johannes Schramb. He was just a simple scribe in the city hall, like a number of others. But there was a time when I saw Schramb almost every day."

"And when was that?" Magdalena asked.

Jeremias took a deep breath before answering.

"That was at the time of the witch trials. Johannes Schramb was at that time a scribe for the so-called Witches Commission."

"The Witches Commission?" asked Magdalena, frowning. "Like the one they've set up because of this werewolf?"

"Something like that," Jeremias nodded. "The members of the Witches Commission at that time were the so-called *Fragherren,* or 'inquisitors,' and they alone decided who looked suspicious and whom to question. They were also present every time a suspect was tortured. The Bamberg Witches Commission ruled in cases involving life and death. They were appointed by the bishop, and there was no one in the city who could question their decisions."

"A small circle of powerful men who could decide whether

people lived or died," Magdalena murmured. "They must have felt like they were gods." She stopped short. "Wait!" She pointed excitedly at the other pieces on the chessboard. "Were any of the present victims members of that Witches Commission?"

"The members of the commission changed from one trial to the next," Jeremias replied with a shrug, "but there were some who served every time, and I can remember very clearly who they were. "One of them was Klaus Schwarzkontz, and I think also Thadäus Vasold and Egidius Gotzendörfer, the husband of Agnes Gotzendörfer." He sighed. "But old Egidius is long gone, and all the other victims are naturally much too young. After all, all this happened nearly forty years ago."

"What about the scribe, this Johannes Schramb," Jakob asked. "Is he still living?"

Jeremias shook his head. "Surely not. Even then he was no youngster. I think he died more than ten years ago."

"But his daughter . . . she passed away just recently," Jakob replied, taking another deep drag on his pipe. He glared at old Jeremias. "Do you think there's a way we can find out whether the two other young women had a father or grandfather who served on this commission? If they got married, then their surnames would be different, of course."

Jeremias thought for a while. "It wouldn't be especially difficult to find out their maiden names. Perhaps Berthold Lamprecht can help us with that. As the tavern keeper of the Wild Man, there isn't a soul in Bamberg he doesn't know." He shrugged. "But whether their fathers or grandfathers were members of the commission then . . ."

Georg couldn't contain himself any longer and jumped up excitedly from his stool. "Let's see if I've got this right. Do you seriously believe there's someone out there deliberately targeting these former commission members? And once he'd disposed of them, he strung up their spouses, children, and grandchildren?"

"Good Lord, how often do I have to tell you to keep your mouth shut when adults are talking," Jakob scolded, looking at Georg so angrily that his son meekly returned to his seat.

"He's fifteen, Father," Magdalena objected. "Georg is no longer a little boy. Besides, we have a lot to thank him for," she said, giving her younger brother a sarcastic look. "Even though he's unfortunately worthless as a nursemaid."

Jakob grunted his disapproval, then offered an explanation.

"I told you before, there are two possibilities: this alleged werewolf could be a madman who kills people indiscriminately, or he could have a plan. If he has a plan—and I'm beginning to believe he does—then there's some connection between all these murders. It can't be an accident that among the victims there are two former inquisitors, the widow of another, and one of the scribes. The other murders no doubt have some connection to it all, as well, and that's what we have to find out." He turned back to Jeremias. "So what can you tell me about the names of the commission members?"

Jeremias sighed wearily. "I already told you. There was not just one commission, but many: a new group was assembled for each trial. I can remember Schwarzkontz and the two old councilors, as well as the scribe Schramb, but as far as the others are concerned . . ."—he hesitated—"for the life of me, I can't remember who they were. Those were uncivil, barbaric times, and, moreover, it all happened ages ago. You'd have to look at the old records to find out what lists all those inquisitors were on."

"But why should we do that?" Georg asked, confused.

"How stupid are you, you numbskull?" Jakob snapped, pounding the table so hard that the chess pieces flew off in all directions. "If we can find the one trial where all of these inquisitors were present, we can perhaps prevent another calamity."

"And you say this because . . ." Magdalena started to say.

"Because I sense there are a few more people on this list," Jakob interrupted. He pointed at his nose. "And my nose here tells me our unknown suspect won't stop killing until he's gotten to the end of the list."

"You can just forget about that," replied Jeremias, shaking his head. "Those lists are ancient. No doubt they're rotting away somewhere in the bishop's archive. You can't just walk in there and start looking around. The place is crawling with guards. Besides you don't know your way around there. You might just as well go looking for the needle in a haystack."

"We got into the dungeon in the Old Residence, and we'll make it into the bishop's archive, as well," Jakob replied firmly. "There's always a way." He pointed to Jeremias. "And you will help us in the search for the right document. I know that hangmen, too, often search the documentation about the questioning of condemned men. That's what we do in Schongau."

"And if I refuse?" Jeremias asked.

"If you refuse, we'll turn you over to Captain Martin Lebrecht first thing tomorrow as a confessed murderer who is probably also the werewolf they're looking for."

Jeremias groaned and raised his hands in defeat. "Very well. It's possible I might find the list in the archives, but as I said, we'll never get in there. Never. You can forget about it." Then he hesitated. "Unless . . ." A grin spread across his face.

"Unless what?" Magdalena and Georg asked at the same time.

"Well, perhaps there is a chance," Jeremias replied, enjoying the moment, as the others looked at him expectantly. "It's really a dreadful thing, and if we decide to do it, we'll need nerves of steel."

The hangman nodded. "Don't think twice about that. My nerves are as strong as a seaman's rope."

For a long time, Barbara and Markus Salter remained silent, cowering down on the floor of the little room that smelled of mold and decay. The crates and chests all around them were covered in dust and had evidently been standing there for years. On the opposite side of the room, next to the archway that led down into the sandy tunnel there was another door, which appeared much newer.

"Where are we?" Barbara asked, as she felt her strength coming back and the trembling gradually subsiding.

"Probably in the Carmelite monastery on the Kaulberg," Markus replied. He pointed to the brown monk's robe he was wearing. "In any case, I found this here in one of the trunks, along with a few old crucifixes and altar cloths. Most of the things have seen better days."

Now Barbara noticed that there was a dark spot on the side of Salter's robe, and she assumed it was blood. Evidently his injuries were worse than she'd first thought.

"What happened?" she whispered. "The last time I saw you, you were outside in the courtyard just after everyone had fled the room."

"They chased us like animals," Salter responded in a monotone. "They caught fat Matthäus first, out in the courtyard. Karl and skinny Bruno made it out to the street. I tried to help them, but it was hopeless . . ." Salter sniffled as he wiped the blood from his nose. "Finally, I ran up the Kaulberg and crawled into this wretched hole." He pointed to the low archway and the rubble-strewn staircase. "I looked around a bit. The entire hill is like a piece of cheese; the Bambergers are digging up the sand here for all their new building sites. You can be glad that none of the tunnels have collapsed, or the monastery overhead."

Apprehensively, Barbara looked up at the damp ceiling and the water dripping down from it.

"Did you say," she asked, "we're probably the only actors to have escaped this madness? What happened to Sir Malcolm? Did he perhaps also . . ."

Markus Salter sneered. "Don't worry about him. He always

saves his skin. Malcolm has played so many roles in his life that he can easily play the part of the curious onlooker, a member of the angry mob, or God knows what—anything that crosses his mind. You don't have to worry about him."

"I'm much more worried about you," Barbara said, pointing hesitantly at the dark spot on his robe. "It seems you had a hard job saving yourself, too."

Salter waved dismissively. "Oh . . . that will get better. I'm just glad I was able to get out in one piece. You should put on a monk's robe like this, too. It scratches like hell, but it's warm. It looks like we'll be spending a while down here. No doubt the devil is at work down in the city."

"Or, rather, the werewolf," Barbara replied bitterly. Anxiously, she glanced at Salter. "Did the suffragan bishop really turn into a werewolf during our performance? He looked so horrible." She shuddered. "How can anything like that happen? Perhaps these incidents do have something to do with the actors. First the pelts in Matheo's room, and now this."

"Well, I'm reluctant to say so, but I've had my suspicions for a long time," Salter replied. "I had to wonder when I first saw the wolf pelts in Matheo's luggage, but now . . ."

"What are you saying?" Barbara asked.

He hesitated but finally replied. "I've got to say it's not the first time we've encountered a werewolf." He wrapped his arms tightly around his chest. He clearly was freezing despite the heavy robe he was wearing.

"There were a few strange incidents after our performances in Cologne and Frankfurt, as well," he continued gloomily. "Peaceful citizens suddenly attacked others in the street for no apparent reason; a vagrant is said to have stolen an infant from its cradle and eaten it; a few young girls disappeared without a trace . . . I've had my suspicions for a long time, and then three days ago in the wagon I caught him red-handed."

"By all the saints, who?" Barbara whispered.

"Sir Malcolm." Markus took a deep breath. "Actually, I just wanted to ask him which costumes still needed mending. There was a strange, sulfurous odor in the wagon, and when I addressed him, he quickly stashed something away in a chest. He seemed very annoyed. Later, I went back to the wagon and looked inside the chest . . ." Salter hesitated, then after a while continued in a strained voice. "Inside there was a silver pentagram, a chandelier with black candles, and a skull so small, it could only have been that of a child."

"My God," Barbara gasped. "Is Sir Malcolm a warlock?"

Markus Salter shrugged. "Later, he even showed us the chandelier and the pentagram, saying he needed it for our performance of *Faust*. The whole time he was looking at me so strangely, and didn't say anything about the child's skull. Naturally, I can't prove anything; all I can say is that whenever Sir Malcolm and his troupe stayed very long in a city, strange things started happening."

"How long have you known him?" Barbara asked anxiously.

"Around ten years. Back then I was a student in Cologne, and I was broke. I was as fascinated by the theater as you are now." Markus smiled, then he winced and pressed his hand against the wound in his side.

Barbara pointed to the bloodstained robe. "Can I have a look? I know a bit about treating wounds."

Salter looked at her suspiciously. "Barbara, you are no doubt an excellent actress, but at your age, I can't see you in the role of a doctor."

"Believe me, I really know something about it," she answered a bit snippily. "My father, as you know, is an executioner, and we Kuisls know a lot about healing."

Salter winced again, and this time she wasn't sure it was because of the pain. "I'd completely forgotten that," he said. "Your uncle is the Bamberg hangman, isn't he?"

Barbara nodded sadly. "Almost our whole family is engaged

in this horrible profession, and has been for ages—Father, my uncle, my brother-in-law, my grandfather, and others. We're scattered all over the Reich and all related to each other in some way. That's why executioners all greet each other as 'cousin.'" She sighed. "My great-grandfather was the famous—or infamous—Jörg Abriel, who tortured and killed hundreds of people. Perhaps you've heard of him."

Salter shook his head and looked a little paler now. "No, my dear, I . . ." It looked as if he was struggling to say something, but once again he was overcome with pain.

"Don't be that way. Show me your wound," Barbara said.

With a look of determination, she ripped the robe off. There was blood on the side of Salter's chest, and in one place it was still seeping out. Carefully, she examined the area.

"Someone obviously stabbed you there with a dagger," she said in a professional tone of voice. "Thank God the wound isn't very deep, but it must be cleaned at once or it will become infected."

She ripped off a piece of her wet dress, then looked around the room. In one corner she finally found a small keg of communion wine.

"I don't know if the wine here still tastes very good," she said, opening the stopper and soaking the cloth in it, "but for cleaning out a wound it's a lot better than this filthy water."

Carefully, she wiped away the blood, and after the wound was clean, she made a temporary bandage from a long piece of cloth ripped from one of the robes. Markus Salter remained quiet, except for a few soft groans.

"I can't do anything more for you now," Barbara said finally, "but perhaps tomorrow we can go together to my uncle's house . . ."

Salter laughed bitterly, but his laughter soon gave way to a fit of coughing.

"Are you out of your mind?" he gasped. "If those idiots out

there just stop to think for a moment, they'll figure out you're the niece of the Bamberg executioner. They've been looking for you for a long time. Does anyone here in town know you? Did anyone see you before you appeared on the stage with us?"

"I just don't know," she replied hesitantly, all of a sudden feeling exposed and helpless. "I visited the marketplace a few times with my sister, and then there's Katharina, Uncle Bartholomäus's fiancée, of course, and old Jeremias, the custodian of the Wild Man . . ."

"No doubt the tavern was ransacked a long time ago," Salter interrupted. "After all, that's where the actors were lodged. And they surely asked Jeremias about us." He looked at her attentively. "Do you really think this Jeremias wouldn't betray you to the guards to save his life?"

"Oh, God, I don't know," Barbara wailed. "Probably not, but that means that I can never return to my family."

"At least as long as they live in the house of the Bamberg executioner." Salter nodded with determination. "After everything that happened tonight, neither of us can show our faces in Bamberg again. It's likely that all the guards in the city are out looking for us actors."

"But where can we go, then?" Barbara wailed. "I want to go back to my family."

Markus patted her on the head. "I'll think of something, Barbara, I promise, but first we should get some sleep. You'll see; tomorrow things will look much better."

Barbara didn't believe him, but nevertheless she put on one of the warm robes and laid her head in his lap as Markus hummed a little tune for her. It sounded sad and dreary, but it calmed her down, and soon thereafter she fell asleep from exhaustion and grief.

14

That morning, as the Kuisls assembled in
the house of the Bamberg executioner, there was a strange mood
of despondency mixed with tense expectation. Until then, they
had scarcely had a chance to talk with one another. The injured
Matheo was still upstairs in the bedroom, catching up on his
sleep as he recovered. The wine mixed with herbs that Jakob had
given him the night before finally gave him relief from his bad
dreams — a good fortune not shared by most of the others present. All of them were pale, and the dark rings around their eyes
bore witness to the strenuous days and nights preceding.

Now they were all seated around the scratched table in the
warm main room while the boys were outside playing hide-and-
seek along the city moat with the neighborhood children. The
boys' new friends came from a family of dishonorable gravedig-
gers, so the parents had no objection to them playing with the
Kuisl boys.

Magdalena rubbed her tired eyes. She had fervently hoped
her sister would come back to them after that chaotic night, but
Barbara hadn't returned either to Jeremias's or to the execution-

er's house. Simon and his friend Samuel had taken the deranged suffragan bishop back to his room for observation. Later that evening he had quieted down and lay there motionless. Bartholomäus later found an exhausted Simon in the area around St. Martin's Church, and they'd both finally returned long after midnight. Magdalena was relieved to learn that Simon hadn't been bitten by a werewolf, but what he told her about the horrible transformation of Sebastian Harsee had deeply shocked her. Was it possible a person could change into a beast in the presence of all those witnesses?

"Last night, the whole city went mad," said Bartholomäus, who until then had been quietly eating his porridge out of the communal bowl. He had just returned from a brief check of the city dungeon. "But at least the city guards have gotten everything under control," he continued. "They gave these young thugs a good spanking and sent them all back to their mothers. But people are also saying that at least two of the actors were killed last night and then strung up like dead cats, to the general amusement of the crowd. Now, no one will admit to doing it, and Captain Martin Lebrecht evidently has better things to do than to look for the perpetrators." He sighed deeply. "The rest of the actors have been thrown in the dungeon, and no doubt I'll have to deal with them soon."

"Is Barbara among them?" Magdalena asked, her heart pounding. Simon had already told her and the others that Barbara had been in the performance the previous day. Jakob had groaned and cracked the knuckles of his huge fists but otherwise seemed astonishingly calm.

Bartholomäus shook his head. "Barbara has disappeared without a trace, as has a certain Markus Salter, by the way, the hack who writes or copies the plays, for all I know." Then he turned serious. "Things look really bad for the director himself, this Malcolm. They found a few magic items in a secret compartment of his chest—a pentagram, black candles, and a human skull, and now they're saying he used them to conjure up the werewolf."

"Sir Malcolm probably used the objects in one of his plays," Magdalena speculated, "perhaps for *Doctor Faustus,* which involves sorcery, after all."

"And then he locks them in a secret compartment?" Bartholomäus frowned. "I'm not so sure about that. The council in any case doesn't buy a word of it," he said, then turned to Simon. "You attended the performance yesterday, didn't you? Was Malcolm behaving strangely?"

"Uh . . . not that I was aware of." Simon looked up from a book he'd been paging through until that moment. It came from Bartholomäus's little collection of books in the main room. "In any case, I don't think Harsee's madness has anything to do with the actors," he added. "It's probably some strange illness. The poor fellow is almost completely paralyzed, and only his eyes keep flitting nervously back and forth. If that's a werewolf, then it's a pretty pathetic one." He rubbed his temples with exhaustion. "But it's still strange that such an illness, if that's what it is, breaks out at the very moment everyone is talking about werewolves here."

Simon sighed and put the tattered book aside. "I've spent half the night racking my brain over this, but unfortunately all the books here are about veterinary medicine, and that doesn't help."

"Don't disparage Zechendörfer's *Hippiatrica,*" Bartholomäus interrupted. "That's one of the best books on medicine ever written."

"Yes, when you're treating horses with stomach gas from eating too much hay or shodding them because of a broken hoof," Simon replied, nodding toward the other room. "That applies also to the certainly excellent works about rearing, training, and treating dogs, but here we're dealing with something more complicated, with a human element."

"You can learn all sorts of things from animals, Herr Medicus," Bartholomäus shot back. "For example humility and modesty."

Jakob was about to give him a harsh rebuke, as well, but Georg, who was sitting next to his father, put his hand on his arm to calm him down.

"I know myself that we Kuisls like to fight," he said in a firm voice, "but now isn't the time for that. Let's think instead about whether to pursue the course that old Jeremias suggested yesterday. Since Barbara has disappeared, we should probably be using all our resources to find her as quickly as possible. Everything else is secondary."

Jakob Kuisl looked at his son in astonishment, not knowing what to make of Georg's newly acquired confidence.

"Well, I'll be damned, you're right," he said a bit less gruffly. Then he pointed up toward the ceiling. "On the other hand, the young lad that Barbara is so crazy about is lying up there in bed, while his friends are sitting in the dungeon awaiting their execution as alleged werewolves. What do you think Barbara will say if her own uncle whips their battered bodies to death perhaps as early as tomorrow? Well?" He looked across the table at Bartholomäus, who grimly returned his gaze. "Have you thought about that?"

Despite the grave situation, Magdalena couldn't suppress a slight smile. She knew that her father had always been driven by a boundless curiosity. Without a doubt, he wanted to find out what was really going on here in Bamberg, and until he did, he wouldn't sleep soundly.

"Perhaps you could tell us again everything you learned from Jeremias last night," Simon said, turning to his father. "I must confess I haven't been able to make sense of it all yet."

Jakob cleared his throat, then briefly retold the story of Jeremias's fate and what happened during the witch trials when he was known as Michael Binder, the executioner of Bamberg. He also mentioned Jeremias's murder of the young prostitute. Meanwhile, Bartholomäus sat there thinking and sucking on a stick of kindling he'd broken off a piece of firewood.

"I've heard a bit about this Michael Binder," he interrupted his brother, while still chewing on the kindling. "He must have been a good hangman. Sometimes young people think I'm his son, because the job is usually passed down through the family. Well, whatever . . ." He shrugged. "If law and order still prevails in this city, Jeremias will have to be hanged. I can't say I'll be glad to do it, but I probably won't have any choice."

"I've given him my word we won't report him if he helps us," Jakob replied. "Look at him—the man is a wreck. Scarred forever for his deeds, which he wants to atone for now, including the one that happened so long ago," he added grimly.

"You mean his torturing his fiancée?" Simon shuddered. "That is unpardonable. Even God cannot forgive that."

"Just cut out this nonsense." Kuisl suddenly sprang up and glared angrily at Simon. He looked like a dark thunderhead towering above his son-in-law. "How can a no-account little medicus understand what's going on in the minds of us hangmen? Have you ever hurt someone just because you had to . . . because your hungry family was waiting for you out there and you would be stoned to death if you didn't? Did you ever put a noose around a condemned man's neck as he pleaded and cried, while your blood-lusting fellow citizens stared at you from behind? Have you?"

"No, you are right; I haven't," Simon replied meekly. "I'm only a medicus who wants to heal."

"Who is *permitted* to do that," Jakob growled, then he sat down. "And now let us continue. Georg is right, there are in fact more important things to discuss."

He told them about his hunch that all the victims were some-how connected in the past, that they—or their husbands or older relatives—had many years ago been members of a Witches Commission that determined whether others would live or die and if they would be tortured and burned.

"If we succeed in finding a document listing the members of this commission, we may be able to prevent further disaster. There are no doubt other people on the list, and most important, the name of the accused."

"But all that happened decades ago," Bartholomäus inter-rupted, as he threw a singed piece of kindling straight into the open fire. "Do you really believe there's someone lurking around out there interested in such an old case?"

"I don't know, but I'd like to find out, and Jeremias will help us." Jakob lowered his voice and turned to Simon and Bar-tholomäus. "The old man told us about a half-buried passage-way leading from the cathedral to the bishop's archive in the next building. Evidently, in ancient times the cathedral faced in an-other direction, namely northward, and it was at the time that the passageway between the two was built. It's said to be a pretty weird place. The corridor is an ancient crypt with piles of bones and skulls." He grinned. "I love skulls. At least they can tell you no lies."

"Since our visit to the residence yesterday, the area around the cathedral square is crawling with guards," Magdalena said in a worried voice. "Do you really think we can simply walk into the cathedral and enter the corridor without anyone asking what we're up to?"

Jakob nodded. "I was worried about that myself, but then it occurred to me that today is All Souls' Day, and in Bam-berg, just as in Schongau, there is always a High Mass in the morning in memory of the dead. The cathedral is more crowded then than at any time except Easter." Confidently, he looked around the table. "If we act during the mass, no one will notice us amid all the activity. We just have to get back on time."

"And you intend to climb down into a crypt full of bones on All Souls' Day?" Simon groaned. "I'm not sure if I—"

"Who said I wanted to take a little coward like you along with us?" Jakob growled. "You can just go back to your suffragan bishop possessed by the devil. Maybe you'll learn something there pertaining to our case." He shook his head. "No, Jeremias and I will do that alone, and in the meantime the rest of you can look for Barbara. After all the uproar, I hope she's found someplace to hide in a barn or empty shed. Later, I'll come to you, if you—"

There was a loud hammering on the front door, and Jakob stopped suddenly. A moment later the door flew open and an agitated Katharina rushed into the room. She was as pale as a corpse, her full head of hair was disheveled, and she was still wearing the splendid gown she had on the evening before, but it was now soiled from running through the street.

"Bartl," she began breathlessly, "you . . . you must help me . . . My father . . . has disappeared. Oh, God . . ." She leaned against the wall, crying. Magdalena ran to help her, led her to the table, sat her down alongside the warm stove, and took hold of her shaking hands.

"What happened?" she asked gently.

"This whole wedding is cursed," she blurted out. "Ever since Bartholomäus and I decided to get married, all these dreadful things have been happening. Perhaps the suffragan bishop was right after all when he disapproved of the ceremony. And now, he is a werewolf himself. Oh, I should never have gotten engaged to an executioner, and this is my punishment."

"What nonsense you are talking, woman," Bartholomäus shouted angrily. "The devil has robbed you of your senses." He tried to moderate his voice. "But I'll excuse you, because I see this is all too much for you. But tell us, now, what is this about your father?"

"I lost sight of him last night after the terrible events," she began, calmer now. "We were standing outside in the courtyard, and all around us people were screaming as more and more of them came rushing out of the hall, pushing their way past us. And suddenly he was gone. I waited for him, but it seemed like the earth had simply swallowed him up. Finally I went home, hoping to meet him there. But he wasn't there, either; he was simply gone." Again she broke out in tears. "I waited for him until this morning, but he never came. No one knows what happened to him. Perhaps . . ."

Her words turned into a long wail. Magdalena looked anxiously at Simon, and he returned her gaze. He'd told the whole family about Hieronymus Hauser's peculiar behavior, and Katharina had also told Magdalena that her father had been acting strangely in recent days.

"Is there anything in particular you noticed about your father yesterday?" she asked the tearful Katharina.

She looked up, troubled. "Well, he . . . he was very anxious," she mumbled. "During the play he kept looking around as if he expected to see someone he was very afraid of, but when I asked him about it, he didn't answer." Fearfully, she looked around the table. "Do you believe this werewolf took him away?"

"Believing is something you can do in church," Jakob answered grimly. "What I want are facts. You should all get moving now as fast as possible to look for my Barbara and also Katharina's father. What's clear is that too many people are disappearing in this city." He stood up and cracked his knuckles one last time. "And today, as a good Christian, I intend to go to mass. I'll say three hallelujahs if I can finally get a bit closer to the truth."

. . .

Just a few moments later, Simon was hurrying through the little streets of Bamberg to the rectory of St. Martin, where the suffragan bishop lived. It was a simple, middle-class house adjacent to the church and connected to it by a passageway. As he approached the door, he noticed that someone had drawn a large pentagram on the ground. From the door handle hung a small bouquet of dried St. John's wort, which, according to ancient tradition, would ward off witches, demons, and evil spirits.

He looked around carefully. A few people walked by with their heads down, making a wide arc when they passed the house, as if fearing an infection. In the meantime, Simon had again donned his old medicus's robe, as the splendid outfit he'd borrowed from Samuel was much worse for wear after the attack by the deranged suffragan bishop. At least now he wouldn't attract so much attention from the many people in the church square.

Bells rang out over the city, summoning the faithful to the mass for the dead up in the cathedral. Simon was sure the service would be well attended that day. In times like these, as he knew from experience, people always looked to the church for consolation.

Besides, they no doubt are looking forward to a fiery, bloodthirsty sermon, he thought. *Hatred and fear of Satan are always good adhesives for holding a city together.*

He tapped cautiously on the door, and at once Samuel appeared in the doorway. The Bamberg city physician was unshaven and white as a sheet and looked as if he'd kept watch by the sick man's bed all night. Through the crack in the door, Simon could smell the strong fragrance of incense.

"Come in," Samuel said, looking exhausted, and beckoned for Simon to enter the vestibule. "His condition has not changed much. Unfortunately, none of the servants are here except for a single lackey and the fat maid, both of whom you met yesterday.

All the rest fled in terror. So you will have to do without your morning coffee."

Simon smiled wanly. "I'll survive, even though I admit that the dark devil's brew would help me to think. I've been racking my brain for half the night trying to make sense of all this."

They went up to the second floor, entering a dark corridor whose walls were lined with votive pictures and paintings of saints and with many doors leading off it. From his visit the day before, Simon knew that the patient's room was at the far end of the corridor, and he could have found it blindfolded, as the fragrance of incense became stronger, almost sickening, the closer they got.

"Don't be surprised at how things look in there," Samuel warned him as he opened the tall door. "None of this is mine. But the maid, this superstitious harpy, insisted or she would have left."

They entered the darkened room, and Simon thought he could already smell the stench of death — the familiar mixture of incense, burned herbs, sweat, feces, and disease so familiar to him from his countless house calls. Just as outside the house, here, too, a large pentagram had been drawn on the floor, bouquets of St. John's wort were tied to all four bedposts, and crucifixes of all sizes had been hastily hung around the room. The windows were covered with heavy curtains.

The old maid sat slumped over on a stool in the corner and seemed to be sleeping.

Samuel cleared his throat, and she awakened with a start and let out a sharp cry. For a moment she looked like she was going to faint, but then she recognized the two men standing in the dark room and crossed herself with a sigh of relief.

"Ah, it's just you," she sighed. "I was afraid that—"

"Don't worry; the werewolf rarely uses the door," Samuel interrupted. "He jumps through the window, howling. Isn't that what you yourself said yesterday?" He pointed toward the hall. "Everything is fine, Agathe. You can go to mass now, and we'll care for the patient."

Agathe nodded gratefully and dashed out of the room. As soon as the door had closed behind her, Samuel ran to the windows and tore open the curtains.

"Damn, damn, damn," he cursed. "She thinks she can ward off evil this way."

The bright light of morning came flooding into the room and onto the bed, and only then was Simon able to get a look at the Bamberg suffragan bishop. Under the many blankets, Sebastian Harsee looked like a little puppet, an impression reinforced by the waxen expression on his face. It took a while for Simon to realize that was because all the muscles in his face had tensed up and the only things moving were his eyes, which darted back and forth like those of a nervous mouse. A thin stream of saliva was oozing out of the corner of his mouth.

He can see us, I'm certain of that, Simon thought, *and he can probably hear us, too. What a horrible condition. It's as if you're buried alive.*

"Last night he quivered a bit and even moved a few times," said Samuel as he pulled off the covers, revealing the pale body of the suffragan bishop dressed only in a thin nightshirt. "But in the last few hours the paralysis has spread to his entire body—except for his eyes, and he still can give you a grim and threatening look."

"And how about his teeth?" Simon asked. "Yesterday they looked so long and sharp. Have you examined them?"

Samuel nodded. "They look quite normal. I think that was because his lips and the muscles around them were pulled back due to the cramps. But the reaction we witnessed yesterday was certainly interesting . . ."

The doctor took a cup of water and brought it toward the patient's face for him to see. Suddenly Harsee's body began to tremble all over. Though he couldn't move, the aversion he felt was evident in his eyes. Every fiber of his body seemed stretched to the limit, and white foam formed on his lips. Samuel set the cup down on a table a bit farther away, and then the suffragan bishop became visibly calmer.

"He's afraid of water," Simon whispered.

"Any liquid," Samuel corrected him. "As I said, extremely interesting. I've never seen anything like this before." He sighed and wiped the saliva from Harsee's mouth with a cloth. "Unfortunately, our dear Agathe sprinkled him with holy water this morning, and he thrashed about like a fish on dry land. So now, of course, the old woman is completely convinced the suffragan bishop is a werewolf."

"In any case, he jumped at me just like a wolf," Simon mused. "What terrible illness is it that . . . ?" Suddenly he paused.

"What is it?" Samuel asked, puzzled.

Without replying, Simon leaned over the patient and quickly examined the spot on his neck. The small puncture wound was still there, as well as the red circle around it. Something his uncle-in-law said kept going through his mind, like the murmuring of someone reciting the rosary.

You can learn all sorts of things from animals, Herr Medicus. For example, humility and modesty . . .

Outside, the bells rang for the last time, and after that an eerie silence fell over the city.

You can learn all sorts of things from animals . . .

"We were so foolish," Simon finally murmured, "so incredibly foolish. The whole time the answer was right before our eyes."

"What do you mean by that?" Samuel asked. He, too, had now approached the patient and looked at Simon excitedly. "If you can solve this riddle, don't torture me any longer."

Simon grinned. "How many bags of coffee beans do I get if I can?"

"A whole storehouse full, if I can find them, you buffoon."
Samuel raised his arms to the ceiling. "Why has God punished
me with a friend who's such a joker? Say something, will you?
Speak up!"

Simon cast one last look into the eyes of the suffragan bishop,
who glared at him with a mixture of hatred and infinite terror.
Another thread of saliva ran down Sebastian Harsee's mouth
and trickled into the pillow.

Then the medicus gave his diagnosis.

Wrapped in a simple, wide cloak and with his hood pulled down
over his face, Jakob Kuisl stomped up the steep hill to the cathedral square. A gentle drizzle had set in, so his garb didn't attract
attention. Even though hardly anyone in this city knew him, the
hangman considered it a good idea to be as inconspicuous as possible. He knew that for a man of his size, that was a difficult un-
dertaking.

Some people were already making their way to the cathedral. Many of them had first visited the graves of their deceased
relatives and left behind a fresh-baked loaf of so-called soul bread
in the shape of a stag or a little man. It was said that on All Souls'
Day the dead returned from purgatory for a day of rest. Jakob
clenched his teeth and hoped that at least the ghosts would not
harass him down below in the crypt.

Looking around the square, he soon spotted Jeremias who,
as agreed, had been waiting for him at the Adam's Portal on the
east side of the cathedral. He, too, was wearing a nondescript
cloak with a wide hood, which Jakob considered a good idea,
given Jeremias's badly scarred face.

"All hell has broken loose here," grumbled Jakob when he
reached Jeremias.

The old man giggled. "Or rather, an angry God. Fear has always driven people to church, just like in the time of the witch

trials." He winked at Jakob. "Let's just go along with the crowd, and we won't attract so much attention," he said, hurrying ahead.

They entered the cathedral through the east portal and joined the long line of worshipers. Jakob was amazed at the splendor in this church and others, especially in the cathedral. Here in Bamberg, there were precious statues of saints, bishops, and martyrs; the altars were decorated in gold leaf, and silver and gold candelabra encircled huge sarcophagi. Bright morning light fell through the tall windows onto the many columns, arches, and niches.

Even if the world outside is going to hell, Jakob couldn't help thinking, *the church in any case is a window on the paradise to come, and for that reason, this wretched life doesn't seem so terrible . . .*

They passed a statue of a king riding a dapple-gray horse and were soon crushed between praying old women, crippled old men, and also many young people and children who were all pushing their way forward to the pews in the nave. It seemed to Jakob that all of Bamberg had come to attend the All Souls' mass. Clouds of incense drifted past the pillars, giving off an intoxicating fragrance, while deep, hypnotic tones emanated from the organ. In the pews, some people knelt in prayer on the cold stone floor, still holding the empty baskets they had used to take bread to the cemeteries.

As Jakob looked toward the front of the cathedral, he noticed that this church had two chancels, one facing east and one toward the west, unlike the church in Schongau, which had only one. Jeremias followed his gaze.

"The service today is in front of the east altar," he explained in a soft voice. "That's good for us, since we are going to the opposite side, and hopefully no one will be looking in our direction."

They continued to push their way through the crowd and finally took a seat in one of the back pews. The organ fell silent, and then the ministrant, the vicar general representing the suffragan bishop, appeared in his clerical vestments swinging the censer. People rose to their feet, there were some words of greeting in Latin, but soon the vicar digressed from the usual order of the mass. With a serious mien he turned to the congregation.

"Dear fellow Christians," he began in a quavering voice. "You all know that our beloved suffragan bishop, Sebastian Harsee, has . . ."—he paused to cross himself—". . . has fallen victim to the werewolf. As I have been told, his soul is still struggling with the devil, and let us therefore all pray for him."

The faithful knelt down and murmured their prayers. Some cried, while others rocked back and forth as if in a trance. In order not to attract attention, Jakob also muttered a quiet prayer. From what Simon had told him, he knew the suffragan bishop was an unloved, evil son of a bitch, but nonetheless the people mourned for him as if he were the Lamb of God incarnate.

Finally the vicar continued with his sermon. "I stand here today," he droned, "in the firm hope that this suffering inflicted on Bamberg will soon come to an end. I hear that our highly esteemed prince bishop will now tackle the root of this problem. Some citizens who have given their souls to the devil have already been arrested. Each one of you is now summoned to do his part to throw light on this problem. Look around. Witches, druids, and magicians often disguise themselves as the most charming fellow citizens. Indeed, it could be your own neighbor . . ."

Jeremias, standing alongside Jakob, groaned. "I can't listen to this rubbish any longer," he whispered. "That's just how it all began back then. Anyway, we've got to hurry. The mass lasts about an hour, and we'll have to finish by then. So let's get going."

The next time the faithful knelt down and lowered their heads in prayer, Jeremias and Jakob quietly stood up and headed as inconspicuously as possible toward the western side of the cathedral. With their black robes and their hoods still drawn over their heads, they looked somewhat like Franciscan monks on a pilgrimage, and thus no one paid any attention to them as they passed the rear altar in the northwest part of the transept. No one stopped them here, where the murmuring of the faithful could be heard in the distance. As they passed by, Jeremias picked up two burning candles and handed one to his companion.

"We'll soon need these," he whispered. "Let's go; the time is right."

Just as the congregation struck up a loud hymn, Jeremias beckoned for Jakob to come to a stairway that seemed to lead down underneath the western altar. Once they reached the bottom, they found themselves standing in front of a locked door.

"And now?" Jakob asked impatiently.

Grinning, Jeremias fetched a rusty key chain from his pocket. "It's lucky for you that I kept a few other things along with my executioner's sword from my former life. Before the bigoted zealots built the House of the Inquisition, many trials took place in the Old Residence. With all the torturing, I was soon one of the most sought-after men in the residence—I was needed and respected—so at some time or other they gave me this ring of keys allowing me unrestricted access anywhere."

Jakob looked at him suspiciously. "Perhaps also to the crypt in the cathedral?"

Jeremias giggled and jingled the ring of keys. "They needed me, but they also wanted to avoid a fuss; too many patricians had already died at the stake. Every time I walked through the Schöne Pforte and into the residence, everyone in the city knew what was up, so eventually they came up with the idea of smuggling me in unnoticed—through the cathedral. So come along quickly."

He opened the door and led Jakob into a cube-shaped room with stone walls and a floor that appeared to be located directly beneath the western altar. The floor was strewn with rubble, rotted beams, and old sacks of mortar as hard as stone, making their progress difficult.

"Long ago, this was the crypt of an earlier cathedral," Jeremias explained. "During the construction work it was excavated, but then the part above ground was renovated and what was down here was forgotten. Lucky for us."

He climbed over the rubble until he finally reached a low archway with blocks of stone and beams of wood piled in front of it. Panting and puffing, the old man started to pull away some of the lighter beams of wood.

"Come on, big fellow, lend a hand," he said to Jakob. "It's been more than thirty years since anyone cleaned up down here."

The hangman moved the heavy stone blocks aside as if they were small chunks of plaster, and before long, the doorway was cleared, revealing a narrow, dark corridor.

"Now comes the unpleasant part of our trip," Jeremias announced, picking up the candle he'd set down on one of the pieces of rubble. "Just make sure your little light doesn't go out, or things could become rather unpleasant."

Once again, he giggled, then climbed over the last few pieces of rubble and entered the narrow passage. Jakob followed, ducking so as not to hit his head.

Otherwise, there was not much to see, since the candles illuminated only a small circle of light around them. The tunnel was straight at first, and dense cobwebs hanging from the ceiling kept striking and clinging to Jakob's face. Again and again, the tall hangman bumped his head on the ceiling and walls, throwing up clouds of stone dust.

"Please be careful," Jeremias scolded, pointing at the walls covered with damp mold and saltpeter, "or the crypt will soon have two new inhabitants."

Jakob looked around carefully. Only now did he notice how brittle and crumbling the walls of the corridor were. He now also noticed niches, until then hidden in the shadows, from which the empty eye sockets of human skulls glared back at him, surrounded by splintered arm and leg bones and a few ribs cages covered with moss and mold. As they continued forward, these niches became more numerous, and soon the two intruders were surrounded by crowds of the dead waiting in the stone rooms for the life to come. Jakob couldn't help thinking that today was All Souls' Day.

It's been a long time since anyone brought any soul bread down here to these poor wretches. Will they rise up out of purgatory today just the same?

"We're now in what is probably the oldest section of Bamberg," Jeremias whispered to him. "There was a castle on this hill long before King Henry II, the last of the Ottos, built the first cathedral here, and no one knows how long these bones have lain here. Perhaps even a few of the first Babenberg counts are among them. They must have been a rather debauched crowd."

"I don't give a damn who's here as long as they don't get in my way with their bones," Jakob growled. He pointed ahead, where some of the bones had evidently fallen out of their niches. Skulls and large thigh bones were piled up, blocking the tunnel.

"What a hell of a mess," Jeremias hissed. "As I said, it's been a long time since anyone cleaned this place up. Evidently, the tunnel has been completely forgotten in the last decades. Well, all the better for us." He kicked the bones aside, and his feet made a crunching sound as he moved ahead. Suddenly he leaned down and picked up a skull.

"Well, look at this," he said, turning to Jakob and pointing to a fist-sized hole in the back. "What's your professional opinion, my dear cousin and colleague? Was it a club, a morning star, or . . ."

"Didn't you say we only had an hour?" Jakob interrupted. "Quit fooling around and keep moving, or you can lie down and join them."

With a sigh, Jeremias dropped the skull and moved ahead. Twice more they had to climb over mounds of bones, then they came to a winding staircase with worn steps that led upward. Finally they found themselves before a weathered wooden door covered in cobwebs.

"Thank God, the door is still here," Jeremias exclaimed with relief. "Now I can tell you: I was afraid they'd walled it up in the meantime."

He took out a ring of keys and groaned as he struggled to open the lock.

"I'll bet no one has oiled this in a long time. I don't know if I . . ."

"Get out of my way," said Jakob, pushing Jeremias aside. He turned the key, the lock creaked and finally gave way, then he pushed against the door. It opened with a hideous squeal.

"Jesus, not so loud," Jeremias moaned. "I hope they're all up there at the mass, but you never know with these pale, work-addicted archivists if they'll ever take a break."

They entered a paneled corridor that branched off in two directions. When Jakob turned around, he could see that the door they'd closed behind them was almost invisible between the individual wooden panels, with only the door lock to indicate a hidden passage.

"The corridor to the right goes to the council room," Jeremias whispered, "and the one on the left to the bishop's archive. Keep moving now; we don't have much more time."

He hurried ahead, and soon they were standing in a wide corridor with boxes and shelves full of parchment rolls, notebooks, and tattered documents on both sides. By the dim light of the candles, the corridor looked endless.

"Damn! How are we going to find an individual document here?" he cursed. "This is worse than a needle in a haystack."

"Not really," Jeremias replied. "The inquisitors in those days were perhaps cruel but also extremely conscientious. Several times, I myself had to deliver the minutes of individual sessions here. They're arranged by year. See for yourself."

The old man had been shuffling along, past the shelves and boxes, but then he stopped and pointed at a tiny brass plaque affixed to the side of one shelf and bearing the number 1625.

"At best, we have only until the cathedral bells ring again," Jeremias warned him. "Then we'll have to go back. So let's get started. What do you think: in what year might the trial have taken place?"

"How should I know that?" Kuisl replied. "For God's sake, you were the hangman then."

"Just calm down; you're right." Jeremias raised his hand apologetically, then put it to his scarred nose. "So, just let me think. The first great wave of persecutions was, I think, in 1612, but at that time I was just a young boy, and my father was the executioner here. So, it must have been later, at a time when the present victims or their ancestors were already in the Witches Commission. Do you have the list with you?"

Jakob nodded and pulled out a sheet of paper from his shirt pocket. Just that morning he'd made a list of all the victims of the supposed Bamberg werewolf. There were six names on the list:

Klaus Schwarzkontz
Thadäus Vasold
Agnes Gotzendörfer
Barbara Leupnitz
Johanna Steinhofer
Adelheid Rinswieser

"Let's have a look," Jeremias murmured. "So the first two victims were in fact commission members at the time, I'm sure of that, and so was Egidius Gotzendörfer, the deceased husband of Agnes Gotzendörfer. Barbara Leupnitz was the daughter of Johannes Schramb, one of the scribes at the time . . ."

"We know all that already," Jakob interrupted impatiently, tapping his gnarled finger on the two remaining names. "What about Johanna Steinhofer and Adelheid Rinswieser? Could you find out anything about them?"

"Well, guess what?" said Jeremias with a grin. "I asked Berthold Lamprecht, the tavern keeper of the Wild Man, as I told you I would, pretending I felt bad about the two young women, and asking about their parents. And, lo and behold, Johanna Steinhofer also comes from a good family. She's the granddaughter of Julius Herrenberger, a very influential patrician at the time, who died some years ago. I can remember that he, too, was on some of the Witches Commissions."

"And how about the last one," Jakob asked, "this Rinswieser?"

"Got it." Jeremiah nodded his confirmation. "Adelheid Rinswieser is the youngest daughter of Paulus Braun, now deceased, but at one time a social climber who, despite his youth, managed to get a position in the city council with trickery, money, and cunning. I assume he also sat on one of the commissions, but honestly I can't remember him. Oh, and by the way, Johanna Steinhofer's fiancé and Adelheid Rinswieser's husband are once again on the council." Jeremias grinned and rubbed his thumb and index finger together. "Money is attracted to money."

Jakob frowned, without commenting on Jeremias's last words. Looking around, he discovered a small desk in a niche with a quill and ink pot. He quickly unfolded the note, crossed out some names, and in each case wrote new ones alongside.

Klaus Schwarzkontz
Thadäus Vasold
Agnes Gotzendörfer, Egidius Gotzendörfer
Barbara Leupnitz, Johannes Schramb
Johanna Steinhofer, Julius Herrenberger
Adelheid Rinswieser, Paulus Braun

"This is the group we're looking for," he said finally, handing the sheet of paper to Jeremias. "Can you make anything out of that?"

"I think so." Jeremias thought for a moment and nodded. "That must have been during the last wave of persecutions, or the name of young Paulus Braun wouldn't have been there. Let's have a look . . ."

He walked along the shelves until he reached the number 1627. "I think we need to begin here. That was the year they built the last Inquisition House. I remember it well."

"It's more important for you to remember who was on the commissions at that time," Jakob insisted, as he himself began searching the individual drawers and pigeonholes on the shelves. Dust swirled up as he leafed quickly through the documents. The hangman found an almost endless number of lists and trial transcripts, each of them documenting the cruelty. In the dark dungeons of the Inquisition, suspects were set down on chairs heated until they were glowing; they were given a mash of salted herring and pepper that made their thirst almost unbearable, immersed in a bath of lye that stung their eyes, or locked into tiny enclosures of sharp, wooden pyramids until, screaming and wailing, they confessed to the most outlandish crimes.

Jakob Kuisl found yellowed transcripts and sentences so horrifying that even for a hangman it was enough to make his hair stand on end. On some pages, rust-brown specks of blood were still visible.

". . . the woman was beaten with switches, then put again on the rack, and the entire day she lay there, confessing nothing . . . the arm and leg screws were tightened, but she still screams she knows nothing . . . she is put again on the rack and whipped but still confesses nothing . . . continues to show no remorse . . . *in carcere mortua* . . ."

"Died in the dungeon." Jakob translated the final Latin words. He shook his head in disgust, then turned to examine another dusty record.

"... it is thus duly noted that the woman has given herself heart and soul to the Evil One, and will therefore be tortured with red-hot pincers applied to her breasts, and since she has repeatedly dishonored the sacred host, her right hand will be cut off, whereupon with the other women she will be burned alive at the stake ..."

Jakob cast a surreptitious glance at Jeremias, who was also rummaging through the files. Jakob wondered what the former Bamberg executioner could be thinking as he read about his deeds many years ago, but Jeremias remained remarkably calm, attentive, and he concentrated, untroubled by anything they saw.

Would I be like that if I'd broken, beheaded, and burned hundreds of people? Or am I perhaps already a bit like Jeremias? What is it that makes monsters of us?

The strange thing, actually, was that Jeremias wasn't a monster at all. He was a kind old cripple, a lover of animals, and a learned man who had relieved others of having to do this filthy work, and was now peacefully spending the last years of his life. He didn't even seem much concerned about murdering the young prostitute. Jakob frowned. Perhaps Jeremias was so hardened by sorrow at the death of his fiancée back then that he could no longer feel anything.

In his position, would I have done the same?

Inwardly, Jakob had just answered his own question, when Jeremias standing nearby, suddenly let out a cry.

"Here," he said, holding up a thick dossier. "I think I have it. It was right up on the top shelf. Here are the names we're looking for. And now it all comes back to me." He shook his head in disbelief. "How could I ever have forgotten this trial? Well, I'm getting along in years."

"What do you mean?" Jakob asked, still lost in his gloomy reveries. "Was there anything special about this trial?"

Jeremias grinned. "Ha! Anything special? It was perhaps the

most sensational trial that Bamberg had ever seen, and our candidates were all, in fact, part of it. Here, see for yourself."

He handed the report to Jakob, who quickly perused the pages.

It didn't take the Schongau hangman much time to realize they were on the right track.

Magdalena, her brother, and her uncle were wandering through the streets of Bamberg in a desperate search for Barbara and Hieronymus Hauser.

Since Georg was familiar with the town, he searched the eastern part as far as the Green Market, while Magdalena and Bartholomäus combed through the western section. At first, Katharina intended to take part in the search, but then she quickly realized she was much too confused and upset to do that. She therefore volunteered to remain at their house by the Sand Gate and keep an eye on the two boys. Magdalena hoped that the monotonous children's games would calm her aunt down a bit.

In contrast with the preceding days, the little streets were calm now. A heavy November fog had settled over the houses, so it was impossible to see farther than to the next corner. In addition, it was drizzling slightly. Everything sounded strangely muted, as if buried under a wet blanket. Occasionally, heavily clothed citizens carrying baskets came toward them, evidently on their way home from the cemetery, where they had taken soul bread for their deceased. Some freezing beggars were standing behind empty bowls in front of the small churches in town, but otherwise half of Bamberg seemed to be at the mass in the cathedral. All Souls' was a high feast day on which work was strictly forbidden, and for many an opportunity to sit in their warm houses by the fire, knitting, baking, or repairing broken household items.

Magdalena watched as her uncle, with a grim expression,

hobbled along beside her. It was astonishing how quickly he moved along, despite his crippled foot. They'd briefly cast glances inside empty buildings, looked under bridges, and asked the rag picker Answin and a few beggars, but they hadn't had the slightest lead. During the entire search, Bartholomäus had seemed strangely disinterested, and Magdalena assumed Katharina's rude remark was still bothering him.

I should never have gotten engaged to an executioner . . .

As a hangman's daughter, Magdalena knew all too well how it felt when people looked away when they saw you and secretly crossed themselves. How hard it had to be when his own fiancée apparently regretted her decision, and if she believed a curse hung over the hangman.

"That nonsense that Katharina said earlier," she said, looking her uncle straight in the face, "you mustn't take it seriously." They were heading down Lange Gasse toward the city wall in the hope of possibly learning something from the city guards. "She's just saying things like that because she's afraid."

Bartholomäus glared at her. "How do you know about . . . ?" he began to say, but then he waved it off. "Oh, what difference does it make? Katharina's right, you know. A curse does seem to be lying over this wedding. Executioners should marry executioner's daughters and not put their noses up too high in the air. That's unbecoming to us."

"My father also didn't marry an executioner's daughter," Magdalena said, "nor did I, but I married a bathhouse owner who'd studied medicine. So you can do it."

"Your father always wanted something better," Bartholomäus grumbled, "even as a child. You probably got that from him."

Magdalena rolled her eyes. "Tell me why you're always so angry at Father. I understand he made a bad mistake back then when he abandoned you, but that's ancient history, and he was still almost a child. Why can't you just let it go?"

"There are some things that just keep seething inside you that you can't forget. It's there to remind you, sometimes every day." Bartholomäus pointed at his leg and pulled up his trousers. "This foot here, for example. You weren't there, Magdalena. You didn't look into his eyes when he left me behind on the roof, like an annoying burden too heavy to carry. The damage was too great to repair."

"Perhaps you expect too much of people, Uncle Bartholomäus. You have to learn to forget..."

Bartholomäus interrupted her with a sardonic laugh. "Is that what your father says? He himself can't forget. Why do you think he burned the magic books belonging to Grandfather Jörg Abriel back then? Because they reminded him of our family and everything the Kuisls and Abriels once represented. We were good hangmen, but we were also good healers and magicians — a strong, feared family. And my brother takes off and becomes a ... mercenary." Bartholomäus practically spat out the last word. "He not only betrayed me, but all of us. Do you understand now why I cannot forget?"

Magdalena nodded hesitantly. "I understand. But if you don't at least try, how will you ever know you can't?"

"Believe me, I've tried. Why do you think I agreed when Katharina pleaded with me to invite my relatives from Schongau? Jakob is my big brother, and at one time I really loved and respected him." Bartholomäus sighed. "But he doesn't exactly make it easy to forgive him. He's so pigheaded."

"In that regard, you're both alike," Magdalena replied.

They walked along silently side by side until they'd reached the far end of Lange Gasse. The fog was now so thick that only the outlines of the houses were visible. The gate to the city had to be somewhere nearby.

"I think we can call off the search," said Bartholomäus, who had now regained his accustomed self-confidence. "With fog like this I couldn't even find my front door. How can we be expected to find two missing persons under these conditions? Besides, the dampness and this damned drizzle is bothering my stiff leg."

"Let's just go as far as the city gate," Magdalena suggested. "Then we'll go back to your house and see if Georg has found anything yet."

She tried to sound confident, but she was finding that hard to do. By now, even she was convinced that the search was in vain. Did they seriously think they'd find Barbara and Hieronymus this way? Earlier, they'd called from time to time into the dense fog, as if looking for two children who had forgotten how late it had gotten. But their search of the empty sheds and dilapidated houses was basically nothing more than an act of desperation. If Barbara was really just hiding somewhere out of fear, she'd eventually show up again on her own, and if the two had been abducted, then . . .

Magdalena didn't even want to think about the second possibility.

"We're turning back," Bartholomäus said suddenly in a firm voice, interrupting her dark thoughts. He pointed ahead, where the outlines of the city gate appeared out of the fog. "See, here's the city gate. Let's go back home to Katharina. She needs our help now more than —"

At that very moment they heard a muffled cry nearby, and then a second.

"What . . . what was that?" Magdalena asked.

Bartholomäus shrugged. "How should I know? In fog like this you can't even see your hand in front of your face, much less —"

"Help! Help!" someone cried again, this time clearly and nearer to them. "The werewolf! It's after me! Help me!"

"Has the whole city gone mad? For God's sake . . ." He let out another unspeakable curse, then hobbled forward toward the shouts. With clenched fists and ducking down as if ready for a fight, he said softly, as if to himself, "Perhaps someone has frightened my Brutus. He could get hurt."

"Nonsense," hissed Magdalena, running alongside him. "How could the dog get into the town through the gate without being noticed. In any case, no matter what it is, we'd better be careful."

The contours of a large building now appeared in the fog. It was one of the last houses on the left and backed right up to the city wall. A figure appeared and came running toward them. As it got closer, Magdalena could see it was an old beggar. Over his ripped shirt he wore a threadbare gray woolen coat that fluttered along behind him. The old man was shaking all over, but Magdalena couldn't figure out if it was because of the cold or the fear. In any case, his eyes were wide open in panic.

"The werewolf," he groaned, pointing at the building behind him. "I have seen him with my own eyes. He's in there. He's got a silver pelt and long pointed teeth. My God, he's horrible. At first, he ran on all fours, but then he suddenly stood up." The beggar's face twisted into a grimace that revealed his nearly toothless mouth, as he raised his hands and flexed his fingers into the shape of claws. "And this is how he looked. By God, I swear it."

"A silver pelt, pointed teeth, and walking on all fours?" Bartholomäus mumbled, stopping to ponder the man's words. "That's just the way the drunk night watchman, Matthias, described the werewolf that night." He scratched his nose, thinking. "Hmm, perhaps they both drink the same cheap wine, or else . . ." He looked sternly at the beggar. "You're drunk again, Gustav, admit it."

The beggar, incensed, held his hand up to his consumptive chest. "I swear, I wish I were. Then it would be easier to bear the horror of it all. I've not had a drop for days."

"Then tell me how large this fearsome beast was," Bartholomäus shot back.

"Eh . . . very large, or perhaps not quite that large . . ." Gustav stopped short to think, picking his nose. "I don't really know. It's dark in there, and besides . . ." Furious, the man with the skinny chest stood up straight and glared at Bartholomäus and Magdalena. "Go see for yourself. The beast is no doubt still inside."

Now, for the first time, Magdalena had a moment to inspect the building from which the beggar had just fled. It was probably one of those abandoned at the time of the witch trials, one that had still not found a new owner. No doubt the half-timbered building had been attractive at one time, but now the paint had peeled off, and the doors and windows had been boarded up long ago. One of the windows, however, appeared to have been broken into recently.

"Sometimes I go there to spend the night," Gustav explained, pointing anxiously at the house, "even if some people say it's haunted. They say the souls of those executed still scurry through the halls. Until recently only mice and rats were scurrying around there, but now . . ." He shuddered and crossed himself. "Never again will I set foot in this house. That I swear, by all things holy. Never again."

"There's no need for you to do that," Bartholomäus replied. "Go now, and fetch the city guards. We'll stand guard here until you get back," he said with a wink. "If it's really a werewolf, you surely have a big reward coming to you."

Gustav didn't need to be asked again, and a moment later, the shaky old man had disappeared in the fog. Meanwhile, Bartholomäus prepared to climb in through the open window.

"You're not going in there all by yourself, are you?" Magdalena asked, astonished. "Suppose the werewolf really is—"

"Do you think then that Gustav would still be alive?" Bartholomäus interrupted. "Come on. I have a suspicion . . ."

Without another word of explanation, he slipped through the window opening.

Magdalena shook her head and climbed in after him. Just as she'd always thought, it seemed the two Kuisl brothers were pretty much alike; in any case, they were both curious, pigheaded, and fearless.

Once inside, she carefully slipped down from the windowsill. There was no fog inside the house, but it was even darker. A few rays of light entered through the partially boarded windows, and there was a repulsive stench of mold, urine, and cheap brandy. Evidently, Gustav's protestations concerning his drinking were not very credible.

Magdalena squinted and looked around. A few broken pieces of furniture were scattered on the floor, and a wardrobe stood in one corner. It might have been very valuable at one time, but now its splintered doors hung crookedly on their hinges. There were sooty smears on the bare walls, and in one place someone had recently tried to light a fire.

Bartholomäus had vanished. Apparently he'd already moved on to the next room, from which Magdalena suddenly could hear an odd sound, like someone clicking their tongue, followed by a strange growl that caused her stomach to tighten with fear.

What, for heaven's sake, was that? The werewolf? Or those ghosts the beggar was telling us about?

Magdalena shook her head, angry at herself. She'd let herself get carried away by all those horror stories.

Again she heard the growling, closely followed by the tongue clicking. Her heart pounding, she tiptoed across the creaking floorboards through the mouse droppings until she finally reached the doorway to the next room. At first she could see only shadows, but after a while her eyes grew accustomed to the darkness.

She was looking out at a broad landing, with what were once grand staircases leading up and down. Her uncle knelt at the foot of the stairway leading up. He had stretched out his hand and was making those strange clicking sounds she'd heard before.

A few steps above him stood the strangest animal Magdalena had ever seen.

It had a silvery gray pelt and what looked almost like a lion's mane around his head, as well as a long snout, like a dog, and two glistening, evil-looking red eyes. The creature had a tail and moved on all fours, but suddenly it stood up on the banister. Magdalena cringed.

It had hands like a human. Now the beast opened its mouth and snarled, showing a row of sharp, menacing teeth. There was only one thing that kept Magdalena from letting out a scream and fleeing.

The creature was no larger than a three-year-old child.

"What is that thing?" she whispered anxiously, as Bartholomäus continued clicking his tongue.

"Sh!" he said. "You'll scare it away. Believe me, the beast is as quick as a fox and agile as a squirrel. Once it took us half a day to catch him again."

Magdalena looked at her uncle in astonishment. "You've seen this monster before?"

"More than I care to. It's one of the apes from the bishop's menagerie, a so-called baboon. From time to time I take meat scraps to the animals up there, or clean out the cages. This fellow comes originally from Africa—a very unpleasant animal, if you ask me. Devious, underhanded, and sly in a bad way . . . almost human. Aloysius and I gave him the name Luther."

"Luther?"

Bartholomäus shrugged. "Reminds me of a Lutheran heathen and itinerant priest I once drew and quartered. All right, Luther, just come here. Be a good little fellow." The executioner kept making the clicking sounds while slowly fetching a piece of dry soul bread from his pocket. "Katharina gave me this earlier. Let's see if we can tempt him with it."

Still almost frightened to death, Magdalena watched as the

baboon's little hands twitched back and forth. It was clear he couldn't decide whether to take the bait.

"You said before you had a suspicion," Magdalena said. "How did you know . . ."

"That it would be Luther? Well, Captain Martin Lebrecht expressed his vague suspicions to me a few days ago. He couldn't say anything specific—the bishop would have forbidden that. Evidently Rieneck ordered him and a few other guards to search for the beast under orders of strict confidentiality. That's why Lebrecht was always so tired. He'd been doing double duty for some time, looking for a werewolf as well as for Rieneck's cuddly toy."

"It looks like a number of people have already made Luther's acquaintance," Magdalena replied. "For example, this drunken night watchman you told me about."

"Matthias?" Her uncle grinned. "Actually, that's what I suspected when he described the animal to me. But then everyone started going on and on about a werewolf, and I myself started thinking Brutus might have something to do with it. Since then I've talked with a lot of people who say they've seen a werewolf in the city, and their descriptions were all more or less the same— silver fur, sharp teeth, suddenly stands up on its hind feet. Yesterday, when I went back to the menagerie to take a few pieces of meat to the old bear, I was surprised to see that Luther had disappeared and his cage was empty. It's possible he'd been gone a long time."

"And is it possible the baboon is responsible for all the terrible events recently?" Magdalena wondered.

"Luther?" Bartholomäus laughed. "Just look at him. He might frighten you to death, but he certainly can't carry people away, torture them, or rip their bodies apart. No, our werewolf is someone else."

Meanwhile, the baboon had become more confident. He

ventured down a few steps and reached out for the soul bread. Despite his evil-looking red eyes and sharp teeth, Magdalena suddenly thought he looked cute.

"Too bad he's not the monster we were looking for." She smiled. "Even my children would like to play with this little fellow."

She was about to reach out to the baboon, when the animal suddenly snarled at her and jumped toward her. The attack came so quickly that Magdalena fell over backward. Little demonic hands tugged at her hair, and Luther's sharp fangs were just a few inches from her nose.

"Do something!" she shouted to her uncle. "The thing is trying to bite me."

"Luther, behave yourself."

Bartholomäus seized the baboon by his mane and pulled him away from his victim. The animal was furious and flailed about with his arms and legs.

"The cellar door!" Bartholomäus shouted as the animal howled and struck out. "Open the cellar door!"

At first, Magdalena didn't know what her uncle meant, but then she discovered a wooden trapdoor at the foot of the stairway leading down. She quickly descended the staircase, found a rusty ring in the middle of the door, and pulled. At first, nothing happened, but after some shaking and tugging, it opened. Bartholomäus followed her, still holding the enraged baboon, and tossed it through the opening, then quickly closed the cover. Luther's shrieking continued from down below, like a voice from the depths of the underworld. Bartholomäus straightened up with relief. His coat was ripped, his hair disheveled, and his face covered with bloody scratches.

"That damned beast," he ranted, wiping the blood and sweat from his brow. "Let Lebrecht try to figure out how to get this beast back to the menagerie. For all I care, he can lock the bishop up in the cage with him, where His Excellency can delouse the beast, and we'll be relieved of the two baboons at the same time."

Angrily, Bartholomäus hobbled toward the front door, kicked it so hard it flew open, and disappeared outside into the foggy night.

"Rabies?"

Samuel looked at his friend, Simon, puzzled. The two were still standing at the bedside of the suffragan bishop, who lay like a piece of dead wood in a pile of soft pillows. The Bamberg city physician slapped his forehead. "You may be right."

"Not only *may* be, I *am* right," Simon replied with a trace of satisfaction in his voice. "It's really amazing we didn't think of this before, but we were thinking only of wizardry and human illnesses and completely forgot animal ones. These werewolf stories can make you dizzy, like bad wine that fries your brain." He shook his head in disbelief. "Actually, I just read about it again this morning. Uncle Bartholomäus has an astonishing collection of works on veterinary medicine, among them some about dogs, which he loves more than anything else. One of the books also discusses rabies. It affects dogs, but also wolves, foxes, cats, and even some smaller animals. If one of those animals bites a person, the victim shows the same symptoms as the suffragan bishop." Simon paused to look down at Harsee. A long thread of saliva was dribbling from the corner of his mouth. "It occurs to me that Aloysius, the hangman's servant, also mentioned cases of rabies in this area several times."

Simon also remembered now that his father-in-law had spoken of it several times, and the furrier had also mentioned the spread of the illness.

"So you think Sebastian Harsee contracted rabies from an animal?" Samuel asked, looking at the paralyzed bishop, who was glaring at him with wide-open eyes, like those of a dead fish.

Simon nodded. "The infection must have come from this bite in his neck. All the symptoms point in that direction. The victim, whether animal or human, becomes very aggressive, there is paralysis, hardening of the muscles, and the victim loses the ability to swallow, resulting in a buildup of saliva. At the end, the victim goes mad . . ." He leaned down to Sebastian Harsee, who struggled to sit up, as if he were being restrained by invisible chains. "Eventually the victim dies of thirst," Simon added. "In the case of dogs, even the sight of liquid is painful, and that's probably true of humans, as well."

Simon watched sadly as the suffragan bishop lay there quivering. He'd known Sebastian Harsee as a power-hungry and almost pathologically bigoted man, but now he felt great sympathy for him.

I wouldn't wish such an illness on my worst enemy—buried alive, as you are slowly eviscerated by madness within.

"All that is described in great detail in my uncle's books," he said, shaking his head. "That is, in various aspects and in several books, in a bombastic prose style. I should have recognized it earlier."

"That wouldn't have changed anything," Samuel replied with a shrug. "As far as I know, there is no cure for rabies."

Simon frowned. "Well, some scholars recommend a Saint Hubert's Key, a sort of branding iron that is heated until it glows and can be used to cauterize the wound. Others believe in the power of certain magical letters. But that is no doubt just hocus-pocus. You're right, there probably is no cure."

Once again, Samuel leaned down over the patient, who was now just trembling slightly. Taking out an eyeglass, he checked the wound.

"The bite is rather small," he said. "It certainly wasn't caused by a wolf or a dog, and even a fox is too big. Was it perhaps a rat?"

Simon mulled it all over while inwardly cursing himself. Would they never get to the bottom of this?

"It's possible," he replied after a while. "I think I recall that bats were also mentioned in the books, but I'll have to check on that. Still . . . there's still something here I can't quite put my hands on . . ." He hesitated.

Samuel rolled his eyes. "Don't start in again with this bashfulness; just speak up."

With his hands folded behind his back, Simon paced the floor, trying to get his thoughts together. Finally, he turned to Samuel.

"It's a strange coincidence that all of Bamberg is going crazy because of a werewolf at the very moment the Bamberg suffragan bishop catches rabies, which in the eyes of simple people makes him a werewolf, too. If this were a stage play, then you could say the playwright really planned the action well."

"Do you think, perhaps, this illness was a plot?" Samuel asked in astonishment. "That Harsee was poisoned?"

Simon nodded. "Poisoned with one of the most horrible plagues that exists. It's possible. Didn't Harsee tell you he had probably been bitten in his sleep? Suppose someone hid a rabid rat in his room . . . or a bat?"

Once more Samuel inspected the wound with a magnifying glass. "I don't know," he murmured finally. "I've seen rat bites before, and they're smaller. And even though I've never seen a bat bite before, I think these animals also are out of the question."

"It really doesn't matter what kind of an animal it was," Simon replied. "At least now we know —"

There was a knock on the door, and old Agathe peered out through the opening. She seemed quite excited.

"Gentlemen . . ." she said.

"What is it?" Samuel demanded angrily. "Can't you see we're busy?"

"You have a visitor," she replied. "A very important visitor."

"Well, who is it?" Simon asked curiously. "One of the councilors?"

Agathe shook her head. "No, no, much more important. His Excellency the elector, the bishop of Würzburg, is standing downstairs at the door. Oh God, oh God," she exclaimed, rubbing her hands together nervously. "He says he would like to speak with both of you."

Simon took a deep breath, smoothed down his hair, and passed his hands several times over the creases in his soiled clothing.

"I'm afraid it's rude to keep His Excellency the elector waiting longer than necessary," he said, turning to Samuel. Then he sighed deeply. "Why must such noble personages always come to visit when I am not properly attired?"

About half an hour later, Simon, Samuel, and Archbishop Johann Philipp von Schönborn stood in the nearby small chapel in the suffragan bishop's quarters. There were three rows of pews in the chapel and a simple house altar with a single wooden crucifix on top, alongside a vase of dried roses and a statuette of Mary.

The sacral surroundings made it easier for Simon to engage in conversation with the archbishop, who was also a German elector and a friend of the kaiser. Old Bonifaz Fronwieser had always hoped his son would rise to a prominent position as a doctor, and now Simon was not only meeting face-to-face with mayors and counts but even with one of the mightiest men in the realm.

If only my father were here to see this, he thought. *How proud he would be of me.* But in the next moment he suddenly felt ashamed of his vanity.

Johann Philipp von Schönborn turned out to be an exceptionally cordial gentleman. Samuel had told Simon earlier that the Würzburg bishop was inclined to liberal ideas and abhorred belief in witches. The seizure suffered by Sebastian Harsee the night before had unsettled him so much, however, that he wanted to speak with the two doctors again. The guards sent for his protection waited outside in the walkway in front of the chapel rattling their swords and halberds. Trembling, Agathe entered with a carafe of wine but was politely dismissed by the bishop.

"I hope you know how it reassures me that this matter can be explained logically," Schönborn said, reaching out to shake hands with the astonished Simon. "I was beginning to think I'd lost my mind. Thank you for that."

Embarrassed, Simon made a cursory bow. "I hope your thanks is not premature, Your Excellency. It's just a suspicion . . ."

"A suspicion based on a careful diagnosis," Samuel interrupted with a smile. "Don't hide your light under a bushel, Simon," he said, shaking his head. "I'm just annoyed I didn't think of it myself. Rabies. I should have known."

At the victim's bedside, Simon had told the archbishop of his suspicion that Harsee was suffering from the contagious animal disease. First he had hesitated to tell Schönborn of his suspicion that the suffragan bishop had been poisoned, but Schönborn's friendly manner had convinced him not to withhold this detail, either.

"And you really believe that the disappearance of all these people and the bishop's rabies are somehow connected?" Schönborn asked curiously. "That they could both be the work of one and the same person?"

Simon raised his hands defensively. "Well, I wouldn't go so far as to say that. I have no proof, but it seems at least more logical to me than belief in a howling werewolf. I believe in any case it was hasty to immediately suspect the actors."

"But they were not just suspected: a few were already killed and hanged." Schönborn pounded his fist so hard on the altar that the crucifix quivered. "This superstitious riffraff really believe they can set themselves up as judges. Admittedly, the judge actually responsible in this case is not much better." He lowered his voice. "Our dear Philipp may know his way around animals, but he wasn't born with the gift of dealing with people. Unfortunately, a bishop's position is not awarded based on suitability but only on noble lineage. One can only hope that Philipp grows into his position." He sighed and collapsed in one of the pews. "On the other hand, he's at least harmless and not a zealot like Harsee, or the former Bamberg Prince Bishop Fuchs von Dornheim, under whom these terrible witch trials took place."

"Is it true there are no witch trials under your jurisdiction?" Samuel inquired.

Schönborn appeared deep in thought, but he nodded. "We must do away with this nonsense in the entire Reich. But we are perhaps ahead of our times." Then he turned to the two doctors. "Are you familiar with the *Cautio Criminalis* by the Jesuit priest Friedrich Spee von Langenfeld? You ought to read up on this outstanding scholar from Cologne. Even back then, Spee was convinced that torture was never useful in finding the truth. Probably after enough turns of the wheel, even I would confess on the rack to having danced with the devil. It's such nonsense!"

"I believe some of the actors are to be tortured today," Simon said softly. "If even one of them confesses to having put a curse on the suffragan bishop, we'll have a hard time presenting our case."

"I see what you're trying to say." Johann Philipp von Schönborn arose from the pew. "Very well; I'll do what I can to see if my friend Philipp will put off the torturing for a while. I'm afraid, though, that there are limits to what I can do, especially since this Malcolm, the director of the group, actually was found in possession of some magical trinkets. By the day after tomorrow at the latest, when I leave Bamberg to return home, you're on your own. By then you'll have to present evidence convincing enough for even the most slow-witted citizens to understand."

"It's hard to fight superstition," Samuel said.

"You are telling me?" The elector extended his hand. When Simon and Samuel tried to kneel before him, Schönborn gently pulled them back to their feet. "Here, where no one is watching, that's really unnecessary, gentlemen. Sometimes I wish there was a little less etiquette and a little more honesty in our daily dealings." One last time he looked deeply into Simon's eyes. "I trust you, Master Fronwieser. Bring me the true culprit, and I'll support you. Philipp needs my money to finish building his bishop's residence, so I have a little influence over him. But you must realize that even I am powerless against a whole city that has gone mad."

He turned away and left the building, where the guards outside reverently bowed before him.

Jakob and Jeremias were standing in front of a shelf in the bishop's archives leafing intently through some papers. The heavy volume in Jakob's hands bearing the inscription 1628 was by far the largest he'd ever seen and was secured both by string and glue. The title of the proceeding was announced in large letters on the leather cover: TRIAL OF THE BAMBERG CHANCELLOR DOCTOR GEORGE HAAN.

"Was the accused in fact the Bamberg chancellor in person?" Jakob asked, turning to Jeremias in surprise.

The old man nodded. "The witch trials allowed the powerful to settle some scores among themselves. No fewer than six burgomasters were executed, along with a few council members." A smile passed over his face. "They burn just the way you and I do, as you perhaps know from your own experience." Then he turned serious again. "But the trial of George Haan was something special. Haan was a smart man and was at first protected by the prince bishop. The other patricians were annoyed that he wasn't originally from Bamberg, and in addition he didn't want to end the witch trials, just cut back on them. Until then, the accuser and the judge had been sharing the assets of the condemned party, and Haan wanted to forbid that. In addition he wanted to disband the Witches Commission."

"The bastards were afraid they wouldn't get their cut," Jakob growled.

"Indeed." Jeremias turned to the next page and pointed to some names. "And for that reason, some of the councilors concocted a plot that eventually led to the downfall of the entire Haan family."

Jakob stared at him in astonishment. "The entire family?"

"They started with his wife and his daughter, accusing them of having an affair with the devil. The ever so high and mighty gentlemen also accused the two women of making an ointment from the bodies of children with which they could influence the weather. And of course, witch's marks were found on their bodies." Jeremias scratched his bald head. "I clearly remember how my servants finally found the marks under the mother's armpit. They pierced them with a knife, but no blood came out, and that settled the matter."

With growing disgust, Jakob stared at the former executioner, Michal Binder, who spoke so casually about his former deeds. Jakob, too, had been ordered one time in Schongau to search for such witch's marks — suspiciously shaped birthmarks with which the devil allegedly branded witches as a sign of their alliance. But he was able to stop the investigation before it got to that point.

"After the woman and her daughter came the chancellor himself and his son," Jeremias continued casually. "I must say that the old nobleman was rather steadfast under torture, but eventually he gave in, too, and confessed he had kissed the devil's anus." He winked at Jakob. "You know yourself, that in the end they all confess, though in his case we had to be pretty firm. We beheaded him before throwing his body in the fire."

Jakob closed his eyes as his revulsion spread like a bad taste in his mouth.

He is only a tool, just like you. He's not to blame.

But it was hard to cling to this conviction.

"What happened then?" he asked, to take his mind off it.

"After the old guy came another daughter and a daughter-in-law—in this way almost the entire Haan family was wiped out, even though they had once belonged to the most distinguished and powerful families in all of Bamberg."

Jakob stared in shock at the large document in his hand describing in matter-of-fact, prosaic words the story of so much grief.

"It's clear someone wanted to do away with the chancellor," he said finally. "But the entire family? What was the reason for that?"

"It sounds pointless and cruel, but it was part of the plan," Jeremias explained. "When his wife and eldest daughter were accused of witchcraft, the chancellor went to the Imperial Court in Speyer to enter an appeal. That was a serious error but one provoked intentionally by his adversaries. The Bamberg prince bishop resented Haan for taking things into his own hands, and refused to support him, and the remaining members of the family were also eliminated so there would be no witnesses later. I believe that after the witch trials, other members of the family also died under mysterious circumstances. In a few years, all the Haans had disappeared."

"Who was behind all that?" Jakob asked.

"Hmm . . ." Jeremias seemed to be thinking it over, then he opened the book to the page where the individual members of the commission were named. They were, in fact, the same people as on Jakob's list.

"Well, presumably they were all somewhat involved in it," Jeremias concluded, "but I'm guessing it was principally the chairman, who, as I recall, had earlier been promised the position of chancellor."

"And who was the chairman?" Jakob clenched his fists, and

he was having trouble keeping his voice down. "For God's sake, don't make me drag it out of you."

Jeremias leaned down to inspect the document. "God, isn't it here somewhere?" He raised his eyebrows in surprise. "Indeed it is, but it's crossed out several times in ink. It's probably someone trying to wipe the slate clean afterward. But wait . . ." He turned the sheet over and found another note. Someone had signed the transcript of the interrogation in a large, flowing script.

"Aha!" Jeremias said triumphantly. "But in this place the good fellow forgot to cross out his name." He stopped and stared at it. "Well, that's certainly interesting. Look who we have here."

Jakob's eyes weren't as good as they used to be, and it took a while until he could make anything of the scribbles. When he finally was able to read it, he exhaled loudly. He knew the name — at least the surname.

Dr. Johann Georg Harsee.

"Well, I'll be damned," Jakob said, shaking his head. "Is he perhaps . . . ?"

"Yes, indeed; he just happens to be the father of our present suffragan bishop," Jeremias said with a grin. "After Haan's death, he became the chancellor, and isn't it strange? All these men and women who in some way were connected with the commission at that time met their deaths, and the son of the presiding judge was transformed into a werewolf. If I didn't know it had to be satanic magic, I'd believe God himself was taking sweet revenge."

"God . . . or someone else," Jakob murmured. Then he pointed to a passage farther down in the notes. "See here — it's signed by the two clerks who transcribed the proceedings."

"Of course," Jeremias exclaimed, slapping his scarred forehead. "There were two clerks, not one. That's something that puzzled me last night. I knew someone was missing. One is Johannes Schramb, isn't it? So I was right."

Jakob nodded. "You'll be more interested is seeing the name

of the other scribe." He pointed at the second name, signed in beautifully flowing letters. In contrast with the presiding judge, this person had not taken the slightest effort to conceal his name.

Hieronymus Hauser.

"I'm afraid I'll have to bring some very bad news to someone today," the hangman said, closing the heavy book. "Our dear Katharina doesn't seem to know her father as well as she thinks."

At that moment, the bells in the cathedral started to ring.

It was time to head back.

15

IN HER DARK, DAMP ROOM, ADELHEID RINSWIESER had spent the worst night of her life—alone with a sniffling, scratching, growling beast that was attempting to dig its way down to her. For the first time the dungeon felt less like a prison than a fortress, and she hoped it would protect her.

The unknown monster vanished from time to time, and the sounds stopped, but it always returned to continue digging, and now a ray of sunlight shone past a wooden panel in a corner of the room.

Outside, it appeared to be a pleasant day. A few blackbirds were singing, and from time to time a jay squawked nearby, but Adelheid just lay there holding her breath, waiting for the monster to return and continue digging. How long would it be before it had dug down deep enough and the wooden panel gave way? How long before it reached her and attacked her? Tied up as she was, she could neither flee nor defend herself.

In these hours of terror, Adelheid could only imagine what the beast looked like. Was it the same monster that had attacked her in the forest? Was it the man who was keeping her down here? Whatever it was, considerable time had passed since she'd last heard the digging and scraping.

Had the animal given up?

Adelheid felt a flicker of hope. She tugged at the leather straps. She was dying of thirst and the cold, but as long as neither the man nor this monster broke into her dungeon, she was safe — for the time being. She used this time to reflect, frantically. Would it be possible for her to flee? Why had the man locked her up down here? Was there anything to gain from her newfound knowledge?

She was sure she knew the man.

Ever since she saw him without his hood, she'd been racking her brain, but couldn't remember where she'd seen him before. It took a long time before it finally came to her, but now she was certain; she recognized those gestures, those eyes, even the shape of the mouth. She knew who it was.

And no doubt he suspected she'd know.

If only for that reason, he couldn't let her go.

But why? Why are you doing this? Why did you cry? How can I convince you not to kill me?

Adelheid went over it again and again in her mind, but she couldn't figure it out. She'd never be able to convince him by pleading and crying. The others had tried that, in vain. She'd heard their screams as they became more guttural and softer, until they finally fell silent. If she could just figure out his motive, perhaps she had a tiny chance of persuading him.

Why? Why is he doing all this?

She cringed on hearing a sound. It was the same tapping and sniffing that had always preceded the scraping and digging.

The monster had returned.

It was prowling around out there, sniffing and panting, and once it growled briefly. Then the noise stopped.

Adelheid listened intently. Would the animal start digging again? But there was no further sound; perhaps the beast had left.

But . . . for how long?

"Go away," she whispered. "Go back to hell, where you came from. Please. Hail Mary, full of grace, the Lord is with thee . . ."

Adelheid prayed the Ave Marias familiar to her from her childhood, one after the other, giving her strength and reassurance.

"Pray for us sinners, now and at the hour of our death . . ."

But for all her prayers, the Mother of God did not intercede.

"I can't understand why the two have been gone so long," Simon murmured, pacing back and forth like a caged animal in Hieronymus Hauser's study. "It's already well past noon."

"Just calm down," his father-in-law responded. "Bartholomäus may be an unpleasant fellow, but nothing will happen to your wife with him at her side. With a heavy fog like this, it takes a long time to do a good search of the city."

"I know you're right, but still, it worries me."

Simon gave a sigh of resignation and continued pacing, his hands folded behind his back, through the room cluttered with chests and shelves, from one corner to the other. He'd been waiting more than two hours, along with Jakob, Georg, and old Jeremias, for Magdalena and Bartholomäus to return. They'd arranged to meet here in Hauser's house, as Simon hoped they might find some clue in Hieronymus's documents to explain his disappearance. So far they'd found nothing. And considering the massive disorder in the room, he didn't believe he'd have any success here, either.

Rolls of parchment, notebooks, and worn, weighty tomes lay scattered around, and a huge tower of files was piled atop a small desk in the corner. In a cursory search, Simon had almost knocked over a pot of ink carelessly left on the floor.

Katharina herself had led them into the cramped attic room. By now, she'd calmed down enough to go back to the kitchen and bake cookies with the boys. Meanwhile, Bartholomäus's servant, Aloysius, was taking care of the injured Matheo in the ex-

ecutioner's house. The Bamberg executioner had sworn Aloysius
to absolute silence, which was not particularly difficult for the
uncommunicative servant.

"At the moment I'm worried about Hieronymus Hauser,"
Jakob said, pulling out his pipe. He searched through his pockets
for some tobacco, but not finding any, sucked on the stem and
continued his musings. Finally, he spoke up: "After Sebastian
Harsee, Hauser is the only one remaining on our supposed werewolf's list. Everything suggests that now he, too, has fallen victim
to the werewolf."

Shortly before the end of the mass, Jakob and Jeremias had
returned to the cathedral without incident, bringing the minutes
of Haan's trial along with them. Now it was lying open on the
small ink-stained lectern in the middle of Hauser's study. Jakob
pounded his gnarled fingers on the entry listing the members of
the commission.

"It's just as I told you," he mumbled, chewing on his cold
pipe stem. "All the victims were somehow involved in the trial of
Chancellor George Haan. And in case a commission member
had died, the murderer blamed a surviving relative and took his
vengeance out on him—and in a rather bloody way, it appears."

"You're right," said Jeremias. "When I think how brutally
we treated poor Chancellor Haan then, all this torturing of the
victims suddenly doesn't look so strange." He poured himself another steaming carafe of hot mulled wine, which made his nose
look even redder. "Basically, the suspect is only treating the torture victims in the customary way." He frowned. "Leaving aside,
of course, the rabies infection. That's so cruel, even we wouldn't
have thought about doing it back then."

"On the other hand, he's being completely consistent," Simon replied. "Turning the son of the former head of the Witches
Commission into a kind of witch himself—this vengeance is especially perfidious, worse than any other conceivable torture."

Simon cast a sideways glance at Jeremias, who had seemed so

kind and innocent. The sensitive medicus still was uneasy sitting in the same room with a man who had probably executed hundreds of people — to say nothing of the young prostitute. But, on the other hand, there were also moments when Simon felt something almost like pity for the old cripple.

"I remember young Harsee well," Jeremias said, after taking a few long sips of the mulled wine. "Sebastian was an ardent student of theology, always carrying around his father's documents for him. It's quite possible that he, too, was involved in the intrigue against the Haans. Something smells fishy here." He put his hand to his nose. "You can't say that about the other members of the committee."

Georg, sitting alongside him, cleared his throat. He'd returned more than an hour ago from searching the eastern part of town, and until now hadn't said a word. It was clear he was upset by the disappearance of his twin sister.

"Isn't it about time we told Katharina the truth about her father?" he asked. "After all, it's quite possible he's already dead."

"She'll learn about it soon enough," Jakob grumbled. "For now, I'm happy she's keeping busy caring for my two walking mouths that are always looking for something to eat. Let's all put our heads together now and try to think about who might be the culprit." He turned to Jeremias. "Did you say all the members of the Haan family died?"

Jeremias nodded. "So far as I know, yes — the chancellor and his wife, their son, two other daughters, and a daughter-in-law. Another son was supposedly poisoned a few years later, and a son-in-law died in an accident. I believe that's all of them."

"And the grandchildren?" Simon quickly chimed in. "All that happened almost forty years ago, and if we're really looking for someone who was alive at that time and is still looking for vengeance, he must have been quite young then."

"You can forget that; there was no one else. The family died out." Jeremias took another deep swallow. "Just be happy I could remember anything at all and could lead you to the documents in the archive. I'm just an old cripple now, and nothing more."

"Oh, come now. You're also the ruthless murderer of a young prostitute, and I'm still uncertain whether to turn you over to Lebrecht's guards," Jakob growled. "If your life means anything to you, you'd better use your head, or you won't have it much longer."

Jeremias groaned. "You're asking too much. I'm neither an archivist nor a court clerk. How can I . . ."

"A court clerk!" Simon interrupted excitedly. "That's it! Hieronymus was the clerk. Katharina said he often brought documents back home to work on them here. Perhaps there are some notes that will tell us something about the Haans. This family, once so powerful, cannot have simply vanished from the face of the earth."

"Such documents would have to be decades old," said Jakob. "Why would Hieronymus keep things like that?"

"He didn't keep them; he just found them again." Simon paced back and forth, faster and faster, waving his arms as he spoke. "Until now I thought Hieronymus had perhaps left a note behind. But that's not the case." He pointed at all the books on the floor. "Just look around you. Katharina's father was looking around for something in the old notes—something he'd forgotten. And I think he found it."

He stopped pacing and turned to the others. "Think about what's happened here. Two days ago I paid a visit to Hieronymus. Clearly something in our conversation about the witch trial jogged his memory. He probably remembered the Haan trial and noticed the connection between the individuals who'd disappeared. At the same time he realized that if he was right, he belonged in the group of possible victims. But he wasn't certain, and that's why he hurried off to the bishop's archives . . ."

". . .where he found the document," said Jakob, nodding as he chewed on the stem of his pipe. "It was on the very top of the shelf, meaning it had just been taken out recently, probably by Hauser. So far, so good. But how does that help us?"

"Now hear me out," Simon quickly interrupted. "Magdalena told me that Katharina was watching her father as he searched through everything up here. That was after he *returned* from the archive, so it's clear he wanted to check something, and after that he was very agitated. During the bishop's reception he kept looking around, as if looking for someone."

"Probably the suspect," Georg added, looking at Simon intently. "You think he discovered something here in this room that put him on the right track to the perpetrator?"

Simon nodded. "But evidently the perpetrator had also found Hieronymus. Katharina told us she had lost sight of her father in the courtyard, so we can guess that this unknown avenger was among the guests and reached out to strike there. Who could that have been? There must be a clue, something . . ." He looked around the cluttered room. "If Hieronymus really found something here, where would he have put it?" He walked through the room, then stopped in front of the bookshelves. "Where?"

Simon closed his eyes and tried to put himself in the place of Hieronymus Hauser. He imagined him running through the room . . .

I'm terrified. I've learned something terrible, and now I want to be certain, so I'll start taking books off the shelves at random. No, not at random: I'll look for something very specific . . .

Simon opened his eyes, bent down, and picked up a heavy volume with a sewn binding lying on the floor in front of him. He leafed through it with trembling fingers. Evidently it was an old accounts book for the city, showing tax receipts as well as expenditures for a new gallows, building materials, and food for the kaiser's emissaries.

... two hundred guilders for eight barrels of Rhine wine, plus five pigs at twenty guilders, a cartload of wood...

Simon reached for the next book, but that, too, just recorded city expenditures—endless columns of figures, and soon his eyes began to swim. Again Simon tried to think about what Hieronymus had told him during their last conversation. Just what were his final words?

I have an order from the city council to recopy a whole mountain of financial lists. The old ones are barely legible...

"He must have found something in these old volumes and receipts," Simon mumbled to himself. "But what? What, damn it?" He put the book aside, closed his eyes, and tried again to put himself in the place of the clerk. The others watched him... and waited.

... I'm grabbing book after book from the shelves, looking, paging through, and finally I find something. I'm in front of the shelves, but the book is too heavy to spend any more time standing here and leafing through it. I can't hold it any longer, so I go...

Simon opened his eyes and looked around.

... to the lectern.

There in the corner stood the lectern with a pile of books on top. A large book lay open at the bottom of the pile, looking similar to the other books on the floor. Simon hurried over to the lectern in the corner, took the books on top and put them on the floor, then studied the opened page of the book that had been on the bottom. At first he was disappointed, for once again what he saw were lists and columns of income and expenses. But suddenly he noticed a certain name, and knew at once he was on the right track.

Confiscation of the property of the Haan family, 4,865 guilders, distributed in equal parts to the commission, the city, and the prince bishopric...

"Did you find something?" Jakob asked, rising from his stool and looming over Simon like a huge shadow.

Simon nodded silently, then continued reading.

> . . . less four hundred guilders to the Carmelite Cloister on the Kaulberg to care for the minor Wolf Christoph Röhm, son of Martin Röhm and Katharina Röhm, née Haan. Attested to December 17, *anno domini* 1629 . . .

Only now did Simon turn to the visitors, looking at them ashen-faced.

"I think we've found our werewolf," he said in a soft voice. "It says here 'Wolf Christoph Röhm,' so in fact, the chancellor had a grandson. What irony." He shook his head. "His parents really gave him a suitable name for his crimes later in life."

Magdalena waited impatiently in the little guardroom of the city prison for Captain Lebrecht to finally release her and Bartholomäus. She was certain their family was eagerly awaiting them and was very worried about them. But there was nothing they could do; the captain was not going to let them off that easy. It even seemed to her he was intentionally taking his time with the paperwork.

"And you come from Schongau, do you?" he asked her for perhaps the tenth time. "Where's that?"

Magdalena sighed. "A few hours south of Augsburg, north of the Alps, but I've already told you that."

Lebrecht didn't answer but continued scratching letters with a quill into a thick folder as Magdalena shifted nervously back and forth on her seat and cast annoyed looks at her uncle.

Just as they were leaving the old house with the baboon stashed away safely in the cellar, the city guards, alarmed by the beggar Gustav had appeared. In a fierce struggle, the men had succeeded in pulling the biting and scratching Luther out of the cellar and tying him up. Three guards had wrapped the animal up in a blanket and taken it back to the menagerie while Captain Lebrecht ordered Magdalena and Bartholomäus to follow him back to the city jail. Ostensibly, the reason was to take their testimony, but Magdalena quickly realized that Martin Lebrecht had something quite different on his mind.

"I want to stress again that nothing—I repeat, absolutely *nothing*—about this incident is to be made public," the captain said, gazing sternly at Magdalena. "This order, by the way, comes not from me, but the prince bishop in person, and I'm telling you this only to stress its urgency. His Excellency fears that the citizens of Bamberg might blame this entire werewolf story on him."

"But it's clear that Luther can't kill or kidnap anyone," Magdalena added, shaking her head. "He's much too small for that, and then the traces of all that torture . . ."

"Perhaps that's clear to you, but for many people such a strange animal is suspected of being an emissary of the devil," Lebrecht interrupted, sounding exhausted and rubbing his temples. "If you don't want to obey the order of the bishop, then do it for me. I've been looking for this beast for days and am elated that the problem has been solved. It doesn't do anyone any good if an outraged mob storms the bishop's menagerie and opens the cages."

Bartholomäus grinned. "But Solomon, the old bear, would be thrilled. The succulent bodies of people would be much more to his taste than the old stinking meat scraps that I bring him when I stop by."

"You'll have plenty of work to do, Master Bartholomäus," Lebrecht answered, pointing back to the entrance to the dungeon. "We have almost a dozen sinners here to be tortured soon, most of them actors from that troupe that performed yesterday evening. I hope they'll confess quickly, so we can finally put an end to this madness." He sighed. "But I've just heard that the torturing will be postponed once again until after His Excellency the elector and bishop of Würzburg, has left the city. These high and mighty gentlemen don't know what to do, and people like us have to pay for it with this chaos."

Suddenly the captain stopped short and turned to Magdalena. "It just occurred to me that the leader of this group, a certain Malcolm, asked about you this morning. He urgently wanted to talk to you. I just put him off, but since you're here . . ." He shrugged. "If you wish, I'll let you in to see him for a few moments. But be careful. We discovered some magical devices in his possession, and he seems to be a warlock."

Magdalena hesitated. She and Bartholomäus should have returned home hours ago. On the other hand, she couldn't turn down this request from Sir Malcolm. She was still convinced he was innocent and that the allegedly magical objects were only props. She could certainly find a little time for him. Moreover, she was curious what Sir Malcolm might have to say to her.

"I'll go and visit him," she said finally. "Where can I find him?"

Lebrecht pointed down the hall. "In the last room. The guards will show you the way. But take the hangman along. Maybe the fellow will soften up a bit when he sees the executioner, and we can spare ourselves a long and expensive interrogation."

Bartholomäus mumbled his agreement, and they had the guards lead them to Malcolm's cell.

It took a while for Magdalena to find Malcolm's crumpled figure in the darkened cell. He lay in a corner like a bundle of carelessly discarded rags. Cautiously, Magdalena walked toward him and bent down to speak. His face was turned toward the wall, and he seemed to be sleeping.

Or is he dead already? The thought flashed through Magdalena's mind. She noticed the bloodstains spattered on Malcolm's cloak. Evidently some of the citizens had already taken out some of their anger on him.

"Sir Malcolm," she whispered. "Can you hear me?"

Malcolm flinched, slowly turned around, and Magdalena stared into his battered face. She put her hand over her mouth in order not to scream in fright or horror. He'd been so badly beaten that his eyes were nothing more than two slits in a pasty mass of black and blue. He looked more like a monster than Jeremias did. Nevertheless, he tried to smile cheerfully, which was clearly hard for him to do with his several missing teeth.

"Ah, the beautiful sister of our most talented actress," he murmured, as if in a dream. "So my pleas were heard. This captain is not as bad a man as I thought."

"Lebrecht probably saved your life," Bartholomäus interjected. "You ought to thank him. According to what I heard, he and his men stepped in to save you just as the mob was about to string you up on the tallest willow on the Regnitz."

"Ah, yes, the fate of a great artist," Malcolm said softly, managing despite his injuries to inject a note of pathos into his voice. "Beloved, celebrated, and then cast out just the same."

"Lebrecht said you wanted to see me," said Magdalena. "Is there anything I can do to help you?"

Malcolm placed his trembling hand on her skirt, to quiet her. "I'm afraid no one can help me now," he whispered. "I'm dying, like Shakespeare's Julius Caesar in the third act—slowly, but with style, but my men have not deserved such an exit from the stage." He coughed. "They're innocent."

"Does that mean *you* are guilty?" Bartholomäus asked. "Speak up, fellow. What do you have to do with all this hocus-pocus? Are you the werewolf?"

Sir Malcolm let out a dry laugh, which quickly turned into a painful coughing fit, and he spat out another tooth. "I'd be a pretty pathetic little wolf," he croaked, "if I let myself be whipped like that by a few thugs. You can bet on it, hangman: if I'd played the part of the wolf, I'd have been the greatest werewolf of all time, fearsome and powerful and with a voice rumbling like an approaching tornado, and—"

"Unfortunately, I'm afraid we don't have much time," Magdalena interrupted. "The guards are telling us to be quick. So, is there something you wanted to tell me?"

Malcolm nodded. "You're right, I should cut the monologue a bit; that's what people keep telling me. Very well . . ." He took a deep breath, then continued in a whisper. "They say they found objects of mine that I used for incantations and magic, but I swear I've never seen these things before. After all, I know how dangerous such props can be in a Catholic bishopric. I'm asking you . . . a child's skull?" He shook his head is disbelief. "Things like that are found only in tawdry farces. At first I thought Guiscard had planted these knickknacks on me—"

"Unlike your troupe, he and his men were able to get out of town in time," Bartholomäus interrupted. "Lebrecht told me that earlier. Evidently Guiscard bribed one of the guards at the gate."

Malcolm flashed him a toothless grin. "Ha! This rabble packed up their things while we were still on stage. I saw it with my own eyes. Guiscard knew he'd lost. What an ingenious move of mine to convince him to put on that boring *Papinian* while we performed *Peter Squenz*. I upstaged them all, and Barbara played her role splendidly. We're the clear winners."

"Guiscard would probably look at that differently," Magdalena replied. "In any case, he's free, and you're sitting here in the dungeon. But you were going to tell us who planted these magical things on you, I think."

"Well, I assume it's the same person responsible for all these murders in Bamberg," Malcolm said, lowering his voice to a conspiratorial hush. "I had lots of time last night to think about that and have a suspicion who that might be. And finally, I put two and two together . . ."

Malcolm started talking, and as he did, Magdalena felt a chill running up her spine.

It looked like they'd finally found their werewolf.

A rowboat was making its way slowly downstream on the Regnitz. Two people sat inside, one pulling hard on the oars and steering the boat past the many islands of mud, gravel, and flotsam. Here in the southeastern part of Bamberg, the forest extended down to the shore, where many brooks and tributaries carrying leaves and branches emptied into the wide river.

Exhausted, Barbara snuggled up in the woolen blanket that Markus Salter had given her before they left. She sat on a wooden box in the stern of the boat, looking out at the marshland with its willows, birches, and little ponds as they drifted past. A light but constant drizzle had set in, gradually soaking them to the skin.

"Is it much farther?" she asked, her arms covered with goose flesh.

Markus Salter shook his head. He briefly stopped rowing and pointed toward a hill about half a mile away, with a few houses on top. "Up ahead of us is the little town of Wunderburg," he said, turning more cheerful. "In the Great War, the Swedes destroyed much of the town, but the bishop's stud farm is still there, so there are a lot of warm stables where we can hide. We can stay there for a while, and when things have calmed down a bit, I'll go back to the city and tell your father you're all right. I promise."

He winked at her, and Barbara nodded gratefully. She was extremely happy to have Markus Salter by her side. For half the night, he'd consoled her when she kept waking up with a start from bad dreams. With soothing words he'd urged her to persevere, that this nightmare would soon end, and he'd even gotten her to laugh a few times with poems and lines from comedies. Without him, she would have no doubt left the crypt too soon and fallen into the hands of the marauding gangs still wandering through the streets of Bamberg in search of witches and were-wolves.

They had stayed down there until morning while Markus told her about his adventurous life as an actor and playwright. He came from a well-to-do patrician family, and his father had been a cloth merchant in Cologne. Markus had studied law, but then he'd seen Sir Malcolm and his actors at Neumarkt Square in Cologne and immediately fell under their spell. On the spur of the moment he left his family and since then was completely en-grossed in the world of Shakespeare, Marlowe, and Gryphius.

Although Markus Salter had clearly led an exciting life, Bar-bara was slowly coming to the realization that she herself was not suited for such an existence. Just the last few days without her family had been painful enough, and the thought of always being alone on the road, without a home, without a family — even a family as querulous and stubborn as the Kuisls — was too much for her. She wanted to get back to her grumpy father, to her sister with the two boys, and to her twin brother, Georg, whom she hadn't seen for so long.

She wanted to go home.

Markus had convinced her to wait until early the next morn-ing, when most of the rowdy bands had finally dispersed and the good citizens were in the All Souls' mass. Around nine o'clock, disguised at Carmelite monks, they snuck through the streets down toward the mills near the castle, where Markus soon found an abandoned boat, and in it he planned to take her to a hiding place he'd learned about during an earlier visit to Bamberg.

At first they traveled downstream past the city. Then they traveled back up the right branch of the Regnitz toward Bam-berg looking for a place to land on the eastern shore near the lit-tle town of Wunderburg. Over the tops of the trees they could see the walls of the city and the cathedral, but except for the occa-sional chirping of a blackbird and the distant sound of men chopping wood in the forest, everything around them was quiet and peaceful.

In the meantime, it had started to rain harder, and despite her heavy monk's robe and the blanket, Barbara felt chilled to the bone.

"Haven't you ever thought of starting a family?" she asked, her teeth chattering, as Markus guided the boat toward a small, reed-choked estuary. The actor still had a slight pain on his right side, but it seemed Barbara had done a good job of cleaning the wound. In an case, when she'd changed the bandage again that morning, she hadn't noticed any inflammation.

Markus thought for a moment before answering. "I'm afraid I have difficulty committing myself," he said finally. "I'm too afraid I'm going to lose the person again. People die, and some far before their time — not just the old ones, but beloved wives and even children. The nagging fear of being left alone again would drive me crazy."

Barbara frowned. "I never looked at things that way before."

"Ask your father or your uncle. They know how fast we can be overcome by death. After all, they themselves are often the cause." His face darkened. Dressed in his monk's robe and with his hood pulled down over his face, the haggard actor looked like a stern, ascetic preacher. "How can anyone ever live with that — all the sorrow and screams a hangman must bear? I couldn't, at least not for long. It would destroy me."

"I think my father and my uncle don't look at themselves at such times as human beings, but as . . ." — Barbara looked for the suitable word — ". . . *tools*. They act on behalf of a higher power, the city or the church."

"Tools of a higher power." Salter nodded. "I like that. I'll use it in one of my tragedies, with your permission." He smiled sadly. "In a very special tragedy, in fact, my best one. All it lacks are a few suitable sentences for a conclusion."

He thrust the oar down with all his strength, propelling the boat toward the shore, where it ran aground and remained stuck in the mud. A dense stand of reeds grew all around them, and the branches of a weeping willow hung far down into the water, blocking their view of the surroundings.

"We're stopping here?" Barbara asked with surprise.

Markus jumped into the knee-deep water and waded the last few steps to the shore, where he tied the boat securely to the trunk of the willow tree.

"It's not far now to Wunderburg," he replied, "and the boat is well hidden here." With a cheerful smile, he reached out to give Barbara a hand. "Come now."

She got up, shivering, and was about to climb over the side when she lost her balance in the rocking boat, slipped on the bottom, wet from the rain, and fell. She landed painfully on her tailbone, and to make matters worse also hit her head on the boat box. As she pulled herself up again, cursing, she caught sight of something she hadn't noticed before in the drizzling rain.

There was blood on the box.

She assumed at first it was fish blood, as this was clearly a boat belonging to a fisherman, who no doubt kept his daily catch in the box. Then she took a closer look. There was clearly too much of it here to be just fish blood, and, besides, the stain had an intensive, reddish-brown color all too familiar to Barbara as a hangman's daughter.

This wasn't fish blood; it was human blood.

Her mind racing, she looked at the partially coagulated liquid streaking down the side of the box.

"For heaven's sake, what . . ." she said instinctively.

The box creaked on its hinges as she slowly opened it. She didn't know what might be inside, but her heart was pounding wildly. She suspected that whatever it was would shake her already deeply wounded psyche.

The first thing she saw were a few wolf pelts, which appeared to have been tossed carelessly into the box, then underneath them the hide of a stag with its antlers, a wild boar pelt, a badly worn bearskin . . .

Carefully, Barbara pushed the stinking pelts aside. When she finally recognized what was underneath, her heart skipped a beat. She wanted to scream, but not a word escaped her lips.

She was staring, horrified, into the blood-covered face of a man. He was gagged, and someone had tied his body up into a net so tightly that the body almost looked like a bundle of slimy fish. She thought she recognized the man, even though his face was almost completely mutilated and covered with blood.

"My God," Barbara gasped in a fading voice, as her strength ebbed from her body.

At that moment she heard a *whoosh* of air, and something struck her with brutal force on the back of the head. With a groan, she fell forward, and even before she hit the bottom of the boat, a merciful unconsciousness came over her. Markus Salter was standing over her, holding the bloodstained oar in his hand like a hangman with his sword.

"The tool of a higher power," he whispered, and a grin flickered across his face. He took off his hood, as the rain streamed down his face, and let out a loud howl—the howl of a wolf.

"I like that, Barbara. I'm a tool, and nothing more."

Then he seized the unconscious girl, threw her over his shoulder, and dragged her away into the nearby swamp.

Hurried footsteps came up the stairway to Hauser's study, and immediately thereafter the door opened with a crash. Simon, still standing at the lectern with the open book, jumped. In the doorway stood Magdalena and Bartholomäus.

"Magdalena!" Simon cried out with relief. "You're back. I was really worried about you—"

"We have no time for long-winded greetings," she interrupted as she struggled for breath. "I think we finally know who our werewolf is. Sir Malcolm just told us."

"Sir Malcolm?" Jakob said, looking at her in astonishment. "But he's in the city dungeon. What in God's name were you doing there?"

"We'll tell you all about that later," Bartholomäus replied. "Now listen to what your daughter has to say. It's just the suspicion of a poor gallows bird who's trying to wriggle his head out of a noose, and perhaps he's just telling us lies, but what he says actually sounds pretty reasonable."

By now, the two new arrivals had entered the small room. Magdalena stood in the middle and looked excitedly at Simon, Jeremias, and her father.

"Markus Salter is the one we're looking for," she declared. "The group's playwright. Sir Malcolm has been watching him closely for some time because of all the strange things he's been doing."

"And what would that be?" Simon inquired, trying to sound very matter-of-fact. He was still so relieved to see Magdalena again that he wanted nothing more than to take her in his arms and kiss her. But at the moment, his wife didn't seem to be looking for that.

"Some time ago," she answered breathlessly, "Markus Salter wrote a piece that he very much wanted to have the actors perform, but it was too bloody and weird for Malcolm's taste. It was about a child from a powerful family, all of whom were slaughtered in a power struggle between patricians. Later, as a young man, the hero takes out his bloody revenge on them. Again and again, Salter urged Malcolm to stage this tragedy. He must have been really fanatical about it, though he didn't want to show anyone the piece in advance and only dropped veiled hints as to what was in it."

"And you believe this play describes Salter's own life?" Kuisl said. "Isn't that a bit far-fetched?"

"I'm not finished." Magdalena gave her father a stern look. "Recently, Malcolm had a chance to secretly read the play. It contains a number of torture scenes, and a werewolf appears in it as a sort of supernatural avenger. Malcolm described the play as even bloodier and madder than Shakespeare's *Titus Andronicus*. I'm not familiar with this tragedy, but it must be one long bloodbath."

"My God," Simon gasped. "Do you think Markus Salter is putting on his own play here in Bamberg? And with real people instead of actors?"

Magdalena nodded excitedly. "The troupe visited Bamberg six months ago, and since then, according to Malcolm, Salter has been almost unapproachable, always working like a madman on this piece. It was Salter who insisted on taking up winter quarters here in Bamberg, and he finally convinced Malcolm. He even took a side trip here earlier in order to prepare everything for the troupe."

"If Salter really did visit Bamberg before," Bartholomäus said, "it's possible he really was responsible for the earlier murders. Until now we always thought the actors couldn't have been involved, since they only came to the city later."

"And that's not all," Magdalena continued. "It seems that Salter originally came from Bamberg—at least that's what he once told Malcolm. In talking to me, however, he said that as a child he'd been involved in the witch trials in Nuremberg . . ."

"Well, if our assumptions are correct, the man was involved in a very special way with the witch trials here," Simon interrupted. He showed Magdalena the document on the lectern. "It appears that Markus Salter is none other than Wolf Christoph Röhm, the grandson of George Haan, the chancellor in Bamberg at the time. All the members of the family, except for Wolf Christoph, were executed during the trials. What we see here is devil-ish vengeance, planned down to the smallest detail."

Magdalena nodded. "It must have taken quite a lot of en-ergy," she mused. "Malcolm thought that in recent days Markus Salter had always been tired and distracted, and he often missed rehearsals."

"If he really abducted and tortured all these people, he was a pretty busy fellow," Jeremias chimed in with a giggle. The old man had been drinking the mulled wine while all this was going on, and evidently he'd finished the entire pitcher. "Just torturing with tongs takes a lot of time," he said with a heavy tongue. "They have to be heated just so much, then you start with the arms and then sloooowly go down—"

"Thank you, that's enough," Simon interrupted. He looked Jeremias up and down, disgusted, before continuing. "Salter could have planted the wolf pelts on Matheo. Also, his age ap-pears about right. According to the documents, Wolf Christoph Röhm was four years old at the time, and if I remember correctly, Salter is now around forty. It seems likely that Röhm and Salter are one and the same person." He frowned. "But there still is the question of how he infected the suffragan bishop with rabies."

Magdalena looked at Simon in surprise. "What rabies?"

"While you were on your little jaunt through Bamberg with your uncle, my friend Samuel and I weren't completely idle," he replied. "His Excellency the elector and Würzburg Bishop Schönborn, with whom we enjoyed a long, very friendly conver-sation, was quite impressed with our observations."

"Just stop this high-and-mighty rubbish and get to the point," Jakob growled.

"Ah, indeed." Simon told his wife and Bartholomäus the horrifying news of the suffragan bishop's illness and what he sus-pected.

"We are presently trying to figure out what animal could have infected Harsee," he concluded. "It certainly wasn't a dog, as the bite is too small, but perhaps it was a rat or a bat. We think it had to be a small wild animal . . ."

"My God. Juliet!" Magdalena exclaimed. "Of course, it was Juliet, or Romeo."

Simon looked at her, puzzled. "I don't know what you're talking about, Magdalena, but let me tell you there was no one . . ."

"Not people, but ferrets." She laughed and turned to the others who stared at her in confusion. "Markus Salter has two tame ferrets—Romeo and Juliet. Some time ago, Romeo ran away, at least that's what he told me. But suppose he infected Romeo or Juliet with this rabies and somehow smuggled them into Harsee's room. Would that be possible?"

Simon let out a loud groan. "A ferret, damn. It actually could have been a ferret. Probably Salter gave it an animal to eat that had just died of rabies. There is no guard at the suffragan bishop's house, and it's certainly possible for someone to slip in at night and put a sick ferret in the bedroom. Later, the animal can disappear through a crack in the wall or a mouse hole. What a devilish plan."

"And now Salter has probably got his hands on Hieronymus," Jakob grumbled. "He's the last one on the committee, so if we don't act fast, then—"

"Father . . ." Georg interrupted in a soft voice.

"Damn it," Jakob snapped. "Haven't I told you a thousand times not to interrupt your father? It seems Bartholomäus hasn't taught you any manners in the last two years."

"How can you ever expect the boy to learn if you talk to him like that?" Bartholomäus shot back. "You treat him just the way you did me. But I'm not going to let you get away—"

"Quiet! Both of you!"

Georg had pounded the lectern so hard that the documents nearly fell to the floor, then he turned angrily to his astonished father and the equally astonished Bartholomäus.

"I'm just sick and tired of your endless squabbling," he scolded. "If you don't stop this, I won't stay in Bamberg nor go back to Schongau, either, but I'll look for a job as an executioner at the other end of the Reich so I don't have to put up with your quarreling anymore. And now just listen to me for a change."

He pointed at the document and took a deep breath.

"You say that Hieronymus is the last one to be involved in this, but that's not correct. There's still someone missing."

"And who do you think that might be?" asked Simon, just as astonished over his outburst as the others.

Georg shrugged as if to say the answer was obvious. "Well, the executioner, of course. He was present at all the questionings, as one of the head people, so to speak."

"You're right," Jeremias concurred, nodding his alcohol-be-fuddled head. "But this Salter fellow doesn't know me, and even if he did read about me in the old documents, he'll only find reference to Michael Binder, and that person has been gone a long time."

Georg nodded. "No, he doesn't know you, he only knows the current Bamberg executioner, Bartholomäus, and naturally he assumes that Bartholomäus is related to the former hangman. And why shouldn't he? After all, the executioner's job is almost always passed down from father to son."

"If this pathetic little werewolf tries to kidnap me," Bartholomäus growled, "I'll show him who I am."

"He doesn't have to kidnap you, Uncle Bartl," Georg said, "because he no doubt already has someone else from the family in his hands." Mournfully, he turned to the others. "I believe the werewolf has captured Barbara because she's Bartholomäus's niece, and we'll only be able to save her if we can finally stop this endless quarreling." One by one, he turned to look at them all. "Please promise me that. We Kuisls have to stick together now, or my sister is lost."

• • •

A sound in Adelheid Rinswieser's cell startled her from her macabre dreams and brought her back to reality.

She'd spent the last few hours half asleep, but with the constant fear that the strange growling monster could return. But everything around her turned silent — as silent as the grave. Even the birds had stopped chirping, and all she could hear was the distant, constant sound of falling rain. The sound of the water made her thirst almost unbearable, but, just the same, she'd been able to briefly doze off. But now she heard something coming from the floor above her, at first a clicking . . .

. . . then a bolt being pushed aside . . .

. . . a squeaking . . .

. . . then the door opening. He was coming back.

Adelheid didn't know whether to laugh or scream in horror. She'd become convinced the man would just let her rot away down here. Too much time had passed since his last visit. But now he was back, and that could only mean it was her turn now. Or perhaps it wasn't him at all? Was it someone else, perhaps someone who'd just come here to check on her, a random visitor?

A savior?

"Help!" she screamed hysterically. "I'm here! Here in the cellar! Please, whoever you are up there, come and let me out!"

Adelheid tugged furiously at her shackles, which still didn't yield even a fraction of an inch, struggling to turn toward the door, where she could hear slow footsteps approaching. They came down the steps, but heavier than usual . . . much heavier. That wasn't the man — it had to be someone else.

"Here! Here!" she called. "I'm in here!"

Again she heard a grating sound as the bolt to her cell slid open. The door creaked and swung open, and Adelheid froze.

In the doorway stood her captor.

Over his shoulder he was carrying a black-haired girl around fifteen years old who was either unconscious or dead. Strangely, she was wearing a monk's cape, and dried blood clung to her hair. The kidnapper also was wearing such a hood, making him look like the high priest of some unfathomably evil sect.

Adelheid's disappointment was so great that she couldn't utter a sound.

"Greetings, my love," the man panted, carefully setting his burden down on the floor. "It took a while, but I'm back. Everything is ready for your final act."

He stepped outside to fetch a torch, which he inserted into an iron ring on the wall, then pulled out a leather strap and bound the girl's arms and legs. Adelheid could see blood glistening in the girl's hair and on her face, but she was still alive, as her kidnapper would hardly have gone to the trouble of tying up a corpse like a bundle of rags.

"Who . . . who is that?" she managed to ask.

"Oh, this?" The man looked up and smiled. It was a gentle smile, though in a strange way also a sad one that seemed inconsistent with his cruel actions. "This is the only one I hadn't caught yet," he said. "A hangman's daughter. The second scribe is lying in the boat, and I don't know if he's still alive. But in any case, we're done now." He made a sweeping gesture. "Curtain up for the grand finale."

Exhausted, Adelheid regarded her captor, whom she thought she recognized now. About half a year ago she'd visited the Wedding House in Bamberg with her husband to see a performance by a wandering troupe of actors. Since then, she'd almost completely forgotten the piece, some comedy with a clown and a few other fools. Her husband had enjoyed it all immensely, but she found the crude jokes offensive. Only one of the actors at that time had awakened her interest—a man with a sort of dark magnetism that didn't seem at all appropriate in the comedy. He was very pale, had thinning hair, and there was a deep sadness in his eyes that made him strangely attractive.

He looked just as sad now.

"Hangman's daughter? Scribe?" Adelheid mumbled to give herself time to think, if nothing else. "I don't understand . . ."

"You don't have to."

He stood up and removed his hood, then wiped off his mud and bloodstained hands on his torn vest. "Basically, you are . . ." He hesitated. "Well, something like bit players. Excuse me. I'm just going to get the scribe. Then I'll be back for you all. Forever."

He bowed, as if before an invisible audience, then went outside, pulling the door closed behind him.

Adelheid closed her eyes and moaned softly. She knew that the end was nigh. Her abductor might not be a werewolf, but there was an almost bestial glitter in his eyes. There was no way out.

After Georg had spoken, it was silent in the study for a long time. Outside, a heavy rain was drumming down on the roof of the house. Finally, slowly and deliberately, like a giant boulder coming to life, Jakob nodded.

"Georg, you're right," he said softly. "We haven't seen the forest for the trees. This madman thinks by seizing Barbara, he has a relative of the former Bamberg executioner in his clutches. He abducted not just Hauser, but also my little girl, and he'll pay a heavy price for that."

Magdalena saw how her father clenched his fists as his face became almost expressionless. She had seen her father before in a situation like this, and she knew he was far more dangerous now than when he was ranting and making a fuss.

That's the way he is just before the executions, she thought. *Clear and cold as rock crystal.*

He turned suddenly to Bartholomäus and Georg. "You two know your way around in this city and the surroundings. Is there someplace around here you haven't checked yet that this Salter, or Röhm, might have taken my daughter?"

Georg seemed to be thinking. "I can't tell you we've turned over every stone in Bamberg this morning. Of course he could have hidden her in some cellar . . . but I don't think so."

"And what do you think, then, O wise one?"

"I think he's hiding her somewhere outside of town." It seemed like Georg was doing everything he could to build up his own courage, and his words now sounded more confident and excited. "Salter could have taken his two prisoners, if they were still alive, out of town in a fishing boat. In this way he would evade the checks at the city gates, and if he hides them under a blanket or something like that, no one would notice. In any case, that's what I would do."

"He'll probably take them to the same place he's hiding his other prisoners, and torture and kill them there," Magdalena interjected. Even the thought of what her sister might be facing there made her sick to her stomach, but she tried to concentrate on what was important. "It would have to be a lonely place where no one would disturb him," she continued. "On the other hand, he can't be too far away, either. After all, Salter had to return to the rehearsals in the Wedding House, especially in the last few days."

Jakob rubbed his huge nose, as he always did when he was concentrating, then turned to Bartholomäus.

"Do you remember our visit to the rag picker, Answin?" he asked. "He told us that he fished out the corpse of the patrician Vasold as well as the severed body parts from the right branch of the Regnitz. It seems logical that they were carried there by the current from somewhere upriver, where Salter had disposed of them, probably close to his hideout, as he had to drag the corpses from the hideout to the river."

Bartholomäus nodded in agreement. "You may be right, but where . . . ?" Now he began to rub his nose, as well.

Simon started counting off on his fingers everything they'd learned to that point. "Let's proceed logically. We're looking for some secluded spot close to the river and also not too far from the city. It must be a cellar, or at least a house, since the madman tortures his victims for a period of time. He needs someplace where he can confine them. He also needs a fire, tools . . ."

"A secluded spot . . ." Bartholomäus stared into space, as if imagining all the possible places. "Close to the river . . . a house . . . or a cellar . . ." Suddenly he let out a yelp. "That's it!"

Magdalena stared at him intently. "What, then?"

"The old hunting house near Wunderburg," he explained. "I was even in that area with Aloysius a few days ago looking for Brutus. But my fear for my dog must have distracted me." He slapped his forehead. "The hunting house would be the ideal hideout. Until a few decades ago the bishop's master of the hunt lived there, but then came the war, and with it the Swedes. Now the house is just a ruin, though it's still well fortified. It's constructed partially of stone and has a roomy cellar."

"That's right," Jakob chimed in. "You told me about it the first time we met in the knacker's cabin, but I didn't attach much significance to it at the time. I just thought you were bragging about the new hunting lodge the bishop had assigned to you."

"It's a gloomy place, and people avoid it because they think it's haunted," Bartholomäus continued. "But as a hideout, it's perfect. The house is close to the river and not too far from the city." He nodded grimly. "If we've guessed right, the old hunting lodge is the place we're looking for."

"It's possible Salter knows the lodge from earlier times," Magdalena added, "or that he discovered it on his last visit to Bamberg. Or perhaps—"

"There's no time for a long discussion," her father interrupted gruffly. "My little girl is in danger, so let's get moving."

"But if it isn't this hunting lodge?" Georg added skeptically. "If . . ."

"If, if, if . . ." Kuisl glared at his son. "Do you have a better plan? Or do you just want to sit around here and brood, while this madman is possibly even now tearing out Barbara's finger-nails?"

"Perhaps we could at least alert the city guards," Simon said. "After all, this man is dangerous. Don't forget that he's tortured and killed seven people."

"If that's all that's bothering you, I can reassure you," Jakob replied. "I've dispatched and sent to their final resting places far more people than this little wolf man." He turned to the others. "So who wants to come along with me?"

Timidly, Georg raised his hand, but Jakob just looked down at him. "You? I'm surprised — this is no job for a bed wetter."

"We'll all come along with you," Magdalena announced in a severe tone. "Barbara is not just your daughter, she's also our sister."

Her father sneered. "Ha! That would be some state of affairs if my own daughter could tell me whom I can take along and who stays behind."

"Do you seriously believe I'm going to stay home with the two boys on my lap while my little sister is perhaps at this very moment being tortured?" she hissed. "You'd have to tie me down."

"Then who's going to take care of the children, and Katharina?" he grumbled. "Simon, perhaps?"

"I'm coming along, too," Simon replied firmly. "And Georg is a brave, strong fellow. We'll surely be able to use him."

"I think it would actually be good for Katharina if we let her take care of the children," said Bartholomäus. "Then she'd have something to do that will distract her from her sorrow. I've also asked her aunt to come over. She's such a chatterbox that Katharina won't even have time to worry."

"Does that mean that you, too—" Jakob started to say, but Bartholomäus cut him off.

"After all, she's my niece," he answered. "You can forget

about leaving me behind. You would be blabbing to everyone that your little brother weaseled out. So let's go."

As he turned toward the door, there was a hiccupping sound from the far end of the room and the scratching of a chair being pushed back. Jeremias had struggled to his feet, swaying a bit, but his voice was clear and determined.

"I'm coming, too," he said, clinging to the table for support. "This madman was out to get me, and not Barbara, so I'll come along and pay him a visit. That's the least I can do for your girl. I'm already responsible for the death of *one* young girl, and that's enough."

"Well, what can I say but don't throw up in the Regnitz." Jakob raised his head and looked each one in the eye. Then he let out a deep sigh. "It seems no one here is going to listen to me, anyway. So be it, and now let's all go out together on our wolf hunt." His eyes suddenly turned to narrow slits. "But I swear to you, if this werewolf harms even a hair on Barbara's head, I'll bring him to the Schongau torture chamber and skin him alive with my own hands."

A dull pain pounded inside Barbara's head as she groaned and rolled restlessly back and forth.

Where am I? What happened?

She tried to sit up, but there was something holding her back. She shook, and pain shot through the back of her head. At the same time, she realized her hands and feet were in shackles. Now everything started to come back to her.

Markus Salter. The man in the boat box. All the blood.

"Help!" Barbara screamed, without knowing where she was or whether anyone could hear her. Her vision was still blurred, no doubt because of the blow with which Salter had knocked her unconscious.

"Help! Is anyone there?"

"You can spare yourself all the shouting," said a hoarse voice nearby. "I'm the only one here, and I can't help you."

Barbara struggled to turn her aching head. She squinted, and after a while her vision became clearer. She was lying on the bare floor of a stone room illuminated by only a single torch. Dressed only in the wet monk's robe, she shivered in a draft of cold air coming through a tiny opening near the ceiling, through which the night sky was visible.

A woman was lying on a cot in one corner. Her blond hair was dirty and matted, her once-beautiful dress tattered, and her cheeks sunken like those of a corpse. Nevertheless she attempted a smile.

"I'd like to tell you not to be afraid, little one," she said in a weakened voice. "But I fear that would not be the truth."

"Where is he?" Barbara asked.

"Our abductor?" The woman groaned as she tried to turn in her direction. Only now did Barbara realize that she, too, was shackled. "I thought you could tell me. He only said he'd have to go and get the scribe."

The scribe . . .

Barbara was shocked. The face of the person shackled and lying in the boat box was so covered with blood that she hadn't recognized at first who it was. But now she knew. It was Hieronymus Hauser, Katharina's father. Shortly after the Kuisls arrived in Bamberg, he'd come to pick up his daughter one night in the executioner's house. A pleasant-looking, chubby man whose features she'd almost forgotten until now. What, in God's name, was going on here?

"If you want to know why he's doing this, little one, I can't tell you," the woman continued, as if reading Barbara's mind. "But you must know we are not the first. He brings all his prisoners here—old and young, women and men—then he questions, tortures, and kills them, as if they were witches. For days I've been racking my brain trying to figure out why he does it, but, by God, I just don't know, any more than I know why he has spared me until now."

"He's an actor," Barbara whispered. "He comes from a group of itinerant actors."

"I know, my dear. Earlier, he was going on and on about how we were coming to the final act, and we were just his bit players. I think we have to assume he's insane." The woman heaved a sigh and suddenly appeared deeply saddened. "So there's probably no point in wondering why he's doing this. We will die . . . for no reason. But who says there always has to be a reason to die?" Then she turned again to Barbara with a tired smile. "If I understand him correctly, you are a hangman's daughter. Is that right? I've never seen you in town before."

"I come from Schongau," Barbara whispered. "That's down by the Alps." She told the woman a bit about herself, especially her experiences in Bamberg. It helped at least for a short time to clear her head and put the nightmare behind her. The stranger told Barbara her name was Adelheid Rinswieser and that she was the wife of an apothecary in Bamberg. Evidently, she was one of the people who'd disappeared, and gradually Barbara came to the awareness that the nice man Markus Salter was indeed the horrible werewolf and that she was now one of his victims.

Suddenly small details came to mind—Salter's constant fatigue, his dark gaze, the wolf pelts in Matheo's chest, and also Salter's sudden decision to take her out of Bamberg just after she'd told him she was the niece of the Bamberg hangman.

Now she remembered how surprised, almost horrified, he'd acted when she told him.

"What is he going to do with us?" she asked Adelheid, after lying there in silence for a while listening to the rain outside, pouring down harder and harder on the roof. "Is he going to kill us, like all the rest?"

"When he's finished with us here he'll take us over to another room," Adelheid replied, darkly. "I've seen it. It's . . . horrible, like something out of your worst nightmares." She looked at Barbara gloomily. "But listen, I've still not given up. Now there are two of us, and soon perhaps three if that scribe is still alive and comes to join us. Perhaps then we'll have a chance. Perhaps . . ."

She hesitated on hearing a bolt being slid back above them on the ground floor. There were heavy footsteps, and something came bumping down the stairs, one at a time. Barbara assumed that Salter was dragging the heavyset Hieronymus Hauser down to the cellar, but strangely the steps were not heading toward their cell, but in the opposite direction. She heard another door squeaking as it opened.

"Oh, God," Adelheid gasped. "He's taking him to the torture chamber and is starting with him right away." Her eyes flickered in the dim light. "I don't know if I can stand that again."

Tensely, the women listened for the sounds at the other end of the hall. Evidently Salter had left the door to the hall open. The women could hear groans, then a rasping and clicking sound, then the steps once again.

This time the steps were approaching.

16

NIGHT WAS FALLING AS THE SMALL GROUP approached the wooden bridge separating the city from the gardens surrounding St. Gangolf's to the north. Earlier, the Kuisls had paid a visit to Aloysius's house and armed themselves. Jakob and Bartholomäus had picked out some heavy cudgels made of ash wood; Georg and Magdalena each carried long hunting knives that Aloysius had given them; and Simon took an old wheel-lock pistol from Bartholomäus, which was so rusted that it probably could only be used as a club. Only Jeremias remained without a weapon.

"My appearance is all the weapon I need," he said with a grin, as they walked along the pier in the rain. "Wait and see: when that fellow sees me in the dark, he'll take off like a shot."

"Maybe we should have brought along Bartholomäus's execution sword," Magdalena said, taking a dubious look at her rusty hunting knife. "In any case, it looked sharper than this old bread cutter."

"To do what? Chop wood?" her father said with a smirk. "Only a woman would make a suggestion like that. Out on the battlefield, a large two-hander like that might be useful—I had one once myself—but not in this dense forest and swamp. If we're going to storm the house, I'd rather have a cudgel."

He swung his club around menacingly, and Magdalena instinctively stepped back. She hated it when men showed off with their weapons. On the other hand, she did feel a bit safer with the hunting knife in her hand. She couldn't help thinking how this nice fellow Markus Salter had probably killed seven people.

And soon perhaps two more.

Earlier, when Magdalena had said good-bye to her two boys, she wondered briefly if she really should go along. It would be dangerous, and as a woman she wasn't much use in a fight. But then she thought of Barbara, and her mind was made up. She could never sit idly at home while her sister was in mortal danger.

So she gave each of the boys a kiss and told them she had to go along with Father and Grandfather to look for Aunt Barbara. The children had given her a serious look, as if they understood how important and dangerous this mission was.

"Then will Barbara come back again?" Peter asked in a soft voice.

Magdalena had nodded and held her boys closely, so they would not see the tears in her eyes. "Of course," she whispered. "You'll see; by tonight she'll be lying in bed alongside you again and singing you a song. Now be kind to Aunt Katharina and help her bake cookies. That will surely make Barbara happy when she comes home."

She wiped a tear from the corner of her eye, then followed the others out into the damp and gloomy streets.

In the last light of day, Magdalena caught sight of the massive wooden piles that supported the magnificent Sees Bridge. The posts stood on islands of gravel surrounded by dark, swirling water. At the first pile they came to, there was a long rowboat rocking in the gurgling stream with someone standing in the boat, waving for them to get in.

"It's lucky for us that Answin is out on this branch of the river today," Bartholomäus said, waving to the old knacker. "I told Aloysius to let him know we needed his boat."

"Answin?" Simon asked hesitantly. "Isn't he that knacker, that corpse collector you were talking about?"

Bartholomäus nodded. "Exactly, but I can put your mind to rest: there are no other passengers in the boat at the moment, at least no dead ones, if that's what you were thinking."

Answin threw them a rope from the boat, and Jakob and Bartholomäus pulled it ashore. One by one they stepped over the side and took their seats in the boat.

"What a lovely bunch you've put together, Bartholomäus," said Answin, smirking at his new passengers. "A cripple, a giant, a dwarf, a wench, and a scaredy-cat. Are you going to the circus?"

"Who's the dwarf?" Simon whispered in Magdalena's ear. "Does he mean—" But Bartholomäus quickly replied, cutting him off.

"You can't always pick your comrades-in-arms," the executioner replied with a grin. "In any case, each one of them is better than a drunken city guard." Then he continued in a serious tone. "We're looking for my future father-in-law and my niece. If you can help me today, I'll be indebted to you."

Answin waved him off. "Just invite me to your wedding; that will be enough. And when you have the time, tell me what the hell is going on here."

"We'll have plenty of time for that as we head upriver," Bartholomäus replied. "Now cast off; we're on our way to Wunderburg."

They had to row against the current, which, however, in November was not very strong. Besides, Jakob, Bartholomäus, and the bull-necked Answin were all strong rowers, who moved them along with vigorous strokes toward their destination.

Bartholomäus briefly told Answin in words interrupted by

vigorous tugs on the oars where they were going and what they planned to do, while Magdalena looked out at the rain-soaked countryside slowly disappearing in the fading light of day. As soon as they passed the city walls, the area turned swampy, traversed by many little canals, pools of water, and streams through the peat bogs. The fog-enshrouded Bamberg Forest extended down to the river, with willows and misshapen birches reaching out greedily toward the water. From far off came the mournful howl of a lone wolf, and instinctively Magdalena cringed.

On their way to the Sees Bridge, Magdalena and Bartholomäus had told the others about their discovery of the baboon that had broken out of its pen. They felt reassured now that there was no actual werewolf prowling around, but that didn't make the locale any less sinister.

And the most evil animal is still man, Magdalena thought to herself.

After a while, they turned into a small tributary almost completely concealed in the reeds. Low-hanging branches brushed against Magdalena's face. Now it was so dark that even the trees on the nearby shore were only visible as dark outlines. Just the same, Answin seemed to know exactly where he was headed.

"There used to be a little dock here, when Wunderburg was still a suburb," he said in a soft voice, "but since the war, the forest has slowly reclaimed the area. Nevertheless, this is still the best way to approach the old hunting cabin. Aha!" He stopped short and pointed ahead into the darkness with his oar. "It seems we're not the first to take a trip here today."

Magdalena squinted and now saw another boat tied up at the shore. Answin steered his boat right alongside, and everyone got out. Bartholomäus limped over to the other boat.

"Just look here," he mumbled, after a quick inspection. He held up his right hand and rubbed his fingers together. "There's blood on the boat box." He cautiously opened the box and stuck his head in for a look. "Here, inside, as well. I'd say we're on the right track."

Magdalena heard a soft, grinding sound, and it took a while before she realized it was her father, standing right next to her, grinding his teeth.

"I'll kill him," he whispered under his breath. "Very, very slowly. And it will hurt very, very much."

"But I don't think our werewolf killed his prisoners here in the boat," Jeremias said, evidently having heard Jakob's whispered words. By now he was more or less sober again. "That isn't the way he's been going about it. He wants to torture them slowly, just the way I tortured his relatives back then. We can only hope he hasn't gotten that far yet."

Magdalena felt like she had to vomit. What in God's name was this madman doing with her sister?

"Then let's not waste any time," she said, looking around. "Where is this damned hunting lodge?"

Bartholomäus pointed to a narrow deer path leading into the forest. "It's not far now. We all have to keep quiet if we want to surprise the fellow."

"I'll stand here by the boat and wait for you," Answin said. "Forgive me, but I have a wife and five hungry young mouths to feed, and they need their father to come back home alive. Besides . . ." He hesitated for a moment. "Well, there are stories going around about this house that I don't like. It's said the master of the hunt back then was a bad character — he had his own way of dealing with poachers. Some of them vanished and were never seen again. So watch out that the same doesn't happen to you."

Bartholomäus nodded. "Thanks, Answin, we'll take care of ourselves. Just one last favor, please. If you hear me shouting, then something has gone wrong. Please alert the city guards."

"We should have done that before," Simon replied gloomily, "but once again, no one wanted to listen to me."

"Exactly. So let's go." Jakob took the lead, and the others followed him into the dense forest.

As soon as they were under the tree cover, Magdalena could hardly see her hand in front of her face. The rain came pouring down. Nevertheless, she refrained from lighting the lantern so as not to alert Markus Salter any sooner than necessary. After a while, the undergrowth disappeared and they entered a part of the forest with tall-standing firs and scattered birches, and the view improved. Somewhere an owl hooted, but otherwise all they heard was the sound of the pouring rain and their own steps through the damp, moldy leaves. Repeatedly they had to find a way around swampy pools of water.

They had made their way perhaps a stone's throw or two from the river, when Jakob suddenly stopped and pointed ahead of them through the trees, where the outlines of a large building surrounded by a low wall became visible.

"Is that it?" he whispered to his brother, who had come up from behind.

Bartholomäus spat on the ground. "That's it. It's dark in the house, but that doesn't necessarily mean anything. There are a few cellar rooms whose windows were all boarded up long ago. Let's sneak up a little closer and perhaps we'll be able to see something else."

"I've seen enough," Jakob hissed. "My Barbara is in there, so I'm going to get her and bring her out."

"Father," said Georg in a soft voice, having approached from behind without their noticing, "it doesn't make sense for you just to go bursting in. Salter could hold Barbara hostage or even kill her, so let's see if there isn't some way we can get in without being noticed."

Jakob grunted, which evidently was tantamount to a concession. They passed through a rusty gate in the crumbling wall, then crept toward a large thornbush just a few steps from the building.

Magdalena could see now that the building must have once been a stately hunting lodge. It was two stories high and built of sturdy pine and beams of dark oak on a stone foundation. The remains of a terrace extended along one side of the building, ending in a neglected, overgrown garden of fruit trees and overturned statues. Shingles had fallen off the roof, and some of the siding had broken away, but the building still looked huge and solid.

Like a gloomy old castle, Magdalena thought, *with an evil warlock living inside.*

Some of the stories she read to her boys told of terrifying witches' houses, mostly small and dilapidated, but for the first time Magdalena had the feeling of really seeing such a house.

And it was a very, very big one.

Suddenly something strange happened. The rain stopped and a strong wind arose, howling and whistling as if to warn the house of possible intruders. Magdalena began to shiver, and it wasn't just because of the cold. She remembered what Answin had just told them.

There are stories going around about this house that I don't like.

"The front door appears to be locked," Jeremias whispered, pointing to the massive two-winged portals leading from the terrace into the house. "But a few of the windows are open. Besides, there's probably a back door for the servants, which they can—"

He stopped short on hearing a long drawn-out scream that chilled Magdalena to the bone.

"Barbara!" Jakob howled, standing up from where he was behind the bush.

"For God's sake, be quiet," Bartholomäus hissed. "We're trying to surprise him, so . . ."

But the hangman had already stormed off like a mad bull toward the building.

"Stop this jackass before he ruins everything," Bartholomäus demanded, turning to Magdalena. "You may be the only one he still listens to."

"I'm not so sure of that," Magdalena mumbled, closing her eyes briefly and saying a quick prayer.

Then she ran off after her father.

Barbara froze when she heard the bolt on the cell door being pushed aside. Drenched in rain and sweat, Markus Salter stood before her in the doorway, with that familiar sad smile on his face, but now he didn't appear melancholy anymore, simply crazed, like a dark angel that had just fallen from heaven.

"It's time," he said in a hoarse voice. "Let's get it over with."

Without saying another word, he went over to Adelheid Rinswieser and loosened her shackles in a few places. He lifted her up, almost tenderly, until she was finally standing unsteadily, as her feet were still bound. He held a gleaming dagger up to Adelheid's throat.

"Now, very slowly, we'll go over to the other room," he ordered her. "Please don't resist, or I'll have to hurt you prematurely, and I don't want to do that."

Adelheid cast a final, warning glance at Barbara, then disappeared with Markus into the corridor. Barbara heard a high-pitched, anguished shout, but it didn't seem to be a woman's voice, but that of a man.

After some time, Salter returned alone. He removed Barbara's shackles and helped her up.

"Why are you doing this?" she asked.

"I'm restoring the balance of justice," he said. "An eye for an eye, a tooth for a tooth. That's what it says in the Bible."

With astonishing strength, he pulled Barbara down the dark stone corridor to another room illuminated by a number of torches. Instinctively she let out a little cry. Adelheid Rinswieser had not exaggerated.

Spread out before her was a veritable nightmare.

Barbara had seen the torture chamber in the Schongau dungeon and had even helped her father clean up a few times. But this was something different. The room did not look like an ordinary torture chamber, but one dreamed up by a madman.

Or a demon.

There were the usual instruments, like the rack, a rope and pulleys, tongs, thumbscrews, and a brazier in the far right-hand corner of the room that gave off an almost sickening warmth. Scattered among them were strange devices that Barbara had never seen before—a bloodstained wooden device, spherical on one end and coming to a sharp point on the other; a tub filled with a whitish, caustic liquid; a cage in the shape of a head on a shelf; and a few iron boots inlaid with spikes and screws. Other instruments were so bizarre that Barbara couldn't figure them out even after studying them for a long time. Bales of hay were strewn around the room and had reddish brown spots where blood had congealed on them.

The worst, however, were the paintings on the cloth panels that hung from the ceiling like backdrops in a theater. They reminded Barbara of paintings of hell depicting tortured sinners bleeding from their many wounds, their mouths open in silent screams. They stared at Barbara from every corner of the room — hasty sketches of human cruelty, like the first building plans for a new cathedral. Everything in this room expressed a single human feeling.

Pain.

Moaning and in chains, was Hieronymus Hauser. The old scribe appeared to be unconscious. His eyes were closed, and he quivered like a fish on dry land, but he was still alive. Crouching along the opposite wall on a bale of straw was Adelheid Rinswieser, shackled, and with a leather cord around her neck attached to an iron ring in the wall. She was staring straight ahead, but Barbara could see that her whole body was trembling with fear. Barbara was still so paralyzed by the horrible sight that she was completely devoid of emotion. Like a lamb being led to slaughter, she let Markus Salter guide her over to the wall, where he gently pushed her down to the floor and tied her with a strap, as he had Adelheid. With other ropes, he tied her feet and hands. Then he stood up and dragged Hieronymus Hauser to the rack while continuing to smile gently at the two women.

"We are coming to the end of the performance," he said softly. "The scale is coming back into equilibrium." He passed his hands playfully over the wheel used to tighten the chains at the head of the rack. "I asked Malcolm to have my play performed, but no matter how often I asked, he wouldn't. It's too bad; it would have been a great success, a very great success. Do you know what is the driving force in every good play?" He looked at the two women questioningly. When they didn't respond, he continued. "Love and revenge. Everything else is derived from those two. All of Shakespeare's great tragedies are based on it. My play begins with love and ends in revenge, a great deal of revenge. Do you want to hear a summary?"

"I do," Barbara whispered, hoping to put off the inevitable for a while. "Tell us."

"Well, the play is about a young boy born into a large happy family—father, mother, aunts, grandparents. His grandfather is none other than the Bamberg chancellor himself. The boy is safe and secure in the arms of his mother. That's the end of the first act, the end of love." Salter's smile died like the light of a candle that was suddenly snuffed out. "Because now, a few powerful people want to destroy this family, an ice-cold calculation based on their sheer lust for power. They have a diabolical plot, and the little boy watches as first his grandmother, then his mother, are convicted of witchcraft, tortured, and their bodies burned. He clings desperately to his father, but he, too, is executed as a warlock, as is his grandfather, the Bamberg chancellor. The boy is four years old, and bit by bit his world crumbles. As soon as he seeks comfort in a new family member, that person also is cruelly tortured and killed. He goes to live with his uncle and his aunt until they too are taken away by the executioner. In the end, the boy is completely alone. That's the end of the second act." Salter paused and stared blankly into space.

"From this boundless sorrow, a much stronger feeling emerges," he finally said in a monotone. "Hate. Even before he says his last farewell to his tortured aunt, bleeding from her many wounds—she is the last close relative he had in Bamberg—she gives him the names of those who were paid blood money for destroying his family. He will never forget these names, not a single one . . ."

Tears gleamed in Salter's eyes as he slowly continued turning the wheel of the rack. Each time, Hieronymus Hauser moaned loudly.

"Harsee, Schwarzkontz, Vasold, Gotzendörfer, Herrenberger, Hauser, Schramb, Braun . . ."

On hearing the last name, Adelheid Rinswieser let out a muted cry. "My God, Braun! That's my father."

"The orphan is brought to the Carmelite monastery on the Kaulberg," Salter continued, without paying any attention to the moaning and shouting. "The monks there don't care for him; they believe he is a witch's offspring. They torment him with words and prayers, they beat him day in and day out, they lock him in a cell deep underground. And there he recites the names of the guilty like a prayer: Harsee, Schwarzkontz, Vasold, Gotzendörfer, Herrenberger, Hauser, Schramb, Braun . . ." Salter started slowly turning the wheel again while the moans of the nearly unconscious scribe became louder. "But one day the boy discovers an escape route through a mountain of sand . . ."

"The crypt under the monastery!" Barbara gasped. "You already knew about it, and that's why you went there to find shelter . . ."

Markus Salter didn't even seem to hear her. He just kept going on and on. "So the boy flees from the monastery, and once he's out he learns that the last of his relatives has been killed, to wipe out any trace of the crime. There is, however, a distant relative, an uncle in Cologne, who takes him in. The boy begins studies at the university there; he takes on the name of his uncle in order to forget, but he can't get these names out of his mind: Harsee, Schwarzkontz, Vasold, Gotzendörfer, Herrenberger, Hauser, Schramb, Braun . . ."

The next time Salter turned the wheel, Hieronymus Hauser let out a shriek, a high-pitched, anguished cry, almost like that of an animal.

Barbara closed her eyes, but she couldn't escape the screams.

"Why me?" she shouted. "What do I have to do with it?"

Markus Salter just smiled.

"Can't you see, Barbara? You're a hangman's daughter. Your family, too, assumed part of the guilt back then, which you must atone for now. The needle on the scale is swinging back to the middle; we are approaching the last act."

When he turned the wheel the next time, the victim's joints cracked sharply, and Hauser's scream no longer sounded human.

Magdalena rushed toward the building, where her father had already arrived and was pounding on the door. She could still hear the horrible screams coming from inside the building. Behind her, above the sound of the storm and wind, her uncle was shouting.

"No, Jakob! Don't do this!" But the hangman paid no attention to him and kept slamming his body against the massive door, which did not yield an inch.

"Damn it! It's locked," he cursed, as Magdalena ran up to him. He kicked the door several times, but it didn't move.

"Just stop, Father," Magdalena pleaded. "You won't get anywhere that way. We must pull ourselves together . . ."

"Barbara!" Jakob shouted, as if he hadn't heard his elder

daughter and kept hammering on the door. "Can you hear me? Are you inside?"

Hearing no answer, the hangman raced along the front of the house without saying another word until he reached a boarded-up window. With his huge hands, he seized the boards, ripped them off the house, and soon he had an opening large enough to enter.

"You . . . you stubborn damned ox," Magdalena shouted. "At least wait until the others get here."

But Jakob paid no attention to her, heaved himself up onto the sill, and disappeared inside the building, from which only a muffled, drawn-out moaning could be heard. Magdalena by now was certain that the cries were not coming from her sister. But who, then? Perhaps Hieronymus Hauser? She briefly thought she heard another female voice, but she could have been mistaken.

Desperately she looked around for her comrades-in-arms. Georg, Simon, and Bartholomäus were approaching, but Bartholomäus was having a lot of trouble running across the slippery ground with his stiff leg. Only Jeremias was still hiding behind the thornbush staring out anxiously at them.

"Isn't that just wonderful," Bartholomäus snorted when he finally arrived. "In all these years your father hasn't changed at all. He just plunges ahead, hell-bent, come what may."

"Well, at least he ripped out a hole in the window first," Simon said, pointing at the opening. "You might call that progress."

"But what in hell shall we do now?" Magdalena scolded. "Nobody knows what to expect inside."

"I'm afraid your father has made that decision for us. Now all we can do is act fast and pray." Bartholomäus was already hoisting himself onto the sill, and despite his handicap, he was astonishingly nimble. He pointed at Simon, who was standing alongside the window holding his wheel-lock pistol, uncertain what to do. "You'll stay out here with Jeremias in case the fellow somehow gets away from us. Do you at least know how to use that weapon?"

Simon looked at it doubtfully. "Uh, my father-in-law gave me a quick explanation earlier. I think it's loaded, but . . ."

"Fine, then everything is all right." Bartholomäus slipped into the house.

Once again, there was loud moaning from the depths of the house, and by now it no longer sounded like a human wail. Magdalena looked at Simon, who was staring at the pistol as if it were a poisonous snake.

"You probably won't even need it," she consoled him, "and if you do, just hit the fellow over the head with it."

"Magdalena," Simon pleaded, "don't go in there. It's enough that your uncle and Georg are risking their lives."

Magdalena hesitated, but then she stood up straight. "Simon, you don't understand. My little sister is somewhere inside there, in the hands of a madman. I can't stay outside. If anything happens to her, I'd never forgive myself." She attempted to smile but it looked strained. "Everything will work out—you'll see."

Then she climbed in after Georg and her uncle.

Inside it was as dark as in a rotting coffin. Magdalena thought she saw some dust-covered furniture wrapped in blankets, and some places on the walls were a bit lighter than their surroundings—presumably doorways leading into other rooms. A few steps in front of her she could see the outlines of her uncle and her brother.

"If your father hadn't been so stupid as to come crashing in here, we could have lit a torch or a lantern," Bartholomäus hissed. "Now we're standing here blind as bats. Why couldn't he wait for us?"

"His daughter is being held captive in there, and perhaps being tortured. Don't forget that," Magdalena chided him. But basically she had to admit her uncle was right.

Sometimes Father is like a little boy, just a lot stronger and with a lot less common sense.

She had just reached one of those lighter sections along the wall, which in fact turned out to be an open doorway, when she heard a rumbling and crashing somewhere in the building. There were more screams, but this time she couldn't have said whose voice it was. Near the back of the building, someone shouted Barbara's name, followed by silence.

"That was father, I'm sure," Georg said excitedly. "Then he's already found Barbara."

"It sounded more like something happened to him," Bartholomäus said, as he rushed into the next room. "That's what he gets for being so impatient."

Magdalena followed him, squinting as she groped her way forward. They were standing now in a sort of reception room or parlor, with the main entrance visible on the left. A faint ray of moonlight fell through a crack in the entrance, while the wind rattled the boarded shutters. In front of them, emerging from the shadows, a rickety stairway led up to a balcony, underneath which there were two other doors, both of them open.

"And now what?" Magdalena asked. "We have no idea where Father is. Perhaps he's already headed off in another direction."

"I'm telling you, we need a light," Bartholomäus grumbled. "I left my lantern outside with Jeremias. I can still get it and light it."

"We don't have enough time for that, so let's just keep going straight back." Georg turned to the door on the right underneath the stairway that appeared to lead to the back of the building. "One way is as good as the other. If we don't find Father there, we can always—"

A sudden sound caused Magdalena to spin around, and looking up she saw something black swooping down on her and Georg. At the last moment, she threw herself to one side, dragging her brother along with her. There was a crash, and Georg let out a loud shout.

"Damn!" he gasped. "What is that? That hurts like the devil."

Magdalena, alongside him, smelled a sharp, biting odor that made her cough. Choking, she turned and bumped into something metallic.

"Be careful, that's lime!" Bartholomäus shouted. "It seems there was a tub of it up there that fell down. Quick, get away. The stuff is as sharp and biting as devil's piss."

Magdalena felt a burning spot on her hand. Quickly, she rubbed it against her skirt, and the stinging subsided. Then she moved cautiously away from the balcony and was just barely able to make out Georg and Bartholomäus standing along the wall on the opposite side of the room.

"I nearly tripped over something," Georg whispered, as he also rubbed his hands. "I think there was a wire leading up to the balcony. This bastard set traps here to frighten off intruders." Then he turned toward his sister. "I really have to thank you. If you hadn't pushed me away, I'd probably be blind now."

"So would I," she mumbled.

Magdalena couldn't help thinking of Jeremias and his scars. If she or Georg had gone just one step farther, they would have no doubt looked just like him.

Did our werewolf use this caustic lye on his victims? she wondered with a shudder. *Is that how he disposed of them?*

"We've got to be careful," Bartholomäus said. "Perhaps my brother ran into a trap like that a few minutes ago. God knows what's still in store for us. From now on, we'd better think about every step we take."

They passed through the door on the right under the stairway into another dark room that seemed just as large as the first, and that led them to two additional hallways. By now, Magdalena's eyes had grown accustomed enough to the dark that she could see more than just dark outlines. The walls were lined with deer antlers covered with dense cobwebs, and, alongside them in wooden frames, faded paintings so horrifying that even the marauding Swedish mercenaries didn't want to take them along. Something scurried between their feet, squeaking, perhaps a rat or mouse that they had startled.

Again there was a loud scream. The voice seemed to be both nearby and very distant, and Magdalena's heart skipped a beat. Then she heard her father calling.

"Good Lord," she whispered. "If we want to help Barbara and Father, we really must hurry. I'm afraid we have to just disregard any other traps."

They all ran to the next door.

"Barbara? Where are you? Barbara?"

Jakob's voice rang through the dark rooms and hallways of the old hunting lodge. The hangman had stormed blindly into the building and had made it through the first room when he realized he had badly miscalculated. He should have waited for the others, as now he had to fend for himself. He couldn't hesitate a moment longer after he'd alerted Barbara's abductor of his presence through his own shouting. He was struggling to think it all through, clearly and precisely, as he always did, but his fear for his daughter's welfare simply made it impossible for him to think straight. Where had this madman hidden her?

Barbara, my little Barbara . . .

He groped through the darkness randomly, running through rooms, falling over rotted pieces of furniture, getting to his feet again, and kept looking. Strange beasts lurked in the corners — or were they just wardrobe closets and chests? He felt as if he were in a dream. He continued onward, through doors and corridors. Once he heard a metallic snap alongside his feet, which he ignored, and another time a voice calling. It sounded like his brother's voice, but perhaps it was someone else. Perhaps the madman?

Barbara . . . Where is Barbara?

By now he'd gone almost all the way through the first floor of the house and had to be somewhere in the back of the building. He bumped into a table, hard, and there was a tinkle and clatter of broken dishes. As he was about to turn back to the rooms in front, he saw what looked like a black square opening behind the table. He approached it cautiously and saw it was the entrance to a stairway leading to the cellar. The wooden hatch was open, as if someone had just entered the staircase.

The cellar. I'm on the right track.

His suspicions were confirmed when he heard shouts again from down below. He had already entered the stairwell when his sensitive nose detected an odor he knew only too well. Something was burning down there, and he was sure it was no cozy fire in the hearth.

Grimly he reached for the oak cudgel he'd been carrying on his belt and hurried down the steps. Now that there was not even a ray of moonlight coming through the cracks in the walls, it was as dark as the inside of a coffin. The stinging odor became stronger now, his eyes began to tear up, but still he continued running down the dark steep stairs.

Suddenly he felt pressure on his right shin, then something thin and very hard cut through his trousers. A searing pain passed through his leg, as if someone had struck it with a whip. Thrashing about, he staggered like a shot and wounded bear, trying to grab onto the wall to keep his balance, but it was like trying to stop a mighty oak from falling after it had been chopped down. He plunged down the dark staircase, turning head over heels several times on the way down.

A wire, was the thought that flashed through his mind; *it must have been a wire. This devious bastard, this . . .*

Then he landed hard at the bottom and darkness flooded over him like a warm bath.

Hieronymus Hauser writhed in pain on the rack and screamed like a lunatic while his torturer watched him with interest. Barbara and Adelheid lay shackled in a corner, paralyzed by the horror taking place before their eyes.

"Is that the way my grandfather screamed, back then?" Salter asked, turning the wheel a bit tighter. "Tell me. You were there. You were the scribe and wrote everything down very carefully. Did you make a note of how long he screamed, how loud, how shrill? Did you? Tell me!"

"Oh, God, please stop," Hauser whimpered. "I was just the scribe. I-I had no choice."

"Yet you took the blood money, didn't you?" Salter persisted. "A part of our family fortune went to you, as well. I've seen your house at the Sand Gate, Master Hauser. A simple scribe can't afford anything like that. Tell me: you bought your house with the blood of my family, didn't you? Well?" Once again he turned the wheel a bit, and Hauser's joints made a crunching sound like a dry hemp rope.

"Yes! Yes! I did!" the scribe screamed. "And if I could, I swear I'd pay it all back to you. Believe me, I have suffered, too. Every night I've dreamt of these tortures. They've never let me go."

"And they've finally caught up with you," Salter replied in a whisper. "You knew they would, didn't you? I could see it in your face in the castle hall. I enjoyed your fear as I looked down at you from the stage. You thought you could get away from me, but in the general confusion it was easy for me to strike you down and bring you to the boat." Salter's face darkened. "When I came back to plant the magic props on Malcolm, the crowd seized me. That was not part of my plan, but in any case, that's how I found the little hangman's daughter. God sent her to me."

"It's not yet too late to return to God's just way," Hauser gasped. "If you release me now, I promise you—"

"You disgust me with your begging," Salter interrupted. "I'm certain that my grandfather, my father, my mother, and all the other Haans and Röhms died with far more dignity than you will. Let's end this pathetic farce."

He was just turning to the brazier in the corner where a tong was already glowing red hot, when they heard a loud hammering overhead. Right after that, Barbara heard a deep, muffled voice, coming most likely from up on the first floor, though all she could understand were random words. But she did recognize her father's voice.

"Barbara!"

Her heart leapt for joy. It was her father calling. He'd found her.

When Markus Salter heard the noise from the floor above, he cringed. Then he suddenly stopped, stood still as a board, like a fox in an open field, and shook his head in disbelief.

"This . . . this is impossible," he stammered. "This can't happen now. The play isn't over yet, or . . ." Suddenly a smirk passed over his face, he reached for the tongs, and walked toward Barbara.

"It's your uncle, isn't it?" he said. "Or your father. In any case, someone from your accursed clan of hangmen. Well, whoever it is, he will soon get a big surprise. The audience likes that, doesn't it? Surprises . . ." He listened intently as if waiting for what would come next, but as he didn't hear anything else, he turned back to Barbara and Adelheid with a shrug. "Your family has destroyed mine, and now they'll have to watch how I deal with their relatives. An eye for an eye, a tooth for a—"

There was a metallic crash, and from the corner of her eye Barbara could see that the heavy brazier had tipped over and the glowing pieces of coal were rolling like stones across the floor. Adelheid, who had been crouching along the wall directly next to the brazier and until then had remained silent, had given it a violent kick with her shackled feet. The room immediately filled with an acrid odor, and some of the pieces of coal rolled into the bales of straw, which immediately began to smoke. Flames rose up along the hanging paintings to the wooden ceiling. Stunned, Salter stumbled back a few steps.

"What . . . what are you doing?" he stammered. "Why . . ."

"Here we are!" Adelheid yelled. "Down here in the cellar! Help us, whoever you are!"

Again, there was a crash outside. Evidently something heavy had fallen down the stairs. Barbara was still paralyzed with fear.

What's going on outside, for heaven's sake? Where is Father? He should have gotten down here already. Is it possible he didn't hear us?

She looked back at her torturer. The overturned brazier had given them no more than a brief respite. Salter seemed to have already gotten control of himself.

"If that's what you want, then burn!" he bellowed. "Burn just like my parents and grandparents. Burn, all of you!"

Red and blue flames rose from the bales of straw. One bale stood close to the rack, and flames reached out eagerly to devour the dry wood. Hauser gasped and writhed on the rack, whimpering softly, then turned his eyes away and lost consciousness again.

Markus was about to run to the door when he stopped and turned back to Adelheid with a look of determination.

"You're coming with me," he said. He rushed over to her, pulling her up by the hair so hard that she screamed. "The hangman's girl and the scribe can burn, but I still need you. Who knows what's waiting for me outside? You're my hostage." He stared into her emaciated, ashen face. "You were always my favorite, Adelheid, so strong, so full of the will to live. I almost let you go, but it can't end like this. Not yet."

As he spoke, he removed the leather strap around Adelheid's neck, loosened the shackles on her feet, and dragged her to the doorway. The young apothecary's wife cast a last, desperate glance at Barbara, then disappeared with him into the corridor, and the door closed with a loud bang.

Smoke crept like a bitter potion down into Barbara's throat.

"Father," she gasped, trying to crawl across the floor toward the door with her shackled feet, but the leather strap around her neck held her back, and every time she moved, the noose closed tighter. "Father. Here . . . I . . . am . . ."

Then the clouds of smoke finally blocked her sight.

Jakob Kuisl didn't know how long he'd been unconscious. For a moment? For hours? When he raised his pounding head, there was nothing around him but heavy smoke and darkness. He coughed and tried to sit up. From his experience with execution fires, he knew the smoke was always the densest and the most deadly at eye level. "If you want to die fast, keep your head up," he had sometimes advised condemned men. "Then it's almost as if you're going to sleep."

But I don't want to die—not yet. I'm looking for my Barbara . . .

Every bone in his body hurt, and his head felt like a soaked sponge, but evidently he hadn't broken anything in falling over the tripwire. The smoke was no longer as thick, and he could breathe more freely, but he still couldn't see anything in the darkness. He assumed he was somewhere at the bottom of the cellar steps.

As he was trying to get his bearings in the swirling clouds of smoke, he heard muffled screams off to one side, and shortly thereafter a door swung open with a crash, suddenly revealing a corridor illuminated by the blazing light of a fire. A man came out, dragging a shackled woman behind him. Jakob squinted, but then the door closed again, and once more the corridor lay in darkness. He blinked several times and shook himself, trying to pull himself together. The fall had shaken him more than he'd first thought.

"Barbara!" he rasped. "Is that you?"

A woman's voice cried out but was cut off so suddenly it seemed as if someone had put his hand over her mouth. Still, Jakob was sure it was Barbara. He'd finally found her, and she was still alive.

"Barbara! Here I am!"

The hangman groped blindly toward the place he'd just seen the two people, reaching out into the darkness like a drowning man, when suddenly something bumped into his side and footsteps scurried past. Then he heard a sound, someone gasping nearby, like a disembodied ghost. He reached out frantically in all directions, but there was nothing there, and a moment later he heard another door squeaking somewhere behind him.

This time Kuisl resolved to be absolutely quiet. He wanted to be sure this madman wasn't lurking for him in some dark corner and wouldn't find him an easy target. Intuitively he reached for the oaken cudgel on his belt, but it appeared he'd lost it in his fall.

Then I've got to go with what I have . . .

Slowly and ponderously, like a golem that had sprung to life, he moved toward where he'd heard the squeaking door.

His hands stretched out in front of him, he groped his way down the smoke-filled corridor. For a moment, he thought he heard a hoarse voice behind him, but that was probably just his imagination. On his right there was a rough wall, then an opening.

The door. That bastard left the door open. Now I'll get you.

Blindly, Jakob entered the room and felt a fresh breeze blowing toward him driving away the clouds of smoke. There had to be a window somewhere. But how was that possible? He was deep down in the cellar. He desperately tried to remember how the house looked from outside. Was there perhaps an escape tunnel? A trapdoor he had perhaps overlooked in his haste?

Something hard and cold brushed against his face. He reached for it and could feel a chain with an iron hook on it. There was a second hook within easy reach. He shook the chain, and the links jingled as they swung back and forth. His eyes were full of tears from the smoke and he still wasn't able to see anything but dark outlines.

Where am I, for God's sake?

He strained to concentrate on his other senses: sound, touch, smell. His fine nose detected, amid the clouds of smoke, something else—a fragrance of something that had been there long ago and that had eaten its way into the walls. It smelled of blood and salty smoked meat, haunch and saddle of venison, wild boar's leg . . . Kuisl flinched.

The meat cellar. I'm in the storage area for meat from the hunter's kill, and there's a shaft here that they used to lower the disemboweled animals. Where . . .

Suddenly a shadow jumped at him from out of the darkness. The hangman felt a sharp sting as one of the hanging chains hit him on the cheek. He fell to the ground and rolled to one side to escape a possible second blow, but it didn't come. Instead, he heard fast, shuffling steps disappearing into the darkness.

A moment later he heard the muffled voice of a woman, a bolt was pushed aside at the top of the shaft, and a trapdoor opened up.

Jakob shook off the pain, looked up, and saw moonlight streaming into the room through an opening. After all this time in darkness, the faint light seemed almost as bright as the light of day. The wide shaft ended up above at the trapdoor, which now stood open. A narrow stairway no more than a foot wide led up the side of the shaft, and two figures were standing just below the trapdoor. One wore a dress that fluttered in the wind. Before Jakob could see anything else, the trapdoor slammed shut and the two figures had disappeared.

"Barbara!" the hangman shouted up the shaft. "Barbara!"

He raised his fist threateningly and sent a curse up into the night sky. "I'll get you, you bastard, even if you run to the ends of the earth, and then not even God will be able to save you! No one kidnaps my daughter—no one!"

Jakob struggled to his feet and hobbled, groaning, toward the stairway, which was now once more enveloped in darkness. He thought he heard a soft, hoarse cry coming from far down the corridor behind him, but it was too faint to tell exactly where it came from.

Once again, and not for the first time that day, the hangman felt he was far too old for such adventures.

Coughing and with tear-filled eyes, Barbara tugged on the leather strap that bound her like a dog to the ring on the wall. The smoke was now so thick she could hardly see anything in the room. The rack had to be on her right, where old Hieronymus Hauser was lying, not making a sound. Perhaps he'd already suffocated from the smoke.

"Help!" Barbara cried. "Help, Father! I'm here!" But there was no answer.

Flames crackled all around her, moving up the hanging tapestries to the wooden ceiling, where they licked at the beams. It got hotter by the second, and the only reason Barbara's clothing hadn't burst into flame was that she was still wearing the rain-soaked monk's robe. In her present situation, the robe was like a protective shield. Just the same, Barbara knew it was only a matter of minutes until she would die an agonizing death down here in the flames.

If I don't suffocate first like old Hauser.

Once again she struggled to loosen the knot in the strap with her shackled hands, but it was tied too tightly. She looked around in panic until she noticed the glowing poker lying on the floor not far from her. Could she sever the strap with it?

She stretched her leg out and was just able to reach the glowing poker with her toe. There was a soft hissing sound as the fire ate its way through her shoes. She groaned, clenched her teeth, and tried to ignore the pain. She pulled the poker close enough to reach with her shackled hands. Carefully she picked it up at the far end, which was not so hot, but still the heat was enough that she almost passed out. The poker seemed to practically stick to her skin, but she persisted, pressing the poker against the leather strap she could see only faintly in the billows of smoke, and at the same time tugging at the strap, which gave off a stinging odor.

Finally, when the pain had become almost unbearable, the strap gave way and Barbara fell backward.

Barbara knew she had no time to lose. Gasping, and with her hands and feet still shackled, she crawled through the clouds of smoke toward the place where she assumed the door was. She knew this was her only chance. If her sense of direction failed her, she wouldn't have a second opportunity to look for the exit on the other side of the room.

Please, please, dear Lord, don't let me be wrong.

With shackled hands, she felt her way along the stone wall, recoiled from the burning tapestries, and finally felt the hot wood.

The door. She'd actually found it.

With agonizing slowness, on the verge of passing out, she rose to her feet, groped for the door handle, and found it. Barbara was so happy she barely noticed the heat from the poker. She pressed the handle, threw herself against the door, and with a loud crash it flew open. The dark corridor on the other side was also full of smoke, but nowhere near as dense as in the room she'd just left. Nevertheless, it was enough to rob her of her sight and breath.

Father . . . Father, she wanted to cry, but her throat was so dry that only a soft wheeze came out. Nearly blind, she moved ahead a few steps into the darkness, banged into the opposite wall, and found another door slightly ajar that she pushed open. She entered.

Where . . . where am I?

She turned around looking for another way out, but there was none. The room was tiny, a former storage closet full of old odds and ends. A ray of moonlight fell through a narrow open window far above her, allowing just enough air into the room that she did not suffocate.

Smoke swirled into the room from the corridor, and the crackling flames seemed to be drawing nearer.

Tears ran down her face, where they quickly dried in the soot and ashes.

Her father had not found her.

One floor above, Magdalena, Georg, and Bartholomäus were still groping through the dark rooms as the wind whistled through the cracks in the windows and the rotted roof of the old hunting lodge.

Shadows lurked in the corners, large forms that looked like petrified monsters but which on closer examination were nothing but pieces of furniture covered with dust and cobwebs. They had just walked past a moth-eaten stuffed bear that seemed to glower at Magdalena with an evil eye. Once again they heard muffled cries coming clearly from the cellar beneath them, but they couldn't locate the stairway going down. The entire house stank of mildew, ancient mold, mouse droppings, and . . .

Magdalena stopped short.

"Do you smell that?" she asked her two companions in a low voice. "It's smoke. There's a fire somewhere in here."

"Damn, you're right," Bartholomäus growled. He lifted up his nose and sniffed the air. "Where do you think it's coming from?"

Magdalena squinted and looked around. How could she find anything in this damned darkness? She couldn't see a fire anywhere, but the smoke was getting stronger and stronger. Looking down toward the floor, she suddenly thought she saw a gray, undulating cloud, and now she noticed other little clouds of smoke rising toward the ceiling, where they became more visible in the moonlight coming through the cracks in the windows.

"Good God, the whole floor is smoking," Georg cried out in horror. "There must be a fire down in the cellar."

In just a few moments, the smoke became so thick that Magdalena started coughing. Earlier, she had at least been able to see dark outlines, but now she could hardly see a thing.

"Let's get out of here!" Bartholomäus shouted. "Perhaps the smoke isn't quite so heavy yet in the back of the house."

Her uncle raced down another corridor, and Magdalena followed close behind. She had no idea where Georg was. Smoke was everywhere now, stinging their eyes and making breathing harder and harder.

She heard a metallic click followed by a sudden, anguished cry, this time very nearby. Georg! Bending down, she saw him indistinctly just a few steps away. He was writhing around and seemed to be in great pain.

"What happened?" she asked anxiously.

"Something grabbed me by the leg," Georg said through gritted teeth. "I think it was another of those damned traps. It . . . hurts . . . so much."

Magdalena crawled over to her brother, passing her hand down his leg until she felt something metallic and sharp that had clamped down on his right ankle. The fresh blood stuck to her fingers. While she was examining Georg, Bartholomäus crawled over to them. He coughed, rubbed his eyes, and bent down to have a better look.

"By all the saints! That's a wolf trap," he gasped. "This madman actually put out wolf traps here." With his powerful fingers he pulled apart the two jagged jaws that had clamped down on Georg's ankle. Georg let out a short cry, then just moaned softly. "We've got to get Georg out of here as quick as possible and care for the wound." Bartholomäus said, throwing the trap into a corner with disgust.

"But what about Father and Barbara —?" Magdalena started to say.

"Forget both of them," her uncle interrupted. "If we want to save Georg, we've got to get him out of here right away. Everything will be going up in flames here in a minute. The floors are dry and crumbling, and there is a cellar under the entire house. When it starts to burn down there, the wind will come roaring through the halls like in a chimney." He held Magdalena's hand. "You must be strong now. If Barbara and your father are somewhere down below, there's nothing more we can do for them. But we can help Georg."

"Then you take care of Georg," she said, as another fit of coughing shook her entire frame. "I'm going to keep looking for them."

"Girl, come to your senses. There's nothing more you can do here. Your stubborn father made a mess of it all. Now we've got to salvage what we still can." Georg moaned as Bartholomäus began pulling him away. "Now hurry up and help me. With my stiff leg and all the smoke here, I won't be able to get this heavy fellow out fast enough by myself. The windows are nailed shut, and we'll have to go all the way back to the front of the house."

Magdalena bit her lips and clenched her fists. She'd never in her life felt so helpless. Did she really have to decide between Georg and Barbara? The twins, so different from one another, were like her own children. How often she'd given them a good-night kiss or sung them a song. She'd watched them grow up, and now she had to decide their fate in this lonely house in the forest. Was this really the end?

What shall I do? Oh, God, help me. What shall I do?

Bartholomäus had pulled the groaning Georg to his feet, but it was clear he couldn't walk by himself.

"Hurry up!" Bartholomäus yelled, tugging at her dress. "This whole place is about to collapse."

"I . . . I can't," she mumbled, as the wooden floor beneath her got hotter and hotter. The first tongues of fire were already licking through the cracks.

"You must." Bartholomäus gave her a shove. "Do you want to burn to death? Is that what you want? Do you want Georg to die along with you just because you can't decide?"

"Georg won't die," she replied in a flat voice. "I'll help you take him out, but then I'm coming back to look for Father and Barbara. I'll never . . ."

At that moment a form emerged out of the smoke from one of the doorways. The man coughed, but he stood up straight. He waved the smoke aside with his hands and staggered toward them. For a moment, Magdalena thought it was a ghost.

But then the ghost started to speak, and she knew who it was.

"Out! Get out, all three of you," Jeremias said. "I know where Barbara is, and I'll get her out, just as surely as I am the former executioner of Bamberg." He shuffled quickly past them. "And now, please get out. This is my job."

Somewhere far below, several timbers could be heard collapsing.

17

Outside, in front of the house, Simon nervously clutched the pistol in his hand. The wind had become stronger, the tops of the trees creaked and groaned, and the howling of the wind made it almost impossible to hear what was happening inside the house.

It had been quite a while since Magdalena, Georg, and Bartholomäus had entered. Simon had thought it best to stay behind the thornbush and wait to see what happened. From there he could keep an eye on everything, and if necessary he could . . .

He hesitated.

Indeed, what can I do?

It was his job to stop the abductor if he should leave the building, but no one had told Simon how to do that. Suspiciously, he eyed the loaded weapon in his hand. He probably wouldn't have any luck with the old firearm unless Salter was standing directly in front of him, and even then it was questionable whether it would fire.

Simon sighed and wiped a few raindrops out of his face. Until just a while ago, at least he had Jeremias at his side, but during the long wait, the old man had had less and less to say. He had just stared at the dilapidated hunting house, shaking his head from time to time and mumbling softly to himself. It looked like he was thinking it all over. Once or twice, during brief lulls in the wind gusts, Simon thought he heard muffled cries coming from the house. What was going on in there, anyway? Should he go to have a look? He never should have let Magdalena enter the house. But once his wife had put her mind to something, it was very hard to get her to change.

Impossible, actually . . .

Just as he'd made up his mind to sneak up closer to the house, smoke had suddenly started pouring out of some of the windows, and flames suddenly burst out of them.

At that moment, Jeremias stood up and ran toward the house, where he disappeared through one of the other windows.

Leaving Simon alone.

The iron pistol in his hand felt cold and in a strange way reassuring, but his fear grew nonetheless, as well as a gnawing uncertainty that tormented him and paralyzed him. Almost his entire family was over there in that strange building, which was burning down before his eyes. He couldn't just stand idly by. He had to help. But how? Should he perhaps rush into the burning house hoping to find Magdalena and the others there? But what if . . . ?

Suddenly, very close to him, there was a menacing growl, deep, almost like an approaching whirlwind.

The werewolf, Simon thought.

But then he scolded himself for being such a fool. Good Lord, there was no such thing as a werewolf, there was only a madman taking his cruel revenge—and he was over there in the house and not here in the thornbush.

But what was it then?

Again he heard growling and a rustling sound as if something large was creeping through the thicket.

Right toward him.

That was more than he could take. With the pistol in his hand, he ran toward the building, where smoke was now pouring out on all sides. He turned around a few times but couldn't see anything in the darkness.

But he did see something right in front of him.

Two figures, a man and a woman, came crawling out of a cellar door. At first he thought they were Jakob and Barbara, but as they came closer, that hope vanished. The man was far thinner and shorter than the hangman, and the woman at his side was considerably older than his sister-in-law. He didn't know either of them, but he guessed the man was Markus Salter. He was holding a knife to the throat of the woman and pushing her in front of him.

With a determined look, he pointed his weapon at the abductor. Finally he knew what he had to do. He was trembling slightly and hoped Salter wouldn't notice it.

"Stay right where you are, you rotten scoundrel," he shouted, "and drop your dagger if you value your life."

Only now did Salter appear to notice him in the darkness. With a calm, relaxed demeanor, he turned to Simon. Simon was astonished. The man in front of him looked sensitive and intelligent, not anyone Simon would expect to commit such a dastardly crime.

"When my life ends is something I'll determine myself," Markus said so softly that Simon could barely understand him over the sound of the wind and the raging fire. "And the final curtain has not fallen."

Not until now did Simon have a chance to look more closely at the woman whose hands were clearly shackled. She looked haggard and drawn, and her dress was soiled and ripped. She was no doubt one of the people Salter had abducted. Were there others trapped down below in the burning cellar? If so, they had little chance of making it out alive.

"Where is Barbara?" Simon demanded with a trembling voice. "The hangman's girl? What did you do with her, you devil?"

"So *that's* what you want to know?" Salter smiled. "Are you one of her relatives? It must really be a large family, almost as large as mine was once." The smile vanished. "I'll make you an offer: I'll tell you where Barbara is, and you'll let the two of us go."

"By God, if she's still down there, I'll shoot your head off," Simon replied grimly, pointing at the barrel of the gun.

Salter gave him an innocent look. "Who says she's there? Perhaps I've taken her somewhere else altogether."

"She's . . ." the woman started to gasp, but Salter pressed the knife closer to her throat.

"Don't say another word, or you're dead," he hissed, then turned back to Simon. "Well, what do you say? Throw the pistol away and I'll talk."

"And suppose you don't? What do I do then?" Simon asked.

Markus Salter smiled. "That's just the risk you have to take."

Simon took a deep breath. What should he do? Accept the madman's offer? He was about to go into a long-winded reply just to buy time, when out of the corner of his eye he saw someone climbing out of the shaft. And this time he was quite sure who it was.

It was Jakob Kuisl.

Salter couldn't see him, as his back was to the building, and Kuisl was still a good thirty yards behind him. The hangman raised his hand in a warning, as he evidently had recognized Simon.

I've got to stall him, Simon thought. *Just a bit, until Jakob is close enough.*

"What a splendid hideaway you have here," he said, while continuing to grip the pistol firmly. "It's too bad it's all going up in flames."

Salter shrugged. "I don't need it anymore; my work is done, though I do regret the loss of the . . ." — he hesitated — "let's just say the *props*. Some of them were valuable pieces I was able to acquire from experienced smiths in Forchheim, but most of them were fortunately already there."

"You mean the torturing tools?" Simon asked with surprise.

"I prefer the word *props,*" Salter smiled. "I discovered this house on our last visit to Bamberg. People avoid it because they think it's haunted, and for that reason no one has searched the old cellar, not even the Swedes back during the Great War. The former owner had a strange hobby. I found a rack down there, thumbscrews, Spanish boots, tongs . . . It was like God was giving me a sign. My revenge could finally begin."

Simon carefully looked behind the actor, where Jakob approached, step by step. He seemed to be limping. Apparently he'd had an accident in the house, and Simon could only hope his injuries weren't so serious that he couldn't overpower Salter.

"But why now?" he asked. "So many years have passed. Why couldn't you forget? Why . . ."

"I wanted to forget!" Salter interrupted, still threatening his struggling victim with the knife. Beads of sweat stood out on his forehead. "Believe me, I didn't want all of this. But then half a year ago I came back to Bamberg. I saw these fat patricians at the performances, some of them the same men responsible for killing my family. They'd made comfortable lives for themselves with my family's fortune, while I scraped along as a poor actor. But I learned all about them — where they lived, their habits, trips, political intrigues. I assumed many disguises to get close to them, and, lo and behold, old Gotzendörfer actually lived in one of our former houses that he'd acquired for next to nothing, and I surprised greedy old Vasold in front of a house that once belonged to our mighty family. What a stroke of luck." He smiled, but then his face turned serious and grim again. "It was hardest with Sebastian Harsee. This son of the former chairman of the

Witches Commission, this swine, had made it all the way to the post of Bamberg suffragan bishop, even though his father was the mastermind behind the plot to destroy our family."

"You had to make sure Sebastian Harsee would die in this unspeakably horrible way," Simon said.

"Ha! You figured it out? You know the true story of Romeo and Juliet?" Salter's mouth twisted into a grimace. "The suffragan bishop was my masterpiece. It all began with him. A few months ago I came upon a dying fox here in the forest and got the idea of poisoning my two darlings with rabies. With Juliet it didn't work, but it did with Romeo. I sold some religious writings to Harsee, and in this way gained access to his rooms. Then Romeo kissed him." He giggled. "I made Harsee my werewolf, the one responsible for all these horrible murders. It took a long time, almost too long, but finally he got sick just at the right time. The suffragan bishop, this bigoted zealot, finally became a warlock himself, and people believed he was prowling through the streets in the animal pelts. But it was always me — the last heir of the family that his power-hungry father destroyed."

"Harsee almost found you out," Simon replied. "He sent his guards to watch your actors, and that's when you planted the pelts on Matheo."

Salter shrugged. "I'm sorry about Matheo, but what could I do? They were hot on my heels. Later, I steered the suspicions toward Sir Malcolm. I smuggled the child's skull and other odds and ends into his chest, just in case they were looking for a suspect."

Jakob was now just a few steps behind Salter and beckoned to Simon to keep talking.

"I can understand why you wanted to take revenge on the members of the Witches Commission," said Simon, "but why these innocent women . . . ?"

"They are just as innocent as the members of my own family!" Salter screamed, squeezing the blond woman's neck until she started to suffocate. "Their only quarrel was with my grandfather, but they went ahead and killed the entire family, because they were afraid of our revenge. Now I'm taking my vengeance out on them in the same way." His eyes narrowed to tiny slits. "The only one who had disappeared without a trace was the former hangman. It was said he left no family. Then Barbara and I crossed paths. She told me that all hangmen are related and view each other as cousins. Michael Binder and Bartholomäus Kuisl, for example, so she, his niece, had to die as a member of the great family of hangmen. An eye for an eye, a tooth for a tooth."

Simon was stunned. What had Salter just said?

She, his niece, had to die . . .

Did that mean that Barbara was in fact already dead? And how about Magdalena and the others?

At that moment, Jakob reached the unsuspecting Salter, jumped on him from behind with a hoarse shout, and all three fell to the ground. The woman began shouting now, too, as Salter was still holding her like a shield between himself and Jakob. The knife disappeared in the tumult.

Frozen to the spot, Simon stood just a few steps away, observing. He felt the cold iron of the pistol in his hand again. Had the moment finally come to use it? But what would happen if he shot the wrong person?

"Stop!" he shouted desperately as he fumbled around with the pistol. "Stop at once or I'll shoot!"

But the two men had no intention of stopping. Simon saw now that Jakob looked battered, almost numbed. The smoke in the house must have made him dizzy, and he was bleeding from several wounds to his head.

Finally, the woman, still in shackles, managed to squirm free of the two unequal opponents and rolled to one side, where she lay huffing. Next to her, the fight continued. Markus was nowhere near as strong as the hangman, but he was nimble and had a very athletic build. The hangman, weighing nearly two hundred pounds, was sitting on top of him, but just as he prepared to throw a punch, Salter picked up a handful of dirt and threw it in his face. In the following confusion, he slipped away from Jakob, but instead of fleeing, he angrily attacked the blinded hangman with all the power of a madman.

"You . . . are . . . really a big, damn family," he panted, as he punched the dazed hangman again and again. "How . . . many . . . of . . . you do I have to send to hell?"

Now Simon could not wait another moment. Holding his breath, he aimed even as Salter seemed to be jumping in all directions, then finally pulled the trigger.

"You can go to hell yourself!" Simon cried, trembling and panting, expecting a large explosion.

There was a soft click, and nothing else. The powder had not ignited.

Salter stopped briefly, then broke out in loud laughter.

"You would make a good actor," he giggled. "I almost thought the weapon was loaded. That's the reason I seldom use a pistol, except on the stage. Sometimes just a stone is enough, and just as deadly."

He reached for a large rock, raised his arms, and was about to bring it crashing down on the groaning hangman when all of a sudden there was a threatening growl.

Simon cringed. It was the same growl he'd heard earlier in the thornbush.

A deep rumble, like that of an approaching whirlwind.

"What in the world . . . ?" Salter mumbled, looking around.

Out of the darkness a vague shape came charging at the two combatants. It was bright, almost white, and was as large as a calf.

The werewolf! Simon thought. *So there is such a thing.*

Like a monster from hell, the beast attacked Salter, who was paralyzed with fear, and tore him away from Jakob. The flames were not very bright, so all Simon saw was the outlines of a very unequal fight. Salter screamed as the beast, with its powerful jaws, ripped off his jerkin and shirt and finally tore open his chest. With flaring nostrils, the beast sniffed at the blood-streaked upper torso of his victim and finally located the throat.

Markus's screams stopped abruptly as the huge fangs clamped down on his neck. He twitched violently a few times, his legs thrashing uncontrollably, as the beast ripped apart his throat and drank his blood. Finally, Markus lay there motionless.

The creature raised his head and stared at Simon.

For the first time, the medicus looked at the animal and realized how huge it was. It had short, pointed ears, a stubby face, and a wide mouth with jowls that hung down over a row of sharp teeth. Its red eyes glowed faintly like tiny jack-o'-lanterns, and its rib cage was much too large and wide for its head, as if the creature had been cobbled together from differing races of hounds. Its fur was a grayish white with massive forelegs and huge paws. It was the size of a young bear and spattered with blood. It seemed to have been created with just one purpose.

To kill.

Simon regarded it with a mixture of horror and awe. It wasn't a werewolf, but clearly some kind of dog.

But it was at least just as dangerous.

Once again, the animal gave that threatening growl. Jakob was still lying stunned and motionless on the forest floor just a few steps from the monster, which approached him now, sniffing loudly.

Simon felt his whole body quiver. What would the beast do to his father-in-law?

"Hurry up and shoot!" screamed the woman, who had sought refuge behind a bush. "Shoot before it kills us all!"

Simon was going to reply that his weapon was old and useless, but he took out the gun again and aimed.

*I have to try, at least, before the beast eats my father-in-law alive.
I have to try. Lord, help me . . .*

He pulled the trigger.

This time there was a loud report, a bright flash in front of
him, and a recoil that traveled up through his hand like a whip-
lash. He shouted and dropped the burning hot pistol, thinking
he'd gone blind, but then he heard a whimper, opened his eyes,
and saw the monster in spasms on the ground. Blood flowed over
the white fur of the animal's chest. It gasped, and its legs kicked
as if it were running through an imaginary meadow.

Then suddenly it froze.

I hit it. The realization went through Simon like a shot. *I actually hit the beast.*

For a few moments, the world seemed to stand still. In the
background flames shot up even higher toward the roof of the
hunting lodge, the wind howled, and the firs bent and groaned
under the force of the howling wind.

Then he heard a cry from inside the building.

"Brutus! My God, Brutus! What have they done to you?"

Simon looked toward the burning main entrance, where
Magdalena and Bartholomäus were standing, holding a stunned-
looking Georg between them.

Bartholomäus let go of him and hobbled toward the dead
dog.

"Brutus, my dear little Brutus," he wept. "Why did you have
to run away from me?"

Magdalena was in the clearing with Georg, who stood there
moaning as the flames slowly crept up to the roof of the lodge.
The wind had died down a bit now, but it was still blowing hard
enough to turn the building into a fiery inferno. The events of
the last few hours had shocked Magdalena. As if in a trance she'd
helped Bartholomäus carry her injured brother through rooms

full of fire and smoke, past stuffed, mice-infested heads of stags and wild boar, smoldering furniture, and wall hangings full of holes, with flames licking up them toward the ceiling.

She shouted, cried, wailed. Barbara and her father had to be somewhere in the house, but she couldn't help them. The only one who might still save them was a crippled old man, but he too had presumably already been consumed in the flames or had suffocated in the smoke.

They'd finally reached the front doorway, coughing, when they heard a shot outside. Some distance away, Magdalena saw Simon and a woman she didn't know, but the man on the ground had to be her father. Alongside him was something white that she couldn't quite make out. A wave of relief came over her. Her father had escaped the hellish flames.

And Barbara? How about Barbara and Jeremias?

Bartholomäus let go of Georg and ran toward the group, so Magdalena dragged her brother the last few steps by herself, finally letting him down gently on the ground.

"Everything will be all right," she mumbled, almost like a prayer she was saying just for herself. "Everything will work out."

Shortly after, she was standing around the canine cadaver with the others, while Bartholomäus leaned down to it as if it were a dead child, stroking the blood-spattered pelt and speaking soft words of consolation. Simon, in the meantime, had run over to care for Georg and stanch the blood coming from the wound on his leg with a few strips of material from his torn shirt. Markus Salter lay a short distance away, ripped apart like a wild animal slaughtered in the hunt, but no one paid attention to him.

"I can only do the most basic things for your brother," Simon said grimly, turning to Magdalena as he tightened the bandage. "The wound is quite deep. The boy urgently needs medicine so the wound doesn't become infected." He also pointed to Magdalena's father, sitting silently and dejectedly on an overturned tree trunk nearby. "And your father also needs bandaging. That crazy scoundrel hit him hard in the head several times. But he won't let anyone help him."

"Don't you understand? He's thinking of Barbara," Magdalena snapped, as her whole body began to tremble. "We're all thinking about Barbara. Except you, apparently."

"Perhaps she's not even in the burning house," Simon ventured, trying to console her. "Salter indicated he'd possibly taken her somewhere else."

"She's inside," said a soft voice alongside them. It was the blond woman who'd introduced herself earlier as Adelheid Rinswieser, the Bamberg apothecary's wife who had been missing for more than a week. "Barbara was his last victim," she continued sadly, "along with that old scribe." Timidly, she placed her hand on Magdalena's shoulder. "I'm so sorry."

Magdalena felt something wet on her cheeks—tears, running down her face in streams. She felt as if someone had kicked her hard in the stomach.

"I must go and see Father," she mumbled in a flat voice. "He needs me now."

She stood up and walked over to Jakob, who was still sitting alone on the tree trunk, looking like a craggy boulder in a forest clearing that had been washed up there ages ago. She sat down alongside him, and together they stared into the crackling flames now rising over the roof of the old lodge.

"It's my fault," the hangman said suddenly. "I was so . . . angry. I went charging in there all by myself, like a wild bull. Bartl is right. I am a good-for-nothing."

"Father, what are you saying?" Magdalena replied in a soft voice. "You couldn't have stopped it. All of us—"

She stopped short, suddenly seeing another figure staggering out the front door. Burning wooden beams from the roof came crashing down, and glowing shingles flew through the air, but the figure staggered on. Only now did Magdalena see it was Jeremias, holding something in his arms carefully, like a treasure.

It was a delicate human form, wrapped tightly in a blackened monk's robe, but Magdalena knew right away who it was.

"Barbara!" she shouted, running toward the two.

Magdalena's cries tore Jakob out of his profound grief.

He thought at first his mind was playing tricks on him, but then he looked up and could see Jeremias stumbling toward the group, holding the motionless girl in his arms. He jumped up, rushed the few steps over to the two, and took his daughter in his huge, muscular arms. He hadn't cried since the death of his wife, but now tears ran down over his bearded, smoke-blackened face.

"Barbara, Barbara," he sobbed. "My little girl, I'm so sorry."

Magdalena and the others had come running over as well. Barbara's hair had almost all been singed away, and her face and fingers were covered with soot and little red burn blisters. Her hands and feet were still in shackles, though the ropes were singed. Her chest moved rapidly up and down, like that of a sick little bird. "At least she's still breathing," Simon said, carefully examining her. "This heavy monk's robe apparently saved her life. The material must have been soaked with rain and kept the worst of the heat out." Carefully he helped Jakob lay the unconscious girl down on the forest floor, and together they removed the steaming robe, singed at the edges.

"Bring me some water," the medicus cried. "Quick!"

Jakob ran to a nearby pool of water and scooped up some water in his hat, then they washed Barbara's face and gave her a bit to drink. She opened her eyes, looked briefly at Jakob and the others, and a smile spread across her face.

"Father," she murmured. "You didn't abandon me. I'm thirsty . . ." Then she passed out again.

"You will have all the water in the world, my little girl, if you just stay with us," Jakob whispered, moistening Barbara's dry lips with a few drops he squeezed out of a wet handkerchief.

"I think she'll make it through," Simon said after carefully inspecting her burns. "But I do need a few healing herbs both for her and for Georg as soon as possible, and we can only get those back in town." He sighed. "For the time being, I'd be happy if we could just find a bit of shepherd's purse or a handful of elderberry leaves to prevent an inflammation."

"I can get you elderberry leaves," Magdalena interrupted excitedly, pointing back at the burning building. "I think there's a big elderberry tree alongside the house that still has some of its leaves." Without saying another word, she disappeared in the darkness while Simon and Jakob continued caring for the wounded.

This now included Jeremias. Along with his old scars he now had some burn wounds, and he wheezed with every breath.

Jakob bent down and gently took his badly burned hand. "Thank you," he said, his voice trembling. "Thank you for saving my daughter."

"I owed that to our Lord God," Jeremias groaned. "One life for another. I never should have killed Clara, even if she would have betrayed me, that devious, calculating wench. I had no right to do that."

"Only God has the right to take a life," Jakob replied. "We hangmen are only his tools."

Jeremias smiled. "If that's the case, I'm an often-used tool, ragged and old and beyond repair." He coughed dryly.

"How did you know where Barbara was in there?" Jakob asked. "How could you find her, and I couldn't?"

Jeremias had another coughing fit, this time spitting out blood mixed with soot. "I . . . remembered," he finally croaked. "Long ago I was here, as a very young hangman's servant. The master of the hunt at that time was a cruel man. If he caught poachers, he liked to string them up himself, but sometimes he tortured them beforehand, in order to learn something about their accomplices. He had his own private torture chamber down in the cellar. My father and I helped him set it up." He gave Jakob a sad look. "I've seen so much evil in my life, cousin, and there are many things I've tried to forget, but I wasn't always successful."

"I have nightmares myself sometimes," Jakob admitted, almost inaudibly. "Like my father, like Bartl, like all of us who have to do this dirty work for the patricians. We must never let our bad dreams weigh us down."

He looked down at Jeremias almost sympathetically. The horrible events in his earlier life as Michael Binder had robbed the old man of all feeling, and possibly made him a bit mad, but now, at the end, he appeared to be returning to what he once was, a young man in love with his Carlotta.

"I couldn't save the old scribe," Jeremias gasped, again and again interrupted by dry coughs. "The entire room was already in flames. I found Barbara in a little room across the hall. It seems she had sought shelter there, where the flames were not so . . ." He shuddered and grimaced with pain. "Damn! This hurts almost as much as before, when I threw myself into the trough of lye."

Jakob wanted to remove Jeremias's shirt to get a better look at the wounds, but the blackened material had eaten its way into the flesh. The hangman saw that it was too late for any help.

"Just forget it," Jeremias murmured. "Sooner or later the end will come, even for an executioner. Look after your children instead." He smiled. "You've got such great children. You can't say enough about them. I wish I had such wonderful children myself." He clung to Jakob as another wave of pain coursed through his body. "Just one more thing," he said. "I've got to know it before I go. Would you have turned me in to the city guards? Tell me, would you?"

Jakob hesitated. "I think I would, yes," he finally said. "Every crime must someday be atoned for."

Jeremias let go of him and closed his eyes. "You're . . . a . . . good . . . man, Kuisl," he whispered. Then his head fell to one side.

Jakob listened to his heart, then took his own singed coat and laid it over the old man, as if he were just sleeping. There was still a smile playing over his lips.

He looked as if he was at peace.

With a sigh, Jakob turned to the others. Barbara was in a deep sleep, but her breath was now more even. Simon had washed her, so her skin no longer appeared as black and burned. Alongside her, Georg groaned loudly in pain, but evidently the wolf trap at least had not severed a tendon, and he was able to hobble around. Jakob himself still felt a bit dizzy from the smoke and the blows to his head, but he'd gotten far worse beatings before in bar-house brawls.

Just the same, this jackass nearly killed me, he thought. *By God, I'm really getting too old . . .*

Simon knelt down alongside the cadaver of the dead dog, examining it with Bartholomäus. The medicus looked like he was thinking it all over, trying to find some idea lurking in his mind.

"I think Brutus really was rabid," he told Bartholomäus, who appeared to have somewhat gotten over his sorrow at the loss of his pet. "All the foam around its mouth, this sudden attack, its rage, its trembling legs . . . And Salter's prisoner, this apothecary's wife, just told me the poor animal had been prowling around the house for a long time, rooting around and digging."

"When I went looking around for him here with Aloysius, he must have been very close by." Bartholomäus paused to think, then stood up and washed his bloody hands carefully in a puddle nearby. "God knows where it picked up that infection, but if Brutus had rabies, that would explain his random, savage killing of animals in the forest and why he attacked Salter in such a rage." He winked at Jakob. "But it's possible the dog mixed up the two of us and thought his master was being attacked."

"I always knew dogs were stupid," Jakob answered dryly. "Who could have mixed up the two of us?"

"You're more alike than you want to admit. When will you two squabblers finally realize that?" It was Magdalena. With a broad smile, she returned from the burning house holding in her hands her scarf, knotted together and full of leaves and herbs. "Here's good news for a change," she said, holding the scarf up triumphantly. "I found not just elderberry shrubs in the wild garden, but also an old overgrown patch of herbs. Now, in late autumn, there wasn't much there, but the flames from the house were so bright I was able to find some dried shepherd's purse and buckhorn." She gazed over at the hunting lodge, where the upper story had collapsed. Black smoke rose up into the night sky like a giant, admonishing finger. Magdalena suddenly pursed her lips.

"But even these herbs weren't able to save Hieronymus Hauser," she said darkly. "Katharina's father burned to death in there. What a terrible end for the old man." She handed the folded scarf full of herbs to Simon and helped him and her father as they crushed them in their hands and laid them on Barbara's and Georg's wounds. They also tore Bartholomäus's coat into long strips to serve as bandages.

"I don't think the old scribe suffered for very long," Adelheid Rinswieser replied after a while. She had been given Magdalena's woolen coat and stood off to one side shivering and still looking dazed. "He was already unconscious when Salter dragged me out of the room. He may have suffocated without ever regaining consciousness."

"A merciful death for someone who bought his fortune with the blood of others," Bartholomäus growled, staring wistfully into the burning house. "As the scribe for the Witches Commission, Hieronymus made a lot of money back then during the trials, and I see now how he could afford that beautiful house by the Sand Gate. Basically, I never really liked him; he was a very calculating person."

"But he did agree to his daughter's engagement to the executioner," Jakob reminded him.

Bartholomäus gestured dismissively. "If Katharina will even take me anymore," he said sadly. "After everything that's happened in the last few days, I'm not so sure."

Suddenly the sound of a hunting horn could be heard in the distance. Jakob looked around in astonishment.

"Damn! Who is that? At this time of day it's certainly not the bishop out hunting. Perhaps good old Answin?"

"Ah, not exactly," said Simon, as he cleared his throat and applied the last bandage. "I must confess I told Captain Lebrecht and the city guards before we left. Aloysius was kind enough to tip off the guards, and now it seems we can put them to good use here," he said, pointing at Barbara and Georg, "if only to transport the injured and put out the fire before it spreads to the forest." He rubbed his nose in embarrassment, then grinned. "They could also help us with a plan I've been thinking about for a long time that might end this miserable werewolf story once and for all."

"A plan? Ha! I thought you were just scared," Jakob replied with a smile. "Why do I have such a pussyfooter as a son-in-law?" He chuckled. "But then you went and killed a real live werewolf. What silly old bathhouse medicus can say that of himself?"

A few minutes later, the guards arrived. There were almost a dozen of them, led by Bamberg's Captain Martin Lebrecht.

Meanwhile, Simon had been trying to figure out how to win over the captain. The plan he'd thought up while investigating Brutus's cadaver was quite risky, and it all depended on Lebrecht going along with it.

Him—and the apothecary's wife.

The captain nodded when he saw the burning building.

"Maybe it's better that this building is finally going up in flames," he said, mostly to himself. "There was always something evil about it. I've heard that all sorts of riff-raff and weird people hung out here. I should have had it torn down long ago."

He gave a sign to the guards, and they fanned out to extinguish some small fires smoldering in the woods despite the heavy rain they'd had earlier. Only then did he turn to the small group of wretched-looking people in front of him. Simon had quickly covered Salter's corpse and the dog's cadaver with brush in order to avoid premature questions. Jeremias's corpse, however, still lay there, covered only with Jakob's coat, alongside Barbara, who had passed out again, and Georg, who propped himself up on a makeshift crutch, pale and with clenched teeth.

"Jesus, Mary, and Joseph!" the captain burst out. "What the hell happened here? And whose corpse is that lying there?" He leaned down, holding his torch.

"Well, ah . . . it's a long story," Simon replied. "Perhaps it would be better if we talk about it in private first."

"When you first called for us, I wasn't sure if we should even come, but now . . ." He frowned and looked at the victims as if trying to make sense of it all. "But why not? My men have other things to do now, anyway. Tell me what happened."

Simon took a deep breath. Now he'd see if his plan would work.

"We caught the werewolf," he began in a firm voice. "Actually two of them—one an animal and one human. Come and see for yourself." He took Lebrecht off to one side, where Markus

Salter's corpse and Brutus's cadaver lay underneath a brush pile. Simon pulled the branches aside and the captain blanched.

"My God," he gasped. "*This* is the werewolf? And the man alongside it is one of those actors. Did that monster mangle him? And what brave fellow finally killed the beast?"

Simon blushed. "Ah . . . that was me. But allow me to start at the beginning."

He tried to explain as briefly as possible — the witch trial of Chancellor Haan and his family, Salter's former life as Wolf Christoph Röhm, and his plans for revenge that cost the life of the suffragan bishop. In conclusion, he explained how the trail led to the old hunting lodge, where there was a life-and-death battle.

"Salter often dressed up as a werewolf to spread fear in the city. First he observed his many victims, then he abducted them, and finally tortured and killed them in this abandoned hunting lodge," Simon concluded, as the captain listened in astonishment, his mouth agape. "As a former law student he had precise knowledge of the different degrees of torture, just as they are described in the Bamberg *Constitutio Criminalis,* the criminal code. Salter punished his prisoners exactly the same way members of his own family had been tortured, tit for tat . . ."

He pointed at the pale Adelheid Rinswieser, who up to then had been standing in the background. "The honorable wife of apothecary Rinswieser and my young sister-in-law are the only survivors, and they can confirm all of this for you. There was no werewolf, only a man in search of revenge. Markus Salter *alias* Wolf Christoph Röhm wanted to incite a panic in the city, just like the one back then during the witch trials in which everyone in the city would point a finger at his or her neighbors. You must admit he succeeded."

Lebrecht looked around suspiciously. "Do you mean to say this Röhm fellow duped my men up in the old castle by present-

ing them with a dead wolf and putting on a show of hocus-pocus?"

"Ah, well . . ." For a brief moment Simon seemed uncertain,
but Magdalena came to his defense.

"Evidently he wanted to free his friend Matheo, because he
knew he was innocent and the wolf pelts actually belonged to
him," she suggested with a straight face. "The dead wolf was
only a distraction, and your night watchmen promptly fell for it.
It's quite possible they had a bit too much to drink." She winked
at the captain. "They say people who make their own schnapps
at home sometime meet the devil in person."

"Hmm . . ." the captain scratched his unshaved chin. "That's
possible. In fact, I found an empty bottle in the guardhouse, and
the horror stories the fellows came up with made it seem too
much like they had a bad conscience. I thought—"

"—that it was the bishop's baboon you'd been looking for
for so long?" Magdalena interrupted. "Well, the baboon could
hardly have killed the wolf."

Lebrecht looked at her severely. "Didn't I tell you not to reveal a word about that in public?"

Simon raised his hands apologetically. "Trust us; we'll be
sure to keep this little secret, as I'm embarrassed I didn't realize
earlier what was going on. I visited the bishop's menagerie along
with Master Samuel and saw the empty monkey cage there. But
at the time I was too occupied with other things."

"This damned monkey has been driving me crazy," said Lebrecht. "I'd like to put a stone around his neck and throw him in
the Regnitz, but then the prince bishop would probably throw
me in after him," he sighed. "Oh, well, now the beast is back in
its cage." He shook his head in amazement. "And His Excellency
Sebastian Harsee was indeed infected with rabies, you say?
Damn, and I thought he'd been bitten by a real werewolf." He
gazed across the clearing, now illuminated by torches, where the

guards were still on the lookout for smoldering fires and pulling apart some of the burning timbers. "Actually, the bishop's master of the hunt told me just last week there had been an increase in rabies cases in Bamberg Forest. He had to put down a few foxes and wolves."

Lebrecht hesitated, then pointed at the huge dog cadaver. "That brings me to the matter of this dog. You said there was no werewolf. So what is that? And what's a beast like that doing here in the forest so close to the city?"

"That's something you should hear about from someone else."

Simon stared at Bartholomäus, waiting for him to speak up, but he just stood there defiantly, his arms crossed. After a while, Jakob gave his brother a kick in the shins. Bartholomäus glared at him briefly, then hesitantly started talking.

"The dog is an alaunt, an ancient race, which I have reintroduced," he said. "It escaped from the knacker's house and somehow got infected with rabies, the poor animal."

"*Poor animal?*" Lebrecht scoffed. "It's a damned monster, Master Bartholomäus. Do you have permission from the bishop to keep this animal?"

Bartholomäus lowered his eyes. "No, I don't. No one except us knows it even exists."

"You see, that's just what I was getting around to." Simon beamed, as he always did when he had what he thought was brilliant plan. He turned to the Bamberg executioner. "So nobody knows about this dog?"

"That's right," said Bartholomäus, folding his arms. "Didn't I just say that?"

"Well, then I'd like to introduce you all to the real werewolf." With a dramatic gesture he pointed at Brutus, with his huge body, muscular chest, and long teeth, still looking very dangerous, even in death. "Here it is."

Martin Lebrecht looked at him, confused. "Now I don't understand a word. You just said there was no werewolf."

"Correct, there is no such thing, but we still need a beast like that for the people, because until they see it lying dead in front of them, they'll keep looking for it. That would mean more suspects, more trials, and more innocent people thrown into prison, tortured, or even burned at the stake."

Simon leaned down to the dead Brutus, grabbing him by the neck and struggling to lift him up, so that the dog's eyes seemed to glare diabolically at the group.

"The people need evil. It must lie dead in front of them or they will never believe it has been vanquished," he continued. "Brutus is our werewolf. He's big, looks strange and dangerous, and above all, he has already been captured and is dead. We'll never find a better scapegoat."

"Just a moment," Bartholomäus interrupted. "Do you think my dear Brutus abducted and killed all these people?"

"Yes, a truly horrible beast." Simon nodded, with a dark, theatrical look in his eyes. "And not just that. Brutus prowled the streets of Bamberg and put a curse on the suffragan bishop, turning him into a werewolf as well. Believe me, when we show Brutus to the citizenry, many of them will remember having seen him—in the night, in a dark corner of the city, on their way home from the tavern . . . They'll remember how they barely managed to elude him, and even the guards up in the old castle will be convinced this is the real werewolf."

"You can just forget about that," Lebrecht sneered, shaking his head. "You'll never get away with it. The Bamberg bishop will never . . ."

"Suppose I told you we had His Excellency Bishop Johann Philipp von Schönborn on our side—a real, living elector?" Simon interrupted sternly. "Just today, Schönborn assured me he completely supports us. He wants to make sure this case does not turn into something like what happened forty years ago. *How* we prevent that is entirely up to us — those were his words exactly." He smiled with pursed lips. "And Bishop Rieneck certainly won't oppose Schönborn's wishes, especially since he depends on the money he gets from his powerful friend to finish his palace. Don't you agree?"

There was a tense silence, and Simon thought he could hear Jakob and Bartholomäus suddenly inhaling between their teeth in surprise.

"You have the support of the elector?" Martin Lebrecht swallowed visibly. "Well, that's naturally something else. We, ah . . . could at least give it a try."

"How nice." Simon winked, then clapped his hands with determination. "So I'll ask you now for the following, Captain: call your men to come over, and tell them about this terrible werewolf. Tell them we killed the beast in a heroic struggle in which we suffered some injured and dead. Then we'll tie the beast to a heavy branch, carry it to the Green Market in Bamberg, and put it in the stocks for all to see, so they will know it's dead and this horrible time has finally come to an end."

Lebrecht hesitated, then pointed with concern to the unconscious Barbara and to Adelheid Rinswieser, who had been following the conversation closely, as had the others. "But how about those two? They know that's not the truth."

Simon turned to Adelheid and looked at her intently. He was sure Barbara would keep quiet, as it was even doubtful she had heard much of what was going on that night, but what about the apothecary's wife?

It all depends on that, he thought. *Will she help us? Will she understand how important this plan is for the future of the city?*

"I shall keep my silence," Adelheid finally said in a soft voice. "Everything will have happened just as you said. The werewolf abducted me. It cast a spell on me. I only awoke today in this hunting lodge, and that will be all I have to say."

Simon breathed a sigh of relief, but the captain still appeared uncertain, biting his lips and studying the huge, bloody cadaver.

Suddenly Jakob Kuisl stepped forward, seized the beast in one hand, and held it up like a light bundle of fur.

"Damn it! Just cut out all this foolishness," he growled. "I seldom compliment my son-in-law, as you know, but this time he really has a sensible idea. I'm telling you, string this beast up on the gallows in Bamberg for everyone to see, and then we'll finally get back our peace and quiet—and I can return to Schongau." He dropped the carcass as Bartholomäus, standing behind him, groaned.

"On the gallows? A dog?" A smile spread across the captain's face, then he burst out laughing. "Damn! That's the craziest thing I've ever heard, but since we have the blessing of a real elector and the experience of two executioners, let's try it. *Men!*"

He motioned to the guards, who quickly gathered around Brutus's cadaver and began talking excitedly. Some crossed themselves or murmured a prayer, while others bent down carefully, tore off a piece of the hide or dipped their fingers in the congealing blood of the massive hound.

"There he is, our werewolf," Martin Lebrecht proclaimed theatrically. "The hunt is finally over. Thank God! Now let's take the beast to Bamberg and tell the people what has happened here."

The men cheered even as they cast furtive looks at the cadaver, as if fearing it might suddenly come back to life and attack them.

While the soldiers looked around in the forest for a suitable branch to transport the carcass, Jakob carefully picked up his daughter and made his way down to the river, where Answin's boat was waiting, and Bartholomäus looked after Georg, who came along behind. It was a strangely moving scene as the Bamberg executioner and his nephew hobbled away together into the night. When Adelheid Rinswieser had also said her last farewell, Magdalena turned to Simon with a knowing look.

"Tell me, that business about the Würzburg bishop," she asked in a quiet voice. "Is that true? Is the elector really on our side?"

Simon smiled and shrugged. "Well, I think Johann Philipp von Schönborn will support us if I tell him about it. In any case, he told me he will support us as much as possible. The Würzburg bishop is a reasonable man who doesn't believe in magicians and witches, nor in werewolves, either. But so far . . ."—he winked—"well, he doesn't know any more about it than the rest of Bamberg."

He laughed and embraced Magdalena. "Simon, Simon," she said. "You're a scaredy-cat, a swindler, and—"

"And a brave killer of werewolves," her husband interrupted with feigned severity. "Don't forget that. And now let's leave as fast as we can and go to check on the children. I think they have earned themselves a bedtime story or two."

"But nothing scary," Magdalena pleaded.

"Nothing scary, I promise. For the time being I've had enough of scary stories."

Arm in arm they walked down the dark path through the forest, while behind them the last of the flames in the sinister building died out.

Epilogue

Bamberg, November 5, AD 1668,
in St. Mary's, the Upper Parish Church,
on the Kaulberg

Ⓣhe bells of St. Mary's church rang out loud and clear that Friday morning for the newly wedded Bamberg executioner and his bride. There was a slight drizzle, and fog drifted through the streets, but it couldn't dampen the spirits of the attendees.

Hand in hand, Bartholomäus and Katharina stood under the stone canopy in the so-called bridal entryway, where for ages couples had exchanged their vows. The fact that a dishonorable hangman was permitted to do this had much to do with the influence of the bishop of Würzburg, Johann Philipp von Schönborn had left the city two days earlier, but at Simon's request had put in a good word with the priest there, and thus the church wedding was finally permitted, though not on Sunday, the holy day. Beneath the famous sculptures of the wise and foolish virgins, the priest had placed rings on the fingers of the couple and pronounced his blessing.

Magdalena, Simon, and the other wedding guests stood at the foot of the church stairway. The boys' trousers were more or less clean, and for this festive occasion Simon had also borrowed a fresh shirt from his friend Samuel. Magdalena fanned herself as she watched her future aunt in her low-cut dress standing proudly under the canopy, looking like an aging, blond cherub. Though it was clear she was still mourning the loss of her father, at this moment joy seemed to prevail.

On hearing of her father's death, Katharina had at first collapsed and had wept all night. The next morning, however, she arrived, pale and red-eyed, at Bartholomäus's house and in a firm voice consented to the marriage. That was two days ago.

"My father would have wanted it this way," she said, looking lovingly at her future husband. "Life goes on, and Father never wanted me to spend the rest of my life as an embittered old maid. I'm sure he's in heaven looking down on us and sending us his best wishes."

Bartholomäus thought it best not to tell her how her father actually had died, and he also spared her from hearing that almost their entire fortune had been bought with the blood of the Haan family. Things were bad enough for her as it was.

"I don't think Bartholomäus has anything to complain about," Jakob muttered as he stood alongside Magdalena at the foot of the stairway. In his brother's honor, he'd worn a fresh shirt and even put away his stinking pipe. "Katharina is perhaps a bit fat, but she has her heart in the right place," he said, studying his future sister-in-law like a cow for sale in the market square. "If she'd just stop that constant puttering around, cleaning and moving furniture . . . Bartl will have to cure her of that. It's enough to drive you crazy."

Magdalena grinned. "I think a woman in the house would do wonders for you as well," she said with a wink. "Who knows, perhaps you'll find someone in Schongau who can put up with you."

Kuisl let out a dry laugh. "God forbid. You and Barbara are almost more than I can take. Why would I need another female around who can't keep her mouth shut? Torture on the rack is a pleasure compared to that."

Magdalena was ready with a fresh answer, but at that very moment the couple started down the wide staircase, and the small party of wedding guests broke into applause, which Bartholomäus acknowledged with a nod. He was clearly proud: before him, no Bamberg executioner had ever been permitted to step through the bridal portal.

"If Bartholomäus gets puffed up any more, he'll fly away," Jakob growled, spitting on the ground.

"What did we say? No nasty words on the wedding day," Magdalena glared at her father. "You don't have to marry your brother, after all; Katharina is doing that, and tomorrow we'll be on our way home."

Jakob Kuisl grumbled something incomprehensible into his beard. They had in fact decided to leave right after the wedding reception, as Jakob, and especially Simon, were anxious to get back. The hangman's house and the bathhouse had been empty far too long, and in recent days Simon had complained more than once about how the new doctor in town would be taking his patients.

After a last look at the church, Magdalena joined the small motley crowd marching through the streets of Bamberg in the direction of the city moat. Now that the scheming suffragan bishop was no longer able to interfere, the city councilors had allowed Katharina and Bartholomäus to celebrate in the Wedding House after all.

But surprisingly, Katharina had changed her mind and decided to have a small party in the executioner's house. After the death of her father, such a big party no longer seemed appropriate to her. Perhaps, though, she had come around to the realization that it was more important to celebrate with a few real friends than with a crowd of almost total strangers, who would just start gossiping afterward and in any case were only interested in the wine and the meat pasties.

Together they crossed the city hall bridge on their way to the Green Market, which on this foggy Friday morning was not nearly as busy as on market days. The few people who passed them in the street stared at them with a mixture of fear, disgust, and respect. Ever since the soldiers had carried the dead werewolf into town a few days ago and had told the first horror stories, rumors had swept the city. A short traveling scholar, well versed in the field of alchemy and magic, was said to have shot the beast with a silver bullet, the only way to kill a werewolf. Others claimed to know that the Bamberg executioner himself had cast a magic spell and then quickly strangled the beast. And some spoke of a giant stranger, evidently the brother of the executioner, versed in the art of transmutation, who had vanquished his greatest enemy in an epic battle. Almost no one spoke of the dead Jeremias or Markus Salter. Adelheid Rinswieser also kept her silence, even though her husband and other meddlesome busybodies urged her to speak. All she would say was that the werewolf had dragged her off and cast a spell on her. Magdalena had come to know Adelheid as a strong woman, and she was certain the apothecary's wife would remain silent, for the good of the city. Since then, there hadn't been any arrests, and even the actors were released after it turned out there weren't any witches among them. Evidently, the influence of the enlightened elector was far-reaching, and Magdalena assumed that one or more of his contributions for the building of the Bamberg bishop's palace had a role to play in that.

Bartholomäus never gave the slightest hint that his dear Brutus was involved in any of this, and only once did Magdalena notice a tear in the corner of his eye. The dead beast remained on the gallows, but soon nothing much was left of him, due in part to the time and the weather but primarily because of the many

Katharina had gone to lots of trouble to decorate it as fes-
tively as possible, with mistletoe and ivy branches over the front
door, fragrant dry flowers along the walls, and fresh reeds on the
floors. There was a fragrance of braised meat, onions, and dump-
lings in the air. Hungrily, the guests helped themselves to the
food. Laughter was in the house, and quarreling; the boys raced
through the room whooping, and somewhere there was the
sound of a glass breaking. Magdalena cut into a steaming dumpling, smiling inwardly. It was like every other family party, and a
chance visitor would never suspect he was in the house of an executioner.

He'd find a mix of guests gathered around the large table. In
a back corner sat the rag picker Answin, who in honor of this festive day had actually taken a bath, and Berthold Lamprecht, the
tavern keeper of the Wild Man, who appeared to be enjoying an
animated conversation with him. When Lamprecht heard the
news of Jeremias's death, he paid a decent sum to assure a respectable burial for his old custodian. The former Bamberg
hangman now rested in the city cemetery next to St. Martin's, not
far from the gravestone marking the spot where his former fiancée was buried.

At the far end of the table sat the hangman's servant, Aloysius, silent as always, enjoying Katharina's roast, and even the old
furrier arrived and was once again telling the story of how Jakob
had bought the fox skin from him for Katharina's wedding dress.
"Believe me, I would have advised badger fur," he announced
to everyone, though no one seemed to be listening. "By God, the
badger fur makes you look like royalty. But no, he said it had to
be fox hide. And then Georg came later and bought all those

stinking hides from me. God knows why the boy wanted them."
He shook his head, then took a spoon and, smacking his lips,
spread caraway seeds on his spicy sausage.

Magdalena had to grin watching how her father's face
flushed with anger and shame on hearing the furrier's story. Jakob still hadn't completely gotten over how the actor Markus
Salter, disguised in a beard and a floppy hat, had gotten away
from him while he himself foolishly fell into the river.

Alongside the furrier sat Georg, talking to his twin sister. At
that moment she laughed out loud. Apparently she had recovered well and except for a few scars would have little lasting
damage from the horrors in the old hunting lodge. The burn
blisters would heal, and her beautiful black hair would grow
back in — and in the meantime she was wearing a trim headscarf. Georg, however, appeared grimmer than ever, though perhaps older and more mature. The wolf trap had injured him
more than they'd first thought, and he would probably always
limp a bit, making him look astonishingly like his uncle. Just the
same, Georg had decided to return to Schongau after one more
year as an apprentice in Bamberg, in order to one day take his
father's position.

Magdalena wanted to speak with Simon about that, but he
was talking shop with his friend Samuel about some new theory
of blood circulation, which practically put Magdalena to sleep.
Not until the discussion turned to the Bamberg suffragan bishop
did she sit up and take notice again.

"Harsee is still as stiff as a board," Samuel was saying. "But
his eyes look at you full of hate. That's really strange. Perhaps
he's not really conscious anymore. I hope he isn't, for his sake, as
that would be hell for him." He sighed. "I give him some water
from time to time, but his body shrivels up more and more every
day. I think he has only a few days left, and the Bamberg bishop
is already planning his funeral."

Simon shook his head sadly. "It's really terrible there's no cure for rabies, and I hope very much that the learned doctors will find one someday."

"Let's not give up hope," Samuel replied. "After all, it took William Harvey a long time to gain acceptance of his theories on the circulation of blood. Even good old Galen . . ."

The conversation veered once again to veins and arteries, and Magdalena turned to her father on her left, who was chewing sullenly on his meat patty.

"I'd really like to have a good pipe now," he grumbled between bites. "With lots of smoke so I'd no longer see this bunch of blabbering people."

"Don't forget you promised Katharina not to smoke in her house today," Magdalena admonished him. "And this tobacco really smells bad. It's enough that you stink up everything at home in Schongau."

Kuisl grinned and picked his teeth. "You sound just like my Anna, God bless her soul. Do you know that?"

Magdalena changed the topic. "Whatever became of Bartholomäus's other two dogs?" she asked. "He certainly can't keep the alaunts now that people think Brutus was a werewolf."

"Aloysius thinks Bard found a buyer for the beasts, some nobleman in Franconia with a large dog kennel." Kuisl shrugged. "My brother will certainly get a pile of money for the animals, and perhaps then he can buy himself an even bigger house, or his citizenship, the old showoff."

Magdalena sighed. "Now enough of that, Father. Anyway, you wanted to have a beer together and talk, you and Bartholomäus. You promised me you would." She looked at him, pleading. "So how about it?"

Jakob poked about sheepishly at the dumpling on the plate in front of him. "Hmm . . . well . . . we had a big fight about the venue for the wedding party, then we both went our separate ways and got drunk. I doubt Bartholomäus and I will be getting together anytime in this life."

"Oh, don't talk such nonsense. You don't have to hug each other every day, but it isn't asking too much for you to make peace with one another. Even if it's just for Katharina's sake."

Magdalena nodded toward her aunt, sitting proudly alongside her bridegroom looking out over all her illustrious wedding guests. On her left, her cousin, who was just as fat, was taking one of Bartholomäus's veterinary books from Peter's greasy little fingers. "She doesn't want any quarreling in the family," Magdalena said softly. "So pull yourself together and have a talk with him before we finally leave town."

"I don't know . . ." Jakob grumbled.

"You'll do that, by God, or I swear I'll clean up the living room and move the furniture around every day."

Jakob groaned. "Now you're being just like my Anna. All right, I promise, but just leave me alone now."

Grinning, Magdalena turned to her two boys, who were begging for some more doughnuts spread with honey. Just as she was leaning down to them, there was a knock on the door.

"Well? Who could that be?" said Katharina with surprise. "I don't expect any more guests."

"Perhaps it's the bishop himself," Berthold said with a laugh. "I think he owes all of you here a big thank-you."

Shaking her head, Katharina got up, and when she opened the door she let out a loud shriek of delight.

"Good Lord—Matheo! Along with your esteemed director in person, if I'm not mistaken. Isn't this a surprise. I thought you'd left town."

Barbara quickly jumped from her seat, wiping the gravy from around her mouth and blushing.

In the doorway stood Sir Malcolm, who, with his tall, haggard stature, had to stoop in order to enter the low-ceilinged room. He was followed by the delicate, diminutive Matheo, who still looked rather battered after the beatings in the Old Residence, though the welts on his face would no doubt heal in the weeks and months to follow. Just the same, he smiled brightly. Sir Malcolm had used powder to try to cover the many bruises on his face that he'd suffered in the dungeon, and with his wig he looked like a sad image of a decadent Parisian courtier, carrying a bouquet of dried autumn crocuses, which he handed to Katharina with a deep bow.

"Before we take our leave forever from this glorious city, we wish to pay our humble respects to the beloved bridal couple," Malcolm said in his usual flowery language. "Milady, I am profoundly indebted to you for having taken in one of my principals and returned him to health."

"Anyone would have done the same," Katharina replied, embarrassed, as she accepted the flowers. "But I thought you had already left the city."

Malcolm waved dismissively. "There's a lot for us to do first. Our equipment was badly damaged in this whole affair. No, we're still camped outside the city walls. It's safer there now that this, uh, werewolf has finally been destroyed." He grinned mischievously, and Magdalena could see one of his incisors was missing since she saw him last in the Bamberg dungeon.

"When we finally have all our provisions together, we'll head for Würzburg," he continued with obvious pride, though with a slight lisp due to the new gap in his teeth. "The Würzburg bishop and elector personally invited us. We'll perform in his palace and be a real sensation." He straightened up to his full height, like a giant scarecrow, and spread his arms out theatrically. "Sir Malcolm's troupe will be famous in the whole realm, and soon everybody will have forgotten Guiscard. What did Shakespeare say? 'All the world's a stage, And all the men and women merely players.'" He winked at Katharina. "Or as it says in another passage: 'Many a good hanging prevents a bad marriage.'"

"I never doubted that in the least," said Katharina, pointing to the last two remaining chairs. "But please take a seat, and eat and drink with us."

Malcolm peered at the steaming meat cooking on the hearth, and licked his lips.

"I believe we do have a bit of time. Matheo, what do you think?"

The young man winked at Barbara, then let Katharina fill his plate, along with Malcolm's.

Magdalena leaned across the table and looked intently into the eyes of her younger sister. "So tell me, you and Matheo . . ."

But Barbara waved her off.

"You don't have to act as if it's such a secret," Barbara said with a shrug. "Matheo and I had a heart-to-heart talk yesterday. I was with him all night out in the actor's camp, and . . ."

"You were *with him* all night?" Magdalena had trouble controlling herself. "Good heavens! What does that mean, and why am I just learning about this?"

Barbara looked at her peevishly. "Now you're sounding like Mother."

"Strange," Magdalena mumbled. "Somebody else just said the same thing to me. But go on. What were you doing with Matheo out at the actor's camp?"

"Well, we said good-bye, that's all, and nothing more." Barbara hesitated. "I think our relationship is . . . platonic. Matheo told me what that means—that we love each other, but in another way we don't. Anyway, I can't imagine spending my life wandering around, even if Sir Malcolm told me again yesterday that I really have talent." She looked severely at Magdalena, but then her face softened. "When I ran away and hid in the castle garden after that horrible event in the theater, I felt more alone than ever before in my life," she said softly. "I realized I need my family more than I thought."

Magdalena smiled. "Well, someday you will probably get married and have a family."

"Yes, but there's plenty of time for that still, and until then I'd like to spend time with all of you." Barbara leaned back and looked at all the chattering, quarreling, laughing crowd, then winked at her older sister.

"Basically, we're really a great family. God knows life with us will never be boring."

AFTERWORD

Warning to curious readers who always read the end of the book first! As Jakob Kuisl would say . . . : Keep your hands off, Himmelherr-gottzehfxsakrament!

When people ask me why I like writing historical novels, I usually have the same answer: "History always writes the best stories!"

And, in fact, in the course of researching for my stories, I keep coming upon more hair-raising, bizarre, fantastic, or simply comical facts than I could hardly have invented on my own. Often, my wife just shakes her head in checking my manuscript and tells me I've exaggerated a bit too much. And I'm happy as a lark whenever I can tell her it's something that actually happened.

In gathering materials for this novel, there were two tales that awakened my love of storytelling (and if you don't want to spoil the fun of figuring out who's the culprit, you shouldn't be reading this until you've read the story . . .).

The first discovery was a short reference in an old article to the so-called "werewolf of Ansbach." In the year 1685, a man-eating wolf terrorized the Bavarian city of Ansbach, killing two children and a young woman. The citizens were convinced the huge animal was the reincarnation of the deceased mayor, Michael Leicht, a swindler who allegedly roamed about dressed as a werewolf. People even claimed to have seen him at his own burial service!

Shortly thereafter, the real wolf was found in a pit and stoned to death, but people still believed in a devilish monster. They flayed the beast, set a human face made of paper on its shoulders, as well a wig and a cape, and to the accompaniment of loud

A werewolf in Bavaria? I started doing some research and soon found other cases. In 1641, for example, a whole pack of these beasts was said to be lurking in the Bavarian Forest near Straubing. In Bedburg, near Cologne, a certain Peter Stump, nicknamed Stubbe Peter (*Stubbe* = "stump," perhaps because his left hand had been severed, leaving only a stump), was executed in 1589 on the wheel. He was accused of the dreadful crime of dressing as a wolf and killing and eating more than a dozen children, including his own son, whose brain he was reported to have devoured.

There actually were many so-called werewolf trials all over Germany, and particularly in France, in which people were accused of having changed themselves into man-eating monsters. The numbers vary, but some experts say there were up to thirty thousand presumed cases in Europe just between the years 1520 and 1630, a fact that is often pushed into the background because of the dreadful witch trials.

Of course there were never any real werewolves, and the suspects were often simple shepherds or charcoal burners living in the forest and for that reason alone objects of suspicion. There may have been a few mentally ill people among them, since people back then viewed any form of mental illness as proof that the person had signed a pact with the devil.

One interesting theory is that "werewolves" may have simply been people infected with rabies, at that time called *Hundswut*, or "canine madness." The characteristics of the disease, still largely incurable today, actually made the victims look like wolves. They ran around biting people and other animals, they sometimes howled, their teeth looked longer due to spastic paralysis in their face, and they were terrified by water. The disease was transmitted at that time, just as it is now, by dogs and wolves, but also by small predators like foxes and ferrets, even by bats.

When I read about this connection between werewolves and rabies, I knew I'd come across an interesting murder weapon — for crime writers, always an exciting moment.

The second historical inspiration behind this novel was the Bamberg witch trials of 1612 through 1630, in which around a thousand people met their deaths. These two trials, along with the Würzburg witch trials, are considered to have been the most cataclysmic in all of Europe. In the neighboring town of Zeil am Main, a special oven was built just to cremate the many corpses. Many houses in Bamberg stood empty for decades afterward and fell into disrepair because their owners had died at the stake. Ruins, haunted houses, the decline of a once wealthy city — in my novel, this provides a gruesome backdrop based on historical facts. Many years ago, I came across an article about the so-called Bamberg Malefiz ("malefactor" or "criminal") House, or Druden ("druid") House. The building was probably the most modern prison and torture facility of its time, sort of a Guantanamo Bay of the seventeenth century. In addition to the usual means of torture, victims were immersed in caustic lime, fed a salty mash of fish, forced to sit on iron chairs over a hot fire, or placed in tiny enclosures whose bottom was covered with small, sharp wooden pyramids. Historical reality was often much more cruel than any writer's imagination.

When the Swedes invaded Bamberg in 1632, during the Thirty Years' War, the citizens learned about the atrocities committed there. The last of the ten prisoners were quickly released and the Malefiz House torn down in an effort to erase all evidence of the cruelty perpetrated there.

An online museum (http://www.malefiz-haus.de) offers a gruesome picture of the interior of this horrific building, as does the graphically remarkable nonfiction work *The Factory of Death* by Ralph Kloos and Thomas Göll (available at http://www.amazon.com) from which I took a short passage from a Bamberg sentence for witchcraft. For anyone interested in the period of the Bamberg witch trials, I especially recommend Sabine Weigand's well-researched novel, *Die Seelen im Feuer*, from which I have excerpted a short description taken from the trial minutes.

I've often wondered what effect these witch trials had on the Bamberg hangmen at the time. After all, they had to torture and execute hundreds of people. How does anyone process that psychologically? Does the constant killing turn one into an unfeeling monster? Did the hangmen have nightmares? Anyone who wants to learn more about torturing at that time should visit the terrifying torture museums in Siena and San Gimignano during a vacation to Italy. I'd like to emphasize, however, that these museums are definitely not suited for small children! I only mention this because in my research trips I keep bumping into families with small children licking ice-cream cones and looking very upset.

The only way one can exercise this bloody vocation with a good conscience in the long run is to be like the Bamberg executioner Jeremias (alias Michael Binder) in the novel, who was modeled after an actual, historical person. The last German hangman, Johann Reichhart, beheaded almost three thousand persons just during the Nazi period, presumably a record for executioners. He also continued working for the American occupation forces after the end of the war. The GIs beat him up before giving him the job of hanging war criminals in Landsberg, and after that put him in a labor camp. Reichhart always performed his dirty work professionally and above all quickly, no matter which side the criminals were on. Nevertheless he died poor and impoverished at the age of seventy-nine. He insisted he never regretted the work he did.

The trial of Chancellor Haan and his family, by the way, is something I didn't make up, either. His name is recorded in the city archives. Most of the members of the so-called Witches Commission also appear in the official documents, so they also really

existed. Whether, decades later, there was still one last living sur-
vivor plotting revenge . . . very well, I did take a little artistic li-
cense with that. Also, at that time, Sebastian Harsee was not the
suffragan bishop of Bamberg.

And to the best of my knowledge, there never was a werewolf trial in Bamberg, though it surely is a possibility.

Just a word about the group of actors in the novel, which I
really enjoyed writing about—after all, I studied theater as a mi-
nor subject "with great passion," like Faust, for my own enjoyment. Yes, there were such groups of traveling actors in the
German Reich at the time, presenting plays by Shakespeare,
though in edited form. The focus was clearly on the action, and
poetic form, plot development, and complex characterization
were secondary—just like in Hollywood, 350 years later. According to information from the German Shakespeare Library
in Munich, it isn't certain these works were performed under the
name *Shakespeare*, but it's quite possible my Barbara would be
able to find such a book.

Otherwise, as I said, history always writes the best stories. Do
you know by chance the story about the collapse of the latrine in
Erfurt in the year 1184, in which practically the entire German
nobility in that city fell into the cesspool and almost literally
drowned in its own excrement? No? Or perhaps the Fourth
Crusade, which ended in folly when it got to Constantinople,
where Christian knights plundered and torched the Christian
city? Or the execution of the pirate Störtebeker, who . . .
Well, you see, there's plenty of material left for books yet to
come . . .

As always, I'd like to thank many people who contributed to the
creation of this novel, first of all the art historian and city guide
Dr. Christine Freise-Wonka, who patiently and helpfully told
me everything I needed to know about Bamberg. The same is
true of Rita Hoidn of the Bavarian Department of State-Owned

Palaces, Gardens, and Lakes; Anna-Maria Schühlein of the Bamberg Tourist Office; and the kind people at the Bamberg Municipal Archives.

Petra Nerreter showed me her master's thesis about Bamberg executioners; Dr. Thomas Löscher of the Institute for Infectious Diseases and Tropical Medicine at Munich University told me all I needed to know about rabies; and Dr. Bettina Boecker of the Shakespeare Research Library in Munich helped me with my questions about the acceptance of Shakespeare's work in seventeenth-century Germany.

Thanks also to Christine Hartnagel, whose guided tours of Bamberg are outstanding, and who gave me a valuable tip for my next Hangman's Daughter novel. Likewise, sincerest thanks to my esteemed colleague and writer, the erudite Richard Dübell, who helped me a number of times with my research.

Have I forgotten anyone? Naturally I am deeply indebted, as always, to Gerd Rumler and Martina Kuscheck at my literary agency for their proofing and encouragement, Uta Rupprecht and Nina Wegscheider for edits, the always energetic Stephanie Martin at Ullstein Publishers, and to rights director Pia Götz, who helped to introduce the Kuisl family into more than twenty languages all over the world.

Special thanks to my American translator, Lee Chadeayne, who has done a wonderful job translating the Hangman's Daughter tales. And of course also to all the people in publishing, editing, and marketing who cared that my books became so successful on the American market.

Last but not least, thanks go to my brothers and my father for medical matters, Christian Wiedemann for the desk with a view of the Eiger North Wall—and my wife, Katrin, who's always lent an ear when I reach a dead end. Thanks for all your tips, and I love you even if I sometimes grumble like a Kuisl! And as always, all the errors are mine. If you find some, let me know. You never stop learning.